THE MALLOW YEARS

It seemed neither could look away. Their eyes were locked in a strange and cautionary fashion as though each was sizing up the other and yet that was not it entirely for they were both well aware of who the other was, of what the other was and of the antipathy between them. It was more than that, more than the yawning gulf of class, of prejudice, more than the conflict which existed in each of them to fight and wound, to hurt in the protection of what was theirs, he for the people who looked to him for leadership, she for her father's mills. It was quite simply the look of a man and a woman taking the measure, *as* a man and a woman, of one another.

She snapped her fingers and the dogs lay down and one yawned. They lowered their muzzles to their paws, giving the impression they were about to doze off but neither took their unblinking eyes from Joss Greenwood.

'So,' she said softly, 'here we are again, Joss Greenwood. I wondered how long it would be before we met up with one another.'

About the author

Audrey Howard was born in Liverpool in 1929 and it is from that once-great seaport that many of the ideas for her books come. Before she began to write she had a variety of jobs, among them hairdresser, model, shop assistant, cleaner and civil servant. In 1981, out of work and living in Australia, she wrote the first of her novels. She was fifty-two. Her fourth novel, *The Juniper Bush*, won the Romantic Novel of the Year Award in 1988. She now lives in her childhood home, St Anne's on Sea, Lancashire.

The Mallow Years

Audrey Howard

CORONET BOOKS
Hodder & Stoughton

First published in Great Britain in 1989 by Hodder and Stoughton
A division of Hodder Headline PLC
First published in paperback in 1990 by Hodder and Stoughton
A Coronet Paperback

20 19 18 17 16 15 14 13

A CIP catalogue record for this book is available from
the British Library

ISBN 0 340 54294 2

Printed and bound in Great Britain by
Clays Ltd, St Ives plc

Hodder and Stoughton
A division of Hodder Headline PLC
338 Euston Road
London NW1 3BH

For Marjorie
and Jim
with love

Author's Note

1. The cotton plant is a member of the mallow family.
2. In 1832 John Fielden and William Cobbett, radical candidates for Oldham township and out-townships of Royton, Crompton and Chadderton were returned as Members of Parliament with tremendous majorities over their Whig and Tory opponents. The addition of Joss Greenwood is purely fictitious.

Part One

1

The day they were to march was hot and sultry. It was barely daybreak and already Joss could feel the sweat soak into the back of his shirt and collect beneath his armpits. It would be like a furnace by noon when the sun was at its highest but in his enthusiasm he did not really care. He was not yet nineteen years old and about to embark on the most exciting day of his life. The knowledge that he was to tramp twenty miles to Manchester and the same back was of no particular significance to the young man. He was strong and more than a match for a challenge such as this. He had on many occasions walked thirty miles in one day, up on the high moors of the South Pennine Heartland, striding out easily, eating up the vast distances with his long and powerful legs. And today he would be at the side of the man who was, in his opinion, the most dauntless in the world, his own father Abel Greenwood.

Joss Greenwood's grey-green eyes, the colour of wild mignonette in May, became soft with a deep and reverent love and he stood for a moment, one wooden clog on his bare foot, the other still in his hand, looking beyond the small window of the room he shared with his brother, beyond the drystone wall which enclosed his father's small-holding and out to the sweeping folds of moorland and the deep, wooded valleys of the hills which surrounded the cottage that was his home. The building was the last in the row of old 'laithe' houses which were to be found in the hillside valley, half home and half work place with a loom-shop above and stalls on the ground floor for cattle,

9

though these, of course, were long gone. His view of the rugged landscape was uninterrupted. He could see to the top of Dog Hill in the clear morning air and hear the roar of the mountain stream tumbling on to the more placid waters below. But though his eyes encompassed the vast stretches of tussocky grass, the moor heather and blazing bracken of the wild hills, the picture he looked at in his head was that of the man who was his father. Though he listened to the music of the waters which had sung its song for as long as he could remember, the sound he heard was that of his father's voice as he spoke to the men who followed him. He would be downstairs now in the kitchen, putting on his clogs as Joss was doing, ready for the march, watching Joss's mother stirring the pan on the fire which contained the oats mixed with water that was to be their breakfast. His eyes, the exact colour of Joss's own, would be serene, the expression on the passive face uncomplaining. But Joss knew that behind the quiet face and eyes blazed a mind which was sharp and far reaching, courageous and compassionate. Inside the thin, hollow chest, formed to that state by the nature of his work, beat a heart like that of a lion. Though he was no more than five feet six inches tall and weighed only an ounce or two above nine stones, he was a giant of a man, and to Joss and the men who listened to him, only a degree or two below God Himself.

The door opened and Joss turned and the man who was in his thoughts entered the low-ceilinged room. His father smiled the slow, sweet smile which was peculiarly his and his eyes crinkled at the corners and the lines which cut his thin cheeks deepened. His lips parted on big, uneven teeth and he spoke quietly, the broad dialect of the north country-man rich on his tongue.

'Are't not ready, lad?'

'Aye, Pa. I've nobbut me clogs to put on.'

'It's a grand day for it.'

'It is that.'

'Yer Ma's got t'porridge on't table. Men can't march on empty bellies.' Abel Greenwood winked and his son's heart

10

swelled with pride for it seemed his father made no distinction between himself, a lad of almost nineteen and the gallant company of men who had been with him since the hated 'Combination Acts' had been passed in 1800. That was the year Joss was born and though he was not the passionate believer in the righting of the wrongs done his fellowman, that his father was, never having suffered what they did, the prospect of the day's escape from the routine of his life made him willing, eager to march for them. Nineteen years, and before that, and still the battle went on. Today this demonstration by workers from the whole of Lancashire, and beyond the county's borders to Yorkshire and Cheshire, would show those in authority that something must be done to alleviate their suffering and Joss Greenwood was thrilled at the prospect of being a part of it.

'Will they all come, Pa?' he asked, not really caring who came since he would be there.

'Aye. Weather's on our side.' The answer was short. Only when he was addressing a meeting did Abel Greenwood allow his natural gift as an orator to flow from him and even then he spoke quietly so that the enormous crowds who gathered to listen to him stood like silent statues in order not to miss a word of what he said. But at home with his family his remarks were brief, just as though he must save his strength and his eloquence for what had become his life's work.

''Appen they'd not march if it was raining, Pa,' he said scornfully, since he would go whatever the weather.

''Appen not, at least not in such great numbers.'

The younger man's eyes were brilliant in his thin face and his immeasurable enthusiasm for this day's outing put spots of crimson in his cheeks. He was tall, six inches above his father's height and reed thin but he held himself as straight as an arrow. His dark head was proudly set on his broadening shoulders. His hair was thick, tumbling with rich, brown curls on to his forehead, uncut and unbrushed. He wore threadbare breeches and a shirt to match, no stockings and the wooden clogs he had just put on.

'Will there be a great crowd to see us go, Pa?' and pretty girls, too, he would have liked to have said.

'Aye, lad, but that's not the purpose of t'march. We want to show t'maisters rightness o' what we ask for and the more of us go the better they'll see our determination.'

Joss Greenwood looked suitably crestfallen but his father smiled, laying a hand on his son's shoulder. He knew how he felt. He himself had been involved in the often hopeless, sometimes patient but always courageous struggle of the working man for almost twenty-five years. He had fought in the bread riots of Oldham in order to feed his growing family. He had watched helplessly as his own wages declined. He had seen the appalling effect of the 'Combination Acts' which had taken away the working man's right to congregate with others of like mind. But changes had come about slowly. The 'flying shuttle' and the 'spinning jenny' had seemed to him, and other hand-loom weavers and spinners, to be the miracle which would bring, if not prosperity, at least a decent standard of living for them all.

Abel Greenwood, and his father before him, rented the cottage which lay on the hillside of Edgeclough village. It was built on land belonging to the local squire and for the building and the acre of tough-grained soil on which it stood they paid the sum of two guineas a year. It was well built of local stone in the traditional manner by those who had been employed for generations in the spinning and weaving of cloth, first wool and then, as trade increased, cotton. The workroom or 'loom-shop' was on the first floor so that it might obtain the maximum light, with a 'taking-in' door set on the same level with steps on the outside of the building leading up to it from the ground.

They had worked side by side, Joss and Abel Greenwood, since Joss, at the age of eight had proved to his father that he was capable of operating the hand-loom alone, and had been allowed to weave his first 'piece' of cloth. There were two hand-looms, each able to produce a length of cloth measuring forty yards a week, or more, if they wished but the father and son were their own men, weaving when they had a mind to, or working on the smallholding which surrounded the cottage, growing what vegetables the harsh climate of the Lancashire uplands would allow.

It was a good life. Martha Greenwood and her eldest daughter Jenny would often take their spinning jennies – after which the girl had been named – and sit by the cottage door while father and son worked the vegetable plot. Younger children were put to opening the bales of raw cotton, cleaning and carding the fibres and thus the whole family was profitably and satisfyingly employed. The raw yarn was brought to them each week by the merchant from Manchester and the two lengths of cloth which had been woven were sold at the Cloth Hall in Crossfold.

But by this time Joss and Abel Greenwood were among the dwindling number of men who could call themselves independent. The supply of raw cotton on which their livelihood depended was fast disappearing as the factory system, begun in 1806, took a firm hold. Men like James Chapman and his son Barker Chapman, the merchants who had once supplied their yarn for a commission, built their own spinning mill and had not the time nor the inclination, now they were spinning for themselves, to bother with the likes of Abel Greenwood. Those men who had depended on the firm of Chapman for their yarn began now to weave Chapman cloth on an 'outworker' basis but Joss and Abel between them, with a third weaver called Enoch Butterworth, who was also unwilling to give up his emancipation, managed to fetch the raw cotton they needed themselves. One pack pony could carry enough for three weavers, though it was a long trudge to Manchester and back. They took a pride in themselves and in their craft and were determined to manage despite the difficulties.

But many did not and today they were to speak up for themselves through the voices of men like Henry Hunt, John Knight and Abel Greenwood. His eyes softened as

13

they looked into the excited brilliance of his son's and he squeezed his shoulder lovingly, the only demonstration of his feelings he would allow, then he turned away briskly.

'Come, lad. They'll not wait on us if we're late.'

John Knight gave the signal at nine o'clock on that hot and cloudless morning for the columns to swing off Oldham Green and on to the road to Manchester. He had organised the Oldham assembly and Joss Greenwood, as the son of one of the movement's leaders found himself marching directly behind the great man's back.

He looked straight ahead at first for this was the first time he had been so far from his hillside home and the excitement was almost too much for him to contain. He did not look at the thousands of people who lined the route, flinging wide their windows and gathering on their doorsteps to watch the great column of men and women march through the town and out on to the moorland route which led through Failsworth and Chadderton to Manchester. For the first few minutes he stared unseeingly at the low-crowned, broad-brimmed hat worn by John Knight, but he was a young man with a young man's susceptibility to admiration. The shouting, cheering spectators, the joyful sound of the band which kept them in step, the soft excited laughter of the two hundred white-gowned young women, who formed the centrepiece of the procession at his back, was too much for him and he began to smile, then to grin broadly, waving his hand jubilantly at all those who had come to see them off. The white silk banner emblazoned with the inscription "Universal Suffrage", "Annual Parliaments", "Election by Ballot' and "No Combination Acts, Oldham Union' flew high above his head, like a great and glorious bird in the depthless blue of the sky and he knew that by the end of that day, they, the cotton operatives of Lancashire, would have these things. He could see the sprig of laurel in his father's hat, placed there to signify that he was a leader and as a token of amity and peace. The small splash of green gave Joss a

14

feeling of such joy for what it represented he felt his heart expand to accommodate the wealth of his emotions.

They passed through sun-filtered woods, up mossy banks and down into sheltered valleys until they came to the toll-gates at Harpurhey and Joss saw his father stretch up to speak in the ear of John Knight. The distinguished gentleman looked about him as though expecting some mishap for it had been rumoured the magistrates might try to stop them here but there was nothing to be seen except the excited cheering faces of the people.

They had reached Newtown by now and the predominantly Irish population of this worst area of the slums came out to greet them. Row upon row of cheap, back-to-back houses with no visible sign of ventilation or drainage and with every scrap of space overflowing, or so it seemed to Joss, with apathetic, black-haired people. The street through which they marched followed the course of a ditch overflowing with the most appalling mass of human garbage, from the contents of the previous night's chamber pot and bucket, to the remains of dead animals. Children played barefoot, wearing next to nothing in the hot sunshine. Dirty, noisy, quarrelsome, half-starved and half-wild, and strangers, it appeared, to the pump water and privy at the end of the street which was shared by twenty houses. Every patch of land, scrubby and wasted, between the rows of houses themselves, carried a festering heap of filth. There were broken windows mended with oilskin, rotting wood in the doors and frames and the stench from the open drain and underground cellars made Joss Greenwood's head reel.

The men and women who cheered, or stood silently staring, depending on their disposition and state of health, were of low stature, thin and pallid with bowed legs and crooked backs. Their hair was lack-lustre and patchy and their eyes had a curiously dusty look about them as though for want of sleep. They had a spiritless and dejected air but they had been made aware that this blithe company which passed their door was on its way to better their lot and though they had no great hope of it the music and pageantry

15

made a pleasant change in their drab lives and there was a smile or two and even a tentative wave.

Joss held his hand to his mouth as he gagged on the putrid air.

'Look to't front, lad,' his father's voice told him steadfastly. 'Remember 'tis to do away with this that we march.' Joss Greenwood took heart, averting his eyes from the horrors about him, looking to the laurel spray on John Knight's hat and to the bright day ahead it signified.

The band began to play 'St Patrick's Day in the Morning' to please those who stood to watch them pass by and the noise of shouting voices became louder, ringing in their ears until at last they reached the centre of Manchester and their destination.

St Peter's Field!

The marchers were singing now, laughing and filled with spontaneous gaiety, but disciplined just the same. Children clung to their fathers' hands or were lifted on to their shoulders and one might have been forgiven for thinking they were all to attend a country fair rather than one of the greatest political meetings the country had ever known. Joss thought he would burst with excitement and pride to be part of such a good-natured multitude. They were near to starvation, many of them, scarecrow men and women with scarecrow children but still they remained good-humoured, walking the twenty miles, some of them without a shoe to their foot or a bit of gruel in their bellies.

It was midday before the word came that Orator Hunt was to arrive accompanied by the Manchester female reformers, dressed, like the Oldham women, all in white. The sun beat down and the heat became oppressive for no breath of cooling wind could reach the thousands upon thousands who crowded the great field that day. It was estimated later that six per cent of the total population of Lancashire was there, upwards of sixty thousand people and as the massed bands rendered 'See the Conquering Hero comes' sixty thousand voices roared their approval and Joss Greenwood's was surely among the loudest.

At twenty minutes to two the cheering was allowed to die down and Henry Hunt, the great Radical leader whom they all waited eagerly to hear, began to speak.

The Manchester and Salford Yeomanry Cavalry trotted briskly down the length of Cooper Street, intent, as they had been ordered, on arresting the leaders of the seditious meeting which was taking place in St Peter's Field. Henry Hunt's name was on their list, as was that of John Knight, Richard Moorhouse, Joseph Johnson and Abel Greenwood.

The horses of the troopers were restive and hard to control, raw and unused to the field and when the last galloper had gone by, his head still dazed by the amount of ale he had consumed before mounting, the woman and her two-year-old child, who had come to see the procession and with whom his horse had collided, lay still and bleeding in the gutter, unnoticed and unheeded except by those who stood beside her. They were the first casualties of the day.

The first intimation that something was wrong was conveyed to Joss Greenwood by the sudden look of alarm on his father's face. Joss had climbed on to a window-sill, clinging to a drainpipe, which ran down the wall, so that he could see over the heads of the great press of people to where his father stood at the hustings. Abel had been smiling, turning his attention to Henry Hunt, clearly moved by the splendid occasion and the support and loyalty shown by those for whom he had fought so long and hard. Joss smiled too, and hoped his father would be allowed to speak for there was no more fluent and heart-warming orator in the whole of the land. Abel believed passionately in the need for change in the lives of his fellow workers, as did all those congregated there that day, and yet, though his soul burned with it, his way was to speak quietly, simply, movingly and the people who listened to him loved him and did what he told them. No one broke machinery nor wrecked mills in their aim for reform under Abel Greenwood's direction and though he was a fervent radical

17

he did nothing with violence but preached peaceable change through education and the ballot box.

As Joss watched him he saw his father turn sharply away from Henry Hunt, his expression changing from smiling accordance, to dismay and Joss turned also, trying to make out what had alarmed him. He could see nothing but the crowd was beginning to surge and he heard someone cry out ' . . . soldiers . . . there's soldiers . . .' He saw Henry Hunt raise his hands to those before him and the great man shouted something as though beseeching them to stand firm then, surprisingly, there was laughter and Joss relaxed. He saw the soldiers then. They were mounted, appearing enormous above the heads of the people on the far side of the field. Quiet, it seemed to him, orderly and imposing no threat to the bewildered crowd but as he watched, idly wondering if perhaps they had come to join the march, a fine sight in their splendid uniforms, his heart jumped sickeningly to his throat, choking the words of warning he would have spoken. He watched in growing confusion as they drew their sharpened, glittering sabres and began to advance towards the hustings. He found his voice then.

'Pa,' he shouted. He could see the terrified horses begin to rear, surrounded as they were by thousands of men, women and children. The soldiers were trying desperately to maintain order for, at that precise moment, they meant no harm to the crowd. They had come only to arrest those who were breaking the law. The people about them could take themselves back to wherever they had come from for all they cared; but the frightened, panicking multitude did not know this. They only knew sudden fear, the smell and taste and feel of it, which was as thick and oppressive as the mid-afternoon heat. Men and women fell back from the plunging horses, knocking over those behind them and bodies began to go down like dominoes, the first being the cause of the last to fall. The cavalrymen tried resolutely to follow their officers in line abreast but the further their mounts were forced into the solid wall of the throng the less their riders could control them and finally the ranks broke.

Joss's mind became a terrible seething mass of unco-ordinated thoughts but one overruled all others. It was that his father, not afraid as he himself was, but concerned only for those about him would wade into the sea of screaming, panicking women and their children and pick them up in his protective arms, as many as he could carry, taking them to safety and Joss was desperate to be beside him when he did so.

'Pa,' he shouted again. 'Wait for me, Pa, I'm coming.' Many of those between him and the hustings had turned in his direction and away from their leaders, instinct herding them, like sheep, from the approaching danger to the safety of the dozen narrow streets which radiated off the square. Suddenly there were detachments of foot soldiers and Dra-goons blocking their way and Joss found himself held fast in the iron grip of the swaying, panic-stricken crowd. They were packed tight together, as close as matches in a box, gasping and choking. Those women who could draw breath began to scream. Already dozens had gone down as they lost their footing, disappearing beneath the trampling feet of men and horses.

Again Joss was lifted up above the bobbing heads of those still on their feet and he could see the cavalry officer, backed by a handful of mounted soldiers approach the hustings. The officer spoke to Mr Hunt who stepped down obligingly, his hands spread to show he meant no harm but two other gentlemen, Joss could not recognise them, were dragged from the platform with little or no ceremony. One of the ladies with the company tripped and as she jerked herself upwards again a cavalryman slashed across her body with his sabre, for what reason Joss did not know since she posed a threat to no one, and he saw the first blood spilled that day. Of his father there was no sign.

Those who had not yet moved, amazingly unaware that something appalling was happening were standing on tip-toe, craning their necks and asking one another what was

19

to do. However, the yeomanry, having enjoyed a rout of destruction at the hustings and filled with the bloodlust which comes upon those who seek glory, turned their horses in the direction of the silken banners which flew defiantly about the field and within minutes hundreds of those who stood before them were crushed beneath the animals' hooves. They charged again and again, those brave Hussars, their sabres making a fine, flashing sight in the sunlight.

Fresh troops, trained in the removal of the enemy had arrived and at a signal from their officer began the systematic clearing of the square. It was then that the real panic began, the panic of sixty thousand bodies packed tight together and caught in the open with nowhere to go to avoid the stiff-necked, stiff-backed soldiers, the trampling, rearing horses, the flashing, slashing sabres – from where had they come, and why? – were the last thoughts of the bewildered masses as they went down and the sounds grew more appalling with every second.

The dust rose up, drifting beyond the rooftops towards the hot, sun-drenched sky. Those who were still on their feet were forced this way and that in a horrid unison but the piles of bodies, women arched protectively over fallen children, grew higher and more bloody. Joss saw one young woman lift her arm in a mute appeal to a trooper to spare her child and watched, mad with shock and terror as the limb was struck from her body. Though his eyes could not believe the sight nor his mind arrange his thoughts to coherency, instinct had him inching his way towards her over others just as seriously injured and in need of his help. There was blood and soft, damaged flesh beneath his hand, eyes glazed in shock and horror and pain, even death, moans and screams and in the midst of it young Joss Greenwood fought, quite senselessly, to go to the aid of the mother whose body was by now completely covered by others. Men were shouting and pushing, fighting to get out of the square, leaving their comrades, those with whom they had just marched, to lie in their own blood, or crawl desperately to get out of the way of the horses. They were ridden down with as much compunction as an ant's nest which had been kicked over. The soldiers on horseback were screaming as loudly as those they attacked, screaming words of abuse . . .

'. . . damn you reformers . . .'

'. . . bloody radicals . . .'

'. . . the devil take the lot of you . . .'

. . . and the tide of humanity was swept on as relentlessly as waves upon a shore, towards the streets which were their only means of escape and with them went young Joss Greenwood. When they came up against the Quaker Meeting House on the outskirts of the field it was there that those who were still capable of it took a stand. There had been a strong fence about the house made of sturdy pieces of wood and, though he had no recollection of even taking one up, Joss found himself standing, legs braced, shoulders hunched defensively, side by side with the men and women who had survived, swinging a fierce section of timber as though it were a cudgel. The others with him were blood-stained, bruised, caked from head to foot with dust, eyes flaring from maddened faces, mouths opened wide on screams of despairing rage.

For ten minutes they fought, those brave souls, defending themselves and the dream they had set out with that day, unseating several of the yeomanry with sticks and stones and anything else they could lay their hands on and even, though no one could say from where it came, a loud shot from a pistol. But when the Hussars rode in, pushing the defenders back against the walls of the house, the resistance was ended and it was all over.

In twenty minutes the field, which had been thronged with sixty thousand exuberant, joyous, laughing, singing persons, come to show their masters that their cause was just, was emptied.

But for the dead and dying!

Joss Greenwood found his father no more than fifteen paces from the hustings. He lay on his face, his body protecting

21

that of a small boy who cried lustily for his Mam. The child stood up shakily when Joss lifted his father's body from him and began to run, like a small dog after its own tail, in search of his mother and for several moments Joss watched him, his concern for the boy keeping at bay the frightful knowledge of what they had done to his Pa. As long as he concentrated on the boy's distress he could pretend that the heavy body – why was his Pa so heavy? – was no more than knocked unconscious and that soon, when his senses returned to him, his Pa would stand up, a bit shaken and bruised perhaps but whole, and Joss would give him his arm and together they would walk back to Edgeclough, this battle lost but the war still to be won.

'Pa,' he said gently, looking down into the face he loved so well. But his father's eyes stared somewhere over his own shoulder and the blood ran from his ear on to Joss's own bloody hand.

'Oh Pa, please, Pa . . .' Joss lifted the dusty head into his lap and stroked his father's cheek and began to rock him back and forth. For the last time as a boy he wept and it was as his youthful, anguished tears fell on the beloved face that he became a man.

He would let no one help him. They found him, those who had set off with him from the village that morning, those who had survived and crept back to look for friends, and when they would have shared his burden he turned on them, snarling like a cornered beast.

'I'll carry him, damn you. Leave him be.'

Back the way they had come they went, a small band of injured, shocked and dazed men and women, some with silent children, hovering at Joss Greenwood's back, still following their leader even though the one they had begun the day with was dead. Joss stared ahead of him, putting one foot in front of the other, his arms cradling the increasingly heavy weight of his father. Through the long summer evening, warm and sullen with an impending thunderstorm, they tramped until they reached the rutted turnpike between Manchester and Oldham. Some way along was a turning

22

on to a bridle-path, lined on each side with banks of wild honeysuckle and roses. The fragrance drenched the senses of those who had about them the dreadful odour of blood, the acrid smells of sweat-stained human and animal flesh, of dust and smoke and the stench of fear, and of death, and the company stood for a moment, drawing the sweetness into grateful lungs.

It was full dark now and the little band lay down to rest but none attempted to approach young Joss Greenwood whose brain had surely been turned by what he had seen that day. He sat with his back to the broad trunk of a canopied oak tree, his father's body held in fierce, protective arms. He cradled the greying head to his chest and those nearest to him swore they heard him speak to the dead man through the short night though none heard the actual words and not one could guess the depth nor the intensity of his feelings.

The sky became clear and bright with stars towards morning and Joss Greenwood lifted his gaze from the burden in his arms and looked up into the radiance of the fading night. He felt the beauty of it enter his soul and though his heart was breaking in anguish and guilt (for had he not failed to stand by this man he loved?), he held its splendour to him a moment longer before he let the bitterness set about its work. It was then it began to harden within him, like the frill of ice which edges a lake, creeping towards its centre until the whole is frozen, covering the life which lies beneath. Under the ice is the vital force, the growth which will blossom when the thaw sets in, but warmth and the light of the sun are needed and none touched Joss Greenwood at that darkest hour of his young life.

He carried his father into his mother's kitchen at noon and when he laid him gently on the table she had prepared for him, for word had gone ahead of him, Joss Greenwood could not straighten out the arms which had carried his father's body for almost twenty-four hours. They remained bent, held to his chest as though in self-protection and when his mother with a soft cry of grief would have pulled him to her in comfort, he stood stiffly rigid, silent and staring. His eyes had sunk into deep, plum-coloured bruises in his grey face and those of the villagers who had stood respectfully at the roadside to see their leader come home for the last time had not been completely certain that the thin lad who carried him was his son. His face was quite expressionless, indecently so, they were inclined to think, since a show of grief was surely called for. It conveyed neither pain nor sorrow and those who looked into his pale eyes stepped back uncertainly beneath their gaze, for the manifestation of what he was to be glimmered in their cold depths.

2

They met for the first time on a stretch of moorland above Friars Mere and though they were alone and unknown to one another she did not drop her eyes when he drew near as young ladies of her age and station were trained to do but stared boldly and with lively interest directly into his face. Her eyes were the blue of the bellflower which grew in the hedgerows and woods surrounding Edgeclough, a violet-blue, shading almost to purple round the pupil and framed by extravagantly long black lashes. Her skin was a pale gold, like honey, pinked at the cheekbones by the biting cold. Her hair, what he could see of it beneath her close fitting bonnet, was as dark as his own with a gloss on it like that of a horse-chestnut and she was tall. He had an impression of colour and vibrant life, of vigour and defiance and a compelling self-esteem which showed in the way her black-booted feet stepped out confidently from beneath the hem of her warm woollen skirt and the determined thrust of her hands into the pockets of her three-quarter length coat. Her back and shoulders were graceful but straight, uncompromisingly so and her head was tilted high and proud. She was obviously not of the labouring class, the quality of her clothes would have told him that, if her attitude had not, and as he stared back at her, astonished at the strangeness of seeing her up here on the wild moorland, alone and so far from anywhere, he was further amazed when she spoke.

'Good morning,' she said cheerfully. 'Is it not a lovely day for a walk?' She stopped, fully expecting him to do the same and he hesitated since he had never in the whole of his life spoken to, or been addressed by a woman who was not of his own class. It was not that he was afraid, nor shy, nor even overawed by the enormous gulf which gaped between them, it was simply that he could see no reason why she should wish to engage him in conversation. Perhaps she imagined it might be intriguing to pass the time of day, of which she would have more than enough to spare, with one of the working classes. One of those strange creatures which crept from their refuge each morning as soon as the sun was up, or before in the winter, to make their way to their employment which demanded they stay there until their master said they might leave which was often after the sun went down again. They were a curious breed, she would think, and nothing to do with her, or her like. A different race one might say, and so, on this cold sunny morning with nothing else to do she had taken a fancy to address one of its number.

'I spoke to a man from the lower orders today,' he could hear her say laughingly to a friend over the teacups, 'and had a marvellously refreshing conversation with him. He was quite ordinary, and clean, with clogs to his feet and could speak the King's English as well as one could expect of such a person. Really, it was *most* amusing.'

His expression of unsmiling contempt did not alter, despite the graciousness of her greeting. He hated with all his heart the class from which she obviously came, the class

25

which had killed his father, and if he could do them harm he would. But this girl was merely a lass trying out her hand at a bit of condescension to, in her opinion, an underprivileged lad, and nothing to do with the concepts which now governed his own life. She obviously thought a lot about herself. One could tell that by the way she raked him with those haughty blue eyes of hers, imagining herself, likely as not, doing him a favour by noticing he was on the same bit of earth as herself, but she was harmless and a touch of mockery on his part would put her in her place. Take her down a peg or two, as they said in his part of the world.

'Aye, 'tis an' all. Fair gives a chap appetite fer 'is snap right enough. Ah trek over yon 'ills every day 'bout this time, or 'appen a mite later. Let streets get aired, like an' t'sun up then ah get mesen out o' me bed. There's nowt like a bloody good walk ter set a chap up fer 'is breakfast and tha porridge tastes a fair treat, tha' knows wi' a reet big plate o' bacon an' eggs ter foller. We 'ave us a clack round t'fire 'til openin' time then a pint or two o' ale at t' "Wheatsheaf" then another stride on't moor an' 'ome fer us tea. Eeh, there's nowt like it.'

He smiled maliciously, watching to see how she would react to his broadly exaggerated Lancashire dialect, or if she would even understand it. Would she perceive his obviously sarcastic jibe at her expense regarding the nourishing breakfast — or lack of it — that a working man could expect, and his election to walk the hills as a form of exercise and enjoyment when he barely had the energy to get himself from his bed to his place of work. Joss was ready to turn away scornfully and continue his journey to the meeting on Friars Mere but without hesitation and with no lessening of her queenly bearing she answered him pertly.

'Yer reet, lad, an' does tha' know summat, I feel exactly t'same. There's nowt like a good tramp on't hills ter perk up a finicky appetite. 'Tis a reet good tonic an' puts roses in tha cheeks. Sets me up fer't day, I can tell thee.'

She began to laugh then. Her eyes sparkled as the sun caught in their depths, narrowing between the tangle of her long lashes. Her lips spread over her white teeth and he could clearly see the quiver of her pink tongue as her mouth opened wide. She threw back her head in an uninhibited way he had never seen before, delighted by his expression of amazement and a certain truculence at being the butt of her humour. But there was no spite in her laughter, just the unspoiled enjoyment of knowing she had been quick enough to see through, and beat him, at his own game. She had realised instantly that he had been 'having her on' as they said in Lancashire and though she did not know why she felt she had evened the score.

'I only bade you good morning,' she went on in her normal voice, 'and you had only to return the greeting and walk on but if you wish to continue in this amusing vein you have but to say so.'

She grinned engagingly and Joss felt a reluctant amusement stir within him, but she had not done yet.

'I don't know who you are or why you are walking up here and I really have no particular interest in either and if you wish to go on, please do so, but really, can you honestly tell me it is *not* a lovely day and that the view at your back can be equalled anywhere in the world?' She turned her astonishing eyes from him to stare out at the splendour of the wide, wild open moors and down to the deep, tree-covered valleys which lay below them. There was an isolated farmhouse far away on the fringe of the moor, smoke from its chimney painting a line of pale grey straight up into the sky and below, huddled against the glint of a river, a small valley town was almost hidden beneath the pall of smoke which covered it. Drystone walls spread their webs across great swathes of green and grey and brown, and the pale coating of hoar frost which had come in the night. The stepped profile of the hillside on the far face of the valley was alternated with bands of tough gritstone and softer shale, and gently on the air was the sound of the tumble of water falling to the valley bottom.

Joss turned to look, ready to stress witheringly that he had been nowhere beyond Manchester and could not therefore, like her it seemed, compare what lay before him to any other part of the world, but the austere beauty silenced them both for were they not Lancashire born and bred with a common love of this beautiful part of unspoiled England which was home to them? They shared nothing beyond this but for the moment it was enough and they stood in quiet harmonious contemplation of their heritage. Forgotten was the inordinate cleverness with which Joss had thought to put this lass in her place and her own quickness in answering it. He stood, tall and lean as a young sapling. His clothes were worn and patched but scrupulously clean for water was plentiful where he lived, as was the fuel – peat for the most part – which was needed to heat it. She stood beside him, almost as tall, slender and strong and dressed in the best that money could buy. Stout boots of the highest quality leather, a coat lined with some soft fur against the cold and her full skirt was made from the finest Yorkshire wool.

For a full five minutes they leaned comfortably side by side, their backs against a waist-high rock, absorbing the crisp air into their lungs, delighting their ears with the singing of the streams as they fell from a dozen hidden places into the waters of Hull Brook far below, delighting their eyes as the sun picked up a reflection of itself in the diamond snap of the hoar frost on the peaks.

'You shouldn't be up here on your own,' he said suddenly.

'Why not? Who is there to harm me? I have been coming up here for years now, ever since I was twelve or so.'

'What difference does that make?' he asked scornfully. 'I bet your Pa doesn't know. No man of sense would let a lass of his wander about the moors by herself. It's asking for trouble.' He was mindful of the closeness with which the gentry kept their womenfolk protected but perhaps her family was different. So high and mighty it did not consider any dare harm one of their own. They were like that, the upper classes, capable of believing in their own superiority,

28

their infallibility and even immortality it seemed to him. Look at this girl, strolling about where no girl should be, of any class, for there were desperate folk tramping these hills. Men on the lookout for work, rough men going from town to town, village to village, begging, starving, and likely to strip a lass, especially this one, not only for the fur lining of her coat but for a bit of sport with her slim girl's body. It was well covered, shapeless he would say beneath the layers of clothing she wore but he had no doubt it would be delectable enough to a man who already had nothing to lose. Fourteen she would be, if that, but not unattractive and she was putting herself in the gravest peril by traipsing about on her own along this moorland path.

For some reason the idea made him irritable and he was quite perplexed by his own impatience with her. She was nowt to him, a silly lass, a different and altogether alien species from the one to which he belonged and yet she made him smile with her compelling and quite unquestioning belief in herself and her right to be up here, just as he had and it took him, for a moment, from the deadly seriousness of his own world.

'My father is no concern of yours,' she was saying. Her tone was lofty and her mouth firm, a little prim even, a young lady being taken to task by one who had no right to criticise. She had been about to take herself off in the direction of Crossfold, diverted and intrigued by her encounter with the tall, strange youth on the path to Friars Mere. Until this moment she had imagined the working classes to be inarticulate and stunted creatures with no thought but the contemplation of herself and her family as the providers for their very existence. But this young man had shown her how wrong she had been. Her sharp mind had been stimulated by what she had sensed in his. She had no real conception of what it might be exactly for she had met no one like him before, but his eyes had told her he was quick-witted and shrewd with a reluctance to suffer fools gladly. They had barely spoken. A joke really, a teasing of one another which had been enjoyable, fun, she supposed, and she got little enough of that in her life but his mocking humour had appealed to her own and his love of this land, matching hers, had drawn them close for the space of five minutes.

She whirled about to face him. Her full skirt flared round her ankles and as though she could not bear the obligation to wear it for a moment longer she untied the ribbons beneath her chin and whipped off her bonnet. Instantly her hair fell about her shoulders and Joss drew in his breath sharply. It shimmered in the pale winter sunshine, the light caught in its silken thickness and though it was so dark, chestnut, russet, copper and gold were captured in it, a breathlessly lovely cape almost to her waist, straight and heavy and unmanageable. With an impatient 'tut' she pushed it back behind her ears.

'And what kind of trouble could I meet up here?' she went on. In truth Joss Greenwood did not know since for the life of him he could not remember what he had said to her. He was rendered quite speechless and could do no more than stand and stare at her dramatically altered appearance. With her bonnet ribbons firmly tied beneath her chin and its brim partially concealing her face she had been no more than a personable young girl. Now, in a breathless moment she had changed from a headstrong impudent girl into a woman of strange, almost foreign beauty. There was certainly none like her in the chapelry of Oldham, Shaw or Edgeclough, or none that he had seen and he had for many months now travelled a long road and met a great multitude of his own class and trade in the course of his days.

'Well . . .' he said lamely, '. . . there's many a chap . . . rough and . . .' He had been about to say as tactfully as he knew how, for it was obvious she had been delicately reared, that her contempt for caution might lead her into more trouble than she could handle but as he spoke she pursed her lips and almost soundlessly a whistle escaped from between them. Instantly two large dogs padded silently from behind the rock on which he and the girl leaned, slipping across the frozen ground to stand beside her full skirt, one on either side of her. They were like no dog he had ever seen before, black and sleek with brown markings on the head, and virtually no tail. They were tall, almost on a level with her waist and they made no sound but their eyes stared unblinkingly into his, flat and dark and baleful.

'Bloody hell . . .' he whispered.

She smiled and tossed back her swinging hair, the gesture at once arrogant and yet amused. Her eyes challenged him, filled, not with contempt exactly but with the complete recognition that if there were to be a confrontation, not only between herself and any 'rough chap' she happened to meet, but between herself and him, there was no doubt who would be the loser!

'This is Joby . . .' she indicated the dog on her left, '. . . and this Blaze and though they are friendly enough, when their tempers are not roused, they can be . . . impetuous. I trained them myself. My father gave them to me when they were pups, realising I suppose, that if I were to roam these tops, as I was bound to do, I would need protection. "When they will obey you without question and when you can control them to my satisfaction you may go," he said. It took me six months, in the fields about the house and when he saw what I had made of them he gave me permission to go about alone. I am well aware, as he is, that we are considered . . . unusual, but then we can do no more than make the best of what we are given in life and that is what my father has done with me. He knew the day would come when I would need to get about unescorted and so he has given me the means to do it. If he had not done so I would have found some other way to achieve my freedom and he knew it, of course.' She laughed impishly with a further toss of her proud head. 'We made a pledge, he and I and it had to be honoured and so it has been. He knows I am quite safe with these two. They are completely harmless, believe me, except when I tell them to be otherwise. I have

31

had no cause to do so yet for it seems their appearance is enough to deter the most courageous. I imagine you can see why!'

For the first time in many months Joss Greenwood felt the young and completely spontaneous desire to laugh out loud. He really had very little idea of what she was talking about in her description of her strange relationship with her father but the need to throw back his head and let out the light-hearted merriment this girl inspired in him was more than he could resist. She was watching him, her eyes alight with mischief, knowing perfectly well that she was unique, that her father and the arrangement she appeared to have with him was staggeringly unprecedented in this world of male dominance and female submission to it and her expression challenged him, if he dared, to question it. She laid a hand on each of the dog's fine heads and immediately they turned to lick her fingers, gentle as doves, their eyes worshipping, their bodies straining against her skirt.

'Call to them,' she said to Joss. 'Call them by name.'

'Give over! I don't want me damned hand taken off.' He took a step back, his laughter fading away, his eyes never leaving those of the dogs who had both turned to look at him peaceably.

'Well naturally, if you are afraid.' Her eyes gleamed in the flaunting frame of her gypsy dark hair.

It was a throwing down of the gauntlet, of course, and he was not surprised for this girl was clearly out of the ordinary. Like a boy, she was, a young man daring another to some mad show of courage as he had done many times with his peers in the rough and tumble of play, but this was different. Boys did this, and full grown men sometimes, demonstrating their superiority to one another, recklessly hurling the gage and defying anyone to pick it up. But by God, he'd not be shown up by some slip of a girl, not he! She might turn her bloody dogs on him, with a word or a snap of her fingers, since he was manifestly aware as he looked into her smiling face that she was not to be trusted. She'd win at any cost, her expression told him, but be damned to that, she'd not see him show lack of courage. He *was* afraid since he'd never seen the likes of these animals before, great glowing-eyed beasts who gave the appearance of one moment being prepared to lie down with babes and the next, there was no doubt of it, of tearing a grown man to pieces, and which was it to be with him, he had time to wonder!

'Call them to you, if you are up to it,' she said softly and her eyes smiled, sweet as you please but her teeth showed between her rose pink lips and he saw her hand move slightly in some secret command only the animals knew.

He drew in his breath, acutely conscious in that moment that it was to be of some strange importance to him. A test he must pass. A test *she* was to set him. A bit of a girl she was, nothing more, but Goddammit, she'd not find Joss Greenwood wanting.

'Joby, Blaze, come here. Come here to me,' and he lifted an imperious hand, his manner implying that there was no question that they would not obey him, indicating to the two dogs that they were to lie at his feet.

Instantaneously, as if they were motivated by one mind they moved gracefully across the frozen ground, standing quietly before him. For a second they had glanced at their mistress and again she made some minute hand movement.

'Lie down, both of you. Lie down, I say.' Joss was aware as he gave the command that it had not come from him but at once the great dogs lay down at his feet. He had seen her control them. They had obeyed *her*, held where they were by her training and if she should tell them they would spring up without hesitation and take out his throat.

He knelt down before them, his face but six inches from theirs, hearing her indrawn hiss of breath. Putting out his hands he laid one on each enormous head, holding them firmly, staring with his own eyes into the black depths of theirs, steady as a rock, his will combating theirs. His fear had gone and his voice was quietly commanding.

'Good boys, good old boys. Now stand,' and at once they stood for him. They looked up at him for a moment, their eyes serene as though to say *this time*, then they turned and padded back to stand watchfully beside their young mistress.

She let out her breath on a long sigh and there was genuine pleasure in her eyes. He had pleased her with his fearlessness, he could tell, and she liked to be pleased. Not many would do so for she would be difficult to beguile or impress, her attitude said. She had questioned his male superiority and he had found approval with her and though he could think of no reason why he should care, one way or the other, he found himself to be quite immeasurably satisfied.

'You are the first person beside myself who has handled them,' she told him admiringly.

'There's nowt to it really.' His tone was self-deprecating, making light of his own bravery and his boyishness shone for a moment from the man he had become on St Peter's Field, ' . . . besides, they were watching out for you most of the time.'

'No, not in the least . . . well, perhaps in the beginning but you showed them you had no fear and they respected you for it.' As I do, her shining eyes said.

'Well . . .' He shrugged, grinning amiably, shoving his hands in his pockets. He was awkward now, unused to decent female company beyond that of his mother and sisters. He had known only the light-hearted women who had, in his past, flirted with him, responded to his own masculine banter. He had no aptitude in the art of small talk and he turned away to stare out again over the valley.

'Do you walk this path often?' she asked, settling herself companionably by his side, quite at ease it appeared in his company.

'Oh aye, when I'm on me way to Saddleworth or Dobens.'

'And what do you do there?' Her face was bright with interest.

'Oh . . . well . . .' She had caught him on the wrong foot again and he stumbled over his words for he had no wish, nor entitlement, to tell her of his movements on these hills

34

of the South Pennines and beyond, nor of the men he met there from the dozens of villages which were scattered over the hinterland. They were secrets which were held close by those who were involved in them and certainly not to be shared with this girl. But he must say something, give her some reason why he was walking this path, some believable reason which would satisfy her sharp curiosity. His brain, sharpened by the years he had listened to, and tramped with his father and those others who even now were awaiting trial for their part at St Peter's Field, sprang readily into action. He was as arrogant and as proud of his heritage as this girl was of hers but he must protect his companions in their great venture. They would be gathering now as they had in the past, illegally, on Tandle Hill and Buckland Castle Moor. Meetings had been broken up in the past when the military had opened fire on them but today they were to be but a dozen or so men, those who were leaders and were to march to York for the trial and if they should be discovered they would all go to gaol. 'The Six Acts', the consequence of 'Peterloo', as it had come to be called, made it illegal for any person to attend a meeting and should he do so and be caught, he and those with him were liable to transportation for seven years.

'Well, I don't always go to Dobens or Saddleworth, or any particular place, really.' He smiled winsomely, allaying her suspicions, if she had any, that he might be lying. He was rewarded by the interest in her face. 'It doesn't make any difference as long as you find a decent burrow.'

'Burrow?' Her voice was sharp.

'Aye. A rabbit burrow.'

'What on earth for?'

'Rabbits! What else?'

'But why should you . . .'

'Have you never heard of rabbit pie?'

'Well, of course, but . . .'

His face became hard for a moment since now he was telling the truth and he did not care to be revealing the domestic deficiencies in his own family but he had no choice. He had started the invention, the only one he could think of on the spur of the moment and the fabrication must be brought to its conclusion if she was to believe him.

'We don't get a lot to eat, me and me family. I have a brother and sister no more than babies. Me . . . me Pa died last year and I'm provider now . . . well . . . main one so . . .' His mouth worked, for the mention of his father still had the power to pain him, '. . . if I can bag a hare or a rabbit for the pot we get a bit of meat in our bellies. Of course, Squire don't like it. It's poaching, you see, and he don't take kindly to having his rabbits snared so I'd be obliged if you'd keep it to yourself.' Better to be caught for poaching, though that could be a transportation offence as well with a severe magistrate, than breaking the law in other, more serious misdemeanours, his memory reminded him!

She smiled broadly, leaning closer to him. He caught the delicacy of some fragrance as she did so, something sharp and yet sweet which drifted from her clothing and though he could not recognise it since none of the women of his association could afford to wear perfume, it reminded him of the woods in summer, of the trees and the tangy smell of grass and new leaves.

'I don't think I have ever eaten rabbit. Is it good?'

'Oh aye, with a few taters and an onion. Ma puts a crust on it . . .'

'A crust?'

'Yes, you know, pastry.'

'Pastry?'

He was laughing now for the very idea that here was a girl who seemed not to know what a pastry crust was, who had never heard of nor eaten rabbit pie or hare stew, was quite unbelievable. It was no lie that if he could snare one or the other he would do so, for food was scarce and expensive as prices continued to rocket and wages plummet, but that was not his objective today though she had been made to believe it was and that was all that mattered.

'Dear God, where have you been all these years? Never eaten rabbit or hare and you a Lancashire lass!'

'We have potted hare for luncheon on occasion but I believe it is not to be eaten after the end of February.'

'Is that so!' He was laughing all the more at her quaintness for really food was food and did it matter what the month was to an empty belly. 'And who told you that?'

'My father.'

'Oh aye, and who's he when he's at home?'

'Barker Chapman.'

The ground beneath his feet seemed to sink quite incredibly and he was afraid he would vomit.

Barker Chapman. It was a name which was ever on the lips and in the tortured minds of those he called comrade, a name which was spoken so often by those with whom he associated they felt they knew the man and what he stood for as well as the members of their own families. It represented, more than any other, all the ills of their lives and if the man should ever put himself within the range of their hatred it was doubtful he would survive. And this was his daughter!

He looked into her startled eyes and the revulsion he felt for the name of the man who was her father rose like a bitter tide. He stood up, stretching to his full height and the whiteness of his face and the loathing which flowed from him, must have alarmed not only her, but also the animals. They sensed the sudden change in him and she put out a warning hand to restrain them as they rose slowly, but menacingly, to their feet.

'What is it?' she said, her goodwill dissipating suddenly, the haughty manner of a young woman of the privileged class returning. Her expression said she must surely have forgotten herself for the space of half an hour, forgotten who she was and where she belonged, in the novelty of speaking to this young labouring man, but really, if he was going to act in such an uncouth way, staring and speechless at the mention of her father's name she had best be on her way.

37

She clicked her fingers to the dogs. 'Come Joby, Blaze. It is time to get on. We have lingered far too long already. Good morning to you. It has been most pleasant chatting.' She nodded imperiously in Joss Greenwood's direction and as he watched her, frozen from head to toe in the implacability of his own venom she put on her bonnet, pushed her hair up beneath it and without waiting for an answer began to walk towards the village of Crossfold.

3

Barker Chapman came from a family concerned mainly with banking. A younger son here and there had gone into other businesses, mining, canal building, the constructing of turnpike roads but it was his own father who had been the first to look with interest at the textile trade.

Between 1776 and 1811 there were forty-two cotton mills built in Oldham where the Chapman family lived, the overwhelming majority being put up by men with capital and most had a great deal! James Chapman, son of a banker's son was one. In 1771, Richard Arkwright invented a spinning machine designed to be powered by a horse but quickly adapted to water. It became known as a water frame and he set up his own factory in Cromford, Derbyshire, well away from the troublesome operatives of the Pennine heartland, home of the cotton industry. James Chapman, then thirty years old, was quick to see the potential of such a machine and the means to increase his own already considerable fortune. He built his first cotton spinning mill in Crossfold, a few miles out from Oldham. It was no more than a sleepy hamlet then with two or three cottages, a church and a coaching inn to serve the stage-coaches which passed through from Manchester to Huddersfield.

He brought in whole families from every part of Lancashire, women and children to spin and men to labour, housing them in frail, back-to-back boxes he threw up in a matter of weeks, eight, ten, twelve persons to each, all standing in rows like spokes from a wheel radiating out from his mill and so close together there was scarcely room to walk between them.

He took more trouble with his mill! It was sturdy, six storeys high and the machinery he put in filled every floor. It was set deep in the Penfold Valley, serviced by the plentiful supply of soft, fast-flowing water which tossed and tumbled down the hillside, flooding through the sluices to turn his giant wheel and give power to his machines.

He prospered, he and his son Barker, employing over a hundred persons at Crossbank Mill, as it was called, to spin the yarn which was then 'put out' to hand-loom weavers living and working in their own outlying cottages. Samuel Crompton had devised the 'Spinning Mule', a combination of the old 'Spinning Jenny' which could produce sixteen threads at once and Arkwright's 'water frame' which could spin thirty-eight, and the new machine provided a firm, yet soft, yarn and was capable of operating twice as many spindles as those before it.

James Chapman was one of the first manufacturers to have one in his second mill, built beyond Crossbank and higher up the stream which powered the first and when it was completed he named it Highbank Mill and began to think of not only spinning the yarn but of weaving it as well for he was not a man to put money in another's pocket when it could go just as well into his own. The inhospitable climate of the damp Pennine air which helped the fibres to cling together, reduced the strain placed on them by the new machinery and his production costs fell even lower and his profit grew.

His raw cotton came laboriously from Liverpool by pack-horse on the turnpike roads and by the new canals and was returned by the same method in a 'piece' of completed cloth to Manchester where it was sold.

But James Chapman was never to see weaving-looms in his shed. He died in 1815 and it was his son, an only child, Barker Chapman who built the Chapman weaving-shed on the outskirts of the now bustling township of Crossfold. With the advent of the steam engine and with no need of the water which drove his wheel he could afford to choose a site wherever he pleased and the long tramp his new operatives must take to get to their looms was of no concern to him. He employed in it men who had once worked in their own cottages, and in their own time, weaving a 'piece' as and when they pleased, which did not please *him* and by the end of the year he had forced many of them to give up their independent way of life and become chained, if they wished to feed their families, to his new power-looms. Some chose to remain ungoverned, struggling resolutely for the right to call themselves their own men. They did not care for the factory system, they said proudly, with its harsh discipline, its rules, its fines if they were broken, the peremptory summons of the factory bell and the long hours of labour, as many as seventy or eighty in a week. Mill-master Chapman could afford to let them go their footloose way since he had the vast resources of the unemployed to work his weaving-looms and spinning mules. On this fine day in May when the loveliness of spring was in the air he prepared to set off to the mill to supervise the installation of his latest 'self-acting' spinning mule into his mill at Highbank. It would, without a doubt revolutionise the cotton industry when, set with another in a pair, have in common usage at the same time 2,500 spindles!

Barker Chapman was an impressive man, tall, well built and inclined to overweight, handsome in his youth and living now only to see what he had built carefully placed into hands which would carry on his work, making it grow and prosper as he had, accumulating wealth and prestige for the Chapman name, someone of vision and strength and the dedication to give their life, as he had, to the mills. A son, many sons he had dreamed of in his youth, sons to carry on when he was gone and with this in mind he had married Miss Isobel Townsend, the bonny twenty-year-old daughter of a calico printer from Accrington but in their ten years of marriage he had nothing from her but a string of stillborn infants, one each year until the day she died, delivering to him another.

Not a man to be thwarted he married again. He was forty-three when he took Miss Hannah Baxter, eighteen years old and as healthy and buxom as a farm wench and certain to bear him many fine boys. But it seemed in this one aspect of his life he was to know only disappointment. Nine months after their wedding she gave birth to a girl, as sturdy as he would have wished had she been a boy and encouraged by this sign of his capability to father a living child he and his young wife tried again and again and again until, approaching the age of sixty he faced the appalling truth that he was to have nothing but this one girl child.

Katherine Chapman! Kit! In the far off days of her infancy when Hannah Chapman had been in sole charge of her pretty baby daughter and Barker still had the hope of a son, when she had played with her and nursed her and called the child her 'little kitten', the endearment had seemed appropriate but as she grew it had become shortened to Kit, even by her father. She herself preferred it to Katherine, which in her opinion was formal, whereas Kit spoke of family affection, the fondness of a father for his daughter. She had been disappointed.

On the day he turned his attention to her she was twelve years old, almost as tall as he and quite unremarkable as far as he could determine on the occasions when they met. On this day she was in the garden of Greenacre, walking rapidly across its wide lawn, turning as she came to the high wall which surrounded it in an explosion of movement, then striding back to its furthest corner, her skirts swirling quite indecorously about her ankles. Her bonnet, which should have been on her head was hanging from her hand by its ribbons. Her pace was like that of a man and the little woman who did her best to keep up with her was almost running.

He smiled, amused by the sight which reminded him of a tigress, prowling up and down a cage followed by a small and harmless tabby.

It was Sunday. The mills were closed, for on this day his machines were cleaned and oiled, and he was bored. His wife was resting on her chaise-longue in her pretty sitting-room, at thirty-one years of age so delicate and of such a nervous disposition after several failed pregnancies – her only success the girl he now watched – she considered herself to be an invalid. She was of about as much interest to him as were the domestic arrangements of his home.

On a whim he stepped from the french windows of his study and began to walk in a leisurely fashion down the stone steps which led to the lawn, a cigar held in his right hand, his left pushed into his trouser pocket. The sun was warm, it was April and the massed swathes of wild daffodils which crowded the base of every tree were beginning to fade but the fragrance and beauty of a flowering almond, just coming into bloom made a splendid splash of colour against the grey cobbled wall which surrounded the garden.

His movement attracted his daughter's eye as he saun-tered towards her and though he could see the effort it cost her she stopped politely and the round little woman caught up with her, her breath ragged in her throat, her eyes apprehensive in her high coloured face.

'Good morning, sir,' she said and he wondered who she was.

'Good morning,' he answered, not really caring, for he left all household arrangements to his wife, '. . . and good day to you, Kit. You appear to be in a great hurry. May I ask what you are doing?'

'Exercising.' Her reply was only a fraction short of rude and the woman beside her gasped and began to splutter nervously, evidently afraid that his daughter's forthright manner might offend. It did not and Barker Chapman felt a small bud of interest begin to grow in him. She was as strained as a young dog on a leash, her body taut with some passion, some energy which was clamped within her and

42

he wondered quite idly what it might be. He had felt no passion himself for years, beyond that of his business ventures, and he was quite intrigued by this tall and barely contained child, who was his daughter.

'Exercising?' he questioned smilingly. He had breakfast and sometimes luncheon with her on most days of the week and had held short conversations with her on the subject of her studies and had even perched himself on his wife's drawing-room chair and listened to her play the piano. However, when he thought of it, he had never actually *noticed* her before.

'If you can call it by that name,' she snapped and her eyes flashed vividly in the sun's rays and before he knew what she was about she had reached out and clasped his hands entreatingly with her own.

'Control yourself, Katherine,' her governess, he supposed, beseeched her, looking in his direction in such anguish he thought she might be about to weep, but Kit Chapman took no notice.

'Please, Father . . . please let me leave the garden.' Her whole frame quivered dramatically and Barker Chapman felt a great desire to laugh since melodrama had always amused rather than thrilled him, but she had only just begun.

'Can you not see what you are doing to me? Can you not see how insane I shall become if I am not let out of this prison? Do you not realise what I suffer, day after day, walking up and down, up and down within these four walls with no one but this stupid creature for company?'

The 'stupid creature' gave a small moan of sheer terror since it was clear that her control of this girl was small indeed, and what use was a governess who could not keep order, her manner seemed to ask. Barker Chapman turned to consider her as though he was about to agree then looked back at his daughter who, now that she had captured his attention, freed his hands.

'May I not walk some way on to the moor?' she pleaded with him, doing her best to control what she knew had been a quite foolish outburst. 'I will not go far, *we* will not go far . . .' for even she knew there was not the slightest hope she could go alone, '. . . just up on to the moorland path above the house. I long to . . . to stretch my legs. I will be . . . I won't run, Father' – and he knew she was not to be believed for if ever a girl was made to run it was this one – '. . . or speak to anyone we might meet and Miss Strong will be there to make sure I am . . . circumspect . . . Oh, Father, please allow it, let me leave the garden. I am kept all day at the top of the house in the schoolroom and never allowed beyond its door except to walk in this strip of garden with Miss Strong.' Barker Chapman raised his eyebrows, looking about at the 'strip' of garden which covered the best part of three acres and though she saw the direction of his gaze she went on, 'I know nothing beyond how to sew a seam, and that not very well and the names of the flowers you see about you.' She tossed her head and gave them a shrivelling look and her rebellious hair began to slip and Miss Strong put a hand on her arm, evidently with the idea of drawing her away before her father ordered her to be locked up but she shook it off.

'What *is* over the wall, Father?' she beseeched him passionately.

'You know very well what is there, Kit. I have seen you myself go in the carriage with your mother.'

'Oh, I don't mean that! I mean in this land, in the world, in the . . .'

'You are saying you would like to travel?' He sounded amused.

She turned to him and the radiance of her face blinded him. He had it in his mind to wish at that last moment, when it was still possible to draw back, that his curiosity had not compelled him to step out from his french window and that surely he would live to regret the utter boredom which had led him to it on this fateful Sunday. He had lived for over thirty years with nothing in his life but his passion for his mills and the certain conviction that he would pass them on to his son, as his father had to him. Until the day of his death James Chapman and he had shared this expectation, shared their interest, their home life, their journeying to other parts of the country to find buyers for their cloth and it was not until now, in this first strange meeting with his unknown daughter, did he realise how much he had missed that companionship and shared involvement.

He was sceptical at first. She was a girl, no more than a child but who else was there to inherit what he and his father had built? He could marry her to someone like himself in the textile industry but it would no longer be a Chapman concern for on her marriage she would, with all she inherited become the property of her husband. But he was tempted! By God, he was tempted to let her have her head. Just to see if it could be done! What a stir it would make! He had no doubt at all that she could do it for he discovered over the following months that in her female head was a man's brain, sharp, shrewd and devastatingly quick and in her woman's breast beat the heart of a strong man, filled with courage and the ambition to do more than marry and bear children which was her allotted function in life. She became even more impatient with the restrictions placed upon her by Miss Strong, who, now that Mr Chapman had said they might go out of the ordered security of the garden, was afraid her charge might dirty her gloves, or step in some unimaginable horror or even catch a disease from the often quite rough persons they met on the moorland path just above the house. It did not improve matters when Katherine begged to go further than she had been allowed, to stray from the well-defined path and absorb the haunting fragrance of the heather and see the splendid view she was convinced lay just over the hill, and the freedom her father gave her made her yearn for more.

But not even Kit Chapman knew of the turmoil which she had created in her father's mind. The spring and summer had been the most satisfying she had ever known in her young life and the gratifying interest her father seemed suddenly to take in her had awakened all kinds of longings, unnamed and more than likely, she supposed, to be unful-filled. He had taken to engaging her in conversation, amaz-ingly asking her opinion on many subjects and her own mind, starved and empty, was nurtured by his and she blossomed and grew and though he could not say he loved her, he found he admired her keen, adventurous spirit and even the way she had influenced him.

The dogs decided him. They were a test. One he had devised, God knows why, not only for her but for himself. Take them, he said to her that summer, and make them obey you, make them your protectors against those who would harm you and if you succeed you may go alone to the moor, walk where you please and speak to whom you please for you will have earned the right, as a man earns the right when he becomes a man. It is a risk, but one, if you wish to take it, I will allow. We will make a pact, he told her, watching her soft young face become strong with a beauty and a glow which had nothing to do with her femininity. It will be a pact which we will both honour but first you must let me see your courage, your determination to succeed since these dogs are not for the weak-hearted.

She had done it as he had known she would. She had been twelve when he had begun. She had even then a maturity which had made her an oddity among the young girls which her mother brought to the house and when she begged him, he put a stop to it. The gossip began to bud and grow then but he found he cared nought for it since her future lay not with them and the female lives they would lead but with him and, God help him, in his mills. For the first time in years he felt a surge of excitement.

All that was nearly five years ago, and today, the twenty-eighth of May was her seventeenth birthday and she was to go with him to watch the installation of his new self-acting spinning mule.

She was sensibly dressed as she came down the wide staircase to join him. A plain walking dress in dark green merino since she had been told that the mill floor would be cluttered and dirty. The waist was high and the skirt narrow, the bodice plain and uncluttered with a small, turn-down collar and containing her slipping hair was a small chip bonnet with broad ribbons of the same shade as her gown. Her half-boots were of black kid and her gloves of doeskin and she carried a reticule with a draw-string neck. She was perfectly composed and for a moment he felt a pang of disappointment since he had expected her to be aflame with eager excitement, overawed and trembling with emotion on this incredible day, then she turned to look at him and it was there in her eyes. They were feverish, brilliantly shot with wondrous blue and in them was her deep and ardent gratitude, not love, for it was too late for that between them but an enduring thankfulness which said she would never forget this gift he was about to give her.

His managers and overlookers had been told that Miss Chapman was to visit the mill on this important day and though there was really no need of it — for which among the pale and hollow-chested women spinners and crooked shouldered, bow-legged children who thronged the enormous rooms would dare give offence to their employer's daughter? — they had been warned to be on their best behaviour. They must have a thorough wash before presenting themselves at their 'mules', an insurmountable feat when the water supply in each lane was turned on for half an hour each day, and the smaller children also. Those who worked beneath the machines as 'piecers', twisting together threads which had broken, and as 'scavengers', cleaning up the waste which gathered beneath the mule, were to be made decently presentable.·

It was hot in the big room and though Kit had been prepared for it by her father the furnace-like blast which enveloped her the moment she stepped through the doorway brought an instant slick of sweat to her armpits and collected uncomfortably in the small of her back. She was immediately deafened by the noise and could do no more than walk blindly beside her father, his hand guiding her, standing when he did to talk to the manager of the room. Her eyes and mind could make no sense of what she was

47

experiencing for neither had been subjected to what was about her, but gradually some tiny piece of the scene would take shape and become sharply focused, then another and another until she had the whole.

There were dozens of men, women and children working ceaselessly before the machines they attended. The men were clad only in a shirt with the sleeves rolled up and a pair of thin white drawers to the ankle and were barefoot as were the women since they picked up from the floor, with quite amazing dexterity, the threads and cotton waste, using their toes. The women wore a short skirt to just below the knee and a kind of bodice and all had their hair well tied back for there was always danger that it might catch in the frantic machinery into which they leaned. It was ten-thirty in the morning and all of them, she had been told, had already been at their machines for five hours and would continue industriously for another ten or eleven. The spinners stood in the midst of 400 whirling spindles, every thread of which must be incessantly watched and if one should break a shrill cry would go up for one of the smaller children – *children*, my God, for a ghastly moment she had thought them to be small deformed monkeys – would crawl beneath the horrifying wheels and bands and swift-straps, which would, she was convinced, snatch off a limb during a second's careless inattention, to piece together the broken thread. The spinners moved about constantly from one end of the machine to the other, their bare feet sucked into the slick of oil and waste which coated the floor, walking, her father told her, fifteen to twenty miles in each shift, the exercise doing them enormous benefit he added, for it kept their limbs, which were inclined, as he was sure she would notice, to slight deformities, supple and straight.

There were half a dozen 'tacklers', or overlookers, each bearing a thick leather strap who prowled about the long room so that the operatives were constantly under supervision, on the lookout for any infringement of the rules, which were posted on the walls – despite the fact that none could read – and to ensure that there was no time-wasting.

It was not uncommon for a child who had worked for ten or twelve hours or more, to doze off while in charge of a machine and for their own safety these men were here to keep them awake. They were rough often savage these illiterate labourers coming, as many of them did, from agricultural areas where there was no work to be had and from Ireland where it was known insolence abounded. They must all be kept under strict control. They could be violent and had been in the past, rioting and even breaking their own machines which they were convinced would put them out of work, her father said, so low was their intellect! Over all mill-masters hung the spectre of 'General Ludd' and the ordinary folk he had incited until they became a rabble, ripe for revolution and destruction.

But these spinners seemed to have no such thought in their heads as they bent unflaggingly over their machines. The women bobbed an awkward curtsey as she paused to watch their nimble fingers move but they did not stop since it was of the greatest importance, not only to them who were paid for the yardage they spun, but to their master, to keep the spindles turning and the yarn spinning no matter what! A young bobbin-carrier, no more than five or six years old, ran past her at such speed she was afraid he would slip in the oil, taking the roving-bobbins to the mule and bringing away the bobbins of spun yarn, but he did not lift his eyes to look at her. She might have been a fairy princess – if he knew of such a being – or the Squire's lady from Crossfold, it was all the same to him. The overseer's strap awaited him if his slowness caused some holdup in the changing over of the bobbins.

'We will go to Broadbank later in the week, Katherine,' she heard her father shout in her ear, 'to see the weaving-sheds but for now I think a rest in my office,' and she smiled in agreement for really half an hour in this heat and noise and the sudden difficulty she found she had in breathing, were quite enough for one day. She would grow used to it; she knew she would for she must learn all the operations in the spinning and weaving of her father's cotton. But her main purpose was in the office of the mill where the business, the *heart* of the concern, was carried out.

They were seated several minutes later in her father's pleasant office, far away from the noise of the spinning rooms, drinking the coffee which had appeared from somewhere, brought by a clean little woman with respectfully downcast eyes. The room was large, wood-panelled and thickly-carpeted. A fire burned brightly in the hearth. The windows were closed and for a few moments the noise from beyond them did not impinge on their absorbed contemplation of a piece of velveteen which had just been sent over from Broadbank for the master's consideration. Her father was explaining the merits of the cloth, his eyes bright with unexpected pleasure since her fascinated attention gave him a forgotten satisfaction, when the commotion became more insistent and he raised his head to listen.

'It's the new machine arriving,' he said, and he stood up eagerly, surprised by his own enthusiasm and she stood with him, ready to go where he did, wherever that might be, to welcome this incredible innovation which was to make *their* mills the wonder of Lancashire, but he began to frown, moving hurriedly towards the window overlooking the mill yard and she went with him. There were men below, hundreds of them, it seemed to her, none of them with any particular purpose since they milled about like cattle at a market, all going in different directions, getting in one another's way, jostling and pushing and shouting, raising clenched fists and, she could see it now, *fighting*. In the middle of it all on a sturdy waggon pulled by four huge horses was her father's new self-acting spinning machine. Men, strong rough men, with cloth caps and mufflers and all wearing masks on their faces began to converge on the waggon, held back at first by Barker Chapman's labourers, who had come to unload the machine and place it where the engineer directed them but the interlopers were hazardous in their intention, grim faced and dangerous and when they raised their huge iron hammers, not caring it seemed, whether they fell on man or machine, Barker Chapman's men moved back and stood quietly at the side of the yard since they did not care to be injured in a fight which was not theirs.

There had been reports of rioting in many places during the last two years, of mills and warehouses having their windows broken, of bales of cotton set alight. There was talk of the resurrection of General Ludd, for the gang was organised now and led by a man of control, no longer the shouting, undisciplined mob of rabble-rousers who had once destroyed the machinery which had put out of work the very ones they had pledged to support. It had become an underground revolutionary movement led by masked men. They left alone, as the Luddites had done, the spinning frames and weaving-looms of simple hardworking cottagers and even one or two of the mill-owners, those whose operatives worked in decent conditions and who were paid fair wages. And wherever they went, it was rumoured, they collected money for men who had been thrown out of work and for families who were starving. From Colne down to Oldham they marched and they had begun to be called by a name that was spreading wherever men and women were engaged in spinning and weaving. 'The Onwardsmen' were spoken of reverently, hopefully. From Lancashire, where it had first been whispered, as far north as Glasgow, down to Lincolnshire and Nottinghamshire and south to Somerset, the name, and the men who had coined it, was on the lips of men driven to despair by their inability to earn a decent life for themselves and their families.

Petitions to Parliament asking that a minimum price be fixed below which the manufacturers could not go had been ignored. They had, in desperation, struck work to enforce better wages and even, not knowing of any other way to stop the looms of the mill-masters which had stolen *their* living, taken away the shuttles of those who continued to work in a Rochdale mill but the men involved in the insurrection had been arrested and imprisoned.

Now, it seemed, it was Barker Chapman's turn!

'Father . . .' Kit's voice was but a whisper in the sudden hush but her eyes were on fire with anger. 'Father . . .' Her voice was stronger now, '. . . they mean to break the machine . . .'

'They do, Kit.'

'But are we to let them?' His daughter was surprised by Barker Chapman's acceptance of the destruction.

'How are we to stop them? It seems the men I employ are unwilling to fight and if I was to send for the militia by the time they got here from Oldham it would be too late.'

'There must be men who will stand by us.'

'Look at them. They are in the yard.'

The hammers clanged against the metal of the machine and the men who wielded them, strangely quiet and composed, did not waste a blow and Kit Chapman felt each one as though it fell on her own flesh as she watched helplessly beside her father while they destroyed what was not theirs. She hated them for it and if she could have called down a charge of cavalrymen to slash them to pieces with their sabres she would have done so. If she had a rifle she would have shot each one and should the militiamen come on the scene and arrest each and every one she would have gone gladly to see them hanged. They were not only smashing this splendid machine which belonged to her father and therefore to *her*, but despoiling this day which was to have been the beginning, the foundation on which her life would be built. This was *her* world, to be handed over to her she knew, though he had not yet said so, by her father when the time came and they would not do this to her and what was hers.

They would not!

Her feet skimmed the stairs as if she had wings in her heels and her father's warning fell on deaf ears. Her skirt was held high to her knees showing an immodest amount of her leg as she burst from the doorway into the yard and for the space of fifteen seconds they stared in amazement, their hammers poised above their heads. Her hair had, naturally, come down, for unless she sat perfectly still or wore a bonnet it always did. Thus she gave the appearance of some wild, woodland creature in her forest green dress and swirling cape of midnight dark hair. The men did not wish to continue while she screamed some gypsy curse at them for surely, if they did, they would be damned.

'Get away from that machine. All of you. Stand back, I say or I shall call the militia and have you all arrested. Stand away at once and drop your weapons. Do you not know this is a hanging offence, you fools? Now stand away, I say. Go back to your homes and I will say no more about it. But let just one of you touch that machine again and I swear he will live to regret it for the rest of his life which, let me assure you, will be short or spent on the far side of the world in the Australias. I mean what I say. Drop those hammers and be off with you.'

If it had not been for him they might have fallen back, so fierce was her anger, so great her determination, so strong her will. Her nostrils flared and her mouth opened wide on her screams of outrage and her eyes flashed vivid blue sparks at them. One or two, Irish and superstitious, crossed themselves hastily but the one who led them came forward and stood in her path. His face was masked but his eyes were visible and they were scornful, amused, for she was no more than a bit of a girl, the expression in them said. She should be at home with her mother and not interfering in *men's* work.

'Get on with it, lads. It's only Chapman's lass in a tantrum and nothing to us.' He reduced her with those words to a spoiled child who was making a fool of herself.

'Get out of my way,' she hissed, raising her hand to strike this impudent lout who had the effrontery not only to address her in front of these other louts but to make mock of her, of her father's name, but he caught her wrists and held them, laughing, not displeased she could tell, to show the others there was nothing to fear here.

'Smash it up, lads. We'll show him how we deal with men who lower other men's wages so that they cannot even eat. Men cannot live on six shillings a week, and *by God* they *will* not. He takes the bread out of the mouths of our children with his greed but he'll not do it with this machine.'

They broke it up before her eyes and she could have wept for she had loved, if not the machine, the idea of what it meant to her, the symbol of what it stood for in the start of her new life. But the tall and slender young man stared audaciously into her face and she would give no one, least of all this hated intruder, the satisfaction of seeing her humiliation.

'I shall not forget this,' she said to him softly.

'Will you not, Miss Chapman? I certainly hope not. And do not think to frighten us with your threats. We are fighting a just cause, my men and I, and we will win. We are no rabble, but soldiers. Yesterday some of our comrades, Hunt and Johnson, Bamford and Healey were sentenced to long terms of imprisonment merely for meeting and attempting to talk to others who think as they do. That is all, Miss Chapman. Not for thieving or violence, but for talking. So we are done with talking, my men and I. We are to fight now. We are to fight men like your father who are murdering other men, murdering women and *children* in the name of progress. This machine is the first, but tell your father and other men like him that it will not be the last.'

His green eyes gleamed through the slits of his mask, fiercely contemptuous and in some curious way they were familiar to her, as though she had seen them before though she could not have said where. They were as clear and deep as the water which cascaded over the moss into the pool at Sherbrook Falls, but wild, challenging, dangerous.

'I know you,' she said, narrowing her eyes speculatively.

'Do you indeed, Miss Chapman? Perhaps we met at a ball in the Assembly Rooms in Oldham . . .' The men at his back laughed delightedly, '. . . or was it at a dinner party given by one of your father's manufacturing acquaintances?'

'I know you,' she repeated softly, ignoring his men's derision. 'I don't know how but believe me I shall remember and when I do you will regret it. I shall hound you and your . . . your rabble until I see you all hang.'

He laughed and she felt her skin prickle. He was no more than nineteen or twenty but he was evidently held in some respect by these men, many of them older than he. For when he had done he drew them up in formation, called over a roll, each man answering not to his name but to a number, then giving a great shout of triumph they marched off in regular military order with him at the head. And because she was but seventeen, still a child in many ways, as she climbed the stairs to her father's office she hung her head in her curtain of hair and wept.

4

They had not gone at once to their homes, his men and himself, for they were still intoxicated with their own success and the ease with which they had achieved it. When they were out of the town and away from the enthusiastic cheers and applause of the labouring poor who lined the streets to see them go, they could not resist all talking at once, laughing and jostling one another like boys let out of Sunday school; all attempt at column and file, which they had drilled, vanishing with their exuberance.

'They'll not find it so easy to displace our womenfolk now, eh Joss? My Janet's spinning wheel's been still these past three years but by God, without this new machine there's bound to be "putting out" again . . .'

'Aye, he'll not manage wi'out . . .'

'. . . our women'll get a look in, 'appen . . .'

'. . . us'll beat 'em now, yer reckon, Joss . . .?'

'. . . 'appen 'e'll think twice about takin' over this valley with his blasted machinery . . .'

'. . . a few more knocks like this 'un an' we'll all be our own maisters again, what d'yer say, Joss . . .?'

'. . . an' just let 'im try bringin' in power driven looms an' it'll be't same fate for them as 'appened with this 'un . . .'

They had climbed the rough track up to the 'Five Pigeons', an inn which was set on the junction of the Lancashire and Yorkshire roads, deep in the moorland. Surely they deserved a celebration, they said to one another and the landlady was a known sympathiser with their cause. Many of her customers worked in the factories in Oldham and along the Penfold Valley and though they had barely enough to feed their children, once in a while they had the few pence for ale and the talk, which went with it, of the good times to come Joss Greenwood had promised them with a fierceness they could not help but believe.

It did not seem in any way unusual to these men, some of whom nearly ten years ago had marched with 'General Ludd' ready to smash and burn, not only in Lancashire but over the Pennines and into Yorkshire in their fight to keep what they cherished, to turn now to Joss Greenwood as their natural leader. It appeared to them as they marched shoulder to shoulder with him, their pale faces flushed with triumph, their narrow backs stiff with pride that the father lived on in a more full-blooded, more *satisfactory* way in the son. They had loved the father, believed in every word he told them, every benefit he had promised them but it had occurred to many as they had stood to listen to him, how much more gratifying it would be actually to *do* something! Most had walked with him to St Peter's Field and not a few had been injured, or even killed and now they were on the move again, done with accepting their lot and merely waiting passively for it to better itself. Joss Greenwood, in these last two years had welded them together with one purpose and whether it be wrong, or even foolish as some were saying, by God it felt good to be

56

in action at last. They were exploited, they knew that, by this new breed of manufacturer, and their women and children more so than they themselves and the injustice of it could scarce be borne. Today had put a stiffener in their spine and if Joss Greenwood, who was the son of the great man himself said it was the only way, then that was good enough for them.

All the men who marched that day had once laboured only for themselves, in a small way, of course, working their plot of land and selling at the weekly market the piece of cloth woven that week, the woman at her spinning wheel, the man, the 'aristocrat' of his trade, at his hand-loom and their children helping in all the processes of cloth making. They had the freedom to decide on the rhythm of their own lives and they were prosperous in their own class.

But the burst of mechanical inventions which had usurped the domestic spinning wheel and the cottage hand-loom had taken their old ways from them and they simply could not understand why they were thrown into such turmoil. Once their families had earned thirty shillings a week and sometimes, when a weaver was involved, as much as fifty and why could they not go on as they had done, they and their fathers and grandfathers before them, they asked? Was there not enough to go round, they asked? But the answer, it seemed, was no for the mill-masters took it all, the spinning and the weaving and all the processes before and after. Unless the women and children, who were quick and nimble and compliant and could be paid less than a man, or any of the men who were prepared to do as they were told, came to work for *them*, they could starve to death in a ditch for all the mill-masters cared. They went, the women taking the children they could not see starve, and so the 'factory', a word which had until the previous century never before been heard of, was begun.

But the men, those who would rather starve than work for another, and those women unmarried and without children, were another matter entirely. Were they not free-born Englishmen, and as such, unable to abide the idea of slavery? For whichever way you looked at it that was what it was. They were not prepared, by God, should the mill-owners have been willing to employ them, which they were not, to work locked up for sixteen hours a day, summer and winter, in a heat of over ninety degrees. It was well known that a man could be heavily fined for sending out for a drink of water, needed in the heat in which he was forced to work, for opening a window, or even for the simple act of whistling, unlikely in the circumstances, as he went about his employment! No, parliamentary reform was called for or, if they were not listened to, a revolution such as had broken out in France. They wanted nothing more, they said, than sufficient money to live decently. They did not enquire too deeply into why they could not earn a living, for politics and the pressures which were arising due to the new 'industrialisation' were beyond their understanding. They had Tom Paine's *Rights of Man* read out to them and societies began to spring up on both sides of the Pennines, for the woolworkers of Halifax and Bradford were in the same sorry state as themselves. Luddism was born and men were executed in its name and political unions were formed and the unrest reached its climax in August 1819 with the massacre which was to be called Peterloo. The 'Six Acts' forbidding such foolishness as had been displayed there were rushed through Parliament and the radical agitation, for the most part, subsided.

But Joss Greenwood and others of like mind fought on. Their women, those who worked for Barker Chapman since children must be fed, were all pale and hollow-chested and prone to complaints of the lung due to the cotton dust they breathed for sixteen hours a day. They were undernourished. They were round-shouldered and had bad teeth caused by sucking the weft up in the shuttle and the surprising fact that they bore a child each year, scarcely stepping from their machines to do so, was due not to their husband's love and desire but because the act of copulation was the only moment of pleasure left to them which cost nothing.

Their children who, from the age of four or five worked

beside them grew hardly at all from their introduction into full time employment, remaining stunted and dwarf-like, their limbs crooked, their joints swollen and deformed through constant kneeling and scrabbling beneath the frames. It was required that they be small, the smaller the better since the space beneath the machines would not allow for a normal, healthy, full-grown child above the age of six or seven and yet they were required to be alert, lively even, for only a child who remained awake, remained alive and uninjured. The mill-owners could not be blamed for it, they said, for did they not employ overlookers to avoid such a catastrophe and if they should need to beat a child, or to kick it even, was that not better than to lose an arm, an eye or even a life?

But working beside the local children were the 'parish' children, brought from all over the country in cartloads and 'apprenticed' as labourers in the cotton mills. No one cared much if an unguarded machine tore off a finger or an arm from one of these children nor if they slept in an exhausted tumble of tormented bodies on a pile of waste in some corner nor if they were fed on a diet of water porridge and oatcake day in and day out. It was of concern to no one that they had a bare ten minutes in the middle of the day to eat it, to relieve themselves, nor in fact whether they lived at all for there was a constant supply from parishes who were glad to be rid, not only of them but of the expense of keeping them. The 'Peel Act' of 1802, the first of the 'factory' acts, limited the working of pauper children to twelve hours a day, later extended to *all* children under the age of sixteen, had done little to assuage the lot of those children for the passing of an act means little when there is no way to enforce it. They cleaned the machinery on Sunday, their day of 'rest' and these infants (for what else were they?) became crippled in body and mind. Nevertheless, as the mill-masters told one another complacently, whenever the subject arose, what greater benefit could society bestow on the poor than to provide them with employment? They were kept from vice and degradation and became useful members of the community in their industry and what could any man ask but that? The factory wages were sufficient, they assured one another, to sustain a thrifty family and though with the passing of the Corn Bill the price of bread was high, causing riots in past years, their own profits were growing and trade had never been better, a matter for self-congratulation, they considered.

Joss had kept his hand-loom working though when he looked back over the two years since his father had died he often wondered how it had been done. Without Jenny, his sister, it would *not* have been done. He had taken his father's pack-pony, tramping miles to the Cotton Exchange in Manchester when he could not get supplies from the merchants of the raw cotton he needed for his mother to spin. He and Jenny worked the two hand-looms, weaving a small piece of cloth each but the work was heavy, a man's work and not meant for a lass of sixteen. Two pieces of cloth, perhaps of no more than thirty yards, would earn him ten shillings and still wages continued to plummet. He worked the smallholding, he and Jenny, cleaned and carded the raw cotton before the spinning and weaving and they did not starve though they came damn near it a time or two.

And at the end of the day he and the Onwardsmen would tramp the moorland, moving unerringly through nights which were thick and dark, drilling their force whenever there was light to see by, into a small but efficient body of soldiers. The soft dash of falling water was in their ears and the soft murmur of men's voices, men they met from other districts who were as swift as they in their retribution against the manufacturers.

He would slip home in the dawn, his tread as light and graceful as his mother's tabby. He could barely see a foot ahead of him when the clouds hid the moon and the stars but he knew every swell and fold, every rock and track and dark tree. The moorland heights were as familiar to him as his mother's kitchen and the men he talked to and planned with were as treasured by him as the members of his own family. They kept the bright flame of his father's memory alive and fed the hatred with which he burned for those who had killed him.

Yes, they said, trade was good, those who were involved with reaping the benefit of it and profits were growing. Oh indeed, and this was the only fact with which the men who followed young Joss Greenwood were in agreement as they sipped the glass of ale they could ill-afford in the tap-room of the 'Five Pigeons'. The air in the room was smoky from the guttering fire and the flames of the candles which were its only light. There were men crowded on settles and leaning against walls, their eyes ablaze with excitement for the whole district knew what had been achieved this day.

'What 'appened? Did you break the machine? Was there any trouble?' their genial landlady begged to know and their tongues ran away with them as they vied with one another to tell her.

'It went like clockwork, Abby,' Tom Butterworth's voice was high with the thrill of it. 'We marched in formation just like Joss showed us, right up to yon mill gates an't machine were there, standing in't middle o't yard . . .'

'Were there no soldiers?'

'Not a one! Well, them what were there to lift it from't waggon were that 'mazed to see us they just stood there gawpin' and we were in and up on it afore you could say knife. They started to jostle us a bit, well, they had to make a show of it, 'adn't they, even if they did agree wi' us on the quiet but it was no contest until . . .' Tom's face assumed an uncertain expression and Abby leaned over the bar counter towards him.

'Until what, lad?'

'Well, there was this lass . . .'

'What lass?'

He turned then to Joss, pulling a comical face. They had talked about Chapman's lass on the way to the inn, the other men and himself, and the remarkable way she had acted, speculating on why she and not her father, as they had expected, had been there in an attempt to defend, or

61

at least protest at the breaking of his expensive machine. The other men had been contemptuous saying they would allow no lass of theirs to act in such an unwomanly fashion and her only sixteen or so. What kind of man was Barker Chapman, they questioned, who could be so brutally hard on those he employed in his mill and yet let a slip of a girl speak for him in a yard filled with rough men? They could find no answer and it appeared Joss Greenwood, who had inherited his father's eloquence and could always find words on other occasions, had none to spare now.

'You tell her, Joss.'

'Nay, it's not important.'

'But she might have stopped us. You saw how she was.'

'Never! A spoiled bairn, that's all she was.'

'Come on, Joss, be honest. She had a . . . a way with 'er.'

'Are you saying she would have prevented you from doing what you had gone there to do, Tom Butterworth?' Joss Greenwood's voice was dangerously low and the men about him quietened, looking at him in wonderment for it seemed he was filled with some strange tension they could not understand. They had fulfilled their mission, had they not and returned safe and sound and proud of themselves as they had every right to be since they had done well. Tom Butterworth was only sixteen but he had proved himself a man today. They were all men in their championship of the downtrodden labouring classes who fought, not only to keep alive but to keep their dignity in employment but they were conscious that Joss was impatient with this talk of some girl who had been part of their day and Abby Hobson, being a woman, could not let it pass.

'Who was she, Joss?'

'Chapman's lass,' he answered shortly, and that's the end of it, his attitude said but she elected not to notice.

'Barker Chapman's daughter!' Her voice was incredulous. 'At t'mill?'

'Aye.' Joss turned from her irritably. The only flaw in the perfection of the day had been the way in which Katherine Chapman had almost turned away the will of the men, *his* men, from the job they had come to do. They had stopped what they were about, ready to drop their hammers at the voice of authority, ready to stand back, he was inclined to believe if he was honest, and doff their caps to the master's daughter so ingrained was their habit of obedience to those who were considered to be above them. If he had not overridden her will with his own, if he had not humiliated her, reduced her to her proper place in the eyes of his men she might have done it, but he was not prepared to say so, for if he should how was he ever to lead these men who followed him as they had followed his father?

'But what was she doing there?'

'How the hell do I know? Making a fool of hersen, I'd say.'

'But what did she . . .?'

'Oh give over, Abby. She was nowt. Nowt! The job's done and we've shown 'em what we're made of and that's all that counts. We mean business and no bloody machine is going to stop us. These new machines threaten our livelihood, we all know that. Look at the miles me an' Enoch have to tramp for raw cotton. Once over the merchants used to bring it to us, begging us to spin it and weave it for 'em. Maybe those days will never come back, Abby. Maybe we'll have to accept the factory system but by God, things will have to be different. We'll have us a decent wage, and conditions, or we'll not work and the only way to let the owners see how serious we are is by serious methods. That's what it's all about, lass. We've to fight, you know that, don't you? We all do, and nothing and *no one* is going to stop us.'

'Aye, tha's right, Joss.'

'Buggers'll 'ave us all under . . .'

'We'll not be stopped . . .'

'Us'll show 'em . . .'

There was jubilation among the younger men, their hot blood deeply satisfied by what they had done, and by Joss's words. The older men smiled, tolerant of them. They had been in the fight for twenty years and more, some of them and had seen many failures but today's success made it all worthwhile.

There was more deliberation on the splendid outcome of the day and of those to come which Joss and his Onwardsmen were planning. They were at ease, the tension, exhilarating as it had been, replaced by relaxed companionship. They were surrounded by the brotherhood of men who were as deeply involved as they and who, if put to the torture would never give them away. It was a moving moment, almost mystical in its significance for now they were no longer rioters, a mob, but a core of hardened fighters, drilled and led by Joss Greenwood into a small army of hit and run soldiers. The moorland was wild and a man could get lost on the desolate stony tracks, the vast outcrop of rocks which could hide a whole battalion, and hostile to those who did not know it. They were safe up here, safe from the militiamen and the troops which had been brought to subdue them and the small inn could scarce contain the triumph of the men it held. They were charged with it, flushed with it and Tom Butterworth who was but a boy and unused to the drink, which was forbidden in his father's Methodist house, could not control his wandering feet nor place them to move in the direction of the path, which led down to Edgeclough. He was a tall lad and, though slender, was heavy-boned. Hard as Joss tried to lift him when the time came for them to leave, Tom slipped through his hands like mist.

'Put 'im on t'settle,' Abby told Joss amiably, her warm, experienced eye studying Joss's tall, graceful body as he struggled, laughing, to contain Tom Butterworth's harmless befuddlement. 'Let t'lad sleep it off there. 'E'll come to no 'arm.'

Her voice was husky and her hand on Joss's arm was warm with a meaning no man could mistake. She had liked the broad sweep of Joss Greenwood's shoulders and the slim length of his waist and hips and legs ever since he had first come up to her inn and her eyes told him so now. His skin was flushed and in the warmth of the tap room he had opened his shirt neck to reveal the brown hollow of his throat and the fine mat of dark hair which led down from it. Abby was a bonny woman, a widow of thirty-three or -four, with a deep breast and fine curved hips, ample and womanly. When Joss turned to her after laying Tom on the settle she was waiting for him, her own buttons were undone to reveal the creamy whiteness of her breasts and Joss sank into them with a murmur of pleasure.

Joss was nowhere to be seen when Tom awoke in the soft dawn, his body cramped from the hours he had spent on the wooden settle. His head ached and his mouth was like the gritty cavity which cut the granite on the moorland. He decided he'd best be off since his father would be waiting for him with his Bible under his arm and a sermon on his lips. He couldn't escape it. He put his head under the pump in the yard, hoping to clear it somewhat for he could remember little of what happened last night or how he came to be on Abby Hobson's settle. Where was Joss, he wondered?

He was quiet as he let himself into the cottage in which he lived with his father and sister. The soldiers who were waiting for him, and anyone else they could lay their hands on in the villages along the length of the Penfold Valley, were disappointed when they trapped only one unsuspecting and confused young lad since they had hoped for the whole gang but he was better than nothing.

He did not see them immediately. His head hurt and his stomach was uneasy and he was thinking of nothing but the comfort of his own bed this Sunday morning and some peace from his father who would be bound to speak, if he learned of it, of the dire sin of drunkenness. The soldiers had hidden themselves in the tall bracken beyond the wall of the laithe house, only one remaining in Enoch Butterworth's kitchen and though at the last minute Tom's sister, Mercy, had shouted a warning despite the brawny arms which clutched her about the neck and shoulders, her young brother walked dazedly into the trap which had been set him. In each of the half dozen cottages which formed the tiny hamlet of Edgeclough a soldier had been posted for it was well known these outlaws hung together and if they were not prevented a villager would be sent to warn them.

Mercy Butterworth wept as her brother was knocked senseless to the floor of her kitchen. She was ready to dart to his assistance but she was held back by the grinning soldier who had her in his grip.

'Fetch the rest of the troop from the cottages, Private,' the Sergeant who entered the kitchen barked. 'I'll watch the lad and the woman. This is all we're to get 'ere, it seems.'

Tom Butterworth was dragged semi-conscious to the door of the cottage. The Sergeant was of the opinion that it did no harm to let the rest of this disorderly rabble of women and children and old men with their lunatic ideas of equality see what would happen to them if they should step out of line as this one apparently had. It would be the penal colony for him, or a couple of years' hard labour, no doubt and if an example was made of him perhaps the rest would toe the line. It gave him a great deal of satisfaction to have netted this one since, to the best of his knowledge not one of the 'reformers' as they liked to call themselves, had ever been caught so great was the conspiracy of total silence among those who supported them. This lad was young and inexperienced, coming in as he had from some obvious overnight wrongdoing but it would be his last fling for the time being, the magistrate would see to that. The spirit of the Luddites lingered on, as the Sergeant well knew for he himself had been involved in taking some of those who had murdered William Horsfall, a hated mill-owner from Huddersfield. He had seen some of them hanged at York gaol, the rest transported, but still the legends of their heroism, as *they* called it, lived on in the songs and stories and secrets of the Luddites themselves. They had been proud men and proud of their involvement in the underground movement which had begun this unrest in the lower classes, but there was one less now to carry on the tradition.

Tom Butterworth's head was ringing from the blow it

66

had taken and for several minutes he allowed himself to be shoved here and there by the jubilant soldiers. He was aware of a noise somewhere, a woman whimpering and the laughter of men. They had not yet put the manacles on him though he could see through the blood which ran down his face a grinning soldier approaching with them dangling from one hand. He felt quite, quite paralysed, numbed with the sudden horror of what was happening and already he was blindly holding out his hands, prepared to let them lead him away to wherever it was he must go. But the woman — who was it? — had begun to moan in terror and her voice was familiar and he turned in confusion and the blood which dripped from his brow ran hot and mad with outrage. They had Mercy, the soldiers, one holding her arms, the other leering at her uncovered breasts. He had her nipple between his thumb and forefinger and as Tom watched in horror they began to drag her towards the back of the cottage. He looked about him in anguish for the Sergeant, instinct telling him which man to seek for help but he was nowhere in sight.

He screamed then and sprang forward and even before any of those who were watching the 'bit of sport', the soldier was dead, his neck snapped cleanly by the strong right arm of Tom Butterworth.

5

Tom Butterworth, just two days short of his seventeenth birthday, was hanged at Lancaster gaol on the twenty-first of July, 1821, for the murder of a soldier.

Though she had sworn to those who had wrecked her father's spinning machine that she would not only see them all hang but would rejoice in it, Katherine Chapman found the day extremely trying to get through. She and her father breakfasted together as usual, served by the same self-effacing maidservants who waited at table every day, but from the moment she walked into the morning room, the door held open for her by the head parlourmaid, she had sensed the tension which charged the atmosphere. There was no apparent change she could put her finger on. Ellen bobbed her usual curtsey and wished her good-morning and Betty and Flora stood ready to offer her collared or potted meats, cold game, poultry or veal and ham pie. There was whiting or herring, if she wished for something hot, broiled sheep's kidneys, sausages, bacon and poached eggs, omelets, toast and muffins, and marmalade and fruit preserve. There were freshly gathered flowers arranged on the table and sideboard, and fat, red strawberries from her father's garden, piled in a luscious tumbling heap on a silver serving dish.

The sun shone in a golden stream of floating dust motes on the shining breakfast table, laying a path across the thick, flower-patterned carpet and she walked along its length to her chair beside her father.

He smiled, not warmly for that was not his nature, but in the pleasantly friendly fashion which had grown between them in the past five years. It was a smile a gentleman will bestow on a lady of whom he approves, not perhaps a lady with whom he is on more than a nodding acquaintanceship, but one he respects and admires. He stood as she approached and asked her how she did on this hot and sultry morning for though it was barely five o'clock the temperature was already rising above sixty degrees. He enquired politely, as he resumed his seat, if she had slept well. As she replied that she had, helping herself to a small piece of whiting from the dish Ellen held out to her, he congratulated himself on the decision he had made five years ago to take her into the business. Though she was a female, his daughter, he had, in all respects given her the rights a man would automatically pass on to a son, and what a success it had turned out!

68

As he had expected, there had been talk and his wife had sworn that they would be ostracised, cut off from polite society since who amongst it would entertain a woman, a girl yet, but soon to be a woman, who was to mix daily with the riff-raff whom he employed! No . . . no . . . she would not agree that the men and women in his mills had more respect than to dare address her daughter for she had herself seen them from her carriage in the streets of Crossfold, the women huddled in shawls with sullen faces peering balefully from beneath thin and dusty hair, the men grim-faced and grey and watching her most perilously. And the overlookers were as bad. Though they were forced to keep a civil tongue in their heads in the presence of their master she had seen the way, when they thought themselves to be unobserved, the way their eyes slid about . . . well, they were not respectful . . . not at all! And her friends, the wives of the bankers and solicitors, of professional men and of other mill-owners would not care to be in the company of a lady, *their* daughter, who must, in the course of the day, put herself forward in a most unladylike manner as she addressed those uncouth persons at the mills.

'She *is* my daughter, as you say, and as such wherever I am received so will she.' Barker Chapman's voice was thin and dry. 'I do business with these men, my dear, and it is to their advantage to know which side their bread is buttered. She is not the only woman to go into business and still be considered a lady. These are modern times, Hannah. The commercial world is expanding rapidly and with it, our outlook on the proprieties is changing. Katherine will conduct herself properly at all times, I can vouch for that and there will be no scandal. She is the most level-headed woman, yes, *woman* despite her youth . . . in fact I will go further and say the most level-headed *person* I have come across in business and I assure you she will cause no gossip. She is too . . . determined to succeed to risk it. She will go about with me and believe me, there will be no talk, not in my hearing.'

'But behind your back, Barker. What of the gossip?'

'They will get over it, Hannah. They will become accustomed to it. They will be forced to if they wish to do business with me.'

She could run it almost as well as himself. Though he had jibbed at taking her into the spinning and weaving sheds at first, she had insisted that unless she learned at least by what means the machines worked and the way in which the operatives *operated* them, how was she to take over the running of the business when the time came.

'Did you take off your coat and roll up your sleeves when you were learning, Father?' she asked impishly.

'Good Heavens, my dear, hardly! I leave that to my engineers.'

'Well then, may I not do what you did which I believe you are telling me was to watch and be instructed by others who *do* such things.'

She could tell a fustian from a velveteen and how each was woven and where the markets were for the finished cloth and like himself and his father before him could shrewdly make one penny do the work of two and, moreover, could pare down production costs until she made a profit of *two* pennies where before there had been only one! She proved to be an able scholar and he was growing confident that when he was gone his mills, under her guidance, would continue to flourish. She still had much to learn in experience and the snatching of opportunities when they arose but she had the best head on her shoulders – Chapman shoulders – since the death of her grandfather. Though she had not had the benefit of a good education, as a son would have, it seemed not to have reduced her capacity to use her brain, quick and lightning sharp, as he himself did. She had no objection to rising at five in the morning in order to be at the mill as the gates opened, nor to working far into the night when necessity demanded and her ability to hold her own in the often sharp practices which were the custom among manufacturers did not go

70

unnoticed by his rivals. She had nerve and was not afraid to speak out if she disagreed with some action he took, but at the same time she was always willing to admit a mistake.

There had been but one truly difficult moment and that had been on the first occasion he had taken her into the Cloth Hall at Crossfold, that innermost and absolutely male sanctum of the cotton industry. They had been met by an appalled silence which had lasted for the space of five long minutes, broken only by the polite greetings Barker addressed to his business acquaintances. They had not exactly turned their backs on her, Barker had far too much influence for them to dare to do that, but their faces were stiff and cold and their voices, when they found them, icy. But Kit Chapman seemed to know instinctively how to conduct herself, keeping well in her father's shadow, speaking only when spoken to and as the weeks went by and they became accustomed to her she was accepted and the day came when it was as though she had always been one of them. She was as wily as her father and grandfather they grudgingly told one another, and they admired her for it since it was the highest praise one businessman could apply to another in these parts.

'Will you read *The Times*, my dear?' he asked her courteously.

'Thank you, Father, no.'

'It seems the Coronation was a splendid affair. Our new King is apparently exceedingly fond of show and pomp and determined his own crowning should outshine anything in history.'

'Indeed.'

'Would you not have liked to be there, Katherine?'

'No, Father. Such things do not greatly interest me.'

'It says here that the Queen looked very fine . . .'

'Really.'

Barker Chapman sighed and folding the newspaper neatly to the precise pattern into which it had been ironed that morning by his housekeeper, placed it beside his plate.

He sat back in his chair and regarded his daughter thoughtfully as she picked at the fish on her plate. She had matured in the last twelve months and now, as a woman of seventeen, was, he knew, considered quite a beauty among the gentlemen who had been angling for her hand since she was fifteen years old. She was tall, almost as tall as he, a disadvantage in this era when small and dainty was so much admired, and very dark, when fair ringlets and pink cheeks were the vogue but the gentlemen who had asked for her were prepared, it seemed, to overlook these faults in consideration of the fortune she would inherit. Her wilful hair was brushed into a silken smooth chignon at the back of her head and with the help of two tortoiseshell combs and the lady's maid she had been allowed on her seventeenth birthday, she had curbed the wayward strands which had once slipped about her ears. She wore the gold earbobs he had given her and a soft coffee and cream gingham day dress, very simple and elegant with a long sleeve and a sash of taffeta about her waist and though there was no special gown suitable for a lady to wear in a cotton spinning mill (for who would expect to see one in such a strange place?), she was decently and modestly dressed.

'What is it, Katherine? You seem somewhat preoccupied this morning. Are you not concerned with their Majesties' new state?'

'No . . . I . . . I cannot seem to find it of particular interest.'

'You mean in general, or merely . . . today?'

She looked sharply at him then since they were both well aware of what was to happen today and though the belief that the man should hang for the crime he had committed was shared by them both, he knew and was sorry for it, that it was affecting her more deeply than she cared to admit.

The maids at the back of the room had become still and the tension deepened, snapping almost, for Tom Butterworth was a local man and there would be many who would sympathise with his state today, saying he had been driven to it. His, Barker Chapman's own servants could, no doubt, be acquainted with the man's family, whoever they might be, but that was nought to him and should be nought to his daughter. The man had committed a crime for which the penalty was death, and he must pay the penalty.

'It is to be today,' she said abruptly. 'Seven-thirty, I believe.'

'I am aware of that, Katherine.' At the back of the room there was a small sound followed by a soft flurry of skirts and one of the maids left the room but he did not turn to see who it might be.

'Does it not . . .?'

'. . . affect me?' he finished for her. He paused, looking deeply into her eyes and was quite bewildered by a look of what he could only call confusion there. 'No, it does not. Why should it? Because it was *our* machine the man helped to wreck? Is that what you are asking . . .?'

'No . . . no . . .'

'Then why do you concern yourself?'

'I do not . . . but . . . he is so . . . young.'

'He killed a soldier, Katherine. A man who was doing his duty. The man deserves to hang despite his youth. I heard you say so yourself when they smashed the new machine. You were quite adamant about it then. If I remember your words you swore revenge on all of them, including the lad who is to hang today. Do you now say they were right in what they did . . .?'

'Oh no, Father . . .' Her eyes had become the vivid blue of her anger, the anger she had known then.

'As I recall, you told them that what they did was a hanging offence and you meant what you said. You cannot change your mind because that is now to happen and the one who is to be punished is but sixteen. You are only seventeen yourself and know exactly what you are about and in what you believe. Do you not think he is the same?'

'Yes, of course!' Her chin rose and her colour was high again with remembered outrage.

73

'Then does it not follow that he must pay the penalty if it is proved he was breaking the law. That he must pay the price, the ultimate price for the crime he committed?'

She nodded her head in agreement and though she did not smile for what the man was to suffer was not to be smiled at, in her eyes was the warm and positive belief that what her father said was the truth. She had indeed done all she could, with her father, to get the man convicted for he had been there, it had been proved to the magistrate's satisfaction, when the machine was smashed. Was it not unreasonable now to shrink from the truth, sad, but implacable, that within two hours the man – dear Lord, he was no more than a boy – would be dead! She must not let sentiment, stupid *female* sentiment, soften her otherwise clear-headed thinking. She was her father's heir, pledged to the task of carrying on what the Chapmans before her had built, to defending what was theirs and she must learn to deal with these men, these wicked men who would put the clock of progress back with their destruction and riots. They were no more than rabble, most of them, a mob of base-born, coarse and brutish labourers who could not see that improvement would never be halted and that she, Katherine Chapman, would never be halted either.

They discussed the merits of a new cloth her father was experimenting with as they drove from Greenacres to Crossbank, and the advisability of having troops to supervise the second new 'self-acting' mule they were to install there in the next week or so. The machine which had been wrecked was to be replaced naturally, since nothing must stand in *their* way, the Chapman father and daughter agreed, and though he did not say so to Katherine, Barker Chapman was aware that the young man who was, at this moment, being led to the gallows, was to die for nothing, since his cause had *gained* nothing. They talked of other matters concerning the business. Barker Chapman was not satisfied with the hand-looms which he had put in his new weaving-sheds at Broadbank and what did Katherine think to trying out one or two power-looms now that the steam engine was so readily available to them. Their heads were close together, their rapt attention with their own bright future and that of their mills absorbing them as they drove through the mill gates at precisely five-thirty. The factory bell pierced the air and from every direction scurried frail shadows of men and women and children, running to be through the gate before it was closed to latecomers since, if they did not get through now they would not only be made to wait a further two and a half hours until it was opened again at eight o'clock, but also would be fined for their tardiness. They crowded, women in shawls despite the heat, into the yard, children still half asleep on their feet whose eyes were sunken shadows in their candle-pale faces and men, thin and haunted, but fierce eyed, nevertheless, and bitter.

Without warning, as they packed into the yard with a clatter of clogged feet on cobbles and the soft hum of voices on the air, there fell a menacing silence, a hostile stillness that was louder than the clamour which had preceded it and Barker Chapman and his daughter turned in the carriage to look in bewilderment at their operatives who had suddenly become as frozen as the marble statues in their own garden at Greenacres.

The carriage drew up to the staircase which led to the offices. From inside the mill came the singing of the machinery, the machinery which never stopped except on Sunday for as one 'gang' finished another began and those who had worked through the night came quietly down from every floor, their feet still bare, standing shoulder to shoulder with their companions until the whole yard was a massed sea of white faces. Behind them, their voices raised warningly, their thonged straps swinging, followed a score of perilous overlookers. From the office windows faces stared in amazement as Barker Chapman's managers came to see what was amiss and but for the harsh sound of the overlookers' shouts and the 'thwack' of their straps as they slapped them into their open palms, there was a complete and eerie silence.

75

Barker Chapman stepped down from his carriage, reaching as he did so for his cigar case. He extracted a cigar, and with the casual air of one who has all the time in the world and is no more than an unconcerned spectator to someone else's drama, he lit it. When it was drawing to his satisfaction, the fragrant smoke curling about his top hat he turned to Kit.

'Will you step down, my dear, and go on up to the office. Tell Mrs Plank to make us a pot of coffee. I shall be up shortly.'

His words could be heard clearly in every corner of the silent yard for even the overlookers, truculent and smarting at this contemptuous disregard for their authority, had ceased to shout orders. Katherine felt her heart fill with some vast emotion which she had never known before. She herself had stood up to a crowd once before. She had been in hot temper, fearing none of the rough men she had confronted and though her father then had known it was useless, accepting that there was nothing to be done to save his machine, she had been wild, undisciplined, giving those men the satisfaction of sneering at her. She would not do so again, nor would her father. He was superb at this moment. He might have been in the tranquillity and seclusion of his own garden, surrounded, not with the hostility and aggression of a silently staring crowd who could, as the expression on their haggard faces seemed to indicate, tear him and trample him, and herself, into the muck of the yard, but among his own rose beds and green lawns. He was smiling imperturbably, his cigar clenched between his teeth and there was no trace of fear on his face. She had never admired him . . . no, *loved* him more than at this moment. She smiled too, and their expression of disdain, of arrogance, was identical. They might be forced by sheer weight of numbers to back away from this confrontation, they said, but they would pick their time to retaliate and they would always win in the end!

As Barker Chapman turned to face the mob, for surely that was what it was, his daughter thought, just like the one which had ravaged France, she stepped deliberately from the carriage, and just as cool as he himself was, opened her cream taffeta parasol and moved slowly and gracefully around the carriage to stand beside him. She slipped her hand through his arm, a gesture which said quite plainly to this riff-raff that if they were to take him, then they must go through her to do it!

'What is the meaning of this gathering?' Her father addressed his remark to a bony-faced, weak-eyed man, tall and quite straight of frame, unlike those about him, who he had decided must be the leader since he stood in the centre of the front row of the crowd. The man stared, not at Barker Chapman now, but over his shoulder directly at the wall of the mill building and Katherine began to realise that not one soul looked at her, or her father, but into blank space, into the air in front of them, into *nothing*. They were expressionless, their eyes clouded now, as though someone had mesmerised every last one of them.

'You all appreciate that you are losing wages by standing here, I suppose?' her father went on, but no one answered him and no one moved.

'I'll get 'em back, Mr Chapman,' a voice at the side of the carriage said and a burly man stepped from behind Barker Chapman's sleek and well-nourished carriage horses, swinging his overlooker's thonged strap gently to and fro. 'A touch with this'll get 'em on the move and I'll guarantee to give you the reason for it before the day's out, so I will.' His tone was perilous, for with every moment the machines were not operating the size of his own weekly bonus was reduced. He had a few nice little sidelines going in the mill, many of which brought him more than his own wage, but he'd not be defied by this motley assembly, and certainly not before the master himself. They were terrified of him, those who worked on his floor, especially the women, and even more, the women with daughters! He began to jostle the drab who stood before him, moving threateningly on the child who was with her but she merely

77

held it closer to her though her face became even whiter in her terror.

'What the devil is this about?' the man began to roar, taking hold of another, pulling and shoving until the man he had picked on fell to his knees, but still no one moved.

'Leave it, leave them be, if you please, Ellis, for I have a few words to say.' Barker Chapman's voice was soft and pleasant but the steel which lay beneath it was obvious to them all, from the oldest there, a mill hand who had come as a parish apprentice with a cartload of others when the mill first opened, to the youngest, a 'piecer' just five years old and with no shoes to his feet. 'If they wish to lose wages they may, and for each five minutes they do not work they shall be fined threepence. I shall go up to my office now and I expect to see this yard empty of everyone except those with legitimate business in it within five minutes. See to it, will you, Ellis.'

The hazy sunshine, yellow and burning above the roof top fell about the yard. The shadow of a vagrant cloud sighed across the metallic blue of the sky and the faces of the men and women who stood passively beside Barker Chapman's spinning mill, darkened, and Katherine felt the touch of an icy finger run across her warm skin. It was unearthly the absolute quiet, and the huge gathering seemed to float like disembodied ghosts, frail, insubstantial, scarcely human at all in their complete silence and lack of movement.

'Come, my dear,' her father said softly at her elbow, bringing her from the strange trance-like state into which she had fallen. 'They will be gone within five minutes, you will see.'

But the silent assembly was still there five minutes later, and ten minutes, and half an hour, and though all the overlookers pushed and jostled and threatened, not one of that vast crowd would move except to fall over when forced to it and Barker Chapman became afraid that serious damage might be done them. Not that he cared a great deal about that, but he had no wish to be held responsible for the mass savaging of his workers at the hands of his incensed overlookers.

He was standing at his office window, watching them, marvelling that a great multitude such as this, without apparent leadership or support could remain so fixed and without movement for so great a length of time. Not one had moved, nor spoken as far as he could tell for more than an hour. They merely stood, each one staring at the back of the one in front or into the space which contained them, until suddenly, as though at a signal, they bowed their heads in complete unison for several long moments then, with a humming like bees which have been stirred with a stick they moved slowly, going quietly towards the door-ways which would lead them to their machines, or, those who had just come off shift, through the gate and into the street. Within five minutes the yard was empty except for the waggons and horses, his own carriage which had been unable to be moved among the press of people, and the labourers who worked there.

It was five minutes past seven-thirty!

'It is because of him,' he said incredulously to Katherine who had come to stand beside him.

'The man who has just been hanged?' She had known it, as he had, though he had not admitted to it, for the past hour since why else would these people, all of them barely above starvation level, have risked all that they had. It had been a demonstration of their loyalty to the men who were fighting, and *dying* for them.

'Yes. They have stood for two hours in his honour. They have each lost four shillings and fourpence, two weeks' wages for some of those children.' He shook his head in wonderment. 'The man murdered another but they have made a martyr of him this day!'

For a moment, a bare fraction of time, Katherine Chapman felt a thrill of awe tingle through her body. She had known no great emotion until this day beyond the single-minded devotion she had begun to give to her father's mills. No one had seemed inclined to show her affection as a child beyond the rough embraces of the woman who had helped in the nursery, and she had given none, for who had wanted it? Today her admiration for her father's courage, her loyalty to him, had turned, she thought, in that moment, to love, but now she had seen something else and it was an emotion of which she had no knowledge, no understanding and she could put no name to it. Perhaps constancy? Allegiance to another? A ruthless discipline to a cause which had given them the willingness and the strength to risk the loss of their jobs in its name, and she found she could only feel a sense of baffled admiration. She did not like it, for these people were rebels who were attempting to upset the authority put over them by the laws of the land. They were trying to stand in the way of progress with their antiquated methods of spinning and weaving and their dogged determination to preserve them. There would be work for all, a decent standard of life for all if they would only allow it to happen in this great industrial age which was to come. One day they would realise it, they must, but today had shown her the true temper, the spirit, if not of this crowd who were but the tools of the movement, but of the men who led it.

Her thoughts seemed to draw her eyes to the gateway which opened out from the yard into Weaver Street and for several seconds the identity of the man who stood there escaped her. He was tall, with a big frame, and thin, almost to the point of emaciation. He had a shock of uncut dark curls and even from where she stood she could feel the compelling fierceness of his eyes. They were filled with a spirit of harsh challenge, a throwing down of the gauntlet at her feet, *her* feet, they seemed to say. Would she take it up? His skin was burned by the sun and his bare arms were folded across his chest. He stood, his legs wide apart, a warrior who has done battle and won, in the exact centre of the gateway and those who were in the yard turned and stood, like him, to watch her. *She knew who he was then!*

Her heart began to pound and though she was acutely

aware that she should call her father, who had returned to his desk, she found she could not. They looked into one another's eyes across the width of the yard and the stillness which enveloped them, a stillness which spoke as loud as words, declared their enmity and, at the same time, the curious bond between them which had nothing at all to do with what had just happened here. He lifted his hand in greeting, perhaps a declaration of his dangerous intentions, though there was a certain sardonic mockery in it, then he was gone, slipping into the shadows of the high wall which surrounded the yard.

Katherine Chapman leaned for a long time at the window. There was an emptiness inside her which she knew she must fill and it must be filled with an understanding of what was to happen in her life from this day. She was her father's daughter, a Chapman, and committed to nothing beyond the continuing of his business, to its growth in the industry of cloth-making. The man at the gate was nothing to her. He was from another class, another culture and yet he seemed to acknowledge a link, a binding of their lives which had begun on the moorland path to Friars Mere when they had been scarcely more than children, a boy and a girl, even then on separate pathways. She had been drawn to him, she recognised it. She had seen him only twice since that day and on each occasion he had been the instigator in some dispute against her father and his mills. He was her protagonist in what must surely come, that was beyond doubt, as the mill-workers wreaked their revenge, for surely that was what it was, on her father and other mill-owners, for what they saw as the loss of their livelihood. If that was so, then why did she feel such a sense of loss as she looked at the open gateway where, for the space of a minute, the man had stood?

6

Mercy Butterworth was tiny, a dainty flower of a girl, her father called her, like a snowdrop with her pale, luminous skin and silky brown hair. Her eyes were soft and grey, fringed with fine brown lashes and though she was just over eighteen, her figure was as slight as that of a twelve year old. She wore homespun, plain dove grey with a snowy white collar and apron, and though she was a child of Methodism, not given to adornment, she had a natural sweetness, a shining laughter about her which needed none.

Her father Enoch was fifty years of age and a staunch Methodist boasting that he had once in his younger days been present at a fieldside sermon when the great and much loved John Wesley, himself an old man then, had spoken to the massed multitude. He had given each of his sons the name of John before they died as infants, from the mysterious and various ailments which his God chose to inflict on them and it was not until his wife, now dead, had timorously wondered if perhaps they might chance the sixth with another name should a child of his survive. But the child was a girl and he called her Merciful Goodness for that was what his God had shown him, shortened in the first year of her life to Mercy.

His son, named Thomas, since his wife, filled with superstitious dread of the name John, had begged it, was born a year later. He was a merry imp of a child, much loved by his sister and mothered by her as they grew up together. Their mother had died at Tom's birth.

Their cottage was the first in the village of Edgeclough,

as the Greenwoods' was the last and the two families were close. Enoch was a weaver, like Abel had been and between them, Abel, Joss and Enoch, they had undertaken and achieved the task of providing enough raw cotton for Martha and Jenny Greenwood, and Mercy Butterworth to spin the yarn for the three men to weave, thus keeping the two families from the starvation which struck at so many others.

Mercy, with Tom, was a staunch believer in the movement to better the lives of the families who, like her own, were concerned with the cotton trade. Though she did not undertake the walk herself since that was not her way, her heart and soul went with Jenny Greenwood and Joss to wherever there was a meeting, or a march as they walked many miles to support men from towns where cotton was woven or spun. To Saddleworth, to Todmorden and Nelson, to Colne, Burnley and Shaw. They walked the old pack-routes, once known as 'salt-ways' because of the salt which had been carried along them, going by night, and even on one occasion moving by the Long Causeway which led from Burnley down to Halifax in Yorkshire to a meeting of hand-loom weavers in the wool trade.

There had been attempts to form a 'General Union of Trades' with men travelling from Nottingham, those in the lace trade, from Birmingham and Liverpool and weavers from Somerset, and wherever men were exploited. Joss was invited again and again to speak, to take up the leadership as he had before the arrest of Tom Butterworth, of not only the Lancashire Reformers, but of those of many counties.

Wherever he went a thousand weavers and more would be massed to hear his impassioned pleas for the support of their fellow workers who were without work but he would not, though many cried out for it, use force or resort again to machine-breaking. He told them that he was afraid that any such destruction might jeopardise the possibility that Tom would be sentenced, not to be hanged, but to transportation to the penal colonies and surely, Mercy begged him, that was better than losing his young life. He did agree to

83

join a parade which moved through the streets of Blackburn, accompanying three thousand others in protest at the
lowering, yet again, of wages, marching in regular order in
files of four abreast and though all those in the ragged
crowd knew of him and what he had done at the Chapman
mill, he was a hero, a legend, the son of the man who had
been the symbol of the dream to which most of them clung,
and they would not inform on him to the militia.

The mill-owners were saying yet again that power-frames
and power-looms alone could save the cotton trade and
those who were made to work them longed for nothing but
their return to their simple domestic life and both sides
were prepared to uphold their own desires and beliefs to
the bitter end. But there was to be no more rioting, Joss
Greenwood said during that month of June, until Tom
Butterworth's fate was decided but that did not mean their
protesting voices could not be heard. The machinery which
was reducing their wages, or their chances of earning any
must not be tampered with, the manufacturers said, or they
could not compete in the foreign markets, but the labouring
class, those who marched with Joss Greenwood, would not
have it. They had been told to 'stand firm, live on air, burn
your looms and bear any extremity rather than work for
the mill-owners' and that is what they intended to do under
Joss Greenwood's leadership.

Enoch Butterworth grieved silently for his son, upheld
despite his grief, in the firm conviction of his God's mercy
and that Tom, should he be punished in this life for the sin
he had committed, would be forgiven in the next. He prayed
a good deal in those last weeks of his son's life, more than
he had ever done and was filled with sorrow when Mercy
would not kneel with him. He could not understand her
bitterness, though he recognised that Tom had killed the
soldier in her defence.

'He did it for me, Father,' Mercy said passionately. 'He
didn't mean to kill him but they had . . . had me by the
arms . . . they meant to . . . to harm me . . . you know
what I am saying, and to stop him Tom put his arms round

84

the man's neck, holding him . . . tight . . . and . . . his neck broke!'

Her voice which had told the tale a hundred times to others, and to herself became soft with despair and Joss, who sat at the kitchen table beside her, put a gentle hand on her arm. He had seen what flesh she had fall from her small frame in the month they waited for the verdict and the dullness of guilt blight the soft grey of her eyes and he knew that since the day they had taken Tom she had not slept for more than an hour at a time.

'He killed a man, Mercy. There is no excuse for it,' Enoch Butterworth said gravely, his own eyes moist for he loved his easy-going, engaging young son, despite his laxity in the ways of Methodism. 'He has always been a good boy and hardworking. He was abstemious as our religion orders us to be and a good son and brother, but no matter what the cause he had no right to take another man's life.'

'Even in my defence, Father?' Mercy asked wildly, but the father would not agree and when they got word a week later that Tom was to hang on the following Friday and his young and healthy body was afterwards to be delivered to the surgeons for dissection, a custom with dead criminals, Enoch merely picked up his Bible and went out of the cottage door, disappearing along the valley bottom into a stand of trees by the water's edge.

Joss and Mercy stood side by side, the flesh of their ashen faces stripped away from the bones, like the wax of a melting candle, their eyes wide and staring in the black hollows into which they had fallen. The man who had brought the message looked about him uncomfortably, saying nothing more, for what was there to be said? He had been picked by the others to bear the dreadful news and now that he had done so he longed to be away from the suffering that was here.

He had gone when Mercy began to weep. Her rich, sweet mouth opened wide on a cry of anguish and though he felt as though his own heart was being torn, still beating, from his breast, Joss shivered away from the desolation of her.

She lifted her hands to her head and before he knew what she was about to do she had grasped a handful of her own hair and began to tear it, quite literally from her scalp until the blood ran.

'Jesus! . . . aah, don't . . . don't, Mercy . . .' He gripped her arms, appalled, then in the only way he knew how to stop her he pulled her against his chest, holding her writhing body to his own. She would not be still. Her cries were piercing and her face ran with tears and she threw her head from side to side in an effort to be free of him. She would hurt herself if he let her go, for her mind had fallen into a pit of suffering, from which there could be no escape for a long while and so he held her, saying nothing for she was deaf to his voice.

Through the pain, and the disbelief, since surely they would have shown clemency to one so young, another feeling was struggling to free itself from Joss Greenwood, but that was for later, that was for the day when Tom died, that would be brought forth and examined then and he would allow it to drown him in its fierceness. Now he must concentrate on this girl in his arms. That was all he was at this moment, a pair of arms to keep her from falling down and never getting up again. Not the leader, not the son of a mother who grieved for him in his wild ways, not the son of a father who had died for his beliefs but the man who must get this girl, this woman through the days of torment which would follow up to next Friday and beyond.

All night he stayed with her. She swooned against him, her emotions weakening her so dreadfully she could not stand and he carried her slight figure to the small bed upstairs where he knew she slept. He put her on it and lay down beside her, the first time he had held a woman in his arms without lust, and when she finally slept he listened to her ragged breathing and when she woke, crying harshly that was it not enough that they should hang him but they must mutilate his body as well, that he would have no grave, no resting place where she might mourn him, he soothed her again to troubled sleep.

He left her at dawn when her father returned, slipping back after dark to see her, to hold her in his arms, for it seemed only when she was close to him did she get comfort.

She was mindless in her sorrow, doing her household tasks like a machine which has no thought but will, when the correct lever is pulled, go about its function. Her father stayed with her, his face grim and haggard, but in his eyes was the serenity which his religion gave him, the true belief he could not seem to pass on to his daughter. He watched her with Joss in the candlelight, holding his hand, sitting close to him as she had once done with Tom, in the communion of two hearts which feel the same pain and he did not speak now though something would need to be said soon.

And at seven-thirty on Friday, the twenty-first of July, as Tom Butterworth's life was throttled from him, Joss Greenwood stood in her mill yard and stared into the lovely face of the woman who had helped to put the rope around his neck and though he had lifted his hand to her in some greeting, the hatred he felt, the hatred he felt for her and her father and all the men like him who exploited others for gain, hardened, became fast set and unbreakable in that moment.

Mercy was at her spinning wheel when he returned to the cottage that night. The wheel had belonged to her mother and grandmother before her going back to the days of the 'Spinning Jenny', fifty years or more. Her grandmother and mother had spun the yarn on it, with other spinsters for their husbands to weave and the movement of the wheel, the action of the bobbin and spindles soothed her tortured spirit and gave her hands something to do. Tom had worked a hand-loom at Abbotts, a mill-owner in the Penfold Valley, and with the 'piece' her father had woven on his loom on the top floor of the cottage there had been enough to feed the three of them. Like most of the hill dwellers they had a tiny smallholding to augment their earnings and with this they had managed to keep her from the work of a mill girl.

She rose as Joss came quietly into the room and at once he could see the calmness in her eyes. Enoch was there, his Bible on his knee, his pale face coloured to a healthy hue by the glow of the fire. There was fresh baked bread on the table and a pitcher of milk. There was a plate of oatcakes, one of black puddings and another of tripe.

'People have been,' she said simply and he knew that the women, destitute many of them, had managed somehow to fetch the customary condolence on this day of bereavement. It was their way up here in the barren wilderness of the moorland of sharing her sorrow and he could see she was eased by it.

'Sit down and eat. You must be hungry. See, take off your jacket and get by the fire since it's turned cold. And you've a tear in your shirt. Let me have it later and I'll mend it. You can put one of Tom's on. He won't mind, will he, Father?'

And so Tom Butterworth was put to rest, to lie in peace in his sister's heart though his body would never have a resting place.

'I came to see if you were . . . all right,' he said when he had eaten.

'Aye, I'm all right. He's . . . sleeping now and knows no more pain, or fear and it comforts me.' She made a brave attempt at a smile and reached out to touch his hand. Though she was more at peace now, despite her sorrow, knowing that Tom's suffering was done with, she still needed this man's strength. She looked into his lean, brown face, seeing the hard, flat planes of his cheeks, the fierce swoop of his dark eyebrows and deep and complex expression in his eyes, watching as they softened for her and her heart was moved with the tenderness he aroused in her. She was not clever, nor especially pretty though she supposed the velvet grey of the eyes she saw briefly in her mother's mirror each morning were well enough. She was made for the raising and caring of a family, for marriage and children and Joss could probably provide her with neither. He was concerned so passionately with the men and *their* families, with injustice and exploitation, with the cruelty done them and would have no time for what *she* needed but she loved him just the same and would have no other but him.

'Did it go well?' she asked, knowing what had been planned. She had said her own farewell to her brother up on the 'tops' he had loved, alone and inconsolable, not really knowing at what exact moment he had died but with him nevertheless when he did and it had occurred to her afterwards as she walked slowly towards her home that her father's God, a God of love, he said, had separated their family as nothing else could. They should have been together at this moment of grief, she and her father, and yet he mourned alone the son he had lost, as she did her brother. He was a good man, Enoch Butterworth, eager enough to give help to anyone who asked him for it, whatever it might be and yet now, when *she* needed him, he was off alone praying and exorting God to take their Tom into Heaven just as if it wasn't a complete certainty that he would go straight there anyway. The only one, beside the women who had come up quietly to put an arm about her, to help her healing, was Joss.

'Aye, they all stood. Brave they were, Mercy, everyone. The tacklers tried to move them, shoving them, even the children, knocking them down . . .' His voice was harsh with his hatred, '. . . but they wouldn't be moved. How they'll manage, whole families losing more than a week's pay, but they did it, all't same. They're strong, love, just like you an' me are strong when it's needed, but by God, it took a bit o' doing. Sorry, Mr Butterworth, I know you don't take kindly to hearing the Lord's name spoke lightly but sometimes it needs to be remembered that *He* seems to take *us* lightly.'

'Nay, Joss Greenwood, I'll not have things like that said in my house. The Lord is here with us. It's not for the likes of us to question His ways nor what He has put us in this earth for. Tom is . . .'

'Tom is dead, Mr Butterworth, and no matter what the

Lord put him on the earth for He had no right to let him suffer what he did. It was not his fault that the soldiers were waiting for us but mine, *mine*. I organised the machine breaking and it was *me* they were there for. Tom paid the price, and Mercy here but you can tell your God the next time you speak to him that they'll not go unpunished, those who took his life. He's a strange God, that one of yours, Mr Butterworth, that lets some men live on the fat of the land while children, no more than babies really, grow old and crippled before they reach the age of ten in the bloody mills. Have you seen them, Mr Butterworth, have you? Little old men and women, they are, with their legs bent under them and their shoulders stooped, coughing their lungs inside out with the dust? Their arms are broken and their eyes taken out and I heard tell of one or two, pauper children nobody gives a damn about, who killed themselves rather than go back to their machines. Little girls get dragged into the machinery by their hair, they get headaches and pains in their bones and all they want to do when the factory bell goes is fall on to the nearest pile of waste and sleep until it rings again to tell them it's time to get back to work. No wild beast treats its young as we treat ours, Mr Butterworth. They are paid, along with the women, wages which have been reduced to starvation level and the pauper children, the "apprentices" as the mill-owners quaintly term them, do not even get that. They work sixteen hours a day in stench, in heat which would fell a grown man, forced by the blows of the overlooker to keep going. They are fed on food you wouldn't give a pig. They try to run away, some of them and so they are chained to their machines, boys and girls alike and I'm sure you are not unaware of the fate of many of the girls. They are slaves, Mr Butterworth, no more than slaves and we should be ashamed that we have allowed it to happen, so I say this to you. Though Tom is dead I know he would be glad, if he had to die so young, that it was in trying to free these children. He didn't die for nothing, I tell myself and I suppose it comforts me to think so. He died to get better conditions for these little slaves, to give them an education so that they can lift themselves up from where they have been kicked, and the men and women who are slaves with them. I could let Tom's death stop me, since, as you seem to think and I agree with you, that I am responsible in some measure for it but I will go on. I will fight and fight and *kill* if I have to, to stop this bloody mass murder, this torture of innocent children and if you, or your God, has anything to say on the subject then let me hear it now.'

His breath heaved in his chest and his eyes glared like those of some tormented beast and Enoch Butterworth stepped back from him, not afraid but astounded to see such passion in a man. Since his father had died at the Battle of Peterloo, Joss Greenwood had become wild and uncontrollable. He had gone about with other fighting radicals, stirring up the people against the manufacturers, speaking of injustice and reform and he had done it hot-bloodedly as one would expect of so young a man and Enoch had not liked it, nor the involvement of his own son. He believed himself in freedom for all men, though he had heard tell that the great religious leader, John Wesley himself had gone so far as to recommend child labour as a means of preventing youthful vice and really, there was something to be said for that.

No, Joss Greenwood was anathema to a man like himself for he seemed in some way, though he fought to right the wrongs done his fellow to go against everything Enoch Butterworth believed in. Joss Greenwood had never worked in a factory and neither had Enoch and so he supposed they could neither speak from first-hand experience as operatives, as men who had suffered the factory system. Joss had worked a hand-loom all his life in his own cottage. They had kept a pig and a few hens and grew vegetables. Martha and her daughter still spun the yarn on their dom-estic spinning wheels and young Charlie could 'card' now and they lurched, like many families, from crisis to crisis, but they managed. Joss Greenwood had no first-hand knowledge of labouring in a mill when he ranted of injustice and Enoch was not awfully convinced that Joss fought, not for the cause he vowed he believed in, but for the fighting itself. And Enoch did not like to be taken to task by a bit of a lad who knew nowt about 'owt in his opinion. Neither did he like the way he made free with Mercy, his daughter. A good girl, she was, half daft with grief these last few days and not knowing what she was about but he'd not see her handled again by Joss Greenwood like she had been this past week. Not without a ring on her finger as was decent.

Joss had regained his composure now. He had moved to stand at the small window which looked out at the slope of the hillside across the narrow valley. A pack-horse bridge crossed the stream below Enoch's cottage, the track leading from it vanishing into the carpet of heather which climbed it. A blue shadow moved down from the tops, sinking visibly until it reached the valley bottom, then climbing again as a stretched band of cloud moved across the moor. He could hear a dipper call as it circled its nest against a high slab of limestone, alarmed by a buzzard which hung in the sky. He could smell the aniseed fragrance of the Sweet Cicely which submerged the drystone wall which surrounded Enoch's cottage and the beauty and peace almost destroyed the calm he had forced upon himself. Today a young man had died quite savagely at the hands of the hangman. He would never see this again, nor smell the wild flowers nor hear the cry of the bird and it almost broke Joss's heart to think of it. But he must go on. He had been fond of Tom Butterworth in a casual, masculine way and he felt the same way about Tom's sister. His responsibility to them both had kept him here this last week but now it was over and he must get on with his work. He must go wherever he was needed to organise mass meetings and strikes, marches and protests which would lead to the extinction of the system which had created the men, and their mills who were destroying the vast multitude of the working men and women of this realm.

Enoch Butterworth stood up slowly, his great shaggy head of grey hair turning with some deliberation to his daughter. His face was set in a mould of grim determination for though he was not a man with a forceful will, being too engrossed in the unworldly rather than the practical, he could be trenchant on matters which concerned what was right, and decent.

'Go outside, our Mercy,' he said firmly. 'There's summat Joss and I must talk on. See to the hens, now look sharp, there's a good girl.'

'But father . . .' Mercy's face was bewildered.

''Tis man's talk, lass. 'Twill take no more than a minute or so.' His face gentled for the girl, who was as pale as death itself, with great dark, sorrowing eyes sunk deep in their sockets. She was brave, fighting the desolation and harshness of her brother's death. She had got through this day with the steadfast strength of a north country woman who had the capacity to bear all she must. She would recover, he knew that, but he'd not have her trifled with, no, not by his new Majesty himself!

'We have to say a word about the lass, Joss Greenwood,' he said sternly when she had left the room. His eyes followed her as she wandered across the plot of coarse grass to the drystone wall and climbed up to sit on it, gazing sadly across the stream to the hills beyond.

'The lass?' Joss was clearly puzzled.

'Aye. There's been a deal of . . . of contact between the two of you these past few days and I'll have to ask you your intentions, my lad. When . . . when we heard about Tom . . .' he swallowed painfully and a spasm of anguish crossed his face, '. . . well, I'll be honest with you, I was . . . knocked sideways and I . . . I had to get up to the . . . to where I could be on me own with God.' It was said simply and Joss was finally made aware that Enoch's God was as real to him as the girl who sat on the wall outside the cottage, perhaps even more so.

'Well . . . maybe I was at fault, leaving her, but she was with you . . . Tom's friend and . . . well, to tell the truth I wasn't thinking straight. When I got back you were in her bed, Joss Greenwood, and that means but one thing to a

93

man like me!' His voice and face were like granite, accusing, but ready to forgive as his God said he must if Joss was ready to do the right thing.

Joss had an urgent desire to laugh and if the circumstances had been less tragic he might have done so for Mercy Butterworth was nothing to him *in that way*! She was Tom's sister, for God's sake, no more and though he had held her through that dreadful night, soothed her desolation and absorbed her shock and disbelief, she might have been his own sister, or mother or any woman who needed his pity. She was soft and sweet, gentle as a dove, good and innocent as a child and that was all. A child to whom he had given comfort and protection when it was needed.

'Did you hear what I said, lad? I'll not see my lass dishonoured, not by you or any man. They all know here-abouts the way things have been between you . . .'

'Between us?'

'. . . aye and I want to know the way of it before you take yourself off again on your path of violence. I'll admit you're not the man I would have chosen for our Mercy but 'appen a wife and children will take the fire from you. You an' I can make a livin' wi' the looms your father left. With your mother an' sister an' my lass to spin, with young Charlie, an' Daisy, when she's old enough to "comb" and "card" if you shape yersen we can weave a piece or two each week. One of us can fetch the raw cotton from Manchester like we did when your Pa was alive an' take the finished cloth to the Cloth Hall in Crossfold. That young brother of yours is growing and between us we . . .'

Joss began to laugh then. He could see that Enoch was deeply affronted but he could not stop himself. Enoch Butterworth was mapping out the lives of not only Joss Greenwood but his whole family as well and though it was far from amusing he found he could not stop since the sheer effrontery of the man was scarcely to be believed. Marriage! He was talking about marriage between himself and Mercy with the absolute certainty that Joss was bound to agree. And he had not even kissed the girl! He had not even *thought* of kissing the girl, *ever*, when he and Tom had skylarked about the place – a hundred years ago, surely? – and she had watched him with a flush to her cheek and a shine to her eye. He had sensed in a casual kind of way that Mercy Butterworth *liked* him – he would admit to no more than that – and now it was marriage. *Marriage!* It was sheer lunacy. His life could not allow for wife, nor child, not for years, if ever. He was dedicated to . . . Oh Jesus, God . . . he could not be saddled with . . . even if he loved her . . . she was sweet . . . and . . . but Enoch was not smiling and he had, he admitted it, shared her bed with her that night but with what innocence. It had been no more than pity for the terrible grief she suffered, that was all.

'I . . . I'm sorry, really I am, Mr Butterworth. It is no laughing matter . . . but . . . when you spoke of what there was between Mercy and myself, well, I couldn't help myself. You see there is nothing, she will tell you herself. She was distraught, you must understand that, and I couldn't leave her. She was alone, which was your fault, not mine and I couldn't leave her. She was out of her mind, for God's sake . . .'

He found he was beginning to raise his voice for Enoch was looking at him, grim-faced and disbelieving. 'It's true, Mr Butterworth, we did nothing . . .'

'Are you sayin' you don't want my girl, Joss Greenwood?'

'No, I'm not saying that though . . .'

Enoch's face cleared. 'Well then, a day must be set for the wedding.'

'Wedding! Jesus Christ . . .!'

'Now then, lad, before you become a member of this family you'll 'ave to get it into your 'ead that I'll not 'ave the Lord's name . . .'

'For God's sake, man, I can't marry your daughter, or anybody's daughter. I lead the life of a gypsy and that's not for a woman. Tramping from village to village, going to meetings and organising protests and strikes. Living as best I can on the cloth I manage to weave, when I can. My mother will continue to spin what raw cotton I can fetch and with Charlie as he gets older and when I am able, I'll weave a piece. It will keep her and the young 'uns fed but our Jenny'll have to go into mill. Aye . . .' He grimaced painfully and Enoch was made aware of how much it pained him to say it. '. . . She suggested it and she knows that if I'm to carry on then that's what she must do. She's a good lass, a sensible lass and she is helping in the only way she can. But I'm fighting a bloody war here, Mr Butterworth, and don't you glare at me because you know that's what it is, and I must be free to get on with it. Don't you think I wouldn't like to have a home, a wife and family, like any other man but what chance have I of making a girl like Mercy happy? She is . . . the loveliest girl I know and brave too, but I couldn't ask her to come with me. Good God, I'm a soldier and if they catch me I shall go to gaol. I never know from one day to the next where I shall be and it's no way for a woman to live. Not a woman like Mercy who's never been used to . . .'

'I'll live it, Joss, and right gladly.'

They both turned and there she was, smiling shyly, radiant and blushing and it was clear from her expression that she had heard no more than Joss's last words. She moved to stand before him and her eyes glowed with her love.

'I'll go anywhere with you, Joss,' she said simply and put her hand in his.

7

Barker Chapman's spinning and weaving mills were plain and utilitarian, the two spinning mills being six storeys high with small windows of clouded glass. The windows were not for looking out of, nor even to let in much light, the object being to hold within the buildings the moisture and heat needed for their economic running. The buildings existed for one reason only, to make money and were not for show, as some owners made *their* concerns, putting in walls of shining Accrington brick to proclaim their prosperity. The Chapman mills were four square, sturdy and ugly.

His two weaving sheds were of one storey only since the six floors in each mill which contained his spinning concerns fed the appetite of one floor of weaving. Those who were put, as many children were when they grew too big for working beneath the spinning frames, into the weaving sheds were immediately aware of the appalling noise. The spinning frames 'sang' as they performed their function but the weaving looms clacked so loudly they caused actual physical pain, and even deafness. The inability to hear even what one's closest neighbour was saying was overcome by the weavers' knack of learning to lip-read, known locally as 'mee-mawing'. An experienced worker could converse with a friend across a busy shed without uttering a sound, if she could avoid the 'tackler's' eye since the fine for 'talking' was twopence!

There was no heating as none was needed but the sheds were badly ventilated and the reek of the gas from Barker Chapman's recently installed and extremely modern gas-lighting made the atmosphere almost unbearable. It had been known for operatives to bore a small hole in the window frame in order to suck in a breath of fresh air from the outside but when they were discovered, those concerned had been dismissed on the spot.

Barker Chapman had an agreement with his overlookers. 'My daughter is to come down to the workroom tomorrow, Ellis,' or 'Miss Chapman wishes to check that cloth we are weaving, Gribb,' and the men would know to a nicety what was implied. It had begun on the day he had taken her there for the first time, the day on which his first power-frame had been wrecked and had continued ever since. He had more than two dozen of the new machines now, each one operated by a woman for it was they, and their children who were the labour force now in demand. They had more quickly adapted to mill discipline and conditions. They were nimble and quick-fingered, cheap and more easily exploited than men, but the sight of an emaciated, probably deformed child, a gaunt, coughing woman, an almost naked man in the weaving shed was not one for a lady's eyes. On the days she went down there only the sturdiest were presented, women who were young and still bonny, older children who were supple and, not having worked in the mill, like the pauper children, since the age of four and five, had a bit of flesh on their straight limbs. No nasty sights for Miss Chapman, then, but cheerfully smiling like monkeys, presentably dressed and clean, the women told to be respectful and in good humour and the men decent in their dress.

She was at her desk in the corner of her father's office comparing the quality between two pieces of cloth which had been sent over from the warehouse for Barker Chapman's approval. The 'cut-looker' had examined the finished length of cloth, looking for faults in the weaving. These were called 'floats' and any man found to have a float in his work was fined, but this was a splendid piece of cloth and Kit was pleased with it. She would put it to one side for her father to see when he returned from Broadbank where he had been called to look at a loom which the overlooker reported was not working as it should. It was powered by the new steam engine just installed and since it had been put in had to be stopped every few minutes to adjust the threads as they unrolled. The threads were not strong enough to undergo the weaving, her father had been told, and so, saying he would be gone no more than an hour he had taken the carriage to see for himself.

The sharp tap at the door was followed immediately by its opening, as though the man who entered had no time for the courtesies towards his employer's daughter his position as manager demanded. His face was the colour of chalk and his eyes snapped with some nervous tension. He flung himself into the room, turning without closing the door in the direction of her father's desk which had been moved into the bay of the window to make room for the one she used.

'Mr Chapman, sir, can you come at once. The . . .'

He stopped, quite bewildered when he saw his employer's empty chair behind the desk where he was usually to be found. He turned distractedly and as if for the first time noticed Kit. 'Oh, Miss Chapman . . . I was just looking for Mr Chapman . . . I didn't see you there for the minute.' He tried a smile.

'Gribb? Is there something wrong?' She smiled herself, putting down the swatch of cloth she held, straightening her back. She had been at her desk since six o'clock that morning going carefully over the weekly accounting, checking the figures with those for the same week the previous year and feeling gratified by the growth of production and profit. The new power-looms had made an enormous difference to their output of cloth and she really thought it was high time another new weaving shed was built as her father had suggested. There was land and to spare at Broadbank for a third building and now they were to finish the woven cloth themselves they might at last call themselves complete manufacturers. The whole procedure of producing a length of cloth, from the raw bale of cotton which was opened in the blow room for cleaning and blending, through carding, combing, spinning, weaving and now the wet and dry treatments such as bleaching and mercerising was to be done in the Chapman mills and every farthing of profit was to be put in Chapman pockets!

There were almost a thousand cotton mills in the land now and trade was excellent. The machine breakers who had caused so much trouble in the past appeared to have given up the fight and nothing had been heard of them since the murderer of the soldier had been brought to justice at Lancaster. The Manchester cotton weavers had sent a petition to Parliament complaining of the low wages they received, no more than subsistence level they said, and sometimes not even that, but Sir Robert Peel assured the House, after making enquiries, that the weavers lived in comparative comfort. So what had they to complain of, he asked. Those from Stockport, who had sent in a similar petition, had been similarly treated. The machinery was starting a new and prosperous era and now was the time to expand, Kit was convinced of it. There were women and children knocking on the factory gates demanding work, and men too, now that their hand-looms were obsolete. They couldn't keep up with the factories, with men like her father who had cornered the market and though many of those same men were willing to work the new power-looms in Chapman's weaving shed it appeared that strength was not needed, as it had been with the old hand-looms and women, who were more submissive and manageable, might be employed instead. Women who were not inclined to wreck their machines and would be more agreeable to take whatever was offered in order to feed their children!

She stood up and moved round her desk, looking enquiringly at Gribb. He turned about him as though expecting her father to be hiding in some corner then, on seeing she was alone he smiled nervously and began to back out of the room, bowing in a most unaccustomed way as he did so.

'Gribb? What is it? Did you want Mr Chapman?'

'Yes, Miss Chapman, but it can wait, really . . .'

'What is it?' she repeated. 'You seem to be in somewhat of a dilemma. I'm sure whatever it is can be put to rights.'

She waited patiently for the manager to tell her what it was that had him in such an obvious state of panic but he had gained the open door by now and was reaching for it with the manifest intention of going through it.

'Gribb!' Her voice was sharp. 'In my father's absence I am his deputy as you well know. Speak up, man, and tell me what you came to tell my father.'

'Really, Miss Chapman, it is nothing. We can deal with

100

it. Some small disturbance in the spinning room . . .'

'Then if it is small and you can deal with it why should you come to fetch my father?'

'Well . . . Mr Chapman likes to be . . . told when . . .'

'When what, Gribb?'

'Nay, Miss Chapman. T'isn't for a lass like yourself to be seeing.' The man was so upset he went so far as to forget her position as his employer's daughter, calling her a lass, for that was what she was to him, no more than a lass with no rights to be here in his opinion. If Mr Chapman, who had given strict orders about the state of the working areas, and the women and children working in them when his daughter visited, knew that she had been called there when they were not ready for her, he would fire the lot of them on the spot but she was already walking towards the door, brushing past him and descending the stairs to the yard.

'Miss Chapman, please, there is really no need. A small accident and we can deal with it, really. Do go back to your office, Miss Chapman and as soon as your father returns if you would be so good as to tell him, or better yet, send for me and I can explain . . .'

'Do stop chattering, Gribb. If there has been an accident it must be dealt with and if Mr Chapman is not here . . .'

'Well, he wouldn't necessarily come into the mill, Miss Chapman. Me and the overlookers can tackle it normally, but Mr Chapman has to be told, of course, and then . . . perhaps . . . compensation . . .'

'Compensation! For a small accident?' Kit turned to look at him in astonishment, picturing a bruised shoulder or a cut arm for there was often a minor injury in the huge rooms where machinery was unguarded and children were careless.

The long room was filled in every conceivable space with humming machinery, and it was hot. There were women, drenched with sweat and smelling quite badly, tending spinning mules, and everywhere, small children, almost naked in the intense humidity, ran about from machine to machine, or crawled beneath it. The shrill voices of the women pierced the air with strident urgency, calling to the tiny 'piecers' to mend the threads as they broke. A scrap of humanity, a girl, Kit thought, her face quite blank, her eyes black holes in it, her frame stunted, crept out at Kit's feet, dragging from beneath a machine an enormous pile of cotton waste and oily dust. She did not look up nor get to her feet but crawled along, like a small, wizened animal, between the rows of machinery, pulling the filthy mass behind her until she reached the corner where she piled it on to a heap already begun. An overlooker, unaware that Kit was watching, idly struck her a blow across her narrow back with his thonged strap and she flinched and crawled faster until she was safely beneath the flying shafts and straps of the spinning mule again.

A woman began to cough, her thin figure bent double, her face, suffused with blood, turning to the colour of a plum. Her shoulders shook and she put out a hand to steady herself, lifting the other to rub at her nose and mouth. She tried to spit and Kit felt her own stomach move in a spasm of nausea, then the overlooker who had still not seen his employer's daughter clinging — it was her only means of support just then — to the door frame, pulled cruelly at the woman's arm.

'Get to't corner, yer daft bitch,' and the woman, still crouched almost double, left her machine and staggered to the corner of the room. There was a bucket there, and beside it a jug in which there was a thin, yellow liquid. The woman, still choking and spitting, reached for the jug and began to drink its contents, then, turning hastily, vomited into the bucket. She straightened up, wiped her mouth and sweating face on a bit of waste and, the whole incident taking no more than thirty seconds, ran back to her machine.

Kit turned to Gribb and though she said nothing, her grey-white face and staring eyes asked the question.

'It's the "fly",' Gribb explained apologetically.

'The fly?' Her voice was no more than a whisper.

'It fills their mouths and noses. From the yard. When

102

they can't get rid of it by coughing or . . . well, they drink mustard and water. It makes them sick and . . . they get it up.'

'Dear God!'

'They take no harm, Miss Chapman, none at all. 'Tis better than choking on it.'

She could not answer and the overlooker, the one who had struck the child, came running then, his own face appalled, at what she had time to wonder, for surely he was well used to what had just happened, and for a moment she had the distinct impression he was about to take her arm and bundle her from the room. His face was thunderstruck and he brushed women and children roughly aside to reach her.

'Miss Chapman, really, you should not be here.' It was the man called Ellis, the one who had offered on the day of the hanging to remove the crowd who had gathered in the yard. She had recovered her composure somewhat and though her eyes still darted feverishly about the room, confounded by the sight of so many whey-faced, stoop-shouldered, undernourished and oddly shaped women and children, where once they had been clean, well formed, even managing a smile or two when she had been before, she had found her lost wits, and voice!

'Why not, pray?' she answered him. 'In my father's absence I am responsible for the mill, and, as a matter of interest, may I ask where on God's earth did these . . . these workers come from. None of them look fit to be in charge of a machine and while you are at it please be so kind as to tell me what is going on. I have been told of an accident so I would be obliged if you would lead me to it . . .'

'Oh no, Miss Chapman, no. Your father would not be best pleased if you were to go up there . . .'

'Up where? What has happened?' She began to walk in the direction his vague gesture had indicated and short of laying their hands on her there was nothing the two men could do to stop her. She strode past ceaselessly toiling women who were hard pressed to keep up with the

103

machines they operated for the spindles and bobbins moved quickly and needed constant alertness. Their feet were never still, their hands the same and their eyes appeared haunted for the mules must never stop except for the cleaning of them which took place during their own 'rest' periods. The machines were often turned on early and switched off late, 'cribbing' it was called so that they were forced to work extra, precious minutes for which they were not paid. The spindles whirred and the hot smell of oil and grease clamped shut Kit's mouth and clogged her nostrils and when she came to the end of the long row of machines, turning to the corner of the room where a group of men stood she was not at first certain what it was she saw. She had been told there had been an accident, though not of what kind for the manager and overlooker were afraid to disclose the details. Mr Chapman would have dealt with it, privately, seeing to the family, if the victim had one. A few shillings for tongues that needed to be kept silent, though really none would dare speak up for fear of losing their own job.

'What is it?' she said sharply, moving towards the group, three or four overlookers and another manager. 'What has happened?' As she spoke she slipped in something on the floor and Ellis put out his hand to steady her. It was dim in the corner since the windows were high and let in little light but what there was fell on the floor and she looked down, narrowing her eyes to see what was there.

It was red, bright and shining and thick. A lot of it, seeping into the wooden floorboards along with the oil and sweat and other unmentionable substances which were deposited upon it. She looked at it and knew that somehow she must raise her eyes to meet what was waiting for her. She heard a child cry out somewhere behind her, the voice sharp above the sound of the machinery and a man's voice could be heard telling someone, 'it was for his own good for if he dozed off and tumbled into the machine like' . . . then she lifted her head slowly and forced herself not to flinch as she looked at what they had laid on the blood-soaked pile of cotton waste.

A small boy. Perhaps five or six. His face was like paper, white and fine, the skin clear beneath the grime. His eyes were closed and she could see the blue veins on his lids and the long sweep of his brown lashes. His hair was a soft tumble of baby curls and his small mouth was open, just as though in sleep he dreamed of something which pleased him. He was not, of course, sleeping, for at the end of his thin arms were no hands, just the jagged . . . Oh dear Lord, dear, dear Lord . . . white bone . . . blood . . . blood . . .

She stood rigid and though she felt the food she had eaten at breakfast rise rapidly to fill her throat she made herself, *steeled* herself not to turn away. This was her father's mill, *her* mill and what went on in it was their responsibility. She must not faint or look away. She must not show signs of female weakness or they would shrug their shoulders and ask one another what else could one expect of a woman? She had chosen this. Her father had given it to her and she must accept it. *Every part of it!*

'What happened?' she asked and was quite amazed that her lips, which she thought to be set forever in a clamped line of self-control, could form the words.

The still life group of men sprang to attention together, their astounded expressions slipping simultaneously into ones of horror that she should see this, of dread at what Mr Chapman would say when he heard, not of the accident but of his daughter's witnessing the result, and of anxiety that they might lose their jobs over it. The child had simply been in the wrong place at the wrong time. No one's fault, not even his own. He had slipped on the oil, put out his hands to save himself from falling and . . . well, the machinery had been waiting there, as it always waited for those who were not constantly alert. He had been dragged into it and only for the quickness of his overlooker, might have suffered far worse mutilation than the loss of his hands. He would have still lost his life, of course, since the flow of blood could not be staunched, but . . . well, life was cheap and it was an ill wind for there would be another to take his place before the day was out.

They told her, their tongues clipping their words in their effort to explain what had happened as blame was laid at everyone's door but their own.

'Who is he?' she asked abruptly, allowing herself to look away now.

'Pardon?' they said, not quite understanding.

'What was his name?' They did not know of any since he had come only that week from Liverpool, they said, in a waggon filled with parish children, half of whom knew neither their own name, nor where they had originated. It seemed there was no one to grieve for him.

'Cover him decently,' and when one threw a bit of sacking carelessly over the pathetic body she turned angrily, her eyes ablaze with some emotion even she did not understand. She sent a man to her office, quite astounded he was and when he had put the soft shawl he had brought into her hands she knelt by the boy's side and covered him, gently patting the warmth and compassion about him, perhaps the first his young body had ever known. Then, standing, turning away, she walked past the women who did not even glance sideways from their frames. Past the silent, blank-eyed children, none of whom seemed unduly concerned about the dead child, nor even to be aware that he was dead. They were like ghosts who are forced to haunt the place in which they had met their end, longing to lie down and rest, simply to fade away, but unable to do other than what they did.

A young girl came through the door as Kit put out her hand to open it. The girl stood back, allowing her to pass but she did not hang her head, nor even lower her eyes respectfully as the others did, but stared, quite unafraid it seemed, by the appearance of her employer's daughter. She was slender but her bones were decently covered by her flesh. Her appearance was neat, her hair drawn back into, surprisingly, a cheerful knot of red ribbon. She was dark, her skin fine and retaining a colour which said she was used to the outdoor life. But it was her eyes which drew Kit Chapman's startled glance for they were a shining pearl grey, pale and cat-like, gleaming and bold. She was no more than sixteen or so, pretty, and those eyes bored into hers with unconcealed contempt.

'He's dead, then.' It was not a question but a statement of fact.

'I beg your pardon?'

'The little lad. The one who had his hands ripped off.' It was said brutally, meant to hurt, to accuse.

'Yes, I'm afraid he is.' Why should she feel the need to answer this impudent girl? She had no idea why she did, nor why she had the urge to explain that she had been unaware of the true conditions in which her father's spinners worked. That she had heard of their grievances (as who hadn't?), but she had imagined them to be exaggerated, blown up out of all proportion in their demand for higher wages. Profit must be made. Production costs must be pared down to make it, and if they could not compete in foreign markets they would *all* be out of a job for the mill would close and then what would they do, all those clamouring for a better way of life? Surely any job was better than none and all the time her thoughts fluttered like moths inside her head the girl stood silently by to watch her.

Then, 'I ran to fetch someone. A woman I know. She has a way with herbs, potions, splints and such. I thought if she could stop the bleeding . . . but they said he was gone so I'm on me way back to me machine. Of course, they'll stop me pay an' fine me into the bargain for leaving without permission but I couldn't just stand there and watch the poor little beggar bleed to death.'

'No.'

The girl's eyes never faltered. They were filled with a fierce, quite devastating emotion, hot sparks of it flashing across the space between them, striking at Kit with the force of a physical blow. There was an angry contempt, an animosity, an unwillingness it seemed to Kit even to share the bit of space in which they both stood, so great was her aversion.

'This wouldn't have happened if you'd fenced them machines, you know that, don't you?'

'I beg your pardon?' she said.

'And so you should, or someone's, for you're the one to blame, you and your father. You should certainly be begging that little lad's pardon for takin' his life, not that it was worth much to him, or to anyone else for that matter, since he lived like an animal and was worked like one.'

'I'd be obliged if you would step aside and let me pass.' Her voice was cold. Her own anger was moving inside her, a somewhat guilty anger for should she really be feeling it in the face of what she had just seen? But it was at this impudent girl it was directed. No matter what had happened she was merely a mill-hand and had certainly no right to be laying blame at her employer's door, not if she wanted to keep her job, nor to be accusing her father of neglect. Fencing the machines indeed, when it was well known that the wooden casings which some of the other idealistic mill-owners had considered, were a fire hazard and therefore more dangerous than the machines themselves.

'Of course! I'm right sorry to have held you up. You'll be busy making the funeral arrangements, I dare say, an' havin' a whip round for his family, if he's got any.'

'I fail to see what any of this has got to do with you. Have you no work to go to? If your machine is standing idle I'm sure someone can be easily found to operate it.'

'You don't like to hear the truth then? You don't want to see what's going on in your father's mill, under his *own bloody nose*. You don't want to be reminded that the elegant dress you're wearing was bought with the sweat, aye, an' the blood, of bairns like that one in there.'

'Let me pass.'

'No, I can see you don't, but if you took a stroll round the mills and the weaving sheds now an' again, you couldn't avoid it but you wouldn't like that, would you?'

'I could have you turned off for insolence and . . .'

'Aye, that you could,' but the girl was not afraid, only drunk with her own contemptuous loathing.

'What is your name?'

'Jenny Greenwood.'

They separated then, one to her machine and another eight hours of racket and stench and heat, to the bucket in the corner and ten minutes' respite to eat her 'dinner' at midday, the other to the peace and solitude, the comfort of her office, the order of her desk, the coffee served in a china cup by Mrs Plank and the certain knowledge that whenever she chose she could order her carriage and go home.

At the end of the week Jenny Greenwood was surprised to find that her wage, all six shillings and sixpence of it had not been 'docked' of the fine she had expected.

That night Katherine and Barker Chapman had their first argument.

'It cannot be necessary, father,' she finished after she had given him a graphic account of what she had seen that day, and though he had heard it from Gribb, his manager, who had thought it expedient to put forth his own version first, Barker listened politely as was his way.

'Those children were deformed . . .'

'Most are deformed when I take them on, Kit. Their parents are often not as diligent in feeding them as they should. You have only to tour the town on a Saturday night after they have been paid to see them lolling in gutters and on doorsteps. Gin, my dear! That is what they spend their money on and not on nourishing food for their children.'

'But they are so young. Surely they should not be forced . . .'

'Forced! Who told you they are forced?' Her father smiled and his voice was smooth. 'They beat on my gate every day, mothers and their children begging me to employ them, more than I can take, but I let them in, for really, their families need the wages or they would starve . . .'

'But surely . . . there must be some way to allow them to . . .'

She faltered and her hands gripped one another in her

lap but her father reached out and placed his own about them, a rare demonstration of his regard for her.

'To what, my dear?'

'To work, if they must, but in some decent occupation.'

Her father stiffened and withdrew his hands, sitting back in his armchair. His eyes became steely in his grim face and his mouth was tight-lipped with outrage.

'Are you saying that the work I offer these people is disreputable in some way, Katherine. That it is not honest labour for which they are paid?'

'No, no, of course not, but that child . . .' She could not shut out the image of that waxen-faced child, the blue-veined vulnerability of his closed eyes and her own voice was harsh, '. . . the one who died, he came from the workhouse in Liverpool, I was told and really, Father . . .'

'There are hundreds of children who are taken from the workhouse, where, let me assure you, my dear Kit, they are not as well treated as in my mill. Do you not think, if they are to work, and work they must, either here with us, in the mines or up the chimneys, they are not best served in a factory. The work is not heavy. They are warm and fed and clothed. They have Sunday free and many are taken to Church where their religious needs are catered for.' It was evident that Barker Chapman was making a great effort to be patient.

'I know all that, Father, but . . .' She knew what her father said made sense, that it was all perfectly true but she had received a bad shock this morning and she was still flayed by the sights she had seen. They must work, all of them, women and children or they would starve but the look of animal-like docility, the feeling that inside each skull was nothing more than the intelligence to move hands and feet in the necessary operation of the machine; the weariness, the dull acceptance, the very appearance, though she knew her thoughts to be exaggerated, of dying by inches, had harrowed her. Were they alive, but breathing and eating a slow death? Did they long to see, did they even *know* of a flower, the green of the grass, the vast blue . . .

110

Dear God, she must stop this torturing of herself and listen to what her father was saying.

'Kit, my dear, do not look at me with those reproachful eyes.' He smiled and the face she had come to know so well, was smooth, untroubled. 'Look at it from another point of view. These children are learning a trade. They are apprenticed to us and at the end of their indentures will call themselves spinners, or weavers and, if they wish, will be at liberty to go anywhere they choose, anywhere spinning and weaving is done. They will owe me nothing.'

'Yes, I know that to be true but the child . . .'

'Katherine.' His voice clipped through hers and she looked up, startled.

'Yes . . .'

'Perhaps I have made a mistake.'

'A mistake?'

'In believing you to be capable of running a mill.'

'I don't understand.' Her voice was uncertain and her eyes were wide.

'Yes! You do! If you cannot accept that there will be a certain amount of . . . disagreeable, even distasteful aspects to this business world we are in then perhaps it would be advisable for you to return to the one which is really yours. The one your mother and her friends occupy. I am running a business, not a charitable institution. I must do it in the way which makes the most profit or I will go under. I am asked to employ not only men and women, but their children. No one else is small enough to go under the machines or I would not take them since I care for it as little as you. They are necessary, Kit. The machinery is dangerous, I grant you that but the overlookers are there to ensure the younger children do not fall into it . . .'

'Then what was Ellis doing to allow that child to be so near the machine?' Her voice was passionate and she reached out to him with her hands. She had been appalled by her father's words, knowing that he meant what he said and she could not bear to return to the empty life she had once led but she could not let the horror of this morning

111

go by her without a word. She knew it was true. Profit must be made but not, surely, with the crippling and deaths of young children.

Her father stood up and moved towards the door, his face cold, pinched almost, for he was deeply disappointed. He had known from the start that the mill floor, the weaving sheds would upset her but he had hoped, with time and the growing fascination she found in the business, the satisfaction of knowing that one day it would be hers, she would grow to accept it, as they all did. He went as seldom as he could himself, to the work floors, leaving the managers to see to the running of them. He knew exactly how much each machine produced but he really did not care to see how that production was achieved and Katherine must learn to be the same, or stay away from it altogether.

'If you are to take that attitude then there is no more to be said. I shall go alone to the mill tomorrow and you can remain with your mother and . . . sew, or whatever women do all day long.'

'Father . . . don't . . . please . . .'

'I can see no alternative, my dear.'

'I could not stand it, not again.'

'Then . . .' He shrugged his shoulders expressively, then turned back to her. 'I cannot change the system, Kit, whether you are there or not. The managers run the sheds and I run the business. If you are not prepared to do the same, then you must stay away from it.'

'Father . . . please . . .' She stood up and her lovely silken gown fell about her slender figure. It was the colour of a golden guinea, soft and shining, enhancing the pale gold of her own skin. Her glossy hair was held in place at the back of her head with a looped knot of gold satin ribbons and he thought, for a brief and marvelling moment, what a waste it was to put such splendour in a mill, in the masculine environment his son, if he had bred one, would have taken, since there was no doubt she would be an asset to grace any man's table, his bed, as the breeder of magnificent children. Her face was lit by the intensity of her emotions.

'Father, I cannot just ignore what I have seen. It has been a . . . shock. I must be allowed to . . . to consider it. There is the funeral to be seen to . . .'

'Funeral!' Her father laughed harshly. 'What funeral?'

'But the child . . .'

'Is already buried.'

'Dear God . . .'

'As you say, Kit, dear God indeed!' Now, if you will excuse me I shall leave you to . . . consider, was that the word? . . . your future. You must, of course, do as you think best. If you are not in the carriage tomorrow morning at the usual time I will understand but remember, whatever you decide, nothing will change in my mill!'

He closed the door quietly behind him.

8

He saw the dogs first. They were lying, one on either side of the path, low in the coarse grass, their ears flat, absolutely motionless, two silent menacing forms barely visible against the harsh black and grey of the winter landscape.

It had snowed in the night, a light dusting which had laid a pattern of lace on the tops but he was below the snowline, half way between the peaks and the valley floor and there was nothing here but tough, gritstone rocks, the harsh remains of summer heather and bracken, brown and snapping underfoot and the endless miles of walls, little more than piles of stones which had come with enclosure when much land along the moorland fringes had been turned into a field system.

It was bitterly cold with an east wind blowing straight from Scandinavia whipping across the Pennines, searching out every patched and thin place in his jacket and breeches.

He shivered and clutched his arms about himself, then beat them fiercely across his chest to get the blood coursing, stamping his feet on the ground as he walked for surely they were frozen solid inside his clogs.

It was steep where he walked and the upland track of causey stones, almost obliterated now, but once used by pack-horses, was slippery, the moisture which coated it frozen during the night. A thin mist lingered in the valley beneath him, wisping about the oak woods, leafless and skeletal and outlining the stately conifers. He could see the roofs of a cottage or two and the shape of Abbott's weaving mill but it was Sunday and, apart from the cleaning of the machinery by the pauper children Abbott employed, there would be no work done this day. In front of him, behind him and above rolled the vast expanse of moor, rising and falling in splendid isolation to the far horizon, its dark and sombre mass flecked with snow. Here and there where water had settled were sheets of ice and down through the mist patterns he could see the dull gleam of the flowing river in the valley.

He hurried on, picking up his heels and stamping down his feet in an effort to warm them, wishing to God he had the price of a new pair of clogs for though Mercy had packed these as best she could, with paper and some cotton waste, they were still as thin as air. He smiled sadly at the thought of her and the frozen skin of his face almost cracked with the pain of it. He had, for the past six months courted Mercy Butterworth with all the propriety a girl of her station deserved, going whenever he could to Enoch Butterworth's cottage at the end of the village street, tolerated as his future son-in-law, and sitting as patiently and decently as he was able under Mercy's loving gaze as Enoch read from the family Bible. Joss was to move into the cottage when they were married since there was more room than in the one in which his mother, his sisters and his younger brother lived and he wondered, as he sat and listened to Mercy's father extol the virtues of 'turning the other cheek' how he was to manage it. Mercy protected him from Enoch as

114

much as she could, knowing Joss's explosive nature and impatience with such beliefs, but her dove-like meekness and bowed head could not always quench his fierce need for action, for the getting up and throwing off of the delicate chains which bound him to her. But how could he? She loved him and thought he loved her. Her brother was dead because of the cause Joss fought for and he felt responsible for it. He owed her something and he was paying his debt as his conscience bade him. But he found it hard. Mercy could not seem to get enough of 'seeing to him', as she put it, mending and washing his meagre wardrobe of clothes, much to his own mother's disapproval making him nourishing dishes to put a 'bit of meat on his bones', fussing over whether he was too cold, or too hot, or tired, and in her new found dignity as his betrothed – he quailed at the word and all it conjured up – she found peace and acceptance as she prepared for their wedding day in the autumn, loving and maternal and yet shy with him in their new roles as man and woman. She would be waiting in the cottage, not far from the window so as not to miss his arrival. On the fire would be a pan of something hot and as tasty as she could make from the scraps she garnered. Carrots, grown in the summer and stored in one of the rooms above the kitchen that had once housed hand-looms, potatoes and an onion or two though these did not keep as well, even a bit of rabbit if Charlie, who was five years old, and handy, had been lucky with his traps.

He loved Mercy, did Charlie and was made up with the coming wedding. Though he spent each day with his mother and four-year-old younger sister, carding the raw cotton his mother was to spin, whenever he could he was up at the Butterworth cottage, doing an odd job or two, those Mr Butterworth found increasingly difficult to do as he grew older, or out on the moor setting his traps or checking to see if a rabbit had been snared. A wiry lad, bright and already longing to follow his brother and dead father in the ways of radicalism, he had the natural independence and plain common sense of the north country lad, a readiness to learn, to 'get on' as their Joss was to do. Mercy's brother had been a martyr to the honourable and just cause in which the Greenwood men were involved and Joss, as its leader, was Charlie's idol. To Charlie he was a warrior who had bested the enemy. Tom had been a soldier too, but he had fallen which did not in any way denigrate him in Charlie's eyes. They were both heroes and Charlie wished for nothing more than to emulate them. To be a spinner, even a master spinner or weaver was well enough, he told Mercy, conscious of the status of her father, but one day he meant to be known as something, *somebody* in this world. He was learning to read and write, taught, as Joss had been, in the village Sunday school, as all the village children were, if they wished it. Whereas most would rather spend their precious free time in more pleasurable pursuits, playing the children's games which had passed from generation to generation, he, and Joss, who had encouraged his younger brother, had persevered.

The dogs rose slowly to their feet as Joss approached. They did not snarl or even move a muscle. Their ears were laid flat and their eyes were still and watchful and their rigid stance warned him that should he make a move they did not like he might have cause to regret it. He stopped and his heart began a sharp tattoo in his chest. His breath shivered in his throat and he held it for several seconds before letting it out. He remained perfectly still for he remembered her words.

'They are completely safe except when I tell them to be otherwise!' she had said, then invited him, challenged him to command them to him, and though he had done so, *she* had allowed it. Two years almost to the day and in that time he had seen her twice. Her spirit had been uncompromising on each occasion, her extravagant courage defying the men he had sent to wreck her father's machine, defying those who, though she had not known of it then, had meant her no harm on the day of Tom's hanging. These were her dogs, Joby and Blaze she had called them, and where they were she would not be far away.

He took another step and one of them growled warningly. Not much of a sound really, just enough to let him know he really was dicing with death and should think twice before chancing another move.

He drew in a deep breath of the lung-searing cold and turned his head cautiously since he had no desire to have it torn from his shoulders. There was a group of stones thirty yards from the track, just on the edge of a drop which went almost vertically down into the valley. 'Badger's Edge' it was called since it was known that a 'badger', one of the men who had once hawked goods about the district, using the pack-way as a means of getting from Edgeclough to Crossfold had gone over the clough in a snowstorm and fallen to his death. The stones were as tall as a man, a dozen of them and they formed a sheltered circle in which anyone seeking solitude could not be seen from the track.

She stepped out quietly from behind the rocks, her back to the edge, saying nothing. She was wearing an outfit which was identical – perhaps it was the same – to the one she had worn then and her hair hung about her face and tumbled down her back as it had on that other day. Her hands were thrust deep into her pockets and beneath her skirt, though he could not see her legs, he knew she stood with her booted feet wide apart. As a man would stand, bold, defiant, declaring that this was *her* bit of earth and what right had he to invade it?

It seemed neither could look away. Their eyes were locked in a strange and cautionary fashion as though each was sizing up the other and yet that was not it entirely for they were both well aware of who the other was, of what the other was and of the antipathy between them. It was more than that, more than the yawning gulf of class, of prejudice, more than the conflict which existed in each of them to fight and wound, to hurt in the protection of what was theirs, he for the people who looked to him for leadership, she for her father's mills. It was, quite simply, the look of

117

a man and a woman taking the measure, *as* a man and a woman, of one another.

She snapped her fingers and the dogs lay down and one yawned. They lowered their muzzles to their paws, giving the impression they were about to doze off but neither took their unblinking eyes from Joss Greenwood.

'So,' she said softly, 'here we are again, Joss Greenwood. I wondered how long it would be before we met up with one another.'

'You have been looking for me then, Katherine Chapman?' His voice was mocking and he felt a surge of triumph as her eyes narrowed in sudden anger. Then she smiled sweetly.

'Only to see you caught and, hopefully, hanged.'

'Like Tom Butterworth?' He felt the acid of his hatred burn his throat and he took a step towards her. The dog, Joby, raised his head.

'Really. Was that his name? I had quite forgot.'

'That doesn't surprise me. What could he possibly mean to you except as some rough, cloth-capped working lad who forgot his place and got his just retribution.'

'Well, so he did. I could not have put it better myself. He killed a man in cold blood and deserved to die.'

'Did he indeed? And were you there to witness it?'

'No, and neither were you or you would have been hanged beside him.'

'*Instead of,* actually, Katherine Chapman, since it was my fault the Redcoat died, not Tom's. He was protecting his sister from the soldiers you sent to find me, damn your rotten soul to hell, and I should have been protecting *him* instead of ... of ...' His face worked with something which looked curiously like guilt, guilt and shame, and a deep sadness. 'He was only a boy, trying to do a man's job ...'

She looked surprised then recovered from it, drawing breath to attack again.

'Really, but then from what I have seen of you, you were ever a violent man. First in the wrecking of my father's machine and then, so you say, in the death of a man who was doing no more than his duty in apprehending a criminal. It appears that you thrive on destruction and interference in the affairs of others.'

'If you mean by that I fight for what is rightfully mine and for those who try to make a decent living for themselves, then you are right.'

'By destroying what is *not* yours. By taking away what will eventually give them prosperity . . .'

'To the mill-owners. Not to those who work for them.'

'It will take time to move from one era to another . . .'

'And what era is that, Miss Chapman?' His voice was cruelly mocking.

'The industrial era. You cannot simply ignore it. You cannot stand in the way of . . .'

'Progress! Yes, I have heard all the arguments the ones who are to benefit from it put forward to justify that claim but I am yet to be convinced.'

'You do not give it a chance . . .'

'Do I not? Perhaps the men who are out of work would like to be given a chance. A chance to feed their children on more than water, oats and potatoes . . . if they are lucky enough to be able to afford even that . . .'

'But they will. If they will accept this changeover from the domestic industry to power looms. A hand-loom weaver can weave only 172,000 picks a week while a power-loom weaver can weave 605,000 on two looms. Does it not seem reasonable that eventually that man will be capable of earning so much more than . . .'

'It is the power-looms that take the bread out of their mouths and it is this for which we are fighting. Not against progress, for any man of sense can see it must come. The men will work at anything for a decent wage, a wage they can *live* on, bring up a family on, but until that day comes I will fight you and your father with every means at my disposal. Did you know that in the barracks at Burnley they house two hundred soldiers, all to keep in order the *dis*orderly populace? Even if the poor weaver dies at his loom, his useless loom, they must maintain the soldiers. There were disturbances there four or five years ago, you see, and so there they sit, doing nothing – unless they have me and my men to chase – ' he smiled maliciously, 'since nothing happens for them to take up arms against, but it will change. I warn you now that though we have been quiet since Tom's death we will come back and if we don't get what we want we will force the mill-owners in any way we can, violent or not, to deal fairly with us. So be warned. Tell your father. I have an army of men behind me and by God . . .'

'Have you no softer side, Joss Greenwood?'

Surprise showed in both their faces, hers at herself as she asked the sudden question for why on earth should she have said that, or even thought it, his at the strangeness of it, but his savage oath, the lunging step he took towards her, the lifting of his clenched fists brought the two dogs to their feet and she raised a finger, no more than that, to bring them to her side.

'A softer side, Katherine Chapman? You dare say that to me?' His face twisted in repugnance and he stepped closer to her and the dogs began to growl deep in their throats. He was no more than ten yards from her. He could see the deep flaring blue flame in her eyes, the outraged dip of her silken brows and the soft pink of her angry mouth, just on the inside of her lips where the moistness was. Her three-quarter length coat was open at the neck and the pale golden smoothness of her throat, the fiercely beating hollow at its base was plainly visible and he felt a tremor run from his belly down the inside of his thighs and he hated her, hated her for it. His bitterness was such that he could have taken told of her, put his hands about that lovely neck and squeezed and squeezed until . . . dear God . . . until . . .

'You speak of softness . . .' His voice was ragged, '. . . you . . . and yours who would sacrifice a child . . . aah yes, I heard of him, Katherine Chapman, from my sister who saw him . . . a baby, no more, being dragged into the frame, and you dare to ask me of softness. How do you sleep sound in your bed at night knowing you are responsible for it . . .?'

'Aah . . . please, don't . . .'

For a moment he was taken aback, not believing what he had heard. He lowered his threatening fists and the shoulders he had hunched, just like those of a bareknuckle fighter about to take on an opponent, slowly fell and the madness in his brain subsided. Without another sound she sank painfully to her knees, an arm about the neck of each dog and her upturned face was anguished and for a dreadful second he felt his heart move in his breast with pity for her. She was so obviously in pain, torn by some great conflict within her and it was almost more than he could do to restrain himself from going to her, putting his arms about her, holding her, soothing away that tangled web of hair from her face, cupping her chin to look into her eyes for the truth. Her mouth was open, so soft and sweet and vulnerable, and her eyes looked up at him, enormous and haunted, begging. Sweet Jesus, what was he thinking of? She was the symbol of all he hated the most. Proud, disdainful, arrogant in her fur-lined coat when his own mother had but a thin shawl, in her expensive leather boots when his sisters trudged the moors in worn out clogs, with her firm golden skin, her fine straight body, her bright-eyed look of glowing health when he moved among men and women every day who were no more than living skeletons, with children who could scarce walk on their stunted limbs. What did she want of him, for Christ's sake, looking at him like that, just as though she was asking him for something? What did he know of the life she led, though he could guess at its splendour. It was evidently one of freedom not known by other women of her class since it was well publicised now that one day she would inherit her father's mills and not only that but would run them, as a son would. She was not a *real* woman, how could she be for she lived the life a man would lead? There was no gentleness in her, no sweetness and soft warmth as there was in Mercy, and yet . . . and yet there was something, something as basic as the earth on which they stood, as deep rooted as the trees in the valley, as unyielding as the moorland itself. She was not feminine as Mercy was feminine, but by God, she was all *female*.

He turned away from her, afraid if he remained he might go to her, put out his hand to help her to rise, and that, he knew, must never happen.

Kit felt the dogs as they licked her face and hands, distressed as her strangeness conveyed itself to them and she stood up abruptly, steadying herself on their strong backs. She flung up her head, pride stiffening her spine for was she to let this . . . this stranger see the secret guilt she had carried for the past week since the death of the boy? She had gone back to the mill with her father the following day, telling herself that she would, somehow, do it differently, that she would convince him that, surely, there was some way to replace the children, but when she had tried he had taken her down to the gate, rough with her in front of the men who watched, and begged her, if she could, to inform these women, indicating the patient, shawled creatures who stood there that from now on there would be no more work for their children.

They had set up such an outcry, beseeching the 'maister' to reconsider for they had other bairns at home to feed and if these they had brought were not suitable, too big perhaps, they could fetch the others. Their men had no jobs, they cried, not for a year or more, some of them longer, and if the children did not work how were they to manage? She had seen their eyes, those haunted eyes for even as they spoke they had hated themselves and her for forcing them to it, in offering these scraps of humanity as the only providers of the family, but what else could they do, those eyes pleaded to know.

She attacked with venom. 'You go about the country preaching your sermons on justice for the labouring man, on a fair wage for a fair day's work but you know nothing about the *real* working of a mill . . .' Her voice was harsh, unforgiving.

'Damn you, my own sister works in your father's mill. Don't tell me I know nothing of what goes on there.' The pity was gone as if it had never been and he turned gladly, ready again to fight her since that was safe and all he knew how to do, all he could allow himself to do.

'I have seen your sister. She looks none the worse for working in my father's mill.'

'That's no thanks to your father. It was a man like him who abandoned her . . .'

'Abandoned her . . .?'

'Aye. She was what's known as a pauper brat. I'm sure you know what that is, Miss Chapman. Brought from some poorhouse to work in his mill and when she didn't suit . . . My father found her on the moor. She was holding the hand of another child, a girl about six years old, my father said. She was dead. Her legs were deformed, stunted and weak. Some mistake had been made at the poorhouse, deliberately, to get rid of them. A mill-owner who couldn't be bothered with a crippled child and another who was too young to work. Jenny . . . she was only about two years old, my mother said, and they had been abandoned, like a couple of unwanted pups . . . She was sixteen when my father died and . . . she was kept at home before that . . . with her mother . . . safe. She had food . . .'

Dear God, why was he telling her this, explaining the roots of Jenny's beginning and the reason for her look of good health . . . 'just as you do, Katherine Chapman. Your father, as a father should, provided for you, as mine did for us . . . as is their right as fathers. But the men I know cannot provide for their own, *as is their right,* with decent work, *as is their due* . . .!'

They glared at one another wildly, gripped tight in the madness and inevitable clash of their single-minded wills. There was nothing more to be said. They had fought and neither had won and what was the use of going over and over the same painful conflict. She knew, he had seen it in her eyes a moment ago that the employment of children, and their mistreatment, was wrong but it seemed she was prepared to turn a blind eye to it, for the sake of her father, he supposed. She was not without feelings for he had heard of the incident with the shawl, but perhaps that made it worse. To know, to sympathise, to bear compassion and yet to go on must surely be more wicked than to be as her father and the other mill-owners who genuinely believed they did no wrong.

But they might stand here forever and spit at each other. He might sense her indecision, her uncertainty but there was no getting away from the truth, that she, or her father and the rest of the mill-owners had killed Tom Butterworth. He must cling to that for it was a fact. He must not let her pain, if that was what it was, deflect him from the hatred he felt for the system her father and others like him and through them, *she* had created.

'Your father is the murderer, Katherine Chapman, and should have been hanged in Tom Buttworth's place.' He said it quite without emotion, passionless and therefore more chilling and rejoiced to see the hot flame of her enmity, her hatred of him and her loyalty to her father burn in her eyes.

'And what of you, Joss Greenwood? When are you to hang? The militiamen cannot seem able to catch you or your men as you go about looting and burning and destroying. Well, you can be sure I shall tell them it was you who wrecked my father's machine. It seems you are quite elusive, but one day you will make a mistake, or perhaps one of those underdogs you champion will give you away. You cannot win, you know. We are too strong for you, or perhaps it is you who are weak and not quite the man you seem to think yourself.'

She laughed and tossed her head and her hair flew back and rippled almost to her buttocks. She placed her hands on her hips and the bitter cold flew ribbons of scarlet in her cheeks. 'I despise a man who promises much but cannot seem to carry out what he declares so loudly he will. Fight you say, and win, you say! How, and with what? You cannot return your followers to their rural activities since

124

time will never march backwards. There are laws to restrain you, made by those who rule the land. There are those who are meant to rule and those who are meant to be ruled . . .'

'So you see yourself as Queen, then, Katherine Chapman, and we are your humble subjects to be ground beneath your . . .'

He stopped suddenly and his panting breath clouded about his head. His chest heaved and his fists clenched yet again by his side, but slowly his brain cleared, then he sighed slowly, sadly, and the madness left his eyes.

'Really, I do not know what I am about.' It was as though he spoke to himself. 'I stand here in fierce argument with a woman who knows nothing of the distress and disaster in this land. She is like a child in a tantrum. She is as ignorant as the rest of the country to the true predicament we are in. All these years, fifty nearly, since the first water frame was invented we have tried. They have banned us from meeting together, from forming a trade union to protect ourselves and still we fight on.' He laughed softly and she found herself listening to him as she had not listened to him when he shouted. He spoke well, with little of the broad dialect of the north countryman. She was not to know of the hours he had spent in teaching himself to erase it, since, when he addressed the crowds, not only of his own Lancastrians, they must understand him. He must be understood by the gentry, the squirearchy, the millocracy, and even those up in London when the time came for him to go there.

'I need my head seeing to.' He shook it gently, as though at his own folly, turning away, ready to set his foot on the track again, ready to deliver himself to Mercy's loving arms and sweet and modest kisses for she understood him, and the passion of his work, as this woman did not. Then he looked back at her, grinning quite good-humouredly over his shoulder.

'Go back to your playing, Katherine Chapman . . .'

'Kit,' she said unexpectedly.

'**Pardon!**'

'My name is Kit.'

'Is it indeed! Well then, *Kit* Chapman, go back to the toy your father has promised you if you do as he says. That is what you want isn't it? If you are a good girl and behave yourself and close your eyes to what is distasteful, you might even be as rich and successful as he is, though I doubt it. I doubt you have the stomach for it, since that is what you will need. A strong stomach!'

He tipped his cap impishly and in that moment she forgot the ideal for which they both struggled, so diverse and yet, though neither was aware of it, the same, and, marvelling at the light of laughter in his eyes, the engaging tilt to his dark eyebrows, wondered how they would have been, Kit Chapman and Joss Greenwood, if they had known one another in different circumstances.

She heard him begin to whistle as he stepped out jauntily on the path and she could have sworn that the violent exchange they had shared had done him the world of good!

9

The three men sprang to their feet when she entered the room and for a second she was startled since she had thought her father to be alone. She hesitated at the door, raising her eyebrows enquiringly in his direction and her father moved round his desk and came across the carpet to take her arm.

'My dear, I was under the impression you had gone to Crossfold with your mother. Did I not hear her say something about a new gown for your birthday?'

'It did not take long, Father. Miss Cavendish is clever and knows exactly what I require.'

'Well then, in that case, come and meet an old friend of

mine.' He turned, leading her forward, his face reserved, his smile cool and Kit Chapman received the distinct impression that she had caught her father off guard. She had indeed been into Crossfold, spending an hour of her precious time, time when she might have been more profitably employed going over the monthly accounting, listening to her mother and the rest of the clientele who crowded the salon owned by Miss Cavendish, gush approvingly over the high waisted, ivory silk gown which was being created for her to wear at the ball her father was giving to celebrate her eighteenth birthday the following week. It was a lovely dress and the occasion would be splendid but she really did begrudge the time that was needed to be pinned and prodded and told to stand this way and that, when Miss Cavendish knew her exact measurements and requirements and could so easily make and deliver the gown without Kit even having a fitting!

Her mother had been most put out when she had said so, telling her she was unnatural and really, she should have been a man since she had never yet met a girl who was so disinclined towards pretty clothes. It was not exactly true for Kit dressed well. She had a talent for creating a look of understated elegance, a simple, uncluttered style which made the decision of what to wear each day so easy. Day-dresses of white French lawn in the summer, with gigot sleeves, which were then fashionable, and a sash of soft apple green, of lemon or biscuit or rose pink, and of long-sleeved gowns of cashmere or merino in winter. Simple lines, pleasing colours, misty blue, poppy red, crisp lime green, with her straight and shining hair arranged in an Apollo knot. Many ladies were forced to add false hair of plaited loops to thicken the effect but Kit's abundant hair made this practice unnecessary and with a jewelled comb to hold it in place the style made her look even taller and her pale golden neck long and slender.

The man who was appraising her with a cool and interested expression was half a head taller than she was. His fair hair was cut short and brushed smoothly about his head and his eyes, a deep and chocolate brown, narrowed for a moment before they began to smile. He had a self-assurance of manner that suggested he had generations of gentlemen behind him. As though his ancestors had been among the privileged, a condition which had continued until it reached him, but Kit was not taken in by the charm of his smile which revealed his fine, white teeth, nor the courteous bow he inclined towards her. She had met many gentlemen just like him in the course of her new business career, and at the functions she attended with her mother and father and she had very quickly come to recognise an opportunist when she met one. Those who believed that an heiress was fair game, and this was one of them!

'My dear,' her father was saying, 'may I introduce Mr Samuel Atherton. Samuel, this is my daughter, Katherine.'

'Mr Atherton.' She extended her hand and the older gentleman took it, bowing gallantly, but in his eyes, as brown as those of the younger man, was an expression of quizzical interest.

'Miss Chapman, this is a delightful surprise.'

'Surprise, sir? Did you not expect to meet me, then?' The gentleman faltered and shot a strange look at her father, then smiled suavely. 'We hoped to, Miss Chapman, we certainly hoped to, but first, may I present my son, Harry. Harry, this is Miss Katherine Chapman.'

'Miss Chapman.'

'Mr Atherton.'

His manners were exquisite, his education obviously expensive and despite his air of superiority, which, she supposed was one that all men of his class had, she found she could not help returning his smile for it was impudent as though to say he knew his own worth and how could she fail to recognise it.

For several moments there was a small confusion of who was to sit where and which of the gentlemen was to be allowed the honour of holding her chair, but at last they were all seated.

'Mr Atherton and his son are staying in the area for a week or two, Kit. They are . . .'

'Kit?' Harry Atherton leaned forward, interrupting her father, then turned to him swiftly. 'I beg your pardon, sir. Forgive me but I was intrigued when you called Miss Chapman . . .'

'Kit? Yes, somehow my wife and I . . . well, a pet name, you understand, and it has become a habit.'

'And I prefer it to Katherine, Mr Atherton.' He turned instantly to her, his eyes glowing.

'Do you indeed? What a pity. Katherine is such a pretty name. One of my favourites if I may say so. How did you come to be known as Kit?'

Harry Atherton crossed one immaculate leg over the other and sat back in his chair. On his face was an expression of the keenest interest. He smiled encouragingly.

'Well, I hardly think our family idiosyncrasies can be of the slightest concern to someone like you, Mr Atherton.' Kit felt a small kernel of irritation bud inside her. Only the need for good manners in the presence of her father's two guests kept her from telling this arrogant stranger to mind his own damned business, but he merely grinned imperturbably and as though they were alone, leaned forward once more to say quietly, almost conspiratorially, 'Oh but it is, Miss Chapman. Anything you do would concern me and I would dearly love to know how you came by the . . . endearment!'

She turned, quite astonished, to her father, for surely he would not care to have his daughter spoken to in such a . . . a familiar manner but the two older men were smiling paternally. She felt the irritation become a prickle of anger, and something else, she could not really put a name to it, came to keep it company and she knew a decided longing to attack what was evidently this man's inflated sense of his own self-esteem. What was her father thinking of, letting this . . . this upstart speak to her as if they were old friends. How dare he question her on what was a private family matter, but her father interrupted smoothly.

129

'Come, Harry! You are teasing my daughter and she does not like to be teased.'

She turned to stare in amazement at her father for in all the years she had known him and she could really only count the last five or six, he had never once been jocular. Her mouth popped open quite foolishly and the three men began to laugh and for the first time in her life she wished she was one of those women who could command a man's thoughts with the teasing and pert ways of a pretty flirt. Some had the knack of being able to divert with a capricious look, a fluttering of eyelashes. To turn what might become too serious into something amusing. She was at a disadvantage and she did not like it, nor did she care for the way her father had placed her there!

'I hardly know Mr Atherton, Father,' she protested, conscious of the amusement with which Harry Atherton was regarding her.

'Come, my dear, do not upset yourself. Harry did not mean to embarrass you. He has always been known as a tease.'

'Has he really?' Her manner was disdainful as though the very last thing she wished to be acquainted with was Harry Atherton's teasing and she could sense her father's sudden disapproval, and wondered at it, for he, like her, did not suffer fools lightly. These men must be important to him or he would not act so strangely, nor so out of character. She had never heard mention of the Athertons, father or son, and yet it appeared that Samuel Atherton was an *old* friend of Barker Chapman's. In what way she could not imagine. Certainly not in business for he was a product of the class known as gentry and her father was not. Perhaps they had gone to school together but whatever their connection it seemed they were pleased with one another now, smiling and nodding benignly, smugly even, she would have said.

'Are you visiting friends in the district, Mr Atherton?' She directed her polite social question at the senior gentleman, hoping to amend the somewhat bad impression she had made, since the indolent smile of the younger made her decidedly uncomfortable.

'Why no, Miss Chapman. Your father and I were discussing the possibility of . . .'

'Mr Atherton and his son are here to . . .'

'Yes?' She looked from one to the other, quite perplexed since it seemed to her there was some flickering undercurrent here, into which, in a moment, she was to be flung. Her eye caught the polite smile, the amused eye of Harry Atherton and her heart missed a beat for she knew quite suddenly that the tension was to do with him.

'Would you think me rude if I were to ask you if this is a social call, Mr Atherton, or does it concern the mills?' Her voice was cool, imperious, 'Because if it does, as I *feel* it does, then I think I should be consulted.'

Her father answered. 'It does concern you, my dear and believe me I would have talked it over with you but you seemed intent on the dressmaker and your new ball gown . . .'

'*Father*, please, you know that is not so!'

'Katherine, can we not continue this when Mr Atherton and . . .'

'Of course.' At once she turned courteously to Samuel Atherton. 'Forgive me, sir. My manners are appalling. May I give you some tea, or perhaps coffee. You and your son will have a long drive, no doubt. I do beg your pardon but I cannot even claim to know where you are from, or where you are to travel today . . .'

'We are come from Cheshire, Miss Chapman. My family have a property there, and no, we will not take tea though it is gracious of you to ask.'

'A property in Cheshire, really? You are in business there?'

Samuel Atherton smiled. 'No, we have . . . land, an estate, farming land and a bit of shooting, you understand, but with four sons . . .' He shook his head and his smile deepened, '. . . that is why your father's offer was so welcome.'

'My father's offer?'

'To take Harry into the business.'

She felt the air about her move, lightly brushing against her, cold and quite painful. The smile she had pasted on her face to accommodate her father's guests remained there but the coldness in which she sat chilled her to the bone.

'Into my father's business,' she said and her voice was light, the voice of a lady holding a conversation with a gentleman, one she did not know very well but to whom, nevertheless, she must be polite.

'Yes. That was what we were discussing when you came in,' rudely, he might have added, she could see it in his face, and where you have no real right to be but his mouth smiled urbanely and she continued the charade, for that was what it had become.

'In what capacity, may I ask?' She did not look at Harry Atherton, nor Samuel Atherton but at her father and her eyes, though *she* still smiled, were like chips of blue diamonds.

'In the capacity in the first place as . . .'

'I do not think I should be given a title, sir. Not until I have earned it.' Harry Atherton lifted his well bred head to smile at Barker Chapman. 'I have a lot to learn, I am sure.'

'Indeed you have, Mr Atherton.' Kit's voice was soft, but not at all warm. 'The work of a mill-master is not for the weak.'

'Oh, not mill-master, Miss Chapman.' He put his hand to his brow languidly. 'Heaven forbid!'

'What will you be then?'

'Really, I cannot say. I shall be an apprentice. What do you think to that?'

The picture of the 'apprentices' in her father's spinning mills flashed vividly across her eyelids and for a moment she had the most unladylike desire to scream with hysterical laughter. The last apprentice she had seen had been dressed in nothing more than cut-down ragged breeches, no shirt, no shoes . . . not even hands! She remembered the smell, the unbearable heat, the veil of cotton 'fly' which hung in the air and crept into the mouth and blocked the nose, the damp which had come through the soles of her shoes, the noise of the machines, the shouts and the sharp crack of the overlooker's strap. Where would this handsome, this faultlessly dressed gentleman fit into that picture, she thought frantically.

'You are familiar with the cotton trade then, Mr Atherton.'

'Oh hardly, but I have some skill with figures and, which is more to the point for that is what your father needs, I am rather good at selling whatever you have to sell to those who do not always wish to buy it. I remember once at school I had a number of . . .'

'You are not at school now, Mr Atherton.'

'How perceptive of you, Miss Chapman, but please, allow me to tell you what I am to be employed in. You and your father are, I have been told, completely indispensable at the mill.' He looked as though he found this hard to believe, in her case at least, but he continued smoothly. 'Someone must find new markets for your cloth, would you not say?'

'Really, Mr Atherton?'

'Really, Miss Chapman.'

'Are you accustomed to working for sixteen hours each day, whatever else may come along to distract you?'

'I am sure if you can do it, Miss Chapman, then so can I!' He smiled engagingly. 'It seems we are entering an age of machinery and if one is not to be left behind, one must accept it. My eldest brother does not require me to help him collect the rents from our tenants on the estate which will one day be his, nor does he need the services of my two brothers who are already become soldiers. I must support myself, Miss Chapman, and your father being good enough to come forward with an offer of honest employment . . .' he bowed in her father's direction, '. . . I seized the opportunity.'

And what other opportunities are you likely to seize,

given the chance, Kit Chapman thought as she looked at the quite calculating, completely agreeable smile of Harry Atherton.

'You do not trust me,' she said to her father when the carriage bearing Samuel Atherton and his son had been politely waved down the drive. They had taken tea with Hannah Chapman since, as hostess she had insisted, and had promised, as Kit had known they would, realising bitterly it must have been arranged beforehand, to attend the ball for her eighteenth birthday the following week. Samuel would bring his wife and daughter and . . . well . . . if Mrs Chapman insisted . . . really, it was most gracious of her . . . they would be delighted to be weekend guests.

Harry Atherton had smiled, tilting a sardonic eyebrow in her direction as though admitting quite blatantly – to her – that he was thoroughly enjoying himself, at her expense, she imagined since why else should he keep grinning at her like some supercilious cat. A cat from Cheshire which had just been allowed to lap the dish of Lancashire cream which had *her* name on it!

She had waited, her nerves frayed to raw and painful edges until she and her father were alone, her mother gone to summon the housekeeper since, with important guests to be prepared for and with no more than a week in which to arrange it, Hannah Chapman would be hard pressed to spare an hour even to lay her head on her pillow.

'Of course I trust you, Katherine. You are being foolish . . .'

'Foolish! I imagine if I had been your son and not your daughter you would not have used that word.'

'Katherine . . .'

'Please, Father, let me speak. I had supposed, as I am one day to be your successor, indeed I had been led to believe I was to run the mills, as I am well able to do, whenever you are absent, that all decisions, all actions to be taken to do with the mills would be shared with me. Does this not predispose one to imagine that if this was the case I should be consulted, not only in the manufacture and selling of

134

our cotton, but also about the men we employ to achieve it. I am acquainted with all our staff, all the overlookers and managers, the factors who buy our raw cotton, who ship it from America, the agents in Liverpool, in fact *every man* concerned with the spinning and weaving of our cloth. If that is so, why was I not informed of this . . . this Harry Atherton?'

She threw up her head and was quite mortified when the splendid Apollo knot which her maid, Janet had devised for her, began to slip, and a smooth strand of hair fell across her cheek. She brushed it back angrily, her hands going to the back of her head to adjust it and her father smiled.

'My dear, you speak of sons and daughters and your rights as my successor but really, one can never forget you are a woman!'

He had meant it kindly, a compliment, but her face blazed to crimson fury and her eyes glittered ominously.

'For all your bold comments about my fitness for the role you are preparing for me, you do not really think me able to do it, do you? You are to put in this popinjay to supervise what I do . . .'

'Come now, Kit. You already know more than he will ever learn. How can he possibly supervise . . .'

'Then why is he to be employed, and, more to the point, Father, why did you not tell me?'

'Katherine . . . Kit, sit down, please and do me the honour of listening to me without jumping down my throat every time I open my mouth to speak. You are hot-headed, daughter, and must learn to control your emotions or you will never make a business man. You allow everyone to know exactly what you are thinking and that will never do.' He sat back and studied her and though she lifted her chin in that haughty way she had, like a princess who is to inherit the crown which was no doubt the way she saw herself, he knew she was paying attention.

'Harry Atherton will be very useful to us in our business, Kit. He knows nothing about commerce and less about the manufacture of cottons but he has something which you will need . . .'

'I?'

'Yes, when I am gone!'

'Good Heavens, Father, how can you . . .?'

'Do not be foolish, Kit. There, I have used the word again and if it offends you then I must apologise but let us be realistic. You are to take my place, my business, my *mills* when I am dead, Katherine, and that is why we are preparing you for it. You will do splendidly or I would not allow it. I would sell the lot to George Abbott or Albert Jenkinson, both of whom would give me a good price but, quite frankly my dear, we do not need the money. I hate to seem . . . mercenary but if I were to die tomorrow, mills or not, you and your mother could live in style and luxury for the remainder of your lives. But you see I have this hankering to think of my mills, *our* mills, spinning and weaving and turning out the best velveteen and fustians for another generation, and even beyond. But there is a new age coming, you know that. Harry Atherton knows it, too, and it is to be the age of the machine. It will be, quite simply, an industrial revolution. We shall be turning out more cloth in one day than my father did in a week, a month! And that cloth has to be sold! Markets must be found, all over the world, and someone must find them, and get our cloth to them.'

'Harry Atherton?'

'Harry Atherton.'

'But he knows nothing about it.'

'We shall teach him, you and I, and when he knows *almost* as much as we do we will allow him to work for us.'

'I still do not understand why you told me nothing of this.' Her face had cleared and returned to its normal colour but her eyes were still watchful for she had the feeling there was something her father was holding back. She had known a sense of discomfort when Harry Atherton had teased her about her name, a sense that there was more to him, more

136

to the words he spoke, than was apparent. Her father had been . . . strange, unlike himself and Mr Atherton senior, positively arch in the way he had studied her.

'I wished to sound out Samuel, and Harry, before putting the proposition to you. They are not "trade", you know, as you and I are considered to be.' He smiled at his own small joke. 'The Athertons are landowners near Chester with three hundred years of privilege and authority behind them. They do not work, my dear Kit, and though I was at school with Sam Atherton, we do not quite come up to their considered opinion of what constitutes a gentleman.'

'Rubbish!'

'Rubbish indeed, but then you and I are practical people and have been brought up to believe in the satisfaction of a full day's work, and the profit it brings us. We live a satisfying life, in our eyes, but they, of course believe theirs is better than ours and that we are mad to do it, particularly as there is no need of it since I am an independently wealthy man. But now they are forced to reconsider. There are four sons, you see, and the estate can only support one so, Harry Atherton, being a sensible and ambitious young man must look elsewhere for the wherewithal to support the expensive tastes he has been reared to consider his due. And, my dear, I think he will earn his keep. He is a personable young man, do you not think so?'

Barker Chapman watched his daughter keenly. He did not appear to be doing so as he lifted the lid of his silver cigar box and selected a cigar. He took his time lighting it, studying, or so it seemed, the smoke wreathing slowly to the ceiling, but his heavily lidded eyes watched and waited for her reaction to his question. He and Sam Atherton were both opportunists, in a completely different way, naturally, and the delightful solution to both their difficulties was an opportunity neither could ignore. Though Barker Chapman could quite easily have the pick of any young buck in the county for his lovely and wealthy young daughter, he knew the man must be exactly the right one for his Katherine. She was self-willed and self-opinionated and would need a strong man, if not to steady her, for the man who could do so did not exist, at least to pull in the same direction as herself. He must be a gentleman, naturally, but one prepared to realise that *she* was the 'mill-master'. There would be a pre-marriage contract to ensure this for Barker Chapman's mills must remain *Chapman* mills. No fortune hunter would get his hands on them, or on Katherine, but *somebody* must be found to marry her. Despite his quite liberal ideas, his madness, some would say in allowing his daughter to inherit and run his mills he believed that she must be married and before he died. A woman not married was an unnatural thing, in his opinion, but he must choose, as far as he was able the man who would be Katherine's consort in marriage. He must supervise its setting up, train the man who was to stand beside her, or more probably, if he knew Kit, just *behind* her, since, though he would not admit it to anyone but himself, to put a vast fortune in the hands of a woman, even one as shrewd as Kit, was not *quite* like leaving it to a son. Not that she would squander it for that was not her style, but with someone standing, looking over her shoulder so to speak, she would more carefully guard it.

And Sam Atherton's Harry was the perfect man, with the added bonus of being a superb salesman. Had he not sold himself as husband for Barker Chapman's daughter? Sam needed the generous amount of money Barker was prepared to put into his estate. Harry required some activity into which he could funnel that bright and enormous energy, that self-seeking ambition, greed, if you like, which was the reason Barker Chapman approved of him, and the rewards he knew would be his if he kept his nose clean!

Kit shrugged carelessly, apparently unimpressed with Harry Atherton.

'I suppose he has a certain . . . style.'

'Style? What does that mean?'

'He will appeal to those who like to be flattered.'

'Then he will do well since who does not? Is that all you can say about him?'

'What else is there to him?' She turned away, uninterested

138

in Harry Atherton's charms but Barker Chapman was not deceived. An attractive man, not only to women but liked by other men was an asset to any concern, and Kit was not as immune as she pretended to be. He had seen her confusion under Harry's teasing scrutiny, her concern with her hair and the smoothness of her gown, all indications of a woman's interest in a man. She had not perhaps been aware of it herself but to a man of experience it had been there to see. No, Barker Chapman was quite satisfied with it all and with the way in which she had been distracted from her original question. He had not told her about Harry Atherton because, despite his protestations to the contrary, quite simply, being the man he was, he told *no one* everything he did!

He came from a family which had for generations been in banking, but was still considered 'trade' by polite society. He owned spinning and weaving mills and all the processes associated with the textile industry. His father had been a wealthy man when he built his first spinning mill at Crossbank and in the past fifteen years or so the Chapman family fortune had grown to such a size Barker could count himself one of the wealthiest men in Lancashire. He owned land in both his own county and in Cheshire, farming land, mining ventures, a share in the family banking concerns in Oldham, Manchester and Liverpool.

But his heart, if he could be said to have one, was devoted to his mills, and now, surprisingly, to his only child.

10

Barker Chapman, it was well known, was not really a gentleman. Like most of his family, and indeed, many another with wealth, had married wisely, love rarely being a matter for consideration, following the trend of the gentry, aristocracy and royalty.

Barker had loved neither of his two wives. What regard he had now went to his daughter and on this day which was her eighteenth birthday his expression might almost have been described as fond as he watched her open the gifts she had been given.

A gold filigree necklace linked with pearls and earbobs to match. A ring set with amethysts and a bracelet of the finest opals. Mother of pearl combs for her hair inlaid with tourmaline, satin slippers and a butterfly brooch created in turquoise and an aquamarine.

She smiled, composed and unastonished, since she had been used to seeing such jewels on her mother and now that she herself was a woman it was her turn.

'Thank you, Father. They are delightful.'

'The slippers and combs are from your mother.'

'I shall thank her later.'

'I have another gift for you, my dear.' Barker Chapman smiled and there was a gleam of gratified approval in her eyes as he placed the slightly worn velvet jewel box on the table in front of her. Really, she had done so well since the unfortunate incident of the child killed in the mill six months ago, putting it behind her with a resolution which he had hoped, but had not been absolutely certain she possessed. She no longer went into the spinning-rooms and weaving-sheds without prior warning to the mill-manager which was only sensible, leaving the running of the machinery to those in charge of it and when Harry Atherton came into the mill, as he was to do within the month, there would be no need for her to venture any further than the office block, perhaps the warehouse or into the design room where he himself and more lately, Kit, worked on experiments with new cloth. Harry would stand as a buffer between her and the rougher side of the work for Barker still harboured a seed of doubt about her . . . well, he could only call it her womanly sensibilities regarding the conditions of the work force.

He watched her as she opened the box.

She moved through the evening on a drifting cloud of enchantment which turned her from an attractive young girl into a creature of radiance and light, her happiness blazing from her like the hot, golden flames of a furnace and those from Crossfold and Oldham and Manchester who had come to celebrate her eighteenth birthday told one another they had never before realised what a beauty Barker Chapman's girl had become. She wore the ivory silk Miss Cavendish had made for her, a clinging, high-waisted gown as light as thistledown with a low neckline and a tiny sleeve and scattered on the bodice with cream silk embroidery. Janet had dressed her hair into a heavy, intricate coil in the centre of which she had placed half a dozen ivory silk rosebuds and around her neck was the magnificent rope of ivory pearls, given to her by her father.

'They were your grandmother's,' he said 'and worn by no one since.' From that she deduced that neither of her father's two wives had been considered worthwhile enough to wear them but that she, his daughter, was! 'I saw your gown and . . . well, can you deny that they are not the perfect match?'

He led her out in the first dance, to the astonishment of those who knew him, since Barker Chapman used occasions such as these, not to be sociable, though he was never less than the perfect host, but to do business with many of the manufacturers who were his guests. Of course he took his wife on the floor and then the wife of the gentleman who was his house-guest, as was only polite, but his face as he presented, as it were, the treasure of his daughter to those who had come to celebrate her birthday was really almost fatuous, they thought.

She danced every dance. Squire Longworth of Longworth Hall, set between Shaw and Oldham – the Squire only consenting to mingle with the manufacturing classes on account of Barker Chapman's house-guests, with whom he was acquainted – took her from her father's arms with an eagerness which, as the ladies watching agreed, was unseemly in a man of his age, whispering in her ear and

141

most reluctant to let her go when some young sprig came to claim her.

There was Jonathan Abbott, the son of George Abbott, who had spinning mills over Edgeclough way, ready for a flirtation, ready to make love to her if it could be managed and she was willing, but, prodded by his father, who could make neither head nor tail of Barker Chapman's madness, in letting this lovely child anywhere near his mills, really ready to marry her.

'By God, you look fine,' he said, his eyes undressing her, his florid face pressing close to hers, his heavy body blundering most uncomfortably against her own and his polished boots crushing her satin slippers.

'Thank you, Jonathan. You are most kind.' She tossed her head and smiled so brilliantly, for was she not worthwhile in her father's eyes and what else mattered? He missed a step as he whirled her about the floor and, no longer obeying his father in his instructions to 'make himself pleasant to the Chapman girl' he began to do it for his own sake, for really, Kit Chapman would be more than adequate in any man's drawing-room or in any man's bed!

He had no time to expand upon his sudden realisation of her charms when she was whisked away once more, this time by Ritchie Jenkinson, the son of another mill-owner, Albert Jenkinson, a baize and dommet manufacturer from Rochdale, who was for several minutes struck quite speechless as the delightfully bubbling Miss Chapman captivated him with her sparkling wit.

'May I take you on the floor, Miss Chapman, before you are carried off by another of your admirers. They are like bees to the blossom this evening and who can blame them!'

It was Harry Atherton. She had seen him earlier, of course when he had arrived and been installed in the luxury of the guest rooms Hannah Chapman had had prepared for them, with his parents and sister, Diana, a well-bred, languid young lady of her own age who, though her father had

142

barely a shilling to his name, knew her own value. A thoroughbred then, Miss Atherton and quite ready to be bored with the bourgeois 'tradesmen' with whom, for her brother's sake, she was to mingle. Mrs Atherton, an older version of her daughter, said quite clearly by her attitude that the idea of her son going into the business of cotton spinning and weaving, despite its financial rewards, would bring nothing but dishonour to the family name, since she herself was niece to a baronet!

They took the elegance, the comfort, the hospitality of Greenacres quite for granted, summoning maids at all hours of the day and night for hot water, hot towels, tea trays, supper trays and anything their aristocratic minds could devise, and here they were, the masculine Athertons quite prepared to be gracious if that was what it took, the females, ordered by their menfolk, doing their duty.

'Your sister does not care for dancing, then?' Kit said sweetly as he whirled her beneath the chandelier which held forty candles.

'Why yes! She loves it the best in all the world, after hunting.'

'Is that gentlemen, or the fox?' Her smile was malicious.

'Miss Chapman!' One fair eyebrow arched and his eyes gleamed with sardonic amusement. He was taller than she was by eight or nine inches and as she looked up into his handsome face she could feel his warm breath, wine- and cigar-scented, fan her own. His eyes were dancing now, a warm brown dancing that said how immensely he was enjoying himself, enjoying the luxury, the superb food her father's chef served, the warmth and the comfort and the beauty of her father's home, and ready to enjoy her, like Jonathan Abbott, if she were willing.

'You really are an attractive woman, Kit Chapman.'

'And what is that to you?'

'Can you not receive a compliment without beating a man about the head with it?' He leaned nearer to smile more warmly into her face.

'It would depend on the man, naturally.'

'You know how to wound, Miss Chapman. Come, accept what I say as nothing but the truth.'

'Not from you!'

'And why is that?'

'Because I wouldn't trust you to the top of Friars Mere, that's why. There is some reason for this . . . this claptrap and I have a fair idea of what it might be.'

'Have you indeed, Miss Chapman. Could it not be that your charms have quite bowled me over and, as a man, I cannot help but spill out my innermost dreams to you when I have the chance.'

'Fiddlesticks!'

He threw back his head and roared with laughter and every head in the room turned to stare.

'I like you, Kit Chapman.'

'And you are showing me up with this silly exhibition. Furthermore, I do not care to be held so tightly.'

'Ah ha! You are afraid of me, then?'

'Don't be absurd and if you don't stop this . . . this stupidity I shall walk off the floor . . .'

' . . . and insult your father whose hospitality mine is enjoying. Why, Miss Chapman, where are your manners?'

'And where are yours? I was given to believe you were a gentleman.'

'And so I am, so come, smile at me and at least pretend you are enjoying my company.'

She drew in a deep, infuriated breath.

'What is it you want, Mr Atherton?' she asked him as they floated for the umpteenth time by her father and his father, standing side by side in communal gratification to watch her and Harry Atherton take the floor.

'I really don't know what you mean, Miss Chapman.'

'You know exactly what I mean. You have insinuated yourself into my father's good graces . . .'

'Insinuated! Good Heavens, what a dreadful word, Miss Chapman, or may I call you Katherine?'

'No, you may not and insinuated is the word which describes exactly what you are doing, not only with my

144

father but with me. I do not come with the deal, you know, Mr Atherton.'

'Miss Chapman, *the deal*, what a way you do have with words. My, my, you really are rather . . . what is the word I search for?'

'Inaccessible I think would describe it precisely.'

'Oh, I don't know.' He narrowed his eyes, letting his gaze linger on her mouth and she felt the flush of warmth begin somewhere in the region of her knees and move upwards until her whole body, including her face and neck was rosy. His lips curled in an amused smile over his white teeth and she prayed the music would not stop at that precise moment, for if it should and she was forced to walk coolly across the floor to her mother she was absolutely certain her legs would not support her. On and on they went, round and round, their eyes locked in a clash of wills. He was a superb dancer, holding her firmly, guiding her expertly in the precise steps of the dance and she began to respond to it, to sway when he did in the lilting rhythm which had somehow got inside her head. Dip and sway, her dress flowed about her as smoothly as water and though it appeared she had no room in her head for thought it occurred to her that she could float on like this forever. His eyes smiled warmly into hers, holding her glance, his smoothly brushed head nodded slightly in time to the music.

Suddenly people began to clap, a gentle and polite coming together of white-gloved hands, then, as the music played on and she and Harry Atherton swung round and round beneath the sparkling chandelier, it became more enthusiastic and a man's voice cheered. There was laughter and colour, dazzling light and soft shade, and to her horror she became aware that she and Harry were the only couple on the floor.

'Bravo, bravo . . . how enchanting they look . . . what superb grace . . . she is a credit to you, Barker . . . indeed . . . what a lovely couple . . .'

There was nothing for her to do but to curtsey, first to

the grinning Harry Atherton and then to the applauding spectators who crowded the edge of the floor, to affect a blushing modesty and embarrassment at her own boldness when really all she wanted to do was to stamp her feet and smack Harry Atherton's silly smirking face with all the strength she could muster. She could tell by their faces what her father's guests were thinking. What else could they assume when Samuel Atherton and Barker Chapman stood side by side smiling like two old foxes who are in the hen house, their children, she and Harry Atherton, so evidently made for one another and so obviously approved of. So that was the way of it, they would be saying, Barker Chapman's girl spoken for by the son of an *old* family, and what chance had their sons, their expressions said quite clearly.

'I'll never forgive you for this,' she hissed through clenched teeth and brightly smiling lips.

'I? What can I have done now, I wonder?' Harry's warm, carressing hand held her elbow as he guided her politely back to her mother. His arrogance and high-toned opinion of himself was beyond believing and her own body's response to *his*, appalling! She didn't even *like* him, for Heaven's sake and as for being paired off with him, as seemed likely by the look on the face of her father and Samuel Atherton, she would see him in hell first. Not a word had been spoken about marriage, ever, by her father, nor even hinted at and she had been glad of it. She supposed one day, when she had achieved her dream of running her father's business concerns, of being free and independent *as men were*, she might consider marriage, children, providing neither interfered with her professional life. She was lucky, she knew that, for women were not considered in this man's world, did not exist above a certain level, had no rights, no responsibilities, no obligations except in the home, no entitlement to property, no claim on society bar what their menfolk felt was proper. She, if her father had considered it more beneficial to himself, might have been married at sixteen to a man of *his* choice, but she had been allowed to leave the secure and protected world of a lady and move into the exciting, challenging, quite relentless world of a man, and she was not, absolutely not going to put what she had been given into the hands of this fortune-hunter at her side.

'If you will excuse me . . . I must . . .' She pulled her arm quite rudely away from his restraining hand and turning swiftly to avoid both her mother and *his* mother, who sat together with the precious Diana, whose airs and graces had frightened away a score of young men who had approached her. She moved as quickly as was circumspect from the salon, and along the gallery which was thronged with guests, down the stairs and through the first door which opened to her hand.

It was her father's study. It was empty and she sighed with relief. Thank God, just a minute was all she needed, a minute to get over the swell of rage Harry Atherton had aroused in her and then she would go back and face them all, her father, his father and the fool who thought she should not only be glad to receive his attention, but also honoured by it.

She wandered towards the window, drawn by the shaft of moonlight which lay across the terrace and which bathed the whole garden in a sheen of misty silver. It was almost the end of May and everywhere shrubs and trees were budding riotously in the eagerness they showed each year to be out of the hibernation winter cast over them. She could see the shadows on the rippling bark of the trees, and even the separate leaves, lovely and ethereal, on each bough. Her hand reached for the catch of the french window and in a moment she had stepped stealthily, smiling and quite ridiculously pleased with herself, down the stone steps of the terrace and on to the lawn.

He saw her coming and the torch of wood he had ready in his hand felt foolishly heavy and out of place and without his being consciously aware of it, it fell from his hand on to the uncut grass behind the summer-house. The reason he had come slipped easily out of his head, like the hard ice on the moors which must give way to the warmth of the sun. What possible purpose could such things have on a night like this, his bemused senses begged of him, with the loveliness, the grace and sheer magic of the woman who walked across the grass in his direction. His eyes saw her and were dazzled and his heart saw her and grew grave with the truth of what lay there and his mind saw her and was filled with the despair of it for what could she and Joss Greenwood ever share, beyond the enmity of that which lay in the past and the violence which would come in the future. The summer-house had been his target. Just a small reminder on this day when the big house was full of guests that his people were still here and when the time for it came round, as it surely must for the manufacturers would not listen, they would strike, not merely at their playthings as this summer-house was, but at their mills and their looms and their warehouses, until they *did* listen.

But tonight it was out of place. It was her birthday, he had been told for he had spies everywhere and the present he was to bring her seemed somehow inappropriate now. No longer as clever as he had thought it. His own personal gift, he had imagined from his world to hers, but it would not do now.

He stepped out of the shadows and let her see him. She was not afraid, though tonight she had no dogs to guard her.

'What do you want here, Joss Greenwood?' she challenged him but there was nothing in her voice but a strange softness and he felt himself sigh sadly for what might have been.

'God knows now. A present for your birthday.' He bent to pick up the torch and held it out to her. 'I was to light it. Set fire to the summer-house but I give it to you unlit, so, my birthday present to Kit Chapman.'

She looked like a statue carved from marble but her eyes were alive and in them, as though she had sensed what was in him, was a curious expression, one which he thought he recognised.

'Why did you not do it?'

'Again, I don't know. I saw you there. It no longer seemed appropriate.'

The silence was long then, and somehow speaking, threading them together quite naturally though neither would ever be able to explain it.

'We have not heard from you for some time.' Her eyes held his and still he felt no amazement at this that was suddenly between them.

'No, but you will.'

'I suppose so.'

The darkness away from the house enclosed them in a world far from the one they both knew, a fresh and quite separate world in which only the two of them existed. The house at her back was soft with light from every window and it flowed out over the heath garden and the flower beds close to the wall, but here only the stars lit the space about them. Two silhouettes cut out of the darkness, no more than a yard or two between them, each face straining to the paleness of the other.

'I don't quite know what to say, not that it makes much difference. I didn't expect to see you, or anyone out here. The music . . . the noise, it's from somewhere I've never been, another world really, so I stood for a moment to listen, I don't know why . . . and then you came.'

'I was escaping . . .'

'You like to do that.' She saw the gleam of his teeth in the darkness as he smiled.

'You know I do. And don't you?'

'I am not . . . captured.'

'Not even by the life you lead. The things you do for those you . . . fight for.'

'I choose to do it . . . but let us not . . .'

'No.'

There was silence again, but it was not repressive. For that time in which fate had decided to bring them together, not as enemies but in a tentative curiosity in one another as individuals, they were without animosity.

'You look . . .'

'Yes . . .?'

'You look well in your frock,' he said lamely, quite unable to turn his gaze away from her, awkward, almost a boy again in his bewitchment.

'Thank you, Joss.' She was grave, completely without artifice as she spoke his given name for the first time.

'Do you still walk up to Badger's Edge?' he asked softly.

'Sometimes.'

'It is on the track to my mother's house.'

'I know.'

It seemed the magic would never be broken and they took a step towards one another then from somewhere a man's voice called her name and a wide path of light shone through the window of the room from which she had come, not quite reaching them.

'I must go.' His voice was almost regretful.

'Yes.'

'Goodbye, Kit Chapman.'

'Goodbye, Joss Greenwood.'

11

He was waiting in the same circle of stones, his back to one of them, his arms folded across his chest, his face serious as he stared out over the valley. Almost at his feet was the edge of the cliff face going down and down to the swathe of grass and the scattering of rocks far below.

He heard her call to the dogs, her voice clear on the quiet air and he swung round immediately. As she walked towards him the dogs bounded in great joyous circles about her, quite unconcerned by his presence because she was the same and he found he was aware of every turn of her head, of every breath of air she drew into her lungs, every movement of the muscles of her face and neck as she smiled at him and each sound and intonation of her voice as she called to the dogs. It was completely segregated from the logic and plain common sense with which he addressed himself to life but somehow he accepted it as part of the strange fascination she seemed to hold for him. The glow in his heart when he looked at her was simply there. One moment it had not been, now it was. Beyond reasoning so why try to explain it. Irrational, he knew, just as he knew what he felt for Kit Chapman was madness and that he should throw on his cap and without another glance, nor even a greeting, stride off in the direction of Edgeclough and sanity, but of course he did not.

There was mist up here and she had appeared out of it like a blurred and dissolving shadow. The damp had traced itself about her uncovered hair, decking it with dew-drops and loosening the usual flowing strands of it from her chignon. She pushed it back behind her ears and came to stand beside him, looking out over the misted landscape, the gully below into which the traveller had fallen, or so it was said, hawking his goods to the remote cottages in the area. Here and there the top of a tree protruded through the drifting grey, the breeze moving the mist about in wisping strands, like her hair and they could hear the everlasting music, which was never far away, of the mountain streams.

'Good morning,' she said after a moment. 'A splendid day for a walk,' and because his heart hammered at her closeness and he was suddenly afraid of her and of himself, he was sharp.

'What's good about it?'

'My word! What a grumpy lad he is then!' She was laughing but he could see quite clearly in her eyes that she was as afraid as he was.

'Why did you come?'

'I often walk up here. I told you that the last time we met on this path. And I might ask you the same question?'

'I am on my way to a meeting.'

'Really.'

They both knew the other was lying and without conscious thought they leaned side by side against the tall rock and both sighed in unison.

'I didn't want to come, no, that's not right. I wanted to come but I knew I shouldn't. I have been here an hour, telling myself with every minute that passed that I must get on, that I had things to do, that there was no sense to it. You do see that, don't you?' He did not turn to look at her as he spoke but he could feel her eyes on his face.

'I know. I said the same thing as I walked up. I could so easily have gone the other way, up to Sherbrook Falls, anywhere but here but . . .' Her voice tapered away, almost sadly and he turned then to look at her. She was eighteen, not a beauty certainly, but beautiful nonetheless. Her mouth was wide and strong, but there was something about it which said it could so easily slip into laughter if allowed. She had been brought up a solitary child and from the age of twelve, she had told him, trained to take over her father's business. His heir, a wealthy and much sought after young woman and it had made her serious, intent on only serious things, not much given to the giggling to which young girls of her age were prone. Her eyes looked dubiously into his, uncertain and not awfully sure she approved of this strangeness between them. They were enormous in the dampness of her pale golden face, brilliantly blue, the violet in them washed out like the skies above. Her dark eyebrows dipped in a frown, almost of annoyance and she bit her lip.

'I think I had better get back,' she said, trying so hard to be the haughty Miss Chapman, daughter of Barker Chapman who was unused to speaking to rough fellows such as he.

'I think so too,' but still they continued to look at one another. The dogs had lain down, several feet away, but something of the tension between the two people conveyed itself to them and one — was it Joby or Blaze he remembered thinking dazedly — began to bristle.

'I can't seem to think straight,' he said, running a distracted hand through the rough, damp tangle of his curly hair and as he did so her own hand lifted, quite involuntarily to his forehead, smoothing where his had just been and he took it and very gently put his lips to the inside of her wrist and she felt the touch of them move through her whole body.

'Joss . . . I'm scared . . . I do not understand . . . all my life I've known exactly what I've wanted. I've understood what . . . my feelings were about . . .' She took a deep breath, '. . . about life and . . .'

'About men?' He smiled deeply into her eyes, his hands still holding hers.

'Well no, not really, but . . .'

'You don't want complications.'

'No.'

'Then you must turn round and walk away right now, Kit Chapman. We are not meant for one another, you and I. Dear God, there could not be a more mis-matched pair. Our background, our beliefs, our needs are as different, as separate as any two species of animal could be. I hate you, you know that. I hate your people, your class, your careless unconcern with . . .' He stopped and threw back his head and his laugh was false and strident. 'Complications. Dammit to hell . . . what are we doing here . . .?' His voice was shaking now and, her heart going out to his pain for it was answered in hers, she leaned against him putting her forehead to his lips to stop the flow of words which hurt them both.

'Don't . . .' she said sharply, seeing the working of his mouth and throat, so near to her own and without thought, as naturally as she had known, deep down, that it would be with him, she lifted her mouth for her first kiss. Their lips dovetailed, cool and damp from the misted air, sweet and soft and when he lifted his head to look into her face the sharpness, the rough and spiky corner of his anger had gone and they both smiled in delight.

153

'Do it again,' she whispered and he did and this time it was longer and deeper and she leaned into his arms, wanting more, though she did not know then what it was.

'Kit . . .' he said and his voice was shaking and he held her close, his cheek against hers and she knew what it was, and so did he.

'We should run away from one another as quickly as we can and not look back, you know that, don't you?' he said softly.

'Yes, but it seems I cannot.'

'I know.'

'What are we to do?'

He put her from him, smiling ruefully. 'What do you suggest, Kit Chapman? Just look at us.' He held her arms out wide and his eyes swept over the rich soft wool of her three-quarter coat. It was a lovely blue, with deep pockets, simple but serviceable enough for walking. Her skirt was of the same colour, wide and also easy to walk in and her boots were of a supple leather, black, highly polished. He could see a froth of lace at her throat pinned with a brooch in which some jewel flashed and he marvelled at her folly in coming up here alone, despite the protection the dogs afforded. He found he was suddenly afraid for her, afraid she might be hurt, accosted in some way, insulted by some rough fellow and he was quite amazed by the overwhelming sense of protectiveness he felt towards her. Some rough fellow . . . dear God . . . could not that description apply to him when put beside the elegant, expensively dressed Miss Katherine Chapman?

'Look at us, Kit,' he repeated and her eyes now roamed over him, over the worn and patched breeches which had once been his father's, the thick woollen socks his mother had knitted, his wooden clogs, well made and serviceable but the mark of a working man, the cap he had thrown on the rock beside him.

'What do you see?' he asked her gently.

'Joss . . . don't . . .' since how could she deny it?

'We must. We must look at what we are.' His smooth

brown face, freshly shaved since he had known she would come, his warm, firm, sweet lips curled up at the corners even in repose. The deep, cat-like green and grey of his eyes, the wings of his eyebrows tilting up towards the rough tumble of curls on his forehead. She looked and he watched her and saw her eyes become soft and dreaming in contemplation of him and he wondered where the wild Kit Chapman, the one who had threatened to see him hanged on the day he had wrecked her father's new machine, had gone. She was surely not this soft, sensual woman who was looking at him with her whole female yearning in her eyes for him to see.

'Sweet Jesus . . . we must be mad. We have nothing to give one another.'

'No . . .' and her mouth found his again, carefully, like a child experimenting with something new and exciting, something which grown-ups did, but the feel of her body under his hands was not that of a child, nor the taste of her lips and her tongue.

They spent an hour, dazed with the wonder of it. They stood, her back to the rock, sheltered from the wind and the rain which came down to blot out the valley beneath them and when they were both wet through, laughing, kissing the rain from eyes and mouth and chin, they parted, the dogs padding after her, turning all three again and again to look at him until she disappeared into the mist from which she had come.

They met almost every day at some time, marvelling on how each mind knew when the other was there. No matter what time of the day it was, he or she, would be at Badger's Edge.

'Have you been here long?' he would say, sweeping her into his arms.

'I have just this minute got here,' she would answer, her lips reaching hungrily for his.

The next day or the next he would be leaning against the same rock his face peaceful and as she ran to him she would ask, 'Have you been waiting long?' and his answer, 'No,

I've only this minute come,' did not surprise her. There was something in her, and in him, some magic which spoke over the miles so that quite often, when she was with her father or Harry, their commercial minds deep in profit and loss, in turnover and yardage she would lift her head and smile, then shake it in amazement.

'What is it, my dear?' her father would ask, a smiling question in his eyes but she would shrug her shoulders and pretend a forgotten errand, some female excuse to put him off and within the hour, for perhaps no longer than five minutes, she would be in Joss Greenwood's arms, desperate for the feel of his body and his mouth against hers.

'Those dogs of yours get an inordinate amount of exercise these days, Katherine,' Harry remarked lazily as she whipped them through the back gate of the mill yard one morning and up in the direction of the moor. 'They must be the healthiest beasts in Lancashire and why have you suddenly decided they must come to the mill with you.'

'Not that it's any business of yours, Harry, but I feel it does them no good to be shut up in the stables at home all day.'

'Could not one of the grooms exercise them?' He tilted his fair head in her direction whimsically, 'not that it is any concern of mine, as you pointed out, but it seems to me . . .'

'It seems to me, Harry Atherton, that every time I turn round to do something I find you looking over my shoulder. Have you nothing else to do but spy on me?' Her colour was high, unusually so and her eyes glittered in a quite amazing violet flame. The skin of her face was smooth and had become tinted in the summer months to a deep wild rose on her cheekbones, the rest a delicate golden amber. She looked quite lovely, alive and glowing, more than he had ever before noticed and he looked with renewed interest at her.

'I? Spying on you? My dear Katherine, perish the thought!

156

I have more than enough work to do in my day without keeping an eye on your comings and goings.'

'Well, do it then, and let me get on with mine.'

Each time they met Joss demanded, and took a little more of her until they were both like the dry, crackling, sun soaked bracken in which they lay, ready to be consumed by the slightest spark into an inferno. Their passion for one another was slow burning, barely discernible on the surface of their separate lives, well tamped down with only a wisp of smoke and a strange warmth to warn those about them that there was some difference in them and yet underneath it raged, in Kit more slowly since she was untouched, inexperienced. But Joss was a man well used to satisfying his physical needs. From the age of twenty when he became acquainted with Abby Hobson's welcoming body and since then with more than a few willing young working lasses he had met on his travels, his body had been pleased, pleasured as often as he desired. Now he was in love. He loved Kit Chapman. He wanted no other and he could not have her! She allowed him small liberties, afraid, so afraid not of him but of herself. This was so new, this delicate unfolding of her woman's desires, her delight in her own body's response to his. She did not know where it would lead, indeed if it should lead anywhere. She did not know where she *wanted* it to lead. It was as fragile as the cloudberry which made a sweet pillow for her head, and as fragrant. She wanted, at that moment, to do no more than hold it to her, to savour it, to take it out in the dark of the night and marvel at it, but she needed to keep it secret, in a place of concealment until she had grasped the implications of her love for Joss Greenwood.

Yes, she loved Joss Greenwood and it terrified her.

'I want to make love to you,' he said to her on their third meeting. They had moved away from the track which ran along Badger's Edge, walking hand in hand, a man and a woman accompanied by two dogs, in the vast, empty stretches, for as far as the eye could see, rolling hill upon rolling hill, of the South Pennine moorland. There was

157

nothing. No cottage, nor farm nor shelter of any description, just the sudden winding of an old pack-horse track leading to Denshaw and on to Huddersfield, or a turnpike abandoned with the coming of the new canals. It seemed as endless as the ocean, an ocean without sailing ships, divided by the deep troughs of gulleys, steep cloughs and the gentle flow of a stream which became a roar as it cascaded over a ledge to become a waterfall.

They were content then, as they walked, their faces turned to the sun, or to one another which was the same thing. They shared little in their lives, not heritage, class, culture or beliefs, little but this, this love of the 'tops', the rugged, rocky hills, the deep, sheltered, wooded valleys. It was harsh, the upland climate at times, waterlogged in winter, scourged by winds and snow, gripped by ice that crackled underfoot, fog-ridden and desolate, but now as summer laid her gentle, sometimes treacherous hand upon it, it was majestic, shaded by a dozen colours from palest green, lavender, gold and bronze, softened by trees in the valleys that were a carpet of multi-coloured lace from this height, but this man and woman who had been born to it, who had known it in every shade of temper, loved it and in it their love for one another flowered, not softly, nor slowly but with the vigour which marked them both. They would lie in the bracken hidden from everything but the skylark above their head and their ardour grew at each encounter. His hands could not be restrained from caressing the smooth skin of her face and neck. His lips explored the curve of her ear, his tongue its inner softness and his teeth its lobe. He became bolder, more peremptory, more challenging in his eagerness knowing she was as willing as he, since he was a man used to women and her body told him she was not prepared to wait. His fingers were restless, ardent, moving to the buttons of her bodice then turning ill-humoured when they did not open easily.

'Help me, dammit,' but she would sit up and toss back her hair which he had loosened and her rosy face would become pale and strained for how was she to allow him what he wanted, what *she* wanted at that moment more than anything, *anything* she had ever before wanted in her life? They were Kit Chapman and Joss Greenwood. They lived both of them, *now*, for the hours they stole from their separate lives, nothing in the past, nothing in the future but could she take that final, irrevocable step, which would change her from what she was, *just*, a marriageable young woman, a virgin, which a husband would require, into this man's mistress. She loved him. God, how desperately she loved him but the risk she took was appalling for what could he give her? What could she give him?

'I want to make love to you.'

'I know.'

'And you do not?'

'Joss ... dear God ...'

She left him, running, the dogs at her heels, her face wet with tears, the content, the sheer joy of living gone, it seemed forever, for this must stop.

But the next day, or the next, she would be there at Badger's Edge and so would he.

'I know nothing about you,' she said on another, quieter occasion.

'Nor I, you.'

'Tell me.'

He turned to smile at her. The sweetness, which had almost soured in him, shone in his eyes for her. They sat on a flat rock above Friars Mere, shoulder to shoulder, their minds and hearts and bodies gentle on this day. It was almost the end of the summer and it was in both their minds that with the coming of the winter they would be faced with the impossibility of meeting up here on the winter moorland which had been their sanctuary for over three months.

'What d'you want to know?'

'What did you do as a boy?' she asked with the eternal feminine yearning to know the boy who had become the man she loved.

159

'I worked with my family. My father was a weaver and my mother spun the yarn for his loom. I did the cleaning and carding . . .'

'By hand?'

'Of course by hand. There were no machines to do it then. I picked the bits out of the raw cotton and untangled it ready for my mother to spin. When I was big enough my father let me use the hand-loom which had been his father's.'

'And were you a good little boy?'

'I don't suppose so,' bending to kiss her.

'And your sister, the one I met in the mill. How old is she?'

'Jenny's nineteen and should have been a man.'

'Really! Why do you say that?'

'She is like you. Though she does as she is bid, a woman who has her place in the order of things.'

'Like we do in . . .'

'In your class, yes. There is the same set of rules among our women too.'

'Really, I did not know.'

'Oh yes, and though Jenny abides by them she is as rebellious as I am underneath. In a way she is stronger than I am for where I have thrown off the conventions because I am a man and I am allowed to do it, she is forced to stay in her place. A woman must have strength to do that. She would dearly love to come on the tramp with me to . . .'

'Yes?'

'Wherever I go.'

'Aah . . . yes . . .'

He told her about the days when his family had been independent and free, secure and confident in the knowledge that they were craftsmen who counted for something. He described to her the day on which his father had died and of his own devastation, making the massacre at St Peters Field come alive for her, nurturing the seed of doubt which had been planted in her on the day the child had lost

160

his hands in her father's mill and she became quiet then, lost and uncertain, the grand beliefs with which she had grown, which her father had bred in her that profit was a virtue of which to be proud, that loss was a mortal sin, sitting uneasily on her shoulders.

She told him about Harry and for the first few moments as she spoke he felt as though she had flung him into a lake, deep and dark, its bottom wild with weeds which grappled to hold him down. He could see the light on the surface of the water and hear the sound of the life which was above him but as he struggled madly to get back to her, to hear what she said, he could not catch his breath.

'. . . as a salesman originally,' she was saying. 'There will be markets all over the world for the cotton which is manufactured in Lancashire and someone must travel to them and find the buyers. I was scornful, really I was for he is . . . his father is of the landed gentry and his mother, well, one might have been forgiven for thinking her to be related to His Majesty so imperious was she, but for some reason my father believes that Harry is the man to expand our growth.'

Her voice was lazy, her eyes dreaming in contemplation of the pure pale blue of the sky above them. Her head was on his chest and she could not see his face.

'He came to us just before my birthday and I must say I was suspicious. It was so evident that his father and mine were up to something so naturally I began to imagine they were making a match between them. For Harry and me. My mother would love to be allied to a family who can claim kinship with nobility, even the minor kind and it would do my father no harm for it to be known he was related to the niece of an Earl or whatever he is. He is a mill-master, an industrialist so of course they would not receive him at the moment but if I were to be married to one of them, who knows what contacts might be made. But Harry is an idiot, really. So charming, so completely a member of the privileged class one wonders how he can bear to consider a union with one of us, but he loves money

161

and sadly, his family has none. Land, oh yes, for shooting and hunting and whatever else they do in season, and a bloodline which goes back into eternity, but he would dearly like to be rich, one suspects. I suppose he could be considered good looking and his manners faultless but I am pleased to say he has made no move to which I could take exception and I suppose when he has learned the textile trade, as I learned it, in the factory for twelve or more hours a day . . .'

He sat up so violently she was thrown to the ground and her expression of amazement might have been amusing in other circumstances. She looked up at him, ready to smile with her skirts above her knees and the sprig of heather which he had laughingly, lovingly put in her hair fell over her eyes.

'Joss?' she said, leaning on her elbow, shading her eyes against the lowering sun but he sprang up his whole body snarling with the force of his emotion and the two dogs rose to their feet, catching his fierceness, beginning to growl in the back of their throat.

'Joss . . .?' she said again. She sat up and arranged her skirts more decorously as though instinct told her this was not the moment to be seen as a hoyden. She watched him warily.

'Dear sweet God,' he hissed, his back to her, unable to turn to look at her as he spoke. 'Do you ever listen to yourself, do you? Have you no idea of the world outside the bloody gates of your fine house and your splendid mills? Do you give a thought to the men and women . . . and children too . . . who are killing themselves . . .' He turned on her then, his eyes dark with his jealous hatred, for that was what it was, '. . . yes, my fine lady, killing themselves quite literally so that you can . . . what was the word . . . *expand* your growth! Thousands and thousands of them marching to London with bleeding feet to hand in petitions which no one reads, or if they do declare as rubbish. Starving, deformed children . . . Jesus, I must be mad to sit here with you . . . lolling in the grass . . .' He was in torment with his guilt and his shame and the blazing inferno of his jealousy which he loathed himself for feeling.

She stood up slowly and the expression on her face began to harden into the same one he wore.

'. . . and so they are to marry you to this . . . this sprig of a gentleman, are they? who is to work in the factory for twelve hours a day. Poor sod, one wonders how he will manage it!' His voice was a parody of her own, '. . . but then if he is to dip into your fortune and into your . . .' For a sick moment he nearly used the coarse expression men use among themselves for such things and doubtless if he had she would not have understood but in that moment he stopped himself with an effort which was so violent she could visibly see the sinews of his face and neck, his arms and hands, struggle for self control.

'You are all the same, all of you, scrabbling for every penny . . .'

'And you do not? Why are there strikes and . . .?'

'They need to eat to stay alive, damn you.'

'Dear God, are we always to have this . . . this diatribe on every occasion that we meet. Starving children, unemployed men, women who are forever producing children so that they might put them in the mill. Why do they not contain their families to one or two so that they do not go under in the deluge of babies they have year after year . . .'

'It is the only pleasure they have, making love to one another but then you wouldn't know about that, would you? You're keeping that fine body of yours for someone worthy of it, I suspect and it must be given where it will do most good for your father. Christ, do you and your kind ever do anything just because you want to or must everything be bought and sold to the highest bidder . . .'

She sprang at him then, reaching for his face but he knocked her away with the back of his hand and without the slightest sound both dogs leaped at him together and he saw it in her face, the longing to let them tear him to pieces. It lasted for no longer than a second but it was

163

enough to carve itself into his mind with an anguish which he could barely withstand.

'Joby . . . Blaze, down, down, I say,' and immediately the dogs reared back, dropping one on either side of him, each muzzle lifting a little to reveal their bared teeth, each head that had allowed him to fondle it affectionately during the summer months stiff with hatred.

'You had best take yourself off, Joss Greenwood,' she whispered, 'before they do you an injury.'

'So I had.'

'I shall not come this way again,' she said but in her eyes was the beginning of something which begged him not to let this happen, not to let her go. God knows what she wanted of him, her own mind agonised since this madness must finish but the endless days before her without him in them could not bear thinking about. She hated him for what he had said to her, for what he believed in, but how could she live without him? It was as simple as that, her eyes told him.

He looked at her and he saw it and the violence left him. He felt it drain away in the hopeless dread which her going would leave and though he simply could not bear the hurt he must inflict on her he knew the time had come when he must. She was so young, surely, his desolate heart said, she would get over this. She would marry this man her father had picked for her. She believed she could resist it, she pretended it was nothing but a business arrangement but deep down she knew it was not. They were alike, despite the difference in their class, this man whoever he was, this man and Katherine Chapman. The bridge could be crossed between them as it never could between her and Joss Greenwood. Though he longed for it, demanded it, had taken masculine offence when she had hesitated, though he would have carried the picture of it forever in his heart, he had it in him to give thanks she was to leave him as she had come. He had loved her, loved her now and always would and the gift he had given her, reluctantly, was the gift of her virtue. For a whole summer they had pretended, perhaps built fantasies in their innermost hearts, of marriage, of children, of the years ahead together, but that was all they were, fantasies, dreams which children dream and now the time had come to put an end to them.

'Joss.' She could see the indecision in his eyes and the true power of his love for her and her heart lightened and her eyes became soft for a moment before he delivered the thrust.

'You must go back to your father, Kit Chapman.'

'Joss . . . please . . .'

'I cannot meet you here . . . again . . .'

She stepped back from him, her body sagging though she was upright. She did not know what was to come but the pain of it hit her even before he spoke.

'There is a girl . . . you see . . .' he continued agonisingly.

'Please . . .' She put out a hand as though to stave off a blow.

'. . . and I am to be . . . married to her next month.'

It was as though her body had become filled with some substance which ran along her veins to limbs which had been weak, to her shoulders which had drooped, to her head which had wilted on her neck and she stood tall, erect, proud of who she was with no need of the support, or love of any man. Her eyes darkened to a sombre purple and though every scrap of colour receded from her face, it was alive, vital and threatening.

'Then you had best get back to her since you are not needed here,' and with a click of her fingers she called the dogs to her and strode away towards the track which led to Crossfold. Her steps were firm and her head high and as he watched her go he had never loved her so much as he did at that moment.

12

Joss and Mercy were married on an autumn day on which the sun shone from the pale sweep of an eggshell blue sky, over the moors, which fanned out from the tiny Methodist Chapel, where Enoch Butterworth and those of like mind worshipped, laying a great slumberous haze of warmth and lassitude. It would be the last of the summer, they said, those who had come to fill the Chapel and the surrounding burial ground and beyond that even, spilling out on to the moor itself. They could smell the winter in the air, they said. It was the middle of October and amazingly warm but it would not last, for these parts were well known for the ferocity of the weather from now until April or May.

There were more than a hundred there, the men and their wives, those who followed Joss Greenwood on, some said, his violent path of destruction or, as was more likely, they were inclined to believe, those who had known him four years ago, of revenge for the death of his saintly father. It was well known he had no interest in politics before then. He had been no more than a lad, skylarking about, often seen in the company of a pretty lass or two and though he had done his work as conscientiously as any father would like he had certainly not appeared to have a serious thought in his head. His eyes had always been laughing with more than a hint of impudent mischief curling the corners of his mobile mouth and his mother had loved him more than she should for how could anyone resist his merry and engaging flippancy?

Now he was a leader of men, a challenger of authority.

He had lost that jaunty charm which had endeared him, not only to pretty girls but to all those who had seen him grow up in the village of Edgeclough. It had been replaced by a bold defiance of authority, a dangerous shortcoming which, though it brought chaos to the mill-owners, often frightened those who sympathised with his beliefs. The Onwardsmen were known now from Liverpool to Halifax, from Glasgow to Somerset and their name had only to be mentioned in the presence of a mill-owner and he was putting up his barricades, calling in the soldiers to protect his mills and his weaving-sheds and his machines. Surely, they asked, those who wanted an end to it all and a return to peace and some decency in their lives, it must be resolved soon?

Mercy Butterworth, Mercy Greenwood now, left the Chapel to no joyous pealing of bells since such frivolity was frowned upon by those who worshipped there, her hand through the arm of her husband, as lovely and serene as a spring snowdrop, her head shyly lowered as a snowdrop should, though her face was radiant. She wore no bridal gown, nor her husband a bridal suit but in her hands and in the buttonhole of his frayed lapel was a mixed spray of freshly picked wild flowers, red and white Campion, Maiden pinks and white Rock Rose, tied with a delicate froth of white ribbon. Her family, her new family clustered about her and Charlie, greatly daring kissed her cheek, making her blush and then her new husband did the same, deepening the colour in her cheeks to flame and they all agreed they had never seen a prettier bride. There would be no wedding feast, how could there be? It had taken many weeks to scrape together the fee for the parson since even a shilling was hard come by these days. Many of the men and women who had come to wish them well had probably never been legally married since the finding of the fee was often beyond them and anyway, what did it matter? They had no property to leave their children, should they have any and should those they have survive, so why go to the bother of legalising a union which was much more

167

convenient to consummate in the simplicity of a bed?

He kissed his mother goodbye and promised her he would see her the next day since, though he was to live with Mercy and Enoch now he would continue to weave on his loom which had once been his father's and grandfather's before him. Mercy would spin for as long as there was raw cotton available but it was getting more and more difficult to come by, as the machines of the mill-owners, Barker Chapman, George Abbott, Albert Jenkinson and half a dozen others in the town and along the valley ate up the supply. The raw cotton was brought by canal from Liverpool and on to Manchester and as far as Saddleworth before the waterway carried on through Standedge tunnel to the other side of the great Pennine chain to Huddersfield. It came in great quantities, swallowed up by the factories to feed their power-frames and power-looms, stored until they needed it in vast new warehouses, stored, the woven cloth, in other warehouses just as enormous ready to be sent on the same route back to the great seaport and across the oceans of the world to the buyer. Calicos, ginghams, fustians, sateens and velveteens, thousands upon thousands of yards of cotton cloth, making the North, the whole of the country one of the most prosperous in the world and though a great number of the population were at or below subsistence level, those who were not were intoxicated with it.

Joss Greenwood took his new wife to their marriage bed that night as gently as he knew how. He was twenty-three, a man who had been offered and taken more than a few women in the past three years. Abby Hobson, who still good naturedly accommodated him whenever he was in the region of the 'Five Pigeons' had taught him what pleased her and what she liked he had found was acceptable to all women. A bit of decent wooing, kisses and soft laughter and the belief he gave them that they were worthwhile to him, not just their female bodies but in their complex female minds which needed so much more understanding than many men knew of. He had loved many women in the fleshly sense and liked some of them too, particularly the brazen-hipped Abby who asked nothing of him but that he gave her as much enjoyment as she gave to him.

Of the other one he would not allow the smallest whisper of thought to infiltrate his mind for she no longer existed. She had been an abstraction, a shadow without substance, which had, for a lovely moment delighted him, dazzled him but, like illusion, had vanished with reality.

Mercy loved him. Her eyes adored him through the soft candlelight as they and Enoch ate the simple meal she had prepared early that morning. She knew nothing of men beyond the gentle and modest kisses they had shared and the almost brotherly embrace he had enfolded her in as he left at night. He did not love her. He did not desire her and had found the idea of undressing her, of laying her on the bed and covering her naked body with his own, quite unnerving, since she was like a child to him. Just eighteen and virginal as a nun and he was to take that from her.

She began to tremble quite violently as he closed the bedroom door. They were to sleep in the bed Enoch had shared with his own wife since it was the largest in the cottage, and this was enough to alarm Joss Greenwood since the idea of Enoch who was never parted from his Bible, doing to his wife what Joss was about to do to his daughter, and in the same bed, was enough to douse the fiercest passion!

He took her clothes from her one by one, not allowing her to slip into a dark corner and undress herself as she would have preferred since if they were to be man and wife they must know one another's body, take pleasure in it and in the act of love, and this, as he had learned, was the sweetest way to start it. She allowed it, standing like a forlorn child in an agony of embarrassment as he slowly took her garments from her one by one, kissing her frail white skin, here and here, his hand lingering at the curve of her small, exposed breast, smiling as fondly as he knew how, allowing her to know he held her, and her woman's body in the highest esteem, taking his time in bringing her to the rightness of her own desire. Her long fine hair drifted

169

in a soft cloud about her face and shoulders and she shivered at his touch. She hung her head, her eyes staring at her own feet through it all, not once raising them as he shed his own clothes and when he finally put his arms about her she became rigid. He soothed her gently, putting his lips again to her ear and neck, finding the places where experience had shown him a woman is most vulnerable, responsive, smoothing his hands down the length of her narrow back, pressing her tiny body close to his own. She made no protest when he laid her on the bed, lying beside her, careful with her, taking his time in his inspection of her smooth flesh, her tiny pink-tipped breasts, the satin of her inner thighs, with his hands and his lips and his own strong male body. He was mindful not to bear down upon her too heavily for she was as light as thistledown, as insubstantial as a handful of air and he was afraid to hurt her. She cried out sharply as he penetrated her and his mind was so fixed on her frailty it almost unmanned him.

When it was done he lay back with relief. The next time, he told himself, would be easier since she would know him and what was expected of her but in the days and weeks that followed it was always the same. She loved him so much in the day, following him with eyes which shone with a light which said he was the centre of her world, that he *was* her world but at night she withdrew herself, not bodily but in her mind, from his rough demands, his coarse and inexplicable ardour, the strange sounds which came from him, only holding him tenderly when it was done with and the stranger he became for those few minutes, was her Joss again. He was patient. He made love to her so gently, so delicately, he often found he could not himself become a man, to love her as a man loves a woman, and so he began to try less and less. Her sweetness defied him for how could he hurt it? Her gentleness overpowered him since he felt himself to be less than a man in their bed but she was his wife.

It was April now. He and his men had been meeting regularly with other members of radical reform societies, mainly at the 'Five Pigeons' which along with other public houses was being used more and more as a meeting place. Trade Unions were under the ban of the law and though frightened Tories had tried to put a stop to it, denouncing the inns as places where the lower orders talked sedition and mill-owners had called upon the authorities to punish publicans for allowing the illegal trade unions to collect there, Abby Hobson was afraid of no one and was certainly not concerned with the possibility that she might lose her licence. Every night they crowded there, the men who had nowhere else to go bar their miserable hovels and the everlasting sight of downtrodden women and starving children. They could do nothing about it, though it broke their hearts, so they escaped it by mingling with other men in the same condition but with the hope Joss Greenwood and other militant radicals put in their heart. They often did not drink since they had no money. Sometimes, when the 'Benefit' clubs or 'Thrift' clubs of which 700,000 of them were members, gave them a 'hand-out', or the poor relief, the outdoor relief some of them were granted, contributed a small amount to the family welfare, they might have the price of a jug of ale and it was not unheard of for the open-hearted landlady to slip a jug over the bar counter to a man who had nothing but the company of other men to comfort him.

They had all gone. The night was very dark, the thick, low cloud cloaking the moorland in a blackness which could almost be felt, but it was mild. The air gently caressed the cheeks of the flushed men as they stumbled away in every direction, cheerful most of them for they had been uplifted by the plan Joss Greenwood had outlined to them, excited with the prospect of being about something after the long torpor of the winter months. Abel Broadbent fell into one of the cold little moorland streams which tumbled noisily down the hillside to the valley bottom where it met the River Penfold and there were a few amiable curses mixed with their high laughter since, for once, they felt optimistic and what did a dousing in the water matter?

171

Joss watched them go, his own face softened with a smile for he had grown to love these hapless men who looked to him for leadership. He was younger than most of them but the last four years or so had matured him, made him into a strong and compelling man, a man accustomed to being obeyed, to have other men follow him without question. He went to meetings in Halifax and Huddersfield to hear Mr Richard Oastler, a man involved in the abolition of colonial slavery and now taking up the cause of factory children, to Blackburn to listen to William Cobbett who had been imprisoned after the massacre at St Peters Field and as far south as Nottingham to sound out the ideas of others who thought as he did. He was much respected though still far too wild for some of his followers. He was about to threaten Barker Chapman again and though what he had said made sense and had the majority mad with excitement, one or two of the older men had it in them to wish he was a little more like his father. He had incited the younger men this evening, promising them with fire in his eyes that the blow they were to deliver the Chapman mills would be repeated up and down the Penfold Valley and into Crossfold and Oldham itself. Fine talk and bold, but that was his way.

He was still rangy without an ounce of spare flesh on his big-boned body and his shaggy hair was cut only when his wife could get him to sit still long enough for her to get at it with the shears. There were fine lines in the skin around his eyes and the shadows of clefts beginning on either side of his mouth. His skin was brown, even in the winter since he walked for miles in all weathers across the moorland paths and his step was springing and graceful. He had a magnetism now that was undeniably male, arrogant and headstrong for his authority had for so long been unchallenged, drawing not only the appreciative eyes of the women, most of them young and fancy free and ardent in their support of the cause, and ready to show it to the one who led it, but also Joss had the championship of the men.

Abby Hobson was stirring the fire with the brass poker

when he returned to the tap room. Her movements were slow and unhurried and as she turned to smile at him the weight of her splendid breasts fell forward, straining against the fabric of her bodice. Her nipples were peaked and brazenly full and as he watched she undid the top buttons one by one, allowing him to see the magnificent valley of fine white skin which divided them. Instantly he felt himself become erect as he had not done for months in his bed with Mercy and the cloth of his tight breeches was uncomfortable against his thighs.

'Tis 'ot in 'ere, lad,' she said, 'and that there smoke don't 'elp none. Mind, I do like the smell of tobacco and brandy. Will you 'ave one fer the road, Joss?' She smiled, offering him more than a glass of brandy if he cared to take it and if he did not, letting it be known he would not give offence. A woman of ease, of comfort, a woman made for pleasure, not only of herself but of the man of her choice. She gave the abundance of herself, the bounteous goodwill of her body where it pleased her to give it and woe betide any man who tried to help himself, but of all the men she knew and had known, none moved her like Joss Greenwood. He was ten years her junior but he was a man for all that, and not since Matt Hobson had she recognised such a man. Her husband, the publican of the 'Five Pigeons' had died some years ago and she had taken the inn over, keeping order when men grew unruly, as easily as he, a bareknuckle prizefighter, once had done. She had loved him well and been faithful to him while he lived but she was a woman of appetite and liked to eat when she was hungry.

Joss sighed and shook his head though he ached, quite literally in the region where Mercy's submission could not touch him, to take what he knew Abby offered.

'Nay, lass, I must be on me way. It's an hour's walk and Mercy'll be waiting.'

'Aye, 'appen it'd be best.' She smiled quite gently at him and her great dark eyes, gypsy eyes from the man who had probably fathered her were filled with compassion. 'You'll not want ter be worryin't lass.'

'No . . .' but he did not turn away from her.

'She's a lovely little thing, Joss,' she said sincerely, but not giving you what you need, her eyes continued and though she made no movement her body seemed to sway a little and the lift of her breasts drew him another step towards her.

'Abby . . .' His voice was thick and a fine film of sweat broke out on his face.

She sighed deeply. 'Eeh my lad, there's no need to be uncomfortable with me. I've seen it all and there's many a young girl needs time . . .'

'She cannot . . .'

'Joss, there's no need, not with me.'

She opened her arms and he sank into them, pressing his aching flesh against the warm softness of hers. She raised her rosy face and his lips found hers, moving hungrily from them to the flesh beneath her chin and the hollow of her throat. His hands rose to take her bodice from her and the chemise she wore beneath it and his hands cupped the magnificence, the lovely rose-tipped bounty of her breasts. But it was not enough. Tipping her back until her buttocks rested on the table beside the fire he lifted her skirts until they were bunched about her waist and with a swift movement undid his own buttons and in a moment he was inside her and wave after wave of giddy-paced excitement thrummed through him and into her until she cried out and so did he. It took no more than a minute or so and when it was done he stood between her legs, his breath ragged, his face like that of a mad man, his eyes savage.

At last she pushed him away and stood up, her naked breasts swaying an inch from his chest. She put her hands to the fastenings of her skirt and in a moment it was round her feet and the gloriously female splendour of her was there for him. She reached out and began to unbutton his shirt and when he was as naked as she, she leaned into his arms and began to lick his skin, just below his chin, following the strong line of his throat, the sweat-dewed mat of his chest hair and down to his flat stomach and he groaned

174

with delight, grasping the entangled mass of her hair.

She looked up at him and smiled and her eyes were black in the firelight. 'That was for you, Joss Greenwood, and now this is for me.'

'How did you know?' he said, hours later. She had been, one moment, like mother earth, basic and honest and understanding, allowing him the great and plentiful goodness of her heart and the next, a wild woman, demanding, showing him the secret delights of her body and how best he might please them and only when her pleasure had been attained, and his again and again did they lie in peace together before the dead fire.

'Nay, don't ask me, lad. I'm a woman and I know what drives men. Some men have needs which others don't, and women are much the same. I could see what you were missin' 'cos it was in me an' all.'

'I cannot . . . seem to make her love me.'

'She loves you right enough, Joss, what woman wouldn't?'

'Oh I know what she feels for me, Abb, but she's so . . . so little, no more than a child and I'm afraid to hurt her.'

'Women like to be 'urt a bit . . . now an' again. You weren't exactly gentle wi' me a time or two tonight, my lad.'

He leaned on his elbow and smiled into her face. Her hair was a rich and glowing red, like the pelt of a fox and it was snarled about her head, burnished by the firelight almost to gold. Her eyes were understanding, the eyes now of a friend, the eyes of a woman, complete and uncomplicated. A friend!

'I have a great deal of affection for you, Abby Hobson.'

'So I noticed in the last hour or two, but what else ails you, Joss Greenwood? 'Tis not just that little wife o' yourn, is it?'

'No.'

'Perhaps . . . a woman?'

He sighed and his eyes looked into hers, seeing the

175

wisdom and tolerance there and putting his cheek to her full breast he told her of Kit Chapman.

'She's no good for you, lad, heartless, like the rest of her . . .'

'I know, Abb, but who has made her so?'

'You're defendin' her.'

'Aye, she's his child. She has no say in what happens at that mill.'

'You love her then, Joss Greenwood, or you'd not be takin' up for 'er. You really love 'er.'

'Aye.' His voice was sad and empty.

But as he walked home his face was calm, his body at peace as he listened to the sounds of the moor at night. The soft splash of water against the stones, the squeak of some small creature in the budding heather, the rustle of another as it crossed his path at a run. He had not felt so content since before his father died and he wondered why that was. He had been a callow youth, carefree, careless, ready for any prank his own or his mate's brain could devise and though they had known hard times his childhood had been secure. He had been aware that other children, factory children, pauper children had not been so lucky for he had gone about with his father and listened to men who told them so, but he had not really *known*.

He was a man now with the knowledge burned deep inside him of the desolation which was creeping over this northern land he loved so well. He was a man of responsibility, with a wife at home and his mother and her family to help support. He did not know where he was to get the next supply of cotton for his wife and his mother to spin in order that he might weave his piece but somehow, just at this particular, bewilderingly contented moment, it did not seem to matter. Was it just because his body's hunger had been assuaged – surely not – or was it because he had allowed Kit Chapman into his heart again when he had spoken of her to Abby Hobson?

Mercy was waiting for him when he got home, her face rosy from the heat of the fire. Though coal was readily

176

available, and cheap to all those who could afford it, most of the cottagers cut peat from the bogs which stretched for miles across the moorland basins and which, when they drained, compacted into the fuel which was a substitute for coal and had the advantage of being free. It burned just as brightly and warmly and the cottage kitchen was cosy as he stepped inside.

Mercy smiled, standing to move across the room, lifting her lips for his kiss as sweetly as a child. Her eyes were clear and innocent and if he had not himself taken her as his wife he could have well believed she was no more than fourteen and virgin. His heart was soft for her, protective, but his manhood folded itself away, knowing sadly she was not a complete woman, nor probably ever would be. She was a lovely young girl, eager to help him in his work. Her heart was filled with her love for him and for her father, her dead brother and her new family but physically she was as immature and as naïve as a child. She imagined that she fulfilled her role as his wife, that she did her 'duty' though she would not think of it quite like that, in his needs as a man, and she was happy despite her repugnance for it.

'You shouldn't have waited up, love,' he said, no sense of guilt or remorse for the past hours he had spent with Abby coming to trouble him.

'I wanted to hear how the meeting went,' she replied, bustling about the kitchen, a wife now, as she saw herself. A woman in her kitchen seeing to the requirements of her husband. This was where she felt at ease, washing and ironing his shirts, mending them, creating tasty meals from nothing and watching with great pleasure as he ate them.

'Well, I think, though some of the older men were not convinced.'

'Would you think me disloyal if . . . if I said I felt the same, Joss?' She carefully put the pan she had filled with water on the fire, then stood back to look anxiously up at him. It was a wife's job to support her husband, her expression said, but this one of hers was sometimes an enigma to her. She knew he was fighting for the oppressed and the starving folk who were her neighbours, many of them, but he frightened her sometimes with the intensity of his recklessness, of his daring.

'No, Mercy, you may say what you please. But talk does not always bring about the reforms we need. We must often resort to other means.'

'I know . . . but to . . . well, suppose someone is hurt?'

'We shall make sure no one is.'

'Oh Joss, sometimes I wish . . .'

'What lass?' His voice was patient.

'That there was some other way.'

'Well, there isn't, so how about getting me something to eat? I've been on the tramp all day and I'm fair clemmed. I've had nothing since me breakfast and porridge and treacle doesn't stick to your ribs like . . .' He stopped as she turned away in confusion and what appeared to be distress. Instantly he was contrite since she did her best with what little he could give her. Enoch put the few shillings he earned directly into her hands each week but the hens from which they sometimes had an egg or two had long since gone into the pot and with winter just behind them, the store of vegetables was finished. Of course she could not give him a hearty breakfast and he had not meant his words as a criticism but as a joke. Now she was close to tears and he sprang across the room to hold her in his arms.

'Don't fret, sweetheart, please . . . don't cry. The porridge was well enough and I'll not be wanting to get far, will I?' He smiled and kissed her cheek, bending to look into her eyes. 'Give me some bread and . . . whatever you've got and we'll be away to bed . . .' but the tears still fell and she hung her head as though in deepest shame.

'What is it, Mercy? For God's sake, tell me.'

'Oh Joss . . . I'm sorry . . . but . . . well . . .' She lifted her tear-stained face, her eyes agonised with guilt. 'There's nothing to eat, Joss. I tried to manage, really I did. I went up to your Mother's to see if . . . well, perhaps . . . sometimes Charlie's had a bit of luck with his traps, but there was nothing, and Martha . . . they had nothing either.

178

Oh, I'm sorry, Joss . . .' She might have been frittering away the few shillings a week he earned on gee-gaws and bon-bons, so pitiful was her expression but it was nothing to the despair in his own heart. His wife, and apparently his own mother, were harrowed by the emptiness of their own larders while he himself had been concerned only with the frailties of those others in Lancashire who were in need, who were starving, the men ready to commit murder, the women to go on the streets to earn a shilling to feed their families. Now, at last, that spectre had come to stalk his own family and he had nothing to offer his wife but words. He stared over her head and the glow of exhilaration he had felt as he walked across the tops faded away, going out like a torch leaving nothing behind but a wisp of smoke and he knew, at last he finally *knew* what it was he fought for. All these years he had fought. He had protested and marched, wrecked power-looms, for if the power-loom was broken and the spinning frame was left untouched did it not follow that the manufacturers still producing yarn would send it to the cottagers for weaving? He had broken windows and a few heads. He had put his name to a dozen petitions, preached what was called *sedition*, attended illegal meetings, drilled men in the use of weapons to fight for what was rightfully theirs and now what was rightfully *his*. He had been shouting into the wind, he realised that, liking the sound of his own voice, enjoying the power he had and the splendid way men jumped to do his bidding, but he had not really *known* but now it seemed he was to experience it at first hand. He could not stop now, even though his own wife and mother were in the same plight as the others. He could not stop *because* they were in the same plight as the others.

Now, finally, their fight had become his fight!

13

They were silent as they streamed down the hillside, no more than a dozen of them since that was all that would be needed for what was to be done. They had kept to the wood which sloped down the hill since it gave them good cover, a rush and blur of dark shapes, dropping over the rough wall and into the grassy ditch beyond though there was no one to see them since the watchman was at that moment enjoying the young girl Ellis, the overlooker in the spinning room, had supplied him with. It had cost him sixpence, of which the girl got nothing, beyond the keeping of her job but it was well worth the money for though she had struggled somewhat at first it being her first time, and was painfully thin with no breasts to speak of, being only twelve, she was female, cheap and clean. He never knew what hit him as he slumped across her white body.

'Dear sweet Jesus . . .' someone said, his voice sounding abnormally loud in the dense black silence of the night and for several minutes there was complete confusion since Joss Greenwood had not allowed for this predicament and not being there to ask, those who milled about waiting for him had no idea what to do with the silently weeping child. They covered her decently, averting their eyes, ashamed most of them of their own maleness, wondering what the hell to do with her but, sniffing dolefully she took matters into her own hands, and vanished, it seemed, to wherever it was she slept when she was not on shift.

It was Saturday night and the weaving-shed, for the first time since last Sunday night, was shut down, the machinery switched off and idle, ready and waiting for the factory children, including, presumably, the one who had just been outraged by the watchman, to clean it the next day.

He was there then, quietly appearing from nowhere, a slightly darker shape in the darkness, tall, easy, soothing their jitters just by being there. They grouped about him, unnerved by what had just happened, longing to unburden themselves to him but quelling their instinct to shout about the obscenity of it. They had heard of course, about the plight of many a young girl and of the use the overlookers made of them, those who had no home to go to and no man to defend them. They were often offered to other men who came to do business in the sheds, it was said, an added inducement to the closing of a better deal. Naturally, it was well known that the heat in which these girls worked hastened the process of female development so that in some cases a girl of eleven years might have the breasts of a fully mature woman so who could be blamed, those who took advantage of what was offered them said, when they took it? The girls were clean, free from disease, at least for a while and, if they did well and made no fuss could be rewarded with a penny now and again to spend as they liked.

It was almost midnight, an hour when those who had beds to go to were in them, and only those who screamed and fought and fornicated about the gin-mills of Pig Lane, Boggart Hole and Lousy Bank, tore the peace of the spring night to shreds with their wild cries and their howls of drunken laughter. The bulk of the warehouse stood between the men and the town and only the odd hoarse cry or the wail of some woman, rose above its high roof and they took no notice. It was well known that Crossfold was no place to be on a Saturday night and those who took no part in such goings on stayed in their villas and mansions and kept their doors and windows locked.

The glass made no more than a tiny shattering sound as Joss put the stone through it and when he had wriggled inside the men were eager, ready now to show what they were made of in this war they fought. They were ordinary men, labouring men who asked no more than a decent wage and a dignified way of life but they had been forced to take on the role of soldiers and not all were cut out for it. Joss's white teeth gleamed for a moment in the darkness of his face when he opened the enormous door to them, wide enough and high enough to accommodate the horses and waggons which came to take away the velveteens and fustians so beautifully woven by Barker Chapman's operatives.

The warehouse was stacked high. Roll upon roll of carefully wrapped cloth waiting to go to many parts of the world, ready to be put on the canal barges which would carry it away, first on the Huddersfield canal to Manchester and then on to Liverpool by the Bridgewater canal. Barker Chapman's wares would go by 'narrow boat' beyond Old-ham up and down a dozen locks before they reached the sea but these would not make that journey for Joss Greenwood had other plans for them.

The first smoke was no more than a trickle, a vague wisp sneaking through a crack in the brick wall. There was the merest flicker of a flame, not ready yet to take good hold, smouldering and whispering among Barker Chapman's splendid cloth. The men stood uncertainly, the empty oil jars in their hands, quite fascinated really, forgetting for a moment where they were, watching, as small boys, the mishap of another, then Joss's fierce whisper had them on the move, their clogs fetching sparks from the cobbles of the yard, clattering out and into the street and in a moment they were over the stone wall again. Even then it seemed they could not tear their excited selves away but must stay and watch, kneeling to peer over the wall at their own handiwork.

They had wanted to wreck the power-looms Barker Chapman had put in but Joss had been against it. Though he was aware of the logic of their thinking, their belief that if the Chapman weaving-sheds could not weave who else could Barker Chapman turn to but themselves, he himself had begun to doubt it. In theory it was sound, their thinking, but this time he wanted to get at the mill-owner in another way. Those operatives who worked the looms would be thrown out of work if they were destroyed. With the woven cloth itself burned to a crisp, Barker Chapman would have no option but to begin again, with work for carders and spinners, for weavers and finishers and nobody thrown off. And when this was safely alight, burning so fiercely it could never be put out, they were to march on to Abbott's mills, to the Jenkinson mills and as many more as they were able, and do the same there.

They were half way up the hill, their jackets streaming behind them, their arms flailing enthusiastically, their shouts of triumph not pleasing him much since it was not the action of a band of soldiers but of children who have just tied two door-knockers together. But he supposed that sometimes they must be allowed this outlet for their frustration and bitterness or they would go mad with it.

It was then he heard the scream. It was high and desperate, lifting the hairs at the back of his neck and for a moment they all stopped, the memory of the desolate child fresh in their memories. Surely to God she had not gone into the warehouse ... Dear God ... suppose Barker Chapman put the children in there to sleep ... Sweet Jesus ... but then their faces cleared for they were conscious that no man and certainly not one as careful as Chapman would allow a group of children to roam about in a shed containing thousands of pounds worth of cloth.

'Who the hell ...?' one whispered though if he had shouted it is doubtful his voice would have been heard above the increasing roar of the flames. The fire had taken hold with a will now, leaping up above the roof of the warehouse, fed by the easily devoured provender of the fabric within, lighting up other buildings set apart from it since by keeping his sheds well spaced Barker Chapman had thought to avoid the very disaster which was now taking place. Glass was beginning to shatter in the windows and tiles popped and again the scream rang out, nearer this time and it was then he saw her.

Kit Chapman! It was Kit Chapman. A vividly illuminated figure set against the lurid wall of the warehouse, running, tripping, picking herself up, turning about again and again and so close to the burning building he could well believe he could see smoke coming from her clothing. She seemed not to know what she was doing, to be unaware of everything but the flames, uncaring of her own safety, desperately seeking something which eluded her.

They all watched, paralysed with shock, himself included since they had dragged away the unconscious body of the watchman and had believed there was no one else who could possibly be injured. The warehouse was empty except for the cloth, they had been told by Jenny who was an experienced spy for the movement by now, going often where she had no right to be to gather information. The apprentice children slept where the bales of raw cotton were stored and there was no one on the site but the watchman since, it had appeared, no disturbances were expected at Barker Chapman's mills and weaving sheds. Many mill-owners had asked for troops to protect their property in the scattered outbursts which had rippled across Lancashire but Barker Chapman in his insolent belief in his own superiority needed no one to guard what was his!

His daughter darted suddenly to one side, foraging under the disbelieving gaze of Joss Greenwood and his Onwardsmen, among a pile of what appeared to be rubble, then finding what she sought she ran like the wind, carrying something towards a trough which stood by the gateway. It was a bucket. *A bucket.* Swinging it wildly she filled it from the trough, set there to water the horses of her father's callers and, her mission clearly understood now by those who watched, she began to wobble lop-sidedly towards the open doorway of the burning warehouse. Surprisingly there were as yet no flames coming from it, but inside it was an inferno, savage, loud and hungry and she was going in to douse it with a bucket of water!

The others, still frozen in horror, did not even see him go, the first they knew that he was no longer with them was when they saw him from their elevated position above the street, racing across the yard, his long legs eating up the distance from the gate to the warehouse doorway. She had just reached it when he dragged at her arm and even then, with her skirt beginning to smoulder she swung the bucket at him, screaming wildly, maddened, her eyes like those of a warrior defending his territory, cursing and dangerous.

'Leave go, you fool, the warehouse . . .' Her voice screeched insanely with the need for speed and for a moment he thought he could not hold her or, as seemed more likely in her furious strength, she would take him in with her. He held her with both hands now, dragging her, screaming and kicking, spitting in his face, the bucket gone, thank God, or she would have brained him with it. Still she would not let him take her. Her nails raked at his eyes and his cheeks, drawing blood. Her knee came up, ready to plunge into his crotch and he had time to wonder where she had learned that trick then he struck her, not a violent blow but enough to stun her and he caught her in his arms as she fell.

He was half way up the hill, Kit Chapman mumbling against his chest, her hair all over the place, her arms hanging limply when he realised his men were still there at his heels.

'Get home, for God's sake,' he shouted, '. . . we'll have to leave the rest. Go on, they'll be here in a minute, you bloody fools . . .' and in the space of thirty seconds they were all gone and he was alone with Kit Chapman in the blessed peace and coolness of the woods.

He laid her down on a pillow of mosses. There was a thick carpet of dead leaves, dry now since there had been no rain for several days. There was a dense layer of wood sorrel, nourished by the leaf mould, delicate pale green upside down parasols with yellow-centred white blossom. There was a ring of beech and hornbeam about them, all in new leaf and he could hear the whisper of the breeze in the canopy above him and smell the delicate fragrance of new growth.

She sat up slowly and in the pale glow from the burning buildings down the hill he could just make out the blur of her white face and the glitter of her eyes. She put her hand to her jaw where he had hit her and he heard the sharp intake of her breath as she winced. He knelt by her side, his knees deep in the softness of the moss and waited.

She turned her head then, bending it a little to look into his face and though he could see no change in her expression, indeed no expression at all, there was no mistaking her venom.

'You set it, didn't you?' Her voice was like a razor in her throat.

'Yes.' He could certainly not deny it.

'You bastard.'

'No doubt, but it had to be done.'

'*It had to be done!* A week's work . . . a *month's* work. Hundreds of yards of expensive cloth and it all had to go up in flames! Why, dammit? For God's sake, why?'

'You know why, Kit Chapman.'

'Do I? Do I? My God, if I live to be a hundred the logic of this . . . these outrages you commit will continue to baffle me. They spun it, weaved it, these . . . these people of yours. They worked and were paid for that work and in a moment's insanity you have destroyed it.'

'As you are destroying them.'

'Destroying them? . . . We employ them . . . give them work when there is no other to be had . . .'

He stood up, sighing wearily for what was the use? They were saying the same words they had said when they last saw one another nearly nine months ago, which they had said a dozen times before and still it was the same. Both looking at the coin from opposite sides and though it was the same coin they each saw a different face to it.

'Are you all right?' he asked, ready to walk away since what else was there to do. He felt his arms ache with the need to put themselves about her, just once, sweet Jesus,

186

just once more, to hold her as he had last summer, in love, but he must get away from here before they caught him, before *she* caught him again in the deep netted trap of love.

He was half way across the tiny glade then he stopped, taking a step or two back towards her. She was still crouched upon the ground, her arms draped across her drawn up knees, her head bent on her arms.

'It just occurred to me . . . an idle question really since what is it to do with me, but what the hell were you doing at the mill alone at this time of night?'

'You're right.' Her voice was muffled in the crook of her arms. 'It has nothing to do with you.'

'I'll leave you then but perhaps it would be a good idea if your father kept a stricter watch on his daughter in future. Crossfold is not exactly the place to be on a Saturday night.'

'Damn you, Joss Greenwood, damn you to hell! What business is it of yours?'

'None whatsoever, but had you not perhaps better get down there. They will be looking for you. The warehouse is a holocaust now and I presume, if you are missing they will imagine you to be in it.' He kept his voice neutral, without expression.

'My father knew I was in the . . .'

'Where?'

'In the design room. I drove the phaeton in. There was something I wanted to finish. So I left the dogs in the stable . . . then I smelled smoke . . .'

'You drove yourself! My God, he must be mad.'

'He trusts me. I am his son.'

She lifted her head then, proudly and even in the dim light, illuminated now by the flames from down the hillside, he could see the satisfaction that simple statement gave her. 'He allows me to do exactly what a son would do. He knows I will come to no harm with Joby and Blaze.' She made a contemptuous movement with her hand. 'What do I want with dinner parties and evening concerts. I had a problem to be worked out so I changed and came down.'

'You still like to take risks then?' His voice was low almost as though he did not want her to hear.

'And you do not?'

'I am a man.'

'So?'

She tossed back her hair and a sudden explosion of flame lit up her face. There were black smudges on it and her hair was wild. The gown she wore, a riding habit of dark cloth was fitted tight to her body, sculpting it, displaying the lift of her breasts, the narrowness of her waist and the lovely curve of her hips. She was quite magnificent in her newly won womanhood, violent in her rage, dangerous but proud, proud to be who she was and of what she did, hating Joss Greenwood still for what he had been to her.

He grinned sardonically since she must not see into his heart and his white teeth slashed his face. 'You don't look like no son to me,' he said, and his eyes roamed insolently over her body.

'You filthy bastard,' she shrieked and leapt forward, reaching again for his face, for any part of his flesh from which she could draw blood, for his eyes to blind him so deep was her hatred but he caught her wrists, laughing now and in a moment he had her backed up to the wide trunk of the tree under which he had laid her minutes before.

'You see how easy it is to overpower you, my lass? You are a woman, *not* a man and any man who has a fancy for it could take you, and your fine ideas and reduce you to what you are. A *female*! a *woman*! Your father might call you his son, God damn him, but look at you, *look at you*, you are helpless in my hands, in any man's hands . . .'

'If I had my dogs . . .'

'Do you take your dogs to your bed with you, my fine lady, for that's what you need to make you see what sex God made you. A man to tame you, to make you into the woman you are . . .'

'And you are that man, I suppose? Well, you were not man enough up on the moors that summer, Joss Greenwood, so tell me what has changed?' As she finished speaking she spat full in his face but he did not release her to wipe the saliva away. Bending his head he put his face against her straining breasts and with all the time in the world, or so it seemed, rubbed sensuously against them, with his cheeks and his mouth until he felt her nipples harden, then swiftly, as she gasped in outrage he lifted his mouth to hers, taking her lips beneath his own. Brutally he captured them and they trembled and though for the space of a heartbeat she would have turned her head away, they opened under his and the softness, the fire, the sweetness surprised neither of them.

They were both breathing hard, both fighting, though neither of them could have said why, or for what since they were both fully aware of what they wanted.

'Don't . . .' she whispered against his mouth and he let go of her wrists and felt her hands lift to cling to his shoulders.

'Oh Jesus . . .' His mouth slipped down her arched throat and her eyelids fluttered in the straining pleasure of her body's response but from down the hill the sound of men's voices drifted on the tide of flames and billowing smoke and as they at last penetrated her bewitched mind, she stiffened and her eyes opened wide. His dark head was beneath her chin, his lips warm at the hollow of her throat and he was whispering her name.

'Dear God!' Her voice was a shriek of pain, of horror, of abhorrence and he fell away from her in confusion. 'Oh dear God . . . you bastard . . . get away from me . . . get your hands off me . . . my father will have you horse-whipped for this . . .'

He was stunned, overpowered by the strength of his need for her which he had thought to be dead, of the dangerous emotion she had disturbed in him. His senses were as sharp, as raw as though they had been exposed to the fire down the hill. His breath hurt his chest and every part of his body was acutely aware of hers but she was looking at him with such loathing he could not bear her to know it. His face strove to smile coolly for she must *never* know it.

189

'Your father, my dear Miss Chapman, would be wise to have you locked in your room for if you are to go about bestowing your favours on all and sundry as you did with me, and delicious they were if I might say so, well . . .'

He managed a smile of amused contempt, feeling at last the black, snarling anger he needed to expunge the memory of her body and her lips and sweetness of the moment from his brain.

'You . . . devil . . . I'll see you hanged . . .'

'So you have been telling me for the last three or four years and yet I am still here, my lass.'

'Not for long . . . dear God, if I have anything to do with it, not for long. No one has known who it is that leads this mob which goes about burning and looting, and raping for all I know . . .'

'Oh no, not raping, Miss Chapman.' He raised a sardonic eyebrow. 'I had no need of rape here tonight for you were more than willing, I would say, wouldn't you?'

She struck him full in the face and, unprepared for it, it rocked him on his heels but he only laughed and she thought she had never hated any man as much as she hated this arrogant devil.

'You are as foul in your mouth as you are in your deeds and if you cross my path again I will kill you . . .'

'Really, Miss Chapman, such melodrama. Come now, a little kiss! Where was the harm in it? You were not unwilling the summer before last as I recall, and don't tell me you didn't enjoy it tonight?'

'Don't . . . don't push me too far . . .'

'I have no intention of pushing you anywhere, nor will any man from what I have learned of you. A man likes a woman to *be* a woman, you see, and you . . . well . . .' His dark eyebrows tilted wickedly, '. . . but I really must go since I hear a hue and cry coming up the hill . . .'

'I know you now, Joss Greenwood, and your family since your sister works in my spinning mill . . .'

Instantly he had her in the vice of his two hands again, holding her wrists agonisingly in front of her face and she was afraid then, shrinking back from him. He was black-faced with anger and his eyes beat her down and his voice was icy, chipping away the apparent amusement he had felt, telling her that what had gone before had been no more than child's play.

'You threaten my family, you bitch ... you touch my family and you won't be the only one to talk of killing. Do you understand? They have nothing to do with this, nothing, and if a hair of their heads ... any one of them is harmed I shall know where to look.'

'Go ... oh for dear Christ's sake ... go ... I cannot bear you ...'

He threw off her hands, then turned slipping away through the trunks of the trees without a backward glance and she leaned against the tree, her face quite blank, her eyes empty and staring, though her mind was alive and crawling with the imagery of her thoughts. She hated him and all his kind and no matter what they did she would not give in. She would punish them and through them, *him* and if it took her to the end of her days she would make sure he was hunted down, imprisoned, transported if she could arrange it so that she might never see his face again. She had known some sympathy for their plight, those frail children who worked in her father's mill and had wondered in the secret recesses of her mind whether, were she to be in the place of those women who put them there, might she not feel the same sense of grudge, the same sullen resentment. Might she not have fought beside the man who had just, she realised now, saved her from an unthinkable death, clawing for the right to share in what the mill-masters had? She had heard them say so often, these faceless men and women that if the manufacturers tried to increase their own profits through wage cuts and sweated labour, then, through machine breaking, they would make sure there *were* no profits. It had a certain plausibility but why could they not see that if the mill-masters closed their mills, as they would be forced to do, it would be the labouring man who would suffer. Why did they not accept ... Oh dear

God . . . it was *him*, that damned radical reformer . . . *Joss Greenwood* . . . Joss . . . aah . . . how she . . . no . . . no . . .! At each confrontation he made her think, made her wonder and question and it did no good. She had a mill to run, a profit to be made, workers to pay, a responsible position in the economy of the country. She was part of what made the country great, and he was no more than the breaker, the destroyer, the instigator in the tearing down of what men like her father and grandfather had built up.

Her body was still in a tumult, fiercely consumed with the energy she remembered so well and understood so little, an energy she had known only with him. She wanted to stretch langorously and at the same time beat on the trunk of the tree at her back with angry clenched fists. There was something stirring in her body's core, something she did not recognise but which she was desperate to discover and her lips still burned with the touch of his. She rubbed them frantically with her hand and her heart was dazed and despairing.

'Kit . . . Katherine . . . Katherine . . .' Her father's voice, almost unrecognisable in its desolation, floated up from the road and there were other voices, hoarse and urgent and getting louder. She turned to look dully and on the slope of the hillside, coming up towards the trees, were the figures of men, dozens of them.

'Kit . . .' Her father, still dressed in evening clothes was in front of them, shouting to them to spread out, to go round the back of the buildings and in a moment she knew she must go to him for he was distraught, believing her, perhaps, to be in the burning warehouse.

'Get the dogs . . .' she heard him shout, '. . . they'll find her if she's . . .'

She must face him, make up some story to explain how she came to be up here, so far from the mill site, dirty, dishevelled, but unharmed and as the hurried speculation of what she must say slipped through her tired brain, her heart grew still and cold for she had realised that, without

192

conscious thought she was preparing, quite instinctively to protect Joss Greenwood.

She turned her face to the rough bark of the tree and wept.

14

Harry Atherton watched his employer's daughter cross the mill yard, admiring the way in which her skirt swung, almost but not quite brushing the cobblestones. Though he knew she would not do it deliberately, for it seemed Miss Katherine Chapman was impervious to a gentleman's admiring glance, her hips moved in a way that was infinitely sensual, and her arrow-straight back constrained her to lift her breasts quite splendidly. She had left her bonnet in the office and her hair caught a sultry beam of sunlight, turning it to the superb glow of a chestnut, so shining it looked as though it might just have been polished. She stopped to talk to one of the workmen, the foreman who was in charge of the rebuilding of the new warehouse and her face was impatient and her hands lifted, cutting through the air, and presumably his excuses, as though to pour scorn and disbelief on whatever it was the man said, and Harry chuckled. She would, no doubt, be telling the poor beggar his own business, demanding to know why since it had been a week ago that the first brick had been laid, the building was not complete. Already the foundations were down and the walls waist high and it would probably be no more than a week before the roof was ready to go on since Katherine Chapman seemed blindly determined, almost obsessively so, he thought, to have the new building filled with finished cloth as it had been before the fire.

His sharp brain wondered why. There was no doubt that

the Chapman mills stood to lose an enormous amount of profit, not to mention the cost of rebuilding the warehouse but it did appear to him that this was not the only concern on Katherine's mind. It was as though the horror of the night of the fire could only be scourged from her by the act of replacing what she had lost, and as quickly as possible, just as though she must have everything exactly what it had been before.

It was a puzzle which set his alert mind humming. He had not been present at the dinner party held that night at Barker Chapman's home. There had been his employer's bank manager and his wife, so Harry had heard, the owner of the local newspaper, *The Crossfold Observer* and his wife, a business acquaintance from Germany who was interested in Chapman fustians, and Albert Jenkinson, his wife and daughter – brought to balance the party.

Harry realised quite early in his new position – and smiled to himself – that Barker Chapman, though the arrangement he and Harry's father had made was firm, would allow no liberties to be taken, not until the final event had been legalised. Harry Atherton had been given the chance, but he must prove himself capable of grasping it before he could consider the Chapman wealth at his disposal. He was Barker Chapman's insurance, if you like, on his daughter's future. He could do her no harm, nor any good, really, since she was completely able now to run the mill alone but he was her *bulwark*, her shield between herself and her fortune, and the rest of the hunters who crowded about her at every function she chose to attend. He was a gentleman. The 'right sort'. He would en- sure that the dynasty – of mill-owners, for God's sake – would not die, in fact he was to inject it with some decent blood!

And he would enjoy the task immensely, he told himself, since Katherine Chapman was – apart from the misfortune of her birth – an ornament splendid enough to decorate any gentleman's home, particularly one as luxurious as Greenacres, which would, naturally, come to him. She was bright and had a malicious wit which would add spice to their partnership. She was elegant and ladylike, quite lovely to look at, and very, very rich. Not for a moment did it occur to him that he might fail and when Kit entered his office he smiled, at his most amiable for the pictures in his head were more than pleasant.

'And is it to be finished by lunchtime then?' he asked, raising a good natured eyebrow and though often he irritated her beyond measure with his flippancy, Kit could not help but smile back at him.

'Perhaps not, but if I have anything to do with it, Harry Atherton, it should be no longer than the end of the month.'

'My heavens, you can get more work out of a man than my old schoolmaster who used to beat us unmercifully if we were not word perfect in our French conjugation.'

'No doubt, but then I should imagine that is the only way to get work out of you,' and she looked pointedly at his immaculately trousered legs, crossed at the ankle, which were propped on his desk.

'How sharp you can be, my dear Katherine. So cutting, my heart is in tatters. And so serious. Do you never relax for a single moment?' His smile was silky and innocent.

She sighed and shook her head. 'Everything is a joke to you, isn't it? I am trying desperately to replace the yardage we lost in the fire, to make up the orders which were to go out the next day while you sit about on your . . . chair, smiling and talking nonsense and getting nothing done. Can you not . . .?'

Quite lazily he picked up a sheaf of papers and moved them towards her. His eyes narrowed almost dangerously but his voice was pleasant.

'Before you dress me down as I have just seen you do that poor chap in the yard, take a look at these will you? They are letters from customers, those whose cloth was lost in the fire. Where do you imagine I have been these past weeks, my dear? Down to Leicester to the hunt . . .?'

'I wouldn't be at all surprised . . .'

'Now then, Katherine, that is not at all polite and quite unworthy of you and if you read these letters you will see you were mistaken in me.'

'Oh for Heaven's sake, Harry . . .'

'All right then, listen to this. Do you imagine I am happy to invest my time and my energy and my considerable talents . . .' he grinned disarmingly, ' . . . into this business of yours if I am to get no return? Hardly, my dear. I have been to call on every man, in England at least, who has lost cloth in our . . . your warehouse, at considerable cost and taking up an enormous amount of my time, assuring each and every one of them that Chapman's, despite this slight setback, will have a new consignment ready for them by the end of the month . . .'

She gasped. 'The end of the month! Harry, for God's sake, you know that's not possible . . .'

'Your father does not agree.'

'But the operatives cannot possibly manage to produce that amount by the end of the month. Two months, perhaps, since we shall have to have somewhere to store it . . .'

'I have rented a warehouse from George Abbott.'

'Very commendable of you but how are we to fill it?'

'Extra hours, extra shifts, seven days a week until we have made up what was lost.'

'Seven days a week! But the machines must be cleaned and oiled and the children cannot . . .'

He sighed deeply and stood up, brushing down the fault-less creases in his dove grey trousers.

Harry Atherton had done well in the year he had worked at the Chapman mills. He had not, as Barker Chapman had, been brought up in the cotton industry. Where he came from the manufacturing classes were held in contempt and though a chap would not be censured for marrying where money was, far from it, they could not understand, and said so, why he should choose the daughter of one of those upstarts, who thought themselves to be as good as they. And on top of that he was to learn, so he said, every process of cotton manufacture, the skills, the difficulties, the

196

stratagems that the damn class got up to! He accompanied Barker Chapman on his daily rounds of the mills and the weaving-shed and was shown the intricacies of the machinery, to the counting house to learn the intracacies of profit and loss. He went often to the Cloth Hall in Crossfold mixing most agreeably with the commercial gentleman who admitted to each other they had not expected him to stay the course as long as he had. He was an 'easiful' man which was not something to be said in his favour since the textile trade was cut-throat and if he should cross swords with one of his competitors, many of whom would slice a bean in half if it could make a profit, it would be interesting to see how he would fare then.

'Look, Katherine. Your father has told me of your . . .'

'My what?' Her expression was perilous since she had found on several occasions that her father seemed disposed to talk of her to Harry Atherton behind her back and it alarmed her since she had not forgotten her eighteenth birthday when she had been quite certain that it had been his and Samuel Atherton's intention to pair her off with Harry. Nothing had been said since and Harry had kept his distance, communicating with her only in the course of business and on the one or two evenings he had been invited to dine with the Chapmans. Then there had been other guests and not by word or deed had there been an indication that he was anything but her father's employee.

'My what?' she said again.

'It does you justice, really it does since it is well known that ladies, or most of them, have tender hearts . . .'

'What the devil is that supposed to mean, Harry Atherton?'

'That you do not care for your operatives to be worked too hard. That you would prefer not to employ children despite the fact that their families cannot do without their wages and the work they perform can be done by no one else for it needs tiny bodies to . . .'

'Stop it. Not another word. How dare you and my father discuss me behind my back, how dare you? I am fully aware that children must be employed and I have said nothing about . . . turning them off. I appreciate that the work they do is important . . . necessary. It was just that . . . well . . . I just felt . . .'

'Yes, Katherine?'

But she would not let him see the slightest sign of weakness in her. She must not allow any of them to say that she was a woman and therefore could not discharge her duties as a man would. Her father, this man, all of them had no qualms about employing children and if she was to compete with them, as her father's heir, then she must do what *they* did.

'I shall speak to the managers this afternoon. Let me know what you need exactly, to make up the orders and I shall see that it is done. Now, if you have nothing further to tell me I must be about my business.'

'There is just one more thing, Katherine.'

'What is it?' she asked defensively, turning back to him.

'You look quite incredibly lovely today, my dear.'

The slamming of the door as she left the room could be heard in every part of the counting house and so could his following laughter.

Barker Chapman's dwellings to house the families which flocked in ever-increasing numbers to beg work at his mill spread like a weed round the factories and to pay for them and for his new warehouse, for someone must, his spinners and weavers had their wages reduced once more by three-pence a cut.

Those who lived in Pig Lane, Boggart Hole and Lousy Bank and were already at starvation level in their Chapman-built terraces of 'company houses' became even more sullen.

'We won't stand for it,' they said and their angry mutterings grew louder and could be heard even above the sounds of their neighbours' brawling, their lust, which they all shared in the back-to-back intimacy which was thrust on them in their one up, one down dwellings. They could be seen in groups of four or five at the tap which was shared by twenty cottages and was turned on for an hour each day, or at the communal privy, used by the same twenty families. Their pinched faces were set between crooked shoulders, their hands thrust deep in trouser pockets or tucked inside the wrappings of a shawl.

'We won't stand for it,' they said, and there was despair and violence breeding in the slums Barker Chapman had created. Those in Pig Lane and Boggart Hole and Lousy Bank and the squalid alleys behind them became surly, knowing as they sipped their water porridge and treacle that, though there was not much they could do about it, since they must work to earn even what little they had, they did not like it at all. They watched the manufacturer, Mr Barker Chapman and his daughter, the fine Miss Katherine Chapman, the mill-owner Mr Albert Jenkinson and the weaving-shed owner Mr George Abbott ride down Jagger Lane in their carriages, their glossy carriage horses better fed than they themselves were and word was carried up to Joss Greenwood at Butterworth's cottage that it was time to be on the move again, to make bloody Barker Chapman hurt again in his pocket, to burn something else he valued, like his mill, or his weaving-shed, or his house.

'We won't stand for it,' they said. They had been promised better things, by Mr Hunt at St Peters Field, four years ago now and still they were starving, still the men were forced to watch their women and children flock to the mill to bring home the wages which fed the family, or not! The price of bread had gone up again and were they to stand for it, they asked one another, when their wages, or more precisely the wages of their women and children had been cut?

Gangs of youths roamed the streets, playing at 'Onwardsmen', looking for mischief and when they found it in the shape of Mr George Abbott they threw stones at him, hitting him on the head, and in Mr Albert Jenkinson's weaving-shed where they smashed his windows, every last one of them. They were men, they said, weren't they, not bloody animals to be worked until they dropped. They wanted the old system back with their wives at the spinning wheel and themselves at their hand-looms and in their own homes and if they could not have it, why not?

'It won't come again, that's why,' Joss told them unsparingly, 'and it's no good shouting for it and saying you won't have anything else. It's gone, can't you understand it? There are power-frames and power-looms and that's the end of it but we'll find something to take the place of what we've lost, don't you fret. We might not work for ourselves any more, we might not even work any more but we'll bloody well fight until we've got a life that's fair and decent. A fair day's pay for a fair day's work . . .'

'It's a bloody long time in coming, Joss Greenwood. They're making us work even 'arder and longer than what we were since that bloody warehouse fire *and* for less wages. What 'ave you ter say to that, then?'

'I know that, Isaac Pickering, but by God if we stick together and wait it out we're bound to win. That's the answer, can you not see it? Fight and more fighting and even more, and when we can say we won't work for what they're prepared to give us, and mean it, then we've got a chance. We need to close ranks, let no one part us for only in strength can we fight with strength. One day we mean to have the vote for every man . . .'

' . . . and woman, eh, Joss . . .'

'Aye, Sarah, for with the likes of you to put in your fourpenny worth how can we fail?'

He and Mercy, Jenny and Charlie had gone up to Ravenstone Brow above Saddleworth, the green and gold and purple infinity of the moorland stretching out for miles on all sides of them and the men had come to listen to him and to other reformers who had come to talk to them. This last blow struck them by Barker Chapman had flung them low and they needed the hopeful words Joss and the others gave them to lift them up again. They had crept up from as far away as Oldham and Bury, from Rochdale and Todmorden and Bacup, the women bringing sickly infants and younger children. The older ones, those who worked in the mill for six days out of seven fell into their beds on a Saturday night and did not get up until Monday.

It was Sunday, high summer and everywhere heather and gorse and bracken bloomed about the knees of those who walked in it. Lapwings beat over their heads, stirring the still air with their wings and the heat wrapped itself about the great crowd, lulling them to somnolence for it was not often they could sit and do absolutely nothing. They were tired, those who had walked ten miles here and must walk the same back and many simply lay down and went to sleep, pillowing their heads on soft grass and sweet smelling clover, shielded by bracken fern and ling and purple moor grass, their eyes closing on the sight of tiny, quite beautiful cloudberry.

But the men did not sleep. They milled about Joss Greenwood and the two who had come to talk to them, remembering Abel Greenwood, the martyr, and Tom Butterworth, who, though he had not died for the cause but in defence of his sister was a martyr nonetheless, looking to the man who was now indisputably their leader. He was speaking of forming a union even though it was illegal, as this meeting was illegal, and of wrecking not the power-looms which were taking their living, but of the wisdom of attacking Barker Chapman and George Abbott and Albert Jenkinson and the other mill-owners who were bringing their trade to the Penfold Valley, where it would do them the most damage – in their pockets! As they had done in the burning of the Chapman warehouse. All along Hull Brook and the waters of the river which had once driven the wheels to power the machinery, these new men were building and if the textile trade was to survive in Lancashire, men like themselves would be needed to ensure that it did. It could not be done without them and the manufacturers must be made to see . . .

They had crept up between the drowsing women and children, slipping past on their bellies like eels, hidden in the waist-high summer bracken, even their red coats invisible in the dense foliage. Joss was standing on a rock, head and shoulders above the hundreds of men about him. He had seen the movement of the bracken, taking no particular notice for there were dozens of children about. Young lads delighting in the hidden depths of the undergrowth, playing the games young lads love so well.

His voice was powerful, mesmeric and the men understood and believed what he said. It made sense and they cheered and clapped one another on the back, saying it would not be long now, surely, since how could they fail to overcome their destitution and misery with a man like Joss Greenwood to lead them?

They rose from the bracken at their very feet, not children but soldiers, no more than two dozen but enough to move in a tight circle towards the ringleaders. They let the others go, those on the edge of the crowd who panicked and ran, stopping some of them to pick up a crying child or a bewildered woman. Those close to Joss, Abel Brigden, Jack Akroyd, stood by him for even if they had been inclined to it they could not have run with the others. They were radicals, leaders of men in other parts of the country where cotton and wool and silk were manufactured and workers were exploited, brothers in arms against oppression, who had come to speak today to Joss Greenwood and his Onwardsmen, to tell the Lancashire spinners and weavers to keep a stout heart and a hopeful one for they were supported by those of Yorkshire and Nottinghamshire. These men and others had marched beside Joss in protest, their faces masked as his had been, but they were not masked today and neither was he and the soldiers had the three of them by the arms, knowing them, it seemed, before the horrified crowd had realised what was happening.

'Run . . . take your families and run,' Joss shouted at the top of his voice and so used to his authority had they become they were away, pushing and shoving and jostling so that the six soldiers who held Joss and Abel and Jack had to be protected by their comrades. They drew their muskets, and the officer-in-charge, his sabre, standing about the three captives, ready, should it be necessary, to shoot anyone who dared a mischief against them or the three men they had captured.

Half a dozen of Joss's men, those who had come alone and were without a family, hung about thirty yards or so from the troop of soldiers, ready to make a dash for it but willing, if Joss gave the word to take on the armed soldiers.

'For God's sake, run! If they get us all there'll be no one to . . .' and they watched helplessly as the butt of a rifle at the back of his head brought Joss to his knees. They went then, hundreds of them, streaming across the moorland like the waves of the sea and the soldiers watched them go impassively since they had the ones they had come for.

It was then Mercy began to scream. She had stood, quite paralysed, beside Jenny and Charlie, unable to comprehend what was happening. The sight of those red coats had plunged her back into the terror of that day when . . . when Tom had . . . when the soldiers . . . when the soldiers . . . had . . . She pulled frantically at Jenny's restraining hand and Jenny was not certain whether it was to run to Joss or away from the soldiers. Charlie, fleet as the rabbits he snared, darted towards the circle of soldiers who were keeping a close guard on their captives until the hostile group of their followers decided what to do.

'Charlie . . .!' Jenny's shriek drew the attention of one of them and before the lad could reach his brother the man had scooped him up, kicking and swearing, under his arm. He ran like the wind, carrying him back to where Jenny and Mercy hovered, his long legs leaping like a hurdler and though the boy still struggled, begging to be let loose, tears streaming across his ashen face, the man would not release him.

'Come on,' he said roughly to Mercy and Jenny, grabbing Jenny's arm with his free hand since she seemed to be the one most likely to respond. Joss's wife was still screaming, her voice shrill, demented but beginning to fade into the moan of an animal in shock and when Jenny was dragged along so was she.

'We just can't leave them,' Jenny agonised, but the momentum of the slope of sweeping moorland, down and down and down, carried her with the others until the little scarlet-splashed group behind them was no longer visible.

'Please . . .' she cried to the unknown man, her breath breaking in agony from her tortured lungs, '. . . please . . . can't we . . .?'

'There's nowt to be done, lass, nowt . . .'

'But . . .'

'They've got bloody muskets . . .'

Within five minutes the stretch of moorland beneath Ravenstone Brow was empty, every man, woman and child who had come to hear Joss Greenwood, Abel Brigden and Jack Akroyd, gone and all that was left was the bright splash of colour where the soldiers still stood defensively about their captives.

The officer lowered his sabre then returned it to its scabbard, his careful eyes still sweeping the moorland about him. There was nothing to see but the miles of empty bracken, the stretch of the hills above and the long decline below him into the Penfold Valley. The sun which warmed his back painted a blue shimmering haze above the long and lovely sweep of the heather which minutes before had made a fragrant bed for those who had the stink of the factory in their nostrils for six days a week. There was nobody, nothing but a bird rising from the shadow of the far side of the valley and the sound of its cawing.

'Right, sergeant' he said smartly. 'I think we may proceed now. They have all gone.'

'Aye, lad, 'tis safe to move on as you say. They've all gone now. It would look bad to be overcome by women and children, fine soldiers like you.'

Jack Akroyd suffered the same fate as Joss Greenwood as his laconic, smiling remark reached the ears of the officer and he fell against Joss who was still struggling to rise. Blood flowed from behind Joss's ear, dripping on to the whiteness of the shirt Mercy had ironed for him the night before and his head rang with pain but he was determined to stand. With a great effort, his thoughts jagged and piercing, the swiftness of the attack still dazing him, he stood straight, his hand reaching to help Jack.

'Get your hands off that man,' the sergeant barked but Joss took no notice, stooping a little now to raise Jack to his feet. Abel took his other arm and at last all three stood tall, staring boldly, arrogantly, the officer would have said, at the circle of soldiers.

'You are under arrest,' he said arbitrarily, 'for contravening the Combination Acts of 1801 and 1819, one of which states that a seditious meeting such has been taking place here today where more than seven persons have gathered is illegal. You three, as its leaders will be tried and sentenced. Right, sergeant. Manacle the prisoners, please and we will get them down to the lock-up at Oldham.'

Jenny Greenwood stared into the dying embers of the fire in Enoch Butterworth's grate. She leaned forward in the chair, putting her elbows on her knees and cupped her chin in her hands, her eyes unfocused, her face strained and weary. Upstairs, induced by the draught of valerian which Sarah Pickering, one the village women, had brewed for her, Mercy slept at last, still trembling fitfully as her dreams carried her back to the moment earlier in the day when she had seen her husband clubbed to his knees and to three years ago when she had seen her brother knocked almost senseless in the same way. They would hang Joss just as they had hanged her brother, she had screamed again and again until Martha Greenwood, the mother of the captured man but herself composed had sent for Sarah who knew every herb which grew and what each was capable of.

'She will do herself an injury,' her mother had said when Jenny had turned on Mercy, shouting at her to be quiet. 'You have not loved a man yet, Jenny Greenwood and cannot know how she suffers. Her brother was hanged and it has . . . made her . . . delicate . . . more anxious.'

'We are all anxious, Mother. Good God . . . oh dear God, what are we to do?' It had been the turn of Enoch then, reprimanding her sternly for taking the Lord's name in vain, telling her it was possible to save her brother only through God and prayer and to get down on her knees and beg His forgiveness and to intercede for the life of the man who, in his own opinion had lived lawlessly, mocking God in his . . .

'Oh for Christ's sake be quiet, old man,' Jenny had shouted nearly off her head with worry and Enoch, bitterly offended, had left the cottage swearing he would go up into the hills to speak on her behalf and on her brother's behalf to his God. He had known of Joss Greenwood's disposition when he had married his Mercy and the hopes he had nurtured that the love of a good woman and the begetting of a family, which he had prayed would bring an end to the violent ways of his son-in-law, had come to nothing and now look where he was. Rotting in Oldham gaol with others like him and with transportation staring him in the face and what was to happen to his young wife, Enoch's daughter then, he asked?

The cottage was quiet. Charlie and Daisy had been put in with Sarah's young ones, though Charlie at seven years of age had protested wildly, asking why they could not go, all of them, all of Joss's men and break him out of the gaol like they had done for others, who had been taken? Jenny had been inclined to ask the same but Martha had soothed them both, begging Jenny to be cautious, to wait and talk to the others for no good would come of breaking the law a second time that day.

'What will they do to him, Mother?' she asked now and Martha leaned into the firelight, her own face drawn and haggard for she had known this upheaval so many times since she had married Abel Greenwood. So often he had been apprehended, fined, once three months in prison for 'disorderly conduct' though a more peaceful man had not existed. Her son was violent, disregarding the peaceful ways of his father, marching, drilling the men who followed him up to the moors, breaking machinery and, she was well aware, though nothing had been said to her, that he had been involved in the burning of Barker Chapman's ware-house.

'I don't know, lass.'

'What will they do without him?'

'They'll manage, Jenny, same as always. Like we've man-aged since they brought the first power-looms into the valley.'

'But they depend on him. They look to him for leadership and a bit of hope.'

'There'll be others to carry on.'

'Dear God, Mother, he's your son. Are you not concerned that they might send him to the colonies?'

'He'd still be alive.'

Jenny sprang up, her hair springing up with her and her mother marvelled that these three children of hers could be so wayward for even their Charlie, at his age, was heading the same violent way.

'I'll get the men together. There's a hundred of them'd be willing. We'll have the three of them out of that gaol by nightfall tomorrow. It's been done before . . .'

'And have him a wanted man, on the run for the rest of his life.'

'I'll go down now to Isaac Pickering's. He'll fetch the others.' She reached for her shawl throwing it like the wings of a bird across her shoulders her face vivid now she was on the move. She had gone as far as the door when Martha's voice stopped her.

'You'll do no such thing, my girl. You'll sit down and stay here with me.'

'Give over, Mother. I can't hang about and do nothing . . .'

'Why is it always what *you* can't do, or what *Joss* can't do? Why is it that whenever there is trouble, whenever someone is *in* trouble, the pair of you must be off some-where, doing something regardless of what the one *in* trouble needs?'

Jenny hesitated then, looking back at her mother, her eyes saying she could not bear to sit here doing nothing, begging her mother to let her go, and yet, admitting in her heart that she could not, that she *should* not go, that Martha Greenwood was right. She wanted to be off for her *own* sake, because *she* was frustrated and needed to be doing something. If Joss was freed by his men, which it was more than likely they could manage, since there would be no more than half a dozen soldiers guarding the gaol, he would not be free at all. He would be a man wanted by the law, his name on the magistrate's list as a criminal and what good was he to them then? He would be unable to move about freely as he did now. He would be forced to hide, to dodge and run at every alarm, disorganised, hunted, never able to stop in one place long enough to speak to anyone, let alone the crowds who came to drink up his strength, to take hope from his power. He must be a free agent and if he must go to goal to be free again, then so be it.

She moved back slowly, her feet dragging on Mercy's well-scrubbed floor. She sat down again in the chair from which she had just risen and putting her face in her hands began to weep.

They were shut up, the three of them together in a slip of a cell scarcely big enough to house one. There was no window, no light nor air and the stench of other men who had been there before them was so thick Joss thought he would choke on it for it got in the way of each breath he took. He was afraid, more afraid than he had ever been in his life for wherever he had rested in the past, he had been free, out in the open where the sun was, or the gracious beauty of the moon and the stars. He was to stand trial at Lancaster at the next Quarter Sessions before the magistrate, for conspiring with Abel Brigden and Jack Akroyd, to raise the wages of those employed in the cotton industry, which was against the law as set out in the Combination Acts.

The learned counsel said so at his trial three weeks later, remarking sharply that any assembly which endangered the peace and security of other men could only be looked upon with great anxiety, particularly as the object of the gathering was an impossible one. The new machinery, without which there would be no foreign trade had reduced the wages of the labouring man but that gave him no right to disturb the peace of others. The acts of Joshua (Joss) Greenwood, Abel Brigden and Jack Akroyd, the accused, amounted to an expressed and avowed determination to destroy the most fundamental freedom of a man to employ men and to pay wages as he chose. It attacked the very foundation of the government itself and was not to be borne at any cost.

The accused were each sentenced to a year's hard labour.

15

Martha, Jenny and Mercy Greenwood moved wearily up the track leading to the moorland path which would take them to Edgeclough. Jenny carried Daisy who was soundly asleep, her small head lolling against Jenny's shoulder like that of a broken doll. Some way behind them Charlie limped, his feet dragging, his face drained of colour or expression, his eyes staring ahead of him and Martha turned jerkily, clutching at Mercy's arm as though to keep her balance.

'Come on, love, it's not far now,' she called to him anxiously but he just went on putting one foot in front of the other, like a sleepwalker, giving no indication that he had heard her.

'Wait for him, Jenny, or he'll not catch up,' and Jenny stopped obediently. They stood, patient as oxen, almost mindless in their exhaustion, Martha clinging to Mercy until Charlie came abreast of them, then they resumed their journey, not speaking again for it took what little strength they had left just to keep going.

It was distressingly hot and the three women had tied their shawls about their waists, the weight of them too great to be carried. Their wooden clogs made a hollow sound on the stony track and their tread was heavy and flat. Martha slumped against the fragile figure of her daughter-in-law and it was evident in the way Mercy leaned towards her that even Martha's light weight, since she was painfully thin, was a burden to her. Martha's head hung down as though the effort it would take to lift it and look ahead was beyond her. Her face was a pasty grey, lined as the bark on a tree. She coughed continually and when they reached the gentle brow of the hill which led on to the moor, she stopped, gasping for breath.

It was almost dark. The sun was a livid ball of fire in the sulphurous sky, its lower curve already dipping below the horizon, the vast space about it the colour of a hot coal. There was orange and gold and apricot fading at its edges to the palest lemon and in the far distance a tiny star or two pierced the pale pearl grey.

'I'll just sit for a minute, lass,' Martha said when she had got her breath. 'It's that damned "fly". I just can't seem to clear it from me chest. I've been sick three times but it'll not be gone. See, put our Daisy down, love. She'll be all right on the grass,' she said to Jenny, 'an' we'll wait for our Charlie. Poor lad, I'd carry him meself but he's that big.'

'I'll try if you like, Martha,' Mercy said tiredly, but Martha shook her head.

'Nay, love, you can't manage him. 'Appen a minute's rest will perk us up.'

They sprawled on the tufty grass beside the track like so many marionettes whose strings have been cut and Jenny eased her clogs from her bare feet which were as black as the fireback where the soot settles. She wriggled her toes, sighing with relief, then stretched her shoulders trying to ease the agonised muscles.

It was almost nine o'clock and since five that morning

210

they had all been on their feet, she and Mercy and her mother at their spinning frames, Daisy 'piecing' broken threads and cleaning waste from beneath the machines and Charlie as a bobbin boy. Fifteen hours in Chapman's frantic determination to make up the woven cloth that had gone up in flames in the warehouse which her brother had burned. Not that she blamed Joss or regretted for one moment the destruction which must have cost Chapman dearly but by God it seemed sometimes that she, and all the others who worked for him were paying for it. The machines were never still, twenty-four hours a day, even on a Sunday, and the only time they were cleaned was during the few minutes in which the operatives were allowed to eat their food and relieve themselves at the tub in the corner of the yard. It fair turned your stomach taking away any appetite you might have had, up to your elbows in muck and grease, oil and cotton waste but it had to be done.

And how long could they go on like this, her mother and Mercy and the children, she asked herself? She had begged Ellis to allow her mother to sit for five minutes when she had almost fainted in the desperate heat and had been told viciously that if her mother wanted to sit down she was welcome to do so outside the factory gate where three dozen other women were waiting to take her place.

She put a protective arm about her mother's shoulder, hugging her to her. She bent her head to look into her face and her own was worried. Martha Greenwood was in her forty-ninth year, an old woman who should by rights be taking her ease, at her time of life, by her own fireside. She was strong, or had been, since she had lived all her life on the high moorland in good clean air and had fed on vegetables from her own garden, on fowl she had fattened herself, pork from her own pig and when she was a child, milk from the cow her father had kept. A hard life certainly, from dawn to dusk and beyond, but a healthy one, out of doors in the shelter of the cottage wall spinning in the sunshine and though she had lost seven of the ten children

211

she had borne, they had all been healthy at birth. Now, in the three months since Joss had been imprisoned they had all been swept into the factory system, either that or starve, she had aged ten years. It had nearly broken her heart to take her young ones into the mill, against which for so long her husband and son had fought but she had simply no choice.

Enoch Butterworth had died the week after Joss was sentenced. He had taken it hard, fretting on the shame of having not only a son hanged for murder but a son-in-law imprisoned for sedition. It seemed to take the heart from him, rendering him suddenly rudderless without a course to put his feet, a course approved by his God. It was not that he no longer believed in Him but that He seemed to have become disapproving of Enoch Butterworth and it was more than he could bear.

'I'm tired, Mercy,' he said one Sunday afternoon. 'I'll go and have a lie down,' and so he did and never got up again. Mercy, too anguished on the fate of her husband and how she was to manage without his strength, violent and destructive though it had been at times, to spare any for her father, buried him quietly in a corner of the yard of the Chapel where he had worshipped, closed up the cottage where generations of Butterworths had been born and took herself, her furniture and her father's hand-loom up to Martha's, putting the loom in beside those which had once been worked by Joss and his father. It made no sense to pay rent on two cottages, she said tiredly so if Martha didn't mind . . .? Martha had welcomed her daughter-in-law, taking her into her own bed and comforting her when she cried for her husband in the night, wondering as she did so on the mystery of her son's attachment for this delicate little wife of his who never seemed to grow from a girl to a woman.

'Come on, my lasses, we'd best be off,' her tone was cheerful, her face determinedly bright, 'or we'll not be home before dark.'

'Nay, Mother, let's sit for a while. It's nice up here, cooler

212

and the view's lovely. We should've brought a picnic.'

Martha smiled at her daughter's small joke, thanking God for her since she was the life-line to which they all clung now that Joss was not here. She was a strong one, her eldest daughter and with her help Martha knew they would manage until Joss returned. By God, they'd have to! The memory of the day she had just gone through and the anticipation of the one she must suffer tomorrow, and the next day riveted itself into her mind but she tried to ease her daughter's worried expression by standing up and straightening her shoulders, just as though they really had done nothing all this day but enjoy a picnic amongst the sweet grass and heather of the moor. 'Nay, we can't loll about here, can we, lass?' She turned to look at her daughter-in-law, surprised somehow to see her rise to her feet, for if anyone looked as though she could be knocked sideways with a feather it was Joss's wife. Her face had a bleached, quite lifeless look about it, the pale prettiness of her cheeks gone with the appalling smell and atmosphere in which she worked and though she had never been robust what flesh she had had been burned away from her in the mill. Only Jenny looked capable of doing a full day's work without too much trouble and that, her mother decided was because the girl was so like Joss. Tough-grained and ruthless in her determination not to let the mill-master bear her down. Like a tiger she was in her defence of those who worked with her, defiant even of Ellis who was no less than the devil in man's clothing. She had earned herself many a clout with his leather thong though it was in reality only meant to keep the younger children awake and at their employment and to prevent them falling into the unguarded machinery.

'Thought you was about to drop off there, lass,' he would say spitefully, 'so don't look at me like that. And none of yer lip, neither, or you'll be out of that door and on the street with all them others looking for a job. There's plenty more where you came from, tha' knows, aye, and work a damn sight better an' all,' which was not true. Jenny

213

Greenwood was one of the best workers he had and on *her* and all the other women who worked beside her depended the amount of the wage *he* took home at the week's end. The 'tackler' or overlooker might have as many as one hundred and sixty women and their spinning frames, or in the case of the weaving-sheds, their looms in his charge. His wages were assessed on every pound, collectively the operatives earned and so it was in his own best interest to keep them hard at it. An overlooker was very often a man who had been a weaver himself and he was able to strip and re-assemble a Lancashire spinning frame or a hand-loom with ease, though power-looms needed that new breed, an engineer to serve them, but it was on Ellis's efficiency and those of the rest of the overlookers that Barker Chapman's profit depended. The tackler was the most hated and feared man in the factory since his job was well paid and secure and he could do as he pleased with the labouring women and children provided he produced the weekly yardage of cloth his employer required.

'I don't wish to know *how* you do it, Ellis. You are in charge of the machines and I leave it to you and the managers to get the best results,' Barker Chapman had told him. 'I do not employ managers and overlookers and then expect to do the job myself. Do you understand?'

Ellis did, perfectly!

Daisy and Charlie slept curled about one another like puppies in a basket, their heads pillowed on the springy grass and Mercy, who had sat down again abruptly, seemed to have dropped off into a light doze. It was still very warm though it was almost full dark. The sky had cleared of all but a blurred pink smudge over Badger's Edge and a tiny sliver of moon no bigger than a child's finger nail lifted serenely into the pearly grey. The stars had brightened and the smell from the heather curled about the two women who crouched shoulder to shoulder against the sun-warmed face of the rock. It was quiet, so peacefully quiet a small moorland creature ran madly across the bit of ground in front of them, quite unaware of their presence and Jenny

214

sighed. They still had a couple of miles to go to reach the cottage in Edgeclough and when they got there they must turn round and tramp three back to the mill for five o'clock starting. The children would be difficult to wake and even more difficult to persuade to the walk and as she watched her mother's head nod to her chest she knew that they couldn't go on like this any longer.

For almost three weeks since Joss had been imprisoned they had trekked back and forth, back and forth, at first quite strongly since they had been fresh and determined to manage until he was home again but increasingly these past few days she and her mother had been forced physically to manhandle the children from their beds, pushing and shoving and coaxing until they were on the path to Crossfold. Daisy would grizzle until Jenny felt like landing her one, but the little girl was bewildered, frightened, exhausted to a point beyond her own childish strength. The soft flesh had been scraped from her and she already had the shrunken look of the typical factory child and Jenny was ashamed of her own frustrated anger. Charlie did his best, once they had him out of his bed, declaring stoutly that he could easily do the walk there and back but his eyes had become strangely unfocused lately and his submissive manner was so unlike the bright and cheerful imp, who had talked of nothing but following their Joss. He had taken it badly when his brother was sent to Lancaster and though he worked hard, having no choice, he was curiously lifeless.

It's this bloody walk, Jenny admitted to herself as she sat among her sleeping family. The work was killing but she reckoned they could manage it, all five of them if they hadn't this three-mile trek at the beginning and end of each day. It put two hours each morning and the same in the evening on the strain of the already punishing work day. They were allowed no more than four or five hours in their beds each night and the limit of the children's endurance had been reached. What they were being forced to do was more than could be managed by a grown man let alone a child. Her mother would keep going until she fell dead at her machine and Mercy, frail as she was at least understood the necessity of it but Daisy, and Charlie to some extent, were stupified by the sudden and quite terrible change in their young lives.

'Are you awake, lass?' her mother's voice interrupted her thoughts.

'Aye, Mother.'

'We'd best get on, Jenny. It must be nearly ten.'

'I suppose it must.'

'Well then, you get Daisy up and me and Mercy'll give Charlie a hand.'

'No, Mother.'

'No! What d'you mean?'

'You put your head down and go back to sleep.'

'Jenny! Don't be daft, girl, we can't stop here.'

'Why not? It's mild and dry and that grass is soft. Spread your shawl out and get some rest, Mother.'

'Nay, love, we can't . . .' but the argument had gone out of the older woman's voice for the idea of simply going to sleep, of waking up in the morning and having no more than a mile to walk to the factory, perhaps six hours of rest, was very tempting but . . .

'We've got to feed the children, Jenny,' she said, her voice weary and discouraged. 'They can't do a day's work with nothing in their bellies.'

'I'll walk up to the cottage and get something.'

For a moment Martha Greenwood allowed herself the relief and wonder of letting her daughter trek up to Edge-clough while they all settled here in the softness of the bracken which lined the track then she shook her head.

'Nay, you can't do that. It's not fair on you. You need a . . .'

'Come on, Mother, why should we all get no sleep? I'm strong and really not tired' — which was a lie — 'and I'd have to walk it anyway. No, you four stay here. I'll be back in an hour or so,' which was probably true for the weaknesses of the other four held her back. 'I'll fetch something. It'll have to be cold but the sleep will do the

216

young 'uns more good.' Her voice softened and in the darkness she found her mother's hand. 'It makes sense, Mother, you know it does.'

'Aye, lass.' Martha sighed and for the second time that night thanked God for this good girl of hers. 'You're right but I hate to see you go off in the dark on your own.'

'I'll be all right, Mother. Now put your head down and before you know where you are I'll be back. Go on, love, go to sleep.'

They moved into a company cottage in Lousy Bank at the end of the following week, one up and one down, the agent for the landlord cheerfully called it, and to excuse the smell but a family of twelve had been evicted the previous day for non-payment of rent and he had had no time to get it cleaned. He winked at Jenny as he spoke but his little joke fell on deaf ears since they were all too stunned to even notice it. They stood, Martha and Jenny, Mercy, Daisy and Charlie in the doorway of the cottage and behind them was the handcart overflowing with Martha's few pieces of good furniture and what Enoch Butterworth's wife and then Mercy, had cherished, and a place must be found for them and for the one loom they had been able to fetch for when Joss came home he must have some means of earning a living. He might be able to struggle on with a bit of hand-loom weaving though Martha had heard that a 'piece' of sixty yards which once had fetched ninepence a yard in his father's day and for which Joss had last been paid only three shillings had been reduced to a mere ninepence for the whole length, and that was when the work was available which was certainly not a guarantee! The new sophisticated machinery, which was to bring prosperity, was certainly doing just that, but only to those who were already prosperous. There were select committees pondering even now on why it was. Benefit societies had put petitions which argued their common cause and begged the support of men of affairs, before them but still they did nothing. Relief committees gave out rations to those most hard pressed but the

217

textile workers of Lancashire did not want *relief*, they wanted decent wages for decent work done.

Though Martha had lived in the area all her life she had never ventured into the heart of Barker Chapman's network of company houses until this day and though Jenny had assured her that they would not be here long saying it was but a temporary stay, close to the factory and easy for the children, she had been quite appalled as they had walked through from Jagger Lane, which was the main thorough-fare of Crossfold into the maze of Boggart Hole, Pig Lane and Lousy Bank. A dense cloud of smoke pressed down on their heads penetrating the honeycomb of back streets through which they had trundled the handcart, borrowed from Isaac Pickering and to be returned the next day, and the jumble of the hundreds of hovels which lined them. Each house had no foundation and therefore no ventilation or drainage and the walls, what the builders called 'brick-noggin' were no more than half a brick in thickness, giving little or no privacy. They had been flung up overnight, making quick and easy money for the builder and looked — and were — as if each one was on the point of collapsing. The gutters of the streets were thick with some abomination. Children, those who had the will and physical capability for it, swarmed like flies over mouldering heaps of refuse, the odd dead cat or rotting carcase of a dog, the ash heaps which were carted away once a week, or not if the carrier failed to come, screaming obscenities at anyone who passed by, or chucking stones, or mud, or any foulness which came to hand.

'I want to go home,' Daisy wailed and Charlie ran a bewildered finger along the frame where once there had been a door, trying to hold his breath for as long as he could since the rotting floorboards gave off a reek of the previous occupant's careless sanitary habits and he felt his head reel with it. They stood in a tight group, their faces clenched, their muscles rigid, their faces the colour of the ash which spilled from the grate across the sagging floorboards.

'Martha . . .' Mercy whispered, her little work-roughened hand reaching for that of her mother-in-law.

'I know, love, I know,' and what else was there to say. They had been brought down to this now, forced by circumstances beyond their control from the cottage up on the clear, sharp-scented moorland where the wind blew sweetly and the smell of heather and gorse and lavender filled and delighted the nostrils. Brought down to the reality of Boggart Hole, Lousy Bank and Pig Lane where the alleys fanned out like the spokes of a wheel from the factories which grew in Crossfold, over a hundred now, where once there had been green meadows and grassy tracks, weathered cottages snug against the hillside, a church or two alongside a coaching inn and the Cloth Hall. Now there were mean rows, hundreds of them, of what Barker Chapman and the rest of the manufacturers just like him called 'workers' cottages', built to house the operatives who toiled round the clock, day shift and night shift, in the making of his cloth. Each week, or so it seemed to those who remembered Crossfold when it had been a pleasant country town, more were thrown up as out-of-work agricultural labourers and out-of-work weavers flooded down from the hills to find work and now, Martha Greenwood agonised, it was the turn of her family.

But that must be left until later. It did no good to dwell on it. Somehow they must manage here, the five of them and first they would have to set about the task of making this stinking pig-pen habitable.

Far into the night they worked, scouring the cottage from top to bottom so that they could at least put their beds down on a bit of clean floor. They had scrubbed until the standpipes had been turned off at three o'clock and there had been no more water to be had to heat on the fire in the newly cleared grate. Jenny worked like a being demented scarcely able to contain the heat of the thoughts which scorched her brain. Though she had worked for twelve hours or more, scraping filth from walls and floors, shaking rag rugs vigorously in the alley to the blank-eyed amazement of the slatterns who were to be her neighbours, carrying dozens of buckets of water from the standpipe at the corner of the passage, watched by women who did not even *own* a bucket, she had not flagged. There was a trembling to her shoulders and a dark stain beneath her eyes. Her face was pale and strained but there was a look about her that swore she could go on for another twelve if she had to, and in her brain was the resolve that she did this not for herself, nor her family but for her brother and those he fought for. She was a fanatic, as militant as he in the fight for the betterment of her fellows. She hated the tyranny of the mill-masters, the harsh treatment rendered the children who worked beside her, the very concept of children *needing* to work beside her. She was strong and could labour hour after hour beside any man. She was unafraid, reckless some said in her defence of the underdog, in her defiance of the overlookers. She hated them for the vicious thugs many of them were. She hated the repression and the reduction to less than beasts of the women beside whom she spun and had it not been for her mother for whom she was responsible as Joss carried on the fight, and for her brother and sister, she would have become a soldier in his brave army of men, with his Onwardsmen. She would have tied up her skirts and her hair and marched beside them, burning mills and breaking the machinery which, though it gave a meagre wage to many, brought untold wealth to the few who were at the top.

But she would fight on in any way she could while Joss was in gaol. She was a woman and often filled with a humour which she thought to be frivolous but she would fight on until they had the better of those who exploited them. For every step they took forward it seemed two were taken back, but by God it would not always be so. The working class were surfacing through the muck and the filth in which they had drowned for so long, becoming aware of their own identity, of their own importance and Joss had told her that when they understood it they would be a force to be reckoned with, through their unity and by the sheer weight of their numbers. Even now the benefit societies were helping to get many through the hard times and if they could just stick together, hold on, they would win and houses like this one and all its neighbours would be a thing of the past.

Mercy was asleep in the bed by the wall, looking as though she was dead as she lay neatly on her side of it. They would have to be careful with Joss's wife, she mused, as she watched the shallow rise and fall of her sister-in-law's chest. She was not right. There was something gone from her, leaving her as dependent as Daisy, a child lost and frightened and needing to hold the hand of the nearest adult, but that must wait. She had enough to worry about without worrying about Mercy.

She rose from the chair before the fire and her mother awoke from the light doze into which she had fallen.

'What time is it, lass?' she murmured.

'Time for bed, Mother, or we'll miss the five-thirty bell.'

Mercy Greenwood's mind was as simple, as guileless as that of a child. A child brought up in a kindly fashion by an elderly father to believe that the reward for obedience, purity, kindness and generosity to one's fellowman, was a contented, work-filled day and a dreamless, peace-filled night. She had lived by this creed for the first eighteen years of her life and it had proved to be true.

The first crack in her equanimity, no more than a hairline, fine and noticed by no one, even herself, began on the day they hanged her brother.

She could remember, she was sure, though she had been no more than a baby herself, the day Tom was born. She had not, of course, at the time known how he came to be in her mother's arms, she only knew that the wonder of him, the joy of him in the years that followed was like a gift from the God in whom she implicitly believed. She must have been worthy of Him to be so well rewarded, she told herself when she was no more than a child. She tried to do all the things her father told her were the aim of a good Christian girl, a good Methodist girl, marvelling on how

221

easy it was, not aware that the simple goodness of her own soul, the innocence of her heart were the real cause of it. She was happy. She could imagine no other way to be. She could imagine no other way to feel and in the isolated cottage in which she lived with her father and Tom, in the small community of the village where there was really no opportunity for wrong-doing she met nothing to change her conception of how life was for the rest of the world. In her simplicity she imagined that everywhere were villages and towns, though she had never seen a town, where people worked hard, where sometimes they might be one family with less than another but which, when it became known, was helped by those who had more until the bad times were over.

Of course she knew that there were rich people, grand people, a King even in London, who lived impressively splendid lives though having nothing with which to compare it, she could not even imagine what that meant. The word 'wealth' had no meaning. She had all she wanted, so was that what it was? She thought about it as she lay on a carpet of clover and watched a butterfly drift across her vision, a fat bumble bee flounder from flower to flower. The sky was a ceiling of blue above her head, the liquid cry of the curlew filled her ears with its melody, her bed was soft, her body whole and healthy, filled with well-being and only ten yards away her young brother hummed a tuneless song as he dug down between the roots of the bracken for the rabbit he was certain lay waiting for him.

He was ten years old then and she was nearly twelve and surely life would go on forever like this. They worked hard, she and Tom, helping her father with his piece which he took each week to the Cloth Hall in Crossfold, spinning the cotton he brought back into yarn so that the cycle could go round again and her world was secure, protected from anything which might shatter her tranquility.

It was Joss Greenwood who pulled the soft, fleecy, ever so cosy wool from her eyes, but even then it did not harm her, for was not Joss and others like him to put it right?

222

She had never heard of a knight in shining armour, nor of the white horse it was rumoured he rode, since her only knowledge of words came from her father's Bible, but if she had, it was certain Joss Greenwood would have been one! The mill was a dreadful place, Joss told her, where people worked for long hours in appalling conditions. Where children laboured with little hope of escaping it, but when Joss said it she could tell by the flash in his eyes and the strong and determined way in which he set his mouth that he would soon put it right and she was comforted. If she could help in any way she would, she told him shyly and he had said that any help they could get was more than welcome.

His smile when he looked at her made her heart leap like the fish Tom went after in the river which ran through the valley, and she loved him. She longed, though she knew she would never have been brave enough to go through with it as Jenny Greenwood did to stride out with Joss and Tom and all the others who were to free the overburdened mill-workers from their bondage, to meetings up on the moor, to listen to Joss speak as she had heard he did, to listen to others from Yorkshire and Nottinghamshire, who it seemed, were as badly off as the Lancashire weavers and spinners but she knew she would be afraid, even with Joss and someone must stay at home to spin, to cook and clean and mend. That was *her* job, she told herself, her contribution to the cause they fought for, to look after those who fought in it.

She was afraid when the soldiers came. She had not understood what it was they wanted. She had done no wrong. Her family had done no wrong. They lived by the word of her father's Bible, those which said that the meek would inherit the earth and which were, of course, unquestionably true. She was alone and though she longed to run up to Martha Greenwood's cottage, for Joss's mother always gave her a sense of security the soldiers would not let her.

The next few hours were difficult to remember. She had

seen a bird once, a wheatear which had built its nest in a clump of gorse, close to the ground and while she watched, dozing a little in the absolute stillness and quiet which existed nowhere else but high on the moor, a hawk had flown over. Instantly the small brown bird which had been busily mothering its fledglings, fluttering and twittering as mothers do, became as immobile as the rock against which Mercy leaned. The hawk hung lazily in the sky for many minutes, its eyes seeking for any sign of movement far below it but the wheatear had not winked its eye, nor ruffled one feather and the hawk had gone on leaving it unscathed.

Mercy Butterworth did that on the night the soldiers came and it was not until she felt the large sweaty hand of the soldier at her breast did she begin to scream and when she stopped they had gone, the soldiers and Tom.

And they had hanged Tom. Her good, honest Tom who had been hers from the moment of his birth. A soft-eyed, soft-fleshed baby whose hands had reached for her own infant curls, a merry tumble-legged toddler, an engaging, mischievous boy who, though he was never bad, did not always follow the teaching of her father's Bible. An eager, fresh-faced youth, dazzled by Joss Greenwood's ideals, longing, as Joss attempted to do, to ease the suffering of the 'afflicted poor'. A young man then, who had harmed no one in his life. And they had hanged him!

The tear in the fabric from which Mercy Butterworth was fashioned widened a little more on the night of her wedding to Joss Greenwood. She loved him. Oh, how she loved him and the wonder of discovering that *he loved her*, that they were to be married was a joy which almost healed the desolation of losing Tom and would have if Joss had not done to her what he did on her wedding night. It was so *violent* and Mercy found she really could not cope with violence. He became someone else when he climbed into the bed they shared, wanting to look at her shrinking body – as the soldier had – demanding that she should do the same to him. His face became red and dangerous and his eyes wild and the noises he made terrified her. Afterwards, when the dreadful thing he did was over, he was *her* Joss again and she loved him then, and during the day when his tall body was calm and his kiss soft and his eyes kind and gentle, she felt a return to that warm safety of her childhood, her girlhood and the peace of it lapped about her.

It was shattered on the day, when persuaded by the sunshine and the companionship of her family to walk up to Ravenstone Brow and listen to Joss speak to the mill-workers, the soldiers had come again, to arrest her husband, they told her, for the gathering together of a crowd for an illegal meeting as laid down in the Combination Acts. He was put in gaol for it and not long afterwards the last guardian of her childhood, when goodness had been rewarded by happiness, was taken from her when her father died. She knew then that somehow, in some way, she had been so grievously wicked that she was to be punished until she repented of it. Her punishment was the work she was forced to do, by Martha, her mother-in-law, by Jenny her sister-in-law at the spinning frame in the Chapman mill.

'We all have to do it, even Daisy,' Jenny told her.

'But Daisy's done nothing wrong, Jenny.'

'Of course she hasn't. What's that got to do with it?'

'Then why has she to work in the mill?'

'Because we *all* have to work in the mill. Because we have no other way to stay alive, that's why.' And Jenny had cried that night though no one had heard her but Mercy.

She hated the spinning room but she accepted it as her punishment for the badness she must have done. She accepted it and the black exhaustion of the long walk from Edgeclough to Crossfold and back again. She clung to Martha as the only steady, unchanging reality in a world which had gone mad, a world from which everything she had loved, everyone she had loved, except Martha, had been taken from her. There was no stability except Martha and the only way to escape from where she had found herself was to shut it out. It was easy when you learned the knack of it. By concentrating hard on the little brown moorland bird, by pressing the picture of it firmly into her brain, everything else faded away and the hawk passed over. She could do this at five o'clock in the morning when she stepped up to her spinning machine and when the engine was switched off fourteen hours later she would be bewildered but immeasurably relieved to find the day had gone by without her suffering it.

The day they went to live in the cottage in Lousy Bank had been too much, even for the little moorland bird which was her friend and it refused to come and help her. The stinking, decaying refuse-heaped alleyways through which they had walked with the handcart to Lousy Bank had terrified her. The sore-eyed and misshapen children who screamed abuse had her shrinking against Martha for protection. The slatternly women, who had given up the fight against the filth, which lay not only on the rutted track but also on their own children, their homes and themselves, since water was needed to keep them clean and they had none, leaned indifferently in doorways, waiting for the standpipe to be turned on in order merely to drink. They watched her, it seemed to her, knowing she was sinful, their eyes following her progress through the filth which oozed up over her clogs and when she had passed by they would tell one another she was suffering only what she deserved.

'I want to go home,' she wept, when Daisy did. 'I don't want to sleep upstairs in that dirty room with Daisy and Charlie. Please don't make me. If I must stay here and I suppose I must, please let me sleep down here with you and Jenny . . . please . . .'

Martha, too appalled by her own and her family's misfortune to see the strangeness which was developing in her daughter-in-law, perhaps too close to it and its day-to-day familiarity, sighed impatiently.

'See, take this bucket and go to the standpipe at the corner and fill it. Charlie, you see to the fire and we'll get some water heated when Mercy comes back and start scrubbing out the . . .'

226

'Martha . . .' Mercy whispered, the thought of going out alone among those dreadful people who would jeer at her, too awful to contemplate and Martha, seeing the blankness settle in her daughter-in-law's eyes, took pity on her.

'I know, love. It's a bit strange . . . never mind, Charlie will go and you can do the grate . . .' and when, hours later, it was done she had allowed Mercy to share her bed the little bird came to comfort her. It was all right then.

16

They were walking across the yard the next day. Jenny had Daisy by the hand, and Mercy and Martha, with Charlie, were close behind. She was one woman among hundreds who moved in their shawls and wooden clogs, their rough homespun skirts, to their spinning frames, but those about her bowed their heads and shuffled, their hands folded patiently, while she strode out like a man, her uncovered head held high, her riot of curls spangled with raindrops, her breasts thrust proudly beneath her shawl and the man in the office saw no one but her. He liked the way she looked about her as though she owned the place and was considering what she could get for it, the way her glance passed over every man in the yard, all those who were looking at *her*, as though they simply did not exist, and he liked the way her hips swung and her breasts peaked and the strong straight arrow of her back. His eyes narrowed speculatively. He drew on the cigar which was clamped between his strong white teeth and he began to smile.

Though he stood in the bay window of Barker Chapman's office with all the assurance of the man who owned the mill, though he was in charge of Crossbank, of Highbank and Broadbank while Barker Chapman and his daughter travelled about the country on business, Harry Atherton was not exactly satisfied with the position he held and though he fully expected in the near future to start on the wooing of Katherine Chapman now that he had insinuated himself into her father's good graces, he was restless, a mite irritable, for the damned mills and the weaving-sheds did not really seem to have need of him. They ran themselves in fact, with the excellent managers, the engineers and overlookers that Chapman had put in and Harry realised sourly that what he had thought of as a position of some importance, of responsibility with the authority to make decisions during the weeks Barker Chapman was away, was no more than that of a figurehead, a man at the top who had no function at all and that Chapman had known of it when he left his mills, supposedly, in Harry's charge.

Harry Atherton was bored and when he was bored he was inclined, as his mother well knew, to get into mischief. He turned away from the window and the now emptied yard and shouting for his clerk told him to look sharp and fetch Ellis the overlooker, from the spinning room at once.

Ellis was all smiles and good humour when he entered Mr Atherton's – Mr Chapman's office in truth. He had obliged Mr Atherton – the young Squire as those in the mill called him – with what he wanted several times in the past. He liked them young and free from disease of course and Ellis had the pleasant task of ensuring that they were both. He kept the best for Mr Atherton, wondering quite often why a man who was wealthy – or would be, for they all knew which way the wind blew – and handsome and presumably well able to obtain his own women, should trouble himself with mill girls. Still it took all kinds to make a world, as Ellis well knew and some men had strange tastes and it was nothing to do with him. He was well paid for what he did and if a girl refused, as some did, it was no trouble to get rid of them and set on one who was more willing. He was always amazed by those, not many it was true, who showed independence, shouting they would rather starve, but if that was what they wanted, to hell with 'em.

Mr Atherton raised an imperious head as Ellis stood before his desk. He had never in his life spoken to someone in trade and certainly not to their underlings until he had been introduced to Barker Chapman. Ellis was an unknown quantity to him, a servant and yet not at all like the servants, as one of the landed gentry, he had known all his life. They were something he understood, voiceless unless addressed but at the same time members, in a curious way, of his family. Old retainers who had served his family, *their* forebears serving *his*. This kind of man, this overlooker, the managers and engineers with whom he worked, were a breed unknown to him and he found it hard to address more than a clipped word or two to them. Still, this one was very useful, and discreet too, which was convenient.

'Yes, sir?' he said.

'There is a particular girl I wish to speak to.'

'Speak to, sir?' Ellis was clearly bewildered.

'Indeed. I saw her in the yard just now. I will describe her and you will bring her here.'

'Nay, I don't even know their names, sir.'

'She is quite distinctive . . . tall with short hair . . . curly, quite . . . unusual . . .'

Ellis's face cleared and he beamed for the description could fit only one girl, then it clouded again and he pulled at his lip with grubby fingers. He shook his head doubtfully, for if there was one girl in all of Barker Chapman's mills who would spit in the face of the young Squire, soon as look at him, it was this one. Blast her eyes and blast the eyes of this young fool for fancying her since it was going to be difficult to get her to comply and Ellis did not like the taste of failure. A proper firebrand, she was and if she had not been such a tireless worker, earning money for him he would have got rid of her long since. Always taking up for someone, she was, giving him a mouthful if she saw him so much as raise his strap to a child. Not that she could do

229

much on their behalf and if he wanted he could have her out in a jiffy but if he were honest he supposed he would have to admit that he quite enjoyed the exchanges he had with her and if he could find a way to do it, which meant if *she* was willing, had meant to have her for himself.

'Well, sir, much as I'd like to oblige I'm afraid this one might be difficult.'

'Difficult! Don't be ridiculous,' but there was an excited gleam in Harry Atherton's eyes.

'No, sir, really. She's a . . . well, if you'll pardon the expression . . . a hellion . . .'

Harry Atherton began to smile and Ellis smiled with him for he could see the way of it now. He was not a fanciful man, brutal and coarse, taking his pleasures where and when he pleased for the most part. He exploited the children, the girls in his care, the mothers who would do anything to feed their children, telling himself that most of them would finish up in a brothel or on the streets in any case and if they were to do it they might as well do it with the commercial gentlemen he sold them to. Some preferred the independence of prostitution to the discipline of the mill but as he watched Harry Atherton's face he was aware that this one had a partiality for the . . . well, he could only call it . . . the unusual!

'She'll not come willingly, sir,' and he knew the statement had pleased the man on the other side of the desk.

'Fetch her.'

She was at her frame when Ellis walked towards her down the length of the noisy room. She wore nothing but a sleeveless bodice and her skirt was tied up in a way which, should she slip in the oily filth on the floor, would not hamper her movements nor catch in the machine. She was bathed in sweat, her bodice soaked in it and the round aureoles of her nipples were clearly visible through the wet fabric. Her feet were bare, and her ankles, and they were slim, neat and the skin where the muck had not reached was white and fine. She darted up and down the long frame, her eyes constantly on the look-out for broken thread, moving the carriage by turning the driving wheel, her whole body always in motion, graceful as a bird and yet without a single wasted movement. There was a child beneath her machine, deftly avoiding the whirling straps and wheels as she swept up the waste and he saw Jenny Greenwood lean down and smile at her.

'All right, Daisy,' she said, 'that'll do,' and the girl crept out and for a moment leaned against Jenny quite fearfully.

'Go on, love,' he heard Jenny say, 'go and do Mercy's machine. You know you can't stop with me.'

She whirled about when he tapped her on the shoulder and when she saw who it was her expression of surprise turned to one of truculence.

'She's new,' she said defiantly, 'but I'll see she does her work.'

'You know 'er then?' he asked pleasantly.

'Aye, she's my little sister but she'll do well as a piecer. We're used to hard work in our family.' Her manner was proud and though she held a conversation with him not once did she still her hands or her feet and he was forced to move up and down the machine with her.

A boy darted up to them with a creel of bobbins. He was too big to crawl under the machines and would, in a month or two be taken on in the weaving-sheds where a loom would be found for him but in the meanwhile he would work as a bobbin carrier.

'Thanks, Charlie,' Jenny said and Ellis was struck by the likeness between the boy and the girl.

'It seems your whole family is employed here, Jenny Greenwood.'

'Aye, and all doing a good day's work, Mr Ellis.'

'Of course you are, lass.' He grinned maliciously, 'But there's another way for you to earn a few bob if you've a mind. Want me to tell you about it?'

She turned and her machine fell idle. She put her hands on her hips and glared at him, her lip curling distastefully as though he was something unclean she had narrowly missed stepping in.

'You can take your foul mouth and your foul ways and get out of my sight, Mr Ellis. There's many a poor lass with no one to defend her gets dragged into your filth and if there was something I could do about it I would, but I'm not one of them! One day buggers like you'll be strung up for what you do and it's not far off, believe me. Until then, leave me alone for you'll not terrify me into messing with your sort, or the men who pay you.'

'Will you not, Jenny Greenwood?'

'No, now leave me to get on with my work.'

'Oh no, lass, you can leave that for now. Put your clogs on for Mr Atherton'll not like his good carpet messed up.'

'*Mr Atherton!*'

Her heart, pumping vigorously in her outrage, missed a beat but she was not afraid since what could *he* want with her. She worked well, she knew she did though everyone knew whose sister she was and whose daughter she had been. They did not believe her to be involved with the Onwardsmen. So what did Mr Atherton want, her quick mind asked and the answer was so ludicrous she began to laugh since she was nought but a common mill girl with dirty feet and a sweat-stained bodice and he was a fine gentleman who was, if the rumours were correct, to marry the mill-owner's daughter.

'Go on, Jenny Greenwood,' Ellis was saying softly, 'and don't bother to get cleaned up. It seems he likes 'em rough!'

On the night before they were to go on their travels Barker Chapman and his daughter Kit had dined Harry Atherton at their home, discussing prior to his arrival his fitness to undertake the running of it in their absence.

'Do you really think he is capable of managing it all, Father?' Kit asked anxiously.

'I should not be going if I had any doubts, Kit,' her father replied mildly, drawing on his cigar. Harry was to dine alone with them that night, Hannah declaring petulantly that she could not abide the boredom of listening to them

232

discussing the mills and the frames, the weaving-sheds and the looms, the rising cost of coal and all the trivia of business which seemed to be of such vital interest to her husband and daughter. How any woman could bear to think of such things, was even *capable* of thinking such things when there were so many other quite fascinating pursuits available to her was a constant source of wonder and irritation to Hannah and she said so constantly. As a result Barker and Kit were not a little relieved to dispense with her company on their last evening.

They dined on vermicelli soup followed by a superb salmon with turbot and lobster sauce. There was a choice of trout or whitebait, no more than a sliver on bone china so fine and fragile it was possible to see the pattern of the white damask tablecloth through it. There had been a roast saddle of lamb, larded quail, roast duck and turkey poult, whichever was preferred and Harry Atherton wondered at the magnificence of the food which was barely tasted by the master, which one assumed was eaten in the servants' hall. A green salad followed with mayonnaise of chicken, tomatoes and green peas *à la française, suédoise* of strawberries (from the Chapman hothouses, naturally). Charlotte Russe and compôte of cherries, Neapolitan cakes, pastries and Madeira wine jelly and all to cater to the appetites of three people. Harry, accustomed, despite his family's penury to the superb tables found in his mother's dining-room and in those of their friends thought it all to be somewhat ill-bred, a little too vulgar and ostentatious and though the thought of the enormous waste did not trouble him unduly since if one had money it was only sensible to spend it, it really was unforgivable to feed one's servants, who came from the lower orders after all, on such delicacies.

Barker Chapman's wine cellar was just as magnificent, old and venerable and exceedingly rare, each bottle chosen by his butler, whose excellent training had taught him to complement each course. There was brandy and cigars and when Harry had stood, expecting Katherine to withdraw as was the custom at the end of the meal to take her coffee

233

in solitary ease in the drawing-room, he had been quite amazed when she shook her head.

'Sit down, Harry. I'll take a brandy with you but I think a cigar would be beyond me, and don't look at my father like that, either, since I have no intention of leaving you and he knows it. Really, Harry, you are so hidebound in your ideas of what constitutes good behaviour in a lady. I had no idea you were so conventional.'

She said it mockingly, laughing at his upbringing and for a moment she saw the longing in his eyes to order her from the room, as his mother would her own daughter should she be impertinent enough to wish to remain with the gentlemen.

He smiled disarmingly, quickly hiding his expression, reaching languidly for his brandy glass and shaking his head as though she was a child who was up to some mischief and of no concern to her elders, quite innocent, of course, as children are but in need of a good spanking just the same.

'Really, Katherine, where on earth do you get your ideas? I am the most unconventional of fellows . . .'

'Where *fellows* are concerned, I suspect, but not the ladies.'

'How . . . charming you are,' he murmured and she knew that though he smiled sweetly it was not really the word he would use to describe her. Wilful. Wayward. Arrogant. Self-opinionated. Obstinate and damned exasperating, but not charming!

'I am afraid you must blame me for her impudence, my boy.' Barker watched the smoke from his cigar which his butler had just lit for him, drift to the ceiling. 'She is as I have allowed her to be, in fact, as I have made her, are you not, Kit?' and you will just have to make the best of it, his eyes said as they met Harry's. '. . . And she is more in touch with what goes on in the mill than I am,' which was not true for nothing went on in Barker Chapman's mills that he did not know of, nothing! He was well aware of Ellis's little sidelines, those involving girls who were in his charge and of Harry's involvement and as long as it did not interfere with the smooth running of his mills he turned a blind eye to it. Ellis was an excellent tackler and he knew where to find men like himself who were needed to keep it all in order and running as efficiently as it did. If he made a few shillings on the side, good luck to him and if Harry liked a bit of sport with young women it was only natural. He was a man after all with a man's needs. It was what Barker Chapman would have done in his place.

Harry had gone, murmuring his hopes that their journey would be not only delightful but might reap rich rewards in the obtaining of orders for their mills. They were not to worry about the business, not at all. It was in his good and careful hands and though Kit was doubtful about his choice of words since his facile good humour was to her not the characteristic best suited to run a mill, to deal with managers and overlookers and customers since it spoke of a careless disregard, a flippancy which did it no good, she must take her father's word that Harry would be equal to it.

'Come, my dear. We have taken him on to help us build our overseas markets and that is what he will do when the time comes. But he must know the cotton trade to be able to convince potential buyers that what we are selling is the best and the ideal way to do that is to be in charge of it, to manage it himself. He is keen and intelligent and has learned quickly. Believe me, my dear, Harry Atherton will rise beautifully to the occasion. He wants to make money, Kit. That is his most important quality. A man who is as ambitious and as ruthlessly determined to have wealth as he is will not let us down. Now, shall we retire? We have a long journey ahead of us tomorrow.'

And now they were home again and at the ball Barker Chapman had given to celebrate their successful venture Harry watched Kit Chapman from where he leaned indolently against one of the fluted columns in the ballroom. She was surrounded by a group of ladies and gentlemen, friends and business acquaintances of her father who thought it expedient to keep on his right side by deferring to his daughter and who all, without exception had the glazed look of a congregation which is burdened with a long-winded parson. One or two of the ladies tried to turn the conversation to other more feminine matters, concealing yawns behind their fans for really this constant talk of warp and weft was most unladylike and the gentlemen, who wanted nothing more than to retire to Barker Chapman's study and the secluded masculine environment to be found there, tried desperately to edge away from her, wishing to God the blasted band would resume playing so that they might give the excuse of waiting partners.

What a bore she is! What a pompous bloody bore on the eternal subject of the textile trade and but for the fact that she was one of the wealthiest heiresses in Lancashire he'd pack his bags and go back to Cheshire, Harry thought. She looked magnificent, of course. Though a lady never exposed her skin to the sun, since to be freckled or brown as a gypsy was quite unacceptable, her already golden skin had been tinted by the sunshine in which she walked on the Pennine moorland to a glowing, peached amber. Her gown of aquamarine silk was cut on simple classical lines and it fell from her gleaming shoulders to the floor in a fluid sculpting of her body, lovingly accentuating her breast and hips. She wore sapphires at her neck and wrist and in her ears and her dark hair was unadorned, dressed to the back of her neck into a heavy coil which tilted her head to a proud and haughty stare.

Dear God, what a woman she would make if only she were not so obsessed by her mills, by the spinning and weaving of cotton, which though it had made the fortune she would get, was driving him quite simply to the mad-house. He must get away soon. He had learned all he needed to know to sell Barker Chapman's piece goods and now, after nearly two years he was ready, and entitled, surely to get into those rich markets, those luxury hotels, those splendid cities in which beautiful women were lavish with their favours to the man who had the money to buy them. And he would sell Barker Chapman's velveteens and fustians, make no mistake. He would do well for him, make him another bloody fortune. That was his game, his function in this ill-bred process of manufacturing, not addressing himself to profit and loss, to the stink of machinery and weaving-sheds and the mass of sweating humanity who worked in them. He would travel, like a young lord he would travel but first he must guarantee his place in Barker Chapman's world of commerce by marrying his daughter.

The buffet supper table was still buzzing with dozens of the hundred persons who had been invited to the ball, heaping their delicate bone china plates with lobster salad, roast fowl, garnished ham, ornamental tongue, roast pheasants, trifle, fruited jelly, charlotte russe and custard in crystal glasses. There were two enormous epergnes weighted down with fruit, bowls of flowers, candles and the tables were draped with ivy in which pink rosebuds and white satin ribbon were threaded.

'Katherine, you have not eaten yet. Let me fill a plate for you.' They all turned as one as he approached, their faces slack with relief and bowing their adieus, for the moment, they said, they each found they had some urgent matter to which they must attend, a chignon to be rearranged, a flower come loose, a lady who really must not be left alone for another second.

'What a lovely time you are having, Katherine. I declare you really do enchant everyone with your splendid achievements in the cotton exchange in Manchester and Liverpool and your description of Mr Whitney's gin-mill, which is used so extensively in the cotton trade had me quite spellbound. I had no idea the seeds of the cotton were such awkward little devils and how much of a boon it was when he invented it.'

He grinned audaciously and raised his eyebrows and Kit Chapman drew in a deep breath, her face taking on the bright glow of the rosebuds decorating the table. Then she began to laugh, a deep and merry laugh, throwing back her head, careless of the lively shining knot at her neck and the scattering of a pin or two.

'You are saying I'm a bore, Harry Atherton.'

'Heaven forbid that I should be so rude.'

'You are the only man who tells me the truth and so you shall take me to supper. I have not yet begun on the system of cotton planting an American gentleman, whom I met in London, told me about and I mean to share it with someone. While we drink champagne and sample some of those strawberries for which I have a fancy I shall tell you all about it.'

'You will do no such thing. I want to hear . . . other things about you. But you shall have your strawberries and champagne, and more if you wish.' His mouth curled in a rich and sensual smile and the deep brown of his eyes whispered something to her, something which had nothing to do with food and she felt a small spring of curiosity well in her to find out exactly what it was. If she liked it she would taste it, if not she would discard it, spit it out laughingly, pulling a face as she had once done as a child over a dish of prunes.

'Go and sit in that little alcove by the fireplace on the landing and wait for me and if anyone else should try to sit beside you tell them . . .'

'What?' she asked laughingly, quite intrigued by this new and boldly masterful gentleman who had, it seemed, replaced the carelessly indifferent one she had known for over two years. His indifference had not annoyed her, in fact she had found it reassuring after her first fears that her father might have organised him as a husband for her. But he had quite done away with her suspicions in his obvious concern for the mills and his eagerness to learn the trade and with the hours, as many as herself and her father, he had put in each day. And now, if she cared to, she thought she might find him amusing, perhaps a pleasant way to make her forget . . . someone else . . . and she could hardly come to harm on the landing of her father's house in the company of a hundred guests!

He was quite a fascinating man, she thought, an hour later as he regaled her with humorous tales of his boyhood and the — to her — quite ludicrous code of conduct imposed by the landed gentry. She listened to his recounting of glorious days in the saddle, of men called whippers-in, of earth-stoppers and coverts. Of what it cost — dear God she could scarcely believe it — for his father to keep his own personal stable and private kennel, of his home which had almost gone with Cromwell since, naturally, his own family had been for the King, of the long gallery and the medieval great hall, of his own 'Grand Tour' which his father had managed somehow, putting her own quite ordinary trip about the country in the shade.

They sipped champagne, a whole bottle and more, glass after crystal glass and she felt the lovely peaceful warmth slip through her body and her head told her heart, quite bemused by the wine that she really did not care what happened since Harry Atherton's eyes, brown and smiling and his lips which were an inch from her bare shoulder were really very nice indeed.

'You are quite delicious, Katherine, when you can be winkled out of that commercial shell of yours. There's not a girl here who wouldn't be in your shoes and not a man who wouldn't be in mine and those eyes of yours! They remind me of a jewel my mother has, not blue nor purple but somewhere in between and your skin is . . . it brings to mind a golden retriever I once had, golden and smooth as cream . . .'

'Come on, Harry, can you do no better than that,' she said lazily though she had to admit that he excited her with the closeness of his warm lips.

For an instant there was a curious prick of light in his eyes, an almost fox-like fierceness, then reaching out quickly he drew the curtains across the opening of the alcove and before she could protest, should she have wanted to which she was not even certain of, he placed his lips lightly on hers, moving them just a little, breathing his warm, wine-scented breath against them until, quite amazingly she felt her own open and his breath was in her mouth. Only one man had kissed her before, like this at first, then fiercely,

239

hungrily and she had responded as naturally as the earth opens and takes in the rain. This was nothing like it, nothing at all since she knew enough now to recognise the difference between love and simple lust, but it was decidedly pleasant, none the less. His mouth slid effortlessly across her neck and with an expertise which told her he had done it a time or two before, explored the curve of her ear, the small hollow beating beneath it and the smooth line of her jaw. He did nothing to which she could take exception and when he stopped and lifted her chin to smile at her she smiled back quite naturally.

'Did you like that, Katherine?' he asked impishly.

'I must admit I did.'

'Would you like to try something else?' His smooth face was confident, telling her he was quite sure of her answer.

'I don't really think so, Harry. I have had enough excitement for one evening. Now if you will take me back to my mother I must fulfil my duties. There are a dozen men with whom I must dance. Oh, and thank you, Harry, for pointing out to me how tedious I am becoming. It is a lesson I have learned well. I shall not repeat it, believe me.'

Harry Atherton was smiling as urbanely as only he knew how as he seated her next to her mother in the ballroom. There were rows of delicately carved, gilt-legged chairs on which those disinclined, or not invited, to dance might take their ease and though Hannah as was her duty made certain that no young unmarried lady was a wallflower for long, she did love to exchange gossip with those of her neighbours and acquaintances who had marriageable girls like her own. She could not help but preen as Harry bowed to her and the rest of the ladies when he returned her daughter to her and her sharp eye noted the glow and sparkle which emanated from the girl. She looked meaningfully at her friends, Mrs Abbott and Mrs Jenkinson, who both had girls in the marriage market, her expression asking triumphantly could they not see which way the wind was blowing for if ever a girl had the look of someone who had just been kissed it was Kit Chapman. Of course it was quite scandalous that

240

she should have allowed it but the fact that she had could signify only one thing. Penniless he might be, her expression said but they could not help but agree he was a catch for a mill-master's daughter. They were of the industrial classes, many of them only a generation away from a weaver's loom in a moorland cottage and he was of the landed gentry and she meant to have him, one way or the other, for her daughter. She might, if she had been an astute woman, one who was not blinded by the outer trappings and background of Harry Atherton have had some reservations if she had seen the peril in his eye as he sauntered in the direction of her husband's study where the serious drinkers, all male naturally, were gathered.

'He wants our girl, Hannah,' Barker Chapman informed his wife the next day in the privacy of Hannah's bedroom, a place he rarely visited. 'He says he has served his apprenticeship and feels he should now be given the chance to present himself as a serious suitor to Kit. He has fulfilled all the conditions of the agreement made between his father and myself, so he tells me and the time has come to honour it. He even went so far as to tell me of the feeling which our daughter had aroused in his breast, quite filled with ardour he was, and which has grown over the months and he feels it is not quite fair to expect him to wait much longer. Most forthright, he was and quite determined that Kit returns his devotion though I must admit I have seen no sign of it myself . . .'

'But I have, Barker.'

'Really, my dear.'

'Oh yes, last night at the ball they were missing for at least an hour and when he returned her to me she was . . . well, I can only describe her as . . . glowing . . .'

'Glowing. Good God . . .'

'Indeed, Barker. I was seriously disturbed, not only by the embarrassment but by the knowing looks which were exchanged between Sarah Jenkinson and Emma Abbott. Things like that can ruin a girl's reputation, you know that, Barker. But let us give thanks that the announcement of their betrothal will subdue any gossip which might have arisen.'

'Betrothal! I did not mention the word betrothal, Hannah, though I am seriously disconcerted by what you have just told me. Why did you not say something before? If I thought he was taking liberties . . .'

'Oh no, Barker. He is too much of a gentleman to . . .'

'And knows which side his bread is buttered, by God.'

'. . . but do you not think it might be wise to speak to her. Let her know what you have in mind.' Hannah could scarcely contain herself, rehearsing already the way in which she would tell, no, not tell, *hint* at what was afoot when she took tea with Sarah and Emma Abbott tomorrow afternoon. She would be very secretive, letting drop a snippet here and a snippet there, just enough to have them pleading to be told what it was that delighted her so but she would smile and shrug her shoulders and shake her head and beg them not to press her further for really it would be no more than her life was worth if it was to get out before . . .

She was deep in her day-dreams of a wedding in spring attended by the aristocratic relatives of Harry Atherton, scarcely hearing her husband's answer.

'Certainly something needs to be said and I shall see to it immediately. I cannot believe that Kit would act in a manner which would bring discredit to her or her family. To be truthful, my dear, I find it hard to conceive of her . . . er . . . dallying with Harry Atherton at all. She is quite scornful of him, when she speaks of him at all and seems completely preoccupied with the business.'

And high time she became preoccupied with something else, his wife thought, though naturally she did not say so.

'. . . but if there is something afoot I wish to know of it. I would be delighted with a match between my daughter and Samuel Atherton's boy but if she is not willing, Hannah, I would not try to force her.' The lie sat easily on his lips and he believed it. 'We employ Harry in the mill, pay him handsomely too and one day soon he will be off to sell our

242

piece goods in many parts of the world where previously there has been no market. I have trained him myself and he will be an asset and, I must admit, more concerned with making a profit if he were married to Kit. So we will see. I shall speak to her tonight and find out what, if anything, is going on between them.'

Kit Chapman dined with her mother and father that evening and her attention was captured at once by the curious undercurrent, an air of something not quite as usual between them. Her mother appeared excited, her father rather more severe than he normally was and when Hannah excused herself the moment she had eaten her iced pudding, fluttering like an overweight butterfly from the room, Kit turned questioningly to her father, her eyebrows raised.

'What on earth is wrong with mother this evening? She seems to have an exciting secret which she is determined to keep to herself.'

Barker smiled, nodding to the butler to light his cigar. When it was drawing to his satisfaction he stood up and held out his arm to her.

'Shall we go into my study? There is something I want to discuss with you.'

She began to laugh when he told her. He had seated her before the fire, poured her coffee which was unusual, asked her if she would care for a glass of madeira, perhaps a brandy since, though it was not the drink for a lady he knew she liked a sip now and again. He took a moment or two to let the masculine calm of the study, the completely male surroundings which they both enjoyed, lap round them, then, knowing there was no need to beat about the bush, told her what Harry Atherton had asked for.

'My God, he doesn't waste time, does he?' she said when her laughter had subsided. 'He kissed me . . . oh yes, Father, why pretend it shocks you since you know very well it meant nothing to me, or to him, just a bit of mischief which, as an unmarried girl I am not supposed to indulge in, but that was all it was. He is a rogue, a charming rogue and . . . well . . . we drank champagne and . . . he kissed me.

There was nothing more to it than that. I'm afraid I laughed at him a little, but really, the idea of marriage is ridiculous. I will admit that when you first introduced him and his family I was afraid that was what you had in mind but the last two and a half years seemed to have proved me wrong. Nothing was said. He got on with what he was taken on for, worked well and he surprised me with his conscientious attention. But as a husband . . .' she began to laugh again. '. . . really, I would rather take Jonathan Abbott or Dick Jenkinson . . .'

'You may have either.' Her father's face and voice were quite serious and she became still for it appeared there was no room for laughter here.

'I want neither,' she said quietly.

'Then whom?'

'Father, I cannot believe what I am hearing. You know I do not want marriage . . . children . . . at least not yet . . .'

'A woman must be married, Kit.' His voice was gentle. 'I am not telling you that you may not run the mills when I am gone but you would do better as a married woman than as a . . . spinster. If you married you would have status, protection, a security from the attentions of other men, a position in society . . .'

'I have that now.'

'My dear, as long as you remain unmarried you will be at the mercy of every fortune-hunter from London to Edinburgh. You will be an enormously rich woman and they simply will not let you alone. While I am here you are under my protection. I stand between you and them but when I am gone . . .'

'Dear God, Father, you have years . . .'

'I am sixty-four, Kit. I am no longer young.' He was being enormously patient with her.

'But . . .'

'Harry is my choice but you may have any of the . . .'

'Please, Father . . .'

'Katherine, listen to me. Let us approach this in an intelligent and practical way. You are not without judgment. You have a cool head on your shoulders and you have an understanding of business I have met in no one before. We are to do great things now we have got those damned radicals behind bars and the constant threat of machine breaking and burning lifted from our shoulders. Believe me, my dear, it has been a constant worry since the warehouse was destroyed and the cost of guarding the mills ate seriously into our profit. Things will die down now, there will be a steady pattern of growth and an increase in our production which will need our . . .'

His voice moved steadily through her head. She could hear exactly what he was saying and if it had been demanded of her could have repeated his words to the letter but ask her what they meant and she could not have said. The last understanding she had ended at the precise moment her father said, '. . . behind bars.'

Behind bars! Behind bars! Behind bars!

'. . . and so you see, Kit, it would really be to your advantage if you were to . . . well, shall we say, not exactly encourage Harry Atherton's proposal but at least do not turn it away out of hand. He is very useful to us, or will be. He is a very pleasant, personable young man and it is known he comes from an excellent family. He will give a good impression among business men abroad. He will know how to make buyers feel important since he is well-mannered and well-bred. He knows the cloth now and really, when you consider it, is quite an asset to us in the business. Heaven knows how he will take it if you turn him down without hope. That is all he wants, I believe, the hope that you will consider him. Is that too much to ask, my dear?'

'No indeed, Father.'

He looked slightly surprised since his daughter was well known for her argumentative turn of mind. He had expected somewhat more of a show of opposition from her so perhaps she really did have a fancy for the boy, despite her earlier laughter. Females really were so unbelievably hard to understand, even Kit Chapman whose mind was more masculine than many a gentleman he could name.

'You will . . . take him, then?' he asked tentatively, 'or at least listen to what he has to say?'

'Yes . . . but . . .'

'What is it, my dear?'

'You mentioned that . . . you said some radical reformers had been . . . imprisoned . . .'

'Did I?' He looked perplexed.

'You said that with these . . . these men behind bars . . .'

'Oh yes, I remember now. It was while we were travelling. I myself have only just heard. Three were captured at an illegal meeting up on Ravenstone Brow, I believe. They were tried for sedition and convicted . . .'

'Convicted?' Her face was as white as his own shirt front and her eyes stared into his with such . . . well, he really could not describe how they looked, they were so strange, so wild, so . . . then he remembered! She had been there on the day one of them had smashed his new spinning frame. She had been consumed with rage then, threatening to see them all hang, violent in her hatred of them. Now she must feel a sense of triumph, of elation that at last they were being brought to justice and he could not blame her for they had been a thorn in the side of the manufacturers for years. Onwardsmen, they had called themselves. Well, they would be broken up now for their leader languished in gaol, he had been told, and two others, and if they hanged them it was no more than they deserved.

'Who . . . do you know who . . .' Her voice was no more than a thread of sound in her throat.

'No, I did not concern myself with names, Kit, though I believe one came from Edgeclough which has long been known as a hotbed for their particular brand of nonsense.'

'They . . . they are to . . . hang . . .'

'No, but by God . . . Kit, my dear, you look . . . what on earth . . .'

'I am perfectly well, Father, really.' She looked at him and her eyes were steady and quite without expression. 'I will have that brandy now, if I may.'

'Of course. Now, may I send Harry in to see you. He is waiting to . . .' He was at the decanter and did not see the violent shudder which passed quickly through her body and when he turned, though she was still pale she was perfectly composed.

'Why not?' she said and raised her glass to his.

17

Jenny Greenwood walked along Jagger Lane, the springing step with which she usually moved quite gone. It was January. The new year had just begun, coming in with a bitter cold which had frozen the standpipe at the corner of the passage and hung icicles from every rotting roof-top in Lousy Bank. All along the foul street and in every back alley people were freezing to death. There were bodies propped against doorways, those who were homeless, new ones every day waiting for the watch cart to come and haul them away to their paupers' grave. The rutted lane which led from Lousy Bank to the main thoroughfare was all white with rime, hiding pleasantly with its thick hoar frost the unmentionable substances which with the coming of summer would fill the nostrils with its stink.

It was a glorious morning. Sunday and the belching smoke which formed an arch above the town on every other day of the week was gone today to reveal the high clear blue of the sky, shading from delicate pink in the east to the deep winter blue above the town.

Jagger Lane was empty. The shops in which the wealthy purchased their goods, which came each day on the coach from London, were all closed and shuttered. Where the street ran out from the town's centre to the long winding lane of the residential area, those who lived there, managers, solicitor's clerks and the more prosperous shopkeepers in their villas and smart terraced houses, were still in their beds.

Jenny pulled her threadbare shawl more closely about her. She had her riotous halo of curls well covered today and her arms were crossed over her breast, hugging her body. Her woollen skirt though patched in many places, very neatly with material of several colours, was clean and her bare feet encased in their wooden clogs had been washed only that morning in the ice she had melted and heated over the fire. She had washed as much of her body as she could beneath the silent gaze of her mother but it had been difficult with no more than a panful of water and no soap.

'Where are you going, lass?' her mother asked and not for the first time and Jenny gave the same answer as she always did.

'Don't ask, Mother.'

'I must. You're my daughter. Can I let you go out each Sunday, aye and at nights an' all and not fear for you? Tell me, girl, where are you going?'

'I can't, Mother.'

'Let me come with you.'

'You must rest, Mother. You need your rest.' Her voice was calm and expressionless, as it had been for weeks now just as though the vivid, resolute light which had burned fiercely in her had been blown out, to be replaced by something which was just as strong, just as determined but with no warmth in it. Her movements were unhurried. They seemed to indicate that she had all the time in the world to go wherever it was she went each Sunday and Martha Greenwood, from the warmth of the hollow of Mercy's back against which she slept, felt the dread creep over her as she knew the cold would creep over her, and all of them, as soon as she got out of bed. The icy air hurt her face and though there was a small fire in the grate which Jenny had lit half an hour since, the dank frozen chill had not yet dispersed. There were rags to the windows to give some

248

privacy but she knew beneath them the small panes of glass would be a solid mass of ice.

She buried her head more deeply into the pillow and the dread grew. Something terrible was happening to their Jenny, draining the compelling life from her and though she defended them all just as fiercely and worked just as hard as she had ever done, she was not the same girl who had moved with them into Lousy Bank. Perhaps it was that? Perhaps the hovel into which circumstances had forced them to live was too much for a girl brought up in the clean, sweet air of the moors but Martha knew it was not that. Her girl was too strong for that. She had questioned her daughter, sharply at first suspecting a lad but when she had asked her Jenny had laughed, quite hysterically, until the tears had wet her face, denying it and telling her mother she was not to worry, everything would be all right and to go back to sleep.

'Let the fire go out, love. We'll stop in bed today.'

Jenny Greenwood turned then, almost a dancer's pirouette, a gypsy dancer Martha had once seen and for a moment Jenny's face came alive, looking as it had done months ago. It was flushed with emotion, warm with her love for her mother, and the headstrong resolve which Martha had seen on the occasions she had followed their Joss. She lifted her head, tossing her curls, lifting her hands to them in a gesture of defiance, or so it seemed.

'No, you'll not, Mother. Keep the fire in today. Have a bit of comfort for God's sake and to hell with it. See, I'll put a shovelful on . . .' and taking the bucket from the side of the grate she threw some coal on to the smouldering fire watching with immense satisfaction as it caught hold and flared up into a bright warmth which they had not seen for a long time. She stood for a moment to watch it, her hands on her hips then turned again to Martha.

'Now keep it like that, d'you hear and eat those tripe bits you were saving. Give some to the children and Mercy, but eat them all, every last bit. I'll bring something for you to eat . . .'

'Dear God, Jenny . . . where . . .?'

'Don't ask, Mother,' and she was gone.

She turned at the corner where Jagger Lane met Reddygate Way, stopping for a moment or two to watch the frosted sky over the brow of the hill which led out of town to Edgeclough change imperceptibly from oyster to pearl grey. Her face, strong and infinitely enduring, softened as the memories flooded into her mind. Of days, warm and secure in her father's protection, of strong arms and a serene face, of Joss who rotted in prison but who had once carried her 'piggy-back' up this same brow, of her mother, her apron clean and starched, her hands steady as she brushed the long hair which Jenny had cut off. Days of childhood, but now she was a woman with a family who depended on her.

She breathed in the iced wine air and smiled and felt the tension drain away and it was almost with relief that she turned to walk up Reddygate Way. The houses which lined it on both sides were just as substantial as those in Jagger Lane but there was an air about them which spoke not of families and children's laughter, but of well scrubbed commercialism, of better times, of genteel poverty perhaps which had not gone under. Here there were rooms to be had for those who did not care to be put up at the local hostelry, of varying degrees of comfort according to the means of its tenant and it was to one of these that she went.

Harry Atherton's rooms were very comfortable indeed. His landlady had been the daughter of a parson brought up to be a gentlewoman and with no accomplishments beyond a talent for playing the piano, sewing a fine seam and directing her servants in the provision of her father's comfort. When he died he left her a small legacy, not quite enough to live on so, being a lady of some independence and strength of mind and unwilling to take on the only respectable employment open to her, that of governess in someone else's home, she decided, and beggar society's opinion, to take gentlemen lodgers into her home. Respectable only need apply, her advertisement said. She kept her

250

servants, who now cooked and cleaned for three very reputable gentlemen, serving them in their own suites of rooms and keeping to hers, seeing them once a week to collect their rent. Providing they were discreet they could do as they pleased, though not in so many words.

'Come in, Jenny,' he said and she did, stepping boldly into his comfortable drawing-room and before she could lose the resolve which had hardened in her that morning, she threw off her shawl and strode defiantly to the fireplace in which an enormous fire blazed. She stood with her back to it for a moment absorbing its heat, then with steady fingers she began to undo the buttons of her bodice.

Harry watched her with disbelief at first for it was many weeks since that day last October when he had first whispered in her ear what they might do together if she was willing. Then she had turned on him like a wildcat caught up an alley by a prowling tom, spitting her disgust, ready he had believed to scratch his eyes out. He had loved it and almost in his heart loved her for he had always treasured that which was hard to come by and this woman would be that. Since then he had forced her to him many times, threatening if she did not come he would fire her, and the whole of her family and he had meant it, she could see it in his eyes.

'Rape me then,' she had said, 'and be done with it. I'll not be the first mill girl to be taken down by the maister, nor the last.' She had lifted her head in that arrogant way she had, daring him, defying him and he knew, by God, that his days of boredom were over with for the time being. 'Go on,' she had continued contemptuously, the first time he had summoned her to his office, 'take what you want and I'll be on my way and be quick about it for I'm losing money while my machine lies idle.'

'Dammit, Jenny, but you're a rare one,' he said admiringly. 'Are you not afraid of me?'

'What's there to be afraid of? You're a man, I'm a woman. I know what happens and if that's what I have to

251

do to keep my family from starving then get on with it.'
Her lip had curled in contempt.

'You have done it before then?' he asked later, in the
comfort of his rooms, lounging against the fireplace in the
indolent pose of a young gentleman quite at ease and why
should he not, for was that not what he was? He wore
immaculate dove grey trousers, a coat of claret and his shirt
frill was white and crisply pressed. His fair hair was brushed
smoothly and his brown eyes were warm and approving in
the well-shaved symmetry of his face. The contrast between
them was quite startling and she could not help but marvel
that this handsome, faultlessly tailored young gentleman
should want her. She was not even particularly clean since
it was hard to be fastidious when the water was turned on
only once a day and that when she and her family were at
the mill.

'What I do, or have done in the past is nothing to you,'
she went on scathingly.

'Oh but it is, Jenny, and please feel free to call me any
name you care to lay your tongue to. I can see you are
longing to. I must say I find this highly diverting. The . . .
the others . . . were so . . . submissive . . .'

'Oh for God's sake, let's get it done.'

'No, oh no, my dear, not like that. Not at all like that.'
He smiled disarmingly then reached for a cigar, lighting it
lazily, his eyes never leaving hers and for the first time she
felt uncertain. She had come, that first time, to be used
against her will by this man who Ellis had told her liked a
bit of 'rough'. He had said many other things to her on that
day concerning how she might best please a man such as
Harry Atherton and her flesh had crawled and the inner
core of her woman's body had shrank from it for she had
known no man's touch, but she had come. She had no
choice.

'You see, my dear,' he went on, casually letting his eyes
roam over her, 'I want you to enjoy it also.'

'Then you'll have a long wait.'

'I don't think so.' He grinned and she was quite fascinated

by the glowing firmness of his well fed flesh and the whiteness of his teeth. When he smiled two deep creases appeared in his cheeks, dimples they would have been called on a girl.

'What d'you want with me?'

'I've just told you.'

'You're mad.'

'Only for you, Jenny Greenwood,' and his smile broadened.

'Then get on with it.'

'Only if you're willing.'

'Well, I'm not.'

'Then when you are we will enjoy it all the more. Until then you will come here when I tell you.'

And now that time had come for she could no longer stand against him. She would not waste herself though, nor the indignity, the humiliation she was to suffer. She would get everything she could from him, make him pay for what he was about to do to her, make him *sorry*, by God, in the end that he had done it. She would not sell herself lightly. She would earn it, the money she meant to obtain from him would buy food and warmth for her family. Week after week she had spat in his face, clawed his face in her effort to madden him into *taking* her for then she could have told herself that what was done, was done against her will but now she was to be forced into offering herself. To be shamed like any street whore. Well, so be it. He could try, he could damn well try to cheapen her but by God she'd lead him a merry dance before she was through with him.

When she was completely naked she stood before him, without shame, without humility and when he touched her she did not flinch. Her eyes locked with his, savage and bitter and for a moment he hesitated, not unwilling, far from it, but not convinced that she was.

'What are you waiting for, Mr Atherton?' she said silkily. 'Here I am just as you said I would be, offering myself to you. Let me see what you have to offer me.'

They were sitting by the fire, her mother and Mercy, Charlie and Daisy when she arrived home. The room was warm, almost cosy by the standards they had known during the past weeks. Daisy leaned against her mother, her sunken face quite rosy in the fire's glow, languid with the warmth. Martha had been cleaning, polishing with the last of her home-made beeswax the incongruously lovely blanket chest, the table which had been her mother's and the dresser which was stacked with the crockery they had brought from Edgeclough. The room smelled of it. On every side was the stench of years of filth, seeping through cracks in the walls, through broken and split doors and windows and up through the rotting floorboards and by the end of the day the smell of the beeswax would be gone but for just that moment it brought back memories to Jenny of the kitchen in the cottage which she still called home.

They turned to look at her when she entered the room, bringing in the raw chill of the January day and her mother's eyes questioned her sadly but she avoided them. She put the basket she carried on to the table, turning to smile brightly and the children stood up expectantly for she had a look about her that said something unusual was about to happen.

'Now then,' she said, 'who would like a piece of . . .?'

'What . . . what, Jenny?' Daisy's face flowered with excitement.

'A piece of custard pie?'

The child's face fell for their Jenny's joke was unforgivable, but her sister lifted the cloth from the basket and reaching inside brought out a plate on which was an untouched tart. Daisy's eyes grew enormous and her mouth popped open and a small dribble of saliva ran down her chin. Charlie, older and wiser than she, looked suspicious, since when could they afford such delicacies as this. He knew it took his mother all her time to put the porridge and treacle, the plain boiled potatoes, the stale bread bought when it was almost a week old, the tripe bits, into their stomachs. The rent on these homes was not cheap, despite

254

their appalling state of repair, and with the wages of the three women, himself and Daisy who earned one and six-pence a week, they managed, just, to exist above starvation level. But he was a boy, a boy who had seen nothing like this for a long, long time and when Jenny cut him a large piece and put it in his hands he fell on it, stuffing it in his mouth, laughing with excitement, watching, as the lovely pastry flaked about his chin, the appearance of a jug of milk, a packet of tea, a loaf of crusty bread, cheese, a green cabbage and a ham bone with only a slice or two cut from it, the results, though he was not to know it, of a raid on the larder of the parson's daughter.

'Where . . .?' he managed to say but Jenny shook her head laughing with delight, her heart soft and at peace with herself, everything she had done that day made insignificant by the look in the boy's eyes.

'Ask me no questions and I'll tell you no lies,' she laughed but he was not satisfied. He was the man of the house while his brother, his leader, was in prison and he could not have one of the women in his charge going about alone and coming home with an unexplained basket of food which he knew full well they could not afford.

'Now then, our Jenny,' he said, his seven-year-old voice stern, 'our Joss wouldn't like it if . . .' but Jenny laughed and ruffled his hair then bent to kiss his awkward cheek.

'Don't worry, lad, I've done nothin' illegal. There's this lady in Reddygate Way, a parson's daughter she is. Well, I've been working in her house and I was given this basket of food in payment.' That was the exact truth. No lies and she could look her young brother in the face and say it without shame, without remorse, without regret and the delight, the joy, the look of well-being which was already alerting the faces of her young sister and brother made every moment of it worthwhile. She *had* worked hard today, pleasuring young Mr Atherton and the things she had done and had done to her . . . she could hear his voice yet . . .

' . . . stand just there, with the light falling on your . . .

255

yes, yes . . . that's right . . . now drape this shawl about you . . . no, leave your breasts uncovered . . . put your hand . . . there . . . now, if I lean a little you can reach . . . now turn with your back to me and put your . . . lovely . . . aaah . . .' and when it was done and she had been dressing beneath his satisfied gaze he had said to her carelessly, '. . . and the next time, don't bother to wash before you come. I want to see you just as you are at your machine, do you understand?' She did!

She looked away from her young brother then, the rosy glow of her face not entirely due to the warmth from the fire and her body, aching though it was, throbbed with a curious feeling which was not altogether displeasing.

'Come on, Mercy, don't sit there with your mouth hanging open. Put the tea in the pot and we'll have us a nice brew and a ham sandwich an' all and don't stint because there's plenty more where that came from. I'm to go each Sunday and perhaps a couple of evenings after work so tuck in, oh and Mother, order some more coal, will you. With what we save on food we can manage a bit of a fire now.'

They were in bed, the children as Martha called them, including Joss's young wife among them, the intense joy giving way to the exaggerated weariness of the undernourished, and she and Jenny sipped a last cup of the delicious tea. She felt it put warmth in her and the good food in her belly had strengthened her but her old heart was frail and hopeless, helpless with pity as she looked at her girl. Jenny would not meet her eyes but stared into the fire, sipping her tea, seemingly absorbed in her own thoughts.

'Who is he, lass?' Martha said at last. 'One of the managers?' for who else had the money to give food away such as they had just eaten.

'No one, Mother.' Still her girl did not look at her.

'I'm not daft, Jenny. It must be someone with a bit of cash to send that basket of food.'

'Don't ask me, Mother, for God's sake leave it alone.'

'I can't, lass. I can't bear to think of it but I must.'

'Does it matter who it was?'

'No, I suppose not.' She sat up suddenly. 'Dear God, it's not Ellis, is it? I couldn't stand to think . . .'

'No, Mother, it's not Ellis. He'd not be so generous.'

'Thank God . . .!' She was silent for a moment, watching her daughter, surprised somehow to see the . . . well, the girl did not look chastened, not particularly ill-used. There was a drag of strain about her mouth but her eyes were calm, steady and certainly not harrowed as you would expect those of a girl who had been 'taken down' to be.

'Do you . . . love him, Jenny?' The words sounded ludicrous in the circumstances but they popped into her head of their own accord, just why she could not have said but her daughter looked up and her whole face split into a shout of laughter.

'Love him? *Love him!* Dear sweet Jesus, are you mad? I hate his guts and one day I'll make him pay for what he's done to me but in the meanwhile my family'll eat well and something'll be done about this place too, or I'll know the reason why.'

But in her eyes still was that strange, quite unexplained glow, mysterious and troubling to her mother who had once known the joy of physical pleasure herself.

Kit Chapman lay in her bed and stared up at the lazily dancing shadows on the ceiling. Her maid had built up the fire since the night was as bitter as any they could remember, or so the older servants were saying in the kitchens, and the rosy flames tinted the white paintwork to apricot and gold. It was reflected in the black panes of the window where Janet had drawn back the curtains and in the polished surfaces of the furniture and Kit watched them, her mind empty, quite blank of everything but the stray darting thoughts of the events of the day. Blurred, thankfully and vague and she hung on to the feeling, the insubstantiality of her mood for only in its merciful oblivion could she cope with it.

She breathed lightly, taking in shallow sips of the warm air, afraid to disturb her own mindless tranquillity, the measured pace of her heart, the heavy stillness of her body. Janet had brushed her hair, excited and longing to talk, as she had thought her mistress would, of what had happened this evening since it had been all over the servants' hall within five minutes, but her chatter had trailed away on the wave of Kit's silence and her young face, looking at that of her mistress in the mirror had become sad, compassionate and wondering at the same time on why it should be, since surely this was, *should* be the happiest day in the life of Barker Chapman's daughter.

'Thank you, Janet. You may go now,' Miss Katherine had said, her face set and . . . and lost, somehow, though surely that was fanciful, Janet told herself.

'Will I make up the fire, Miss Katherine?'

'What . . . oh, yes . . .'

'Good-night then, Miss.'

'Good-night, Janet.'

Good-night . . . would she ever know that again? The awful thought was in and out again before she could stop it, just as though it had slyly opened the door for all the others to follow, they flooded in on a torrent of anguish and despair and she sat up in bed. Her hair fell about her in a great silken shroud and she clutched her bent knees with desperate arms, hiding her face in them but still she could see what was there. The peace, the false serenity was gone in a blinding current of pain and she called his name.

'Joss . . . Joss . . .' Her voice caught in her throat, trapped there in silence and there was no sound but the gentle ticking of the clock on the mantelshelf above the fire. Where was he? Please, dear Jesus, tell me where he is. Let me be with him, let me see him, let him hear me, let him know that I am in his heart as he is in mine. Give him strength, give him *my* strength, keep him safe, bring him back.

She lifted her head, then pushed back the covers, padding silently across the carpet to the window. The skies were clear in the frost-trapped harshness of the night and when she pressed her face close to the window she could see the outline of trees and shrubs, each one clothed in a thick hoar frost, white and exquisitely beautiful against the blue-black eternity of the sky.

'Joss . . . Joss . . .' Her mind could not get beyond him, beyond his name, beyond her body's pain and longing and the room she was in, warm, comfortable, soft, could not contain her. In a moment she had flung off her nightdress and her mind still functioning on the level of basic needs, she dressed in the warmest clothing she had, thick boots and woollen stockings, a shawl of cashmere about her long, unbound hair.

The dogs greeted her in silent delight, snuffling ecstatically against her hand. They padded quietly beside her as she let herself out of the stable yard and their noses were a mere inch from the hem of her skirt as she strode up the pasture at the back of the house and on to the track which led to the moors. There was no moon as yet, but the stars clustered thickly in the velvet darkness of the night and they lit her way between crisply frozen bracken and the stiff and cracking carpet of the grass.

The cobbled track once used by pack-horses, was slippery with white rime and she could easily fall and break her ankle, she thought dazedly, left to lie here and freeze to death but what did it matter? Would *he* be warm and so should *she* be?

The track wound in long curves up the steep slope and as she went higher, wrapped in the vapour from the mouths of her dogs and herself, she could see nothing of what was below in the valley for it was Sunday and the mills would not yet be firing up for Monday's first shift.

It took her an hour to reach it, the circle of stones at the top of Badger's Edge and when she did she was gasping for breath in the lung-searing pain of the cold but her body was warm and her muscles had lost the cramp of the despair which had held her since that tangled moment in her father's study. What had gone before was a dim memory, difficult to recall and not important, never important now, and what had come after drifted vaguely, trifling, insignificant, barely remembered through her confusion. Up here she could mark it out, pick the essentials from the turmoil of what had happened, distinguish what was of concern to her and what was not. Up here she could think.

She leaned her back against the same tall rock, imagining that she could feel the warmth that he had left there. She let it in then, she let *him* in, opening the closed doors of her mind which she had slammed shut, forever she had thought, on the night of the fire. They had scarred one another quite disastrously on that night and on others but could she say those scars had healed, that her wounds were gone, that she was whole again, delivered from her deep love of Joss Greenwood? She had told herself that it was so and pretended that she believed it but now, facing the truth, the honesty she prided herself in, she knew she had lied.

She loved Joss Greenwood. Then she had loved him and now she loved him and sadly, could she really envisage the day when it would end? She sighed, somewhat more at peace, accepting the inevitability of it, of him, and of their love. Oh yes, she knew he loved her despite the wife he had and the life he led. It was as certain as the stars which came each night to pierce the dark heavens, as the sun which rose each day and fell each night, hidden many times behind a cloud of confusion but always there nevertheless.

She pulled off her mittens, putting her hands to her face, cupping it as he had once done, then blowing on her cold fingers for even the soft wool could not keep out the bitterness of the January night. The ring slipped round her finger, the enormous jewel which adorned it catching on the knuckle and she became still then, quiet, hiding herself suddenly from the strange unfamiliarity of it, quite bewildered for a fraction of a second on where it had come from, for she had never before seen it. Not that she could see it now, in the pale darkness which fell about her but she could feel its weight, its dreadful weight and as she did, her mind scurrying to hide from the knowledge – too late, too late –

she remembered Harry Atherton's smilingly satisfied face, her father's formal kiss and the ecstatic fluttering of her mother and as she did so she felt the frozen tears slip painfully across her cheeks and the whole horror of it came flooding in on her bent head.

18

'An April wedding, I think, do you not agree, Kit?' her mother said and her father nodded his approval. The sooner the better in his opinion for she had had a strange reckless look about her recently which he did not particularly care for. He could not put his finger on exactly when it had come about or what had caused it, but he had a definite feeling that he would like to see her married by Easter, perhaps a couple of children to steady her in the next two years, sons preferably while he himself was still here to supervise their upbringing. Then, with the foundations of her life securely cemented and herself well protected in the safety of marriage and motherhood she would be a splendid rock on which to continue the growth of his empire. He was fast becoming the most important manufacturer in the South Lancashire textile trade with his three mills, his blow room, his combing and carding mill, his fine new warehouse, big enough to hold miles and miles of cloth; his finishing shed, design rooms and dye-house. And he meant to build again this year. Another spinning mill and weaving-shed, expanding to employ over a thousand workers, since among them Albert Jenkinson, George Abbott and himself hired the near majority of the textile workers in the sixteen square miles of the Oldham chapelry.

'That sounds reasonable, my dear,' he said to his wife, 'then if Kit and Harry are considering a wedding journey,

France perhaps, or Italy, they might spend the summer travelling. I think I could manage without them for a while.' He smiled, one might almost say twinkled if such a word could be used to describe Barker Chapman's serious visage, over the humorous notion of Barker Chapman being unable to run his mills alone and his wife laughed politely, looking to her daughter and her daughter's new fiancé where they sat side by side on the elegant sofa in the drawing-room.

They had dined in the usual sumptuous manner, Kit picking at her food in the way her mother had wished to see her do for years, in the way a *lady* should. She did not look at anyone, her eyes fixed on her plate or the tablecloth or the window opposite. She spoke only when a remark was addressed particularly to her and if one did not know better one might have believed that Harry Atherton was some business acquaintance of her father's, a stranger to whom she had just been introduced and whom she did not care for. And yet she wore his ring. His grandmother's ring, he had told them, bequeathed to him when she died, for his own bride. It was heavy and old-fashioned, of no special value except that of great antiquity and the knowledge that it had been worn by innumerable ladies of the family of gentry.

'Kit?' her father said. 'We are speaking to you.'

'Yes Father, I heard you. I do apologise and must beg you to excuse me for I have a headache.'

'A headache, my dear.' Both Hannah and Barker Chapman echoed her words in amazement since neither had ever known their daughter to suffer a moment's sickness in her life. From the day she was born she had thrived, quite excessively so, her mother had often thought when it was considered well-bred to faint now and then. But now it seemed she was ailing and Hannah looked at her sharply since young women who suddenly developed unusual symptoms were instantly under suspicion. She *had* been alone for more than an hour with Harry, her betrothed, on the night of the ball and heaven knows what had taken place.

Perhaps it might be expedient to bring forward the date of the wedding . . .!

'Really, Father, I am quite well but . . .'

'Katherine, please do go and lie down. I cannot bear to think you are suffering on my account. If I were not here I am sure you would have retired by now.' Harry was possessively smug in his newly created role as her husband-to-be and Kit felt the revulsion rise in her as his hand reached out to touch hers. It took all her self-control not to snatch it away in disgust but instead she stood up abruptly and moved away from him, ready to dart to the door if he should offer to . . . to kiss her goodnight. It was hardly likely in front of her mother and father but when had Harry Atherton ever been bound by rules that, in his opinion, which was that of a gentleman, were those composed by the industrial classes and therefore not worth considering?

'Very well, my dear,' her father said, rather displeased his expression telling her since this was not the stalwart Katherine who had stood among men in the mill and matched her will against theirs but he was willing to allow it this time since the situation was new to her. In his private heart where no one could see but himself he admitted quite frankly that he had pushed her into it with less of a fight than he had expected but it was done now and there was to be no retreat. A betrothal was almost as binding as marriage with contracts and signatures which, without a great deal of inconvenience, could not be rescinded. She had accepted it quietly enough and he would not put up with any female vapours, should she feel inclined to produce any. She would not, of course. She was his daughter, trained to do what was necessary in the world of commerce, to put business before any personal matter and this was a business transaction and well she knew it. It had been explained to her on the night Harry had proposed to her and she had not refused. Now the next step must be taken and this curious pose she had effected must be discarded at once.

'Very well, Katherine. I'm sure Harry is right. You must retire if you are feeling indisposed. We cannot have you drooping at the party, can we?'

'Party . . .?'

'Come now, Katherine.' He was becoming irritated. 'Have you not been listening to *anything* we have talked about this evening? The party on Saturday night for our close friends and relatives. To celebrate your betrothal to Harry. The invitations have been sent out and already your mother has received several acceptances, have you not, my dear?'

'Indeed I have, and Harry's family have consented to be our guests for the weekend. My word, we shall be a houseful! Not that I mind, you understand,' turning hastily to her future son-in-law, 'in fact I am looking forward to it immensely, introducing our family to yours.' More than she could describe, her joyful, triumphant heart sang, for this moment was the pinnacle of all her most treasured dreams, the pinnacle of *all* mothers' most treasured dreams, she was certain. Her daughter was to be allied in marriage to a son of one of the most privileged families in the north and she could hardly wait until Saturday to display it all, to the mothers of girls who had not yet been selected, to her manufacturing friends who had not quite believed her secretive, preening charade of something stupendous to come, to her own relations who, though they were high in the millocracy of Lancashire had not yet achieved an association such as the Chapmans were to be rewarded with.

'I had not realised . . .'

'What, my dear?' Barker Chapman's voice was silky but beneath the benign concern was the rough grit which said she must stop this nonsense at once.

'I'm afraid . . . my head aches so . . . I confess I did not hear your . . . the plans for . . .'

'For the betrothal party?'

Betrothal party! Oh dear God, what was she doing? How had she become entangled in this farce her mother and

264

father were planning so joyfully? What had happened to her? Why had her sharp, quick-thinking brain, her normal ability to be three steps ahead of anyone else's mental processes let her down? In the space of a week, or was it two — Lord, what was wrong with her? she could barely string two intelligent thoughts together — she found she had become engaged to marry a man she scarcely liked, let alone loved. A man who amused her, at times, with his impudent wit, who made her smile and shake her head as one would at the antics of a precocious child, but certainly not someone with whom she could get into bed. She had allowed him to kiss her . . . was that how it had happened . . . as an experiment really, a test for herself to see if she could erase the memory of the kisses of another man, but as he had kissed her, her inner self, the one that loved Joss Greenwood, had shivered away from it. He was a self-seeker, an opportunist, doing business with her father, selling his family name, but more importantly to Barker Chapman, the manufacturer, his own charm and talent for convincing men that Barker Chapman's piece goods were the best to be had. He could mix at any level with men of the business world and over a glass of whisky, or a magnum of champagne, whatever it might take to clinch the deal, he could and did sell her father's cotton. Already he was moving about the country, Manchester, Liverpool, London, using the contacts he had built up, selling the Chapman cotton goods and business was booming. Her father was gratified, she knew, by the success of his plans, those made on her eighteenth birthday, she realised that now, the business deal he had struck with Samuel and Harry Atherton and now it had come to fruition. Everything was flowing as Barker Chapman had intended and on Saturday night, before the whole of the Penfold Valley, and no doubt half of the Cheshire gentry, she and Harry Atherton were to be put on show, the achievement complete, the dream come true, the pinnacle climbed and won.

'My dear, are you to go or are you to stay?' she heard her father ask, his mouth smiling but not his eyes and she knew quite suddenly that she must tread very, very carefully now. He would not take kindly to having his plans destroyed nor allowing the rest of the world (for who in the valley was not aware of his success?), to smirk and whisper of pride going before a fall as that girl of his flung his glory back in his face. The triumph he had accomplished, not just in his business but in his forthcoming connection with a family who had known privilege and authority for hundreds of years, had been worked for, sweated over and should she dash it from his hand it would be the end of her career, her hopes of carrying on his mills, *her* mills then, when he had gone. She would no doubt be given in marriage to a somewhat lesser gentleman in the industrial world and breed a child each year, the mills sold or bequeathed to a cousin, a male cousin, her father's favour in which she had basked for nearly eight years withdrawn coldly, implacably, *finally*.

So, she must play the game, pretend, act out the charade, be as clever and devious as he as she looked for a way out of this dilemma since there was nothing more sure in this life than the certainty that Kit Chapman would never marry Harry Atherton!

She felt the sluggish blood begin to surge through her veins, hotly, defiantly and colour pinked her pale cheeks. Her eyes grew calm, the haunted look of a wild and cornered animal slipping away to be replaced by an almost imperceptible cunning. She felt strong, invincible, her wits returned to her, those that had been swept away when her father had told her of the three felons, one of whom was Joss Greenwood. She would smile, she *did* smile now, and smile again and again as she planned her plans and schemed her schemes and the time to begin was . . . well . . . what was wrong with right now?

'Father, Mother, Harry, I am so sorry. I really do not know what came over me. It was unforgivable of me to be so rude and on such a momentous occasion as this. Perhaps it was the excitement after all since a girl does not become engaged every day and I suppose the sheer . . .' – could she

266

say 'joy' or was that going too far – 'the sheer singularity of it went to my head. I shall go and ask Janet for a draught to clear it and then I shall come right back and we can continue with our plans for Saturday night. No, do not argue with me, Harry, I insist and you should know by now how I do love to have my own way.'

She smiled silkily, her old self again to all intents and purposes and she saw the two men relax and look at one another, visibly relieved by her manner. They were both astute, not easily hoodwinked. They must have been both bewildered and alarmed by the shocked state she had been in – though without it she doubted if she and Harry Atherton would have now been betrothed. Perhaps it was as well for she would have fought her father into the ground and lost what she had anyway. Now, with guile and stealth she would have it all and see Harry Atherton go to the devil!

She dreamed of Joss that night. He was clamped to a wall which sweated damp and his face, haggard, gaunt, thin, was turned up to the light which fell from a barred window. In his eyes was an expression which, though she puzzled and puzzled over it she could not understand. It asked her for something and though she called to him, beseeched him to tell her what it was it seemed he could not speak. He turned to look at her and his eyes, a cloudy mixture of grey and green were dull with misery and pain. Tell me, Joss, my love, my love . . . tell me . . . tell me and the words still whispered in her throat when she awoke.

She smiled and wished her father 'good morning' as Ellen opened the breakfast-room door for her. She discussed the coming day's business, the economic condition which was so good, the possibility of parliamentary reform and the guest list for her betrothal party on Saturday. Through it all she ate a splendid breakfast as she always did, smiled cheerfully and was as matter of fact as her father was used to seeing her.

She had her own suite of offices now at the mill for as her duties and responsibilities had increased and with it the paperwork she must apply herself to, the ones she had shared in the first months of training with her father had not been big enough to contain them both. Harry had his own – just one large room for he was seldom in it – next door to hers and in which he kept his samples, his orders and all the paraphernalia he seemed to require as Barker Chapman's salesman. He was concerned, he said, with fulfilling the constant demand for new products and designs, needing clerks and office boys to run here and there on his business, making a great show of doing it, but doing it nevertheless, and selling Chapman cloth by the thousands of yards.

But she was restless, her mind still dwelling in that dream prison cell with Joss, still haunted by the strange plea which had been in his dream eyes. She prowled about the room, moving from her desk to the window to watch the unloading of bales of raw cotton and the loading of dress goods on to the waggons pulled by huge and patient Shire horses. She played with the ring on her finger, finding it heavy and unwieldy, ready to take it off and put it in her reticule with the excuse that it was of too great a value to her to risk it in the hurly burly of the day. As she watched a girl came out of the spinning mill, tall and fine looking, with well set shoulders and a straight back. Her hair was a cloud of tossing dark curls about her head and though it was still cold and the contrast great between the humidity of the spinning room and the chill of the yard, her shawl was merely draped carelessly across her shoulders, trailing its fringed edges almost in the mud of the yard. It was pretty, the colours of scarlet and rose and deep claret, not at all like those worn by the women in her father's factory and she wondered idly how such a girl had come by it. The girl walked with a springing jaunty step, so different from the rest of the female workers Kit had seen creeping submissively about the place, looking about her with all the indifferent hauteur of a young queen. She cared for no one, her attitude said, and if she wished to loiter in the yard as she was doing, then what was it to anyone else?

Strangely, she turned and lifting her hand to shade her

eyes from the smoke-hazed winter sunshine, which was low above the mill roof, she stared directly up at the office windows, almost as though she expected to see someone she knew. Instantly Kit recognised her and as she did so her heart banged furiously against her breastbone, hurting her. Her dream came back to her with the force of a blow and in it Joss's pleading eyes looked straight into hers and she thought she knew at last what it was he asked of her. This was his sister who stood in the yard so challengingly and somewhere his mother, his young brother and sister were waiting for his return, *and his wife*, her shrinking mind said and how were they dealing with this tragedy which had come into their lives. They lived in a cottage at Edgeclough, Joss had told her, spinning what they could, living on what they grew and what Joss could weave and now, for the past weeks, how long exactly she did not know since she was afraid to arouse suspicions by questioning her father, they had been without his support. What was her name, his sister . . . Jenny, that was it, was a spinner in the factory, he had said and Kit remembered her on the day the child had lost his hands. She had been younger then, three years younger, both of them girls and now they were women, sharing somehow, a common bond of love for the same man. She remembered the way Joss had described his sister, the affectionate humour in his voice when he said she should have been a man, and even this, for should not Kit Chapman have been born a son, gave them unity.

Jenny Greenwood did not see her for her eyes were looking for someone else and later, when the mill-owner's daughter came into the spinning room, standing in the doorway, a lovely bright flower against the drab uniformity of the rest of the room she looked at Kit Chapman with contempt, a sneering look which asked what in hell's name had brought *her* to look them over. She herself must be on the alert, scarcely able to glance up from her frame since if she missed a broken thread leaving the two ends loose she would be in a great deal of trouble.

Miss Chapman walked slowly up and down the

enormous room, waving imperiously away the darting figure of Ellis who had appeared immediately she had come through the doorway, his own face wary for what the hell did this mean? It was three years since she had been here on the day the boy was killed and there had been many accidents since but in that time he had run his one hundred and sixty frames just as he pleased, and the women who operated them. Now here she was poking about again and he'd best look sharp and report it to Mr Gribb, the manager who would pass it on to Mr Chapman. He couldn't have her nosing about not with things the way they were. Some of the lasses, with her on the spot, might take it into their head to speak up, her being a woman.

Calling to a lad who carried a creel of bobbins to 'drop that and run and fetch Mr Gribb,' Ellis watched Miss Chapman's progress.

Kit felt the spongy mess on the floor, cotton waste, fluff and oil, squelch around the soles of the soft leather boots she wore and knew that the hem of her fine woollen dress, a pale harebell blue, would be ruined but she continued regally between the hissing, singing machines, drawn with a fascination she did not try to analyse to find the family of Joss Greenwood. Somewhere in the village of Edgeclough was his mother and his wife. Would she herself be able to look her in the eye, to regard dispassionately the woman with whom he had shared, if not his love, then his fine body, the one she herself had coveted almost from the first day they had met. She did not know! She had been no more than a young girl then, fifteen, sixteen but she had been pulled towards him by invisible threads of need. She had grown to love him, to want him desperately but she had withheld herself and in all of her life she had regretted nothing more.

None of the operatives looked up from their machines and again she was struck by the ill-used, worn-out demeanour of the women who could never, not for a moment, stop their endlessly restless hands and feet. Their backs were permanently bent across the frames of their machines and as they leaned over the hems of their short skirts rose up to reveal the grey white sticks of their legs. They were barefoot, of course, in the sweating heat and filth, forced to keep up with the speed of the machines for while the engine ran so must they. All they needed were 'hands' which is what they themselves were called, and brains sufficient to guide the hands and the wit to keep themselves out of danger. Their minds had no stimulation, stagnating in their aching heads, beyond the care those with their own children about them tried to exercise. Twenty to thirty miles in a day they would walk following the mule carriage and all in the space of twenty feet.

At last she saw the girl from the yard and drawn again by some strange compulsion she stopped, and bewildering herself for what could she say to her, reached out and touched her arm. The girl turned instantly, her hand still hovering about the machine for left to itself it would ruin the yarn she was spinning, then she turned back and with a swift and practised hand, switched off the machine. She stood, head up, eyes gleaming, awaiting her master's, or in this case his daughter's command. She did not bob a curtsey as many would in her place but stared straight into Kit's eyes, revealing nothing of her thoughts, her own face expressionless.

For several seconds Kit was at a loss for words. Indeed she had no idea why she had stopped the girl, nor even why she was here. What should she say to her? What indeed? And what had brought her here? What indeed?

'Excuse me . . .' she said, groping for words, for something to say, well aware that Ellis was watching at the end of the room, that Gribb was moving towards her between the rows of machinery, that Jenny Greenwood's was lying idle, losing money not only for her, who could, she was certain, ill afford it, but for Ellis and Gribb, who she was equally certain, would not care for it.

'Yes?' Jenny Greenwood said. Just that one word. Yes! Her face was quite blank but coming from her was such a strong wave of resentment Kit could feel it wash against her and she flinched a little, stepping back in confusion.

'I wanted to ask you if . . .?' What? for God's sake. What could she say to his sister? What could she ask her? How is your brother, Jenny Greenwood? Have you heard from him? Of him? Does he still live even? Does he survive wherever he is? Does he eat, is he warm, is he injured, does he still love me, when will I see him again?

'Yes?' Jenny said again, coldly, waiting, as all those of her class were expected to wait on those above them and Kit knew she must move on.

'I wished to examine the work you are doing,' was all she could think of to say, coolly, employer to employee.

'There's nowt wrong with *my* work.'

'I'm sure there isn't so in that case you will have no objection to my examining it.'

Why was it that every time she and this woman met they were instantly ready to be at each other's throats, like two bitches neither of whom cares to lie down with the other. Snapping and snarling their black temper, neither prepared to lower their eyes and be the first to step away. Jenny Greenwood was nothing to her, beneath her interest as they all were in the spinning room except as 'hands' to run her machines. She merely wished, in some vague and unthought-out way, to help the family, if it was possible, of Joss Greenwood, to put out a hand, not of friendship exactly, for could they ever know that, but of assistance. But of course it would be taken for patronage by this irritating girl who would rather starve than eat what Kit Chapman might provide.

Jenny Greenwood stepped back resentfully, aware that there was nothing she could do to prevent Kit Chapman from studying the yarn she was spinning, indeed from ordering her out of the mill if she chose, without reason nor reference. She was her 'master'. She owned her. She could lift her up or fling her down, whichever she fancied, and her proud spirit longed to spit in her face, to strike her down contemptuously and grind her into the muck and oil

272

and waste which they were forced to endure for the best part of sixteen hours a day. She glided about the counting house, the spinning and weaving-sheds, the mill yard, scarcely noticing the human ants which scurried madly beneath her feet and certainly not noticing if she crushed one or two in her careless indifference to them. She had the power of life and death over them, the right, if she chose, to end the existence of whole families if a member of one should offend her, or for no other reason than they were surplus to her needs and Jenny Greenwood hated her for it.

'Can you find any fault, madam?' she asked, her insolence making the women about her gasp.

'If there is one to be found I will find it.'

'I've no doubt you would if there wasn't.'

'You step dangerously, Jenny Greenwood,' and they took a stance face to face, both frighteningly close to blows, Kit's former compassion flown away in the teeth of this girl's enmity but a movement at her back drew her away from the confrontation and she turned, finding Gribb at her elbow, Ellis behind him.

'Is everything in order, Miss Chapman?' the manager asked smoothly.

'Of course, Gribb,' she managed to gasp. 'I was merely questioning this girl on the quality of the yarn and I am quite satisfied with it.'

'Thank you, Miss Chapman. Will there be anything else?'

'No thank you,' and without another glance in the direction of Jenny Greenwood she swept from the room.

She waited until the following Sunday slipping from the house as a pale dawn edged the peaks of the hills behind Greenacres. Many of her father's guests had only this moment left, others just fallen into their beds after the party which, in the way of things where young bachelors were present, and ladies retired, had ended in horseplay and a certain amount of cheerful drunkenness, the young gentry the worst of them all. Harry Atherton, assured now of a grand future in what would one day be *his* house had been carelessly attentive for an hour or two to his new fiancée, then gone to join them, believing, it seemed, that as she was now almost married she would be glad to sit and gossip among those who were.

It was splendid up on the moors, not as cold as at the beginning of the year, with a light dusting of snow capping the hills. As usual on a Sunday the air had cleared and the higher she climbed the headier it became and when she reached the hill overlooking the village she could pick out each individual chimney and the pencil straight line of smoke which came from one or two. Eleven there were, eleven cottages and in one of them Joss Greenwood's family lived and again, as on the day last week when she had accosted Jenny Greenwood, she had not the slightest notion of what she would say to them.

They had gone, she was told by the astounded woman who answered her knock on the door of the first cottage she came to.

'Gone . . . gone where . . .?'

'Why, to Crossfold, Miss,' the woman said, eyeing incredulously the fine warm wool of Miss Chapman's clothing – since who in these parts did not know the daughter of Barker Chapman – the stout cut of her leather boots, her shining hair which slipped in a most unladylike, undisciplined manner about her face and shoulders, the healthy flush on her smooth cheeks, the sleek beauty of the two dogs who clung to her skirt, wondering speechlessly what on earth their employer's daughter would want with a family who worked in her own mill.

'But I was led to believe that they lived in Edgeclough.'

'No, Miss, not any more. They couldn't make the walk, yer see, not t't mill an' back, not wi't little 'uns.'

'The . . . the little 'uns . . .?'

'Aye. Daisy's nobbut a baby really and though Charlie's older 'e's not that strong now . . . since . . . well. T'were a bit of a hike after sixteen 'ours in't mill so they left an' rented t'cottage in Lousy Bank.'

'Lousy Bank?' She whispered the name just as though to

speak it out loud might somehow taint her lips with its foulness. *Lousy Bank!* Along with Boggart Hole and Pig Lane it was spoken of as the centre of the dens of vice, of the harbourage of disease, where the homes of those who lived there were foul and damp, rat-ridden, with tunnels leading into a labyrinth of alley-ways where danger and even death lurked for the unwary.

'When ... when did they leave?' she asked and the woman sniffed, somewhat offended to be asked to give out information to a woman who was, choose how, one of the enemies of Joss Greenwood. What did she want with them, her suspicious eyes asked, sorry now she'd divulged as much as she had. She'd half a mind to call Isaac and get him to order this hoity-toity piece from *their* bit of land but common sense prevailed since she *was* Barker Chapman's lass.

'I can't remember,' she replied tartly.

'Could you ... do you see them?'

'No.'

'I was wondering if a message might not be got to them.'

This was too much for Sarah Pickering who had watched with tears in her eyes the departure of the woman she called friend, the mother of the man who was rotting in gaol, put there by the likes of this madam, for trying to better the lot of the labouring poor. It was all their fault, this disaster which had fallen on the spinners and weavers of Lancashire and Yorkshire, their greed which had aggravated it, their callous disregard for the working man's dignity and self-respect and she'd be damned if she'd stand in the cold on her own doorstop answering her foolish questions.

'They work for you, all on 'em. Give 'em bloody message thysen.'

19

He blinked in the sudden blaze of sunshine, blinded by it, shielding his eyes with his arm but blessed by its golden haze and the soft heat which enfolded him. His body felt as though it would never be warm again. The damp and the chill of his prison cell had crept into his bones and even now as he stepped out on the road from Lancaster to Clitheroe with the warm sun on his right shoulder he could hear the crack of his knee joints and wondered if he would ever lose the ache in them. He had been out of the prison on many occasions, of course, for hard labour meant just that and the local quarrymen were glad of the convicted felons to do the work of breaking up the stone. Day after day, week in and week out, in sun and rain and driving gales, in the bleak winter of the north where the cold had entered into his soul, in the fragile spring which had come so late, taken with faceless others to break stone, and his back and almost his spirit, but he had survived and now he was to go home. He was hardened and older. His face was thin and gaunt, he was semi-starved and had been made to pay dearly for his 'crime' but now, with the repeal of the hated 'Combination Acts' he would begin again.

They had got word to him in gaol, those men who had dreams in their heads, as he had, of an immense exchange of ideas and ideals and who needed a man who could put those aspirations into words. Men like William Cobbett and John Fielden, the radical politician Francis Place who believed in one vote one man and who had asked him if he would care to write, being something of a notability now, an article or two in the pamphlets and newsheets which the working man was likely to read. He was a man well known for his sympathies towards those crushed beneath the heel of the new industrialists they said, and might he not have a contribution to make in *another* way beside that of violence towards their cause? Cobbett's *Weekly Register* which had been published for the past twenty odd years was one, and though Cobbett himself wrote most of it himself he would be glad, he said, to print Joss Greenwood's ideas among his own.

The *Poor Man's Advocate*, published weekly, condemning many individual cotton firms, though they could not pay him much, would gladly include anything he might have to say on the matter of reform, which, with his experience and knowledge of the working man, they were certain would be considerable.

And so he was to become a writer, to earn his living at it if it was found he had the knack. A journalist, though this description made him smile as he stepped out towards his home.

He walked five miles that day, following the turnpikes and the pack-horse trails below Tarnbrook Fell, stopping to rest, to sleep uneasily beneath a sweet smelling hedge of hawthorne, waking a dozen times, unused to the night-time peace broken only by the squeak and rustle of small animals, missing, incredibly, the grunts and snores of his cell mates.

There was a farm just off the road, no more than a smallholding, a cow, a pig, geese, reminding him of the cottage in Edgeclough and though the farmer, a dour north countryman with no time for the vagrants and tramping men who roamed the Lancashire uplands told him to be off, he traded a glass of milk and a hunk of stale bread and cheese for two hours' work cleaning out his pig-sty and a pile of logs chopped.

He crossed the River Hodder just before nightfall, thanking the fates for the kindness they bestowed him with the warm weather. Impulsively he stripped off his clothes, jumping naked into the breathtaking iciness of the water, his milk white body like a thread of yarn beneath the clear, silvery grey surface but his teeth shone in a grin of pleasure in his startlingly brown face. Though his clothes were stale when he put them back on he felt exhilaratingly clean, tingling from head to foot and glad to be alive. He was going home!

The restrained grandeur of the hills of Bowland, the forests, the sunken trails waist high in Sweet Cicely were not unlike the spread of hills surrounding his own home and he longed for the miles to be eaten up so that he might be there. He slept the second night in a bed of hedge parsley not having eaten that day and when he arrived in Clitheroe he knew he must find work to buy food.

For sixpence he cleaned out the stables of a coaching inn, sweating and faint as he did it but his handsome smile and courtesy pleased the landlord's wife and she gave him an enormous bowl of thick soup and a heel of bread to go with the money.

He bought bread and cheese, some oats and potatoes and, strengthened, he managed almost ten miles the next day crossing below Pendle Hill and on into the forest towards Burnley. He knew the country here for he had attended many meetings and had marched in protest with the weavers who worked in the northern Pennine heartland. He slept in a bed for the first time that night since he had left Lancaster gaol, the six children who normally crowded together in it swept unceremoniously aside to accommodate the great and glorious leader of their cause and though he had protested to their father, a known sympathiser on whose door he had scratched, it was insisted upon. They had nothing but porridge and treacle bubbling on the spluttering peat fire but what they had was his they told him and were big-eyed, scarcely able to believe it when he brought out the bread and cheese. Their appetites, fed for so long on bland, tasteless food which was cheap, craved a taste of something sharp and they fell on it with such delight, tears pricked his eyes and he pressed them to eat it up unconcerned with how he would manage the next day.

It took him another three days to get through the Forest of Rossendale, working whenever he could for what anyone would give him to eat, sharing what little they had with the men and women, who all knew him now, who had waited, they said, for his return. What would it mean to them, they asked him eagerly, with the repeal of the Combination Acts? Surely things would be better now that it was no longer illegal to meet, to 'strike' or 'turn-out' as it was called in their struggle for wage increases. Food prices had risen again, they said, and something must be done and they looked at him trustingly for they knew whatever it was, Joss Greenwood would do it.

He was growing stronger now. The sweet, wind-ruffled air of Brandwood Moor, north of Whitworth filled his lungs as he tramped and still the sun shone on him kindly and he took off his shirt, letting it warm and brown his prison-white skin.

He stopped a dozen times in those last few days before he began to smell the air of home, to soak and splash in the torrents of clear, stinging water which cascaded down the hillsides and crags into the steep cloughs.

They were waiting for him at Rochdale, word having been sent ahead of his return, gathered in groups at every cottage door and field gate, not speaking much for they were filled with emotion and some of the women wept. They were a scarecrow assembly, thinner than they had been a year ago, with the fight scraped-out of them by hunger and sickness, their children listless, not knowing nor caring who this man was, and he nodded and shook each outstretched emaciated hand unable to speak for he was overwhelmed.

It was almost dark when he began the climb from Cow Heys up to Badger's Edge but he could see her waiting as he had known she would be. The stones were shadowed on their eastern side but where she leaned, her head turned to watch the track up which he would come, the lowering sun struck brilliantly, bathing her in its golden light. She wore a light gingham skirt and bodice to match of pale

279

apple green, simple and uncluttered and she had rolled up her sleeves and taken off her shoes and from a distance might have been some barefoot country girl waiting for her man. Her hair was fastened back carelessly with a dark green velvet ribbon and it was the first thing he took from her as she swayed into his arms. His hands buried themselves deep in her hair before his mouth took hers and for a long, long moment their lips clung together. Their bodies met in enchantment, breast to breast, thigh to thigh and when he released her mouth his eyes met hers, asking the question before he did.

'How did you know?'

'I have come each evening. A year they said, so . . .'

'I knew you would be here.'

'I knew you would know.' She laughed softly and her lips lifted to his, greedily, and her hands went to the buttons of her bodice, some of which were already undone.

'Let me,' he whispered, pressing her back against the tall stone. Slowly he undressed her in the pale blue half-light of the summer evening, each silky shoulder studied and murmured over, kissed with lips which were smooth and increasingly passionate until the bodice lay discarded in the grass and her breasts were cupped, one in each of his hands. The nipples, already hard and thrusting, pressed eagerly into his palms and he took them between his thumb and forefinger, rolling them until she arched her back and her throat and he bent his head, putting his lips beneath her chin, smoothing them down her flesh until his tongue tasted the swollen pink tips, taking each one in turn into his mouth. He pressed his face between her breasts, rubbing his cheek against their firm, soft fullness and in his throat a sound began, a longing, aching sound which was echoed in hers. He knelt then and with the patience and pleasure of the true lover he drew down her full skirt and petticoat, placing his parted lips on the white skin of her belly, moving them delicately across every inch of it, slowly, slowly and when he reached the downy bush of her pubescence she cried out harshly. She was naked, the soft pale gold of her skin glowing in the last rays of the sunlight. He pulled her down to him and her back scraped against the rough stone but she did not feel it. She had but a moment to wait and then his flesh was against hers and the sweetness of the clover-studded grass was beneath them. He raised himself above her before he penetrated her and the tiny budding core of her womanhood throbbed and expanded, glowing and growing until she cried out to him again for she could not wait and he looked down at her, male triumphant and his eyes were the gleaming green of a hunting leopard.

'I love you, Kit Chapman, dammit but I love you,' he cried and then he was inside her and she cared for nothing but the pain of it and the sweetness and rapture and the sudden shivering delight which touched every part of her body. She felt it in her thighs and her belly, in her breasts and straining nipples, down each arm in a languid boneless-ness and when he fell on her, shouting his own masculine pleasure she caught him to her, holding him in possessive arms, showering his face and neck with a score of butter-fly kisses and stroked his back with trembling butterfly hands.

It was full dark when they dressed one another, laughing softly as they struggled with petticoats and clogs, ribbons and breeches, the smoothing of tangled hair, taking a long time, lingering fingers unwilling to leave soft breast, hard muscled thigh, mouths unwilling to give up the smoothness of long silken back or strong throat. The stars came out to lighten the patch of moorland and the stones of Badger's Edge. They could not bear to part and would have started again but from somewhere close the dogs rose soundlessly and became restless. He stared in amazement, first at one black and almost invisible shape and then the other.

'Good God, where did they come from?'

'They've been here all the time.'

'I should have known you would not come this far without them. I'd forgotten about them in my eagerness to . . .' He pulled her against him, his passion for her growing again and she laughed softly, delighted, but the dogs would not be still now, as though they scented danger in the deepening dark of the wild hills.

'I must go, my darling,' she said wistfully. 'I have taken to my bed with a sick headache but if anyone should feel the need to knock on my door and enquire of me, my maid will have a hard time explaining my absence.'

'She knows where you are?'

'Oh yes, but not who I am with. She has been with me for years and is well used to my mad habit of walking with the dogs. She thinks I am quite out of my mind but I fear if I do not return soon she will be alarmed and alert my father. She is devoted to me but she will safeguard her job, and my safety, if it came to the choice.'

'Kiss me again.'

'Just once . . . oh, how I love you. How have I managed all this time without you?'

'I cannot imagine, now kiss me again and while you do it put your hand just there . . . aah . . . and this button appears to have undone itself . . .'

It was half an hour later before she asked the question she had dreaded. She stood within the strong circle of his arms. He was excessively thin, thinner than she had ever known him but he was as hard and strong as a length of steel, the work he had done wielding a pick in the quarries of northern Lancashire fining him down to nothing but skin and bone and hard muscle. They were quiet now. They had known the depths of anguish in the months they had been apart, a great wrenching of their senses that had brought turmoil and disorder to their separate lives. And now they had known love, a supreme physical love which had brought them together in just as complex an emotion as any they had known. It had uprooted all their previous ideas of class and culture, of loyalty to others, of the hopeless past and the unknown future, but now as their bodies rested against one another in a peace which clung about them, soft as mist but strong as the stones against which they leaned, they could speak of it at last.

'Are you to go home now, Joss?'

'Yes. I am anxious about my family. God knows how they have managed without me. But Jenny is a fighter, always has been and will have seen them right. We have friends . . . it is at times like this that we gather round each other . . . our people. They are all hard workers, my mother and Jenny and . . .'

' . . . And your wife?' There was no censure in her voice, only understanding of how it was since had she not herself been pressed unwillingly into the arms of another man.

'Yes . . . she is frail though . . . ' He stared out over her head into memories of Mercy, then looked down into the face of this woman he loved, smiling, '. . . but they have good neighbours in Edgeclough. They will have . . .'

'They are not in Edgeclough.' She made the statement flatly not knowing of any other way to tell him.

'What . . . I don't understand. How do you . . .'

'They had to move. The children could not manage the walk from Edgeclough to Crossfold each day.'

'But why should they need to walk to Crossfold each day?' He was clearly bewildered.

'They had to work, Joss, all of them.'

'But . . .?'

'What did you imagine would happen to them while you were in prison?'

'I don't . . . I had thought they would . . .'

'Would what?'

'Isaac sent a message. He would try to get some raw cotton to them for my mother to spin. With Jenny at the mill and Charlie weaving a piece . . . I was not told . . . A message or two saying they were all right . . . Goddammit to hell . . . why was I not told . . .?'

His throat worked and his hands gripped her shoulders as he stared down at her, his fear beginning to snap and snarl at him, like an animal of prey which circles another. He shook her, his increasing terror for his family making him careless but she stood her ground.

'Where the hell are they?' he demanded, just as though *she* had spirited them away while his back was turned.

283

'They have a cottage . . . in Crossfold.'

'A cottage? What sort of cottage?' since it was well known what kind of cottage was going begging to the likes of factory hands in Crossfold.

'A company cottage, they are called.'

'A bloody company cottage, is it?' he snarled and her head snapped on her shoulders as he thrust her away from him and despair settled quietly, like vultures in a tree, about them. It had been so short, the joy, the love, the understanding and now came the reality. She had him back, whole, strong and it seemed, once again to take up the sword in his fight for those he loved as much, perhaps more, than he loved her. They were his family, as his wife, his mother, his brother and sisters were his family. They needed him where she did not and when they suffered he blamed her. She was one of the other side, one of the 'maisters', the manufacturing class who made millions over the bodies of the labouring poor, *of which he was one*.

'Where in Crossfold?' he demanded to know harshly, not looking at her.

'Lousy Bank.'

'*Jesus* . . .' He lifted his face to the dark blue of the night skies and gripped his thick hair with desperate hands and she could see the glitter in his eyes which she suspected were tears.

'They work in my father's mill,' and her voice could not somehow sound anything but disinterested as though it was really nothing to do with her since she was only the messenger. Inside her chest the pain was almost more than she could bear and she wished she could weep away the tears which threatened to drown her.

'All of them?'

'Yes.'

'Oh dear sweet Lord . . . Daisy . . . Charlie . . .'

'Yes.'

'And you made love to me knowing . . . knowing my family . . . my little sister . . . you bitch, you cold-hearted bitch . . . she is only a baby . . . a baby . . .'

284

He turned on her then and lifting his arm struck her full in the face, leaving an imprint on the smooth cheek he had just kissed so gently, then, torn to shreds by his devastation, by his love and hatred of her he turned on his heel and began to walk in the direction of Crossfold, not looking back and she watched him, holding the dogs lest they go for him. He disappeared into the night and she sat for an hour, dry-eyed, for she had sworn she would not weep for him again.

His mother opened the door to him, her face peeping out suspiciously and when she saw him standing there she let out a shriek of such pure joy, Mercy mistook it for terror and knocked the pan of mutton stew she was stirring into the fire and over the highly polished black-leaded hearth.

'Joss . . . Joss, my son . . .' was all his mother could say over and over again, drawn into the circle of his arms, then they were all there with the exception of Mercy who was weeping, not knowing which way to turn as the lovely stew smouldered on the hot coals and her husband mumbled against his mother's shoulder. Daisy had him by the legs and Charlie held him round his waist, his tear-stained face pressed into the curve of his brother's back and for several minutes nothing was said that made sense. His mother gave up her place in his arms, reluctantly, for his wife but Mercy hung back, confused and when Joss kissed her gently he felt her flinch beneath his touch.

But at last he could look about him, dreading it but knowing he must face what his family had been brought down to because of him.

The room was warm, excessively so, for it was high summer but there was a decent fire in the neat and tidy hearth. The walls had no cracks in them nor mouse-holes, and had been recently whitewashed. The frames of the door were sound, as was the stout door, newly painted and glass in the windows had been mended and were whole with shutters to protect them. Pretty curtains were drawn across them, and on the scrubbed floor were his mother's rag rugs, colourful, warm, clean. Most of the furniture come from Edgeclough had gone to the pawnshop in the first weeks, but what was left was polished with the familiar – he could smell its fragrance – beeswax his mother made herself.

He turned about, looking at the comfortable room, his face bewildered, stunned, then at his family and his bewilderment grew. He had seen too many stunted bodies and haggard faces, those of the work-worn scarecrow poor who never in the whole of their lives had enough to eat and he had expected to see it here. His mother had never been plump for she had worked hard all her life but she had been strong. A handsome girl grown into a mature, not unattractive woman with a clear, well-scrubbed skin and a steady gaze, and now in her fiftieth year she was just the same. The strain was there, the strain and worry of a mother with a wilful son who had fetched up in gaol for his troubles but nothing more. She was an elderly woman, past her prime perhaps, but serene now that her lad was home, and in good health. He turned to Charlie, to Daisy, wondering at the firm flesh on their straight limbs, again not plump but far from the undernourished, malformed scraps of humanity he had seen in the mills and weaving-sheds during the past six years and which he had agonised over as he stumbled from Badger's Edge to Crossfold.

Mercy smiled at him tremulously. Her face was still pale as it had always been but she had recovered somewhat from the shock of seeing him, finding comfort as she always had in the simple domestic tasks Martha set her. She was shy now under his gaze and she turned away to the spoiled stew showing herself in the only way she knew how by beginning the preparation of a meal for her returned husband.

'Get me some water, Charlie,' she said and Joss, still standing in the middle of the room, his head almost touching the ceiling watched, speechless still, as his brother opened the door into the alley and with the jug he had picked up, ladled some water from the rain butt which stood just outside the door. He carried it carefully to Mercy

286

who poured it into a bowl and began to clean up the burned stew.

'I'll have something for you to eat in a minute, Joss,' she said and Martha Greenwood smiled, then unable it seemed to stay away from her son for a moment longer, put her arms about him and laid her cheek on his chest. She looked up into his eyes, studying them, studying the lines of his face, the strain about his mouth, the perplexity, the anxiety which had settled on him as he entered the room and which had nothing to do with his previous torment. He answered her gaze with a smile and a gentle kiss dropped on her brow.

'Are you all right, Mother?'

'Aye, son, and you?'

'Aye.'

'Then sit. You must be fair clemmed.'

They ate fresh bread and slices of ham with pickles, Mercy apologising that she could not give him something hot, consumed with distress at the spoiling of the stew, he thought, and nothing else, and all the while they talked, telling one another how lovely it was to be together again there was a strange unease, a slight air of tension which sat on his mother's shoulder and it told him he must not ask what had happened until he and she were alone. It was understood, the look which passed between them and he waited patiently, wishing Charlie and Daisy would get to their beds and yet dreading it for there was something wrong here and he knew he must face it when they were gone.

He was quite amazed as his mother kissed the children goodnight to see his wife lean over Martha's shoulder and receive a kiss too and when the three of them had climbed the narrow staircase, looking back to him to say good-night again he could not believe his own eyes.

'Mercy?' he said questioningly and she turned back obediently.

'Yes?' Her face was wary. She had only just become used to sharing a bed with Daisy, with Charlie on the other

287

side of a blanket strung across the room, and she seemed suddenly afraid she was going to be asked to do something she did not quite like. Something she had found distasteful in the past though she could not really remember what it had been.

Joss felt his mother's hand on his arm, telling him something, and he understood since he too remembered.

'Good-night then, sweetheart,' was all he said and Mercy smiled like a child.

'Good-night then, Joss. It's lovely to have you home.' He might have been *her* brother too.

'It's good to be home, lass.'

They sat, one on either side of the fireplace, his mother and himself. They had cleared the table and cleaned the dishes, carrying in the sweet rainwater from the butt and it was not until they were settled that he began the questions.

'Where's Jenny?'

His mother stared him straight in the eye as though daring him to dispute her answer.

'She's working.'

'At this time of night?'

'Aye. She cleans for a lady in Reddygate Way. A parson's daughter. She goes a couple of nights and on a Sunday.' And still her eyes looked defiantly into his, why he did not know, since there seemed nothing wrong with extra employment, particularly with a parson's daughter.

'So that's what pays for all this, is it?' He looked about the comfortable room, indicating with his hand the luxuries which he was sure none of the other inhabitants of Lousy Bank enjoyed. Though his mother's room smelled of fresh bread and beeswax, his nose could detect very faintly, now that he had grown accustomed to it, the stench which lay over the whole area in which the mill-workers lived. He had gagged on it as he strode through the alleyways and back passages to this house, asking his way in the maze of streets through which he walked. He had leaped over great stretches of slimy water in which objects not for the squeamish floated, across evil-smelling heaps the contents of which

288

he could not recognise and did not linger to find out. The air was heavy, foetid, so thick he had found it difficult to breathe and his heart had hammered in his chest, with the heat and the effort it took to wade through it and with fear for what he would find at the end of it.

Now, it appeared his terror had been for nothing since his family looked better than they had done since before his father died.

'When will she be home?'

'Soon, but promise me something, Joss. You'll not scold her.'

'Why should I?'

'Well, takin' on another job . . .'

'I don't know how she does it, working for fourteen hours and more in the mill then cleaning in what spare time she's got left, but it's only what I expected of her, knowing the way she is.'

'She's strong, lad. We all are.'

He smiled and leaned forward to touch her hand affectionately.

'By God, you must be. When I see the children who work in the mills about here, poor little sods. I fully expected our Charlie and Daisy to be the same but now I find . . .'

'Who told you they were in't mill?' His mother's voice was sharp.

'Oh . . . a woman who works there. I . . . I met her on the way home. She told me you'd moved . . . Jesus, I nearly went off my head . . .'

'Nay, Joss, you shouldn't 've worried. We're grand, grand.'

'I can see that, but are you not ready for your bed? The factory bell goes at five, not that you'll be there by the end of the week with me home to do some weaving . . .'

'Nay, we've all got part-time, well, me an' Daisy, and Charlie puts in no more than . . .'

'*Part-time*.' He looked incredulous since he and his On-wardsmen with others like John Fielden had been petitioning for part-time, or a shorter working day for children and the age at which they might start work, for many years. The legislation had already been passed by Parliament but with so few factory inspectors the law was difficult to enforce.

'Aye, me an' Daisy work six hours and Charlie does ten.'

'And the rest?'

'What d'you mean, the rest?'

'All the other children?'

She looked saddened, putting out her hand to placate him for his expression said that though he was glad for his own family, he wanted the same humane treatment for *all* of them and why should the Greenwoods be given what the others were denied?

It was like a light seen at the far end of a tunnel when it came, far away and puzzling. He knew what it was, of course he did but he had to distinguish the shape and size of it before he could recognise it clearly for exactly what it was.

He had hit her! He had blamed her for what had happened to them, shedding his own guilt by placing it on her shoulders. She and her father and all the other manufacturers had created the system, helped by men who had invented the machines to make it possible, and thousands had been dragged down with it, his own family, so he had thought, included. But while he had been imprisoned she had protected them for him. He did not know how she had done it, contrived to influence the working hours, the overlookers, the manager of the spinning mill, for though she was entitled to do as she pleased with the men and women and children in her employ, working them for as *long* as she pleased, her father would certainly not have agreed with what she intended for the family of the felon, Joss Greenwood. Jenny and Mercy, young and with good food inside them would be able to manage the work and so she had not drawn attention to them but his mother, too old really to be in the mill at all, and Daisy and Charlie whose soft young bones could so easily be bent or broken, as happened to thousands upon thousands of children, had been spared.

'And . . . this cottage?'

'Nay, some workers came. Said they were doing repairs to Mr Chapman's property but to tell the truth, Joss, they only did this one. They brought the water butt and threatened all them in Lousy Bank with dismissal, or eviction, or both, if they interfered with it, God only knows why,' though of course she was certain she knew in her heart. 'We're not liked round here, Joss, since we've managed where the others haven't, but nobody bothers us and with the extra Jenny fetches we've got through it.'

It was gone midnight when Jenny Greenwood let herself into the cottage and she almost screamed out loud as the figure in the chair by the fire rose to its feet, tall, standing, head touching the ceiling, hands outstretched to take hers. She was still glowing, her hair tumbled about her head, her manner languorous, stretching, sighing, a slow graceful turn of her shoulders, a slow drooping of her long eyelashes and for a moment Joss Greenwood's skin prickled and his heart hesitated uncertainly for he had seen this look before on a woman . . . then the sense of disquiet vanished like smoke in the wind as Jenny's face lit up and her eyes were bright as candles in her joy.

'Jenny . . . Jenny, my lass . . .' and could not speak so great was his emotion.

'Joss . . .' and neither could she. The memory of the man with whom she had spent the last two hours was dashed away as she sank thankfully into her brother's arms.

Martha Greenwood watched them from the bed which she shared now with Jenny. She wore a white cotton nightgown, the one into which she had modestly changed behind the sheet Joss had put up to screen her only half an hour since. She had worn it as a bride over thirty years ago, spinning the yarn herself, her husband-to-be weaving it for her on his own hand-loom. It had stood the test of time as she had, durable as she was and strong. She had not let that strength be taken from her ever, and she had reared children, who were the same. They were alike in their beliefs, in their powerful and unyielding refusal to give in. She had known from the start what Jenny did, Sunday after Sunday and on two or three nights a week and she had not blamed her, knowing, if she had been the right age, she would have done the same herself to feed her children. But she had seen the girl bloom in beauty, an insolent beauty which said she cared for none of the folk who wondered how she came by it. Bold and defiant, careless, for what did it matter, her attitude said, since she had what she wanted, which was security, for her family, tenuous perhaps and not to last forever, but better than most. Someone protected her, and them. Someone had made this home habitable and Martha had a good idea who it was since it must be someone with power. Not enough to let the world see what he did for he had his way to make, but someone influential enough to whisper in the right ear, to grease the right palm when it was held out to him.

And now he was home, her son the fighter and what was to happen? It would not be long before he worked it out for himself and got the name of Jenny's lover out of her. Not for a moment did it occur to her that the man, gentleman she supposed, careless, charming, indifferent to everything but his own needs, was not their protector.

20

'Katherine, I will not be put off again. The summer is nearly over and still you will not decide on a date for your wedding. Your father is not going to like this at all. He allowed you to persuade him that you needed more time to get your work up to date at the mill before taking a wedding journey during the summer, now you are making further excuses and all amounting to nothing. You are not indispensable at the mills, Katherine and well you know it and so does Harry and believe me he will not wait forever. Your wedding dress has been made for months, *and* those of your attendants. People are beginning to talk, indeed Mrs Jenkinson went so far as to ask me if Harry, *Harry*, mark you, had other plans and intimated that now he had become so invaluable to your father he had no need to marry you! I could not refute it, naturally, without telling them that my own daughter was darting from side to side like a rabbit in a cage in her effort to avoid taking that final step. I am at my wits' end to know what to do or say to my friends. Six months' engagement is perfectly acceptable but after that people begin to wonder. I realise that some girls, though not many I do assure you, are not ... concerned with marriage. That some will remain spinsters but they are usually young women with no dowry, no looks and unless they will take a shopkeeper or a tradesman are doomed to remain unmarried. But not you, Katherine. You are the most sought after in the county of Lancashire and cannot escape it. Believe me, you *will* marry and what your apparent objection to Harry Atherton is, I cannot for the life of me imagine. He is of the finest family. He is agreeable, well-favoured and his charm is undeniable. Really, I do not know what is the matter with you ...'

Kit was lounging on the window-seat of her mother's sitting-room which led from her bedroom at the front of the house. It was high and airy with furniture of a gossamer fragility, spindle-legged chairs, small velvet sofas of the palest rose, silk curtains of ivory and a carpet to match. The ceiling was picked out in rose petals and acanthus leaves and straying tendrils of gold and each of the two bays had deep-cushioned window-seats.

Kit leaned her head against the window-pane and stared out across the rolling stretch of smooth lawn towards the towering oak trees, planted centuries ago, the tall pines, the yew trees, the sycamore which had once been part of the vast forest covering the Penfold Valley. The house had been planned and built to stand among the trees, only taking out those which had been necessary. It was as though Greenacres stood in an enormous forest glade, the garden at the front cut in two by the long and winding drive of plane trees.

It was August and the flowering season was at its peak. Great swathes of roses of every shade from palest pink to deepest red crammed beds around which gardeners worked, weeding and taking off the dead heads for Barker Chapman demanded nothing but perfection. There were dahlias, begonias, fuschia in profusion, all surrounded by immaculately trimmed bushes of every shade of green imaginable. A boy was carefully sweeping the stone steps which led down from the entrance porch to the gravelled driveway and two more were on their knees in the hazy sunshine clipping the lawn, watched by the eagle-eyed head gardener who supervised and criticised every snip and cut.

It was Sunday and when her mother had finished lecturing her on the subject most dear to her heart which was Kit's forthcoming marriage to Harry Atherton, Kit would slip away to change from her light morning gown into clothing more suitable for walking, collect her dogs and stride out . . . no, run every step of the way up to Badger's Edge. September, Autumn, then winter would soon be here and what would they do then, she wondered mournfully as her mother's voice droned on at the edge of her mind. She could still walk up there and indeed saw no reason why she should not for the whole household was accustomed to her love of ranging the high moorland and would be surprised if she should stop but soon it would be too cold, too wet for her to show her love, to take his, in the arms of Joss Greenwood.

Her eyes clouded and became unfocused, not seeing the trees nor the garden and the men working there looking instead to the memory of that day, a week after Joss had come home when she had gone, unable to stay away, up to Badger's Edge. It had been grey with a fine drizzle which had shifted in the smooth wind, blurring the track and the shape of the standing bracken, hiding the tops of the hills and the undulating stretch of the moorland on every side. It was a day come suddenly in the middle of weeks of sunshine, when a man could get lost in the wildness, on the faint, almost obliterated tracks, through gorse and heather and strange groups of lowering rock piles. It was a day for staying at home by the fireside, not cold, quite warm in fact with the heat of the summer ground taking the chill from the rain which fell on it, but cheerless in its melancholy.

She did not see him at first. The grey of his clothing blended into the grey of the stones but the dogs' hackles rose warning her that she was not alone and she whirled about expecting some vagrant, some wandering itinerant, homeless as thousands were, sheltering perhaps in the lee of the stones.

He simply stood there waiting for her to speak. The fine drizzle had soaked into his clothing and plastered his hair in dripping black curls to the shape of his head. His hands were stuffed into his jacket pockets and his collar was turned up. As she stared at him he pulled his cap from somewhere and wiped his face with it, still not speaking, his eyes clamped to hers. The dogs stood between them, waiting for her command to attack or to drop down into the heather, ready to do either for though they knew him well it made no difference. They were growing older now, eight years she had been protected by them, but they were still as strong, as defiant, as savage as she had trained them to be if needed.

'Call them off, Kit,' he said at last, softly.

Still she stood, her face as hard as granite. She was hatless but her full length coat covered her from neck to ankle and her stout boots were warm and dry. Her hair, like his, was painted to her skull, but straight and heavy, accentuating the beauty of her high cheek bones, the strength of her firm jawline. Droplets of rain beaded her lashes and her lips and her eyes were narrowed and cold.

'Please. I have come to apologise. Call them off.'

At last she spoke, her voice as cold as her eyes.

'How did you know I would be here today?'

'I have come every morning . . . and waited. I could not let you think . . . I was made aware of what you had done for my family as soon as I got to Lousy Bank. I had to tell you . . . to thank you. That is all. What I did was unpardonable. Not just in striking you but in believing you capable of . . . of . . . being with me while you let my mother . . . my family starve. Will you forgive me? I ask no more of you. I could not rest . . . I must get on with what I do now that . . . well, you will have heard of the repeal of the Combination Acts . . .' He raised his hand wearily to brush back his wet hair which dripped across his face, his smile hesitant, rueful, '. . . I'm sorry, you do not want to hear that and I had not meant to mention it but I could not leave without . . . I had to see you . . . to thank you. I will go now . . .'

But still they stood, face to face with the dogs between them, a strange tableau should someone have passed by to see them. There was a straining tension, a leaning of one towards the other though there was five or six yards between them. The rain misted about them, growing heavier now, sliding in rivulets across each desolate face, then he groaned harshly in his throat.

'For God's sake, Kit, put me out of my misery one way or the other. Go, or stay, as you must, but do something. I love you, dear God, how I love you. I don't want to and if you tell me to clear off I will, but do it quickly for I do not think I can manage this much longer.'

'Joss . . . my love . . . aah . . . my love . . .' and with a soft cry she stepped over the crouching dogs, her hand giving them some automatic signal which they obeyed without question and flung herself into his lifting arms. They were about her then, straining her to him and the rainwater in his clothes were squeezed out against his body and ran down it and he began to laugh and weep at the same time.

'I thought I had lost you. I thought I had lost you,' he said over and over again and her tears and his, and the soft

296

raindrops mingled together in joy and sorrow since this was their life and always would be.

'Forgive me,' he mumbled into her wet hair and her face turned up to his and the brilliance of her smile blinded him for a moment before their rain-wet mouths met, warm, slippery at first but clinging. He cupped her face in his hands, smoothing the cheek he had struck, kissing it in a fever of remorse but she took his hands in hers and put his arms about her again unable to get close enough to him, it seemed.

And so they had begun again, those ecstatic encounters on the 'tops', the top of the world in a world peopled by just the two of them, uninhabited but for the stoat and rabbit and weasel, by cole tit, wheatear and blackbird. Whenever they could they met in that magical August month, unaware of what was to come. Their love was looked kindly on by the gods, they thought, impregnable, unassailable, strong, proved so by the years and by the disasters through which it had come. Days might go by before she could get up to Badger's Edge for as a 'fiancée', her status had altered. She was Harry Atherton's future wife now and he was not awfully sure she should be allowed to roam about in the company of only her dogs. She was to marry into one of Cheshire's oldest families with a tradition of greatness behind it, from the battlefields in which Cromwell took a stand against their King to the latest at Waterloo only several years ago.

'What has that to do with walking my dogs on the moors, Harry?' she asked patiently. She tried so hard to be patient with Harry, she really did, nipping and darting like a hare avoiding a greyhound, diverting his plans for their marriage into other, less explosive channels, making promises which she did not keep, avoiding his sometimes amorous advances though these, surprisingly, were not as demanding as she expected. He was good humoured with her, sure of her she supposed, since there was no way Barker Chapman would allow such an advantageous contract to be broken, allowing her to be foolishly female, allowing her to be somewhat evasive in her last days of freedom. She would be his wife this year, of that he was positive, or early next. His father was becoming as pressing as her own, demanding to know when that 'damned girl' was going to set a date which would not, at the last moment, be postponed, amazed at the indulgence shown her by her father, and by Harry, but Harry had his own diversion which he was not quite ready to give up and it suited him, just for now, to allow Kit her prevarication.

There were times when, running like a child, skipping across the browning bracken, the fading heather, she would arrive to find Joss not there and her heart would falter, beating on his name, anguished sometimes beyond all reasoning since she was well aware he was engrossed now with the forming of a legal trade union to speak for, to act for 'the deluded people' as the labouring poor were called, those who, oppressed by hunger listened to any doctrine which they were told would redress their grievance. He was one of the 'politicians' who were to tour the country, taking up issues which the aristocracy, the squirearchy, the millocracy believed he really did not understand, stirring up the rabble, they said to violent action. She had refused to discuss it with him, refused to let it into their lives which, she said, existed for no more than a few hours each week and what he was to do, what *she* was to do, was separate, apart from what they were, what they did in the sheltered beds of heather and clover they made for themselves in the deserted expanse around Badger's Edge or Friars Mere.

'They will catch you, put you in prison again,' she had wept in a moment of weakness against his sun-browned chest, since it was well known now that Lord Liverpool's government was fearful of an insurrection which it might not easily be able to master. There was a limited number of troops in the Oldham area but she had heard her father say that £500,000 had been raised for the purpose of creating an efficient repressing force, thirty thousand men, he had been told, to protect the district. Parliament had just passed a new Combination Act which permitted the existence of trade unions like the one Joss was forming but strictly limiting their ability to strike, and with the unusually high rise in food prices, the people, the poor deluded people were stirring uneasily once more.

'Don't sweetheart, don't . . .' and he held her close and kissed her passionately for he had never seen her weep before and he was dismayed that he had weakened her. 'They can do nothing, not by themselves. They might catch a man here and there but they will never break the organisation . . .'

'I don't give a damn about the organisation, only you,' but he had kissed her wet eyes and cheeks, smoothing her throat with warm lips which dipped easily into the neck of her bodice. His hands were gentle, then strong as they took her breasts, and her melancholy would fade away with her garments, the argument, the anxiety and the great partition which was erected about each of them when they were apart.

'Harry and I are to go to London for a few days, Kit. I want to introduce him to . . . well, you know them all, those with whom we do business but I am anxious they should become familiar with him before you are married,' her father told her the following week. 'You can manage without me, I know that, my dear but . . .'

'Don't worry, Father, please. I have been your deputy for so long now I am well able to continue while you are away. The mills will not fall down about our ears on account of your absence, not for a few days at least.' She paused, smiling, then sat down in the chair which was drawn up to his desk. Her father had the weekly statement of accounts in his hand and his face looked troubled, the first time, she realised, surprised, that she had ever seen it so. There had been a great many rumours in the newspapers and on the lips of their manufacturing acquaintances of bank failures, of stock exchange collapses, of businesses going bankrupt, the great 'boom' as they had called it in the commercial world of Britain about to languish. They blamed the government, they said, for there was certain to be great privation among the lower classes who were always the first to feel the sharp cold when the trade winds changed. London, Manchester, Birmingham and the agricultural areas of the country were showing already the familiar fruits of distress and, it was whispered, machine breaking was being revived by those radical political societies who had caused so much disruption a couple of years ago.

'Is there to be trouble, Father?' she asked calmly.

'I fear so, my dear. There is a slump coming in the textile trade and only those with the strength to ride it out will come through it, and those with cash behind them, needless to say.' He smiled thinly, for was he not one of those and would manage, but some who worked on a tightrope budget from raw cotton to the sale of their woven cloth would have a hard time of it.

'So you are to go to London . . .?'

'Yes, as I told you and to ensure that our markets are safe. We shall start in Manchester and then go on to the capital. I have many acquaintances in the government who will let me know which way the wind is blowing and how I may keep myself protected until it is over. But it may be a while, Kit, before we see trade become as splendid as it has been these last few years.'

He reached into his pocket and drew out his cigar case. Taking a cigar from it he lit it, then when it was drawing to his satisfaction, he leaned back in his chair, studying her closely.

'And that brings me to another matter which has been troubling me for the past few weeks and I think you know to what I refer, do you not, Kit?'

For a second her heart stilled in her breast, then leapt like a salmon trying for a waterfall up the river. Dear God . . . surely . . .? but he was smiling, coolly but smiling and if he had known of her association, the last only yesterday in the darkening autumn evening of Badger's Edge, with Joss Greenwood he would certainly not be sitting there discussing trade with her.

300

'I am not . . . sure . . .' she said hesitantly, knowing of course, exactly what it was.

'Come now, Kit, let us have done with this maidenly reluctance and get this union with Harry Atherton finalised. You have prevaricated for long enough and I have allowed it since you were . . . well, he was not your choice but mine. But you seem to be fond of him as he is of you and his family are eager, as I am, to see you married. Before I leave for London, and, by the way, I shall be spending a couple of nights at Harry's home in Cheshire where his father will press me, I know, I would like to have a date to give him. Shall we say an October wedding and then in the spring you and Harry can go to Italy as I promised for a month or two. The crisis should be abating by then and . . .'

'Father, I had rather hoped to be a spring bride . . .'

'You had a chance for that this year, Kit.' His voice was crisp and quite determined.

'But the dress, my wedding dress. The one Miss Cavendish made for me, and those of the attendants, will not be suitable since they were made for a summer wedding and it will take time to . . .'

'Nonsense! I am sure Miss Cavendish will manage admirably with others, suitable for winter.'

'Really, Father, the expense . . .'

'Since when did expense bother the likes of you and me, Kit?'

'Well . . .'

Barker Chapman stood and with a swift and surprising movement gripped her forearms, lifting her from her chair. He held her before him, showing his physical superiority for the first time in her life. He had always controlled her before with his quick mind, his sharp intelligence and because, quite simply, he was her father and the only one who could give her what she wanted. Now he held her with hands which hurt.

'It is to be the first week in October, Katherine. I am determined upon it. I have arranged it all, the church and the parson and your mother is to have Miss Cavendish here in the morning for the fitting of a suitable gown and all the other garments you might need. The marriage contracts have been drawn up and agreed, by Harry and his family and by myself so all it needs is the wedding service. You do understand, do you not? Now I shall say no more so you may fetch Harry in here and take a glass of sherry with us. We shall tell him together. The first week in October and no delays.'

Joss was not there on the next three evenings she walked up to Badger's Edge and in her heart, though she was in almost physical pain with her need for him, she had it in her to be glad he had not come for what would it achieve to pour out her desolation to him when he could do nothing to help her. He knew of Harry Atherton, of course and must suspect that her father had some role for him in her life but while it was not mentioned, as *his* wife was not mentioned, Harry had no part in theirs. For three days and nights her mind had twisted and turned, doubling back on itself in an effort to find some plausible reason why, for the moment, she should not marry the man her father had duped her into accepting. She could, of course, refuse point blank to go on with the wedding but as she thought of the consequences her body trembled. Her father would instantly return her to her mother's drawing-room where she would again take up her embroidery and fine sewing and her painting in water-colour, which was the employment of all of the young ladies with whom she had mixed as a girl, those who were not already married. She was twenty years of age, an old maid in many people's eyes and would probably remain so, a 'daughter-at-home', a companion for her mother, unless she married, there to remain until her father's death when she would pass into another man's guardianship, no matter what her age, the guardianship of a relative her father thought suitable. Four weeks, she had little more than four weeks before she became Mrs Harry Atherton.

She leaned back on the stone where so many times she had been taken in love by Joss Greenwood and tried to imagine the supreme act, not between herself and Joss but between herself and Harry and even before the images of it could become properly focused in her mind's eye her female body, that which loved Joss and *his* body, recoiled in revulsion, even the thought of it too appalling to contemplate. But that was only a small part of it, an important part indeed, but the worst was the certainty that she would never see Joss again. He was not a man to share his woman with another man. He had a wife and God knows if he made love to her, for she had no idea and had not asked since she did not want to know, but that would not signify with Joss. *Kit* was his and if he could not have all of her, even for a few hours a week, he would have nothing of her. She knew it. The moment she became the wife of Harry Atherton she would lose Joss Greenwood. She was trapped. Her clever, imaginative mind which had been arrogant enough to believe that somehow she would get out of this, that she would have it all, the mills, her own life to lead as she pleased, and Joss, had been caught in a web from which, no matter how she struggled she could not escape. To have the mills she must take Harry. To have Joss . . . well . . . was there any way in which she and Joss could share a life? Was there?

She felt the hysterical laughter rise in her throat since she knew that whatever she did, whichever way her life went, she could never entirely possess Joss Greenwood. He belonged to so many people, to all those men and women, the children who looked to him for salvation, but most of all he belonged to, was tied forever to . . . his wife!

Turning in a circle, her mind a boiling ferment which somehow she must calm before she reached Greenacres she called to the dogs and walked up to the path which led to Crossfold. She had taken no more than a dozen steps along it when, with a sharp snap of impatience she reversed her step, leaving the path and began to climb towards the higher land above Badger's Edge. It became more barren the higher she got but the landscape suited her mood, desolate, wild and as rebellious as she herself would like to be but knowing in the midst of it all she had no choice. She was her father's child. He approved of her. He approved of what he had made her. He had given her freedom but when she had run, enchanted with it, into the wide open spaces in which men were allowed to range free, she had found, to her dismay, that she wore a rein, a long rein but which could, nevertheless, be pulled short if she went too far. Her father had told her she was to be his son, to inherit his mills and run them when he had gone. It was to be her role but now he had another for her and how was she to play both these roles without being torn in two? She was to be Harry's wife, the mother, she supposed, of his children and yet, her father told her she was to . . .

She threw back her head in a gesture of hopelessness. Dear God, how was she to do it? She could feel the hysteria begin to rise in her and she stopped, her back to the steeply sloping stretch of moorland she had just climbed. She was almost at the highest point and it would be dark soon. It was nearly autumn, the long days of summer almost gone and soon, she knew, she must accept that with the summer would go her love.

She turned wildly, almost overbalancing, her arms flailing about her, ready to scream that she could not, simply *could not* do it, when her eyes caught the flickering movement of a figure on the edge of her vision. A slowly moving figure draped in some brilliant colour which stood out sharply against the windburned green of the grass. She watched it curiously, becoming still, her voice silent in her throat, momentarily diverted from her own despair, trying to distinguish who is was so high on the moorland tops.

At last she could make out the form of a woman. She was some way off, her face indistinguishable in the gathering gloom, but where she had come from, or where she was going, Kit could not imagine since there was no track up here. It was too high for the pack-horse routes which stayed below a thousand feet – and the clouds – so what was she – if it really was a woman and not a figment of Kit's disordered imagination – doing up here?

The woman stopped when she saw Kit, as surprised as she was and Kit lowered her arms, still in the desolate state into which the prospect of her own future had plunged her, willing to believe that this was just a ghost. She had agonised for so long on the dear images of Joss and the living death his loss would bring her that now it seemed that she had conjured up the picture of his sister for that was who the vision was moving towards her through the knee-high bracken. It was Jenny Greenwood.

They looked at one another, each unwilling to be the first to speak, each unsure that they even wished to speak. Jenny was dressed in an ankle length skirt of homespun cotton, a soft grey, serviceable and meant to last. Her bodice was of white cotton and she wore clogs but round her shoulders was a slipping shawl of the finest cashmere in shades of rich red and claret. It was a lovely garment, not something a mill girl would normally wear and Kit could have sworn that in those first moments of awareness Jenny Greenwood blushed as deep a red as her shawl.

She has a lover! How else could a girl who worked in a factory own a garment as fine? And the man was well-to-do, that was obvious and, one supposed, not likely to marry a mill girl. She would dearly like to engage the girl in conversation, to find out his name since the possibility was that it would be one of the sanctimonious gentlemen with whom she herself did business and who considered *her* no better than she should be. How pleasant it would be to sit down with her and pass the time in some . . . well . . . she could only call it *gossip*, the kind of conversation women like to indulge in now and again. Not women like her mother and her mother's friends whose sole interest was fashion and the latest Penfold Valley scandal, but someone with her own heritage and view on life. Why she should imagine that person might be Jenny Greenwood, she did not know but at the back of her mind was the impression that in different circumstances they might have been friends. Or was it, if she were absolutely honest, that she was drawn like a magnet to the irresistible lure of this woman because she was Joss's sister, because she knew him, had known him since he was a boy, and the enchanting possibility that his name might be mentioned?

'You're a long way from home,' she said coolly, wondering as she spoke why she should do so and apparently Jenny thought the same for instantly the uncertain expression on her face changed to one of truculence.

'What's that to you? You don't own the moor as well as the mill.'

There was a familiar tightening of the air between them and Kit felt the hard shell of irritation begin to set about her. It seemed she could do or say nothing which did not immediately raise this girl's hackles. Not that it mattered to her, but really she had meant no offence with her simple remark. Perhaps it was the way she had said it then?

'You seem bent on quarrelling with me whenever we meet,' she said, surprising herself.

'Quarrelling? Is that what we're doin'? Nay, it's nowt to me what you say for the likes of you an' me can hardly *quarrel*, can we? In the first place, you've to be friends to fall out and we're certainly not that and never will be.'

'My word, how touchy you are, Jenny Greenwood. Do you have no conversation that does not involve discord and provocation?' She managed to sound amused as though at the squabbles of a fractious child but Jenny's face remained set in her cold enmity. 'Whenever we meet which I agree has been on two occasions only, you seem intent on attacking me.'

'Don't be daft, woman. You mean *nowt* to me. It's your *sort* I despise and always will so if you'll get off the path I'll be on me way.'

'Certainly. God forbid I should hold you up. You must be on some errand of great importance so you had best be about it. You should not be up here anyway.'

'I see, you're ordering me off your land, are you, an' I suppose if I disobey you'll set those damn dogs on me.'

'Good God, Jenny, I only meant . . .'

'What?' Jenny's eyes were like those of a cat, narrow and venomous.

'That there are ruffians roaming these parts and you are a woman alone. They would have that pretty shawl from you in . . .'

'My shawl's nowt to do wi' you . . .'

'I'm not implying it *has*, only that there are men on the tramp all over these hills who would steal it from you and . . . other things besides . . . They aren't fussy since they've nothing to lose, whereas you . . .' Kit felt the old exasperation, for that was what it was, push them apart, but something led her on. This was the sister of the man Kit loved. If there had been more she could have done without stirring up further speculation, for his family, she would have done so. She had been surprised, pleasantly so, when there had been no repercussions from her reckless inter-ference in the running of Ellis's spinning machines when she had spoken to him privately on the matter of part-time work for Martha Greenwood and her children, telling him nothing, naturally, of her reasons. She had no need, her expression had told him, but he would not be forgotten when promotion, or perhaps a rise in his wages, was pro-posed. She had been in fear for many weeks afterwards that her father, or Harry might notice the three hands who were employed on a part-time basis but Ellis appeared to be a wise man who could see the prospect of advancement when it was offered him, and when to keep his mouth shut. No doubt she would be made to pay for it at a later date but she would face that when it happened. She had not particularly cared for his conspiratorial smile when he had agreed, but that did not matter, nor the way his eyes seemed to watch her as she crossed the yard when he happened to be there.

There was a long uneasy silence while Kit racked her brain to think of some subject, easy for them both, on which she might address Jenny Greenwood.

'You . . . walk up here often?' she said at last.

307

'No. I haven't the time.'

'Of course not,' and how would she, or the energy, after sixteen hours at her frame but still Kit persisted.

'I love these moors. I find great solace . . . peace up here.' She looked about her, her eyes soft now and dreaming as though her communication with Joss Greenwood's sister had calmed her. 'It is so empty with nothing to . . . disturb you, nothing but the silence and the stillness . . .'

'I know.'

'Do you feel the same?' Kit lowered herself into the glowing bracken until only her head and shoulders were visible. She looked down the great sweep of the moorland into the deep wooded valley of the Penfold and Jenny Greenwood watched her with bewilderment. This was Katherine Chapman. This dreaming woman, whose face, moments ago, had been strained with some deep unhappiness, was the daughter of the most hated man in the chapelry of Oldham. She was the fiancée of Harry Atherton. They were to be married next month, Harry had told her and he was not awfully sure that he and Jenny would be able to continue their . . . association, was how he carelessly put it. It would be difficult, he said with a wife to consider and she must expect to support her family without his help from now on, his attitude said. There would be no more baskets of food and, she supposed, the protection and upkeep of the hovel in Lousy Bank would end as well for who else but he would have ordered the repairs to it, the sturdy water butt which was for their exclusive use. He had no further use for her now, though he had not said it in so many words, and suddenly, in the space of time it took for Katherine Chapman's eyes to turn smilingly to hers in some strange communion, Jenny Greenwood saw the opportunity she had been waiting for since that first moment in the spinning room when Ellis had told her that Harry Atherton liked a bit of 'rough'.

Moving with the slow, cat-like grace which had brought her to Harry Atherton's notice she walked over to Miss Chapman and sat down beside her.

'I have always loved it,' she said, then turning to her, she smiled.

21

Barker Chapman was extremely gratified with the success of his journey and even more so with the way in which Harry Atherton had conducted himself among the manufacturing gentlemen to whom he had been introduced during their stay in London. Not by the slightest raising of his often insolent eyebrows had Harry conveyed to them that, though he was of the landed society to which they themselves could never aspire, they were anything but exceptionally fine fellows. He and Barker had dined with several Members of Parliament, those who could be of use to Barker Chapman in the foretold slump in trade, but naturally, these were gentlemen, as Harry Atherton understood the word, for only those of *his* class, at the moment, could hope for such giddy heights.

They had stayed a night or two at Atherton Hall in Cheshire before the run to London since Mrs Atherton had been most insistent that she must return Mrs Chapman's superb hospitality in some small way, even if Mrs Chapman could not personally avail herself of it.

And thankful she would have been too, Barker thought sourly, if she could have seen the massive stone pile which was the ancestral home of the Athertons. Stone walls, stone floors with a medieval hall in which the whole of Greenacres would have readily fitted. Hundreds of portraits of Athertons past staring gloomily at this upstart from the trading classes, a bed hard and smelling of damp despite the fire which burned in the grate and food he would have been ashamed to put before his own servants offered him with an air of supreme indifference, an arrogance which said quite plainly that to be any other way must surely have the stamp of the ill bred. They had drunk an inferior wine, the money which had gone from his own pocket into that of Samuel Atherton obviously not spent on such foolish nonsense as comfort for himself and his family but on the magnificent hunters in the stable, the hounds which were housed more comfortably than Barker himself, but they had drunk the health of Harry and his absent fiancée who would, the following month become his wife.

They had taken the 'Manchester Telegraph' coach from London heading along the miraculous North Western co-aching road which led to Northampton and Leicester. It had been much improved by the immortal Thomas Telford and the first leg of the journey, starting at the 'Bull and Mouth' at St Albans and ending at Derby where they were to spend the night took only a splendid eleven hours. They breakfasted at Redbourn and lunched at Market Harborough, staying overnight at a comfortable post-house, dining on roast duck and on the following evening after travelling eighteen and a quarter hours all told, entered Barker Chapman's own coach in Manchester for the twelve or so miles from there to Crossfold.

It was almost dark as they began the stretch of slowly climbing turnpike road beyond Oldham. The summer had gone now as September gathered momentum in its dash towards winter and the road ahead was a grey misted length of ribbon edged by banks of windblown wildflowers which were retreating as winter advanced. It was bleak country to right and left and up ahead, studded here and there by the pinpricks of light where a village huddled against a hillside, or a lone cottage braved the coming winter in solitary isolation. There would be snow up here, drifts of it twelve feet deep into which carriages and waggons, animals and even humans had been known to be stuck fast, but now, though the hint of the cold to come was in the air it was warm in the carriage and both men dozed a little since the two-day journey had been long and tiresome.

Another hour would see them back at Greenacres and comfort, thought Barker thankfully after the spartan ordeal he had suffered at Atherton Hall, and Harry was busy with pictures of Jenny Greenwood and what he would do to her on the following evening.

They were both considerably startled when the carriage came to a violent stop, swaying most alarmingly as the coachman struggled to bring the frightened horses under control. One wheel almost went over into the ditch at the side of the road and Barker was flung against Harry and both fell into the corner.

'What the devil is it?' Barker shouted to the coachman, though the windows and curtains were drawn.

'God knows, sir. Perhaps highwaymen,' and Harry grinned not at all afraid, finding as always something amusing to say though Barker Chapman did not smile.

'Frederick, what's to do?' he shouted again, considerably annoyed, letting down the window and stretching his head out into the cool air, ready to berate the careless fool who had thrown them into this predicament but his voice died away in bewilderment when he saw them. No more than a dozen, a silent circle of pale-faced men, one at the tossing heads of the horses, the rest, like nightmare figures, merely standing, saying nothing, simply there!

'Now then,' Barker said sharply, not afraid but seriously displeased by this inconvenience. 'What is the meaning of this? Stand aside at once and let me pass,' for you all know who I am, his manner said, but they did not move. They were working men, of the labouring class which was causing such trouble at the moment and would, when the slump really began to bite and the price of bread rose again, cause more.

'What do you want? Why have you stopped my carriage? You realise, I hope, that you are breaking the law, gathering like this. Now stand away or you will be arrested. The penalty for such insolence as this is transportation . . .'

One man stepped forward, a tall man with a thatch of dark hair and an air of assurance about him and the others seemed to sigh thankfully, looking to him to tell them what to do.

'Not any more, Barker Chapman,' he said clearly. 'Have you not heard that the Combination Acts have been repealed? Aye, it's allowed now to gather in groups and talk about how we can manage to get our wages raised by the likes of you. We're not breaking the law any more, are we, lads?'

'No . . .' There was a muttered response from those about him and a voice at the back of the group, well hidden by the others and by the darkness could be heard grumbling sullenly of justice. There was some shuffling which seemed to imply they were not in complete accord with the first man who had spoken and Harry Atherton stepped down from his side of the carriage and walked round it to face them and he was the sum and substance of all they hated most, a gentleman, brushing an imaginary speck of dust from his immaculate trousers, yawning a little behind a languid hand as though the bleating of sheep, or the squabbling of children bored him to the point of tears. They and their forefathers had whipped off their caps to men like him and for a moment the habits of generations swayed them to move back respectfully from him but the man at the front, aware that he was losing control, leaped forward decisively and as he did so Barker Chapman stepped down from his carriage, exasperated beyond measure by this foolishness.

'I've had enough of this. Now stand away at once or I shall be forced to send my coachman for the militia . . .'

'The militia is it? They'll do you no good, Barker Chapman, for they're all over at Crossfold where there's talk of burning your brand new warehouse . . .'

'Who the devil are you, you insolent swine? I'll see you behind bars for this.'

'Will you indeed? There's a hell of a lot of us to imprison. The Onwardsmen are growing stronger with every day that passes and bastards like you will be made to realise that we won't be beaten.'

Harry Atherton's face became taut then, the amusement he had shown at the appearance of this animal-like band of men, slipping away as his outrage grew. How dare they, was the expression, quite amazed, on his face, just as his grandfather and great-grandfather might have looked if one of their peasant labourers had had the gall to address them.

'Stand away from this carriage,' he said, fully expecting to be obeyed at once, but the man braced his long legs and his smile was insolent, swaggering.

'Try and make me,' he taunted.

'Stand away at once or I shall give you the biggest thrashing of your life.' Harry raised his cane and the expression on his face was ugly, dangerous. The crowd of men fell back then and the man who held the horses' heads slipped to the back of the group wishing to be as anonymous as the rest, but still the man laughed and Harry's eyes narrowed to black slits of rage. He moved his hand, his thumb slipped along the cane, there was a sharp click and the cane was no longer a cane but a rapier!

'Now then, Harry, there is really no need for that, my boy.' Barker Chapman was sighing in irritation as he stepped between Harry's snarling violence and the dark haired man. His back was to him and when the man drew the knife from beneath his coat Barker did not see it and when it entered his back, and his heart, the last thing he did see was Harry Atherton's incensed face.

She did not seem able to settle anywhere. All through that first oppressive night when they had put her father's body, not knowing where else to lay it, in the depths of his own curtained bed, when the doctor had gone and her mother lay sleeping beneath the draught he had given her, Kit wandered from room to room trying desperately to escape the horror, not only of his murder, but of who had murdered him. Her mind dipped in and out of it, fascinated, repelled, in and out like a heron's beak into water, studying first one horrendous thought and then another, unable to stop, unable to determine between them for they were all beyond comprehension. There was blood still, on her dinner gown for she and her mother had been still at table when they had carried Barker Chapman across his own threshold, on her hands and on her face where she had scrabbled at it in her anguish, blood from the gaping wound in her father's back.

'It was the Onwardsmen . . .' Harry had told everyone at least a dozen times, his face excited, she thought, by the evening's work and certainly not unaware, even then, of what it would mean to him when he married her. 'A dozen of the swine attacked the carriage. I drew my sword, naturally, but they closed in and . . .' He had bowed his head in remembered despair, a man who had done his best to protect the father of his bride-to-be but overcome by sheer weight of numbers.

She had not spoken since her mother had needed immediate attention, the faint she was in deep and endless. The servants, every one it seemed, had screamed and milled about the hallway, drawn there by the drama, causing more confusion until her mind went quite blank, unable to function without the complete neutrality that was most needed. She moved in a dream world where she was able to fill her role, and did, at a certain level of consciousness, giving rise to the rumour that she was a cold-hearted woman who had neither fainted nor shed a tear at the sight of her father's mutilated body.

She sat by the fire in the kitchen for several minutes, not awfully sure where she was or how she came to be here since she had never been in this part of the house before. She was watched by the bewildered, excited servants, those who swore they could not sleep this night and could they be blamed for their reluctance to go to their beds, they asked one another.

'Will you change your gown, Miss Katherine?' Janet had wept, weeping not for Barker Chapman but for this frozen-faced woman who had shown her maid a careless kindness during the years she had served her, but Kit Chapman, though she heard the voice buzzing like some persistent fly trapped inside a window could make no sense of it. Within ten minutes though they had pressed a cup of tea into her hand which was left untouched, she had risen from the chair, turning her head to look for the way out.

'Come, Miss Katherine dear,' Janet said, 'let me put you to bed,' but ignoring the hand of her young maid, Kit followed the walls of the room until she came to a door and opening it stepped through to find herself in the stable yard. At last, her shocked mind registered thankfully, at last a place which was familiar, and crossing the yard watched by the hovering servants in the kitchen doorway she opened the door to the stables and went inside. The dogs rose to greet her, the stumps of their tails moving in delight but when she dropped down between them, an arm about each strong neck they became quiet, licking her cold face with their warm, loving tongues.

The night went on and on forever. Her whole life was lived in it, lived in tiny, vivid snatches which did not last long enough for her to examine them properly. She found herself on the driveway in one of them, walking determinedly towards the gates which stood open — going where? — to allow entrance to the men — who were they? — who came and went regularly throughout the night. Where was she going, one of them asked most respectfully since Miss Chapman must surely be in shock and should be taken back to her maid, but she had shaken off the restraining hand, turning off into the black void of the garden. Only it was not black for it seemed every window in the house was lit by a hundred candles and the light fell through them in neat oblongs on to the lawns and flowerbeds. Her body was painful, the skin tight and hot to the touch and her eyes ached with tears she could not seem to shed and she prayed that the dawn would come so that she might be released from this silent, bitter grieving.

They all slept now, Harry she supposed, one of them, dreaming of the wealth his bride was to bring him, the wealth which would be unfettered, free for himself to do with as he pleased now that Barker Chapman was dead.

Kit Chapman felt the warmth of her body drain slowly from her, taking with it the finer feelings Joss Greenwood and his family had awakened in her. Taking the girlishness, which, though she was a woman of twenty still lingered in her, an inclination to laughter, innocence, trust, love, filtering away as dawn ended the night on which her lover had murdered her father, leaving nothing but a coldness setting her in a place in which no one would ever reach her again.

She would see him hang, of course, he and as many of them as could be identified. Harry would know them and Frederick the coachman and she would ask if she might be there when they did it. She had said it once before, a hundred years ago now, a young girl screaming at a young labouring lad of how she hated him because he had wrecked the machine she loved. He had killed it before her eyes and now he had killed her father, the man who, if she had not exactly loved him, had been the pivot of her life, the centre of the world she was to inherit. Her father had given her the promise of freedom, given her what no other man had ever given her, even Joss Greenwood, which was a belief in her own self, in her own existence and now he was dead and the man who had killed him would pay with his life.

At last it was done. She was sitting on a low wall at the back of the house when the first pale tinge of pink and gold told her that day was approaching. She saw the sky lighten along the high line of the South Pennine hills in the east and the dogs who were lying at her feet stood up and shook themselves. She could smell the dampness of the soil and the dewed grass and the pungent aroma of the compost in the far corner of the vegetable garden. She was cold and her gown, a simple, highwaisted sheath of pale gold satin was damp and clinging to her body.

She sighed deeply and the rage which had blasted at her in spasmodic waves throughout the night was no more than a cold, hard, tenacious knot inside her, held firmly under her control, holding *her* firmly in control. Her mind was

316

clear and sharp, her thoughts well ordered and presently she would go indoors and change into the black of mourning which was required. There would be many things to order, to plan, the first, of course, her father's funeral.

The thought no longer agonised her. He was dead, her father, and his going, the *way* in which he had died though it had presented her with her first sorrow had also given her an uncompromising strength of will, a powerful resolve that said there was nothing left in her life now but her mills which she must keep running, and the bringing to justice of her father's murderer. She had got through it alone, this night. She had needed no one, only her dogs' company and she had got through the worst. She might have fainted away in sheer horror as her mother had done, as it might have been easier to do, slipped away in a draught-induced trance, letting Harry, or George Abbott, or her father's brother come from Oldham take charge but that would not do. She had known from the first moment that it would not do. She was Kit Chapman, of the Chapman mills. Not Barker Chapman's daughter any more but Kit Chapman of the Chapman mills.

The thought was kind to her. She liked it. She studied it with increasing pleasure, aware suddenly that in all this long night no one had come to her insisting, however pityingly, that she must return to the house. Not one person had been to fetch her, to tell her, to *order* her that it was high time she stopped this nonsense and behaved in a manner befitting her station. No one had followed her, servant or family, to beseech her to come in out of the cold, to take this shawl, to get some sleep, to have a sip of this or a bite of that, to tell her what was best for her!

And they never would! Not now! Not on this day or on any other!

She stood up and smoothed her hands down the skirt of her gown, then lifted them to her hair, habit and the memory of her mother's voice making her fiddle with pins and combs, then, with a defiant gesture which spoke louder than any words she might have uttered she pulled them all out and with her hair in a long, heavy cape, silken and straight about her shoulders she walked quietly back towards the house. The dogs padded at her heels and when she reached the stable yard and the side entrance to the house she did not send them to their usual place but with a click of her fingers called them to her. They were somewhat hesitant for neither had been inside the house before, but obediently they followed her along the passage and into the wide hallway. At the foot of the curving staircase they hesitated again.

'Joby . . . Blaze, to heel,' she said softly and with their cold, black noses pressed to the hem of her skirt Katherine Chapman climbed the stairs of her house.

The funeral, as was expected, had been attended by a great many gentlemen of the manufacturing classes, some from as far away as the Midlands and even Scotland, but what was more gratifying to Hannah Chapman, at least, was the unusually large group from the gentry. Naturally Harry's family was represented, by Samuel Atherton and by his wife and son, since Harry was to marry the bereaved widow's daughter when their period of mourning allowed it, but even the Squire had been there, the dreadful circumstances of Barker Chapman's death, one presumed, requiring his presence at the graveside. Most kind of them to attend, she had murmured into her black-edged handkerchief taking each hand which was held out to her, to steady her, one thought, since she was exceedingly frail beneath her widow's weeds. The Penfold Valley had been shocked and horrified by the event, Mr Abbott and Mr Jenkinson knowing quite well it might so easily have been one of them in the splendid coffin or any one of the industrialists who did business in and around Oldham, and they took their leave of her telling her and Katherine that the bereaved ladies had only to send a message and help with the business of the mills or indeed with anything financial or commercial would be immediately made available to them. Yes, yes, Harry Atherton was able, very able indeed, they said to

318

Hannah, when his back was turned, but he was not *really* one of them. He looked simply splendid in his well cut, well bred coat and trousers of black, his top hat and black gloves and there was no doubt he had a way with him which was inordinately pleasant but could he manage the *mills*? He could sell Barker Chapman's velveteen and fustian and the muslins with which Barker had been experimenting — a new market again — and had already done so beyond all expectations, but could he *manage* those mills and if he could not, what was to happen to them? He and Barker's girl could live very handsomely with or without them, it was true, but there was intense speculation even as the first spadeful of earth fell on the coffin on what Barker Chapman, and now his daughter, was worth.

Kit had stood next to her mother, her head bowed meekly, shrouded from her bonnet to her boots in black, her eyes shadowed behind her mourning veil, her expression unreadable. She listened, when her father's coffin had been put in the ground and the mourners had returned to Green-acres for refreshments, to the flow of conversation around her, to the conjectures and calculations of what her fortune might be, becoming louder as the gentlemen relaxed with a welcome glass of madeira, or even whisky inside them. She did not smile, not even to herself, on how surprised they were to be over the next few days for she did not find their remarks in any way amusing, though she promised herself the pleasure of doing so on the next occasion when they should meet, possibly when one of them needed some small favour her father would unquestionably have allowed them.

She was at the mill the next morning at five o'clock sharp. From head to foot she was in unrelieved black and when Harry arrived five hours later, riding lazily into the mill yard on the bay he had bought himself recently, he was startled to see her carriage in the corner of the yard and her carriage horse in the stable when he threw the reins of his animal to the lad whose job it was to see to them.

'Katherine, my dear.' His face was solicitous and his

319

hands reached out for hers as she stood by the window, a sheaf of papers in them held to the light but she avoided him, returning to her desk, putting the papers on a neat pile in front of her before she sat down.

'Are you unwell, Harry?' she said coolly.

'Why no, my dear. Should I be?' He smiled his charming smile, seating himself indolently on the corner of her desk. 'Why do you ask?'

'Merely that as it is ten o'clock and you are five hours late I presumed you to be ill.'

'Katherine.' His smile deepened at her small joke. 'I must admit to a distinct reluctance to rise from my bed this morning after ... well, after yesterday and to a certain concern to find *you* here at all. I had thought a month, perhaps two, before you returned ...'

'There are mills to be run here, Harry. Business to be transacted ...'

'I realise that. What do you imagine I am here for, my pet? You can leave it all to me.'

'I do not think so, Harry. A mill cannot be said to be well run if the one who is to run it arrives five hours after the engines are turned on.'

'Katherine, really, is this some kind of a joke because if it is I am not amused. I can only suppose you to be still distraught after your father's death, and who could blame you? Why do you not return home? Take at least a few days, my dear, and then ...'

'I am perfectly well, Harry, and perfectly well able to run the mills. Now if you wish to continue in your present employment you may do so for you are good at it. I need someone to sell my piece goods but if you do not work to my satisfaction I will dismiss you as I would dismiss any man who does not come up to my standards. They are high, Harry, as my father's were high. I will not put up with latecomers in the mill and I will not put up with it here. The factory bell goes at five and I shall be here before the operatives come on for the first shift. See that you do the same.'

He stood up slowly, straightening his tall and graceful body, lifting his arrogant head in total disbelief. He was still struggling to hold on to the hopeful notion that Katherine was joking with him, teasing him, that in a moment she would smile and make some remark about new brooms sweeping clean and had he really believed she meant it. She would laugh and call for coffee and they would talk, make plans for the future and he would put one or two ideas to her that he himself had devised like the one regarding this nonsensical fancy that he and she should be at the mill at the godforsaken hour of five o'clock when they had managers who were paid to arrive at that time. He had spent several hours in the arms of his sweet Jenny last night and her lusty demands had drained him to the last drop of his considerable virility. He had almost decided to stay in his bed for the remainder of the morning since Gribb and the other managers who had kept the mills going for the past week were well able to do the same for another day. He really had not expected to see Katherine here, not for weeks and he deserved a day off after all he had been through. Perhaps he would ride over to Greenacres after lunch, he had thought, to enquire on the state of mind of his beloved, dinner at the Old Bull in Crossfold and a game of cards. A pleasant day and one which a gentleman of means could well afford. Only the fancy to sit in Barker Chapman's chair which he meant to be his, had brought him here, and then only for half an hour or so, he had told himself.

He kept well leashed the explosion of anger which grew inside him.

'I cannot quite understand your meaning, my pet,' he said.

'And I should be obliged, Harry, if you would refrain from calling me your pet.'

'Katherine! Have you lost your senses? I can only assume that the events of the last week have shaken you more than we thought. Will you not go home and I think it might be advisable if your mother called in the doctor. You cannot be well, indeed you cannot.'

'Harry, for God's sake sit down and listen to me. I have something to tell you and you will not like it.'

'I do not like *this*, Katherine, and I do not care for your manner. I think it is high time you went home and I suggest you go straight to bed.'

'Don't be ridiculous, Harry.' Her face was still pale but her eyes were clear and lucid. 'There is nothing wrong with me. I have nothing to keep me at home and this past week has not been . . . easy.'

'No indeed, that is obvious from your manner . . .'

'Stop it, Harry. Stop treating me as though I was a foolish child who has not the wits nor the experience to decide for itself. There is something to be said here so sit down and let us be honest with one another.'

'Honest!' His face was white with fury and he lifted his hand and pushed it through his smoothly brushed hair. His mouth curled in snarling temper and his eyes were a hot, hating brown. 'Are you suggesting I have done something *dishonest*?' He put both hands on the table and leaned across until his face was close to hers, his attitude asking quite plainly who the hell she thought she was and how she, no more really than a factory girl, had the gall to question a gentleman's honour. His mask had slipped quite badly and his true feelings were showing and Kit was made to realise how far he had been forced to stoop in marrying her to get what he wanted. But she was not dismayed, rather she felt as though a great load had been lifted from her mind for it made the task ahead of her so much easier. She had felt nothing but contempt for him during the past week, when she had time to think of it. On the night she had met Jenny Greenwood she had known a vast and thankful relief that it was over, the charade her father had pressed on her. It was finally done with when Jenny had told her of the events of the past year and she had been waiting only to tell her father of the true colours of the man who stood before her. She had been too late for her father had died but it was not too late for her.

Now her hostility towards this man who had mocked

not only her father and herself but the virtue of a woman who could not defend herself showed in the disdainful curl of Kit Chapman's lip, the haughty lifting of her head and the expression on her face which said she despised him.

'Do you not think it dishonest to make love to one woman when you are about to marry another. Not only that but to take advantage of someone who has not the authority to refuse what you demand of her. For a basket of food you forced yourself on a girl . . .'

'*Forced*. I have no need of force with women, my girl.'

'Then you admit you have been this woman's lover.'

'I admit nothing. I do not even know which woman you speak of. Who is it who has told you these lies about me? You are talking nonsense, Katherine, and I can only assume you are seriously deranged. Your father's death . . .'

'. . . has set me free, Harry, to do exactly as I please. I may marry, or not, as the fancy takes me and I have chosen *not* to marry you.'

His eyes were almost black now and deep with his hatred of her but in them was a recognition of the dilemma he was in and the care he must use to get out of it. He had allowed her to see, just for a moment, the true Harry Atherton, the one which could when it was needed charm the birds from the trees but who, deep inside him where it had been bred, believed in his own superiority and rank and who meant, when she and her money were well and truly tied to him, to return her to her mother, to her middle-class, industrial background and take up again the life of a landed gentleman. There was enough money to ensure that he lived in luxury for the rest of his life and, his contorted face and bleak eyes said, he was not about to give it up.

She watched him in faint amusement and sudden admiration as he fought to control himself.

'Katherine, my dear, let us not get this . . . this affair out of proportion. I am afraid you have caught me out in a small pecadillo, but really, can you seriously believe that it means anything to me? Gentlemen, my dear, are . . . well, you are a lady and innocent and when I tell you that we have . . . appetites . . . there, I have shocked you, but you will see that it means no more to us than . . . than eating a meal when we are hungry. This girl, she flaunted herself somewhat in the yard, attracting my attention and . . .' He smiled ruefully, a small boy caught with his hand in the jam pot, ' . . . well, I'm afraid, just once I promise you, I could not resist temptation. I was flayed with guilt afterwards, Katherine.' His face was flushed and earnest and his eyes begged her understanding and forgiveness, ' . . . not only for your sake since you know my feelings for you but towards the girl so, knowing how hungry they always are, or so they say, I gave her food . . . sweetmeats. She came to no harm, Katherine, since no doubt it was not the first time . . .'

'It's no good, Harry.'

'What do you mean? I am telling you the truth.'

'I am afraid I do not believe you.'

'Katherine! I cannot understand you, really I cannot. Some slut has been to you crying rape, I suppose, and you are prepared to take her word against that of a gentleman.'

'A gentleman, Harry? Is that what you are?'

'Watch your tongue, Katherine, or I will . . .'

'Will what, Harry? Have me flogged at the cart-tail, or dismissed without a character reference?'

'See here, Katherine. This has gone far enough. You are impugning my word as a gentleman and I demand an apology. I have told you the truth about this . . . this girl . . .'

'You had no option.'

'Blast you, I will not have this. It must stop at once. You are not yourself, Katherine and I insist you allow me to return you to your mother. I will look after the business while you have a couple of weeks' rest and when you are recovered we will set a date for our marriage and no more will be said of this. Come now, where is your pellisse? I will call your carriage . . .'

'No, Hatry.'

324

'See here, my girl. I have had just about as much as I can take . . .'

'Then there is the door, Harry. You have but to walk through it and I think after this conversation I will reconsider my offer of employment. I cannot put the sale of my cloth in the hands of a man I do not trust.'

'Do not be more stupid than you really are, Katherine. *We are to be married.* The marriage contracts have been drawn up and agreed by my father and yours . . .'

'Who is now dead.'

'It makes no difference.'

'But it does. My solicitor informs me that as my father did not sign them and as I am his sole heir I may do as I please. And it does not please me to marry you.'

He lost his control then.

'You bitch. You low class, common bitch . . .'

'Thank you for that, Harry. It confirms that I am doing what is best for us both. Now, if you will excuse me I have a lot to do today. If you call at the office you will be given your wages up to yesterday . . .'

'You have not heard the last of this . . .'

'Oh I am sure I have not, but really, I should not waste your time. It is over, Harry, so I will bid you good-morning.'

22

He thought there had been an accident, or a fight, one of the daily incidents which occurred in Boggart Hole, Pig Lane and Lousy Bank when tempers flared over who was next at the standpipe, a domestic quarrel, a drunken brawl, a dozen urchin children in a flurry of fisticuffs, of no particular interest or concern to those who watched indifferently but this was not like that. There was an air of tension, of something nasty afoot, venomous and threatening and most of the protagonists appeared to be women.

'What's going on here?' he shouted as he turned the corner of the alley into the narrow passage of Lousy Bank. His heart began a rapid tattoo against his rib-cage and his long legs felt curiously weak for the disturbance appeared to be right outside his own front door.

'Get out of my way.' Joss Greenwood's voice was wild with sudden fear and he elbowed aside the sullen women who jammed the passage.

The first thing that caught his eye was his mother's lovingly polished table standing upside down in the pool of water from the overturned butt. There were other objects which he recognised, a rag rug made from odd pieces of cotton, dyed in different colours and sewed together by his mother's careful hand. There was a large white milk jug, smashed into a dozen pieces, a cushion, fashioned again by his mother from what she could salvage from worn out clothing, stuffed with heather and lavender, a framed sampler proclaiming that Sarah Greenwood, aged nine, had embroidered it in the year 1788, several pans, a lovely bright shawl of red and claret and a Bible, the only book his father had ever owned.

'What the hell is happening here?' he demanded to know roughly, pushing his way through the jeering crowd and some woman, without turning round to see who it was who had spoken, unwilling, one suspected, to miss a single moment of what was happening, answered him cheerfully.

'It's them bloody Greenwoods. Bein' thrown out, they are and not afore time an' all. Jumped up hoity-toity besoms . . .'

The room seemed to be filled with shouting, pushing people and somewhere a child sobbed quite piteously. He could make no sense of it, nor of the men who were lifting this and that, a chair, a bucket, whatever came to hand, ready it seemed, to chuck them out in the passage in the wake of those already there and which, not surprisingly, were fast disappearing. A woman hung on the arm of one man who was cursing her obscenely while a second attempted to drag her off. A boy was kicking and biting in the grip of a third and against the wall his mother stood, her eyes enormous in the grey despair of her face. She held Daisy against her breast while her other arm was about Mercy who appeared to have become almost senseless, slumped against Martha's shoulder.

'Put that down, you bastard,' the woman was screaming and with a thrill of horror Joss saw that it was Jenny. Her face was scarlet with outrage and her foot rose again and again as it tried to find a vulnerable place in which to kick the man whose arm she held. He swung her off her feet, aiming a heavy fist at her head and the second man was grinning now, ready to enjoy what had started out as a routine eviction but was promising to become, with this spirited hellion, a bit of sport.

'Hold her, Ned. Get her arms lad, and I'll tak t'other end. Yer little bitch. Like a bit of a fight, do yer . . . see, Ned, 'old 'er properly or she'll 'ave me in't . . .'

The third man put down the trinket he was fingering, turning to watch with growing interest the manhandling, no more than that at the moment, of the girl they had been sent to put out on the street. Her and her family, they had been told by the Chapman manager, and they had no reason to doubt his word, for non-payment of rent. The old woman and the younger one, a good looker an' all, seemed to be out of their minds, senseless with terror, though the lad was a plucky little bugger. It was taking all his own considerable strength to hold him now as he shrieked the girl's name.

For a moment or two they thought the roof had fallen in on them. Indeed the man who held Jenny Greenwood's arms, twisting them cruelly behind her back while the second fumbled at the neck of her bodice, suffered a broken collar-bone as he was flung from the cottage into the alley, landing in the pool of water from the butt and for good measure, splitting his head on the wall of the house opposite. The second and third men, quite bewildered by the explosion which erupted about them and from God only knew where, were convinced at least two, perhaps even three men had attacked them and throwing caution to the wind, darted through the broken doorway and off up the alley, scattering the delighted crowd as they went.

Jenny cried sharply then, her face pressed tight against his chest and the others huddled beside him, finding a small measure of comfort in his presence in this new catastrophe which had come to engulf them. None could speak coherently at first, indeed they had to put Mercy to bed with an infusion of valerian to make her sleep before sense could be made of their weeping, their jumbled lamentations.

'What is it, Mother?' He turned to the one who had recovered first. Jenny still trembled before the fire for though she had fought wildly, bravely, had, while the need was there, defended her family courageously, now that Joss was here and the crisis temporarily averted, she could not pull herself back together again, nor forget the rough handling the Chapman bully boys, those kept for occasions such as these, had subjected her to, nor the terror of what might have happened had Joss not come home when he did. She watched him, seeing the deep grooves which had recently been chiselled in his dark face, the strain about his strong mouth and even, she noticed, the threads of grey in his thick, curly hair. He was only twenty-five and yet he had the quiet maturity now of a man ten years older, all the hot-headed violence of his younger days scourged from him in gaol. He was beginning a new era in his fight for his fellow-man and though he often met with the Onwardsmen and talked to them, sharing his experience and giving his advice he did not always agree with their constant talk of machine breaking, of mill burning, of window smashing. It did no good for the mill-masters merely re-built their mills, or their warehouses, replaced the broken machines and windows and put wages even lower to pay for them. Only by parliamentary reform could the conditions of the poor be improved and to achieve that they must be represented by their own Member of Parliament up in London. Each man, irrespective of his class, his wealth, or lack of it, must be allowed to choose. Each man must have a voice and that could only be made possible when each man had a vote.

'They said we had not paid our rent, son,' Jenny could hear her mother saying, 'but you know that's not true. We shut the door in their faces but they broke it down.' She looked towards the doorway where Joss had propped up the door. 'They began to throw our things out into the street . . . they were all laughing, them out there. They can't abide to see decent folks make something of themselves . . .'

'No, Mother, you know that's not true. They try hard but circumstances are against them. We've been lucky with . . .' He stopped speaking abruptly since he had been about to say her name, to tell his mother who it was who had been their benefactor but she was not really listening. Her face, gone suddenly old, was turned towards the grate. Her shoulders slumped and her hands rested limply, hopelessly on her clean white apron.

'Why have they done it, Joss? We've done nothing to them, the Chapmans. It wasn't one of us . . .'

The voice from the corner was hard and bitter.

'No Mother, it wasn't but that bitch up there thinks it was. They've been here looking for you, Joss. The militia and then a troop of special constables. Quite gave the whole street something to talk about for days and what a thrill, watching them take this place apart and then there's our jobs . . .'

'Your jobs?' His voice was quite bewildered. 'What about your jobs?'

'We haven't got any. The lot of us were told last night we were to find other employment.' Jenny did not add that Mr Gribb had remarked brutally that they wanted no family of murderers working in the Chapman mill.

'But what . . .?' He could make no sense of it, she could see and when Jenny stood up her voice was harsh as she spoke.

'They think you did it, our Joss.'

'Did what, for Christ's sake?'

'You knew Chapman was killed?'

'Aye. By footpads, I was told.'

'No Joss, Onwardsmen, and the leader was Joss Greenwood.'

He began to laugh then, his whole face working in some strange frenzy.

'Dear God, does no one commit a crime which is not blamed on us?'

'They themselves said they were Onwardsmen.'

'Well, I wasn't there and I can prove it. For the past week I've been in Yorkshire talking to men there . . .'

'Working men?'

'Of course! Who else?'

'Will they be believed?'

'Richard Oastler will. I was with him for the whole week, and others who speak for reform . . .'

'Then go and tell them, for God's sake. Perhaps we'll get our jobs back. How are we to manage? Where are we to live? Dear God, I can't stand much more of this, lad. I've twisted and turned, like a bloody vixen with the hounds after it, trying to hold this family together. I've done things I'm not proud of, to feed them while you were in . . . in gaol. When's it going to end, Joss? When?'

'I don't know, lass, but we'll not give up . . .'

'*You'll* not give up! What about me? I'm twenty-two years old and for the past six years while you've been marching here and there, waving your sword in protest at what's been done to the working man, I've been clinging on to what we've got, fighting too, but for the survival of your family. Don't they say charity begins at home, our Joss? Well, how about some for me because I bloody well need it . . .'

'Jenny . . . lass, come on . . . don't weep . . .' He had risen to his feet, moving towards her, his face alive with his compassion but she turned away from him, putting her face to the wall and her voice was empty and quite without hope.

330

'I've kept us fed and dry and warm but I've worked hard for it, Joss. Hard and dirty.'

'I don't know . . .'

'I'll not tell you in front of the children, nor soil my mother with it, but I'm not ashamed. I'd do it again if I had to. I'm strong, Joss, stronger I think than you are and though I could just give up right now, put my face to the wall like this forever, it wouldn't do me any good, nor the child I'm carrying.'

'The . . .'

'Aye, so what are you going to do about it, Joss Greenwood, because I've had enough.'

He was put in the prison barracks at Oldham until they could check his story that on the night that Barker Chapman was killed he was in the company of Richard Oastler, and other men of repute who were fighting for the strange and seemingly amusing belief that children should work for no longer than ten hours in one day. It took a week and when he was released, with no apology or compensation, merely a strict admonishment to keep out of trouble in future, he walked the five miles to Crossfold, just as he was, dirty, unwashed, unshaven and as grim as the prison cell he had just left.

She was sitting in her father's office, *her* office now, her face absorbed as she studied some papers on the desk before her. The two men who had run after him when he passed through the ante-room, through the enormous counting house where her clerks worked, were hot on his heels but he threw them off with a flick of his wrists, his strength, it seemed, as powerful and undefatigable as his rage.

She stood up and the chair in which she had been seated crashed backwards to the floor. Her pale golden skin lost every vestige of its colour and her eyes were a vivid, vicious blue in her alabaster face.

'Miss Chapman . . . he walked past us . . . we did not know who he was . . . took us by surprise . . .' They were only clerks, their faces said and they eyed his menacing strength with some alarm, not really quite sure that even with two of them they could physically manhandle him from the building. 'Shall we call a couple of the yard men . . . ?'

'No . . . thank you, Chambers . . . you may go . . .'

'But Miss Chapman . . .'

'You may go.'

They did not speak for a full thirty seconds, each of them consumed with the heat of their enmity. It was almost a month since they had seen one another. They had made love, then afterwards leaned into one another's arms in peace and the lovely aftermath of it, dreaming together in the last warmth of the dying day. They had known that the time they had been allowed together must surely come to an end soon, but they had not known, on that last day, that it was ending then. They had kissed softly, lovingly, their mouths smiling against one another's, their hands clasped, unwilling to be parted, sighing, smiling again, returning for another kiss, then laughing with the joy of it.

Nothing of that day remained, here in this room as they eyed one another with a hatred as great as their love had been. She was the first to speak.

'Why are you not in prison?' she hissed. 'I know they arrested you. How did you get out? Tell me and be quick about it for you will be back there by nightfall.'

'For what reason should I be in gaol?' His voice was as malevolent as hers.

'For the murder of my father.'

'I did not do it.'

'Liar! You were seen there.'

'No.'

'You and your . . . Onwardsmen.'

'Perhaps them, but not me. I was in Yorkshire with a man whose reputation is above reproach.'

'It makes no difference. The results were the same. You and your . . . rabble. They and you are the cause of my father's death and I shall not forgive you for it.' Her voice was filled with her loathing of him and all he stood for. 'I hate you now, Joss Greenwood, with all my heart and if I can harm you I will. You are a murderer, no matter what your . . . your friends say, if they are to be believed . . .'

'It has been checked and found to be correct.'

'You and they are liars.' Her voice rose in an anguished scream and she threw back her head in pain for she knew he told the truth, but she would not, could not again be at peace with this man and so she chose to disbelieve it.

'I did not come to explain my whereabouts to you, madam.' His voice was as cold as the white hollows of snow which already were beginning to form in the 'tops' as winter approached and his spleen was as great as hers. 'I meant to give you the biggest thrashing of your life, as I would a man who had been as vile as you. That is what you deserve for what you have done to my family, but I . . . cannot. You are weaker than I and could not fight me as I need to be fought so I will content myself merely with saying this. You are not a woman. You have no warmth nor compassion. You have no humanity nor even the mercy of an animal which will put another out of its misery with one quick blow. Because of what you imagine I did to you, you have, without thought, thrown three women, one of them elderly, one pregnant, and two children on to the streets of Crossfold. You have taken away their employment, for what it was worth and consigned them to the workhouse, to poor relief for that is all they can expect now. Because of you and your kind they are to live on hand-outs, on charity, no more than the animals which are put on the earth for you to eat and to work to make you wealthy . . .'

'That is your fault, not mine. If you stayed at home and provided for them, as any decent man should instead of propping up your own arrogance with the "cause" you fight, they would not be as they are . . .'

She could see she had wounded him then and she pressed her advantage home eagerly.

' . . . you go about playing at soldiers, doing good, you tell yourself, stirring up those who know no better, to rebellion, while at home your own family starve for want of a man who is more concerned with his own triumphs than their needs.'

'You . . . bitch . . .' There was a terrible and quite unforgiving blankness in his eyes, a look that said that though he hated her for it, what she said could only be the truth and he was devastated by it. She could feel her own triumph flood through her veins, the joy which had replaced the despair when he had told her his wife was carrying his child. She allowed the strange thought, that which marvelled that in all this chaos, the enormity and strength of their need for revenge, the thing that had crucified her more than any other was that while he had been making love to her, he had obviously given the same pleasure to his wife who was now to bear his child. And *she*, Katherine Chapman, was not, and never would! She could feel the wound going deeper and deeper and even, she suspected, beginning to bleed and she turned the knife a little more in his flesh for he must suffer as she did.

'You call yourself a leader of men, probably a philanthropist, even a saint in your championship of the poor but you do no more than build up your own image playing at soldiers on the moor, killing men like my father . . .'

'I did not kill him.'

'Perhaps not, but your *men did* and that is all the same to me.'

'And so you take your vicious revenge by turning off my mother and sister, my wife . . . by putting two children into the streets to starve. Punish *me*, damn you, not them. If I had not come home when I did they would have raped my sister . . .'

'*Raped* . . . who . . .' She became still then, her face suddenly uncertain.

'Those thugs you sent to throw them into the street . . .'

'Thugs. I . . .'

'Don't pretend you know nothing about it. There were three of them, helping themselves not only to my mother's things but to my sister's . . .'

'Jenny . . . ?'

The virulent flow of his hatred was diverted for a moment, veering away from the narrow gully through which it ran towards only her. His voice faltered as she spoke his sister's name. With it she had brought a new dimension into their conflict and Jenny's voice rang cruelly, as hers did, asking for God's sake, where it would all end? He could feel himself grow weak, brought down, first by his sister, for her words had had the ring of well grounded truth in them, and then by this woman, who did no more than repeat it. But it made no difference. He must go on. He had given as many years as Jenny to this fight for what was rightfully his and theirs and no matter what it cost him he must continue. They *did* weaken him, the women he loved, all of them *because* he loved them but he must not let them divert him from what he knew to be right.

'Yes, Jenny,' he went on. 'They were about to have some sport with her. You see she is no more than a factory girl and who would blame them. As such she would be available to any man who had a fancy to take her down. Now no one would dare lay a finger on Miss Chapman or Miss Jenkinson for if they should it would be a hanging matter. And yet you are all women, all defenceless, the same under the skin and just as easily hurt or humiliated, but they have no defence, you see, the girls in your mill, or anybody's mill for if they should complain they would be turned off to starve. Ask Ellis, Kit Chapman. Ask him how he manages to live as high on the hog as he does and ask yourself how he managed it under your father's sharp eye without being dismissed himself. Ask yourself a lot of questions and you will find the answers in your own weaving-sheds and spinning rooms. Now I say this to you. Leave my family alone. If I find them harmed again I shall know where to look to find the culprit.'

He turned then, leaving her office so quietly those in the ante-room were not aware that he had left and when he was gone she turned blindly and stood for ten shaking minutes with her face pressed close to the wall, just as Jenny had. She did not weep for it was too deep, too shocking for that but her heart wept and indeed every sense in her body, every pulse and muscle and bone ached with the torment of it. He was gone forever from her life since what had been torn open so savagely could never be mended. He would never forgive her for what she had done to him and his family in her madness and in truth she could never forgive him for what he had done to her in his carelessness. He had every right to make love to his wife since she *was* his wife, but not while he was making love to her, her woman's illogical mind screamed. And he certainly had no right at all to incite men to murder others in a cause which though it might, some thought, be just, was definitely not rational.

But she would not dwell on it, she told herself doggedly since she must get on with her life, with the life she had fought so hard to retain for herself. She would not pine nor languish for something which, from the first had been frail and doomed to be short-lived. She had allowed herself once, years ago, nearly three now, to day-dream, but Joss had married and she had been forced on to other realities which had nothing to do with her love.

No, she would stiffen her spine and lift her head and do what she had always intended. She would run her father's mills ... *no, her* mills and it would be enough, she told herself.

She picked up the papers she had been studying when Joss had burst into the room, making a note here and there but all the while she trembled so violently her teeth chattered and the marks on the paper were no more than an illegible scrawl. The sense of betrayal and pain was so fierce it hurt her to breathe, the air about her taut and hopeless and difficult to drag into her lungs. She could not dispel the nightmare pictures from her mind of Joss Greenwood removing his wife's garments one by delicious one – as he had done with her – until she lay against him, her naked body trembling and ecstatic beneath the touch of his hands and lips – as hers had done – and quite simply she could not bear it.

336

But they would not go away, those pictures, remaining inside her head with a vividness which made it ache badly, pressing against her eyes so that the figures on the papers before her ran together. She felt she had lost weight and colour and substance within the last hour, everything she held dear draining from her and leaving her hollow.

A child! They were to have a child, Joss and Mercy Greenwood. Another woman was to give him what she never could and it would bind them together, he and his wife as no wedding vows could, or had. A son perhaps, to be led lovingly, for Joss would love his son, along the paths of reform all the Greenwoods seemed determined on.

She considered it. Joss and his son, and her mind began to slip away from reality, seeing them hand in hand, the smaller figure a replica of the larger and holding the child's other hand was his mother. Joss's wife, the woman who had given him the boy and therefore, dear to him.

The sense that Joss had broken a promise, though he had made none, been faithless, though she had no claims on him was so strong she bent over her desk, winded and gasping and she wished quite coldly that she could die of the pain.

There was, creeping over her, a terrible numbness and she was grateful for it. It would not last, of course but at that moment she welcomed its benevolence. She was suspended above the devastated, deceived woman at the desk, quite amazed by her calm but glad of it as picked up her pen and began to write.

Joss knocked on Sarah and Isaac Pickering's cottage door where he had left his mother and his family on the day he was taken to Oldham. He had not been able to think where else to put them, short of the workhouse and they had all, including Jenny, been in a trance-like condition of hopelessness which seemed to say quite plainly that they did not care *where* they went. A dangerous state of mind which he did not like but Sarah would look after them, she had told him compassionately until a place could be found

337

for them. A bit of a squash but Charlie could go in with her boys next to Isaac's hand-loom and the rest wherever there was a bit of space to put a pillow. He was not to worry, she had said stoutly, though she was glad of the few shillings he put in her hand. Isaac would go to Lousy Bank with his hand cart for the rest of their things, those Joss had not been able to carry and he was not to think about it. What were friends for, besides it would be grand to have Martha back. By, she'd missed her and their Jenny, but her eyes had studied Mercy somewhat warily for there was something not quite right about Joss's child-wife. A right pretty little thing she had been, still was for that matter, but her vulnerability, her strange air of having slipped away for a moment, inside her own head, was quite unnerving.

It was Sarah who opened the door to him and her gaunt, granite face, quite indomitable despite what life had heaped on her strong shoulders, smiled in pleasure. She was not much given to gestures of affection but she had a special place in her heart for the family of this man, and for the man himself since where would they be, all the working families of the cotton trade of Lancashire without the hope first Abel, then his son had given them.

'Nay lad, you're a sight for sore eyes an' no mistake. Come away in an' tell me't news. We'd 'eard you were to come 'ome today an' yer Mam's that excited she's bin backwards and forwards to't end of t'village looking for you. Your Charlie's only just this minute gone 'ome for 'is tea an' you should see't rabbit he caught. Well, your Jenny 'ad it skinned and in't pot before dratted thing was cold. She sent 'alf over to us . . .' She shook her head, marvelling on the generosity of those who, having barely enough to feed themselves will share what they have with others, seemingly unaware that she fell into this category herself. ' 'Ave yer been 'ome yet . . . well, no, you wouldn't, would yer, not knowing . . . eeh, Joss, what a miracle . . .'

He stood just inside the cottage doorway bending his head to avoid the low frame. His face was bewildered and his eyes roamed about the room. There was no fire for fuel must be saved for the winter and the room was cool and empty. Sarah had four living children, those who had survived the 'fevers' which weeded out the weak from the strong but none were in evidence, nor was Isaac and there was no sign of his own family.

Sarah began to laugh then. 'Eeh lad, your face is a picture and well it might be for we all 'ad a look just like yon when the chap came ter fetch yer Mam.'

'Fetch my . . . ?'

'Aye. On the day after you'd gone. 'E 'ad the key an' a bit o' paper which said the rent was paid an' if yer Mam wanted any 'elp she'd only ter say so.'

'Sarah . . . I don't quite . . . who . . . ?'

'Nay lad, no one knows who sent 'im nor why but yer Mam was made up with it an' I don't think she cared. She grabbed that key an' my mop an' bucket and was up the street like a girl. Your Jenny was still standing there, her gob open and Mercy . . . well . . .' The less said about Mercy Greenwood the better so she hurried on with her tale. 'We all went up, me an' Annie Bottomley, Ellie Aspinall an' 'elped yer Mam . . . Well, the place 'ad been empty for a long time an' it was a mess. Isaac made up a bit of whitewash and repaired a broken frame or two. Charlie an' my Jem went up to't tops an' cut some peat, fetchin' it back on't 'andcart an' . . .'

'Sarah . . . Dear God, Sarah . . . ay up . . .'

'I know, it 'ardly seems possible an' what they'll live on God only knows but *He* provided them with a roof over their 'eads so I reckon the rest will come . . .'

'No . . . not God, Sarah . . .'

'What d'yer mean, lad?'

'It wasn't God who gave my family back their home.'

Sarah put out a work-scarred hand and touched his grooved cheek. Her eyes were soft and compassionate. They all went hungry. They were cold and desperate and their men tramped miles across the moors looking for work. They accepted poor relief, many of them, and the benefit given them by the societies set up by the reforming men, a hard and bitter pill to swallow for men who had known independence and freedom. They did not like it and there was trouble coming again it was said, as trade worsened. But this man would not give in! Isaac and many of the others who congregated up at Abby Hobson's place on the moors, lost heart and became sullen, muttering of their grievances, their repeated disappointments but they had not suffered as this man had. He worked tirelessly, sacrificing his own family for theirs. He had gone to prison for them. He held them all together best way he could and never gave up hope that one day he would get for them what his father had told him they should have.

'Nay, Joss, no one's askin' who did it. Same one as dismissed them from t'mill and turned 'em out o' Lousy Bank, I reckon. We all do things in temper, say things we shouldn't when we think someone's done the dirty on us. After a bit we see sense again, when the madness leaves us an' then all we want ter do is make amends. We're sorry! We accept that we've made a mistake an' we try ter put it right.'

She looked at him and her wisdom was infinite and pitying. Throw no stones, Joss, she was saying, not until you're sure some have been thrown at you.

He could see Kit Chapman's face as he strode up the village street towards his old home, his *proper* home, his mother's home and for a sweet moment he allowed his love for her to flow over him and through him, cleansing him of the bitterness and the hatred. She had let him revile her, knowing as he did so that what he said to her was untrue, but she had not told him. She had given his family back their cottage, a place to shelter while he was away. She was a mill-owner now, one of the hated industrialists and as such could never associate herself again with a man like himself but she was fair and just, with pockets of goodness in her which would not allow his family to suffer because of him. She would never, could never allow the fragile emotion which had grown between them to remain, let alone blossom and so she had cut it out quite drastically.

She was *his* enemy but, her action said though *she* had not, that she would not, make war on his family.

His mother was at the cottage door and when he opened his arms wide she ran like a girl straight into them and her tears of joy were enough for him . . . *then*.

23

The man standing on Miss Charlotte Burton's doorstep was soberly dressed in good black and he was clean. His manner was very respectful. He had whipped off his hat when the door was opened to him and the parlourmaid had no reason to disbelieve that he was anything but what he said he was, an associate of Mr Harry Atherton.

'He's not here,' she said politely as Miss Burton required her servants to be.

'When will he be back,' the man said and it was then that the girl felt the first prickle of alarm, well, not alarm exactly, but disquiet for she was not accustomed to men of Mr Atherton's standing, and those others who 'resided' with Miss Burton, allowing their eyes to roam over her body quite so openly.

'I don't know. I think . . . perhaps you had better speak to Miss Burton, sir.'

'Perhaps I better had. Will you tell her I'm here.'

'Who shall I say is calling, sir?'

'Nay, she'll not know me, lass. Just show me in.'

'Well, Miss Burton likes to know who . . .' but the man had stepped inside the hallway, turning round quite boldly to stare at the heavy, old-fashioned furniture, the pictures Miss Burton's father had considered suitable for his wife and daughter to see, the fading splendour of what had once been the parson's fine residence.

'Please to wait here, sir,' the parlourmaid said nervously, not awfully sure she cared to leave this stranger in the middle of Miss Burton's hallway and not a man in the house to protect them should he prove awkward. She did not like the way his eyes assessed Miss Burton's possessions, nor the way they assessed herself since she was not unused to gentlemen's glances and this one was ... not nice!

'Miss Burton says she can spare you five minutes, sir,' she told him a moment or two later, not adding that her employer had told her to stay within earshot.

'How may I help you, Mr ... er ... ?'

'I'm looking for Mr Atherton, Miss ...'

'I am Miss Charlotte Burton, Mr ... er ...'

'Good day to you, ma'am,' and he looked pointedly at the chair by the blazing fire, opposite the one in which she sat but Miss Burton did not invite him to join her. She was a lady and knew instinctively, despite his fine clothes, that this was no gentleman.

'I'm afraid Mr Atherton no longer lives here,' she said distinctly, her hand hovering no more than an inch or two from the bell which would summon her parlourmaid to her. Like the girl, this man made her uneasy though he was polite enough. It was in his eyes, she thought, as though there was nothing he had not witnessed and nothing he would see that would ever shock him.

He looked surprised and then disbelieving, disposed, she thought, to swear, or ask her peevishly if she was quite certain and her hand moved to touch the bell on the table beside her.

'Where's he gone then? I only saw him a couple of days ago.'

'Perhaps you did, Mr ... er ... but he is no longer living here.'

'Well, that was quick. When did he leave?'

'See here, Mr ... er ... What has Mr Atherton to do with you?' for *he* was a gentleman, her attitude said.

'I worked for him, in a manner of speaking and we had

342

a bit of unfinished business to attend to. I hadn't expected he'd take off so soon or I'd a' bin round earlier.'

'Really! Well, I'm sorry I cannot be of more help to you.'

'Well, you can, I'm sure. He probably left his address. Gents like him always do, so if you'll write it down I'll get in touch with him.'

'I am afraid I cannot do that. I had no instructions from Mr Atherton to give his address to anyone.'

'No, but you know it though.'

'Of course, since he asked me to forward any mail.'

'Right, hand it over then.'

'I beg your pardon.'

'I think you heard what I said, Miss Burton. I want to write to Mr Atherton on a very urgent bit of business so if you'll give me his address I'll be on me way and leave you in peace. No harm done and no one any the wiser and if you touch that bell you'll wish you hadn't, believe me.' The last few words were uttered with such smiling geniality Charlotte Burton could only think that she had not heard aright but the man took a step towards her, his highly polished boots making no sound on her threadbare carpet. His eyes narrowed menacingly. They were the palest grey she had ever seen, almost without colour and in the dim light of the afternoon they looked almost white between his lashless eyelids.

'I don't like your tone, my man and I must ask you to leave my home at once or I shall be forced to send for the . . .' Her voice trailed away breathlessly as he put both hands on the arms of her chair, leaning so close to her she could smell the onions he had eaten for his dinner.

'No, I don't think so, Miss Burton, really I don't. Mr Atherton'll be well pleased to hear from me and wouldn't thank you if he heard you'd stopped us getting together. An' neither would I, see?'

Harry Atherton was at breakfast a week later when the letter arrived. It had been a period in his life which he would not like to re-live and as he slumped at the table, alone since the rest of the family had not yet risen, he

343

gloomily contemplated his future. What the hell was he to do, he asked himself, as his father had asked him, snarling, a dozen times since he had arrived at Atherton Hall with, as Samuel Atherton described it, his tail between his legs! He could not believe his ears, his father said over and over again in that first hour. A girl, a bloody mill girl had turned him down, turned him *out*, told him she no longer required his services, not only in business but as a husband. What the hell were you thinking of, boy, letting a woman of her class tell you what you should do, he had thundered. You were engaged, dammit, the contracts drawn up — dear God, the contracts which had stated in black and white exactly how he, Samuel Atherton was to benefit and through him the land which had been held in trust for his eldest son. They had been agreed, by himself and Barker Chapman and though at heart he had despised the man and would not in more favourable circumstances have given his girl a second glance, what that girl now had was morally theirs! And now Harry had allowed her, that was what galled him, *allowed* her to send him away like some mill-hand who had worked for her but no longer suited.

It had gone on and on, round and round in circles until it arrived back where it had begun, and then round again until Harry could willingly have put his hands about his father's throat and strangled him. His brother had been the same. The eldest son who was to have returned his birthright to its former glory with the money Barker Chapman was to pay them for what they had sold him. Now it was in ashes, the grand future, the lives they were to lead, the dowry his sister was to receive to tempt an impoverished but landed gentleman of their own kind into marriage. And his father, it seemed, could simply not get it into his head *how* it had happened, just as though Katherine Chapman was some foolish child, some pretty ninny without two words to say for herself and certainly not the gumption, nor the wit to see through the masquerade which was his son. Harry had sworn, in the heat of his almost senseless rage that he would not let it rest, that she would be sorry

344

that she had crossed swords with him, that he would find some way to repay her and as he opened the letter, idly scanning its ill-written contents it seemed that in his hand might be, must certainly be, the way to do it.

Kit Chapman and her mother were dining in almost complete silence. They had little to say to one another these two women who, though they had been brought up in the same surroundings with the same background of the solid industrial middle class, were so vastly different. During the day, and when the meal was over and she could retire to her father's study – still called that more than two months after his death – Kit could absorb herself in the minutiae of the working of her mills, studying accounts and patterns, balance sheets and designs, but during this trying hour or two in the evening she must do her best to hold a conversation with this woman. She was her mother and Kit had a responsibility to her, a certain fondness but apart from that biological fact they had nothing in common. Her mother was tearfully bewildered by her daughter's stubbornness in running the mills alone and, worse still, her declaration that she was not to be joined in marriage to Harry Atherton after all. It was a bitter blow from which Hannah Chapman could not recover and she was inconsolable. Her mourning allowed her to hide from many of the, she was sure, horrid innuendos which would be bandied about the chapelry of Oldham but her close friends and relatives were understandably concerned at her sorrow, not only for Barker and the dreadful way in which he had died, but for the loss of the splendid son-in-law of whom she had been so proud. Katherine was a heartless, perfidious daughter and disloyal to the memory of her father who had arranged this great match for her and could anyone blame her mother for the unforgiving disappointment she showed.

And so they lived uneasily together, each knowing they had no alternative, and when the butler informed Katherine that Mr Atherton was in her father's study and would be grateful if he might have a word with her when she had finished dining, naturally, their reactions differed so greatly, they each might have been given a different message.'

'Mr Atherton! Good God, what on earth does he want after all this time? I thought I had heard the last of him,' from Kit, and

'Mr Atherton! Oh, my dear, it is Harry. How wonderful . . . oh, how wonderful . . .'

'Tell him I will be there shortly, Winters,' from Kit, and

'Show him in immediately, Winters,' from Hannah and the flustered butler looked from one woman to the other, uncertain which he was to obey. Mrs Chapman had been mistress of the house for over twenty years and he had been here when she came, but Miss Chapman owned it all, and him, down to every last cup and saucer in the kitchen cupboard.

Kit sighed. 'Oh very well, Winters. Ask Mr Atherton to join us for coffee in the drawing-room.'

He was dressed, as they were, in the deep black of mourning and Kit felt a surprising bubble of laughter rise in her throat for really he was the supreme showman, acting the part of the young gentleman of breeding, which he was, still grieving, his demeanour said, which he was not, the loss of a man who had been not only a friend but one who he had hoped, in the future, to call 'Father'. He stood in the doorway of the drawing-room, his hand not exactly on his heart but very near it and Kit had again that strange desire to laugh. He really was absurd and could anyone take him seriously, she asked herself? She forgot the menace of their quarrel on the day she had dismissed him, was ready even to forgive his dalliance with Jenny Greenwood since it no longer had any connection with *her* life, willing to believe his story that – perhaps – Jenny had tempted him for she was an extremely striking young woman and irresistible to a man of Harry's self-indulgent nature. On that day she had been still raw and vulnerable, grieving her father, hating Joss Greenwood, eager to sever her connection with Harry himself and be on her own. She had been abrasive, unsure of herself, wanting to have them all swept away, Joss, Harry and the gentlemen of her father's acquaintance who were resolved to steer her where they thought she should go.

Now, with two months of calm, of running the mills as she wanted them run, of seeing the success with which she did it, she was softer, more forgiving, ready to smile and enjoy his amusing banter. No more than that, of course. She must admit to a certain surprise at seeing him but then he had always been of a shallow nature and quite unmoved by the darts of irritation she had often thrown at him.

'Mrs Chapman, my dear Mrs Chapman. It is unforgivable of me to impose myself upon you in your time of bereavement but I really could not leave the district without calling on you. I had unfinished business . . . a small matter and was about to board the coach to Chester but something held me back. Do say you are not offended.'

'Harry, my dear boy. How could we be offended? Indeed, any offence we might feel would have arisen if you had *not* called to see us. Would it not, Katherine?'

Indicating at once her firm resolve to draw her daughter to the attention of Harry Atherton, and of Harry to Katherine, Hannah allowed him to kiss her hand before almost pushing him towards Kit.

'Katherine, what can I say? These weeks must have been quite dreadful for you.' Her hand was in his and his eyes were brimming over with his concern but about his mouth played a small, disarming, quite impudent smile which was meant to tell her that really, she must not take him quite so seriously as her mother appeared to do. He was, of course, enormously sympathetic towards her in her sorrow and the devastation she must find in running the mills single-handed but if he could lighten her load, her day, this hour with his own brand of sly humour, he was more than willing. His eyes touched briefly, admiringly on the smooth gloss of her chignon and the stark black silk of her gown which, despite its severity was as fashionably elegant as any she wore. A simple sheath, highwaisted, banded just beneath her breasts with a thick cluster of black jet, her

347

pale golden shoulders rising from it, a black velvet ribbon round her slender neck.

'But may I say that your beauty has not suffered from it ... oh my dear, I do beg your pardon. I realise I should not be so forward now that we are no longer ...'

Did his wicked eyes gleam with unshed tears, she thought, or was that a twitch of amusement curling his well shaped lips, and the laughter which had bubbled in her rose to the surface and erupted in a most unlady-like chuckle.

'Oh Harry, will you never change? Why do you persist in this charade of sorrow for my father when the only regret it has caused you is the withdrawal of his money.'

'Katherine. You wicked, wicked girl, how could you?'

'Oh Harry knows what I mean, Mother and is not offended, are you Harry? It took a great deal of resolution to bring himself to work for my father and to engage himself to me but he applied himself to it with great courage. So what could a gentleman such as he, who would make a sacrifice so extraordinary, find offensive in a little honesty. No, Harry, do not look so humble, it does not suit you, nor so aggressive since I do not like it. Tell us what you want and let us have done with humbug.'

'You have not lost your capacity for sharpness, Katherine.' His smile was just as amused, with no glimmer of the affront he must surely feel and she was surprised for the words spoken on the day that they last met were coming back to her. He had told her then that she had not heard the last of him, calling her a bitch and worst of all in his eyes, no more than a factory girl, so why, eight weeks later should he be here, smiling, kissing her mother's hand – herself a factory girl, one presumed – and making himself generally pleasant to one and all. It made no sense for surely he was not naïve enough to imagine he could ingratiate himself back into her good graces after what had passed between them. Perhaps he wanted his job back since he must know he would never get *her*. And what of the 'business' he spoke of? With another mill-owner perhaps? As a salesman?

'So what are you doing back in Lancashire, Harry?' she said as she handed him a cup of coffee. 'Surely the delights of the hunt have not palled already.'

'No indeed, though I must admit to a certain boredom with a life of indolence after being so strenuously occupied in your father's mills.'

'Really.' She smiled disbelievingly.

'Really, Katherine.' He smiled sweetly at her over the rim of his cup. 'When one has been fully employed for as long as I was . . .'

'And well paid for it into the bargain.'

'Indeed, as you say. I found it hard to do nothing but merely drift through the days seeking one pleasure after another to alleviate the tedium.'

'Really Harry. You do surprise me.'

'I surprise myself.'

'And what are you to do about it?'

'That rather depends on you, Katherine.'

'I? What have I to do with it?' A small knot of tension had twisted itself beside her left temple since she did not care for the bright gleam of triumph . . . was that what it was? . . . in his eyes. He lounged carelessly beside her mother on the rose pink velvet of the sofa. The lamplight burnished his fair hair to gold and turned the healthy warmth of his face to a dark brown. The black of his coat seemed out of place on such a glowing, handsome young animal and yet its severity only served to enhance his masculine beauty. He was confident, sure of himself and she wondered uneasily what it was he wanted for his manner said he was perfectly certain he would get it.

Her mother yawned behind her hand, then apologised profusely.

'Dear me, these late nights really do not suit me any longer. I am long past the age when I can stay out of my bed beyond ten o'clock. Would you think me rude if I were to retire, Harry? I know it is not quite the thing but . . . well, you and Katherine have known one another so long I think I might be forgiven for overlooking the niceties.

You are . . . I feel as though you are . . . almost a member of the family . . . well, I'm sure you will know what I mean.'

There was much hand-kissing and bowing, of murmuring of how lovely it was . . . how charmed he was . . . of please *not* to be a stranger, and Hannah was escorted from the drawing-room to the foot of the staircase where her maid waited with a lamp.

'Good-night, dear boy,' she said, archly.

'Good-night, dear Mrs Chapman,' his eyes assuring her that everything would be all right and Hannah went to her bed that night for the first time since the murder of her husband, a delighted and hopeful woman, murmuring in her excitement that she would never be able to sleep.

'Now then, Harry,' Kit said when he had seated himself opposite her again. 'What is it you want?'

'How hurtful you are, Katherine. Why should I want anything? Can I not merely be a caller come to see how you, and naturally your mother, are doing.'

'No, not really, not Harry Atherton.'

'Yes, very hurtful indeed, as you were on the occasion of our last meeting.'

'We both said things in the heat of the moment but they cannot be taken back and nothing has changed.'

'My ambition to marry you has not, Katherine. I will give up the pretence that I have an all abiding passion for you although I cannot deny I find you a very desirable woman. I won't pretend, as I have pretended in the past because you are too intelligent, too shrewd to be taken in by any great spectacle of undying devotion but we could be very affectionate with one another, friends perhaps, lovers, of course and I would not stand in your way in the matter of the mills. They are yours and always will be. Come now, Katherine, admit we would do very well together, you and I. I make you laugh, can you deny it? I am . . . amusing and would make a good host at your table, a shield and protector . . .'

'My father said those very same words . . .'

'There you are, you see,' he said eagerly, 'and you set great store by your father's wisdom, did you not?'

'Harry, please, this is . . .'

'This is right for us, Katherine, you know it is. I am a superb salesman. Your father would not have employed me, had he not thought so. You need a man like me . . .'

'And you need a woman like me . . .'

'That is what I am saying, Katherine . . .'

'It's no good, Harry. I told you weeks ago that I did not want to marry and nothing has changed.'

His expression did, right before her eyes, so quickly she could hardly believe it. From eager, boyish charm to a rigid and absolute oppression which said that Harry Atherton had done his best to be reasonable and if she was not prepared to deal with that he could quite easily turn it about.

'Has it not, Katherine?' he said quietly. 'Are you sure?'

'Oh come on, Harry. How you do love to be mysterious. A boy playing games . . .'

'Not any more, Katherine. I have tried to be reasonable, to bring to you what can only be advantageous to us both, to point out to you in a friendly, gentlemanly fashion that really you are foolish to attempt this . . . this whim of being your father's successor alone. You need me, Katherine, and I intend to show you just how much.' He stood up, the charade of the young and amiable gentleman of breeding, minding his manners in the presence of a lady, slipping away at a quite terrifying speed and the true and dangerous face of Harry Atherton was revealed. His eyes became quite black as the pupils dilated and his face took on more colour with the sudden rush of angry blood to his head.

Why, he is mad, she thought dazedly, wondering why she had not seen it before. How has he kept it hidden so well for all these years unless it was that he had all he wanted, all that he had been promised and so had no need to let it be seen.

'Harry.' Even yet she did not acknowledge the danger she was in. 'What on earth are you talking about? I told you the last time we met that our relationship had ended. My father was the one who wanted this marriage between us, not I, and now that he is dead I am able to decide for myself . . .'

'No, my dear Katherine, you are not able to decide for yourself. I think you do not realise how much you need a man to guide you, to protect you . . .'

'Harry. If you continue to talk this way I shall be forced to ask you to leave. In fact I think you should go right now. We really have nothing to say to one another, have we . . . ?'

'Not even about Joss Greenwood?' His smile had become less of a wolf's grin now. He had her, it said, in a situation which had taken her by surprise and the knowledge had given him the strength to shrug off the rage to which he had momentarily succumbed. It pleased him to see her incredulous face, the shock in her eyes, the colour drain quite dramatically from her cheeks. It gave him a feeling of power and he loved it and quite pleasantly now, just as though the wildness she had seen in him had not occurred, he continued smoothly.

'You have heard of him, of course, Katherine, the reformer who is willing to suffer so dreadfully for his belief that the lower orders are equal to other men. To gentlemen, in fact, and that they should have what you and I have. A lunatic, in other words, who should be incarcerated in an asylum, or transported. What do you say, Katherine?'

'I really . . . I had not . . .'

'Come Katherine. You have such forceful opinions on everything from the morals of your own mill girls to the sorry notion that a woman is able to arrange her own life. Surely you must have considered this rebel who has gone against your own father, I believe. A machine wrecked, a warehouse burned down and if I am not mistaken, Barker Chapman's murder . . .'

'No . . .'

'No, Katherine! I was there! I saw the man and though this radical has drummed up the names of men who will give him an alibi, questionable in my opinion since I could never bring myself to take seriously those who are forever championing their "fellow-man". I do not trust them, nor do I believe that this Greenwood was with them on the night in question. I shall say so . . .'

'No . . .'

'Again no, Katherine. Can you have some information the authorities do not, perhaps?'

'No . . .'

'Then it is for some other reason that you deny his complicity, at least in your father's murder. What can it be? Come Katherine . . .' His tone was silky and as she struggled to regain her composure she could see the frenzy of his joy, the joy which knew no bounds as he took his revenge for her own mockery, her own contempt of him eight weeks ago.

'You know this man, do you not, Katherine? Rather better than you are willing to admit. There is something between you which you thought you had kept secret but you see, my dear, whatever you do, no matter how careful you are, there is always someone who notices that your actions, unremarked by most, are unusual.'

He was completely self-possessed now, in control of himself and her and the enchantment of it had him in a thrall. Katherine Chapman, at whose hands he had suffered humiliation after humiliation was looking at him with eyes in which there was nothing but a dreadful blankness.

'It's true, is it not, Katherine, go on, admit it. He is your lover, is he not? Joss Greenwood. A common labouring man has . . .' Here he spoke words of such obscenity her mind reeled with it, retreating into a place where she could not hear them, could not have him tarnish the most precious things she had known and though his voice went on and on and she could hear the sound and see his lips move, the words were unintelligible. She must pull herself together. She must gather her wits from every scattered corner of her trembling mind, gather them and piece them into a whole, into coherent thought since she must not only defend herself

353

from this madman she must attack him so that he could not do battle again. He had shocked her, stunned her, but not for long . . . oh no, not for long.

She could actually feel the warm blood begin to course through her veins, rushing strongly to her heart until it beat in a tattoo of rage equal to his own and her eyes glittered savagely. As her head snapped up, bringing his words to a sudden halt she had time to realise, and even smile a little inside herself, for was she not as wild as Harry Atherton?

'How did you come by this foolishness, Harry? Who was your informant for indeed he is as mad as you.'

'*He!* I did not say it was a man.'

Dear God, not . . . not Jenny? It could not be Jenny . . . and then her mind cleared and was brilliantly sharp again. Jenny Greenwood knew nothing about herself and Joss and if she had it was not likely she would put the information in the hands of this man who had seduced her. In that first week after her father had been killed and Kit had thought Joss had killed him, her desire for revenge had included his whole family. She had put them out in the street, taken their work from them but she had regained her sense of justice, become aware of her own wickedness and arranged for them to have their cottage returned to them. She had compensated them for her brief lapse into the bitterness and hatred of those first few days, tried to help them in different ways and she was certain Jenny Greenwood would know of it. So who? Who had put her in the hands of this man? Who?

'It does not matter, man or woman. You can go to hell and take your foul tongue with you.'

'Oh ho, my fine lady. So that is the attitude you are going to take, is it? And if I put it about the district that Joss Greenwood has his hand up the petticoats of . . .'

'Stop it, you bastard . . .'

'You don't like that, do you, or at least you don't like to hear it spoken of by me. Well my dear, unless we come to some arrangement, you and I, it will be spoken of by every mill-owner in the Penfold Valley. They will not take kindly to the knowledge that one of their own is consorting with a man who is doing his best to put them out of business . . .'

'What kind of arrangement would that be, Harry?'

'Why, exactly the one we had before your father died, I think.'

'You are willing to take on the well used goods of a working man. A woman who has . . . what was the phrase . . . had the hand of a labourer up her petticoats?'

'If she is as well placed as yourself, Katherine. I am not overly particular . . .'

'You must be insane.'

'No, but you will be if you do not do as you are told.'

'Get out of my house, Harry. Now! Or I will have you thrown out.'

'The wedding I think, next month, but I will return to the mill tomorrow and go through the books with you. We can put it about – I'm sure your mother will help us here – that you have suffered a nervous disorder brought on by your father's death but you are recovered now, your old self again and that you and I are re-united . . .'

She began to laugh then. It was so dreadfully absurd. Could he not see she really did not care what he did, or said? He could do nothing to hurt her. She was not concerned with what people said of her. They had talked about her ever since she was thirteen and her father had allowed her out on the moor with only her dogs for company. She was one of the wealthiest, most influential women in South Lancashire and not one of her business associates could afford to get on her wrong side. She was the foundation on which many of the smaller mill-owners had built their businesses. Dozens of them owed her money and if she called it in they would be unable to carry on. It was a practice her father had begun years ago, astute, shrewd, knowing that a man who is owed money has the loyalty of those to whom it is loaned. She had position and if not exactly the respect of other mill-owners, men of authority in the chapelry of Oldham, for they could make no sense

355

of her determination to run her father's mills, at least she had their ear. They might not care to know that she and Joss Greenwood were more to one another than adversaries on two sides of a battle but there was nothing they could do about it, whether they were to believe it, or not. They could not ignore her, certainly, if she were to make a complaint — defamation of character, was it called? — against Harry Atherton, that is if she cared to, despite his breeding. He was not a Lancashire gentleman, not one of them and though his word might be listened to, would it be heeded? Would they believe, could they really believe that, despite her strangeness Miss Katherine Chapman, daughter of Barker Chapman, would associate in *that* way, in *any* way, with a man such as Joss Greenwood. It was a chance she must take. She must find out where Harry had obtained his information and it would not take long for his accomplice must be silenced too. A man in her own mills to know so much about her — and her connection with the Greenwood family. A man in authority. That must be it, that must be the source of Harry's information and if she put her mind to it there was no doubt that by the end of the night she would have his name.

She turned to Harry who had moved to lounge insolently against the fireplace. He was at home, his manner said, back where he belonged and reaching inside his jacket he brought out his cigar case. Selecting a cigar he lit it without asking her permission, blowing smoke agreeably into his own air, in his own drawing-room, looking about him at his many splendid possessions, not least of all, the woman who sat on the sofa.

He smiled when she told him that if he did not remove himself from her home and her life within the next thirty seconds she would call her men-servants and have him flung into the driveway. He was still smiling as she reached for the bell and even when she told the butler, smoothly, to bring Dick and Jack and Robert for Mr Atherton was leaving and seemed in need of assistance in finding the front door.

He was not smiling as he flogged his bay down the gravelled driveway towards the gate.

24

'You're ter go up ter't "Five Pigeons" but not until after dark, Mr Greenwood,' the urchin said, grinning amiably despite the temperature which was several degrees below freezing, the rag or two he wore for modesty's sake, and his bare, chilblained feet.

'What for, lad?'

'Nay, I dunno. Lady said it were urgent and you was ter tell no one.'

'What lady?' but could there be any other 'lady' up there on the bleak and windswept moorland except Abby Hobson, two years older now but every bit as bounteous and blooming as she had been when she had drawn him into the comfort and release of her body when he had needed it. Not that her favours were in any way directed at him these days, though he dared say they might be if he was to ask. She was not a woman to live the life of a nun though she must be approaching forty and would be taking what she needed, giving what was needed, good-natured and uncomplicated, both in her sexual nature and appetite, and her feminine wisdom.

'I dunno. She gimme sixpence an' said you'd do't same.'

'Don't go, Joss. I don't like it. What's that woman up at the inn want wi' you. There's all sorts go there, thieves and vagabonds, tinkers and wanderin' vagrants . . .'

'Now mother, there's no such folk drink at Abby Hobson's place for she'd not allow it.'

He smiled to himself as he remembered her, openhearted and generous with the occasional free jug of ale to a man

357

who had not two halfpennies to rub together in his trouser pocket but who had come, nevertheless, to listen to the hope, the optimism, the despair, the anger of others like him in the fight for a decent life. Militant radicals. Men like himself who put heart in them. A meeting place then for those who would, had it not been illegal, have formed a trade union, and Abby had allowed it, as many publicans did for were they not of the working class themselves? But thieves and vagabonds, tinkers and wandering vagrants, indeed any man Abby did not like the look of would be shown the door for she'd have no 'riff-raff' in her place.

'Happen there's some trouble. The Onwardsmen would meet there and if they wanted me in on it what better way than to put the name of Abby Hobson on the boy's lips. They could hardly send a message to say *they* wanted to see me, could they? If the lad was questioned and mentioned *her* name they would only smile and take me for one of her . . .'

'Joss! There's no need for talk like that, not in front of your wife.'

They both turned to look at Mercy Greenwood who sat in the chimney corner playing with a marmalade kitten, holding it to her breast, then to her cheek, crooning a little song, her eyes shining in delight, her smooth cheek rosy in the firelight. She looked exactly like some small girl who has been given a gift and cannot express her joy in it. The kitten jumped suddenly from her lap, its sharp claws catching the threads of her skirt, then skittered sideways as she bent to retrieve it.

'Naughty kitten. You mustn't do that or you'll hurt yersen,' she laughed and held the struggling animal to her in a passion of love.

Joss and Martha sighed simultaneously as their eyes met. Not in front of Mercy, she had said, just as though his wife would know what he meant, should he have told her, that once Abby Hobson had been for a short while, his lover.

'I was only implying that to give the child such a message was . . .'

'I know, lad,' and his mother sighed again for really it was almost more than she could bear at times, this creeping about after dark, the mysterious callers her son had and journeys he made to God only knew where. She had hoped after his spell in prison that it might, with his grand new job of journalist, all end and she could sleep snug in her bed knowing all her family were safe where they should be, snug in *theirs* but it seemed her hope was forlorn.

'Give the lad a bite, mother . . .' he turned to the boy who had edged closer to the warmth of the fire and the fascination of the leaping kitten, ' . . . see, here's another sixpence.'

He stepped out across the moor, rough and pitted with rabbit holes into which he might stumble, scattered with rocks on which he might turn his ankle and the icy, moorland streams hidden in the coarse frosted grass which, if he did not move warily would soak him to the knees freezing his boots to his feet and his trousers to his calves.

There was a pallid moon moving in and out of a thin veil of cloud but he could still scarcely see his hand before his face. He walked quickly for, despite his protestation to the contrary to his mother, there *were* beggars and ne'er-do-wells wandering these hills and possibly special constables sworn in to capture those impudent working class men, his own Onwardsmen, who had the ridiculous notion that they were as good as any other man and drilled up here on every moonlit night, forming themselves into an army to fight for it!

He felt a strange sense of urgency, a prickling, crawling sensation at his back and once or twice he looked over his shoulder as though he was being followed, smiling as he did so at his own fancifulness.

The wind got up and he shivered. It was January and as cold as charity up here. There would be snow before the night was out, he told himself as he breasted the brow of a hill and began to descend into a hollow at its foot. There were high, natural stone walls about it, thrown there by the elements and as he reached the bottom the wind parted the clouds, the moon shone brightly and in that moment, a brief moment before the darkness covered them again, he saw them.

Six of them. Big, huge shouldered men, men probably from one of the 'navvy' camps which surrounded each town and sprawled across open countryside where the railway tracks were to run. Men used to manual labour, wielding picks and shovels, with calloused hands and fists, thick, muscled legs. Troublemakers for the most part who would kill or maim, whichever was asked of them, for the price of a jug of ale.

The moon came sliding out of the cloud again and stayed there, hanging in the purple-blue sky, illuminating the moorland and standing some way to the left, his back against a tall rock, indolent, a gentleman smoking a gentleman's cigar, was a man Joss had seen several times in the vicinity of Chapman's mills. An arrogant man with a haughty lift to his head, the hair on it shining a pure silver in the moonlight, his well-bred countenance smiling a little as the six men began to close in on their prey.

'Take him,' he said casually, drawing again on his cigar, settling himself comfortably to watch just as though he was a spectator at a boxing ring where bare knuckle prize fighting was to take place.

Joss knew he must get his back against his own rock. Some protection at least, as the men began to circle him slowly, their eyes gleaming, slit-like in their anticipation of the blood they would spill and the bones they would crack. He felt the stone at his back and his last clear image as he went down was of Kit Chapman's face.

There were too many of them, of course, for as he turned to one or two, the other four or five came at him from his blind side. The fist which crashed against his temple was as big as the hooves of a cart-horse. There was nothing to be done but try to protect his vital parts, his chest, his eyes and his brain, to curl up into the position in which he had come from his mother's womb and hope to God they did not mean to kill him for if they did there was little he could do to prevent it.

There was nothing, once he was down for them to get their fists to so they used their boots instead, not hastily or even with any passion, but in a leisurely fashion which said they knew they would not be disturbed, systematically laying their steel-tipped toe caps from one end of his body to the other until he knew, as his mind slipped away he must look like nothing less than a bundle of bleeding rags. His ribs had gone for his own breath was agony as it scraped in and out of his tortured lungs and the last thing he heard was the well-bred voice of the lounging gentleman.

'Leave him now, lads. That will do. I will pay you . . .'

She was at dinner when the message was put into her hand. It was brought in on a silver salver, a scrap of paper which looked as though it might have passed through several hands before it reached hers.

'This was delivered a few minutes ago, Miss Katherine.' Winters' tone was haughty and not at all pleased for he was not accustomed to having such things thrust at him at the *front* door, mind, by ruffians like the one who had delivered it.

'What is it, Winters?' She put down her wine glass aware that her mother had raised a wisp of scented lace to her nose as though the grubby piece of folded paper was sure to carry some dreadful disease.

'Indeed I could not say, Miss Katherine, but the . . . man who handed it to me was most . . . definite that you should have it at once. Quite . . . offensive, he was, even threatening.'

'Threatening, Winters? Good heavens . . .' and she was smiling as she read what Harry Atherton had written. The blood drained away from her face quite dramatically and Winters told Mrs Batty later that he thought she had been about to faint, indeed he did, and as for Mrs Chapman, well, she began to utter small cries of fear and had it not been for Dorcas, a sensible girl, thank God, would have fallen herself into her bowl of soup.

She was out of the room and up the stairs, the note still clutched in her hand and all the while she was ripping away her lovely evening gown and replacing it with the sensible woollen dress – no petticoats for they would weigh her down – her walking boots and a black, fur lined cloak with a hood against the splinters of snow which were already beginning to fling themselves at the window, she did not once let go of it. It was her link to Joss, one which she dare not break nor cast aside for if she should, might she not lose her sense of direction, the sure instinct which would take her to the exact spot described in it.

No carriage then for the track was narrow, hard and stony and the coachman, a sensible man with concern for his horses, she thought, even more than for his mistress, would probably refuse anyway. She would walk it, run it, fly the distance if she only could, for if she did not get to him in time the cold would finish him off should his injuries have not already done so.

'He has taken the beating for you though I am sure you will suffer just as painfully,' the note said. Dear God, let him live . . . and she had laughed at him, thinking he could not harm her, that there was nothing she cared about that he could destroy. Let him spread his rumours and gossip about Kit Chapman and Joss Greenwood, whisper in the ears of her business associates of her love for the son of a weaver, a convicted felon, a troublemaker, what did she care for none of them dare cut themselves off from her. She was too strong, too wealthy, too influential for him to do her harm. So he had found another way to punish her for what she had done to *him*.

Dear God, let him live, she prayed as she let the dogs out of the stable for even she dare not go up alone on to that sinister night-time moorland which must surely contain in every hole and ditch hungry men who would slit her throat for the boots on her feet. The dogs sensed her fear and clung about her skirts, silent and menacing, protecting her, their attitude saying, from anything which might leap at them from the shadows and which they would quickly dispose of.

It was two hours before she found him, exactly where the note said he would be. A place, if she had not known the moors as well, possibly better than the garden surrounding her own home, she would never have come across. God knows how long he had been there and for an agonised moment she thought he was dead. She could see the congealed and frozen blood on his mauled face, so dark with bruises and whatever other injuries he had received it was difficult to distinguish against the black and frozen ground on which he lay curled. The snow, whipping in hard pellets about her crouching figure had not yet got a hold but she knew that if she did not get him moving in the next few minutes he would die.

'Come alone,' the note had said, 'or the next time it will be worse . . .' *The next time . . .* Oh dear God . . . Dear God, let him live . . .

'Joss, get up, Joss,' she snarled in his ear since this was not the time for patience and sympathy.

He was scarcely conscious and did not know her, or care to be bothered in any case.

'Get up, damn you,' and she pulled violently at his arm, glad in every part of her frenzied mind of his terrible scream.

He began to moan, moving feebly, begging her to let him alone, to let him lie still since the agony was too great to be borne.

'You will have to get up because if you don't you will die, Joss Greenwood. They will be here soon, the men who roam the hills looking for anything that will give them a square meal and a jug of ale. They will have heard you, or sensed you, as animals do the wounding of one of their own kind and they will gather to take their share of the kill. They will not need to choke you to death for the cold will have finished you off. Get up, damn you or I swear I will leave you to them.'

'Leave me then,' she thought she heard him say and again

she tore at his arm, hearing the awful sound of bone grating on bone and the shriek of his pain carved her to her own bone but she would not let him be.

'Get on your feet, you coward. Stand up for I cannot carry you, nor, if I had the strength for it, would I. Come on, Joss Greenwood. They told me you were a leader of men. *You* told me you were a leader of men but I can see no sign of it now since it seems you are prepared to lie here and die like a rabbit in a trap.'

'Kit . . . for God's sake . . . I cannot . . .' it sounded like, but his mouth was torn and a strip of flesh was frozen to his bloodied lips.

'Give me your good arm, dammit.'

'I . . . cannot move . . .' and at her back one of the dogs began to snarl at something, his hackles raised, his head flat, his eyes looking into the darkness which contained a scent, or a movement which he did not like. It might be no more than a moorland animal hunting its prey but it frightened her and her fright gave her strength.

'I don't give a damn how much it hurts you, Joss Green-wood,' she hissed through clenched teeth, '*You will get on your feet.*'

It took ten long minutes to half-lift, half-lever him on to the waist high rock at his back, his own efforts a little stronger now. She took off her warm, fur-lined cloak and wrapped it about his shivering, groaning body, careless of the blood which his movements had started flowing again, feeling its warmth soak into her bodice and drip on to her shaking hands.

'Come on, stand up. You're a hero, you are, to all those men who follow you so let's see your bravery. Stand up. Put your good arm about my shoulder and one step in front of the other. Joby . . . Blaze, to me . . . that's right . . . careful, lean on me . . .' which she really had no need to tell him to do for he was like some man the worse for drink, his weight dragging her down, straining her muscles to the point of agony.

'Let . . . me . . . rest . . .'

'No, keep going, damn you . . .' since she knew that if she put him down she would never get him up again.

'Kit . . . please . . .'

'No . . .' and it seemed to occur to neither of them to wonder, he that she should be there at all; she that she had not hesitated to come.

The path was no path at all, merely the most direct route to Edgeclough, and she took it, her instinct telling her that that was where help would be. She dragged him on to it, that unsteady, hole-riddled, rock-strewn path, making no effort to go slow and steady, no effort to spare him pain since she was shivering violently now without her cloak. *She* was the crutch on which they both depended. *She* was the eyes to lead them to safety and if she fell by the wayside they would *both* go down.

On and on and on. Hours of it, days of it, weeks, and their breath, hers as well as his, rasped, burning excrutiatingly in their throats.

'I . . . can't . . .'

'You . . . can . . . and you . . . bloody well . . . will . . .'

A rock turned beneath her foot and for a despairing second she knew she was about to fall but somehow, though it tore her arm and wrenched a moan of pure and exquisite agony from Joss, she righted herself.

And then there were lights. Just a pinprick or two in the dark fabric of the night. The smell of peat smoke and the drift of pale grey against the blackness, coming from a chimney, a baby crying behind some cottage door and they were at Martha Greenwood's garden gate.

They took him from her, his mother's cries echoing about the cottage kitchen, his sister giving her a look of pure, venomous hatred, knowing somehow that this was to do with *her*. There were half a dozen people, it seemed and an urgent voice telling Charlie to ' . . . keep Mercy upstairs, for God's sake lad, or she'd go out of her mind if she sees this . . .' *And a pregnant woman might miscarry with the shock of it!*

Another, a woman, barked out orders to run and fetch

this, or that, to put that there and hold that here, and to be careful with that hot water, for God's sake and to watch his arm since it looked broken to her.

They did not take him up the stairs to the loom-shop where, apparently, she gathered from the garbled conversation, he slept, since the task was beyond them all but brought down some sort of a truckle bed and without another glance in her direction, stripped him naked, cutting away most of his garments, and laid him on it. His mother wept silently over his white body which, for the most part, was now red and black with bruises.

She stood like some frozen statue, nailed to the door through which they had half-dragged, half-carried him and watched while the woman — dear God, it was the one she had spoken to . . . when was it? . . . who had told her the Greenwoods had left Edgeclough — bathed and stitched him together, cleansed and soothed with some liniment almost every inch of his mangled body, strapped his arm and his chest so tightly she heard him curse her and finally when it was done, kiss him soundly on the cheek.

'I reckon thee'll 'ave a right shiner in't mornin', Joss Greenwood,' she told him fondly, 'but thee'll live.'

'No thanks to you, Sarah Pickering,' he whispered faintly. 'I feel a bloody sight worse than before you got your hands on me.'

'Who did it, lad?' They hung about him; the woman called Sarah, his sister, his mother and his brother and with Mercy off to sleep again, Joss said breathlessly, 'Some gang of footpads, I reckon, who fancied having the gold rings off my fingers.'

'But what of the message from Abby Hobson?'

'I never got to find out.' His voice was fainter now and his glance which had caught hers, slipped away but not before it had told her that this was between the two of them and not to be spoken of now.

'Abby Hobson? What would she want with our Joss?' Jenny Greenwood reared up from the protective position she had taken up beside her brother but the older woman,

Sarah, was spooning some liquid into Joss's torn mouth and indicated vigorously that they were all to step back from her patient.

'Let 'im rest, Jenny. 'e can answer all yer questions tomorrow. 'e'll sleep now wi' this I'm givin' 'im, 'appen for twenty-four hours, so leave 'im be an' get to your beds. The mill gates'll be open in a few hours . . .'

It was as though the words reminded them that the owner of those very mill gates was still standing where they had left her at the cottage door. She was not important. It was because of her, and others like her that Joss Greenwood was lying as he was, mauled almost to death by men who surely must have something to do with opposing the very things *he* fought for, since they had not believed the statement about the footpads for a minute. He had been savagely beaten by men who knew him since *someone* had sent the false message to get him up on the moor in the dead of night and *she* was involved for how else had she known of it and brought him home?

But she *had* brought him home and would you look at the state of her. They did, now that their Joss had been seen to. She was wet through to her undergarments, which would be of the very finest there was no doubt of that, and all over the front of her, down her bodice and dark grey skirt were brown stains which could only be Joss's blood for she herself was not injured. Her long hair had come down and was snarled in a wet and filthy tangle about the chalk white blankness of her face and she shivered so violently the door at her back rattled in its frame.

'Sweet God, get 'er t't fire before she teks a fever. See, Jenny, run up an' get some blankets . . .'

'Not me, for it's her fault our Joss is . . .'

'Don't answer me back, Jenny Greenwood.' Sarah Pickering's voice was like thunder in the small room and already Martha had her arm about Kit's unresisting shoulders, leading her to the warmth of the fire. 'Fetch me them blankets or I'll fetch you a backhander you'll not forget in a hurry.'

Charlie was sent to bed since he had to be up at four, they said, and he could do no good hanging about their Joss who was fast asleep anyway under the influence of the herb potion Sarah had given him, and with Jenny holding a blanket to the fire to warm, she was stripped as unceremoniously as Joss, placed in the rocking-chair without words since they'd none to give her, only the impersonal benevolence they would give any hurt creature which happened by their door. Hot tea was poured down her throat and her flesh rubbed until it was raw but the blood flowed again beneath her skin, tingling until she could have cried out with the pain of it.

'Will you tell us about it, lass?' Sarah said at last, more forthright than Martha, more forgiving than Jenny who could not even bring herself to look at this woman she hated above all others.

'No.' It was only a whisper in her throat but they heard it.

'What were you doin' up theer at this time o' night? Not walkin' them savage beasts beyond yon door, I'll be bound.'

'I had a . . . message . . .'

'Who from?'

'I cannot say.'

'Come on, lass, we weren't born yesterday. Why should someone knock the livin' daylights out o' Joss Greenwood and then send for Katherine Chapman to carry 'im 'ome? You an' Joss are on opposite sides in this bloody war.'

She stood up suddenly, her manner imperious, despite the tangle of her hair and the grey blanket which she held close about her, or perhaps because of it for it was like a Queen's mantle.

'One wonders why anyone bothers to try and help you people,' she said, her voice high-toned and disdainful, 'if this is the thanks one receives. Really it is beyond belief. I drag that man miles over the moor at great inconvenience to myself and instead of a bit of decent gratitude that he has been returned to you in a *curable* condition, perhaps a word of thanks which would not be out of the way, I am

368

cross-examined on my reasons, not only for doing it but for being on the moor myself. Perhaps I was there to meet a lover.' Her eyes flashed blue sparks and even Jenny Greenwood was impressed into silence. 'Or perhaps I was not but whatever it was it has nothing to do with you. I may have been walking my dogs, or myself, or I may not, but whatever the reason for my being there be thankful I was for it saved the life of . . . of the man on that bed. I was there. I came upon your son, madam . . .' this to Martha, '. . . and I brought him home as I would *any* wounded creature I found. That, I'm afraid, will have to satisfy you. Now, if I might have my things I will be on my way. No . . .' this to Sarah, ' . . . I do not need an escort since I have two outside. It would take a brave man, or a very foolish one, to tackle them.'

'They say t'best defence is ter strike first,' Sarah murmured when she had gone.

It was three weeks later – a Sunday and there had been a fresh fall of snow during the night making walking difficult but she managed to get as far as Friars Mere. The dogs had floundered beside her, thrusting their heavy black bodies through a foot of snow, blundering occasionally into a deeper drift, their expressions comical in their amazement and her laughter was the only sound in the vast, white emptiness. She wore trousers beneath her skirt, the fullness of it tucked up into her waistband and though her boots were often up to their tops in the soft and powdery snow she was exhilarated, feeling easier and less prone to the bouts of anxiety with which she had been harried since the night of Joss's beating. She had longed to go down to the spinning room and accost his sister, beg to be told how he was a dozen times each day. To call up her dogs and stride out to Edgeclough, to hammer on his mother's door and beg to see him, to be reassured that he was not permanently damaged, that he was healing, that he was not blind, or crippled but she knew she must not. He was with his family, his wife and she must leave him there now. She had done what she had to three weeks ago for what had happened to him had been *her* fault. Now she must continue in the only way she could for him, for his wife and unborn child and leave him to get on with his life, as she must get on with hers.

The sun shone on the rolling beauty of the white hills, criss-crossed with the tops of crumbling dry-stone walls and in between each stone the snow had blown, making patterns of crystal mosaic. There were shadows cast by the skeleton trees and scattered rocks, blue-smudged, from the paleness of a bird's egg to the deep purple-blue of an amethyst, and the air was so clear and sharp it went to her head like champagne.

She saw him coming up the snow covered track, trudging slowly, his head down, his arm bound tightly beneath his jacket, one sleeve of which dangled empty. His breath curled about his dark head and she could hear it quite clearly in the still air as it moved in and out of his lungs. He was nearly half a mile away and had not seen her but she knew, unamazed by it, as she knew all his thoughts as though they were her own, that he was on his way to Greenacres to see her.

'Joss.' Her voice lifted his head. 'Wait there, I'm coming,' and the snow no longer impeded her as she flew across it, leaping and laughing, her heart singing, her sad intentions all forgotten in the joy of seeing him.

He stopped and waited for her and she could see in his face the effort it had taken for him to walk the two miles from Edgeclough across the wilderness of the snow covered moorland. His still swollen eyes were ringed with deep purple bruises and though the contusions were fading and almost healed his face was pallid with the look of a man only recently risen from his bed.

Her joy brought forth his own, reluctantly.

'I know. I look as though I have just done a dozen rounds in the boxing ring, and lost the bout.' He tried to grin.

'How are you?'

'Healing.'

370

'Your arm . . . ?'

'Will be as good as new, Sarah tells me, and who am I to argue with *her*. Fortunately it is not the one I use for writing.'

'I'm glad.'

'I had to see you,' he said simply.

Could she turn from him as her betrayed heart had told her, weeks ago, that she should, when they faced each other like this, the simplicity and the truth of their love shining between them. She sighed sadly, knowing she was tied to this man and his destiny with bonds which might be invisible but were stronger than the binding of the rocks to the ground on which they stood. But he had not come to smile and gaze at her, as he was doing, she knew that, but for another reason.

'I would have died but for you.'

'I can't tell you, Joss,' she said, knowing what he would say next.

'You cannot expect me to let this pass, Kit. He nearly killed me and I want to know why.'

'You . . . saw him?'

'Oh yes, and saw him smile before I went down.'

'Dear God!'

'Why, Kit?'

'Because of me, Joss. Because I sent him away. He swore then he would make me suffer for it and, having learned somehow about you and me, he did it in the surest way he knew.'

'I cannot let it go, you know I cannot. I am not fit yet but when I am . . .'

'No, Joss.'

'No man does this to me, Kit Chapman. No man, least of all your . . .'

'Please, you know . . . I was forced into it by my father. The moment I was able I told him I wouldn't marry him. He made threats but I laughed at him . . .'

'Where does he live?'

'Let it go, Joss, for God's sake . . .'

'*Let it go!* He damn near crippled me and you tell me to let it go.'

'I know it can't be easy for you simply to ignore it. To pretend it didn't happen, or at least to try, but I will not let it continue . . .'

'*You* won't let it continue.'

'No.'

'Where does he live? If you don't tell me I'll find out somehow.'

'His family is powerful and if you were to harm him they . . .'

'It's all right for *him* almost to kill a man from the lower orders, is that it, but not for that man to seek justice?'

'Joss, he would deny it and he would be believed. They would ask themselves why a man of his . . . standing should bother himself with a . . .'

'With a man of *mine*, is that it?'

They were both breathing hard and she could see the pain it caused him, the simple act of drawing the cold air into lungs which might have been damaged. But she could not tell him. Would not, for if he was to go to Atherton Hall and confront Harry Atherton, which was probably what Harry hoped for, he would arrange it somehow for Joss to spend the rest of his life in gaol.

She turned away from him, her face quite expressionless for he must not see how much it cost her.

'I cannot tell you where he lives, Joss, and I never will. If you wish to do yourself further damage then you must do it without my help. And now, do you not think it wise for you to return to your wife and . . . She will be worried about you. Joby, Blaze . . . to me.'

And with the tears which he did not see, freezing on her pale cheeks, she walked away from him.

Jenny Greenwood had worked until the day her son was born, not caring very much if she harmed him, or herself, at her old machine in Chapman's spinning mill. Surprisingly, when she had asked at the gate for work, having been told by Isaac Pickering that they were 'taking-on', a fortnight after they had returned to Edgeclough, she was told that there was and that if she knew of someone who could 'doff' there was a position vacant in the carding room. A strong boy was looked for, one who was not afraid of hard work, which had amused her for where in the mill was hard work not done? They were 'thronged' at the moment, run off their feet with work, she was told, so the hours would be five in the morning until nine at night, but later, when the work load eased he would work only until seven in the evening. Did she know of anyone who would suit?

Of course she did, surprised that anyone with the name of Greenwood should be considered fit persons to work in the Chapman spinning room for the Greenwoods, after the Chapmans, were perhaps the best known family in the district. Everyone had heard of Joss Greenwood who had led the men of the Penfold Valley in their fight for reform. It was known that his family had, when her father died, been victimised by Miss Katherine Chapman; that they had been evicted from a company cottage and dismissed from her mills but it seemed the persecution was over since it had been put about among the managers and overlookers that should any of them require employment it was to be given to them.

Charlie and Jenny had walked each day from Edgeclough to Crossfold, a good breakfast of oats and milk inside them, their 'baggin' of cold tea, bacon and wheaten bread to sustain them during the day. Charlie, as a doffer was employed to stop the spinning frames and take the 'flyers' off, remove the full bobbins and carry them to the roller, replace the full bobbins with empty ones and set the frame in motion again.

There were a great many frames, all moving so quickly it took dozens of children to keep them in motion and the overlooker's strap made of black leather with six separate thongs, each eighteen inches long and heavy enough to break a child's arm, was very much in evidence. The dust was like a cloud, settling on machines and 'hands' alike, drifting insidiously beneath shirt-collars and waistbands and into tender young ears, irritating the skin and inflaming the eyes, clogging the lungs so that every man, woman and child coughed continuously. The bobbins were tipped into baskets which were dragged the length of the room by the smaller children, a basket which stood taller than a table, large, and when full of bobbins, exceedingly heavy. Many of the children pulled their soft bones out of place, shoulder bones over which their ribs grew until they were so deformed they were forced to adapt strips of canvas to tie about their bodies in the form of a corset in order to stand upright.

But Charlie, despite this, knew he was one of the lucky ones. As he and Jenny walked home together in the black pitch of the winter night he knew he went to a warm kitchen, a soothing bath before the fire if he wanted it, a secret kiss from his mother, a bowl of hot broth with wheaten bread and a restful sleep of six or seven hours in his own clean, warm bed before he need rise again the next morning. He had Jenny to walk beside, to listen to his dreams of working with Joss one day; to get out of the mill before the brutalising effect of the work and his environment crippled him and his young mind. He did not use words such as these, naturally, for his mind was that of a boy, immature and confused, distressed by what he saw and was forced to accept. He knew that their Jenny carried some man's baby, that she was unmarried, not that anyone cared, particularly among the de-humanised men and women with whom he worked. She would work for as long as she was able and again after the child was born, he supposed but it was up to him to bring home what he could – at the moment one and sixpence a week – to feed his mother and Daisy. Joss earned money, he had been told, with the articles he wrote for *The Republican* newspaper and the *Weekly Political Register* but Joss had Mercy, who was not fit to be let out alone, to support.

Jenny's son was born on the day the Power-Loom Riots began. He was a fine healthy boy with his father's fair hair but thick and curling like her own. His eyes, right from the start, were a deep and melting brown and though she had carried him for nine months cursing the day he was conceived, she loved him from the moment her mother put him in her arms.

'A fine lad, our Jenny,' Martha said softly, hesitantly, while in the background Sarah watched closely as she cleared away the detritus of childbirth. The two women were well aware that Jenny had not wanted this child and if she were to reject him now what would become of the bawling scrap of humanity?

It took no more than a trembling, anxious sigh from her mother's throat and the feel of her newly washed son in her arms and the bond was formed between Lucas and Jenny Greenwood. She forgot the days of disillusioned anger, the months of hard and grinding labour when her back had seemed about to break and her spirit weaken. The nights of silent weeping for something she had lost and which was now miraculously replaced, whole and sweet in the form of her child. He cried loudly and when his demanding lips closed over her nipple and silence spread itself about the room, the voices downstairs could clearly be heard. Jenny was engrossed and deaf to what was being said but Martha and Sarah exchanged glances and when Sarah nodded to some unspoken question from Martha, her mother slipped down the stairs and was just in time to hear the words of the lad sent with the message.

There was trouble in Bolton, it seemed, where, as a result of the slump in the cotton trade, foretold by Barker Chapman a few days before he died, several manufacturers had cut their weavers wages by fifteen per cent. The weavers, men whose patience was finally at an end, without waiting for their leaders, one of whom was Joss Greenwood, had begun what was later to be called 'the most controlled riot in history'.

Their targets were the new power-looms which were taking their livelihood from them.

Mr Greenwood was to get to Blackburn as quickly as he could, the excited lad announced, for the hand-loom weavers, some twenty thousand of them, had assembled there. 'They've got pikes, Mr Greenwood and firearms too, I were told to tell thi', some with gret 'ammers an' every-one's got a weapon o' some sort. They mean business this time, sir. Every power-loom in't valley's ter go, they say. They'll not touch t'spinning' frames 'cos if t'manufacturer spins 'is yarn an' 'e's no looms ter weave it on e'll 'ave no choice but ter send it to us. It meks sense, don't it, Mr Greenwood?'

The lad, no more than thirteen or so, hopped from one foot to the other, eager, one supposed, to be off to march with all the other young boys, flushed with the idea that at last they were to be about something worthwhile instead of sitting on their arses talking about it.

'Right lad,' Joss told him quietly. 'Off you go then.'

'Are thi not ter come then, Mr Greenwood?' the boy asked, disappointed, for it would have been grand to march into Blackburn by the side of one of their leaders.

'I'll be along presently,' Joss told him and the lad turned away, quite bewildered, not only by Mr Greenwood's less than fervent acceptance of his message regarding the uprising since, if he didn't look sharp and do something it would all be over before he even got there, but by the sad and weary look of the old woman who had crept down the stairs to join them.

When he had gone Martha looked bleakly at her son.

'So it's to begin again, lad?' she said tiredly.

'It seems so, mother.'

'Will it never end?' Her voice was despairing. For over thirty years she had lived with it, first the father, then the son, two sons for there was no doubt Charlie would follow his brother as soon as he was old enough.

'One day it must.'

'I wonder if I'll ever see it, my son?'

'Perhaps not, but your grandson will.'

Though he and Isaac, and the other Onwardsmen they picked up on the way, marched through the night the great multitude of men had already destroyed almost every power-loom in the weaving-sheds of south Lancashire. The weavers had marched in lines of four abreast, a great long trailing procession of men and boys, and some women, singing one of the popular ballads of the day. 'The Hand-loom Weavers Lament' which told of their poverty, of having nothing to eat, nor clothes to put on their back; of their broken clogs, ending in the downfall of the tyrants of England whose race would soon be run.

Only the power-looms were destroyed that day, the spinning machines left untouched. Nothing was stolen, so controlled were the men and when one over-enthusiastic lad was seen to remove a strap from the gear he was told firmly by the rest of his group that he was to put it back for they had not come here to plunder.

They were striding out across Rake Head towards Higher Mist on the way to Burnley when Joss caught up with them and their joy knew no bounds for though their success had gone to their heads like the finest French brandy, he was their leader, their spokesman, the man who had fought on their side for nearly six years and how much more satisfying it would be to have him with them. When it was done with, he would be able to tell the rest of the country about it in the grand newspaper he wrote in, and then everyone would know of it and how the men of Lancashire had stood up for their rights against the oppression of the masters. They would all be working at their own hand-looms again by the end of the week, they told one another as they marched with light step, fed a constant stream of the yarn the mill-owners would spin but would be unable to weave and their troubles would be over.

They cheered and clapped him on the back as Joss strode past them, making for the head of the column and the men at its front. It took half a mile to bring it to a halt, just near the 'Towneley Arms' inn and those with a penny in their pockets drank the landlord's ale until it ran out.

The man in charge of the column, or so he said, had a strange likeness to Joss. About his age, he was, with a great thatch of dark hair and sliding grey eyes. He was thin, awkward, with elbows which seemed about to break out of his jacket sleeves and two inches of wrist showing beneath. But he was good-humoured and ready to pass over his command to Joss.

'We've bin waitin' on thi, lad,' he said genially, leaning against the wall which surrounded the inn and those about him nodded in agreement. 'We can tek no more, Joss, not after . . .'

'Who are you?' Joss asked quietly.

'Name's Ted Earnshaw. I bin wi' you from't start but we've . . .'

'I don't know you.'

'I reckon yer don't know three-quarters o't lads 'ere today.' Ted Earnshaw looked back to the long, sprawling column of men, the end of which could not be seen on the track as it dipped beyond the brow of the hill. 'Yer away a lot now, Joss and them what followed yer reckoned yer'd fergotten 'em.'

'And you're saying they'll follow you instead?'

'Nay lad, I'm not out ter tek your place. All I'm sayin' is that wi' you so busy wi' yer grand job on't newspaper an't like, 'appen they're glad to 'ave someone give 'em a word or two o' advice now an' agen. Tell 'em what ter do, like.'

'And perhaps lead them into doing something foolish. Something that'll bring our cause into disrepute . . .'

'Nay, give ower, Joss. I were only tryin' ter . . .'

' . . . like waylaying the coach of an important man. Like committing a crime which can do none of us any good. In fact doing so much harm that the names of these men, the Onwardsmen, is spoken of with contempt and outrage.'

'I don't know what yer on about, Joss Greenwood.' Ted Earnshaw straightened up his spiky body, ready to bristle up to Joss in a pose of injured resentment. His pale face had gone even paler and his eyes had a habit of slipping away, then back again to Joss's, never still for a moment.

'I think you do, Ted Earnshaw, and when this . . . this disturbance is done with and the men dispersed, you and me will have something to say to each other. It seems you've a mind to take over my role in this fight we've started and that you'll go to any extreme to get what you want, including blackening my name. But do you and me want the same thing for these men, tell me that? Are you doing this for them or have you some other motive? There is always a troublemaker in every gathering. Men who love violence for its own sake. Men who will inflame a crowd to do something it really has no stomach for, then stand back to watch as heads are broken and buildings burn. I have it in my mind to ask if you are such a man, Ted Earnshaw. That's what I'd like to know and I mean to have the answer. The name of the man who killed Barker Chapman would interest me, or the one who put him up to it, but this isn't the time, nor the place.'

The men who stood about, crowding in closer in an attempt to hear what Ted Earnshaw and Joss Greenwood appeared to be arguing about, looked at each other in stupified silence as the name of Barker Chapman was spoken. One or two nodded, thinking they knew the reason for it since the dead mill-owner had always fought their cause. They turned to speak to those behind and like a darting swallow, the words winged back to those in the column, garbled and senseless, that Joss and Ted were

379

discussing the wickedness of Barker Chapman, though why they should do so at this particular moment was a mystery.

'These men must be turned back,' Joss said, his eyes like flint as they held Ted Earnshaw's.

'They'll not be stopped now, not by thee nor anyone.' Ted Earnshaw's eyes gleamed, strangely pleased, and daring Joss to deny what he said.

'I can try. This isn't the way to go about it. The newspapers will condemn them for it, radical and conservative alike and it will do our cause no good.'

'Mebbe, but we've bin tipped ower th'edge wi' this last cut in wages and these lads are bound on their course. Destroy't power-looms an' we'll get us liveli'ood back.'

'You know that's not the way, not any more. The masters'll only fetch in new ones. You can't stop progress, you know that.'

He turned his back on Ted Earnshaw and began to speak. Great was his magnetism, a quiet thing now but all the more impressive for it. His eloquence was a glorious ribbon of words as he spoke and every man pressed about him in his shadow. They gathered, those who could get near, to listen and as his words reached them they began to hesitate for what he told them made sense and they trusted him. Almost he had them for they were not violent men, just hungry and desperate, exploited even beyond their forebearance and they were ready, if he could have had their attention a moment longer, to follow him back the way they had tramped, to wait again, to trust him to speak for them of the vote for every man, but Ted Earnshaw leaped up on to the wall which surrounded the inn.

'Lads, listen to me. We've come so far, don't let's turn back now. Think, think what we've done today and what it'll mean to us . . .'

'What's 'e sayin'?' The words went along the track from mouth to mouth, each man telling the man behind him that Ted Earnshaw was praising them for how well they had done today and telling them how they would do better tomorrow.

'Is Joss with us?' they asked, for so great were their numbers no more than a hundred or so had heard him.

'Must be. He's standin' at the lead with Ted,' and so they picked up their pikes and their hatchets, their hammers and iron bars, like boys off to a parade, stamping their feet in unison, beginning to move forward in their march to victory and as Joss ran along the line begging them to reconsider they cheered him, thinking he was rallying them on.

'It's no good, lad, they're set on it,' Isaac said to him. 'You'd best fall in an' when we get to Burnley p'raps yer can make 'em see sense.'

So Joss Greenwood 'fell in' with the men who loved him and would, if they had but known it was his intention, turn about and follow him back to Crossfold and Edgeclough and the dozens of towns and villages from which they had come.

The crowds grew bigger as they approached Burnley, thousands and thousands of men and in the centre of it Joss Greenwood was like one droplet in a bucket of water, hemmed in by the men who, gathering about him, thought he was part of it. There was a rumour that troops of cavalry were in motion, being fetched from one place to another, that they had been stoned and that strangely, they had wielded only the sides of their swords and shot only above the heads of the crowds.

'They're on our side, lads,' one marcher chuckled and so it seemed for as they commenced their destruction of the power-looms in the weaving town of Burnley, though the cavalry troops were seen and heard shouting to the men to stop what they were doing, when they were ignored they did little to carry out their orders. Joss stood to one side, a silent despairing figure as doors were broken down and windows smashed and the men swarmed through the factories, leaving alone the singing frames on which the yarn was being spun, the yarn which next week, or the week after at the latest, they themselves would be weaving on their own hand-looms. Their great hammers flew through the air, shattering power-looms and when the foot soldiers arrived, just too late, the weavers escaped through windows on the far side of each building.

Joss tried again when the swelling sea of men came to rest on Dog Hill. He could see his own cottage below him and the straight line of cottages dropping down the fold of the slope which was Edgeclough. His mother was at the door with an arm about the shoulders of Daisy and Mercy and at every doorway and gate women and children gathered for never had they seen so many men in one place. They and Joss had been making their way steadily southward, going wherever a power-loom was used. They were tired and hungry for they had little to eat except what was given them, but the feverish excitement which had burned in them at the start had corroded into their hearts and souls, branding them with a need so great they were no longer men with a mission, but machines, like those they had sworn to destroy. They were quiet where once they had cheered and sung and whistled. They had been harried by soldiers, too few to make much difference and other men had stood in their way, come from the magistrates, it was said, to read the Riot Act but they had been brushed aside like so many quarrelling children.

Joss, exhaustion showing in the slump of his tall, fine body, in the deep lines which ran from his nose to his chin on either side of his mouth, in the frowning eyebrows above deep, sunken eyes, moved about the crowd, crouching to speak to a man, a group of men, to men who dozed or even dropped off to sleep as he begged them to go home.

'You've shown them now that you mean to take no more cuts in your wages. Stop now and go home before the soldiers begin arresting you . . . Oh, I know they can't take you all but they'll not let you go on, lads. You've destroyed hundreds of looms but they'll not let you get away with it . . .'

But Joss knew as he spoke that these men could not stop this clamour they had begun and could not be asked to stop it. They were beyond reason, beyond hope, probably beyond caring. They had begun with the enthusiasm which had believed that with the destruction of the hated power-looms they themselves could be restored miraculously to their former standards and if they could not achieve it, their expressions said they might as well die swiftly by the soldier's sword than by the slow process of starvation. They had contained, fed by the fine beliefs injected into them by their leaders, a brave assurance they would win this campaign but it had dribbled away, bit by forlorn bit as they had tramped, footsore, weary, starving through Blackburn, Burnley and half a dozen cotton towns along the way and now on to Crossfold where there would surely be soldiers waiting for them for property must be protected. The authorities were organised now, the first shock of suprise worn off and the magistrates were taking action. But they could not stop. Not now. They had begun it, the weavers of Lancashire and the movement had gathered speed until it could not be stopped.

'Are thee not wi' us then, Joss?' the men asked.

'Aye lads, every step of the way.'

'Chapman's next, then,' the cry went up and they marched shoulder to shoulder, like soldiers now, their hammers and pikes carried bravely as they had seen the military men do.

She was there at the gate. Kit Chapman. Joss was at the head of the column of men. He carried no weapon. He had broken no windows, no machines. He had destroyed nothing, but, as he had promised he had stood by his men and when she saw him her eyes narrowed for a moment, their message of despairing love extinguished to be replaced by the blazing defiance he knew so well. She held a pistol and the soldiers who flanked her on either side and behind her in the mill yard carried muskets.

Joss stopped and so did the men who marched with him for the sight of a woman, even the hated and feared Miss Chapman was something for which they had not allowed. Men, a man with a weapon, they would rush him without thought, without fear for they were beyond such consideration as death now, but this was different and it brought them to a halt.

'Good morning, Miss Chapman,' Joss's voice was polite. 'We would be obliged if you and your men would step aside. We mean you no harm.'

Her eyes flared into the snapping sheen of ice when the cold winter blue of the sky is reflected in it. Bright and angry flames of scarlet burned in her cheeks and she straightened her shoulders.

'You must kill me if you mean to get in here,' she said clearly so that even men far back in the line could hear her words.

Joss sighed. He was bone weary, desperate to have this over and done with. No one had been hurt. Not one person injured, mill-owners and manufacturers alike, standing aside, some of them in sympathy for the plight of the weavers, as their power-looms were destroyed. There would be consequences, to himself and to the other leaders, that much was certain but the men's determination was petering out and after this he knew he would surely be able to convince them that they had made their voices well and truly heard. This must be the last. It was as though destiny had brought Kit Chapman and himself together for this one last time, to destroy her mills as their love had been destroyed by the vast gulf which yawned between them. It was deep and wide, deepening and widening with every moment they stood, eyes and wills locked at her mill gate and for him to hesitate was foolish.

'Miss Chapman. It might be advisable if you let us through. My men are weary and want nothing more than to do what they came to do and go home. For your own sake call off your soldiers.'

'You must be mad if you think I will allow you to walk in here as you have done throughout Lancashire and break my machines.'

It was as though they were alone, the vast crowd at Joss's back, the soldiers at hers fading into a fine grey mist on the edge of their vision, blurred and silent and still, shades of grey and red with no function but to wait patiently for the outcome of the conflict between this man and this woman. Whoever lost it would step aside, taking those who were with them, allowing the winner to do what must be done.

'You cannot stop us now.' Joss's voice, though quiet, was clear and the men about him lifted their weapons and shuffled their feet, ready to shoulder their way through this woman and these soldiers the moment Joss gave the word.

'I can try,' and he knew she would. If they trampled her into the ground she would not move before their onslaught. She would stand her ground, *her ground*, her head held bravely, her feet planted firmly on her bit of earth and not until she was under their feet would that proud and lovely face lose its challenging courage, would those brilliant eyes become dulled. She would, quite simply, die before she gave an inch of what was hers.

Her eyes glared into his, not wavering to look at those about him. This was a struggle, a clash of wills between just the two of them, a deadly state of war in which there was no one but Joss Greenwood and Kit Chapman. She was the most courageous, the most dangerous woman he had ever known and for a split second he saw what might have been between them if they had been friends and not enemies. The lovers they were meant to be. She was strong and wilful but her femininity was beyond question. She was dressed from head to foot in unrelieved black and yet she was glorious, the vivid colour of her face, the slipping darkness of her hair enhanced by the austerity of her mourning. He had never loved her more than at this moment, the moment in which, to protect her, he must humiliate her.

He moved slowly towards her, his step unhurried, his smile gentle. He kept his hands well away from his sides and though she lifted her weapon, pointing it at his chest, the soldiers did not move and neither did his men. They seemed to know that they really had nothing to do with what was happening here. It was between this man and this woman.

When the firearm was touching his chest he stopped, still smiling but his heart ached painfully for her. Her mouth worked savagely and her teeth showed like those of a cat which is cornered but in her eyes was the desolation of love which knows full well that it cannot kill, no matter with what loathing, the object of that love. Though she died of her hatred of him at that moment she was as incapable of pulling the trigger which would end his life as he was of turning the weapon on her.

At the last moment she made a token movement, her eyes dying a little, the pistol wavering, not towards him but away and when he put his arms about her it was as though she thanked him. She began to kick and scream and bite at his hands but he lifted her easily from her feet carrying her to one side beyond the gate post and behind the high wall of the factory.

'Righto lads,' he called out as he went and with a great cheer his men surged forward, bearing the unresisting military with them and within seconds the clang of the hammers on the power-looms rang out from the broken windows through which the younger men had chucked anything they could lay their hands on.

'Dear God . . . I hate you . . .' she whispered.

'I know . . . I know . . .' and their eyes spoke the dreadful truth of their living love which both had declared quite dead. Then he smiled and she was never to know the effort it took to speak without his voice shaking, to inject that touch of flippancy which was needed if they were both to recover from this.

'I'm afraid I must leave you now, my dear Miss Chapman.' He almost faltered over her name for her eyes which had once been luminous with her love, with the sweetness she held for Joss Greenwood, turned to black hatred for the enemy who had this day defeated her in battle. It was what she needed.

'You can go to hell, Joss Greenwood,' she hissed and her long nails reached to tear out his eyes but he stepped aside, his step jaunty, his grin impudent and daring.

'And you too, Kit Chapman. Perhaps we shall meet there,' as he fell into step with his jubilant men.

The following day, Joss Greenwood, though he had sworn he would get his men home, for enough had been done to bring to the notice of all the land the distress in the Lancashire textile trade, had failed to persuade them and had gone with them to Chadderton where they attacked the factory of Messrs Faulkner, destroying forty looms. So far the rioters had proceeded without opposition but intelligence of their intent — from someone who was never named — had been conveyed to the military who were guarding factories in the town. A party of twenty riflemen and the same number of dragoons, more serious and without the sympathy aroused in the breasts of previous soldiers, probably Lancashire men themselves, and within ten minutes of the Onwardsmen and their followers entering Chadderton seven persons lay dead and dying, one of them a woman.

It was finished.

In Blackburn and in an area of six miles around not a single power-loom survived. A thousand looms amounting to thirty thousand pounds, and the hand-loom weavers in the South Pennine Hills and valleys cleaned and oiled their hand-looms in readiness for the work which would now, surely, come their way, the work for which they had fought so hard to achieve, their objective won it seemed.

Of the sixty-six men arrested for their part in the riots, one was Joss Greenwood. Another was Ted Earnshaw. A third was a man called Paddy Kelly who, when he was threatened with transportation begged to be considered for a lesser sentence if he should turn King's evidence on the matter of the murder of Barker Chapman.

The case quite overshadowed the trial of the rioters, for when the man who was to have been Barker Chapman's son-in-law was brought to identify the accused murderer, Ted Earnshaw, Mr Atherton emphatically denied on his word as a gentleman that this was the assassin, affirming again and again that the prisoner Joss Greenwood was the man he had seen cut down Barker Chapman.

'But the man has an alibi, Mr Atherton,' the magistrate protested, for dearly as he would have liked to oblige a fellow gentleman, it was not in his power to do so. 'Vouchsafed by gentlemen of impeccable character. Not one, but several and at the very hour of the murder which you yourself verified was actually speaking to no less than two hundred people at a meeting in Bradford.'

'They were mistaken, all of them.'

'Come now, sir. Two hundred people cannot make such a mistake.'

'Are you calling *me* a liar?' Mr Atherton was incensed and the crowd was delighted, and so were the gentlemen who reported it in the newspaper the next day, particularly when Ted Earnshaw, who was by some curious mistake put in the same cell with half a dozen of Joss Greenwood's followers, confessed the very next morning to the murder and a month later was hanged for it.

Part Two

26

It was two years and he was to be freed from gaol today, she had been told by the Squire who was also the magistrate, when he dined with her that week, but this time she would not be there to meet him when he passed by Badger's Edge. He was no longer a part of her life and, she told herself, she scarcely gave him a thought these days. Now and again, during her working week some stray event, one that had nothing to do with Joss Greenwood might bring him back for a hurried moment, before she had time to set her mind against it, at first vividly, achingly, as though he stood there with her to witness it but as the months passed, moving to twelve and beyond, crossing the anniversary of the day on which she had last seen him, his memory was beginning to fade . . . she told herself.

She had replaced the power-looms his men had destroyed and to house them she had built a splendid stone weaving-shed, strong enough on its four floors to stand the weight of a hundred, two hundred power-looms. Steam engines provided the power, the engine house erected at right angles to the main building with great arched windows like those of a chapel. It faced north to obtain the best light and had a tall chimney on which the name Chapman was painted, discharging a continuous and massive cloud of filthy smoke over the town.

The machines she put in were of the very latest design, William Dickinson's 'Blackburn Loom' which introduced picking sticks to drive the shuttle backwards and forwards. The mechanism was such that one weaver could attend to two machines without assistance and could weave a million 'picks' a week in contrast to the 605,000 on the old machines, almost doubling production and halving her wages bill! She had begun to experiment with printing her finished cotton, bringing in a cylinder machine which could print almost five hundred pieces a day, designing many of the patterns herself.

She was busy. She was Miss Katherine Chapman, owner of the Chapman Spinning and Weaving Concerns, Katherine Chapman, the innovator who employed a thousand men, women and children in her spinning rooms, her weaving-sheds, her carding rooms, in her finishing and printing processes which were growing in the centre of Crossfold. Her days were filled, satisfying the part of her which had resolved, years ago, that she would be the son her father had wanted her to be. She was a respected business woman, known to be shrewd, hard-headed, with the ability to make a profit before most of her competitors were out of their beds in a morning. She dined with gentlemen of influence and was much sought after by hostesses with sons, even among the landed society of south Lancashire.

Though there had been curious rumours whispered about the valley before the Power-Loom Riots of 1826, ugly rumours gathering momentum of a strange liaison between her and the felon, Joss Greenwood, started by God alone only knew, they had been seen to be the laughable nonsense they were when her weaving-shed was destroyed by the very man whose name was coupled with hers, along with the many others on that dreadful day. Would she have suffered as they did, those with sense said to one another, the gentlemen in the Cloth Hall, the ladies in their drawing-rooms if they had been . . . whatever it was she and Joss Greenwood were supposed to have been to one another? Hardly, and whoever it was who had begun the rumour should be horsewhipped.

Kit had smiled when she had seen their speculative glances, for there was no smoke without fire, was there? –

but it had passed over, the riots turning the mill-masters' thoughts to more important matters than fools' gossip. But she had never discovered the name of the man who had given the information to Harry Atherton, nor how he had come by it, since she could hardly call each of her employees to her office to question them on such a delicate subject without letting everyone know of it! It had irked her and for weeks she had imagined knowing eyes watching her, waiting for her to fall as obviously Harry had hoped but as time passed and her mills continued to flourish she put it from her mind.

She travelled, to America and to the European continent, looking for markets for her piece goods and her name was known for honesty, value for money and reliability. She employed men she could trust, managers and overlookers and had engaged and trained a young man, brought up in his father's textile firm in Rochdale but wishing to make his own way in the world, to replace Harry Atherton. Though it had caused talk – but when had she not? – she had moved about the country with him, accompanied only by her maid, Janet, introducing him to men with whom she did business and had sent him, once she was convinced of his worth and integrity, to buyers found by Harry Atherton in other countries. Her cotton, her velveteens and fustians, her new muslins and piece goods went to a dozen places worldwide and the mistrust with which once she had been treated had vanished.

Yes, her days were splendid, just as she had always imagined they would be. From four-thirty in the morning when she rose from her bed in order to be at her mill gate by five-thirty when the bell was rung, until that moment when, her hair rippling down her back, brushed until it crackled by Janet, she was left alone to face the night.

He came to her then, his grey-green eyes gleaming between narrowed, smiling lids, his mouth curling humorously. Come with me, he would say, up on to the moorland we both know so well. We will follow a track which will lead us to some secluded place where the winds blow soft and free, where the skylarks sing and the scent of the heather will make us tipsy with joy. Leave this burden which you have taken up and I will leave mine and we will be as unfettered as the creatures who roam there. Cut the knot, as I will and come . . .

He would hold out his hands, those strong brown hands and take hers and draw her up into the magic circle of his arms, his beautiful masculine body against hers and her heart would go soft, weak with her need, her love, her anguish. She would move from the chair by the fire, her feet bare, the hem of her nightgown trailing across the fine, rich depths of the carpet to stand before the window, to stare sightlessly across the pitch-black of the night garden where nothing could be seen beyond the dark outline of the hills against the lighter hue of the sky. Her mind, so filled during the day with profit and loss, with production and patterns and yardage was empty and into the emptiness poured the dangerous, tormenting thoughts of Joss Greenwood.

They had given him two years this time. Sixty-six offenders, ten of them, those arrested with weapons in their possession, sentenced to death, the sentence later commuted to transportation and it was said among the manufacturers that one of them should have been, the leader of the mob, Joss Greenwood. Mind you, they said, he was known to have friends in high places who, it was suspected, had spoken out for him and he had been sentenced merely to two years' hard labour in Lancaster gaol.

Two years! She had held her head high, a victim as hundreds of other mill-owners had been victims of the Power-Loom Riots of April 1826 and agreed with them that it was scandalous and that the £126,000 raised by sympathisers in London, not for them, the ones who had lost, some of them, their whole livelihood but for the distressed and afflicted poor of the north, was really beyond belief. She had stood among them, one of them of course, and as she dined on pheasant and salmon and drank the very best French champagne, as she moved in the pleasant and convivial company of the fashionable and expensively dressed; as she carelessly ran up bills for swansdown muffs and lace fans, for velvet cloaks lined with soft fur, fine white kid boots and delicate creamy parasols, she could not, no matter how she laughed and chatted, no matter how she danced, and attended musical concerts in Crossfold, rid her mind of Joss Greenwood in his cell in Lancaster prison. Each night he escaped from that cell and came to claim her. In her mind he was still laughing and reckless, dashing, like a gypsy with his brown tumble of curls and his eyes bright with his hunger for her. Would he still be the same, her mind begged to know and the answer was, of course, that he would not. She remembered the last time he had been released from Lancaster and the shock she had suffered when she had seen the fine bones of him outlined beneath his white flesh, the grey in his hair and the lines about his eyes and mouth. He had suffered cold and damp, gaol fever and a rat-ridden cell, hunger, and had been worked unmercifully, but he had survived; *just!* His robust constitution had served him but he had not learned from his confinement. It had not, seemingly, taught him that his way was wrong. He had taken her looms and smashed them. He had taken her love and smashed it, throwing it insolently back in her face when she allowed him to reach for it. He had humiliated her, not once, nor even twice but time and again and though she felt the ravaged pain and anger of it, she could not use that emotion to stifle the other. The loving would not be destroyed by the hating. It came again and again in the night. As Janet closed the bedroom door softly so would Joss Greenwood open it again.

On some nights she could not withstand it. Tearing the nightdress from her she would fling on her plain woollen walking dress, her stout boots and coat and call up the dogs and walk the moors in the dead of night, her cheeks wet with tears, her heart beating fast with the exertion of climbing up and up to the high point above Edgeclough and the village which sheltered his family. She would crouch on her haunches, her chin resting on her knees and wrap her arms about them as she probed the dark roofs of the cottages, searching for God alone knew what. Peace? A calmness, which came only to her in her work, comfort . . . but from what? Down there lay his wife and the child she had borne him. A son, perhaps who would be walking by now, growing and unseen by his father.

And at five o'clock, as the last of her 'hands' flowed in through the gates in an endless wave of patient be-shawled women, submissive and bowed, with cloth-capped men and children clinging to other children she would be there, ready to close the gates on latecomers who would be forced to wait until they were opened again at eight o'clock.

She would move about her counting house and her design room, confer with her managers, her book-keepers and clerks, attend to overlookers who needed her advice, study patterns and quality, orders and consignment notes, receive business men, lawyers, bankers and all the gentlemen with whom she had dealings and who, knowing her value, no longer required *her* to go to *them*. She was calm then, at peace then, comforted then as the day flowed smoothly over her. She did not *ever* go into her spinning rooms, her carding rooms, her weaving-sheds when the machinery was in motion, nor when her operatives were employed there. She inspected the frames, the power-looms when it was necessary after the engines were turned off and the rooms were still, empty and silent, leaving the hiring of the hands, the management of them to the tacklers who were, after all, employed for that purpose.

She saw Jenny Greenwood that day, with a boy who could only be Joss's brother, walking beside her, her heart lurching at his likeness to Joss. He was tall, fine boned and slender and walked with the same grace. It was June and the sulphurous yellow sky was cast over, pressing down on the town with the smoke and steam from dozens of chimneys. From her office window on the top floor of the building she could see over the high mill wall to the sprawling labyrinth of houses which surrounded it and in which her workers lived. There were blackened church spires standing up here and there, the whole crusted with the soot and filth which poured from the chimneys. There was nothing as far as the eye could see but drab streets, smoky skies, a thick polluted air, the grim monotony of a mill town but she was accustomed to it and did not even see it. Her whole attention yearned towards Jenny Greenwood and the boy, longing to open the window, to call out to them as they crossed the yard and for a dreadful moment her hand actually reached out to the sash, but they turned suddenly, speaking to a girl behind them, a weaver by the look of her. She had bad teeth, caused by sucking the weft up in the shuttle, called by the weavers themselves, 'kissing' the shuttle and Kit knew that soon, when the boy who worked, she had heard, in the weaving-shed, had been there long enough, he would look just like the girl. And yet he appeared healthy enough. He was not round shouldered as many of the weavers seemed inclined to be, nor sallow and afflicted with chest complaints as the carding room lasses were, nor bleached of countenance as those in the spinning rooms became.

How did his family manage, she wondered, as she watched him disappear into the weaving shed, with Joss Greenwood in gaol? What of his mother, of Jenny, the younger one whose name she did not know . . . and of his wife and child? Did they eat well? Did they eat at all? She raised her head suddenly, stepping back from the window, moving to seat herself behind her desk. Dear God, what was wrong with her? It was nothing to her what his family ate, or did not eat and she'd be damned if she'd spend another minute of her day thinking about them.

Charlie Greenwood had a headache. Everyone in the weaving-shed had a headache but they were well used to it by now for the pollution which ravaged the town, the stifling, breathless, airless heat of the sheds, the humidity which sapped the strength of the strongest, spared no one, man, woman or child. He could hear the sound of the engine wheels and the hum of the machinery as it was set in motion. He had removed his jacket and trousers and his clogs, placing them safely out of the way of the flying straps beneath his machine and, barefoot, rolled up his shirt-sleeves and the legs of his thin drawers. He would, for the next fourteen or so hours, apart from two ten-minute breaks be required to tend to two clattering looms with shuttles making two hundred 'picks' a minute, in a steamed atmosphere and a din so horrific the operatives could go deaf with it while at any minute a rebellious shuttle might shoot forth and take out the operative's eye. For fourteen, fifteen, sixteen hours he would not be allowed to sit down since it was necessary while he ate his 'baggin' to sweep beneath and to clean and oil his machine. While it ran he must stand, for the motion of spindles and shuttles cared nought for human pain and woe, nor for the heart and soul of the operative which must be left at home. Hands, and enough intellect was all that was needed to keep the body out of danger for it must keep pace with the machine. The weaver must always be alert for a fault since the loom would go on weaving it continuously until the error was corrected. The looms were packed, as many as would fit into the smallest space, leaving just enough room for the operative to walk sideways between whirring belts and wheels and the ferociously moving picking stick. Each loom had a gas light, the gas turned on at a central point, coursing through considerable lengths of piping while the overlooker walked along the alleyways with a taper, lighting the mantles in an atmosphere that was already thick with escaped gas.

Yes, Charlie Greenwood had a headache but it was not allowed to stand in the way of his joyous thoughts for today Joss was coming home and this time he was not to tramp it as he had done three years ago but would have his fare paid on the coach which would fetch him from Lancaster to Oldham. It had been put up by those radicals, journalists and men from many walks of life who were working for reform and by the Union which had been created as a result of the repeal of the Combination Acts. Tonight when

Charlie returned home Joss would be there and the great burden which had been carried by young Charlie's shoulders as the man of the house these past two years would be lifted. He had worked in Chapman's spinning mill and weaving-shed for over four years now, always with the dream that he would be able to escape it and work with Joss and men like him in the struggle for a decent wage for a decent day's work, one following the other as naturally, as properly as day follows night. He wanted, when he was old enough, to become a member of one of the many committees established in the hand-weaving district of Lancashire for the specific purpose of campaigning for legislation to regulate wages to protect the hand-loom weaving industry. There was a man in Manchester, one John Harvey Sadler, an inventor and engineer who was attempting to contrive machinery which would enable one man to operate two hand-looms at the same time so that he might compete in his own cottage with the power-loom such as the one Charlie ran in Chapman's mill. Charlie would dearly love to see this happen for it would mean that with Mercy and Daisy spinning he might return to the cottage industry that had once been the life of his own father.

He heard the child scream, even above the sound of the machinery. It was a thin scream, like that of a rabbit caught by the stoat but Charlie had heard the frightened, painful cries of children many times before. He knew he could do nothing about it so he gritted his teeth and got on with his own work. One day, he said to himself, one day, repeating it over and over again. One day, one day, one day . . . ! It was something he had taught himself, a kind of hypnotism he put himself under to block out the sights and sounds which went on about him every day. Some of the operatives, after several months, grew hardened to it, too debased and dehumanised themselves by ignorance and by their own poverty to care much for the sufferings of others. Their own domestic comforts were non-existent, their own families as lacking in morals and dignity as animals in a shed. Unlike Charlie, they had nothing with which to compare this existence to the one they left in the morning and to which they returned each evening.

The child cried out again, a long wailing cry of such utter despair and hopelessness Charlie felt the hairs of his arms and legs and on the back of his neck rise stiffly. His scalp prickled and he swallowed several times but his mouth had dried up and his tongue stuck to the roof of his mouth. Still he knew he must not look round. If he so much as turned his head away from his loom, not only could a fault develop but there was a strong possibility he might be fined.

One day . . . one day . . . one day . . .

He heard a man laugh and again the child wailed in anguish, the sound suddenly cut off and as it stopped it seemed to Charlie the absence of it was worse than the sound had been. He could bear it no longer. He was almost a man wasn't he and though he knew he himself would surely suffer for it, since it was known he was the brother of a 'reformer', and as a 'meddler' himself in what did not concern him for he had spoken up in a child's defence before, he deliberately switched off his machine before he turned to see what was happening in the far corner of the weaving shed. All about him operatives, most of them women and children since they could work a power-loom as easily as a man and were willing to work for less bent industriously over their close-packed machines. Not one turned, through fear or indifference, or usage to what was being done to the child who had cried out.

She was no more than three or four, a frail thread of a child wearing a boy's underdrawers and nothing else. Her dirty skin was as thin as parchment and her bones threatened at any moment to break through it. Her head appeared to be too big for her tiny body, ugly somehow and out of shape and Charlie had time to consider that she must be one of the 'idiots', put in a consignment of twenty sound 'apprentice' children, a practice much used by the parishes from which they came. Charlie's face moved in pity and anger at what he saw.

There were three overlookers engaged in their 'bit of fun',

known, all of them for their brutality and for their ability to wring every last scrap of labour from those operatives, and children, in their charge. The child had been gagged. A piece of tow had been twisted into the shape of a cord, put in her mouth and tied at the back of her head and with his leather thonged stick the tackler was 'persuading' her to run round one of the machines which was part of his 'concern'. She was on her knees, her poor vacant face twisted in bewilderment and pain, her narrow back already showing the weals of the thong across it.

'Gerrup looney an' let's see yer run,' the man was mouthing for through the din of the machinery his actual words could not be heard. 'Gerrup on yer feet, yer daft little bugger. I'll teach yer ter fall asleep whilst yon machines goin'. It's the strap fer you an' anyone else who thinks she can . . .'

He got not further as the full weight of Charlie Greenwood took him from the side. They both landed heavily against the wall of the room and it was doubtful who was more surprised, the overlooker or the two who stood, open-mouthed and disbelieving, watching him. The child had scrabbled out of the way, having enough sense to recognise her opportunity to escape the cruelty of the men who owned her and they let her go, ready, as they came from their stunned trance to tackle this new potential for some sport. One of their own 'hands' attacking an overlooker! It was a case for dismissal, naturally but before that they would teach him a well deserved lesson. They didn't hold with rebellion, not among this cringing workforce over whom they had complete authority and this one would really be worth it. He'd given them a bit of 'lip' before, in defence of someone or other, as had his sister who worked in the spinning room and it was well known his brother was a radical who was at this moment serving a sentence in Lancaster for disturbing the peace.

They both began to smile as they pulled Charlie Greenwood from their fallen colleague.

* * *

They were at the end of the village street, every last one of them, to meet him, all the cottagers and even men and women from further up the Penfold Valley and higher still from the edge of the moorland.

His mother had him fast in her arms for she had been uncertain whether she would live to see him again since two years is a long time when you are beyond fifty. They held one another tightly for a moment, mother and son, both without words, her face pressed to his chest, his cheek resting on her grey hair. Those about them became silent, their sympathy reaching out to enfold this man who had suffered so much for them, and for his mother who had, in her way, undergone as much as he. Most of these women about her, though they might go hungry and had often been cold and weary, had a man to give them a hand, to smile grimly with them in the past as they shared a crust of bread among those of their children who survived. They had the comfort of a shoulder, perhaps not strong, nor even broad to weep on when the day just gone could scarcely be borne and the one to come was sure to be worse. But Martha Greenwood had lost one man, a man whose crusading spirit had been snuffed out in the campaign against oppression and she looked to be in the process of losing another if the state of Joss Greenwood was anything to go by. A walking skeleton was a kind description of him and would she ever put a bit of flesh back on his bones, they asked one another, shaking their heads sadly. What was he . . . twenty-eight, twenty-nine and the streaks in his brown curls were thick and white, not unattractive, one or two of the younger women agreed, but where was that glowing, brown-skinned gypsy look he once had, the engaging brightness of his grey-green eyes, the springing, cat-like grace of his long-legged walk?

But he turned to smile and his teeth were still white and whole between his curving lips and his eyes lit up with pleasure as he recognised face after face. He waved a thin hand, then had it taken by a moist-eyed man, then another and another. They followed him down the rutted street, jostling one another to be near him as he walked, one arm about his mother, the other about his childlike wife who acted, they whispered, as though she had no idea who he was but in that sweet way she had was willing to welcome anyone who was kind to her. His young sister, Daisy, ten years old now and, miraculously a kitchen skivvy at Edgeclough Hall with the Squire's family, for which her mother gave thanks on her knees each day, opened the cottage door wide to reveal its spotless, if spartan, homeliness and those who had accompanied him fell back for he'd want a bit of peace and quiet with his family now.

He was seated before the small peat fire, what small store of energy he had spent on the walk from Oldham to Edgeclough, his face almost grey in the last fading shadows of the evening sun. He had managed as much as he could of the appetising rabbit stew his mother had coaxed him to eat and drunk almost a pint of the foaming milk, sent over by a grateful weaver. He had marvelled at the pies, the black puddings, the 'fatty' cake, all prepared by women who had cause to be grateful to Joss Greenwood for the growth of their children in the last two years and though he swore it was none of his doing since he had merely been caught up in the events of that fortnight he, and the other sixty-five who had been sentenced, were venerated as near saints by those who were certain at last, that what they had fought for was surely accomplished. They had their bit of spinning, a 'piece' woven each week, or more if they could manage it and the prospect, now that John Harvey Sadler, the clever young inventor, had promised it of a hand-loom which could do what a power-loom did.

Joss leaned his head on the back of the chair, his two year old nephew on his knee and the last of the suns rays fell about his head. His mother watched him thankfully. He looked right 'peaky' but she'd soon alter that, somehow or other. They had a few pence put by, what with Daisy up at the Hall and no longer in need of feeding and their Jenny and Charlie earning enough to keep the four of them, which reminded her, where were they, her eldest daughter and younger son? It must be gone half-past eight and she had expected them home earlier tonight. Running, they would be, despite the long and unmercifully hard day they had put in, eager to get home to see their Joss. He'd not noticed how late it was becoming, poor lad, his head drooping above the curls of Jenny's Lucas, his hands limp and big knuckled about the sleeping child, as he dozed himself.

She rose to her feet and treading lightly so as not to wake him moved across her kitchen, peering anxiously from the open doorway and along the village street. Long shadows lay in strips across it, banded with muted shafts of sunlight as the lowering sun poured its last rays between each cottage. The slopes of the hills directly to the front of her were a dusky purple, their rims edged with gold and the sky shaded from them, to yellow and peach and the final pale summer blue of the evening.

Martha shaded her eyes, looking in the direction of the track which led from Crossfold to Edgeclough. It curved down through waist high bracken and gorse and she could still see the dark line it made through the vegetation.

'What time is it, Mother?' Joss's voice was drowsy and in the quiet his mother jumped nervously.

'It must be nearly nine.'

Joss sat up stiffly, lifting the sleeping child and placed him in the chair opposite. His body still ached with fatigue but his eyes had become alert and there was a questioning expression on his face.

'Shouldn't they be home by now. Didn't you say they finished at seven today?'

'Aye. I don't know what's keeping them.' She turned abruptly, then seeing his expression of unease, her own face tried a smile of unconcern.

'They'll not be long, lad, don't you fret. 'Appen the overlookers found them something extra to do. You know what they're like. It's nothin' to them if young 'uns are fallin' asleep on their feet. Nay, don't get up, our Joss, rest yourself . . .' but Joss had risen from his chair and come to stand beside her. He followed her gaze up to the Crossfold track, then his eyes swept the length of the soft valley along which it ran, past his own front door and then up again to the far side. The hills were banked all about him, high sweeping moorland, the edges of it starting just beyond the village. It was a lonely place to some, a vast emptiness, a threat to those not used to it but he had lived for the past two years in a cell barely bigger than his mother's larder and he welcomed the feeling of it stretching away on either side with nothing in it but space. He let himself drift away for a moment, breathing in the sweet warm air, the scent of many things, of foxglove and heather, of yellow broom and purple clover and he felt the headiness of it lap over him in healing waves. The stillness, the peace, the calm after the clangour and cries of his imprisonment, rested gently in his heart and he gave silent and humble thanks for his survival and return to it. It sustained him, this often barren and inhospitable land, gave him life and hope and the surety that . . . what? What was it, that feeling of certainty which steadied him to the path he would move along tomorrow and the next day and the next. It was bred in him as it had been bred in his father and grandfather. They were men of the north, a hostile country sometimes but it was their country and they would have it free for the men and women who lived in it.

'There they are . . .' His mother's glad voice brought him from his deep musing. He turned, smiling his pleasure, eager to be re-united with these two who, more than any others knew him and his purpose, his dream, who shared them, who had stood beside him so many times, in adversity and suffering, and in joyful triumph. Jenny. The mystery of Jenny and the baby she had borne. So much to talk about, to tell her and to ask of her, surely, to discover the name of the father of her child. And Charlie. Almost a man now and he would be a fine man, a brother of whom any man would be proud. Despite his extreme youth he had kept faith with Joss, taking on a burden a boy of his age should not have been asked to shoulder, working as a man would work, caring for his mother and sisters in Joss's absence, in a sense *being* Joss.

They were both smiling, Joss and Martha Greenwood, as they watched the two figures come slowly over the brow of the hill. They were too far away as yet to make out their features, just two figures close together, moving down the stony track, leaning together in an extreme of weariness so great it seemed neither would make it to the first cottage.

'Let's walk to meet them,' Joss said stepping out into the last mellow shaft of the sun which showed but a third of its orb above the hills. As he spoke he put up a hand to shade his eyes, looking towards his brother and sister, narrowing them slightly in puzzlement. He put out his other hand to his mother who was following him as though to stop her and she turned to look at him, her expression questioning.

'What is it?' she asked.

'I . . . I don't know.' He had moved to the gate, his eyes still intent on the two figures who had reached the first cottage and as they did so a man and a woman came out of it and hurried down the short path into the street. The woman put her hand to her mouth and quite distinctly on the quiet air Joss heard her cry out. The man, it was Adam Cartwright, took hold of . . . who was it? . . . Jenny? . . . Charlie? . . . and the one remaining sank slowly, quite gracefully into a crouching position against Adam's garden wall.

Joss began to move, first slowly and then, as his heart beat quickened, more rapidly until he was running. Behind he could hear his mother calling his name and on either side of him as he ran cottage doors were opening and heads looked out, voices enquiring what was to do? His feet, he suddenly realised, were bare since he had removed the boots he had worn on his journey from Lancaster and he could hear the slap of his soles against the causey stones which lined the street and the sharp sound of his own breath in his throat. Adam was gently lowering the thin form of the boy he held to the grass verge outside his own garden gate. His face was contorted with horror and his wife was weeping. She didn't quite know what to do in that first moment of shock and kept circling her husband and the figure he held in his arms.

'Oh Lord ... Oh dear Lord ... Oh my God ...' she kept saying over and over again.

'Give over, woman ...' Adam said roughly, ' ... and go and get some help. Fetch Martha and ...' He had not seen Joss who had stopped just behind him and in his compassion he could do no more than rock his burden back and forth, like a mother with a child.

Joss fell to his knees beside them and the groan which wrenched from him brought all those who had followed him in wonderment, to a halt. His mother was among them, her face white and terrified and against the wall where she had fallen Jenny Greenwood lifted her head. She was as grey as the stones she crouched beside. The sweat ran down her face from beneath her hair and dripped from her chin and her bodice was wet with it. She seemed unable to move her arms which were bent awkwardly and there was blood on her. On her breast and on her shoulders, on her arms and staining her skirt and some had even dripped on to her feet.

'Oh sweet Jesus ...' Joss's voice was no more than a whisper in his throat. He did not turn to look at his sister as he spoke since his eyes were nailed to what had once been the engaging face of his brother Charlie. ' ... Who ... what ... who did this to him?'

'His overlooker ... and two others. His arms are broken ... and ... don't let me Mam see his back.'

Martha Greenwood began to scream.

'Oh God ... Oh God ...'

Jenny's voice was like a razor. 'He's got nowt to do with it, nor with anyone round here, I reckon.'

'How did you get him home.'

'I carried him.'

27

He was waiting at the mill gates when her carriage drew up to them, standing, like a statue carved from granite, directly in the horses' path. She heard her coachman shouting and cracking his whip, telling someone to 'get out o't road or 'e'd run 'im down' and was almost thrown from her seat to the carriage floor as it came to an abrupt halt. There were voices yelling and the carriage horses were whinnying and she could hear the crash of their hooves on the cobbles. The carriage rocked again and the commotion outside it grew greater. There was a surge of men and women about it and she could see cloth caps and heads draped in shawls just above the level of the window, a sea of faces swamping the area about the open mill gates all looking in one direction, and hear the sound of the factory bell calling them to work.

'What on earth is going on?' she heard herself say out loud, irritably, since it was almost five thirty and the engines would have been turned on and these operatives who were milling about the carriage and restless horses should by now be at their machines ready to do a day's work. The carriage window was already open for the day promised to be hot again but when she put her head out she did not immediately see what was holding her up. The shuffling feet of her workers had lifted the dust which lay on the road and a fine cloud of it floated on to her horses, her coachman and laid a coating on to the pale green sprigged muslin of her summer gown.

'What is it, Frederick?' she called out.

'Some lunatic in the road, ma'am.'

'What lunatic?' she asked, squinting through the dust and it was then that she saw him. Though her eyes looked at him, a tall, emaciated figure, dressed in breeches and an open-necked shirt, a shaggy mane of greying hair, unkempt and dusty falling in his eyes, they did not immediately recognise him though naturally her heart did. Would it ever forget that familiar beloved outline, the shape of him, the way he stood, the tilt of his arrogant head, for it was still there, the sum and substance of the man she loved, emanating from this man who stood in her path. But this man was – must be – well over thirty years of age. There were lines of weariness and strain about his tight clenched mouth, a mouth which gave the appearance of cruelty, a bitter and menacing threat and surely it could only be directed at herself? This man's eyes were like pale green chips of ice between his narrowed lids and his face was so grey and sweating it might not have seen sunlight, daylight even, for months on end. This man's hands were big, raw and his fingers were like claws, flexing and unflexing. This man was a stranger to her, one she really did not wish to know, and yet, it was he. Her heart told her achingly that it was he.

'Katherine Chapman,' the man, Joss Greenwood, said, and though his voice was not loud it was clear and everyone of the throng about her carriage, slipping through the gateway, milling about her yard, reluctant it seemed, to enter the mill and miss this confrontation, heard it. They knew, of course, all of them, why he was here for those who had witnessed the appalling beating of Joss Greenwood's young brother had told others, who had in their turn spread it about the town, but it had not reached Greenacres, not yet. There would be trouble, those who watched were well aware, for Joss Greenwood, just freed from prison, a fighter in his younger days, a believer in the equality of all men and a detester of oppression would not let it pass.

'Katherine Chapman. Step down from that carriage, if you please.'

The coachman snapped his whip above Joss Greenwood's head but he did not even flinch. The horses pawed the ground restlessly and tossed their heads and though he seemed in imminent danger of being trampled, Joss did not move.

'Get out o't way, yer damned fool,' the coachman cried, his own face indignant for he was severely put out by this defiance of his authority. He had driven Barker Chapman and now his daughter to the mill and back for the past twenty years and always the men and women who jostled the streets of Crossfold, stepped back, some respectfully, some perhaps resentfully, but they had given way to him just the same.

'Step aside at once,' he roared.

Kit Chapman lay back against the velvet upholstery of her carriage and felt the blood drain away from her head. Her pulse beat was thick and heavy at her wrist and temple. She had been busy inside her own active brain planning the installation next week, if she could arrange it, of the new machine which would print the cloth she produced. Simple designs they would be just now but an engineer she had met only last week at the dinner table of Mr Graham, who was her bank manager, had told her that the mechanised roller printing she was to use, though still in its infancy, would by the end of the decade become so sophisticated she might print any design or colour she had a fancy to. The challenge was immense since it would enable her to open up new markets with not only the plain, unpatterned cloth she now manufactured, but light, prettily printed muslins and ginghams, beginning with the raw cotton and finishing with a fabric which would be complete, ready in fact to be made up into a morning dress of the very latest fashion.

She could not seem able to gather the scattered fragments of her pleasant thoughts. Could not even collect her wits to enable her to face this dangerous crisis, whichever way she turned. Scurrying hither and thither, trying to put them into some sort of order, they disintegrated again and again into chaos and confusion. What was he doing here the very day after, she had been told, he had been released from prison? What was his purpose in taking up this challenging stand between her mill gates, his face thunderous, his eyes betraying the enormity of his rage, his finely strung body trembling with it? What had she done since yesterday that had driven him to this madness since, being an ex-convict he would be under the eye of the authorities and one step off the path of lawfulness and the proper behaviour required of him would have him back behind bars before he had time to lose that dreadful prison pallor he had acquired in the past two years. But she could not sit here in the dim warmth of her carriage forever, pondering on the reason for it. She must at least enquire of him the purpose of it. Naturally everyone knew of his championship of the 'distressed and afflicted poor', that was why he had been imprisoned, and, she supposed wearily, he was to be about that championship right away, pressing his ideas of wide-ranging political freedom on to the common man. A militant man, then who had caused, she had heard, the dreadful Power-Loom Riots of two years ago, a man concerned with the repeal of the Corn Laws, of the ten-hour bill for factory children, *any* kind of bill, or law in fact, that would make life easier for the common man and stand in the way of profit for those who employed them.

But her heart plunged and bucketed in her breast at the thought of stepping from her carriage and looking into his face again. She had imprisoned her feelings for him tight inside her, tamed them, forced them, subdued them to manageable proportions, told herself that her life was good now, believed it, and now, with one glance from his piercing eyes and the sound of her own name on his lips it had exploded inside her, firing up and burning as fiercely as her own furnace in her mill. But he'd not see it! By God, she'd not let him know of the tumult inside her. If he wished to roar like a lion, to make a show of his own rage, whatever it was about, outside her own mill then let him, but she would not participate in that performance for all to enjoy.

She would be cool, disdainful, contemptuous. She would let him see how she despised him and all he stood for, by God she would.

She opened the carriage door and stepped down into the dusty area before the mill gates. Lifting her pale green silk parasol she put it up languidly, a lady protecting her fine skin from the already steaming rays of the sun's heat. Her bonnet was held high, a pretty froth of silk and tulle tied beneath her chin with wide silk ribbons and she wore white gloves and white kid boots. She was elegant, stiff-necked with pride, a high mettled, fearless lady who, scarcely able to believe the audacity of this man who was barring her way, was forced to enquire of his purpose in doing so.

'May I ask what you think you are doing? You realise that you are trespassing on private property and that if you do not stand aside and let me pass I shall have no recourse but to summon the constable and have you arrested. Surely you are not so eager to return to gaol. I believe you have only just been released.'

'You bitch! You filthy, vindictive bitch.' His hatred and rage was so great, so malevolent, the words of scorn dried up in her throat and she took a step away from him, not afraid as yet, but considerably alarmed and bewildered. Merciful God, what was wrong with the man? He appeared to have taken leave of his senses, to be quite mad and certainly beyond understanding the words of contempt she had meant to heap on his head. His face was contorted, almost unrecognisable in its loathing and though she was well aware that this scene, these feelings were nothing new between them, that they would never reach a point where either would be in agreement with the other, this was different. This was the roaring of a wounded, tortured animal, an animal that has been ill-treated again and again until at last it can stand no more, until it turns on its tormentors and is ready to tear them to pieces in its agony and violence.

'Joss . . . what is it . . . ?' The crowd were amazed to hear her say. It was uttered uncertainly, every grand resolution she had nurtured flung to the winds in her concern for him, but it was obvious that he did not hear it.

'You are not fit to be called a woman.' His voice was muted as though somewhere deep in his throat he had tamped it down for fear it would escape him in a scream. 'An animal has more compassion than you and I am cursed to have known you. These people are forced to share in your viciousness, most of them unable to stand against it and I do not blame them since they have no alternative but you are a monster, a vile and profane monster who should have been drowned at birth . . .'

'Now look 'ere, you . . .' the coachman began, his face quite scarlet with his outrage. He put his foot on the step of his high seat at the front of the carriage, ready to climb down with his whip and clear a path for his mistress. Already the crowd about them was becoming so enormous it spilled out into the street as far as the corner and in the yard several managers and overlookers were trying to force a way through to the gate. Children and frail women were being pushed to one side, several had fallen and the situation was becoming dangerously out of hand, but Joss Greenwood did no more than turn his eyes on him, a look that said it would be unwise to interfere and the coachman stayed where he was.

Kit stepped back again as Joss moved towards her and her heart banged frighteningly in her breast. The parasol trembled in her hand and for a moment she thought she would stumble as her high heel caught in the hem of her gown.

'Joss . . . for God's sake . . .' she began, her back against the door of her carriage. She was hemmed in, surrounded by the hundreds who longed in some way, in *any* way to see her downfall, whatever that might be. They had all suffered at her hands, at her father's hands, not personally, of course, but at those of the men she employed to subjugate them in the spinning rooms and weaving sheds where conditions crippled them, maimed them, afflicted them with disease and illness, *killed* them sometimes, made slaves of

413

their children and all for wages which barely kept them alive. If they could see her humiliated, perhaps beaten by this man whose brother, it was said, was at death's door, by *her* orders then some quality of redress would be returned to them.

'Don't foul my name by speaking it, you hell-kite and you may do away with the concern for it does not suit you. You would kill a child as we well know to make a profit of sixpence and to carry out your obscene intents you employ men who are as evil-minded as yourself. Or perhaps you had a hand in it. Perhaps you laid on the lash yourself . . .'

In his pain and blind, unreasoning rage he said things which he knew to be foolish, untrue, exaggerated since he had loved her once and perhaps still did and in his anguish over it he was doing his best to trample it into the dust at their feet. She would not personally have supervised the beating his brother had been given and, if he could have blown away the black fog of hatred which befuddled his brain he would have seen the truth but it was doubtful he even wanted to. Someone must pay for it. She was the one who, at best, had turned a blind eye to it, at worst, ordered it and so he was here to collect what was owed him.

'I do not know what you are talking about, Joss Greenwood, and if you think to frighten me with your ravings you are mistaken.'

'Is that so? Then how is it that every man and woman in this town knows of it. Every cottage I passed on my way here had someone at the door asking after him . . .'

Almost he had begun to weep, his pain more than he could contain, the memory burning in his brain, and his heart, of what he had left in his mother's cottage in Edgeclough.

'For God's sake, Joss . . . please . . . what has happened to . . . ?' She put out a hand to him, appalled, but he struck it brutally from him as though her touch might coat him with filth.

414

'Don't put your hand on me, you she-devil. How you can stand there with that . . .'

'For pity's sake, speak more plainly.' She was no longer afraid, nor even concerned for him. Her own rage was rising to meet his, as it had always done, the spark from his igniting the dry kindling of hers. They were like two sticks which, when rubbed together caused such friction everything about them, including themselves was consumed in the blaze.

'I do not intend to speak at all, Katherine Chapman, except to say that your corruption and greed, and that of all the others like you will find its true level one day when you all go to hell. Your inhumanity to those of your own kind . . .' The tears blurred his eyes and again she was pulled towards him for surely he was in need of a hand to steady him but again he stepped back from her in revulsion.

'What in God's name are you talking about?' she cried. 'For a man who swears he does not mean to speak you have a lot to say and I have yet to understand what it is . . .'

'I will show you what it is. Get in your carriage.'

'You cannot order me about like one of your followers. Now, for the last time get out of my way . . .'

'Get in your carriage at once or I shall throw you in. I have but to reach out my hands and put them about your head and within thirty seconds you will be dead. Melodramatic, you say, smiling, but if those men back there, undoubtedly among them the ones who almost killed my brother, should try to stop me, I will do it . . .'

'*Killed your* . . .' Her face had gone paper white and her voice was incredulous. 'Charlie . . . ?'

'Aha, you even know his name.' His voice split on his pain. 'You can look the other way when they beat him almost to death . . . and you know *his name*. Now get in that carriage for I mean you to see what you have done. You sit in your splendid office . . . oh, I know you don't go in the spinning room, or the weaving-sheds . . . they tell me so, those who work there, for though you gloat over the profits you make from them you cannot bear to afflict

415

yourself with the pain they suffer. It offends you to see them, to smell them, to hear them cough their lungs up, to pull out their soft bones, to have them broken and deformed. Your conscience might trouble you, if you have one which I doubt and then it would not be quite so easy to enjoy the wealth you make on their broken bodies. *Now get in your carriage.* We will drive to the edge of town and then we will walk the rest of the way. Call off the men behind me, call them off, Katherine Chapman for though they might kill me, by God, you'll go with me.'

He would not get in the carriage, unable to compel himself to be so close confined with her and when they reached the end of Reddygate Way, he strode out ahead of her, stopping only as she gave instructions to her coachman to wait for her here. Frederick was white-faced now, afraid up here alone on the moors with a madman who was abducting his mistress but help would not be far behind for the managers would have the special constables up to Joss Greenwood's cottage almost before he himself got there.

She was not dressed for walking the three mile track to Edgeclough. It was full summer and the bracken was high and thick, growing across the pathway until it almost met in the middle and the skirt of her gown was full and wide with deep flounces edged in emerald green ribbon. Her boots were soon torn and scuffed and before she had gone half a mile the heel of one snapped right off. It was still early but the heavy yellow sky pressed down on her head. She did not call out to him to slow down to allow her to rest a moment, to gather her breath for her stays were tightly laced, but strode along behind him just as though it was a cool spring morning and she herself was dressed in stout walking boots and skirt. His hostile back moved ahead of her and he did not once speak nor look back to see if she was still behind him.

They lined the streets of the village to see her walk by and though her feet were blistered and bleeding she did just that, her back straight, her head high for even now she had no conception of what she was to see nor of what depths

416

it would plunge her. She was appalled, more by Joss's pain and anger and hatred than by what he had actually said. By *his* suffering and not that of his brother for she had known, naturally, that boys in her mills must receive a flogging or two if they were to be kept in line, or so the tackler told her.

None of the cottagers uttered a sound as they watched her go by but their eyes were bright with their curiosity. They were still, quite unmoving, looking at her as though she was some creature they had heard about but had never seen before, something strange and quite revolting, not of their race and therefore not one with whom they would like to be acquainted.

The small kitchen seemed to be full of women. Joss did not go in but merely indicated with a contemptuous hand that she was to enter. Jenny was there, her face inscrutable, her eyes hot and loathing. There was a slip of a girl, perhaps fifteen, with silken brown hair and confused grey eyes — who was she? — who shrank behind a chair in which rocked an older woman who did not even glance up at her. Joss's mother? And another older woman, greyer, granite faced, tall and stern, guarding this family from further cruelties, it appeared.

And on a truckle bed, face down, was the slight figure of a boy. She moved across the room until she stood over the bed and at once Jenny was there, a sentinel to protect her brother from this woman whose fault it was that he lay there at all. He had a light cotton sheet pulled up to the back of his neck but the left side of his face could clearly be seen against the white sheet beneath his head. At least she thought it was his face! It was so swollen and bruised, so laced with cuts and abrasions it was difficult to tell where his mouth and nose should have been, where his eye actually was in the slitted mask of what had been his face. So deeply imbedded in his swollen flesh, his long eyelashes could not even be seen and but for the breath which whistled between his broken teeth and lacerated lips she could not have said that the hole through which it came was actually a mouth.

'Dear Lord God . . . ' Her voice was no more than a light breath, unheard by them all but Jenny.

'And that's not all, Miss Chapman.'

Jenny gently lifted the sheet from her brother's back and actually smiled, her eyes cold now with hatred as Kit Chapman turned away, white-faced, sweating and sick, sagging against the wall behind her.

'Look at him again, Miss Chapman,' she murmured softly. 'Look at what your men have done to my brother. Three of them there were, two to hold his arms after he had been stripped and one to flay the skin off his back. Then those who held his arms broke them, I was told, quite deliberately before they started on his face. That mark there . . . no, perhaps you cannot see it among the rest of his injuries but it is the mark of a hob-nailed boot. It took Sarah two hours to sew up his face and another two to put splints on his arms but they can do nothing for his back, naturally. And all this for trying to protect a child, an *idiot* child, who had no right being in the mill in the first place.'

Kit's teeth began to chatter and her whole body shook from head to foot as she slipped into shock. She pressed her face to the wall and put her hands to her face, trying to shut out the sight of the red squashed pulp of the boy's back which moved excruciatingly, shallowly with each desperate breath he took. In and out it rasped and in his semi-conscious state he moaned and instantly they were about him, his mother and Jenny, the third woman, each willing, eager to take on his pain, their hands hovering helplessly, their eyes beseeching one another to tell them what to do to ease his agony, their loving pity and helplessness a palpable thing in the kitchen. She turned back to the group then, with all her soul longing to help, to ease the boy's suffering, their suffering, anyone's suffering who should ask it of her and her eyes met those of Joss Greenwood as he hovered by the open kitchen door and she saw in them the reluctant recognition of what was in her heart.

'I did not know,' she said thickly.

'You should be aware of everything that goes on in your mills. You are responsible for this.'

'I did not know,' she repeated.

'You knew of the child who died and you did nothing.'

'Sweet Jesus . . .'

'I cannot ever forgive you and neither will He.'

'I know that. I cannot forgive myself.'

'You should go now.' His face was hard and implacably cold and as he spoke the fragile girl moved from behind the chair and ran to him, her face crumpled in the easy tears of the young.

'Joss, will Charlie get better?' she said, moving trustingly into the outstretched shelter of his arm. 'I cannot bear to see him hurt so.'

The change in Joss was quite dramatic and to Kit, devastating. His eyes warmed and became soft and his mouth curved into a smile of infinite tenderness. He kissed the girl on her cheek and she sighed as she rested like a little bird against his chest.

'Of course he will, Mercy. He is strong and Sarah and Jenny will make him better. Go and play out for a while, sweetheart. Why don't you pick some flowers so that when Charlie wakes up he will be able to see them by his bed, and when you come back Martha will make us all some dinner.'

He kissed her again and she smiled eagerly.

'Oh yes, I know just where there are some lovely violets . . .'

'But don't go far, sweetheart.'

'No, I won't,' and she darted from the kitchen out into the sunshine and as she went Kit heard her begin to sing.

Their eyes met across the room and his answered the wondering question in hers.

Yes, they said, she is my wife and I love her, and the wintry expression in them challenged her to remark on it if she dare.

His wife! Her eyes were huge in her ashen face. His wife! The girl who she had thought to be no more than fifteen, timid and made afraid by what had been done to Charlie Greenwood, perhaps the daughter of a neighbour, *was Joss Greenwood's wife*. And where was the child, the son she had imagined these last two years while Joss had been imprisoned, *his* son. Surely that sweet-faced woman, since she was that, that simple child could not be the mother of a child, the mother of Joss Greenwood's son? The woman she had feared and hated and envied. *Go out and play* he had told her and she had gone, singing as artlessly as a seven year old. Her eyes returned to his and the questions and answers which flowed despairingly, contemptuously between them told her it really made no difference. Not now. He would not allow Kit to come near him again, she could see it in the coldness which had replaced the violence of his rage. This was his home, nothing to do with her, as his wife was nothing to do with her. Her overlookers had almost killed his brother and he had blamed her, brought her to see what had been done, and that was all, and what did it matter now. It was finished. There was nothing more to say, or to be done between them. They were enemies, bitter foes in the war *he* fought and she must accept the fact. She must return to Crossfold, to her mill where the weft and warp of her life lay before her to be woven. This day must surely alter its construction and certainly some good must come of it, or her life up to this day would have been for nothing. She could no longer sit in her ivory tower, a princess who did not recognise the minions who served her, aloof and distant from the men and women and children, the overlookers who had them in their charge and the managers who came each day to tell her how much profit she had made the day before. Her father had been wrong. The other mill-owners of her acquaintance were wrong when they left the management of their sheds and spinning rooms to others.

There is no advantage in employing them to see to these things and then doing it oneself, George Abbott had said to her on numerous occasions, and as long as I get the yardage I want I leave it to others as to how I get it! She had followed the same path, the path her father had set her on. She had not known, had *forgotten*, made herself forget, the two occasions on which she had gone into the spinning room, telling herself that such things were happening all over the country where factories, mines, chimneys were swept, establishments where children were employed, so what could *she* do about it? There was no other way.

But was there? Was there?

She put out a hesitant hand to Jenny Greewood who knelt beside her brother's bed, longing to lay it in sympathy on her shoulder. Her eyes lifted to Martha Greenwood but his mother was consumed with her son's pain and she did not look up from her frantic clinging to the hopeless belief that her closeness to him might ease it. If she could have changed places with him she would have done so, joyfully, her face said as she bent over him.

'Go home, lass. There's nowt yer can do 'ere,' the stony-faced woman bade her, the same one who had mended Joss when Harry's bully-boys had beaten and broken him. How strange it is, she thought, that I should be so closely involved with this family, not only with Joss but with his sister, his brother, and now, in an abstract, quite curious way, with the child he calls wife. I cannot seem to shake myself loose from them, from a concern about them that has nothing at all to do with Joss. There is something in Jenny and Charlie that arouses my admiration and in another time, and place, I might have found affection, friendship, something I have never had before.

She moved from the dim warmth of the kitchen and out into the late morning sunshine and was surprised to see that it was still daylight. What time was it? What *day* was it, her confused and aching heart asked for it seemed an aeon since she had stepped from her carriage in front of her mill gates that morning.

She stopped before the tall figure of Joss Greenwood. His back was to the warm, sun-coated wall of the cottage, his eyes closed, his face held up to the sun and when she put her hand on his arm he jumped guiltily as though he was not accustomed to standing and doing nothing. His face closed up when he saw who it was and he straightened his thin frame to his full height.

'You have had enough then?' he asked harshly.

'They do not want me in there. I am in the way, and besides you have done what you set out to do.'

'And what is that?'

'You have punished me.'

'Is that how you see it?'

'Oh yes. There is no use my saying what I feel inside me here . . .' She struck her clenched fist fiercely against her own breast and her voice was thick and strangled in her throat, ' . . . you would not believe me if I did, so I will . . . will leave you.' She paused, her eyes which she felt she could never raise to any member of his family again, somewhere on the shading of brown hair in the opening of his shirt and was ashamed at her own longing, even then, to put her lips there. 'Would you allow me to send up my own doctor . . . or anything you might need . . . I hesitate . . . I do not wish you to think I am offering charity . . .'

He began to laugh then, a hoarse and anguished laugh, disbelieving, and she felt her heart shrivel up in pain but she did not flinch from him, or from her own desolation.

'You can go to hell, Katherine Chapman, and take your bloody concern with you. My family need nothing from you. None of us need anything from you but justice. Can you give us that?'

28

It made a small sensation when Jenny Greenwood was summoned from the spinning room to Miss Chapman's office and those about her wondered what trouble the family were in now. It was no more than two days since Charlie Greenwood had been flogged by the overlooker in the weaving shed and the lad only alive by the skin of his teeth, what were left of them, they had heard. And nothing had been done about the men who had beaten him, it was said, not even a reprimand, and the three of 'em walking about like 'cocks 'o the north', worse than ever in their brutality.

'Make yersel' tidy, my girl,' Ellis told her, smoothing his hand over her slender buttocks as she leaned across her machine to switch it off. He grinned lasciviously, darting out of the way of her upraised hand, admiring the sweat-stained outline of her pert breasts, telling himself that he would find a way to get her on a pile of cotton waste before long. She might be the leavings of Harry Atherton but what did that matter? The trouble was, she didn't give a damn about anything he might threaten her with. Nothing frightened her and when he thought to control her with the promise that he would tell the world who the father of her child was she had laughed in his face and told him to go ahead. Pity that bit of business with the young Squire had come to nothing but it seemed the high and mighty Miss Chapman was as unafraid as this one and cared nought if her good name was fouled on the lips of the whole valley. It would have been grand to have been carried on the coat-tail of the man who married her. Still, he did all right on the whole, busy with his finger in this pie and that and he'd a few bob put away for a rainy day. He wondered what it was Miss Chapman wanted this slut for. Happen she was in trouble again for there was no doubt the whole bloody family had a talent for it.

Kit rose to her feet when Jenny entered her office and as the stale smell of sweat and oil and the odour which was peculiarly that of a factory in which every window is tight shut, came in with her, Kit resisted a strong urge to put her lavender scented handkerchief to her nose. The girl was unkempt, her hair wrapped about with a strip of torn cotton, her bodice so damp with sweat the circle of her dark nipples were clearly visible. Her skirt was tucked up at one side into her waistband and she wore nothing beneath it but a pair of men's underdrawers. Her calves and ankles were filthy and the clogs into which she had carelessly pushed her feet were crusted with muck and oil.

They studied one another across the vast stretch of deep velvet carpet, across the shining surface of Kit's desk, across the enormous chasm which divided them, not only of class and of privilege, but of the wounds inflicted by Kit Chapman on the family of Jenny Greenwood. They might have come from different continents, worlds even, so great was the contrast between them but as Kit looked into Jenny's eyes she allowed the thought to flit into her mind that if she herself had been born to a cottager, a weaver, to the life Jenny led, to the slavery of a spinning frame or a loom, to a six-mile tramp each day from the mill and back, might she not look as Jenny did, and could not the same be said of Jenny? Put her in a silk gown, perfumed and elegant and might not she and Jenny Greenwood change places without a great deal of bother? Jenny was not coarse featured, nor stunted as many of her contemporaries were. Her hair when it was washed and brushed as it had been on the day they had met on the moor was as dark and glossy as the wing of a blackbird. Her eyes were a pale silken grey, not at all like those of Joss or Charlie and her skin was fine and creamy beneath the layer of oil and filth which now coated it. Her teeth were white and straight, whole and undamaged. She held herself erect and her body was small boned, slender and tall.

She watched Kit now with an expressionless face, standing still and quite relaxed, her hands hanging loosely at her side, no sign of strain or of nervousness, nor of being overwhelmed by her surroundings, by the strangeness of the circumstances, nor of Kit herself.

'How is your brother?' Kit asked quietly.

'Which one?' Jenny smiled slyly and Kit's heart lurched uneasily.

'Charlie, of course?' she answered, hoping that Jenny would not hear the awkwardness in her voice, nor the sudden bumping of her heart.

'Why should you care?'

'There is no reason for you to imagine that I do, but I should like to know just the same. You sent away the doctor so I have . . .'

'He'll mend.' The answer seemed careless, heartless even but Kit had seen the solicitude with which Jenny had leaned over her brother in the kitchen of her home and she was well aware, as who was not, for it was a prodigious feat, that she had well nigh carried him the three long miles from the mill to Edgeclough on her back. A strong young woman, her strength forged in the fierce heat of the fire of life. A loyal, trustworthy woman who would give her life for those she loved, for that in which she believed.

'May I ask how his injuries are healing?'

'What the hell's it to you, for God's sake. You gave him them, more or less.'

'You must believe that, of course, and I make no attempt to defend myself. There is no defence and I will carry his scars to my grave . . .'

'Will you indeed?' Jenny's voice was mocking and she laughed abrasively. 'So will he.'

Kit sighed, watching the amused contempt brighten the deep smudged eyes of the woman by the door. Of course she would act this way. What else had she expected? Her brother beaten to within an inch of his life, his young blood soaking into her flesh as she carried him home, his broken arms dangling about her neck, his screams of agony in her ears as he wandered in and out of the fog of consciousness. And she had been forced by sheer necessity to return to work in the mill of the woman who, in her eyes, indeed in everyone's eyes who worked there was the cause of it.

'Will you sit down, Jenny?' she said, indicating a chair placed before her desk, sitting down herself, smoothing the fine silk skirt of her honey-coloured gown.

Jenny Greenwood was, for the first time since she had

entered the room, at a loss. Her eyes widened in astonishment and her lips parted. She moistened them with the tip of her tongue and Kit saw the uncertainty shadow her eyes.

'Sit down, Jenny. I want to talk to you.'

Jenny laughed then and into her eyes came an expression of malicious enjoyment. Her mouth widened on a huge grin and her eyes glowed.

'Sit down! In that chair? Shall I tell you something, Miss Chapman? I've been in this room before. Did you know that?' She swayed a step or two closer swinging her shortened skirt, almost performing a clog dance in her glee. 'Yes, someone else called me up here once. You and your Pa were away somewhere at the time. I told you about him up on the moor, d'you remember. He did me down, that grand fiancé of yours, on that very table, once he had me . . . where he wanted me. He liked to do it with the door unlocked, just as though the idea that anyone could walk in and find us, me with my skirts up and him with his breeches down gave him an added . . . what's the word . . . zest! Ha, you might well look amazed and so was I, I can tell you. Strip off, he says, that first time I was sent for but I wouldn't, so he never let me alone after that. You'll give in, in the end, he says, and d'you know what, in the end I did. When your little sister's crying for something to eat and your mother's so cold she can't sew on a button, you give in, in the end. He wanted *me* to say I wanted it, you see. He wouldn't force me, he said, but there's forcing and forcing, wouldn't you say, Miss Chapman? After that he'd have me on the desk with the clerks outside . . .'

She bent her head suddenly but not before Kit had seen the desolation in her eyes but she knew better than to sympathise with this proud woman. She wanted no sympathy, no charity. What she had done, what she had taken had been not for herself but for her family, and still her family were persecuted, the cause of it, without doubt, herself.

Jenny lifted her head again and her eyes were proud now, and joyful.

'But it was worth it in the end . . . for the boy. They say good comes out of everything and . . .'

'The . . . the boy . . . ?' and Kit's heart began to pump erratically.

'Aye. He was two in April and . . .'

'You have a son by . . .'

'Yes, and I'm not ashamed of it.'

'Then there are . . . two children . . .'

'What are you talking about?'

'Your . . . your sister-in-law . . . your brother's wife . . . she has . . .'

'What?'

'A child of the same age . . .'

'Mercy . . . good God . . .!' Jenny's face was incredulous and in that moment Kit Chapman felt the joy, the shameful joy race through her and she began to smile, to lift her face to the ceiling ready to shout it out loud but Jenny Greenwood had had enough and she let it be known by the sudden impatient movement of her whole body.

'What is this all about? Whatever it is let's have it over and done with. What do you want with me? Surely not to gossip about my family?'

'No.'

'Then what? Is it the sack, or a fine for missing two days work? There was no need for you to take the trouble to send for me to tell me. Ellis could have done it just as well. Or is it my turn for a flogging? Come on, let's be done with it and let me get back to my machine. I'm losing money while I'm standing here jawing with you, money I can ill afford. There's only me and our Daisy working now until Joss gets going again.'

'I know. It was through me Daisy got her job. I'm not asking for thanks nor gratitude only the recognition that, despite your belief to the contrary, I am not . . .'

'You got Daisy her job at the Hall.'

'Yes.'

'But how . . . ?' Jenny's face had become still, her eyes

wary, just as though the ground on which she had thought herself to be safe, had begun to shake.

'Does it matter?'

'No one said.'

'No one knew, except myself and the Squire's wife.'

There was a deep and shocked silence and into it Kit allowed herself the small flickering hope that a step had been taken to bridge the steep 'clough' that stood between herself and this woman. Jenny's hands clenched against her stained skirt and she looked about her quite wildly since it appeared she did not know exactly what to do with the news she had just been given, and wished in a way that she had not. She hated this woman, though she was aware that in the past they had owed her favours which she had shown them. She had taken a liking to her, reluctantly, on the day they had spoken on the 'tops' but she had not allowed that liking to grow, for Katherine Chapman was the culmination of all that Jenny Greenwood hated most in the world. She had shown no concern for the rest of the multitude who worked in her mills and who lived like wild animals in the squalid houses she, or at least her father had built for them. The Greenwood family had been singled out for consideration others had lacked and why, now that she was here was this woman asking her to sit down, for God's sake, just as though they were two ladies about to take afternoon tea.

'Will you not listen to what I have to say, Jenny Greenwood. You and your brother are forever mouthing vilifications of the injustices done by myself and the other mill-owners, to the men and women we employ. Your brother goes from one end of the country to the other, I believe, begging men of conscience to listen to him and you, I presume, support him in this. You demand to be heard, you radicals. You do not ask, but demand that you be listened to. Now I will do the same. I demand that you listen to me.'

'What the devil can you say to me that I might be remotely interested in?'

'Sit down and find out.'

'No, not in the same room as you.'

'And I took you for an intelligent woman. Very well, but I shall speak just the same.'

'You're the maister in this factory.'

'So I am, and in that case I am within my rights to dismiss you from your work as a spinner in my mill.'

Jenny's face drained of all the colour it contained and her eyes died a slow and hopeless death. Kit felt a great wave of pity engulf her for it seemed a cruel way to make this woman stand down from her blind, deaf attitude of hatred.

'So . . . that's it, is it?' Jenny whispered and though she tried hard to keep the strength of that hatred within her for it supported her, Kit saw the bleak despair gnaw at its base, taking the straightness from her back and shoulders, the proud lift from her head.

'Yes, that's it, Jenny Greenwood. I have plenty of spinners. Enough to fill another spinning room if I wished, but what I have not got is an assistant. A woman to help me in my office, a woman I can trust, a woman who knows the mills as well as I do myself, but from a different point of view. A woman who knows what the other women feel who work for me. What they need, what the children need. Someone quick to learn, eager to learn, shrewd, intelligent, brave, bull-headed. One who knows what is wrong *and can help to put it right*. A woman who is not afraid, of me, of the managers, of hard work and of what people will say about her . . . Jenny? For God's sake girl, sit down before you fall . . .'

She hurried round the desk, her distaste at the unwashed smell coming from Jenny Greenwood gone in her concern. Jenny had put her hands flat on the desk, swaying slightly, her chin on her chest. Her eyes had closed and her breath hissed from her open mouth as though her lungs had deflated in shock. Kit put her arm about her shoulders and led her to the chair and this time Jenny sat down willingly.

'I'm sorry, Jenny, if my manner of offering you a job seemed cruel but I could think of no other way to rip apart that caustic shell of hatred you had built around yourself. Forgive me, but I had to reach you somehow.'

Kit shook her head, then walked briskly back to her chair, giving Jenny a moment to recover her badly shaken composure. Then, impulsively, she rang a small bell on her desk and when the black-gowned little woman who, from a tiny but compact kitchen down the hall, dispensed tea and coffee to Kit's visitors, or even a light meal should Miss Chapman require it, entered the room, ordered, 'tea for two, if you please, Mrs Plank,' just as though Jenny Greenwood was the usual caller Mrs Plank was accustomed to serving. Mrs Plank stared, open-mouthed, quite unable to shift her feet, as she said later to her husband, looking at Jenny Greenwood slumped, all covered with muck and stinking like a pig pen on the green velvet chair she herself had brushed and dusted that morning and it was not until Miss Chapman cleared her throat saying, 'At once, Mrs Plank,' did she find the wits to stagger from the room.

Jenny drank the tea silently, her face turned away from Kit. It was quite blank, pallid with the shock which had her in its grip, but slowly, as the flavour and strength of the beverage she had never before tasted from a china teacup, with milk *and* sugar, penetrated her frozen mind and brought a faint colour, a mere hint of cream in its chalk whiteness crept beneath her skin. For ten minutes neither spoke. They could hear the sound of the engine, the clatter, even through the closed windows, of the looms across the mill yard, the shouts of men loading and unloading waggons and the crash of the hooves of the great Shire horses which pulled them. At last Jenny spoke.

'What makes you think I can do this grand job?'

'I know of no other woman who could.'

'Why?'

'You are Joss Greenwood's sister.'

'And if I say yes . . . what of my family?'

'You will be in a position to safeguard them and their

430

future. You will have a salary sufficient to see to their every need.'

'And my son?'

'Bring him with you.'

'Where to?'

'To live with you at Greenacres.'

'Greenacres . . . ?'

'Why not? You cannot walk from Edgeclough each day with a two-year old strapped to your back. It is, of course, your decision but it would be more practical, I think, if you were to live with me for the time being. There is an empty nursery and more servants, nursemaids I suppose, than I can count. He would be educated, brought up in any way you want. The grammar school at Crossfold . . . but I am getting ahead of the matter in hand. It is your choice, Jenny but before you make it remember that it will benefit not only you and your family but every person in my employ.'

Charlie was awake when Jenny crept into the silent cottage. He was still flat on his face but he could lift his head a little in order that the cheek on which he rested might be turned so that the flesh would not stick to the sheet. His splinted arms lay awkwardly along his body and he could do nothing for himself but with the resilience of the young and the nourishing food which his mother spooned tenderly into him whenever he would allow it, uncaring of the pennies she spent on procuring it, those put by so laboriously over the past two years in readiness for a rainy day, (since was this not *it*?) he was beginning to heal. He could open his swollen eyes to thin slits and Jenny's heart turned over with her love for him as he tried to smile when he saw her.

'Hello love,' she whispered, kneeling beside him. 'D'you want a drink?'

'Yes please, Jen,' he mumbled and when he had sipped awkwardly through the thin bit of tubing Joss had devised for him, for though he could manage to eat from the spoon his mother put in his mouth, whatever cup was put to his lips the liquid it contained merely ran away on to the sheet.

'The others in bed?'

'Aye. Mam wanted to sit up but she was tired and I made her go to bed. Mercy went with her.'

'Aye.' Nothing more was needed to be said between them about Mercy since it was taken for granted that wherever Martha went, Mercy went too, clinging like a child to her hand, weeping piteously when they were parted.

'And Joss?'

'He's gone.'

'He'll do well in that grand job. He's a way with words, has Joss.'

'Aye.'

'And what will you do, my lad, when you're better?'

Charlie's face, though it could not have been said to change expression since there was none to start with in its ferociously distended state, revealed a great sadness.

'I dunno. Not the mill.' He spoke only in a staccato paucity of words.

'You're right there, love.'

'What d'you mean, Jen?'

Jenny leaned her back against the table leg. She was sitting on the floor, her face no more than a foot or so from Charlie's. The fire's glow played on her pale face, giving it a false impression of well-being and in her eyes was a dawning, growing excitement, a spark of something which Charlie found he liked, though he had no idea of what it could be.

'There's to be changes, Charlie, for thee and me.'

'Changes?'

'Aye.'

'What sort of changes?'

Jenny's eyes dreamed into the future only she could see and Charlie felt the gladness, whatever it might be for, pump vigorously through his battered body.

'How would you like to go to school, Charlie Greenwood? Joss isn't the only one to be offered a grand new job.'

* * *

Katherine and Hannah Chapman dined, as they always did when they were alone, at seven-thirty. Kit often brought home reports, accounts of profits, or a sheaf of papers which she had not had time to glance at during her busy day and she would retire afterward to her study for an hour or so. She rose at four-thirty each morning, winter or summer and therefore she liked to be bathed and in her bed by ten o'clock and even then she might sit up among her pillows and study her weekly profit sheet, often falling asleep with the papers in her hand and the lamp still burning. Her mother had grown accustomed to it since the death of her husband three years ago and had learned, as indeed she had learned while he was alive to amuse herself, playing endless games of patience or having her companion, a well-educated, but impecunious, lady named Miss Fryer, slightly younger than herself and of excellent family, read to her from one of the delightful romances of Sir Walter Scott, his very latest published only that year, *The Fair Maid of Perth* being her favourite.

They had eaten a simple meal of salmon trout with parsley-and-butter, tiny new potatoes freshly picked that day from the garden, roast fillet of veal with peas, and gooseberry sorbet to follow. Superbly cooked as Barker Chapman had always demanded, efficiently and effacingly served by Ellen the head parlourmaid and Betty, watched over by the white gloved and critical personage of the butler, Winters, and Kit had seen no reason, because the master was dead that she should not be similarly obliged.

'We are to have a house-guest, Mother,' she remarked casually as she and Hannah sipped their coffee in the drawing-room. Winters had drawn the curtains for though it was midsummer a swirling mist of light rain laced itself against the windows and the evening light had faded early over the almost invisible hills at the back of the house. Kit had ordered a small fire lit, two or three branches of candles cast a pale peach glow over the two women and the room was soft and lovely, feminine with its fragile chairs and delicate figurines, its velvet sofas and dainty, spindle-legged tables.

'Really?' Hannah stirred her coffee glancing with bright interest at her daughter for it was a long time – surely it must have been the Athertons? – since guests had spent a night at Greenacres. 'And who is that, my dear?'

'You have not met her, Mother.'

'Who are her family then? Are they in cotton?'

'You might say that. Yes, I think you might say that.' Kit smiled over her coffee cup and her mother wondered at the small warning prickle which seemed to run down her own back.

'From where? Are they a Lancashire family?'

'Oh indeed. Born and bred for many generations in Lancashire.'

'How interesting, Kit, and yet you say I do not know them. Now that is odd because I could have sworn I knew all the mill-owners and their family connections from Blackburn to Manchester. Where do they live?'

'In Edgeclough.'

The prickle skimming Hannah Chapman's back became decidedly stronger. 'Edgeclough?'

'Yes, you know the village a couple of miles west of here . . .'

'I know the village, or shall I say I have heard of it as who has not, for it is where that troublemaker lives . . . what was his name? . . . the one who went to prison for inciting the riots a couple of years ago?'

'Greenwood?'

'Yes, that is the name. Dreadful man, but really Kit, I cannot recall a property of any size in that direction.'

'There is none, Mother. My guest lives in the village itself.'

'In the . . .'

'Yes.'

'But there are only weavers' cottages there.'

'That is true.'

'Kit, you must be more explicit since I cannot imagine

what you are talking about.' Hannah's face was quite red now and though she really could not believe — it was far too preposterous — that Kit meant to bring someone who was not of their rank to be a guest in *their* home, she felt the prickle in her spine become a painful tremble, almost a palpitation to which she was prone when she was upset, in the region of her heart.

'Very well, Mother. I am to employ a young woman to help me in the mill . . .'

'Not as a clerk, Kit. The men would not like it.'

'No, not as a clerk, Mother. Her precise duties at the moment are vague, but she will work with me. In my office. I intend to train her myself . . .'

'As what, my dear Katherine. There are no women employed in the mills except as machine operatives and you would hardly be . . .' She stopped and her mouth began to tremble. She put her hand to it and that shook too and she placed her coffee cup carefully on the table beside her.

'You cannot mean what I think you mean! I will not have a girl from a weaver's cottage in my home, Katherine, if that is what you are trying to tell me. Do what you like with her at the mill, which I know you will despite what people say about you for you are well accustomed to it, but I will not have her at Greenacres.'

'She will be my assistant, Mother. She is intelligent, ambitious and though she has not been brought up to it, she will learn . . .'

'Not in my house.' Hannah's voice was implacably hard.

'No, not in your house, Mother, in mine.'

'Katherine! How dare you speak to me like that. Though your father in his wisdom, of which, now, I am seriously beginning to doubt he had any, left the house and indeed everything he owned to you, I am mistress here . . .'

Kit's voice was gentle. 'No Mother, you are not.'

'Katherine! How can you be so hard?'

'I had a good teacher, Mother and he taught me how splendid it is to get one's own way. And that is what I am doing now. Our guest . . . my guest, if you prefer, will be to me what Miss Fryer is to you, though I would wish her to dine with us so that she will learn to . . .'

'Oh no . . . oh no, Katherine.'

'Then she and I will dine alone.'

'You are saying I must eat in my room?'

'No, I am not, but if you do not care to share a table with your daughter and her companion, then you are at liberty to eat where you wish.'

'Merciful Heaven, what is the world coming to? To eat with a servant! Your father did not mean this when he left his mills in your care. He would no more have invited one of his mill-hands into our dining-room, into our *home* than he would some Irish peasant from Pig Lane. You must be mad, absolutely mad! What am I to say to our friends? And . . .' Her elderly face crumpled as she dissolved into the easy tears of a woman who can think of no other way to get what she wants, ' . . . are we to include her in our guest list when Emma Abbott and Sarah Jenkinson dine with us. She will not even know which knife to use, if she has even *seen* a knife . . .'

'She will learn. I will teach her.'

' . . . and her nails will be dirty . . .'

'Don't be ridiculous, Mother.'

' . . . and what of her family? Will I be expected to entertain them as well?' Her weeping became more liquid and she reached for the wisp of handkerchief in her sleeve.

'No, you will not. They would not wish it . . .'

'*They* would not wish it! And who are they to say . . .?'

'Their name is Greenwood. The woman who is to assist me is Jenny Greenwood. She and her son will live here in my house . . .'

'*Her son?* And is her husband to come too?'

'She is not married.'

'A . . . widow . . .?'

'No.'

'*You are bringing a whore and her bastard to live in our home?*'

436

The silence which followed dragged painfully from second to second. Kit watched her mother's face disintegrate into lines and sagging flesh which had not been there before and she was sorry. Hannah Chapman was forty-two years old, a pretty woman who spent hours in front of her mirror with her maid and the lotions and unguents she rubbed into her fine skin. Youthful, plump, and even yet looked at admiringly by many gentlemen of her own generation for she would be a fine catch for any man with the wealth of her dead husband behind her. Now, in the space of ten seconds she had aged to a woman of sixty and her voice was the hissing of snakes in her throat.

'If you imagine I will sit down with a woman who had an illegitimate child and who is a member of the family who murdered your father you must be insane and I shall consult my brother to use his influence to have you put away.'

'Mother.' Kit's voice was endlessly patient. 'It was proved that ... that Joss Greenwood had nothing to do with Father's murder. Do you think the man would be walking about unharmed if he had? And his sister is a clever woman, strong and trustworthy. She is not to be blamed for ... her child. She was ... seduced by someone who had a hold on her ...'

Hannah Chapman stood up. Her tears were gone now and in their place was the dislike she had always known she felt for this unconventional, independent, obstinate and in her opinion, quite freakish daughter of hers. Years ago when Kit had been a girl and, Hannah had hoped, malleable, she had run to her father and spurned Hannah's hopes that they might be as other mothers and their daughters were. Kit had taken up the pursuits of a son, become Barker Chapman's son, scorned the dictates of polite society and become, Hannah privately thought, the laughing stock of Crossfold. She had carried on, after her father's death, with the running of his mills and had, her mother was told by the gentlemen with whom they dined, made a success of it, but in the past year or two there had been no more offers

437

for her of marriage. No man wanted a wife, no matter how wealthy, who was a successful *business man!* They had hoped, after her father's death, to see her falter a little, perhaps slip and fall so that one of them might pick her up, kiss her better, send her home to the nursery, and put back to rights the business her father had, foolishly, left in her hands. But she had not fallen and Hannah would never forgive her for it.

And now this! A mill girl, a factory girl with the morals, so it appeared, of an alley-cat, and in *her* home. It was not to be borne and though Hannah Chapman knew she had no choice but to bear it she would let it be known, in her own home and in the Penfold Valley that Katherine Chapman was no longer her daughter.

'You will, of course, do as you please, Katherine. This is your house, as you point out and you may entertain whom you like in it. But not in my presence. I would be glad if you would arrange for me to have my own suite of rooms, my own servants, and only those I invite shall enter them. Good-night, or perhaps it is goodbye.'

29

The town simply rocked with it and Hannah was most gratified by the strong support she received in the beginning from the ladies of her acquaintance who thought they had nothing to lose by giving it. They were unaware of the dreadful position in which she had placed their husbands, most of whom did business with Katherine and who knew it to be only expedient to stay on her right side.

'Dammit, what will the bloody woman do next?' George Abbott thundered to his wife in the privacy of their bedroom, not really distinguishing between Hannah and

Katherine since it made no difference to him who was to share Katherine Chapman's home with her, nor who worked in her office, his only anxiety being the awkwardness the whole foolish situation would create in his world of commerce. Of course, what else could you expect when women were allowed to meddle in the affairs of gentlemen, he begged his wife to tell him? Their damned female emotions were bound to get in the way of their judgment. And did Katherine Chapman have any?

Was that emotion or judgment? His Emma wanted to be told since it was well known that Barker Chapman's daughter had spurned the splendid hand of Harry Atherton, a gentleman of great position, if little actual cash, and anyone could see how much he had been devastated by it and by her coldness to him. Which, to Emma, showed a lack of emotion *and* judgment on Katherine Chapman's part since any girl, particularly of their class would have snapped him up and had him to the altar before the year was out. And now, it was rumoured, he had married a great heiress from Guilden Sutton and Katherine Chapman had lost her chance for good.

'Well, she could finish the Abbott Mills if she had a mind to it,' George said, irritated beyond measure by his wife's female ramblings on a matter which had not the slightest bearing on his dilemma. He couldn't afford to offend Katherine Chapman whatever Hannah might demand of him in the way of loyalty, and there were many gentlemen of Crossfold who were in the same tenuous position. She had only to call in a note or two here and there and not a few men of the textile trade would find it hard to continue so what the hell was he, and they, to do now, he asked Emma to tell him?

'But we can't dine with Hannah in a separate part of the house one week, and with Katherine the next,' his wife wailed. 'Hannah would be affronted though I doubt if Katherine would care. She has no heart at all and no concern for anything but those mills of hers . . .'

'As I have for mine, woman, and that is why you will

continue to call on her and to entertain her in our home and if Hannah doesn't like it then I'm sorry but there's nothing else to be done. I have relied, first on Barker, and now on his daughter for a loan now and again and one does not displease the man, or in this case the woman, one owes money to.'

'But that . . . that factory girl might be there . . .'

'Then we shall just have to grit our teeth and make ourselves pleasant to her.'

'*To a mill girl?*'

'Aye, and don't forget, my lass, your grandmother was nought but a spinner in her father's cottage, as was mine so there's no need to put on that grand air with me. There'll be more than a few gentlemen, and their ladies too, who'll have to toe the line with Katherine Chapman from now on and if that means being pleasant to a mill hand then we'll bloody well have to do it.'

'We must get some clothes for you, Jenny,' Kit said to her briskly on the day it had begun, 'and to do that I think we will travel to London for I mean you to be as elegantly gowned as any of the ladies of this town. Miss Cavendish is all very well but it will take too long for the fabrics and all the rest of the things you need to arrive so we will have a small holiday and fetch them ourselves. It will be an opportunity to get to know one another without . . . other factors intruding.'

'To London?' Kit might have suggested she and Jenny were to go to the Americas to hunt for bearskins to dress themselves in, so confounded was she, and besides, who did she think she was, telling Jenny she was not dressed as she should be? She had on a perfectly decent skirt and bodice, clean and made by her mother only three years ago when there had been a copper or two to spare from Harry Atherton.

'Yes, why not? Don't tell me you have some objection to being fitted out with a fashionable gown and perhaps a bonnet. You will pay for them yourself in the end, you know.'

440

'Then in that case there's nowt wrong with what I've got on.'

'And that's another thing.'

'What?'

'You really will have to make an effort to stop using the word 'nowt'. I appreciate that many of the men I do business with are only a generation away from weavers' cottages themselves but they have learned to speak, or been taught at the grammar school, the language of a gentleman.'

'Meaning I'm no lady. Well, I never pretended to be and if how I speak, *and* dress don't suit, then p'haps you'd better get down to the spinning room and pick someone else for your fine job. I'm a mill girl, Kit Chapman. That's what I *am*, and learning to wear fine clothes and say *nothing* instead of *nowt* won't change it . . .'

'There you are, you can pronounce the word if you put your mind to it. Just listen to the way I speak and watch what I do and you won't go far wrong.'

'Is that so! Well, you may be interested to know that I think *nowt* a pound to dressing and speaking like you and if it wasn't for being able to give my lad and my Mam a bit of comfort I'd tell you to take your bloody job and . . .' The words were hissed through clenched teeth.

'But you won't, will you, Jenny Greenwood?' Kit smiled sweetly. 'You haven't quite the nerve to go that far, have you?'

'It's got nowt to do with nerve and well you know it. I'm doing this to try and get a bit of food in them bairns' mouths down there and a decent roof over their heads, *and for no other reason*. D'you think I want to spend my days, aye, and every spare hour it seems, in the company of Barker Chapman's lass, do you? I wouldn't spit on you if you were on fire, only for *them*.'

'I know that and I must admit the thought daunts me too. But you can be of use to me, you see and so I will make the best of it and you must do the same.'

Jenny had walked from Edgeclough to Crossfold that morning as she had done every morning, leaving the cottage

441

at four o'clock just as the sun was showing its rim above Dog Hill. Lucas was to remain with Martha for the time being but only until Jenny was settled at Greenacres and the nursery had been prepared for him. He was a brown-eyed, sturdy-legged replica of Harry Atherton, with his father's devilish smile but a certain sweetness in his expression which reminded his grandmother of Abel Greenwood, which was strange since they did not share the same blood.

The parting from her son and her mother had been hard, for Martha seemed to think she was to go to the ends of the earth – which was what this new position with Katherine Chapman appeared to her to be – and that she would never see her girl again. She had clung to her fiercely, afraid suddenly since she herself was not young and with Charlie helpless and Mercy no more than another child to be cared for alongside Lucas, how was she to manage?

'It's all arranged, Mother,' Jenny told her lovingly. 'Sarah's to come up each day until Charlie's on his feet again . . .'

'But Sarah can't afford to sit about here all day with . . .'

'Sarah *can* afford it, Mother,' and she was delighted with the grand feeling she had when she added, 'I've seen to that.'

'You . . . ?' Martha's face was bewildered.

'Listen Mother, this new job I'm to do . . . it's responsible work . . .' She tried to remember the exact words Kit Chapman had used when Jenny had told her, brusquely, that she would be willing to take the position offered her. She would give it a try. Yes, she would live up at the big house, she had told Miss Chapman, though God knows how she would cope with it, the stares of the servants, the gossip, the contempt and rejection and loneliness she would suffer, but by God she'd manage it somehow. She could hardly trail each day in her grand frock across the open moorland from Edgeclough to Crossfold and back, could she? Besides Miss Chapman had said she must learn not only the workings of the mill and the changes Miss Chapman envisaged and which Jenny was to supervise, but how to mix with the ladies and gentlemen of Miss Chapman's business and social acquaintance.

'It will take a lot of hard work, Mother,' she continued, holding her mother's hands across the kitchen table, then turning to smile at Charlie who was, as his back healed, almost ready to sit up now. 'I'm to take on duties which need constant watching and can only be given to someone trustworthy.' Could she be blamed for feeling a little bit flattered at that, she had asked herself privately? 'That's what *she* said and if I'm to do anything to help to change what's going on I've no choice but to trust *her*. I can afford to keep you and Mercy, and Charlie *and* pay Sarah to help you . . .'

'Dear God in Heaven . . .'

'Perhaps He is at last, Mother.' She turned to Charlie and leaned forward to touch his still badly swollen face. 'And when you're better . . .'

'Yes Jenny?' He held his breath and his eyes glowed between his slitted eyelids.

'You're not to go back to the weaving-shed . . .'

'No . . .'

'No lad. What would you like to do more than anything else in the world, Charlie, apart from working with Joss?'

'You know, Jenny, you said I could . . .'

'Aye, and I'm to keep my promise. You're to go to the gammar school in Crossfold,' and her voice was hopeful, joyful for had not Joss said that only through education could a man better his station in life and now *she*, Jenny Greenwood, was to give Charlie that chance.

'Will you like that, love?'

'Oh, Jenny, just wait 'til our Joss hears about this.'

'Aye, I wish I could be here when you tell him.' Her face crumpled for a moment since how was she to leave this loving circle which had sustained her for as long as she could remember, then it brightened. Joss had said it time and time again that only through moving on could progress be made and by God she meant to make progress now.

She'd been given a chance, a bite at the good things which were set out on the tables of the privileged and if they should seem sour at first then she'd keep on tasting until she found what she liked. The rest she'd spit out or overcome somehow.

'Watch out for Lucas for me,' she said at the last, burying her face in the soft, sweet smelling flesh of her son's neck, then she was gone.

She was standing silently in Kit's office when she arrived, looking out on to the hurrying crowd of men and women, the fretful children, listening to the incessant sound of their wooden clogs on the cobblestones, watching, remembering, her heart sad for those who were slipping patiently into the sheds and the spinning rooms, there to stay for the next fourteen, fifteen, sixteen hours. She saw Kit at the gate, ready to shut it on the latecomers, then moving across the yard, nodding to a man who touched his cap, a woman who sketched a curtsey and bitterness soured her throat for it seemed, despite Kit Chapman's fine words; that nothing had changed.

'Aah, Jenny, good morning. I won't be a moment and then we can . . .'

'They can't help being late sometimes, you know. They don't do it on purpose. God knows, they can't afford to lose their wages in fines. They've got sick children at home, many of them and have you any idea how hard it is for a woman to leave a child . . .' her face worked briefly in a spasm of pain before she could speak again, ' . . . in the care of another who's probably only a year or two older, or even on its own? They have to work to feed them and so they're left alone and yet when they're a minute late you shut the gate in their faces and make them wait until eight o'clock.'

Kit stood quietly, her face expressionless, her first instinctive anger – since when did anyone take Kit Chapman to task about *anything* – dying away, her hands which had been reaching out to some papers, still hovering above them.

444

'Of course, you are right,' she said at last. 'It has been done for so long it just never occurred to me to stop it. Latecomers have always been fined and I merely carried on what my grandfather began years ago. What do you suggest?'

'Me?' Jenny's mouth dropped open in surprise.

'That is what you are here for, Jenny. To assist, to advise, to help me contrive a business which will still make a profit without exploiting my employees. You see I *must* make a profit or there is no use in manufacturing my cloth for if I lose money I shall lose the mills and those people out there will be without work. Over a thousand of them. I have the expertise. I know *how* to make a profit, but *you* are a spinner, you are a woman of . . . well . . . a woman who has . . .'

'I'm one of the "distressed poor", is that what you're saying? There's no need to mince words with me. Well, so I am, or was. I know how they live and how they suffer in these mills of yours to earn a few bob a week. Well, I suppose you and me, being two sides of the same coin, so to speak, could try to solve not only their problems, but the ones *you* are going to have because you're going to have some, make no mistake about it, Kit Chapman. You'll be despised by everyone in the valley but then, so will I for they'll say I've gone over to you for more money. Well, let me tell you now that I haven't. I'm willing to trust you, for a while at any rate. There will be those who say I'm in it just for what I can get, and I admit that's partly true. Why shouldn't me and my family be warm and well fed, have pretty things and learn our letters like you and yours, but I'd not give you the time of day, never fear, if I didn't think I could do some good for those poor beggars out there. My brother's been doing it for nearly ten years and my father before him. My younger brother nearly lost his life for it. There's not a lot a woman can do but now I'm to be given the chance and I'll take it. So first off, we'll have those gates open again and every one of them outside who has a genuine reason for being late will be allowed in. I can tell a man who's been on the gin and too befuddled to get out of bed on time though he'll pretend it's for some other reason. They can wait until eight o'clock for I'll not stand for them kind of tricks.'

They moved through the spinning mills together on that first day, a strange and unbelievable sight to the spinners and tacklers who stared with mouths agape at the two young women. Kit wore a harebell blue gown of gingham, the bodice high to her neck with small puffed sleeves to her elbow. The skirt was wide and quite unsuitable for negotiating the narrow spaces between the machines and each operative was forced to stand hastily to one side to allow her employer – and her skirt – to pass by. Her half boots were of white-laced kid with high heels and around her slender waist was a wide satin sash the same colour as her dress. Her hair had been arranged by Janet, as it always was, into the style which suited its heavy straightness, an 'Apollo' knot at the nape of her neck and secured with a froth of blue satin ribbons. The use of rouge which had once been fashionable was now declining, since the style was to be languid, listless and pale causing many a gentleman to remark that there seemed to be no healthy females about these days, and Kit's golden skin, peach tinted at the cheekbones was considered to be quite odd. Tight-lacing was the mode but Kit, having no Mama to press her and no concern in the rivalry for a gentleman's interest, did not observe it, indeed had no need of it.

Jenny had washed her abundant hair the night before, taking the scissors with which her father had once trimmed his 'piece' of cloth, and cutting it as she did about once a month until it was no more than three inches from her white scalp and it rioted all over her head in thick, glossy curls. Her plain grey bodice and ankle length skirt were completely unadorned and her feet were pushed stocking-less into her wooden clogs. Her eyes were smudged with weariness since she had slept little during the past week but their colour, not unlike the grey misted skies above Dog

Hill, was clear and lovely. She was clean, decent but beside Kit, a plain grey pigeon next to the brilliance of a peacock. She spoke to Kit almost constantly, pointing a rough, broken-nailed finger to a dozen things in every row of machines and Kit nodded and was seen to touch Jenny's arm, to talk close to Jenny's ear, to stop when she did and examine a pair of the new 'self-acting' spinning mules only recently installed which could spin not only the very finest of threads but double the number spun on the old machines. They tested together the quality of the yarn spun, rubbing it between experienced fingers, both of them and making comments which none could hear. And those about them were quite mesmerised to see Miss Katherine Chapman, their employer, the owner of the mills and of the machines they themselves operated go down on her knees in her beautiful blue dress, just as though the garment meant nothing to her, with Jenny Greenwood, whom they all knew as one of themselves, and draw out a small child who cowered beneath a spinning frame. A little girl of no more than three or four who was plainly more terrified of the creature, beautiful and unimagined in the child's mind, than anything she had ever known in her short life. She was familiar with nothing but the colours of black and grey, with obnoxious smells, which she did not know were obnoxious, with dirt and filth, bricks and smoke, angry faces and the feel of the strap and had not known anything else existed.

She was set on her feet and in her fear her bladder emptied itself down her thin grey leg and when they led her between the rows of machinery, a skeletal hand held in each of theirs towards Ellis who had been stamping his feet in obvious pique at his employer's presence in 'his' room, the child might have been going to the gallows so great was her despair.

No one could, naturally, hear what was said between Ellis and Miss Chapman but those close to them declared later that if looks could kill Jenny Greenwood would have dropped dead on the spot. He had argued hotly, even forcibly with his flint-faced employer, attempting to take the almost senseless child from her but another overlooker was brought over to take his place and the women, those who had the strength to bolster up their usual indifference to anything but the earning of their wage and the feeding of their children, watched furtively as the two women, the man and the child walked out of the spinning room.

'Now then Ellis,' Kit Chapman said crisply when the four of them had gained the privacy of her office. 'I would be glad to hear your version of the event which took place in the weaving-shed a few days ago. I appreciate that you are overlooker in the spinning room and that you are in charge of one hundred and sixty frames there but on this particular occasion I believe you were absent from your work. While you were absent – and I know exactly when that was – this child here . . .' She pointed to the girl who crouched, like some small, dazed night animal caught in the full glare of sunlight, against the wall of the office, ' . . . was considerably abused by an overlooker in the weaving-shed, in fact *two* overlookers, while another looked on. She was gagged, I was told by an observer and whipped round a machine. A young boy who came to her aid had both his arms broken and was so badly flogged it was feared for a while that he might never recover.' Her voice dropped almost to a whisper. 'If he had died, Ellis, those three men would have been hanged for murder. I, personally, would have seen to it. For some reason this child, the child in question, perhaps to hide the evidence, has been transferred to the spinning room and is now in *your* care . . .'

'Now see here, Miss Chapman, if those two in the weaving-shed said I had anything to do with it they are lying. I admit I . . . well, I never laid a finger on the kid, or the lad. It was them that strapped her and flogged the lad . . .'

'Their names, Ellis?'

'Well, I don't know as . . .'

'I wish to know their names, Ellis, so that they may be charged.'

Ellis began to smirk and finger the full moustache he now

affected, believing thankfully that his part in the affair was to be overlooked if he played informer. He lied when he said he had not helped in the beating Charlie Greenwood had received, since he had long harboured a grudge against Jenny Greenwood for her refusal to allow him the liberties he had, if he was honest, almost begged her for; for her scorn, her contemptuous treatment of him as a man; any member of her family would do to work off some of the rage she invoked in him. He had lusted after her for a long time but when Harry Atherton had laid his claim to her Ellis had been forced to relinquish his quarry to a stronger, more authoritative beast of prey. But he had not given up and when Atherton had gone, still swearing revenge on the woman, Ellis's employer who, it turned out had spurned *him*, Ellis had renewed his chase after Jenny Greenwood. Her refusal had made her even more desirable, her contempt more vulnerable, for though he had been hot for her body, his hatred of her had become a cold thing. She was no more than a spinner, a factory girl who he could have dismissed whenever he wanted to, but his resolve, like a certain other part of his body, had hardened each time he caught a glimpse of her as she leaned over her machine.

Now she was watching him, her expression one of withering hostility and he could hardly wait to get her back at her machine for by God she'd pay for this. No doubt she had come running to Miss Chapman, defending that spineless lout who was her brother, demanding that the men involved be punished. It was well known that Miss Chapman was a mite squeamish when it came to the factory floor and it was just like her to pick on this one incident to ease her conscience. For years lads, and lasses, had been flogged in the mill yard for stepping out of line, children strapped to keep them awake and she'd never opened her damned mouth, but, it was rumoured, she had a soft spot for these Greenwoods because of her fancy for Joss Greenwood, he supposed. It was strange how these high and mighty ladies and gentlemen, such as her and Harry Atherton liked to bed with a class inferior to their own, but that was life and nowt to do with him, except when he could make a guinea or two out of it. *He* didn't care who he tumbled, except for Jenny Greenwood. Now she was a bit special and when he had the chance, willing or unwilling he'd have her drawers round her ankles and her skirts over her head and she'd pay for this humiliation she had heaped on him. It was strange the way Atherton had run off three years since, especially after what he himself had told the man about Miss Chapman and Joss Greenwood. Still, he, Ellis had a good spot here in Chapman's mill. A position of responsibility, a decent wage since all his girls worked hard to provide him with it, and as much wenching as he could handle from the fresh girls as they came in. He'd been a bit of a fool to get involved with the flogging Jim and Alfie had given young Greenwood but he'd smooth it over, like he always did. Pity about Jim and Alfie, but then they were nowt to him, were they?

'Their names, Ellis.'

'Jim Briggs and Alfie Jackson.'

'Thank you. I will send for them at once and I would be obliged if you would step into the outer office where the Peace Officers are waiting for you.'

The smirk dropped from Ellis's well-fed face and his mouth gaped to reveal the poor state of his teeth. He'd kissed the shuttle a thousand times before he became an overlooker and those at the front were no more than rotting stumps. The amazement on his face might have been amusing if the situation had been less serious, but it was replaced just as quickly with an expression of such malice Jenny felt her stout heart quail. She had worked in the mill for so long the complete authority of the overlooker had been bred in her and though she had defied more than one they still had the power to frighten her, even if she had not let them see it.

But not Kit Chapman. It was *her* authority which counted here and since the day her father had died she had been opposed by no one. She was in command, supreme and all powerful. They all belonged to her, these men, women and children and they were here because she chose to allow it. She could hire them and fire them at will and her haughty disdain for this one, her absolute belief that, should she want to and she did, he would be behind bars by nightfall was explicit in her face.

'I've done nowt . . .' he began to bluster, remembering at the last moment who she was, remembering that she was no submissive spinner he could have cringing over her machine. 'I was there I'll give you that and happen I should have stopped it but it weren't my place. He was in their charge and he'd taken a swing at Jim. Knocked him to the floor. Like a madman he was and we had to control him . . .'

'An eleven year old boy and *three full grown men*. Tell me, Ellis, who held his arms, who *broke* his arms . . . ?'

'Not me, Miss Chapman. It were nowt to do wi' me.'

'We shall see then, Ellis, when you come before the magistrates.'

'Now look here . . .'

'No, Ellis, you look here. I am the master in this mill and I'll not have my operatives half killed by . . .'

'You weren't so bloody fussy in the past,' he roared, all constraint gone. 'You did nowt when that brat 'ad 'is arms ripped off, did yer? No, you steered clear of t'spinning room when it suited yer. There's dozens . . . hundreds feel t'strap, week in an' week out but you shut yer bloody eyes to it until this bitch 'ere put 'er two-pennorth in . . .'

The child in the corner turned her face to the wall and Jenny called out in a high, appalled voice. The door burst open and in a moment the Peace Officer had him by the arms, manhandling him towards the door. Several clerks craned their necks to see better and Mrs Plank hovered hesitantly at the end of the hallway. Kit Chapman felt her legs give way beneath her. She sat down slowly and her breath sighed out from her in a long expulsion of guilt.

'It's true,' she whispered. 'What he said was the truth, but from now on it will be different, I promise you.' She was looking at no one in particular and Jenny was made aware that she was talking to no one but herself since she was the only one to blame for it and she was the only one to put it right.

'What will you do with the child?' Jenny asked softly after a moment or so. 'The poor thing's terrified out of her wits. Will you leave her for the kitchen maids at Greenacres to fetch up. Or are you to turn her into a skivvy instead of a piecer?'

'No, of course not. She can . . .'

'What?'

'Well, what do you suggest?'

'She could go to . . . in the . . .' Jenny gulped for the word was unfamiliar on her tongue, ' . . . in the nursery with Lucas.'

'Good God!'

'Why not?'

'Well, no reason, I suppose.'

'Poor little beggar will probably feel more secure with another child.'

'Do you think so?'

'Have you no imagination, Miss Chapman, except that which you put to work in the making of profit each week?'

Kit chose to ignore the question, saying instead. 'We are to go on a journey.'

'Where are we going?'

'Home first, and then to London. But you are right. Flora will look after her. She has, I believe, ten brothers and sisters, all younger than herself so she should know how.'

They spent five days there. In a borrowed gown of Miss Chapman's and with Janet, her maid to accompany them, Jenny Greenwood rode in a carriage for the first time in her life, from the mill to Greenacres, which, if she were to be asked, she could have described to no one since her fevered gaze fell on so many beautiful and bewildering objects they all ran together in a kaleidoscope of colours and shapes and she saw none of them. She was vaguely aware of the disdainful faces, of skirts being drawn aside as she passed, of whispers behind gloved hands and the disapproving sniff of the girl called Janet when she was asked to find a gown suitable for *Miss* Greenwood, but it all hurried by on the periphery of her conscious mind.

She stepped, this time in a dark blue travelling outfit which fitted her rather well, and a bonnet to match, a shade too large and quenching the bright, excited spirit of her eyes and tumultuous hair, into the coach for London and shrank for several hours into the protective silence which allowed her to appear composed, unmoved by the desperate speed at which they went. Ten and a half miles an hour, Miss Chapman told her imperturbably, appearing quite unconcerned by it all, but anyone who had been to London before, (as Jenny had been told Miss Chapman had) must find the journey most ordinary.

They reached St Albans the next day, the whole journey from Manchester to London, not counting the night they stayed at the pleasant and comfortable coaching inn at Leicester, taking no more than an incredible eighteen and a half hours. The coach, a beautiful thing in Jenny's wondering eyes was of a dull, black leather with broad, blackleaded nails tracing out the panels. Above these were four oval windows with leather curtains. Upon the doors were displayed in large characters the names of the places from where the coach started its journey and where it would finish it. Jenny read the words carefully each time they came to a post-house where the horses and sometimes the drivers, were changed, marvelling at names such as Portsmouth, Bath, Holyhead and York, Shrewsbury and Dover and where they might possibly be! She tried not to stare too blatantly at the multitude of travellers moving from one part of the country to another as though it was commonplace to them, an everyday occurrence which happened to all, gentlemen in full-bottomed cloaks, beavers and mudstained boots, ladies in wide skirts, wide bonnets, laughing, flirting, drinking, gambling some of them on how long it would take to get from here to there.

The inn at which they were to spend five nights was quite splendid with broad corridors and stairs, elegant drawing-rooms and four poster beds hung with silk, their sheets smelling of lavender. Miss Chapman ordered three bedrooms and a private sitting room since she did not wish to be pestered by bothersome gentlemen, she said and still Jenny Greenwood seemed unable to unclench the tight snap of her jaw, merely nodding and smiling as best she could, trembling at every strange sound, of which there were many, jumping at every loud noise, of which there were even more.

But by doing exactly what Miss Chapman did, by copying every move, every step she took, her smiles and 'good mornings', her courteous 'good evenings', her confident walk and interested gaze, Jenny Greenwood began, little by little, hour by hour, to relax, hesitantly to look about her and actually *see* what went on.

They strolled the length of Oxford Street, Janet a pace or two behind them, boiling indignantly, Jenny was well aware of being made to feel a lesser personage than a mere factory girl. They looked in the splendid shop windows, their facades brightly lit by gas-lamp, their doors open, they were told, until ten o'clock at night. There were shops selling watches, fans and silk, china and glass, crystal flasks every shape and size and colour, the likes of which Jenny had not even known existed. Behind handsome glass windows were pyramids of pineapples, figs, grapes and oranges and when she asked Miss Chapman tentatively what they might be she heard Janet snigger behind her hand. There were shops selling lamps of crystal, silver and brass, slippers and shoes and boots and on Greek Street beyond Soho Square, the magnificent showrooms of Josiah Wedgwood where tables were laid out as though a dinner party was expected at any moment and salesmen hovered discreetly between columns which rose from the polished floor to the plastered ceiling. It was, one of the young gentlemen told them politely, Mr Wedgwood's declared aim to 'amuse and divert, please, astonish, nay, even to ravish the ladies with his display'.

They toured Woburn Walk in Bloomsbury, spending a

day in the first shopping centre designed purposely as a shopping street and at 'The Royal Opera Arcade', a setting of superb shops at the back of the Haymarket Opera House.

But it was in the salons of the great dressmakers and designers that Jenny was made truly speechless. She had, up until then, managed a word or two with Miss Chapman even going so far as to venture an opinion on this or that, but as they ascended the gilt and mirrored splendour of the pale beige carpeted staircase of Monsieur Antoine, just come, they were told, straight from Paris to dress the ladies of London, that she almost lost her nerve.

'We shall have you suitably attired, Jenny and I must admit these peignoirs are quite delicious.' Miss Chapman studied a delicate foamy creation which Jenny could not even recognise as a garment for any woman to wear, or hazard a guess at *when*. 'I should feel decidedly wicked sipping my early morning tea in one of these.'

Sipping tea! Is that what they were designed for, Jenny had time to marvel before being led on to study pelisse-robes and morning dresses, lace petticoats and round dresses, with or without a train, walking dresses trimmed with swansdown, black kid sandals, small black beaver riding hats, York tan gloves, white kid gloves, dresses with 'demi-gigot' sleeves, 'marie' sleeves and 'imbecile' sleeves and evening dresses of satin and gauze with no sleeves at all, and available in Madam's size and any colour Madam might care for, by the end of the week.

And in one of the new evening gowns of which Miss Chapman insisted she needed at least half a dozen, on their last night in London, she and Miss Chapman sat in a private box, as Miss Chapman called it, at the 'Prince of Wales' theatre to watch a performance of 'The Corsican Brothers', a romantic drama adapted from the French, Miss Chapman said. It was, Jenny thought, the most magical moment of her life and she would never, if she lived to be ninety, forget it.

The next day they boarded the coach at St Albans, Janet a mite more respectful of the elegantly dressed young lady

455

who had once been Jenny Greenwood, spinster, from Edge-clough but who was now, it seemed, ready to tackle any-thing from the high-toned butler at Greenacres who had turned up his nose at her five days ago, to the reformation of the whole town of Crossfold and every cotton mill in it.

'And what did you make of London then, Jenny?' she heard her mistress ask her new assistant as the coach pulled out of the mill yard.

'It were all right, I suppose, if you like that sort o' thing but there's nowt to beat a good country fair or a Whit Sunday walk in Oldham.' And her eyes had smiled ma-liciously as she turned her fashionably bonneted head to stare – bored to death with it all, she would have them believe – out of the coach window.

30

They did not recognise her on the first day she appeared at the mill gate with Katherine Chapman and it was not until one of the managers, a young man of about thirty-five who had often admired the flaunting strangeness of Jenny Greenwood's short, glossy curls, remarked on her resem-blance to the mill girl, that it was realised this *was* the mill girl.

'Shall I shut the gate now, Miss Chapman?' the yard foreman said as the clock on the counting house wall struck five thirty, but Miss Chapman shook her head briskly.

'No Sam, not yet. I shall return to my office now but Miss Greenwood will tell you when.'

The man went so far as to utter, '*Yer what* . . . !' before he remembered to whom he was speaking and even then, when Miss Chapman had walked away, her own bare head shining in the early morning sunshine, he found he could scarcely control the habit of a lifetime, his hands fingering the large key, putting it in the lock, edging the stout gates to a slow closing against half a dozen hurrying women whose thin faces shone with relief to see them still open.

'Let them in, Sam, if you please,' Jenny Greenwood had the bloody nerve to tell him and if she didn't watch out he'd clout her one despite her grand frock and the dainty leather boots she had on feet which had known nothing but clogs.

'Who the 'ell d'yer think you're talkin' to, my lass? Dressed up to the nines yer might be but you're still nowt but a factory girl and no right to throw yer weight about at *my* gate.'

But Jenny had taken up a stand in the centre of the arched gateway, addressing a remark to, being answered hesitantly by the dozen or so women who hovered there, smiling, nodding in agreement, touching a sympathetic hand to a bowed shoulder, allowing the women to slip inside the gate and he could hardly shut them with her between them, could he? She was sharp with Jacob Smith, the smell of the gin he had drunk the night before still on his breath and told him to stand aside before she called a man to eject him since only genuine latecomers were to be let in, and surprisingly Jacob Smith did so and at forty minutes past five the gates were clanged shut, not to be opened again until eight o'clock and as Sam crossed the yard he was heard to mutter that old Mr Chapman would be turning over in his grave this day.

'Was there any trouble with Sam?' Miss Chapman asked Jenny as she walked into her office.

'Not really. He would have liked to shut *me* out and make me wait for three hours and see me fined for my cheek but I stood in the gateway and he could do nothing about it.'

'And the women?'

'Most of them had sick children to see to before they left.

457

One of them, her husband or that's what she calls him, though I doubt they're wed, had had an accident and she had to help him out of his bed. Oh, all legitimate reasons for being late so I let them in. It was . . .' She had been about to say that it had been a joy to her to see the slack relief on their poor pinched faces but she could not seem to let herself be natural with this unusual woman. She had begun, at last, to believe that Katherine Chapman's intentions were to be trusted. That she meant what she said, but though they had spent almost a week in one another's company, it did not get any easier. Too much stood between them. They could not, despite good intentions on both their parts, immediately become friends, if they ever would. And if they were to become working partners, for they both wanted this revolutionary idea to succeed, they would have to put aside their past relationship and try very hard to forge a new one for the future, if it could be done.

Kit Chapman leaned forward, resting her elbows on her desk. Beside it, making it double the length, had been placed another which was, for the time being, to be Jenny's. They were to sit side by side and every transaction, every concern to do with the business, every commercial intercourse recorded, profits, loss, meeting agendas, shift rotas, the state of trade, each negotiation Katherine Chapman conducted would include the presence of Jenny Greenwood and all would be explained to her as it happened. She already knew all there was to know about the technical side of spinning and would be invaluable in the organisation of the new work system and the rates of wages which would not only be fair – a decent wage for a decent day's work as Joss Greenwood had dreamed of – but would provide a higher standard of living for all her operatives. But for now the relationship of Katherine Chapman and Jenny Greenwood must be worked out satisfactorily.

'Sit down, Jenny,' she said, her face unsmiling. She watched as Jenny carefully negotiated the wide skirt of her gingham gown round the corner of the desk holding it gingerly until she was sitting down. It was in fine stripes of cream and white with a wide cream satin sash. The bodice was neat, the sleeves close fitting to her wrist, modest and serviceable once she had mastered the art of walking in it, though she had thought the colours chosen by Miss Chapman to be far too light for the walk she intended each day about the mill. It was to be her job to reorganise the placing of the machines so that each operative might have more room and so be exposed to less danger. There was to be stout fencing put about the moving parts of the machines to safeguard against accidents. The windows were to be reconstructed in order to allow for ventilation . . . oh, she could go on all day about the plans she and Miss Chapman had discussed and over which her heart rejoiced, but still, when she lay sleepless between the fine sheets on the bed Miss Chapman's housekeeper had told her roughly was to be hers, the doubts still plagued her for it all seemed too good to be true.

'We must trust each other if we are to make a success of this new venture, you know that, don't you, Jenny?' Miss Chapman was saying, and Jenny nodded brusquely, wishing it was as easy as that.

'I cannot imagine the kind of life you and others like you have known, but neither can I imagine how the King up in London lives for I have never seen it, nor suffered it. Try as I might I can only see your old life through your eyes and because of that you must be patient with me if I seem . . . unsympathetic. I have never known hunger, or cold or discomfort and though I can try hard I do not know what it is like to suffer any of them. I have lived a life of privilege but that does not mean I am without . . . emotion. I suppose I must be honest and tell you that I knew there were young children working in my mills and sheds. I was told by my father that the work they did could be done by no one else, that there was no one small enough or nimble enough to do what they did, that their families would starve if I did not employ them and if you are honest you will agree that that part is true.'

Jenny nodded her head again but the expression on her face was still coolly impassive.

'Until your brother was so cruelly beaten and I was forced to see the results I turned my face from the truth of it. I pretended to believe that it was necessary and could not be changed, that if it were, there would be no profit in it for me. If we work together, you and I, we must be able to devise a way to run a business, make a profit, without killing children, maiming them, turning them into grey-faced, elderly ten- or eleven-year-olds with bowed legs and hunched backs. I don't know how to do it. I need help. I need someone who knows what I am talking about. I need someone to talk *to* and I cannot deal with a woman who I know holds me in contempt in her heart, who does not *believe* I mean what I say. I want you to work as hard as you have ever worked, in becoming that person, for really it is in the best interests of your family, your friends and those you have worked with in the past. Does that not make it worth your while?'

Jenny studied her, her face quite unreadable and Kit felt her heart sink since her expression, or lack of it, seemed to say it did not.

'I will do the best I can,' she said after a long pause, 'but I really can't find it in me to take pleasure in it.'

'Take pleasure in it? For God's sake don't tell me you would prefer to be back in the spinning mill with those . . .?'

'Those what?' Jenny's voice was dangerously quiet.

'With those women who do nothing but move parts of a machine about all day long and whose brains have become dormant because of it. Here you can *use* yours in work that is stimulating, exciting, challenging. Make decisions, when you have the experience, give orders and see them carried out *and* be exhilarated by the results. Does that not excite you?'

'This is your mill and you are the one to benefit from the excitement.'

'But it's not just that, is it?'

'No.'

'What then?'

'I've despised you for so long, I will be truthful, that I cannot get out of the habit. You, and men like you, have been detested by men and women, like *me*, for so long we can't just put it aside because suddenly you say you are different and, because of it, so must we be. You tell me I am to be your 'right hand' in turning this mill into a place where them down there can earn a decent wage and live a decent life. Now *why*, I ask myself, and how long will it last? Is it because of what was done to our Charlie? You say it was. You didn't know what was goin' on, you tell me, but how do I know that's the truth? *I don't know you*, only as a mill-owner and I've always reckoned them not to be worth a great deal. I can't *take* to you, is what I'm saying, and I don't know if I ever will. Happen when you've *proved* to me you mean what you say and this isn't just summat you fancy doing to ease your guilty conscience which, after a while might ease itself anyway, then I might believe what you say.'

'I have the greatest desire to fire you right now.'

'Aye, happen you have, but you'll not find another woman in that mill that'd do what I'm willing to do. I'm not afraid of you, you see, and they are.'

'I might have bitten off more than I can easily chew, you're saying?'

'Summat like that.'

'Why don't we spend the day together on Sunday and discuss it without the work at the mill to distract us. We could take the dogs and walk across the moor . . .'

'No thanks. I like to spend Sunday with Lucas and my family.' She stood up. 'Will that be all then?'

And Kit was dismissed as carelessly, as contemptuously as though Jenny Greenwood was the 'maister' and she no more than a 'little piecer' who had needed a reprimand. Jenny had made it obvious that her privacy and solitude were her own and not to be tampered with by Kit Chapman.

When the day was over, when the nerve-wracking choice of knives and forks and spoons, of glasses and all the paraphernalia the wealthy middle classes seemed to find necessary to eat a simple meal, was done with, her greatest pleasure was to retire to the lovely rooms she and Lucas shared on the first floor at the side of the house and be alone with him. She would sit, peaceful and at rest, her son in her arms, her mind empty and receptive to his child's prattle, and look over the long sweep of the sloping hills in the misty distance.

'I thought you might like these rooms, Jenny, since they have such a pretty view,' Kit had said carelessly, but Jenny had not known they had been given her so that she might look out on, not the immaculate gardens, which were alien to her, but the majestic splendour of the South Pennine heartland she loved so well. She would take her small son from the newly decorated nursery where he spent the day and where already he was the darling of his nursemaid's heart and after she had listened to his amazing accounting of his day among the luxuries he now took for granted, and then tucked him up in the small bed next to her own, she would wonder if she had done the right thing. He was her son, despite the man who fathered him. His family was working class, no-nonsense north countrymen and though her own parentage was not known there was no doubt in her mind that she had the same ancestry as the Greenwood family. Peasant stock, working their land and their looms, the backbone of England and was it right, she agonised, to deny her son his simple, untitled but honest heritage? Or, now that she had the chance for it, would it be right to deny him the privileges he would undoubtedly receive under the patronage of Katherine Chapman? An education, that of a young gentleman, an upbringing that would surely lead to some position of importance perhaps in the Chapman mills.

She was inordinately homesick. It was an ache in her which clawed incessantly, even the 'singing' of the spinning machines as she walked through the mill filling her with a desire, incredibly, to get her hands busy about the flashing spindles, to leave the confusing world of figures and trade and percentages, of business meetings and commercial transaction Kit loved so well, the formal etiquette and stylised way of living at Greenacres.

She would put her arms about her mother almost before she dropped her baskets, in a long, trembling embrace, stubbornly checking the easy tears, rejoicing each time at the improvement in Charlie. His arms were mending and the good food and fresh, clear air of the moorland where he walked each day were restoring him to the robust health and natural high spirits of an eleven-year-old. He would stand awkwardly as she put her arms about him, almost as tall as she was, and would in a week or two take his place beside the young gentlemen at Crossfold grammar school. He had his first, brand new jacket, not one handed down and made over by his mother, new breeches and boots and his books, purchased secondhand from the shop in Crossfold, were already packed carefully in his bag. The moment Sarah told him he was fit to have the splints removed from his arms, he was to be off and he could hardly wait. Joss had promised him a grand job with the newspaper when he was sixteen, or perhaps, with an offer from Miss Chapman if he did well in his studies of a place in her mill, the boy could scarcely wait to start this wonderful life that was to be his. The only smirching of the fresh start he was to have was the giving of his evidence at the trial of Jim Briggs, Alfie Jackson and Arnold Ellis who were all three in Oldham gaol.

Mercy, with eyes for no one but Lucas would reach out hungry arms to him; calling him Tom as she had always done, seeming to confuse him with her dead brother and the boy, cheerfully accepting it for she had called him that since he was old enough to notice, would run to her, loving her, Jenny knew, as much as he did herself. Mercy was endlessly patient with him, absorbed by his bright interest and his tales of what he did at 'home', her own sweetness enfolding him and quietening his vivid excitement to the peaceful contemplation of every fascinating object in the garden from the scattering of the corns to the chickens, the picking of daisies to make a chain for his golden curls, the planting of seed for next year's potatoes, the un-hurried pastimes of a country life with which she filled her day, her life, her very being. She would sing songs and tell him stories and only reluctantly allow Martha to nurse her grandson, and when the time came for he and Jenny to return to Greenacres, would weep piteously for her 'Tom' whom she could not bear to lose again.

The whole of Crossfold was astonished the next week when an army of workmen, Irish most of them and glad of the work, any work which would feed their starving famil-ies, began the renovation of the Chapman mills. Kit and Jenny had discussed at length on whether it would most benefit her employees to have their homes or the place in which they worked improved first. Kit planned to com-pletely demolish, row by obscene row, the mean, ram-shackle houses her grandfather had built for his workers and replace them with small, solid buildings with a bit of garden attached to each, a drain for carrying off every sort of filth and a constant supply of water to everyone from the river, its need gone now with the advent of the steam engine. There would be a parlour and a decent scullery and two or three bedrooms and a privy in the yard, one to a family.

'If they are decently housed and decently fed it follows that they will have the strength and will to do a decent day's work,' Jenny said, 'but put them in new houses before they have a chance to get used to the idea that their station in life is not only to be improved upon but also changed completely and they'll not know what to do with it. They need to be re-educated before they are rehoused or they'll have the new lot as bad as the old. First their conditions and working hours at the mill. A rise in wages, no more slave labour for their children and their outlook will change quite radically. They must be made to see that this is no fraud to trick them into working harder for the same wage, but a genuine consideration of how we can *all* work together to achieve one aim.'

'So, the mills first and shorter hours for better wages. But they must be made aware that I want value for money, Jenny. No more than ten hours a day for each child under ten years of age . . .'

'Right, and a proper dinner hour when they can stop to eat their baggin . . .'

'Whatever that might be. Is it a Lancashire dish?'

Jenny laughed grudgingly. 'No, it's anything you bring to eat at "baggin" time. Dinner time. Or I suppose you'd call it luncheon.'

'We shall have a proper dining-room and . . . what else, Jenny?'

'Special rooms for the female operatives to change their clothes in, proper clothes for them to wear, aprons and such, a washroom with water and conveniences with sewerage to carry off the waste. Proper ventilation . . .'

'And a schoolroom . . .'

In her wildest dreams it had never occurred to her that a decent education for the children might be one of them. And in her eyes was the beginning of a curious expression which might have been an unwilling reluctance to believe that Kit Chapman really *did* mean to do what she *said* she meant to do. 'But if they are to work . . . ?'

'They will be given time to attend classes in the evening. I read about it somewhere, I can't remember now, but it is called the "monitorial" system by which one teacher educates a number of monitors, perhaps among the older children who will in turn teach another group. The system is simple and economical . . .'

'And will they all be able to go, even the "apprentices"?'

'Naturally, and they shall have a proper house in which to live with a housekeeper, boys and girls separately, with decent clothes and food . . .'

'Treat them right and they'll work. My father used to say that, and right willingly . . .' And almost she was ready to believe in it at last!

465

But of course this happened over many months, months in which Jenny Greenwood declared a hundred times to herself that she could put up with it no longer. Her head ached every night as she laid it on her pillow, crammed to its capacity with the knowledge with which Kit burdened it each day. Her body longed for the physical exercise which it was accustomed to, straining inside the elegant gown and petticoats it was forced into each morning, longing to clothe itself in a simple, free moving skirt, a cool, easy, short-sleeved bodice, the homely cosiness of her shawl and clogs. She was a mill girl, brought up to hard work in a hard climate with others like her. She understood that, it was her life but this with Kit Chapman was as foreign to her as though she had been set down at the court of King George. She was neither of one class nor the other and the woman who had put her here, though she was carelessly kind, treating her not as a servant, but neither as a friend, seemed to find nothing strange in the situation. She was talking of entertaining some businessmen and their wives, influential gentlemen from the south who might be of use to her, and she to them and the hardship – and foolishness that it was necessary – of finding two gentlemen to make up the numbers since it seemed there must be an equal ratio of ladies and gentlemen in any party. It was all so . . . unimportant when put beside the genuine hardship Jenny had known all her life.

Though she and Kit had formed a workable relationship based on common need they still moved about each other with the delicacy of two cats tip-toeing across an acre of broken glass. In the three months since Jenny had moved to Greenacres she had not seen Mrs Chapman and had not considered that it was required of her to ask after her. She had known full well what had happened when Kit had told her mother that a factory girl was to be elevated to the position of assistant to the mill-owner and not only that but was to live in the house with them. It was obvious from Mrs Chapman's continued absence from the dinner table that she was living in another part of the house and Jenny smiled wryly when she thought of the upheaval there must have been when Kit announced it, even among the servants. She could see it in their faces when they waited upon Kit and herself. In the insolent slant to their watchful eyes, eyes that told her that they were only doing what they did because Miss Chapman was present, because they had been ordered to do it, but if they had the chance with no risk to themselves, they would not hesitate to insult her. She was a working class girl with no rights to be sitting in the candlelight at the beautifully polished table, in a silken gown, perfumed and elegant as Miss Chapman herself. They watched her, she knew, their eyes malicious, waiting for her to use the wrong fork, or even her fingers but she did what Kit had told her to do on the first night that they dined together and waited until Kit had made a choice, then did the same. Knife, fork, spoon, napkin, wine glass and after a while she no longer had any need to copy her employer. Quite simply, whatever Kit did, Jenny followed suit and even her broad Lancastrian accent began to mellow somewhat, as her brother's had done when he mixed with men of a different class. She would never completely eliminate it but she learned to sound each word separately, not running them together, nor clipping the ends off them. She studied hard to understand and use many words she had not even heard of until she met Kit.

'I have an inordinate amount of paperwork to complete before we can go home, I'm afraid, Jenny. You have a consummate head for figures so shall we go through them together. We will accomplish more in an hour together than I could in three.'

Inordinate! Consummate! Accomplish! They were words no simple, forthright working lass could even get her tongue round, let alone understand but Jenny Greenwood, allowed the full use of Barker Chapman's splendid library, made it her business to find out, and even to try them out, on her own, naturally before her bedroom mirror but it was not until Kit began to laugh, not unkindly one day that she learned that not only must one know the meaning of a word, the spelling, but also the pronunciation!

'Jenny, I am sorry, I am not laughing at you for really, I have nothing but admiration for the way in which you are getting to grips with your new situation and surroundings. If you were not such an intelligent and determined woman you would have given up before the first week was out, would you not? I am not blind, you know, though I might appear not to notice what goes on, unless it is on a balance sheet or a spinning frame. You really are very clever, Jenny and I do not say that in a patronising way, as though I am adding "for a mill girl". You have a good brain and you are using it and you are not afraid of me, or the servants. Oh yes, I have noticed that too, but I decided at the beginning that you must learn to manage them yourself. They will do anything I order them to but you must learn, and they as well, that you have as much right to give orders as I have. You are not a servant here, nor are you a guest. You are a resident . . . no, that is not the word . . . an inhabitant, perhaps . . . *you live here* as I do so you must deal with that role. Now then, these words you are determined to learn. I think it is commendable of you to try, there, you see . . . *commendable*, another one. Do you know what . . . ah, you do, good . . . well, any word I use which you do not understand, stop me at once and ask. That is all there is to it. You must be able to hold your own in the society in which I move, business and social, and only if you have confidence in yourself will you succeed.'

'If Joss can do it, then so can I.'

Kit felt the painful lurch of her heart at the sound of his name on Jenny's lips. It was the first time she had mentioned her brother and though Kit had prepared herself – she thought – for the moment which was sure to come since it was only to be expected that Jenny would speak of her family, the shock was enormous. And she must contain it, not allow Jenny to see that it had affected her in any way. The day, three months ago when he had forced her to see what her overlookers had done to his brother was as alive and agonising as it had been then, and the bitter hatred in his eyes, the contempt, had burned its way into her soul. She should not speak of him, not really, for surely Jenny would hear the strangeness in her voice but she could not stop herself. The yearning to know where he was, what he was doing, was too great to be subdued.

'Your brother is . . . he is living . . . at home . . . ?'

'Good God, no.'

Kit's face was expressionless as she picked up her wine glass and took a sip from its pale golden contents and though her hand trembled a little Jenny was too intent on her own social graces to notice.

'What does he do now? Forgive me, I do not mean to pry or open old wounds but . . . I suppose he still works for the reform he was so vociferous . . .'

'Vociferous?' Jenny looked enquiringly at Kit.

'Yes . . . to utter words . . . clamorously . . .'

'How do you spell it?'

'Really, does it matter . . . ?'

Jenny stared, surprised by the impatient tone in Kit's voice, ready to tell her not to bother with her damned explanations of the big words she used if it was to make her irritable but Kit pulled a face and smiled, replacing her wine glass beside the others.

'I'm sorry, Jenny. I didn't mean to snap but to tell the truth your brother and I have crossed swords on a number of occasions. He was a wild young man, you must admit, and in this valley the manufacturers, including myself had cause to curse him for the damage he did, but surely after being in . . . well . . .' She toyed with the fish on her plate, prodding it with her fork, not looking at Jenny, but Jenny finished the sentence for her.

'In prison, you mean. You reckon it should have knocked all that nonsense from him, is that what you're saying?'

'No, I'm not. But since the Power-Loom Riots the cotton industry has been relatively peaceful and I wondered if he was to . . .'

'Stir it up again?'

'Yes.'

'Well, I'd hardly be likely to tell you, would I?' Jenny smiled in the first genuine moment of shared amusement between them. '. . . and now that he knows what you are planning to do, your mills would not suffer, if he were planning anything, that is,' she added hastily. 'He is very impressed, you know.'

Kit's heart plunged again and the pleasure surged through her, though really, she thought frantically, what was it to her? What did it matter what *he* thought? She was doing this for *her* sake, not his, for her own peace of mind so why should his approval mean anything to her? But it did. It did! The accusation in his face, that grim, relentless face, the curl of contempt on his mouth, the ugly aversion even to sit beside her in her carriage, just as though he could not bear his flesh within touching distance of hers, had been the hardest thing she had ever had to bear in her life. That snarling malevolence had gone with her wherever she went in the last three months. It had hounded her dreams, turning them to nightmares, sat on her shoulder in her counting house, sneering that the profit she made was more to her than the soft flesh, the soft bones of the children she employed. It dogged her footsteps, each one she walked on the moorland up beyond Friars Mere to Moorcroft where she often climbed now since she no longer went to Badger's Edge. It followed her in her loneliness, for she admitted she was lonely, jeering at her, telling her she was fast becoming the old maid Crossfold firmly believed she was to be. She had loved no man but him, and never would, she acknowledged to herself and for the most part she accepted her loneliness, her solitary walks with her dogs, four of them now with the two young ones she was training, and her solitary bed. She found, though it was no surprise to her, that she enjoyed Jenny Greenwood's company but they talked of little else but business, their separate personal lives, their angry past, too fragile to be spoken of between them. Jenny was understandably eager, whenever she could

470

to spend every moment of her spare time with her son and with her family at Edgeclough.

'What is he engaged in then, if it's not a secret?' she went on trying her best to appear only casually interested.

'He has a job now.'

'A job?'

'Aye . . . er . . . yes. He writes for *The Republican*. They pay him a wage,' she said as though the wonder of it could scarcely be believed. 'He's a journalist.'

'How . . . grand.'

'Yes, and he writes articles for Cobbett's *Weekly Political Register*. Have you heard of it?'

'I believe I have. What does he write about?'

'Well, can't you guess?'

'The oppression of the poor. The wickedness of the industrialists. The horror of Lousy Bank and Pig Lane. Low wages. Long hours. Exploitation of children. Am I right?'

Jenny did not smile and her eyes retained that cool speculative look which said though Kit Chapman might have set about the task of transforming her mills, which she undoubtedly had, it did not necessarily follow that the lives of her workers would improve. It stood to reason that should the conditions in which the operatives worked become bettered, their output of work would naturally increase and in that case would not Kit Chapman make even more profit. It certainly did not, in her opinion, make any difference to the relationship which existed between them which was that of employer and employee, cool, impersonal and with not a great deal of trust on her part. She would wait and see, her attitude still said, for was not the proof of the pudding in the eating, and the damn thing not even in the oven yet. She had begun, surprisingly, to find a quiet satisfaction in the work she did, discovering in it, as Kit had said, a certain challenge, but she was not happy, and neither, she knew, was Kit Chapman since she was going against her own class, her own kind, men who believed her to be a traitor, a viper in their bosom which, if they had been able, they would dearly have loved to fling off and trample on, but she was too powerful. They said she was mad, that she would surely lose her fortune, that her workers would loll about all day in their new homes, if they ever got them, that they would make their new homes into *old* homes before the year was out for they knew no better, that they would idle the hours of business away, gossiping with one another in their new *dining-room* – had anyone ever heard of anything so disgraceful? – that their children, with hours in the day in which they had nothing to do, would run wild in the streets and cause untold trouble to those forced to put up with it.

And as for educating them, well, they all knew where that would lead, didn't they? They would get ideas above their station, would begin to believe they were as good as any man, as that fool Joss Greenwood assured them they were. God had put them all on this earth, the Lord in his castle, the parson in his church and the peasant in his cottage.

Somewhere in between stood the wealthy middle class, that new breed known as the industrialist, the manufacturing mill-owner, created not by God but by himself and if he had anything to say on the matter it was that Katherine Chapman must surely soon see the error of her foolish ways. How that was to be accomplished they were not awfully certain, since she was the wealthiest of them all, but if she carried on as she was doing, flinging her father's hard-earned cash about as though it grew on bloody trees, she would not be that for long.

And in the meanwhile Kit Chapman and Jenny Greenwood existed uneasily side by side, not at all sure that even, should their grand new experiment succeed, they themselves could do the same.

31

It was one of those glorious winter days when the eye is
drawn constantly to the window to look out again and
again at the blue of the sky, a clear and depthless blue that
stretches forever with nothing to mar its perfection. When
the book one reads or the papers with which one should
be engrossed no longer have the power to hold the attention,
when the head lifts constantly, when one stretches and
yawns and knows finally that there is no further use to try
despite what is still to be done and that with the eager
enthusiasm of a child shut up too long in the schoolroom,
an escape must be made.

Such a day called to Kit Chapman. It was almost Christmas, a dreaded time for her since it was a day when families
were re-united, a day of joy and merriment, of presents
given and received, of smiles and kisses and, perhaps only
once in the year, of goodwill towards one's fellowman. One
day of blessed rest for those who worked the other three
hundred and sixty-four, a day not to be spent alone but
which she knew she would do since her mother, who did
no more than nod coolly to her should they meet in the
garden, had said in a note delivered by Miss Fryer that she
was to share Christmas with her dear friend Emma Abbott.

But that was six days away yet and Kit Chapman had
learned that, except for the planning she must of course
organise for the future sale of her cotton, it was sometimes
a relief to live only for today. And today told her she was
a fool and a madwoman to sit behind this desk with her
nose in her papers when she could be out striding across

the tops with her dogs. She had work to do, she was well aware of that but nothing which could not wait until after dinner this evening, nothing with which, in an emergency, Jenny could not deal. It was not often that she allowed herself the indulgence of kicking up her heels and acting like a young girl but today was so beautiful, so special, surely she could afford to please herself, to gratify this whim which had come upon her, to throw the whole blessed business in Jenny's lap, call up her dogs and just go. Of course she took long walks each Sunday, often staying out from dawn until dusk with nothing in her pocket but an apple and a piece of cheese but the winter days were so short and once a week was so little. Today was Wednesday, a working day and her manufacturing father and grandfather would turn over in their manufacturing graves if they knew but it called to her, the biting, frosty blue day, the crisp champagne air which would fill her lungs on the top of Moorcroft and Broad Head and she could not resist it.

She stood up abruptly, so abruptly Jenny jumped and dropped her pen.

'Good Lord, you gave me a start. What's the matter? You look as though someone's put a mouse down your back.'

'Not a mouse down my back but wings on my heels. Dammit, I cannot stand this office another minute. I cannot see much of it from here but what I *can* see of the sky tells me the moors will be splendid on such a day. I don't often do it but I am going to play truant. I'll catch up on those papers tonight.'

'You don't have to make excuses to me. You're the "maister" here and if you can't please yourself, who can?'

'You're right. Can you manage without me for an hour?'

'I beg your pardon. Have you not noticed how capable I have become? Say the word and you can take a week off should you care to.'

'Hold on, my lass. You may be pretty good but you're not indispensable yet.'

It had taken years for Kit herself to learn to run the

474

enormous and complicated concern which was the Chapman Spinning and Weaving Mills but Jenny Greenwood, she had to acknowledge, had assimilated in six months what had taken Kit twelve to do. Admittedly Jenny's experience in the spinning rooms had given her a head start on the seventeen year old Kit Chapman but her mind was receptive, just as though it had been empty for years of everything but the mental processes needed to run a machine, dry and thirsty for knowledge and now, as Kit poured it in, it drank it up greedily, always ready for more.

'But that day is not far off Jenny,' she said quietly, then, spinning round with her skirts dipping in excitement she strode towards the door and the carriage which always stood waiting.

She crossed the wooden footbridge which spanned the stream at noon, climbing steadily on the other side of the valley beyond Crossfold. She had put on a rough woollen skirt of dark red, deep and glowing against the winter's day. Her three-quarter coat was of the same shade but checked in shades of cream and white and on her head was a white tam o' shanter. Her black boots were stout and snug, especially made for her for walking and round her neck was a vivid red scarf. She looked magnificent, her eyes a delighted blue, like that of a harebell with a sparkle in them which was brighter than the sun reflected ice which coated every blade of grass, every dried frond of bracken. The blood surged beneath her golden skin, gathering on her cheekbones.

The track up to the high moorland, the *real* moorland which even in summer was dark and rough and uneven, was white with rime and slippery and the stones scattered over the surface made walking difficult. The rough grass was heavy with frost so fine it was like spun sugar and here and there where water lay in the dark, peaty soil, ice gleamed brilliantly. Her old dogs stayed close to her side, still supple and active for even when she had no time to roam the hills with them, one of the grooms had orders to exercise them daily. But the young ones, not yet a year old, frolicked together in the unexpected joy of being out with her, their high spirits and youthfulness making them impossible, just at that moment, to command. But she knew exactly how they felt and she had not the heart to call them in. Let them caper like fools for that was how she felt. She wanted to run across the open spaces, to climb rocks and to jump from them and shout aloud in an exhilaration which was sweet and fast flowing in her blood and which she had not felt for many months.

The sun was not very high and the far side of the valley was in shadow, smudged here and there by a huddle of buildings, isolated weavers' cottages and a farm or two. She could see the glint far below of the river, circling between scattered black patches of leafless trees and where it turned, winding away behind a hill, the tall chimneys of George Abbott's mill. She kept to the faint track for a while, winding in long curves up the steep slope. Hard gritstone bands protruded like a man's ribcage along the hillsides and water dashed over them in great falls, so loud she could no longer hear the excited yapping of her young dogs.

She followed the pack-way, its old flags set deep in the thick, peaty layers of grass, the inheritance of the upland forests which had once thrived here. The pack-horse route had probably been used to carry salt in the old days, and lime which was needed to improve the acid soil of the farmland. A 'white way' it was known as, just as the route which had carried coal was a 'black way' and those along which clay or pottery moved were 'red ways'.

The air was colder up here and she pulled her coat and scarf more closely about her as she reached the highest point at Friars Mere. There was a tumble of stones, the ruins it was said of an old chapel, used by the monks. The ice crackled about her feet and her breath wreathed about her head. She leaned against a massive stone and looked across the vast expanse of moorland, rising and falling in weathered nobility, dissected at a lower level with the regular landscape caused by the encroachment of enclosure. Rectangular fields and orderly access trackways, straight walls which created from this distance an image of a chequerboard of black and white, flecked as it was with snow. Farms crouched right up to the moorland's edges, smallholdings, no more, with a few cattle, a 'laithe house' which included under its roof a barn for storage, a mistal or cow house, space for a horse and cart and living quarters for the hardy moor dwellers.

She noticed the movement just as she was about to turn away. It was too cold to stand and the blood which had coursed through her veins in a hot tide as she had climbed was beginning to slow. The dogs stood quietly now, the two young ones leaning against her skirt, Joby and Blaze in a phalanx of protection a little way out, one to her left, the other to her right, scanning the distance and it was the faint growl deep in Joby's throat that warned her.

The figure was no more than a dark smudged shape against the grey-white background of the winter vegetation, with a thin shadow following, moving slowly, stopping now and then to stare about but as it came nearer Kit could see the slight swing of a skirt and knew that the person who approached was a woman.

'To me Joby, Blaze, lie down. Prince, Barny, stay, stay boys . . .' and all four dogs lay down obediently. It took more than fifteen minutes for the woman to reach the ruined chapel. She appeared either uncertain of her direction, or, like a child, uncaring, stopping to touch this and that, to examine a rock or a frozen plant, her voice, as she got nearer, soft and enquiring as she spoke, addressing her remarks to whatever it was she touched. There was a fey, ethereal quality to her, not quite of this world and Kit felt the hairs on the back of her neck rise as she recognised Joss Greenwood's wife. The last time she had seen her she had hidden herself behind a chair, then, at Joss's bidding had run out to 'play' while the women tended to Charlie Greenwood's wounds. The lad, healed now and completely well apart from the scars on his face and back which would be his for life was attending Crossfold grammar school where he was gaining, besides a fine classical education, a grounding in writing, arithmetic, mathematics and modern languages, a little out of his depth, as yet, among the sons of mill-masters and manufacturers but already showing that ingenuity of which some boys are blessed, gaining a reputation as quite a celebrity by the simple method of revealing to his awestruck peers the scars on his back. An up and coming young man then with the sense to take advantage of any weapon to hand in the battle of life, a fighter like his brother and sister and this elf-like creature who, in a moment or two would stumble over Kit's dogs, was his sister-in-law.

Strangely, after the first warning growl the dogs made no move to bar Mercy Greenwood's way as she came over the lip of the hill. It seemed they recognised this child-woman was no threat to them, or to the one they guarded, and the old dogs merely laid their muzzles on their paws, while the young ones waved a friendly tail.

'Oh . . .' she said, with a little start, not afraid of them, Kit realised and when her eyes rose and found Kit's she smiled in a friendly fashion, the anxiety she had shown on the day at the cottage not apparent in the cold emptiness of the moors. She was warmly dressed with a shawl about her head and crossed over her breast, tied at the back as one would a child. There was another wrapped about her shoulders and her grey homespun woollen skirt was of good quality. She wore stout clogs and heavy, hand-knitted stockings. Her fine skin was flushed with the warmth of her climb, her cheeks pink and like satin but it was her eyes which were her greatest beauty. They were enormous in her tiny face, a soft and velvet grey, set in long brown lashes and in them was a glow of pleasure, of trust, a delight which spoke of her love for the moors in which she wandered so far from home. There was no fear, no hesitancy in her movement. This was her land, her manner seemed to say, her place where there was nothing to hurt her, nothing to fear up here where no people came. Where there was no dirt, no smells, no rotting obscenities to bar her path, no noise but the sound of the water and the call of the raven.

478

Up here she had no need of her little 'bird' and this lady, these dogs gave off no warnings of the perils which lay below.

'Good morning,' she called out. 'It's a grand day,' just as though there was nothing unusual in finding a well-dressed lady in the isolated spot.

'Indeed it is,' Kit answered, not awfully sure what to do or say for the girl . . . woman really . . . seemed so normal, but Jenny had intimated that their Mercy was not quite . . . well, as a grown woman should be. She had given no details, naturally, her loyalty to her family allowing no outsider to pick at its shortcomings but Kit's rebellious heart had missed a beat, glad and ashamed of its gladness, as she had been when she had learned that Joss and Mercy Greenwood had no child, at the hint, not spoken aloud, of course, that Joss and Mercy were not husband and wife in the true sense of the word.

But what the devil was she doing out here, miles from Edgeclough and all alone? The weather had winnowed out the usual itinerants, the wandering, out of work Irishmen, farm labourers, weavers, *any man* and his family who roamed these hills going from town to town looking for work but there was still the chance that some ruffian might happen along, not caring where he slept or how he ate as long as he could find the means, lawful or not, to obtain it. She saw such men herself now and again but they gave her a wide berth at the sight of the snarling teeth of Joby and Blaze and the increasingly protective fierceness, inclined now and then to slip away as their attention wandered, of her new dogs. But Mercy Greenwood had no such protection. What was Martha Greenwood thinking of, allowing her out of her sight for it was clear the girl . . . woman . . . had no idea of her own danger. Jenny had told her that Mercy loved her mother-in-law and never strayed far from her side and yet here she was, on Friars Mere with the look of someone out for a stroll in her own garden.

'Are you alone?' she asked carefully, then drew in her breath sharply, about to cry out a warning, a sharp

479

command to Joby as Joss Greenwood's wife kneeled down beside him, trusting as an infant and laid a small, mittened hand on his smooth head, but the elderly dog merely blinked a tolerant eye in Mercy's direction and allowed her to stroke him, to fondle his ear, as amiable as a cat curled up on a rug before the fire.

'What a lovely dog,' Mercy said smilingly, 'and the others,' looking around. 'Are they all yours?' and then, as the two young ones bounded over, she fell in a laughing jumble of black stockinged legs, skirts and warm petticoats, entangled with the smooth black bodies of Prince and Barny.

'Stay Prince, stay Barny.' Kit laid a restraining hand on the quivering rump of the nearest dog but he was too enchanted with his new friend and it took several minutes before Mercy could stand and the dogs would obey their mistress and the two women were laughing, tidying their hair which had come loose in the tussle, eyes like stars, cheeks flushed.

'I'd love a dog like that,' Mercy said wistfully, eyeing Barny who still could not resist the temptation to lick her hand.

'Will Joss . . . your family not get you one?' His name slipped out before she could stop it but Mercy turned eagerly.

'You know Joss?'

'Well, yes. We have met a time or two.'

'Well, that's grand. I'm his wife, Mercy.'

'Yes, I know.' Kit's voice was gentle for really this child, she was only that, was the most innocent creature she had ever met. 'I saw you on the day Charlie was hurt . . .'

Instantly she could have bitten her tongue for Mercy reared back, her face whitening in fear, just as though Kit had raised a fist to her.

'It's all right, really. He's better now and going to school, so there is no need for you to worry,' Kit gabbled, desperate to take that look of horror from Mercy Greenwood's face and slowly the girl's colour returned and her body relaxed.

The dog nuzzled her hand and she looked down at it and the last of the strain left her. Kit felt her own rigid shoulders settle more comfortably and the breath sighed out of her. Dear God, what *was* wrong with the woman? She was as highly strung as a young colt. A simple sentence, a few words which had no harm nor threat in them had nearly had her over the lip of the mount on which they stood and even yet her hand rested as though for reassurance on Barny's head and Mercy was still not the eager young woman she had been fifteen minutes ago. She watched Kit warily as though she was afraid she might say something else to frighten her, ready to dart away should Kit threaten her peace of mind again.

She shouldn't be here, Kit thought, searching for some innocuous remark, about the weather, or the dogs, anything which had no peril in it for the disturbed child who looked at her from the face of Joss Greenwood's wife. How had she got up here? She was cosily dressed just as though someone had got her ready, put on her shawl and tied it at her back. But she must get her home to her family at once and though she was reluctant to return to that cottage in which there was so much remembered pain, she must. The memory of Joss was there. His eyes hating her, filled with his revulsion for her and what she had allowed to be done to his brother. The memories haunted her still, no matter how hard she tried to erase them, no matter how much profit she ploughed back into the improvements for her work people, his eyes would never let her alone, the expression in them would glare in the night for as long as she lived.

She had done her best, arranged for the youngest girl to work at the Hall, for Charlie to go to school and of course Jenny was invaluable to her, but . . . and here her breath slowed painfully as she prepared to take Joss's wife back to him . . . she really did not think she could fight the despair, the pain, the torment of loving this woman's husband for much longer. She was safe in her mills, in her weaving-sheds and up here on the moors where nobody came but the birds and the moorland creatures, the occasional far off figure of a wandering vagrant but in the village of Edgeclough was the aching, the slow and tortuous death of the ephemeral dream she had once known as a young girl. They had both been young then and filled with the joy of one another. Before Harry, before this woman, before the insurmountable barrier of hate had reared itself between them.

'Would you like to walk with me and my dogs?' she asked at last and even to her own ears her voice was harsh but Mercy's face smiled in pleasure and she looked down, stroking first one affable head then another, first Joby, Blaze, Prince, then Barny, who seemed to be her favourite.

'Yes, if it's all right.'

She went wherever Kit led, amenable to anything Kit might suggest. She threw a stone for the dogs, delighted when the two young ones raced to bring it back to her.

'Tom and I used to come up here,' she said suddenly, stopping to peer at a hollow where the frost lay so thickly it might have been snow. 'Of course we don't now because he's not old enough yet but when he's five or six Jenny'll let me fetch him, won't she?'

'I'm sure she will,' Kit said soothingly. They were at the top of Dog Hill now and far below was the village of Edgeclough. She could even make out the roof of the laithe house in which the Greenwoods lived and she thought of leaving now, of saying to Mercy Greenwood, 'See, there is your home, go on, go down to it . . .' but how could she trust her to do it. She was kneeling as Kit stopped, her gentle face, her soft eyes close to the dogs, waiting to be told what she must do next, quite unaware that she had only to run down the steep hill and she would be home.

'Come on, Mercy, let's get on. I'm sure your . . . your husband will be anxious about you.' Her throat almost closed on the last words and as she heard her own voice speak them she had the urgent need to bend herself double to ease the pain but again Mercy cringed back from her, her eyes flaring in panic.

'Oh no . . . he's . . . no . . . he's away. Martha said he wasn't to be back and really . . . I would rather sleep with Martha . . . please . . . please . . .'

Dear sweet Lord . . . Kit felt her lungs close on the desperate breath she tired to force into them as the pictures which teamed into her head almost paralysed her. Dear God . . . what was this child saying . . . what did she mean? What had he done to her, what had *someone* done to her to make her so afraid of almost everything, and yet so trusting with a complete stranger? She was afraid of hurt and pain, it seemed, of violence, her reaction to the memory of Charlie told Kit that. She was afraid of . . . of the passion . . . was that it . . . of love . . . the strength, the lusty sweetness of sexual excitement. Kit had seen her run trustingly into his gentle arms on that same day so . . .

So what did it matter to her, her mind demanded brutally to know? What did anything to do with this woman and her husband matter to Kit Chapman? They had their life, whatever it might be, and she had hers and what they did with theirs, *in* theirs, did not concern her. She had come to return this poor demented child, this gentle little sparrow who had flown high today among the dangerous hawks and when she had seen her to her doorstep she would be off. Just a simple return of a wandering child which Martha Greenwood would surely understand. But why was no one looking for her then, her logical mind asked, if that was the case, but she refused to answer it, merely taking Mercy Greenwood's hand in hers and leading her down the steep slope towards her home.

He opened the door when she knocked and the shock to them both was so great neither could speak. Eye clung to eye, appalled, both of them refusing to acknowledge that first initial explosion of gladness which came and went before it could be dwelled upon. Mercy still clung to Kit's hand, the dogs to her skirt, ready, should it be needed to defend both these weak females to the death but the two young ones, sensing the lessening of animosity in Joby and

Blaze who recognised the man, snuffled about his knees and hand, willing to be friends if he was.

'Joss . . .' Mercy's soft voice was nervous and she leaned against Kit's shoulder, partly hidden by it. He dragged his tight clenched gaze from Kit's for a moment, staring at his wife as though he had never seen her before and had not the slightest notion of who she was.

'What the devil . . . ?' but his voice, loud, harsh with shock made Mercy flinch and Kit could see him visibly make an effort to calm himself, saw the effort he took to soften his voice and his expression and all the while her eyes filled themselves with him, storing the image of his brown face, the thick familiar swathe of his curly hair on his brow, the shape of his smiling mouth, smiling tenderly now for his wife, the deep clefts one on either side of his lips, his lips themselves . . . aah, Joss, my love, my love . . .

He put out a hand to draw his wife across the step and his expression of gentleness, the soft clasp of his fingers reassured her and she went to him, leaving Kit on the outside, alone, but for her dogs.

'Lass,' he said to his wife and the compassion he showed for this damaged woman brought a lump to Kit's throat. 'Where have you been? How did you . . . ?' He turned to Kit and his eyes became distant. He was in control of himself. The shock he had known when he opened the door and seen her there had subsided and his concern was for his wife, not the woman who had brought her home.

'I found her on the moor. She seemed . . . lost.'

'I hope she was no trouble to you.' His politeness was chilling.

'None.'

'My mother is . . . a cousin in the next village is unwell, so she has . . . She left a note that she had sent Mercy to a neighbour. Obviously she did not go. I'm sorry you have been brought out of your way.'

By looking slightly to the left of his face while he did the same so that their eyes did not once meet they were able to pretend that they were no more than two strangers, one who had done a kindness to the other and must be thanked courteously.

'Not at all,' she answered and though it had all been said and she knew she should move she simply could not. She wanted none of this. She wanted none of him, ever again for the pain was so great she really could not stand it. Just to be near him, though three feet of solid, heavy air stood between them, was the most exquisite agony she had known and she could not, not yet, give it up. A moment more, dear Lord. A moment more to breathe in the scent of the cold air about him, to sense the rapid beat of the pulse in the hollow of his throat, to see from the corner of her averted eye the tight held grimness of his mouth, knowing he meant it for her, but not caring, not caring just as long as she could be here, in his presence for a moment longer. It must last for a long time. It must last forever!

'I'm cold Joss,' Mercy said, shivering a little in the shelter of his protective arms, her head resting against the strong curve of his shoulder and suddenly Kit hated her, hated her, would dearly have loved to smack her silly, simple face, to scratch her gentle dove's eyes, the childish pout of her pink mouth, for she was his wife. This woman was his wife, entitled to share his bed, to love his body, to bear his children. She could, if she had a mind, lean sensuously against him when the door closed and shut out the rest of the world, put her mouth against his, tease him with her tongue, whisper in his ear of what she would do to him and his hard, long man's body, of what she would like him to do to her soft willing woman's flesh if he would care to climb the stairs with her. But she would not. She could not and neither could Kit Chapman and the knowledge tore at her, slashed through the hard shell of the composure she had layered about herself, tore it from her in a severance of agony and her eyes looked directly into his.

She felt the flagged stones of the path tremble beneath her feet as the earth tilted and her own pain overwhelmed her but she could not look away. She felt no shame in allowing him to see her love since she felt none. Her pride,

485

the arrogant pride which had hugged to itself the knowledge that at least he was unaware of the love she could not seem to kill, which he himself could not seem to kill, no longer cared that it was flaring from her eyes, on the breath she forced out of her lungs, from the very pores of her skin for him to see. What the hell did it matter, the defiant lift of her head said? Let him laugh, let him pour scorn on her, let his mouth curl in contempt and revulsion, she loved Joss Greenwood and she always would and there was nothing any longer that she could do to hide it.

But he did none of these things. His whole body became unnaturally still and she watched, wonderingly, the slow, quite incredible chink of light prick the ice green and grey of his eyes. His breathing quickened on the gradual parting of his lips and warm blood ran beneath the brown flesh of his face. His eyes narrowed a little as though at the last moment he would hide it from her, then it came, glowing for her, brought painfully from the place where he had hidden it, buried it, smashed it down into a hole and buried it and was there where she could see it at last, whole, sweet, undamaged, *his love for her*.

She felt the tears brim from her eyes and begin to run down her face and inside her, where the rock had been for six months, the ice riven rock he had put there on the day Charlie was beaten, she felt a gentle warmth dissolve it into her body, releasing it into her arms and legs, her mouth which began to smile, her hands which would have reached for him, her heart which did.

'Joss.' His name was a balm on her lips, a soothing salve which smoothed away the pain.

'Kit,' and it was the same for him as the forgiveness healed him.

They seemed to find no other words necessary, nor to wonder at the strangeness of declaring their renewed love before the sweet and empty woman who clung on his arm and who was his wife.

'Will you come in?' he said, opening the door to her now.

'Thank you.'

'You must be cold,' and I would that I could warm you here, right now, his eyes continued.

'Yes.'

'Mercy, sweetheart, when you have taken off your shawl make Miss Chapman a cup of tea, will you?' and Kit found no hatred in her now for the woman Joss Greenwood called 'sweetheart'.

32

It was easy now for them to become lovers again since what was more natural than that Joss Greenwood should visit his sister, his nephew who had taken up residence at the home of Miss Katherine Chapman? And it was well known that Miss Chapman was a radical sympathiser for why else would she flatten row after row of the perfectly adequate houses her grandfather had built for his workers and, it was rumoured replace them with others which were, in their opinion, those who criticised, far too good for the common man.

He dined with them a week after Kit had returned his wife to him, walking the three miles from Edgeclough to Crossfold in his wooden clogs which he still found more comfortable than the boots he now wore in his daily life. He took them off under the cover of darkness at the gate which led to the driveway of Greenacres, hiding them under a bush, pulling on his boots before beginning the walk up to the front door and when Winters opened it to him he might have been any one of the number of well dressed gentlemen who called on Miss Chapman. A dark green coat, plain, well cut but serviceable buff waistcoat and trousers. His long military boots were of well polished, good quality brown leather and his hat which he handed to Winters as though he were well used to a butler to wait on him, was what was known as a 'Wellington', the crown curving outwards towards the top and the narrow brim curled up at the sides. His greatcoat, ankle length and of good Yorkshire wool was black. It was very evident from his attire that Joss Greenwood was a man of some standing in his own community and though he had, and still did, called himself a working class man, he worked now with his pen in the telling articles his clever brain devised and which were printed in *The Republican* and similar radical newspapers such as Cobbett's *Weekly Political Register*. His wages were small but enough to support himself and his wife, and contribute towards the upkeep of his brother's schooling.

He had been condemned by many for trying to turn simple folk into dupes for his own political ends since it was well known that he had leanings in that direction but men of conscience such as William Cobbett, Richard Oastler and John Fielden held him in high esteem and he was welcomed to speak on the platforms of the meetings he attended on behalf of the working man he still fought for.

But it was not that, nor indeed of anything to do with reform that he thought as Kit Chapman walked across the brightly lit hallway to greet him, her hands outstretched to his, her eyes shining with joy. They might have been alone so vividly did they let their emotion be seen, their love for one another a living glory. They seemed careless of who saw it among the servants who hovered respectfully in the background and Jenny Greenwood who had followed Kit from the drawing-room to welcome her brother when the door bell rang, felt the shock of it hit her just below her breasts in the region where a body blow was most telling.

Their hands clasped, their flesh softly touching and caressing, fingers entwined for a long, long moment, not like acquaintances, nor even close friends but as lovers, reluctant to let go, to part, to become separate again.

488

'Miss Chapman.' He spoke her name softly in a tone of voice Jenny had never heard him use before, even with Mercy, breathed it through lips that curved in a tender half-smile and yet his expression was serious, frowning almost, just as though this was the most important moment of his life and must not be treated lightly. She saw him lean forward, his head bent to Kit's, lifting her hands in both of his and for a fascinated moment she thought he was about to bring them to his lips before the quite spellbound gaze of the deferential gaze of the butler who waited to pass Mr Greenwood's greatcoat to the footman, and the housemaid who had no particular job but to see that the downstairs fires never went out.

It was as though no one would move, could move, not until the mistress of the house gave the order and Kit, Jenny became aware in the midst of the breathtaking silence, was not even conscious that anyone else was there beyond Jenny's brother, Joss Greenwood.

Winters waited, Joss's hat in his hand, his face quite expressionless, his eyes clamped on the portrait of James Chapman which hung above Joss's head. The footman's white-gloved hands waited to receive Joss's greatcoat which was still slung about his shoulders, his eyes, not quite so well trained as those of the butler who had more experience of such things, sliding curiously from the face of the woman whose servant he was to that of the man at whom she gazed so strangely.

Dear sweet Lord! It was all Jenny could do not to spring between them with her hands ready to strike out at their silly faces. She stood in the doorway of the drawing-room, the smile of welcome, the smile of greeting for her brother beginning to turn into an unbelieving, incredulous flare of outrage for it seemed everyone from herself to the influential mill-owners of Crossfold had had the wool firmly pulled over their eyes by this couple. *Joss and Kit Chapman!* Her brother and her employer. It was inconceivable and yet the evidence of it was here right before her eyes. They were standing like . . . like two lovestruck youngsters, starry-eyed, flush-cheeked with the servants looking on, servants who would in the next few minutes be racing back to the kitchens, vying with one another to pour out the details to the rest. It was beyond belief, she could see it even now in the face of the housemaid, she could feel it in her own stunned mind, and how the devil they had managed to conduct what was so obviously an affair of long standing in a community as insular as this was beyond understanding, but that was not the issue causing anxiety here. It was, at this precise moment the delicate task of parting Joss Greenwood from Kit Chapman in the swiftest possible fashion and at the same time making the whole situation seem not at all out of the ordinary. *She* was his sister and therefore should be the one to receive his affectionate embrace, not Kit Chapman who, everyone in the valley had believed until quite recently was the sworn enemy of the radicals. Of course they did not say that now, now that she was taking the working man's side in the fight for what he called justice but that did not concern her at the moment. All that mattered was that Jenny Greenwood loved her brother and must defend him from the gossip which surely must come of this.

'Joss, my word but don't you look grand,' she said loudly, so loudly Winters and the footman and the housemaid who had quite forgotten that she was there at all, jumped guiltily and turned to look at her as she leaned against the door frame.

She wore a simple, long-sleeved afternoon gown of cream muslin edged at the neck and hem with cream challis work. The broad sash was of cream satin and on it she had pinned half a dozen cream rosebuds grown specially in the Chapman hothouses. They had decided, she and Kit, knowing that Joss had no evening suit, indeed had been anxious that he might have no suit at all for neither had seen him in anything but a jacket and breeches, that they would wear their simplest day dresses and not don one of the dozen splendid evening gowns they each possessed. But Joss Greenwood mixed with gentlemen now, with men of

490

good family who, though they were of a higher social class, thought as he did. He appeared on platforms, an uneducated man who had educated himself, through his reading, through communication with men who *were* educated and was respected as an eloquent, plain speaking, forthright and intelligent man. A man of the people then, but one who was rising above his own humble birth. He had skills they could use, the men of reform, skills which were needed when there were elections to be won. He had the mass of the working man behind him. Not that they, any of them, had as yet, the right to vote, but one day they would and Joss Greenwood told them so and they loved him for it and for the education he promised their children. Food for their bellies and food for their minds, he said. Revolutionary ideas certainly, but ones which appealed to those who lived in Lousy Bank, Pig Lane and Boggart Hole.

He turned now, still dazed it seemed, still drowning in Kit Chapman's glowing brilliance, bewildered and not awfully certain who it was had spoken to him. His eyes met Jenny's then and he saw the warning in them and the love she bore him and when she looked away, inclining her head in the direction of the servants, his gaze followed hers and instantly he was aware of what he was about. Kit was still swaying towards him, her face possessed enchanted, ready to sink into his arms if he should hold them out to her, to lift her mouth for his kiss, to lay the length of her body against the length of his. She appeared mindless in her joy, her expression telling him she could not believe that they were together, their minds in harmony and at peace, that after years of hatred and bitterness, their love was holding them in beauty again.

He placed her hands carefully at her sides, letting them go reluctantly and stepped back, clearing his throat which had become clogged with emotion. Turning, he threw his greatcoat from his shoulders and handed it to Winters who passed it to the goggle-eyed footman, then he lifted his arms to Jenny and without a word she flew into them.

The servants all twitched into action, moving towards the back of the hall, disinterested in the public demonstration of the feeling shown by these two who were, in their opinion, completely out of place in Miss Chapman's home. Pearls before swine, they told one another for had they not been born in a weaver's cottage, the pair of them and what Miss Chapman thought she was doing was beyond them. It was bad enough having Jenny Greenwood, no more than a spinner, a factory girl, ordering them about as though she had been born to it, now it seemed they were to serve her brother, a radical reformer and an ex-felon.

Not one of the three could have said what they ate that night. Kit had ordered a simple meal, again considering Joss since she had no wish to embarrass him with a complicated menu to which he might be unaccustomed. It saddened her that she knew so little about him, that in the years they had known one another they had never once sat down to eat together, that they had done none of the simple, ordinary, everyday things which friends, lovers, husbands, wives do together. She had no idea of his tastes, his likes and dislikes, the colours which found favour with him, the books he read, the flowers, the food, the weather, hot or cold, summer, winter, spring, he preferred. They had talked over the years of their respective childhoods, of their love for one another and for the sweeping hillsides and moorlands of the Lancashire Pennines but beyond that she knew little about him. Of course she was only too well aware of his political beliefs and his conviction that all men were equal but now, she prayed fervently, now they surely must have the chance she had waited for to get to know one another, not as lovers but quite simply as a man and a woman.

They talked, he and Jenny, about the startling changes Kit was making in the factory, the better conditions she was creating for her operatives, the new houses which were already being erected for them to live in but Kit just listened, not really hearing what they said, content merely to watch him through the candlelight, to bask in the approval she saw in his eyes, to see the warm smile curl his lips, the constant turn of his gaze to meet hers.

' . . . naturally we did not make the profit we had in the past . . .' Jenny was saying to him seriously, just as though *she* and not Kit were the mill-owner, ' . . . since with fewer hours being worked by each operative and a higher wage given to them, it could not be achieved but the amazing thing, now that a rota has been worked out that is fair and well within the capacity of the women and children, profits are beginning to rise again. They still work damned hard, Joss, but it is as though the . . . the concern Kit has shown, the better conditions, the humane treatment they receive has given them a new optimism, an inducement, even a pride in what they can achieve. Kit has devised a bonus scheme and you could scarcely believe the competition which goes on to win it. And the children . . .' She leaned forward into the light cast by the candles and her face glowed, ' . . . to see them gradually lose that look of . . . of old men and women, to see them begin to smile, to look about them without fear and their faces, when they sit at their desks and suddenly, like a candle lit in a dark room, understand what the teacher is explaining to them, to see their minds *wake up* . . .' She shook her head at her own fanciful description and Kit watched Joss's hand go out to her, then as he turned towards herself, feel the lovely warmth of his love, his respect and admiration flow over her and knew she deserved it. It had taken a great deal of courage and resolution to go against her own kind, against what her own father and grandfather had contrived in the past thirty years or so, but for this man who had shown her how to go about it, she had done her best to enrich the lives of those who worked for her. Would she have acted as she was doing if she had not been so closely involved with the Greenwood family, would she have *cared* about the Greenwood family had it not been for her love for Joss, she had asked herself a hundred times in the six months since Jenny had come to work for her and the answer had been that she did not know. How could she say, she only knew that her involvement had opened her eyes, and her heart. There was a way to run a business, to employ men, women and children fairly, and still make a handsome profit, despite what other men of commerce said, and she and Jenny were finding it, but it was this man who had led her to the start of it.

They drank coffee in the drawing-room and Joss was offered a brandy and cigar by the high nosed butler. He seldom drank brandy since it was beyond his means and had never tried a cigar but now, winking at Jenny, he took both and when Winters lit the cigar with the disdain of an aristocrat forced to wait upon his own servant, he coughed and choked and spluttered and declared he was amazed that anyone could do it for pleasure and that presumably one had to be born to such things since he was not.

But at last the laughter, the conversation, even between sister and brother ran out and the tension, soft and breathless which joined Kit and Joss, the tension of a man and a woman completely aware of one another and of no one else began to invade the room. Jenny could feel it wash against her own flesh, and it prickled, and her woman's body remembered what she had known with Harry Atherton. Not love certainly, nor even liking, but the desire which is born between male and female, a physical attraction which takes no heed of the mind, nor even the heart, but only of the senses. Their eyes were fixed upon one another with a longing so great, so powerful she felt a great need to get up and run from the room, to leave them, she was sure, to fall into one another's arms the very moment she had gone. Should she say something, she agonised. Let them know she had seen – as who had not – what was between them. The atmosphere, with the silence, became more strained until at last she could stand it no longer.

'You would not believe how Lucas had grown since last you saw him, Joss,' she said quite wildly. 'He already knows his letters though he is not yet three years old. I'm sure he will be asleep but perhaps you would like to see him.

Mother would be hurt if she thought you had been here and not visited her grandson . . .'

She was babbling and she knew it but at last she had caught the attention of her brother and filled with some sound, the silent and charged vacuum in which he and Kit were held fast. Immediately, as though he was glad of the diversion, not from Kit herself, but the pressure in him her closeness had created, he sprang to his feet.

'Of course. He must be getting quite a lad now. Three years in April, is it? But I don't want to wake him.'

'No really, I'd like you to see him.' Her face softened. 'He's a lovely boy, Joss, sweet natured, not like . . .' She stopped abruptly and her cheeks flamed and both Joss and Kit held their breath for she had almost spoken the name of the man who had fathered her son and Kit, who had guessed long ago who it was, was well aware that if Joss knew he might be tempted to take his revenge on the man who had not only given him a vicious beating but had 'taken down' his sister. But Jenny turned away, moving towards the door and Joss and Kit followed her, their hands brushing, their shoulders touching, their bodies waiting impatiently for the moment which surely must come.

The nursery was a soft and golden haven of warmth, the light from the glowing fire and from the night candle which stood on a low table filling it with a gentle soft-hued peace. Flora, once parlourmaid but now in charge of the nursery, sat beside the fire, some small garment in her hands and as they entered she rose hastily to her feet, sketching a curtsey, not only to her mistress, Miss Chapman, but to the mother of the boy in her charge who, for tonight, while *Miss* Greenwood entertained her brother, was to sleep in the nursery. Jenny Greenwood, named whore by those who did not know her, had gained the respect and obedience of many of the servants at Greenacres, not just because it was expedient, but for the resolute way in which she had tackled her new life, for her fairness in dealing with them, and others, for her plain speaking and plain common sense and by her refusal to be intimidated by those who considered themselves to be above her in the social structure of the house. It was well known what she was doing for her own class and though some, like Mr Winters, thought she should have remained in the station of life in which she had been placed since her reforms did not better *his* way of life, there were many with relatives in the textile trade who had cause to be grateful to her.

'Don't get up, Flora,' Miss Greenwood said now, putting her fingers to her lips. 'My brother has come to peep at his nephew. We won't wake him . . .'

'Nay Miss Greenwood, t'little imp's awake. 'Tis just as if he knows you've got a visitor an' can I get him to sleep, not on your life! See, will you look at him . . .' she said fondly as the bedclothes on the small bed in the corner of the room heaved convulsively and two shining eyes in a face crowned with a thick mop of fair curls peeped mischievously over them. There was laughter bubbling from the curl of rosy lips, and baby teeth gleamed in the candle-light. The boy sat up, then, enchanted with his own daring, stood up in the bed and began to bounce excitedly, his little nightgown riding up his sturdy legs to reveal his tiny male genitalia which bounced joyfully as well.

Joss and Kit stood side by side as Jenny moved across the room, her whole face wide and smiling her delight. In a moment she and the boy were engaged in a game which consisted of much kissing and hugging, of giggling laughter and rolling on the rumpled bed, oblivious it seemed, to those who watched. The love which bound Jenny Greenwood and her son was like a beacon in the warm room, a lovely thing to see and Joss was reminded of her misery when she was carrying this child who was now the very centre, the pivot on which her world revolved and the strange irony which had decreed such joy should come of so much wretchedness.

He turned to smile at Kit, to share with her his pleasure in his sister's happiness but the expression on her face wiped his smile away and he almost, only the watchful eyes of the nursemaid stopping him, drew her into his arms. He had no need to ask her why her face was so curiously still, so flat and empty, so lifeless and without hope. His love was sensitive now, sharp and wise to her despair since he himself felt it. They were never to know what Jenny knew. He and Kit Chapman. They were never to treasure the joy of a child as his sister did. Never to feel their own son wriggle and squirm in play against them as Jenny's son was doing, never to hold the flesh of their own flesh in loving arms and in that moment, as she looked up at him, her face quite dead, her eyes bright with unshed tears, he felt her desolation mingle with his own. She would never marry, and he, Joss Greenwood, was married to a woman who was and would be forever a child herself and would never conceive one of her own.

The nursemaid had turned away, lifting the poker to stir the glowing embers of the fire, busy with tongs and the coal scuttle. Joss put out his hand, cupping Kit's cheek, caressing it with his thumb, his eyes deep and sad as he looked into hers. There was nothing to say, it was there for her to read in his face, as he read it in hers and she turned her lips into the palm of his hand, kissing it passionately, declaring with that gesture that it did not matter, that as long as she had his love it was enough.

From the corner of his eye as he still looked into Kit's face he caught a movement from the other side of the room where he had noticed there was another small bed. It was tidy, made up, he had thought for the nursemaid to sleep in but as he watched the flat surface moved and on the pillow a small head turned, then rose up for a moment and two eyes peeped over the bedclothes at him. As he stared the eyes vanished and the head seemed to shrink beneath the covers and the bed was still and almost flat again.

'Who's that?' he asked curiously, still holding Kit's hand but the nursemaid appeared not to notice as she looked towards the bed in the corner of the room. Kit had turned to look as well and they both took a step or two in the direction of the bed.

'Nay, don't go too near, sir,' Flora said warningly, 'or you'll scare't poor mite to death.'

497

'Scare *who* to death, Flora,' Kit asked questioningly. 'Who on earth is it?'

'Eeh, I don't know her name, Madam. Nobody does.'

'But who is she? How did she get here?'

'Why, don't you remember? You brought her here yourself.'

'I did?'

Jenny had turned to watch as Kit and Joss, with Flora hovering anxiously at their backs, stood a yard from the bed. Her son was curled on her lap, his bright head on her breast, his eyelids drooping in sleep and for a moment the contrast between the secure, loved, contented boy, safe in his mother's arms and the terrified child in the other bed was quite dreadful.

'She's been here over six months, Kit. She came when Lucas and I did. You brought her from the mill on the day Ellis and the others were arrested. You and I were off to London so you left her with Flora. She's been here ever since.'

'Good God! I'd quite forgotten about her. But why is she so afraid? No one harms her here.'

'Wouldn't you be afraid if you didn't know what was to happen to you next? I suppose she came with a waggon-load of children from somewhere . . .' she shrugged, ' . . . only Gods knows where, or what happened to her before Ellis got his hands on her. She's known nothing but change and fear, hunger and brutality probably since she was old enough to stand, or even before. Can you wonder she trusts no one. She allows Flora to bathe and change her and has been taught how to use a spoon to eat her food. She's put on weight, you'd hardly know her from the child we brought in here six months ago but no one can get near her, not even Lucas. She's been abused not only by adults but by other children as well so . . .' Jenny hugged her own child to her, concerned evidently for the plight of all the children who had known the dreadful life this one had, her expression giving thanks that Lucas would never know the suffering of the child in the other bed.

Kit let go of Joss's hand at last, intrigued, why Jenny or Flora could not have said, and moved towards the bed in which the child cowered. They watched her as she drew back the covers and all of them, with the exception of Flora who was used to it by now, gasped at the rigid, unfocused look of terror in the child's eyes. A little girl, she was, still thin and pale, but quite normal in stature, the dreadful look of the undernourished, the unusually large head, the indecently protruding bones gone with the diet of good food she had eaten for the past six months. Her hair was thick and glossy, a lovely russet with a tendency to curl and her eyes were a soft sea green. But the look in them was appalling, so filled with unimaginable horror both Joss and Kit gasped out loud.

'Good sweet Jesus, what the devil has been done to her?'

Flora bristled. 'Why nothing, sir. She's been as well looked after as Lucas here. She gets the same food and Miss Greenwood has the seamstress make her little clothes just as she does for Lucas. She's warm and cosy but . . .'

'What is it, Flora?' Kit turned to look into the kindly face of the nursemaid.

'She'll not let me cuddle her, Miss Chapman. I've tried times to get her on me knee. We all have. Well, we feel so sorry for the poor little mite but she just goes as stiff as a dead rabbit. Quite give us a turn it did, the first time it happened. She stopped breathing, ma'am. Blue in the face she was, so after a bit we were afraid to touch her. She's no trouble as long as no one touches her, 'cept me when I wash her, like, an' you'd hardly know she was there . . .'

'Does she not speak?'

'Oh no, madam, not a word.'

Kit turned to Jenny. 'Did you know of this?'

'Of course, I'm in the nursery every day.'

'And you didn't tell me?'

'I'll be honest, Kit, but it never occurred to me. You had given her a home, good food, warm clothes. I didn't think you would be . . . be concerned beyond that. Besides, we thought she would come out of it.'

'Well, she hasn't.'

'No, but perhaps with time, and Lucas . . .'

'Has she not been given a name?'

'Well no, poor little poppet . . .' Flora's face was filled with sadness.

'Indeed . . .' Kit leaned over the child and with a gentle hand brushed back the soft hair from her forehead. The gesture brought no response. Kit stood up, her hand still fondling the little girl's cheek, then she turned to the nursemaid.

'I'll come up again tomorrow, Flora and we will see what can be done. I'll not have an unhappy child in my mill and I'll certainly not have one in my home.'

Jenny said she would stay with her son until he slept and then take him to his own little bed beside her own. Joss was to give her love to her mother and tell her she and Lucas would be over on the following Sunday. They embraced affectionately, the sleepy child between them as Kit and Flora watched and as they left the nursery she and Joss heard her begin to sing a lullaby to her boy.

They stood just outside the nursery door in the darkened corridor and as it shut behind them they were instantly enclosed in the world each had waited impatiently for since he had invited her into his mother's cottage in Edgeclough. For over three years they had waited, not consciously perhaps, since neither had believed that it would come again, but their bodies, each one awakened, would not forget, could not be made to forget and they came joyously together now as she took his hand and began to lead him towards the staircase which went down from the nursery floor to her bedroom. When they were inside her last coherent thought was that although they were in a house filled with people not one of them knew exactly where she was – except perhaps Jenny! Winters had seen them all go up to the nursery and Flora had seen her and Joss go down towards the drawing-room. Janet would not come until she was summoned and until then . . .

She sighed as he placed her on her own bed, her mind

500

dwelling sensuously on the hundreds of times she had imagined this moment.

'You break my heart with your loveliness,' he whispered as he put his mouth to her naked breast.

'You soothe my soul,' she breathed as she held his head more closely to her.

'You bring me such joy . . .'

'You always have.'

33

The series of strikes which whiplashed through Lancashire began in Hyde, near Manchester, the leader a thirty-year-old Irishman called John Doherty. Wages had been cut again and though there was talk of militancy and holding out forever, the strikes failed. There was starvation stalking the county since they were out of work for six months, many of them, but the bleak struggle, though it caused hardship and poverty never before known in that part of the land did more to unite the working man than at any other point in his past history. A new militancy appeared, a new sense of defiance and purpose and a new fellowship between the working man's leaders. Francis Place, John Fielden, John Doherty, Joss Greenwood and others were agreed that a National Union, with Doherty as secretary, should be formed. A weekly levy of one penny per head on each working operative was willingly paid, producing a sum which went towards a 'benefit' of ten shillings a week for each family unemployed. Not much, Joss agreed, when Jenny questioned it, but enough to keep starvation from the door and surely a beginning in the great social service which he envisaged for those suffering hardship.

He was often at Greenacres in the spring and summer of

that year, going ostensibly to visit his sister and nephew though there were those who whispered that that was not his only reason for calling. Kit Chapman had been seen with a lean, dark man who looked suspiciously like Jenny Greenwood's brother, striding across High Moor to Badger's Edge with her four ferocious dogs running beside her and what were they doing up there, those who heard the rumours asked each other? And what was Kit Chapman thinking of mixing with the likes of him, a man who had been imprisoned for machine wrecking and mill burning, a man who was the opposite to every conviction her own father had believed in. Turn over in his grave her father would if he knew what was going on and surely it must all be to do with her close association with the Greenwood family? All of them!

There was Jenny Greenwood, tricked out like a lady in her silks and satins, giving orders to men like Ernest Gribb who had been a manager at the Chapman mills for over twenty years. You would think she was the mill-owner the way she went about the newly renovated spinning room, nodding and smiling at the women who worked in it, stopping to speak even, uncaring it seemed of the minutes wasted when the spinning frame was turned off. There was space enough between each machine to hold a dance in, it was said, and a new system of windows which let down from the top providing fresh air into the room and on the side where the sun struck, blinds were put up to shield those who worked there from its heat, and though the children still crawled about beneath the machines to 'piece' and collect the waste, those same machines were so hedged about with guards it was a wonder they could be made to function. And the hours they worked! No child under ten years of age employed and those that were did no more than eight hours at a stretch. *Eight!* Could you believe it and how on earth was Kit Chapman to make a profit, they marvelled, in those circumstances?

But that was not all. At the back of the mill she had

erected an extension in which there was a *dining-room*, warm in winter, wide open windows in the summer, with tables and chairs in which the operatives could sit for half an hour and eat their 'baggin', that which they could now well afford to be nutritious and filling on the incredible, ridiculously high wages she was paying them. There was piped water, clean and cool, brought from the river which ran beside the mill and separate privies for the men and women to use, *whenever* they wished to. No rules, nor fines. Like a bloody rest home, it was and no wonder there were always dozens at her gate clamouring to work there.

And at the end of their eight-hour shift, broken at midday for half an hour, the children of her operatives were given two hours' schooling in the back of the warehouse in a space she had cleared for them, and the new schoolroom and dormitories she was having built – these for her apprentices – were almost ready for them to move into.

In the weaving-sheds another agitator and radical had been made up to overlooker. Jem Pickering, son of Sarah and Isaac Pickering, had organised the same kind of madness as Joss Greenwood's sister in the spinning rooms, treating his operatives as though they were civilised human beings and not the slow-witted, shambling and stunted dwarfs most of them were. They had the same consideration given to them, the same incredible privileges as those in the rest of the Chapman factory, his authority complete, it was understood and him not yet nineteen! It was said he could take to pieces the Lancashire loom and put it together again in the space of an hour. He understood the weaving trade as well as any in the Penfold Valley since he had worked on his father's loom from the age of six. He had devised a method of threading the shuttle by hand, doing away with the arrangement of 'kissing the shuttle' which had lost so many operatives their front teeth. He was a good 'tackler' and they had come to depend on his skill and knowledge. He had a feel for the correct delivery of the cloth and the proper flight of the shuttle but that made no difference to those who were of the opinion that he should be kept in his proper place which was at a loom until he was well in his twenties, as the rest of the overlookers had been. And those who whispered of these things to one another in the drawing-rooms of Crossfold, in the counting houses of the other mill-owners, in the Cloth Hall and 'The Old Bull' in Jagger Lane were bitter and resentful, not that Kit Chapman was doing these things but that she was apparently making a success of them. But then, they comforted themselves, she was mad, out of her mind and what else could you expect of a woman? They forecast it would all turn sour on her, just wait and see and those who were in her debt and had no recourse but to put up with her nonsense, waited.

They moved into their new houses, her pampered operatives, in the new village she had created just on the outskirts of Crossfold where she had bought land. Well lit streets, they had, paved and with adequate gutters to take away rainwater. The rubbish cart came once a week to remove their refuse, for there had been cholera in town that year and it appeared that Miss Chapman was of the opinion that where there was filth and bad water, there could be sickness.

What the community did not know and it was doubtful they could have kept quiet about it if they had was that besides the resident teacher Katherine Chapman employed to educate the children in her mill and the resident physician she retained to improve their health, was that the same doctor, young and with liberal ideas, was instructing the women in a method of contraception which would keep their families to manageable proportions!

The Penfold Valley buzzed with talk. Those manufacturers and their wives who were accustomed to dining with Miss Chapman and her protégé, Miss Greenwood, who had been forced upon them against their will, declared that really, they did not think they could abide it much longer. They had been quite taken aback on the first occasion Miss Greenwood, *Miss* Greenwood, if you please, had been introduced to them by Kit Chapman as her colleague and friend, but short of turning on their heels and walking from the house which Hannah Chapman would have been delighted to see them do, they had no option but to take her hand and smile frostily.

George Abbott, seated next to her at table, told his wife later he had fully expected her to eat the excellent duckling, Kit Chapman had served, with her fingers, but it appeared Miss Greenwood had picked up more than the knowledge of how to wear the exquisite rose-pink silk gown she was in, which any pretty woman could have been put in to resemble a lady, for she used the correct knife, fork, spoon at the correct moment and even congratulated Kit on the excellence of the wine served, just as though she had drunk it all her life.

'You are in the business of spinning, I believe,' she said to him in a voice from which the broadness of Lancashire had not completely gone.

'Indeed Miss Greenwood.' He could not bring himself to say more and his wife, who sat opposite looked as though she might become stuck in the frozen pose she had taken when Jenny Greenwood had the audacity to address a remark to her husband. Put up with her they were forced to do, but converse with her, *never*, but Jenny Greenwood knew her own worth by now and she saw no reason to efface herself in the company of these men and women whose grandparents had been no better than her own.

'And what do you think to the Bill for introduction of the ten-hour working day proposed by Mr Michael Sadler, Mr Abbott?' she asked.

'I think it to be no more than foolish nonsense, Miss Greenwood.'

'Really. Do you not agree with Mr Richard Oastler that our children should be free?' Her face was as innocent as a babe.

'Free, Miss Greenwood. I'm afraid I do not understand you.' His good-natured face, heavy and well fed was turned slightly away from her as though only courtesy to his hostess – and the five thousand pounds he owed her – kept him seated beside Jenny Greenwood.

'You have heard of Mr Oastler, Mr Abbott, and his fight for the abolition of colonial slavery?'

'Indeed. Who has not?'

'You think him an honourable man then?'

'Naturally.'

'Then you would believe his word when he spoke it?'

'Of course.'

'Then what of the letter he wrote in the *Leeds Mercury* several weeks ago regarding the slavery of thousands of children in our very own mills?'

'Come now, Miss Greenwood. You cannot possibly mean it. Those children are free as air itself. They are not forced to work in our mills. They may do as they please, as their parents please . . .'

'And free to die of starvation if they please.'

It was as well that Kit stood up at that moment, signifying that the ladies should retire, leaving the gentlemen to their cigars and port, for George Abbott, as he proclaimed furiously to his wife later, might have thrown caution to the wind and told Jenny Greenwood to take herself off back to the hovel she no doubt came from. It was more than a gentleman could stand and his wife, a lady, agreed with him quite tearfully since her friendship with Hannah Chapman was put seriously to the test by the dreadful strain of being forced to remain on good terms with Katherine. Hannah was cool with her and bitter on the subject of the lower orders who tramped through her lovely home and gardens. Though she was not in the habit of walking in them herself she was often disturbed by the sound of *that child* who romped and squealed on the lawn with his nursemaid and by the sight from her window of *that woman*, his mother and the rest of her horrid family, enjoying what had once been hers alone. She could see her own daughter consorting with a class inferior to her own, laughing and chatting with the woman and more often now as the weather improved, with the one who was her brother.

The very one who had once destroyed dear Barker's machines and burned his warehouse for which crimes he had served two terms of imprisonment. Dear Barker's daughter brazenly flaunting herself, she was, with those to whose level she had sunk and if poor Barker could see what the wealth, for which he and his family had worked so hard, was being squandered on, it would surely kill him all over again.

Kit Chapman was happier than she had ever been before. She would look back to what she had imagined then to be days of perfection. Like the first time her father took her to the mill. The day on which he told her she was to be his sole and complete heir. The day she had been allowed to walk alone for the first time up on the moorland accompanied only by her dogs, but none of them could compare with each lovely day to which she now awoke. She was fulfilled in every need she had. Her mills ran smoothly and efficiently, not as yet making the profit they once had, though her reputation for the best quality cotton was still upheld. Her mind was sharp, her heart content, her conscience clear as she watched the miraculous improvement in the people she employed. They were gaining confidence in her now, realising that this 'experiment' she was proving was no nine days wonder to impress the factory inspectors when they came, but an on-going improvement in their own lives.

And her body glowed with the physical fulfilment Joss Greenwood gave it in her bed, and her heart was tranquil with the emotional fulfilment he gave her every moment of her waking hours. He came to her as often as he was able, sometimes no more than once in two weeks for his work took him all over Lancashire and Yorkshire as he reported on the conditions of those in the textile trades. Though he still wrote articles for several working class newspapers his time was being given up to an increasing demand for his presence at political rallies and meetings. He could command a mighty gathering wherever he went since the men for whom he fought revered him, trusted him, looked to him still as the man who would better their lives. Perhaps not this year, or even the next but one day his revolutionary ideals would come to fruition. Whenever there was a meeting involving a Whig or Tory supporter there would be a great deal of rough heckling, shouted abuse, fights and even garbage chucked indiscriminately, but when Joss spoke they would listen quietly, almost with love, for he was one of them despite his obvious rise in the world.

'You will go to Westminster one day, my darling,' Kit told him.

'And your mother will invite me to dine with her.' He laughed softly, sitting up to look at her in the half light of the candles which stood on the table beside the bed. They had dined with Jenny who had, as usual, excused herself on the grounds that she wished to look in on her son, all three of them acknowledging now, though not openly, that Kit and Joss were lovers and when the servants had withdrawn, told that they would not be required again that night, Joss and Kit had gone up the wide staircase to her bedroom. Though he did not spend the whole night with her, much as they both longed for it, since his mother and Charlie would both expect him home after dining with his sister, they would share an hour or so in the dangerous but enchanted world which was, as yet, just their own, before Joss mounted the rather elderly mare he had bought to move more easily about the immediate vicinity of his home. They were both aware that such a relationship as theirs, carried out in a house where the servants could not fail to realise eventually that Joss Greenwood was more to their mistress than merely Jenny Greenwood's brother, must surely become common knowledge in the community but as yet they were unable, and unwilling to look for some other way to continue it. They would not be parted again, they had both sworn it, but how they were to manage it without destroying not only Kit's reputation which was already a matter for conjecture in the community, though as yet only on the subject of her sanity, but Joss's credibility with those who trusted him in their fight for justice. And how would Martha Greenwood face the truth, if it should come out? She and Kit had met only once on the day Charlie was beaten by Kit's overlookers but Kit knew from Jenny that she was held in grateful esteem by Jenny's mother. Everything they had, the Greenwoods, and many of *their* social group, they owed to Kit Chapman. Not given, most of it, but earned by them because she had allowed them the chance for it and her name was spoken of almost reverently now on the lips of all those who had cause to thank her. But Martha loved her son and her son had a wife who, though she was not as she should be, was still his wife and very dear to Martha. Marriage was marriage, good or bad, in health *and* sickness and what else could you call Mercy's affliction but a sickness? And despite her gratitude to Kit Chapman and Joss's avowed belief that all men were equal there was still in Martha's heart the feeling that the Greenwoods and the Chapmans were not of the same social position. The classes did not mix, not in Martha's world, they did not marry and though she did not consciously consider it, not knowing the situation existed, they certainly did not become lovers.

Kit's golden skin was the rich colour of honey in the warm light of the candles. Her hair a dark and tangled mass on the pillow and she had flung one arm above her head. The movement lifted her breasts, peaking her nipples, amber tinted against the whiteness of her skin and Joss's hand reached to caress each one in turn. Her free hand absently stroked the hairs on his chest and he bent to kiss her, brushing back the hair which drifted across her face. Her lips were warm, parting a little beneath his but it was clear her thoughts which only minutes before had been wholly concerned with his hands and his mouth and what they were doing to her naked body, had flown away to some other place which demanded her attention.

'A fine thing,' he grumbled laughingly, 'when a man cannot capture the interest of his woman when he lies naked in the same bed with her. He pleasures her until she cries out with it then when she has done with him her thoughts instantly wander to other things. What must he do to re-capture her notice, d'you think? This perhaps ... ah ha ...' as Kit squirmed with delight, ' ... or this ...' and she stretched and sighed languorously beneath his delicately probing finger, turning to him at once for there was never a moment when he did not bewitch and enchant her with his touch.

She was watching him dress when she spoke again. The words of love and delight, the whispers and soft laughter, the joyous sounds of their lovemaking were still drifting sensuously about the shadowed room but her head was clear now.

'I meant what I said, Joss.' Her voice was low.

'About what?' He was busy with his boots, his mind concerned with the half hour's ride he must undertake, with the time he must give to his mother, his brother and his wife before he journeyed the next day to Manchester where he was to speak to a gathering of cotton workers, sharing the platform of John Doherty, the secretary of the newly formed trade union. He was torn, not into two parts, but into three or even four, with the commitment he had towards Kit, towards his wife and family, the men who were loyal to him and those who urged him to further his career in the political arena.

'About Westminster. There are to be elections in a year or two and what better man to represent the people than you?'

His hands stilled and he stared blindly into the corner of the shadowed room. It was as though she had read what had been in his mind for many months now. It was believed among his fellow radicals that they could win control at the forthcoming elections even though the right to participate at the polls was restricted to property-holders and ratepayers. The townships of Oldham, Royton, Crompton and Chadderton and the newly created constituency of Crossfold were to be formed into a three-member parliamentary borough and the registered electorate was limited by the property qualification to no more than one thousand five hundred out of a population of just over fifty thousand. But four-fifths of the electorate were composed of men in small businesses, shopkeepers, men who owned smallholdings with a cow or two and all dependent on working-class custom. And the working-class man was solidly behind Joss Greenwood and the other radical reformers. If they were to take it into their heads, as well they might, to boycott these same shopkeepers where else could they sell their milk and their butter, their bread and oats and the goods the working man purchased. Joss Greenwood, if he chose, could become one of the radical candidates for this borough, and he knew it.

He jumped to his feet, stamping them into his boots which had been flung willy-nilly about the room in his eagerness to love Kit Chapman an hour ago. He appeared not to have heard her, or if he had was not prepared to listen.

'Did you hear me, Joss?' she said quietly.

He became still then. 'Aye, I heard you, lass.'

'It's the money, isn't it?'

'Nay, I've no mind to be a Member of Parliament, nor to live up in London. I'm a Lancashire lad and I love a Lancashire lass and I'll not be parted from you, nor my family and besides, there's nothing I can do . . .'

'That's not so, Joss. You've proved time and again just what you can do for these people of yours. They love you. They rely on you. They trust you above everyone because you have never let them down, and because you are one of them.'

'Say that's so, I still couldn't go.' His voice was harsh.

'Because of the money.'

'Aye, because of the money . . .' He turned to her swiftly, his face truculent, arrogant, filled with his frustrated pride, but beneath it in the depth of his clear eyes was the longing. ' . . . and don't you go saying you'll give it to me because I won't have it. You know yourself what the property qualifications are for a Member of Parliament. I've no personal income so how would I live? I'm nought but a hand-loom weaver . . .'

'No, no! It is an honourable trade but that is not all you are.' Her voice was high and defiant and she leaped from the bed, glorious in her nakedness, truly a woman now in the mature roundness of her breast and hip but she might have been fully clothed for all the notice either of them took of her body. 'You are a leader, Joss. There are not many born to be such but you are one of them. You told me your father was one and perhaps he was, but you have drawn these men of the cotton industry into a force to be reckoned with. Only you! And it should be you who speak for them up at Westminster. Let me help you, Joss. Please let me help you. I have more money than I know what to do with. I am spending it now on houses and schools and all the things you have told me they need and what I have come to believe in myself, through you. How much better it would be if you, with your eloquence, could make *others* see it too. Those in Parliament who have the *real* power to change things. Don't let your pride stand in your way, in *their* way. Would you have them go on as they are just because you were too puffed up with your own feelings to consider theirs. You are a bigger man than that, Joss Greenwood. You know it and I know it.'

She could see it in his eyes then. The belief that it could be done. The realisation that what she said was the truth. There was a sudden excited lift to his head and a squaring of his broad shoulders. The very idea that he, a weaver's son, could sit up there with sons of gentlemen, a working-class man, perhaps the first to do so, to speak on behalf of his own. It was so heady he could get drunk on it, his expression said and yet that was surely not what this was about. For a moment he had been carried away with his own joy, his own self-satisfaction, but then was he not human? Was he not allowed to revel for a moment in the pride any man would feel in what he had achieved, what he could achieve in the future if he allowed it to happen? It was his decision and he must make it alone, without the distraction of this woman. She was *his* woman and he loved her for what she was, for what she had done, for what she had already given him of herself but she was bewitchment and he must not be beguiled by the magic she held out to him.

He took her in his arms and held her in a way which had nothing to do with sexuality despite her nakedness. He leaned on her strength, depended on her now, he had come to realise, not just for his bodily easement, for the comfort and joy her love gave him, but for the power of her woman's wisdom, the surety that she was always waiting here for him, for her patience when it was needed, for her stubborn resistance, the ability she had to exhilarate him, to anger him sometimes, to make his life whole. She was his life and without her he would be nothing but this must be considered, not with her to influence him, but on his own. He must decide the rightness of it. There would be no doubt in anyone's mind where the money had come from to send him to Westminster, should he decide to stand for the candidature and those whom he represented must be made to see that he did it for them, not for his own splendid ends which is what would be said of him. A kept man they would call him, and worse. There was his mother, and Charlie, who would have to know. Explanations would have to be made and though Miss Chapman's benevolence, directed at *all* her workers now, and not just the Greenwood family, was an accepted fact surely it would not extend to supporting a man, a grown man, *keeping* him, feeding and clothing and housing him, they would be bound to say. It would not take either of them long to understand the implications. He was a man with a wife, who was *not* a wife. A man, with a man's needs. Kit was a woman, a strong, self-willed woman who also had needs and he and she were together more than was usual. Could he put that burden of shame on his mother, for that was what she would be? Shamed! And yet she was a compassionate woman. Perhaps she might be an understanding woman also, and young Charlie, though still a boy, was mature, experienced, not in the ways of love, but in life. He was a scholar now, with a flair for learning, which was astonishing his tutors, and in his maturity was old enough to know the truth and ready, surely, to accept it. For the sake of the men and women he had always supported, would he not accept it?

'Will you do it, Joss?' she said, her cheek pressed into the curve of his shoulder. 'God knows how I will manage without you if you go to London. I cannot bear the thought and I'm sure I will regret it the moment you are gone but you know it is right for you. I am trying hard to tell myself that I am doing this for the men and women you love so well but if I am honest that is only partly the truth. I love you, Joss, more than any other in the world and whatever I say it will sound priggish, pompous even, but you were meant for this and I am willing to . . . to . . .'

'Let me go despite the pain it will cause you?' He bent his head lovingly to hers. 'Kit. Katherine Chapman. Do you know what you are to me? Do you? Inside you is a fire which warms me, a light which shines from you so that I can see. You are so fine, so good and if that makes you sound saintly that is not how I meant it. I cannot count the times you have tried my patience with your devilish ways until I could take a whip to you. No, you are no saint, my lovely Kit, but you have a good heart. It has been burdened by what your father put in it but you did not allow it to become callous as the rest of the mill-owners in the valley. You are a business-man whose sole aim is profit as your father's was but you have brought a woman's compassion to it, proving something of great importance to the men and women of Lancashire. That fair treatment brings a fair reward, not just for them but for you.'

He threw back his head and laughed. 'By God, will you listen to me sermonise. Saint Joss now, alongside Saint Katherine and the pair of us with more sins on our souls than Enoch Butterworth could shake a stick at.'

'Who's Enoch Butterworth?'

'Someone I once knew. It's a long story from a long time ago but I think old Enoch would approve of my taking this step to help his fellowmen, though not the way I'm to go about it!'

34

Jenny and Charlie noticed the three men on Easter Sunday. She and Lucas had walked the three miles from Crossfold to Edgeclough as they did every Sunday, the small boy running ahead for he was always in a hurry to get to his grandmother's cottage, and to Charlie. He was three years old tomorrow and Charlie had promised to take him up on the moor to show him the warrens where Charlie caught the rabbits which went into grandmother's pot. He was well aware that grandmother had no need of the rabbits Charlie caught, not like she had in the old days his mother had told him about. They had almost starved then, before Aunt Kit had become a 'reformer', though he was not at all sure what that was, and had given the workers, of which his mother and Charlie had been but two, a lot of money, again he was not certain of how much. But the rabbits Charlie caught could be given to other, poorer families who lived in the village Charlie told him.

His mother spoke to him at great length on the wickedness of wrongs done to the 'poor' by the 'rich', among which he often thought they must be numbered since they lived in such a lovely house, and his grandmother did not – so was she not poor? – but his mother said not. It was really too much to understand and though he was well aware that he was better off than many of the boys with whom he played in the village what did it matter when they all had such fun? Sunday was the best day of the week.

He suffered his grandmother's embrace, wriggling like a rabbit himself, but good natured with it, the only characteristic he had inherited from his father, for which his mother gave daily thanks, apart from his handsome face. Aunt Mercy kissed him and would have sat him on her knee, calling him 'Tom' as she always did, why he did not know since that was not his name but he evaded her strange grasp and her strange vacant stare and ran straight to Charlie. They began to wrestle in the way all men did, to show one another their love, and he certainly loved Charlie.

Charlie Greenwood was twelve years old now, growing into the frame which was a replica of his older brother's. Tall, lean, all arms and legs and elbows still, growing out of his breeches as quickly as his mother put him in a new pair, and despite the scarring of his engaging face, agreeable to look on. There was a line across his lips, well defined and deep where Arnold Ellis's boot had split his mouth but already, as he filled out from a scrawny boy to a well set up youth, beginning to fade and as his mother said, he was always laughing these days so you'd hardly notice. The pucker above his left eyebrow, sewed up as best she could by Sarah Pickering, lifted it into an expression of quizzical amusement, of wry humour at the world which Charlie Greenwood now found so much to his liking and fortunately the teeth he had lost were at the back of his mouth, the gap left not visible except when he yawned. He was not much given to yawning since, being a strong and wiry boy he was rarely tired and never, never bored. He had followed his brother and the rest of the Onwardsmen, when he could escape his mother's vigilance as a young boy, but now he was the pride of his family in the grand school at Crossfold and his brother had told him his talents would be needed in other directions as the thinking man he was to be. A lawyer perhaps, but that was in the future and this small scrap who tried to climb his leg and who Charlie loved inordinately, he did not know quite why, was claiming his attention, demanding to be off, like the two men they were, up to the tops to inspect Charlie's traps.

'You'd better not let the Squire hear you say that, my

lad,' Jenny heard him say to her son as they walked up the path towards the track which would lead them to Dog Hill, and the inevitable questions . . . 'Why Charlie?' . . . 'What for Charlie?' . . .'How Charlie?' followed on the air. It was an easy enough climb for the three-year-old boy who had been taught almost from the time he could walk, as they all had as children, the meaning of striding out, of simply going on and up, without whining.

She turned back to her mother, no longer bearing the baskets of food she had once brought for they were not needed. She was proud of her own ability to provide for her family. The soft-hued warmth of the clean, white-washed kitchen, the bright fire in the hearth, the dresser lined with her mother's crockery, the brass candlesticks and herb jars, the rugs, the fresh curtains at the window, the comfortable, highly polished furniture and the saddle of lamb she could smell roasting in her mother's blackleaded oven. Upstairs were three bedrooms made over from what had once been the loom-shop worked by her father and Joss, with comfortable beds and good woollen blankets and white bedspreads crocheted by her mother and Mercy during the winter, bright rugs and curtains. Daisy slept in one on her rare night off and her mother in another with Mercy, while the third was Charlie's. In the stall at the side of the house was the mare that Jenny had bought for Charlie so that he might ride the three miles to school each day and stored beside it was the coal which was delivered now that Charlie could no longer collect the peat for his mother's fire.

It was a joy to Jenny and her heart was filled with it as she looked at Mercy, marvelling at her mother's forebearance with this pretty child who was her brother's wife. She was twenty-six now and looked scarcely older than Charlie. Bonny she was, the firm flesh on her golden with the sun, her brown silky hair springing in fine curls about her smooth face. She had become fuller bosomed in the plenty which had come with Kit Chapman's reforms and Jenny's own elevation in life, a fit wife for any man, one would think and it was only when you looked into her eyes that the emptiness there was revealed.

'And how is Miss Chapman, lass?' It was the first question her mother always asked.

'She's well, mother and sends her regards.'

And perhaps for the very first time since they had met in the doorway of the spinning room on the day the child had lost his hands in a machine, Jenny Greenwood's mind dwelled softly on the woman who was her employer and probably, though she admitted it only to herself, becoming her friend. Certainly the friend of those men, women and children in her mill who had cause, *now*, Jenny acknowledged truthfully, to give thanks for the improvement she had brought into their lives.

'The proof of the pudding is in the eating' she had told herself sourly. Well, she had tasted the pudding and it had proved to be delicious and though she had not yet come to terms, and probably never would with the recognition that her brother and Kit Chapman were lovers, could she really blame Joss when confronted with the woman who was his wife? So, she would try to keep to the adage, held dear in these parts where privacy was valued, that it was 'nowt' to do with her. It seemed to hurt no one, she was the first to admit, indeed Joss had never looked better and as for Mercy she felt no lack of affection in this family where she was treated as a well-beloved child.

They spent a pleasing hour or two on subjects dear to her mother's heart. Country matters, simple and unchanging. Events which had happened during the week, events which happened every week in the uncomplicated and contented life Martha spent with her daughter-in-law, while Mercy busied herself about the kitchen, dusting and polishing objects which she had dusted and polished only an hour since, basting the saddle of lamb in the oven, declaring she would make an apple pie for Charlie and Tom's return, running to the window a dozen times to look out for their coming. Jenny felt her nerves tighten as she watched the constant movement of Joss's wife, wondering how her mother could stand it but Martha seemed not to notice beyond a motherly admonishment to 'watch that oven, lass, 'tis hot', just as though Mercy really *was* no more than a child.

Charlie got out the mare from the stall at the side of the house where once his forebears had housed their few cows, and she and Lucas were lifted on to the animal's back for the journey home as they always did. Strong her son might be but Charlie insisted upon it, walking beside them to Greenacres and then riding back since it was a long walk for the boy who was by now, half asleep against his mother. She leaned down to kiss her mother and Mercy and their affectionate farewells fell softly in the darkening yard as they turned out into the village street. Sarah was at her door, outlined against the soft glow of her fire-lit kitchen and she waved before going inside and the clip of the horse's hooves sounded loud on the quiet cobbled street.

It was at the top of the brow which led out of the village when they saw the men. Three of them striding away in the direction of Beal Moor just as though they had come from Edgeclough. They were no more than dark grey shadows against the pale grey of the evening sky, their faces a white blur as they turned to look over their shoulders at Jenny and Charlie.

'Who are they, d'you think?' Jenny mused. 'They look as though they've been visiting someone in the village.'

'Nay, I don't know.' Charlie stared after them but the men did not look back again, disappearing into the growing darkness of the moorland. He turned again just before they began their descent on the long, winding track to Crossfold but there was no one to be seen.

The lad came to the Greenwoods' cottage door at just gone half past seven the following Sunday morning. He was decently dressed, ready for church, he said, which the Squire insisted upon each Sunday for his servants, but they had all been thrown into confusion when the accident happened and ... well ... if Mrs Greenwood didn't come at once there was a chance she might not see her daughter alive again.

'Daisy . . . oh dear God . . . dear God . . .' Martha reeled against her son, her face ashen and it was Charlie who read the note. Written on the Squire's own notepaper it was, and though he did not recognise the handwriting, never having had a letter from the Squire before, there was no denying the authenticity and gentlemanly hand of the letter. Daisy had fallen, it said, down a flight of stairs. The Squire's own physician had been called but the girl was unconscious and in the physician's opinion, though he did not wish to alarm Mrs Greenwood, her daughter's condition was critical.

'I'll saddle the mare. She'll take us both,' Charlie said, his own face like death and the boy watched interestedly as the mother and son whirled about in the first muddled moments caused by shock before they steadied themselves.

'Mercy . . . Oh dear Lord . . . Mercy . . .'

'Get her up . . .' for Joss's wife was still in the bed from which Martha had just risen.

But Mercy Greenwood would not be 'got up'. She was alarmed by *their* alarm, frightened by Martha's frantic exhortations to be a 'good girl', distressed by the impatience of the woman who had shown her nothing but love and tolerance, whose even temper and steadiness had given Mercy a lifeline to which she could cling.

'Please . . . Martha . . .' she whimpered, cowering beneath the covers, her eyes enormous in her pale face, ' . . . I would like to stay in bed today . . .' for sometimes when her little bird failed her Martha allowed her to lie in the soft feathered security of the bed they shared, to lie and watch the clouds drift serenely across the blue of the sky, to see the wind ripple the tall bracken and the pretty yellow gorse, until she felt the tranquillity soothe her.

'Mercy lass, you must get up and go to Sarah's . . .' Martha was savage now in her anguish for her youngest daughter, pulling at Mercy's shoulders, tugging at the bedcovers but Mercy held on.

'Come on, Mother,' Charlie was shouting from below. 'The mare's saddled . . .'

'She won't get up . . .'

'Leave her then. She'll be safe enough in her bed . . .'

'Please Mercy . . .' Martha tried one more time but the girl was nearly demented now in her distress.

'Will you go up to Sarah's, please Mercy . . .' but blood was thicker than water and this girl was no blood of Martha's and though she knew Mercy should not be left alone since she was incapable of intelligent thought and that given time she should have sent Charlie up the street for Sarah, there *was* no time, and so the choice was made.

The four men watched impassively from the shelter of the little spinney at the back of Martha's cottage as she and her son moved off slowly for the mare carried a double load. Charlie had tried to persuade his mother to ride the animal while he ran beside it for it would have been quicker but she had never been on a horse's back in her life and so, with her arms tight about him they began the seven mile journey to the Hall which lay on the far side of Ashton.

When they had disappeared up the back track which went, not through the village, but in the opposite direction, the men slipped, like silver grey shadows, down through the neat rows of seedlings Mercy had planted the week before and into the cottage, closing the door behind them.

Jenny had stopped for a moment to have a word with Sarah as she and Lucas walked down the street two hours later, remarking on the coldness of the day and the certainty that it would rain before the hour was out.

'Aye, back ter winter it is, that's fer sure. Best round t'fire on a day like this, my lass, an' that's where I'm off right now.'

Lucas was darting ahead, eager to get to Charlie to show him the rough wooden musket, that Dick, the stable lad, had carved for him for his birthday. They could have a good game up on the top of Dog Hill for though Charlie was almost grown up he did not mind playing the games dear to Lucas's three-year-old heart. He lifted the latch, his face, still that of baby, rounded cheeks wreathed already in the joyous grin he reserved just for Charlie, prepared for a moment or two, but no more, to suffer the fond embrace of his grandmother and Aunt Mercy before the serious business of the day began. His mother was but a step or two behind, shaking out the folds of her long, serviceable cloak for the rain which had threatened all the way up from Crossfold had begun, clinging in fine droplets to the fabric.

She felt herself begin to apologise for in her confusion she was convinced she had come to the wrong house, though in her mind of course, she knew she had not. She was ready to back out again, to scream to the three men who stood about the kitchen that she was sorry, really she was, that this was not her house, nor even her mother's and she would tell no one, no one in the whole wide world of what she was looking at, no matter if she was put to the torture if they would let her go, if they would let her son go, if she could be allowed to return and wipe out the last thirty seconds, make them vanish as though they had never been, never happened. If she could be allowed to pick up her big-eyed, open-mouthed boy, take her hand from the latch where it still rested, pull the door to and simply go back to the time, two minutes ago now, when she and Lucas had still been at her mother's front gate. But it was too late. Her eyes had seen what was there, what had been done and it was too late.

Too late for her, and far too late for Mercy whose resting place on Martha's newly scrubbed kitchen table would be her last. Her naked white body appeared to be without bones, her head hanging over the edge of the table until her tangled hair swept the floor. She was on her back. Her tiny breasts were flat, like those of a girl-child and on them was congealing blood about the nipples. She had bruises on almost every part of her body, scraped raw where vicious hands had grasped her tender flesh. Her legs had been held apart so violently she gave the appearance of being almost torn in two and Jenny's demented mind, unwilling to deal with the horror, could not seem to get past the problem of how her mother would remove that vast pool of blood from the table.

'Good morning, Jenny. Come in an' close t'door, lass. 'Tis right cold out, for' time o't year and we'd hate to lose the warmth of yer Mam's kitchen. Please . . .' the voice became sharp, ' . . . close t'bloody door for we want no nosy parkers pryin' in what's not their concern, do we?'

She closed the door, moving automatically closer to her son, her mother's hands pulling him to her, her arms encircling him in a gesture which was already hopeless. Her face was the grey of the pale ashes spilling into her mother's hearth and her firm flesh had fallen in, deepening her eye-sockets to black pits. The bones of her face stood out like a bleached skull as she tried hard not to look at what had been done to her brother's wife.

'Take off yer cloak, my lass, an' come to't fire,' but she shrank back against the door and Arnold Ellis smiled. The year he had spent in prison had stripped the loose flesh from him, revealing his angular frame, the big bones of his hands and wrists, accentuating the cruelty of his thin-lipped mouth. The boy cowered from him in her arms, burying his young face in her skirts and she stroked his fair curls in an effort to soothe him but her eyes would keep straying to what lay on her mother's kitchen table and her terror drove out all thoughts beyond the one which searched for a safe way out for her son.

'Put t'lad to one side an' come 'ere, Jenny,' Ellis said, 'or one o' these lads will tek 'im from yer and they're not over gentle.'

'No . . . please . . . don't hurt the boy . . . please . . .'

'He's a bloody Greenwood, in't he?' Ellis's expression was mild, interested, as though he and Jenny were discussing a diverting fact in the genealogy of Jenny's family, ' . . . as you are, as yer brothers are, both of 'em.'

'I don't know what you mean. Why are you here? What do you want with us?'

'I'm 'ere ter collect summat what's owed me, Jenny Greenwood.'

'I owe you nothing . . . nothing . . .' She was babbling, she knew it as Ellis gestured to one of the other men who began to saunter across the kitchen towards her.

'No . . .' Her voice was ready to rise into a scream and instantly the third man who had slipped up behind her, clapped his hand across her mouth, silencing her. She could smell him, she could smell them all and her stomach rose in horror but she knew she must make no noise . . . Why? . . . Dear God, why not? for a scream would bring the men of the village but there was Lucas . . . Lucas.

'But you do, Jenny Greenwood, you an' that bitch we worked for, me an' the lads. We was doin' no more than givin' that precious brother of yours what he deserved, what many a lad got in the mill yard for giving a bit o' lip, but Charlie did more than that. He struck Alfie 'ere, didn't he Alf, and so we give 'im a licking which was no more than 'e deserved, but what 'appens? You go runnin' ter high and mighty Miss Katherine Chapman an' me an' Alfie an' Jim get a year's hard labour, which we didn't much like, ay lads? But it wasn't until a certain . . . well, shall we say someone else who 'ad a grudge against you and Miss Chapman, came ter me an' . . .'

There was a stirring at the back of the kitchen, just beyond the heavy chenille curtain which her mother drew across the scullery door on a winter's night to keep out the draught, and Ellis stopped speaking abruptly as though he had said too much. Jenny strained her eyes and her ears, for surely there was a fourth person hovering there, but the man holding her pulled off her bonnet and, getting a savage grip in her short hair, forced her eyes back to those of Ellis. They glowed like the coals in her mother's fire, his hatred supreme, his triumph dominating the room. The other two men did not speak but merely stood, watching her, enjoying it, enjoying Ellis's game of making it last for as long as he wished before the final act, whatever he wished that to be.

'So yer see, Jenny Greenwood, me an' the lads're going to punish you for what yer did to us. We're going to punish you and yours because through the Greenwood women

524

we'll get back at the Greenwood men. Both of 'em. Revenge, that's all that kept me goin' in the last twelve months, my lass, an' when I met up with ... well ... the idea was thought up an' 'ere we are. That brother of yours, the one what thinks he's Jesus Christ saving his flock and stirring up folks so that a man can't carry on with a bit of business when he's a mind to, will p'raps think twice afore he goes sticking his nose in where it din't belong, an' as fer Charlie Greenwood, he'll wish he'd died under the lashing we give him last year when he sees what's bin done to his sister. We'll break them both, through you and the other bitch, Chapman. The idiot was a bit of a bonus . . .' He indicated the still figure of Mercy Butterworth, 'we'd forgotten her but while we was waiting for you we 'ad us a bit of entertainment, like, but Alfie 'ere was a bit rough, or was it you, Jim? I forget.'

'No ... no ...' Her head moved from side to side, denying what he was saying, denying the evidence of what had been done to Mercy though the appalling truth of it was sprawled on Martha's kitchen table. Her eyes rolled in her head and the man's hand dragged at her hair, pulling the skin back from her forehead and the smell which was in her nostrils was not of them but of her own terror, for herself, oh yes since her mind and weak woman's body knew exactly what they had in store for her, but for her son, her beautiful boy who was her life.

'Take the lad.' Ellis's voice was a razor slashing her to pieces for she had heard what men did to small boys. They were looking at Lucas, beginning to smile. In his hand was the pitiful lump of wood with which he was to play at 'soldiers' with Charlie and his stunned face, his deeply shocked, mercifully dazed eyes stared back at them. His golden curls gleamed in the firelight and his cheeks were tinted by it to a lovely, rose pink. He was a handsome child, still with the beauty of babyhood on him and Jim Briggs smiled. Jenny saw it and her frozen mother's heart died.

'Don't hurt him,' she whispered. 'I'll do anything you want but don't hurt him. He's only three years old,' but the inert figure of the boy was dragged from her arms, leaving them empty and lifeless. The man who held her breathed some obscenity in her ear, his breath foetid, and pushed himself against her back but she was conscious of nothing but the small figure of her son, his face like a mask, too terror-stricken even to cry.

But the man was becoming impatient. She was quivering against him, just like the other one had and he was ready to start again. He dipped his hands inside the bodice of her dress, gripping her breasts, squeezing until she cried out in pain and the others turned to look at her, speculatively, gloatingly, obscenely, waiting it seemed, but not for much longer, for some signal which would tell them they might begin their sport.

Ellis had turned to look at the child, his face suddenly watchful, the expression on it curious as though something had stirred in his mind, something which chaffed a chord, a memory perhaps, one he could not quite recall. He moved across the room and looked down into the boy's blank face, into his flat brown eyes, then, with a muttered oath he took the boy's arm and began to drag him towards the back of the room.

'No . . . Dear sweet Jesus . . . oh please, don't hurt my baby . . . please . . .'

'What is it?' the quiet voice but sharp now, from behind the curtain said.

'I thought yer'd like ter tek a good look at this lad, sir.'

'Why? What's the brat to me?'

'Can yer not see it, sir?'

'See what, for God's sake?' but the voice had a hesitancy about it which said its owner had suddenly become aware of something quite remarkable in the boy's appearance.

'What d'yer think, sir?'

'I think . . . I think you may have something, Ellis. Something which needs looking into, and I mean to . . .'

Ellis turned back to the men in the kitchen who had begun cruelly to handle Jenny Greenwood's cringing body.

'Right lads,' he said casually, 'she's all yours but

remember what Mr . . . er . . . what you was told. We don't want no 'arm to come to 'er, not like the other . . .'

'Wait.' The voice was soft but peremptory and Ellis turned his head, frowning a little for it was hard to hold back these men of his once they'd got the feel of a woman in their hands. Like dogs they were who have the scent of the bitch, and just as violent if they are thwarted, ready to tear himself and each other into pieces, snapping and snarling over who was to be first.

'Yes sir?'

'I need a moment to think . . .'

'Right sir, but can we get on with . . .?'

'I said wait, man. Tell those . . . ruffians of yours to wait until I give my permission.'

'They'll not like it, sir.'

'I don't give a damn what they like. Have they not had enough?'

'No sir.'

'Tell them that unless they do as I say I shall report the murder of that woman in there to the magistrate and that within the day they will be back in gaol, and you too. You know I mean it, don't you, Ellis?'

It seemed Ellis did.

The man who stood in the shadow of the scullery stared into the mindless brown eyes of the boy. His own were icy and cold, like frozen brown water.

'How old is this boy? Ask her. Tell her not to lie.'

She told the truth. He was her child and she would have said anything, or done it to save him.

'He's three years old, sir, she says.'

'What month was he born?'

She told the truth again. The cruel eyes of the man studied the boy who hung between him and Ellis like some limp doll; his hand still holding his musket.

''Shall me an' the lads get rid of 'im, like we was goin' to, sir?' and in the kitchen Jenny Greenwood began to scream.

'Tell her to be quiet,' he said, and she bit her lips until they bled.

The men moved menacingly at Ellis's back and he re-peated his previous question. They couldn't hang about here much longer. It was a bloody wonder no one had come to investigate that last scream and if they didn't get going soon, someone would.

'No, I think not.' The man spoke thoughtfully and his voice had softened strangely. He put his hand on the boy's head.

Ellis began to lose patience. 'We'll 'ave ter look sharp, sir, if we're ter catch t'other 'un up on't tops. We're not sure she'll even go ter Friars Mere so it might tek a bit o' time ter locate 'er. The lads'll not be long in there with that bitch, but beggin' yer pardon, sir, I want my turn an' all. I've waited a long time fer this day an' I'm not bein' done out of it,' not for you or anyone else, his suddenly cold eyes said.

'Very well. I must admit to fancying a "turn", as you so quaintly put it, myself but I think I'll forgo the pleasure in view of . . . this new development.' He placed a gentle finger on the boy's rounded cheek. 'I must get right away from the district immediately.' He began to fondle the boy's curls and there was an expression in his eyes which, in any other man's might have been described as proud. 'When you've done, get out of this area, all of you. Forget the Chapman bitch, and remember what I said to you. I do not make threats I cannot keep, Ellis, something you'd best impress on those thugs of yours. One word of this and I shall have the three of you back in gaol, and for so long you will all be too old to ever enjoy a woman again. Do I make myself clear? And tell that woman in there that if she wants her boy to live she'd best do the same.'

'Right sir, we'll not be far behind yer,' and already Ellis's hands were at the fastenings of his trousers for he meant to be first. He turned back to the homely kitchen in which so much violence had been done that day, not even seeing the man and the boy slip from the back of the cottage. He watched greedily as Jenny Greenwood's clothes were torn from her body and her mouth was bound with a strip of cambric from her own pretty petticoat. She struggled so hard one of the men was forced to club her with his fist and the other two held her, almost senseless, between them. When she was completely naked Ellis signalled with his hand and Mercy Greenwood's tiny body was tipped carelessly to the floor and Jenny was laid down in her place on the table.

35

The funeral drew the biggest gathering of mourners ever before seen in the Penfold Valley. They came for miles, from Yorkshire and Cheshire, from Derbyshire and Westmorland, from wherever the name of Joss Greenwood was known, from weaver's cottage and from the Hall in which the Squire's family lived. From the working man in his clogs to the black-suited, immaculate gentlemen of the squirarchy, arriving on foot, on horseback and by carriage until the whole area about the small hillside Chapel was black for a hundred yards in every direction with grieving men and women. The horror of it had drawn them all together, high and low, as nothing else had ever done, the Squire feeling himself to be in some way involved as his own notepaper, somehow, had been used, in the carrying out of the crime.

It was said of Martha Greenwood that she would not be long behind her daughter-in-law in her own coffin, but she was the only member of the family to stand with her head held high at the graveside. It had been whispered in the drawing-rooms and factories of Crossfold, of what had been done to Mercy Greenwood before she died, the appalling details spared them in the bare, quite formal announcement of her murder in the newspapers but no one knew exactly what it was, though the men could guess.

Charlie Greenwood was no longer the cheerful, light-hearted young boy who had set his school friends laughing in the classroom. His face had always been good-humoured with a glint in his eye which said it did not take a great deal to turn to easy laughter. Easy going then, and, since he had recovered from the injuries he had received at the hands of the overlookers in the Chapman weaving-sheds, looking forward to his grand future. He would get on, there was no doubt about it, under the patronage of Miss Katherine Chapman, his benefactor. Three or four years at the grammar school, it was foretold and then on to the University for it had been discovered he had a clever mind and an aptitude for learning which was quite extraordinary in a weaver's son and there was talk he might make a teacher, or even a lawyer. A matter of great pride he had been to the Greenwood family and would you look at him now. The anguish in his face was there for all to see since he was the one who had found them, his brother's wife quite naked, it was whispered, his sister tied to a table leg and in a frenzy, and would either of them ever recover from it, they asked one another and the sad answer seemed to be no. He was like a boy grown into a man overnight, supporting his mother and younger sister, she whose imminent death, it was reported, had taken him and Martha Greenwood from their cottage on that fateful day. He was white-faced and sick, standing to attention at the graveside as they shovelled the dirt on to the coffin but surely the worst sight and one the men who followed him could hardly bear was the complete breakdown of Joss Greenwood who was to be, it was rumoured, radical candidate for the constituency of Crossfold.

And but for the quiet presence and continuous support of Katherine Chapman might not the whole family have gone under for it was said Joss Greenwood's grief was terrible. She and Sarah Pickering were the only ones on their feet and in their right minds on that day and it was they who had made Mercy Greenwood presentable enough

530

to be viewed by those who came to pay their respects. Besides the family she and Sarah were the sole persons to have seen what had been done to her and the picture which would be carried with her to her dying day had been savagely locked away in Kit's mind. It would be brought out and grieved over at a later date but quite simply there was no time for it now since somehow she and Sarah, for whom she gave thanks in a hundred ways must get the family through the pain and the horror and the anger until it could be controlled.

Charlie had screamed, she had been told, over and over again, being still a boy then, until every man and woman in the village had stood in the space before his mother's cottage. His mother, thankfully, had lost her senses and Charlie for more than half an hour would let no one in until Sarah and Isaac had overpowered him and Isaac had run all the way to Crossfold for her, with Sarah, almost senseless herself, keeping the doors locked and the curtains drawn for Charlie and Jenny could bear no one to see what had been done to Mercy.

And Jenny, poor frenzied Jenny, still wandering the moorland looking for her son. Calling his name again and again until she could no longer speak, raising the hairs on the backs of the necks of the men who searched with her. She had run out of the cottage, past the weeping women and ashen-faced men and on to the moors behind to look for him, saying only that the men who had killed her sister-in-law had taken him. She was still looking for him three days later, dry-eyed and staring, too desolate even to attend the funeral of her brother's wife, indeed to care that she was dead.

Mercy Greenwood lay by herself at last, dressed in a simple white dress, her face, thankfully unmarked, washed, her hair brushed in soft curls about it, her expression peaceful with no trace left of the violent way in which she had died. She had been tenderly placed on the trestle table the men had put up in the room which had once held Abel Greenwood's weaving-loom. White sheets had been placed at the window and candles lit at the four corners of the room, replaced as they burnt out by others, flowers, masses of them brought up from Greenacres in an effort to expunge the horror of her death with the sweetness and beauty of life, a peaceful haven for her last resting place on earth.

And when he came from wherever it was he had been brought, Joss would not be stopped, though Isaac and the constable had tried, from seeing what had been done to his wife and to hear in a voice which was dead and hopeless, of the abduction of his sister's son.

His cries, like Charlie's were unendurable and the women of the village, as they mourned, covered their ears and drew their children indoors and thanked God it was Sarah Pickering and Miss Chapman and not themselves who had to deal with it. Anything the two women needed in those days before the funeral, they had only to ask for, they were told, just as long as it was not to be with Charlie and Joss Greenwood for the two brothers could not contain, nor control the virulent hatred, the savage and violent pain, the guilt and shame and horror, for surely there was nothing worse a man could suffer than to see the violation and abuse of a woman he loved.

'Thank God Mercy's dead,' Joss cried harshly, the only words he spoke before he ran off into the dark and no one had the heart at the moment, nor the courage to tell him of Jenny Greenwood's missing son. They had searched, hundreds of men from all over Lancashire, from Yorkshire where Joss was known and respected, even loved by those who called him brother in the fight, moving across the moorland from Hind Hill as far south as Tintwistle, from Edgeclough across Saddleworth Moor to Broadhead Moss and west to Tandle Hills but no trace had been found of the boy. Perhaps he was dead, they said but why should the murderers take the body with them? How many men had there been? Jenny Greenwood would not say. More than two was made evident by the nature of Mercy's injuries but why? For God's sake, *why*?

At first it had been thought that a band of passing ruffians had chanced upon the two defenceless women, taking their pleasure, but when Charlie Greenwood became coherent and was able to speak, it seemed a note purporting to have come from the Squire, had been sent to lure him and his mother away. When they had found their Daisy hale and hearty and uncommonly perplexed, as had been the Squire when he was called and shown the note, though he had been inclined to blame practical jokers, *then* Martha and Charlie had ridden home again, the bewilderment and irritation turning slowly to dread, then a cold creeping fear, for the note had been sent for one purpose only; to remove them from the cottage.

'It's too well thought out to be chance, and too well planned to be chance,' the magistrate, accompanied by a Peace Officer told Katherine Chapman, she being the only one with any sense remaining, in his opinion. 'Someone deliberately wanted to get one of those women, or perhaps both of them alone. Why? What reason could they have for wreaking such . . . well I can only call it revenge, Miss Chapman, for what else could it be? It was not chance. There is nothing stolen as far as we can tell so . . .' He shrugged, ' . . . do you know of anyone who could have reason for doing such a thing?'

But Kit had to admit that she didn't and indeed had no time even to consider such a thing. She moved through those heart-chilling, mind-chilling, bone-chilling days before the funeral with an unhesitating willingness to be what anyone asked her to be, to do what anyone needed of her. She had sent a message to Greenacres for Janet to pack a box with clothes suitable for a lady in mourning, plain and unadorned, with necessary undergarments. The gown she had worn on the mad journey up to Edgeclough and in which she had tended to Mercy Greenwood had been burned. She did not sleep except for a light doze in the chair beside the fire and when she did Sarah was there to watch them. She administered the valerian Sarah infused, to Martha, to Daisy who was allowed home by the Squire's lady, distraught and difficult to handle in those first few hours. She lay down beside Charlie and held him in her arms, calming him without words in the way Joss had once calmed Mercy Butterworth when her brother was hanged. He was wild, off his head, talking of revenge and how, if it took the rest of his life he would find the men who were to blame, of what *he* – a twelve year old boy – would do to them, whoever they were, when he did. He was quite inconsolable, his face ugly and swollen, his eyes slits of pure hatred in his once young face for he could not get the picture of that violated body out of his young mind, but when she put her arms about him, giving him what at the moment his own mother was unable to give, pulling his head to her breast as his mother had done when he was a small boy, he slept fitfully.

She held the hand of the dazed and frozen woman who, though she had not given birth to her, was the mother of Jenny Greenwood, who loved her and her son as deeply as though they were her own flesh and blood. Held fast in shock, she was; the potions Sarah administered to her gave her peace. But though she seemed to be far away in a place where the hurt could not reach her she must not be left alone and the women of the village, with Kit and Sarah sat with her in turns as she rocked slowly in her chair, staring out of the bedroom window at the moorland where her daughter roamed in search of her boy, waiting for her to come home with him. Her daughter who had gone quite mad, wandering in circles like a wild woman, dressed in the same garments she had worn for days. Her daughter who could not sleep nor eat but kept up with the men who searched for her boy, unwashed, wild-eyed, snaggle haired, and lost it seemed just as surely as he was.

And Joss? What could Kit do for him, say to him, to bring him from the frenzy, the crazed and dangerously unbalanced state into which his grief had tipped him? He disappeared for hours on end, not looking for the boy as the others were but for the men who had taken him, and the life of his wife.

He sat far into the night before the day of the funeral, in the chair that had once been his wife's, staring sightlessly into the fire, his face black and brooding, his hands hanging limply from the arms of the chair and Kit wondered on the strangeness of the brother and sister, so close in all these years and yet now, in death and sorrow, so far apart. They seemed unable, Jenny and Joss Greenwood, to sit together in the same room, to share their pain and loss as those of a family will for whenever Jenny wandered back to the cottage, which she did now and again to see if there was news of her son, Joss would leap up and go outside, waiting until Jenny had blundered off again into the night, before he returned. What was it, Kit wondered that made them afraid to be alone together, to comfort, if only with a loving hand, the pain they both endured.

Kit knelt before him on that night, saying nothing, offering him her loving compassion putting her hand gently on his arm but he flung it off, flung *her* off and rising, stamped out of the cottage as though it could not contain him, nor he what was within it.

And now she was in her grave, his sweet child-wife and the vast multitude come to mourn her, come to mourn with the man she had loved, had drifted away, reluctantly it seemed as though they would like to offer, if they could, something more to the suffering family, but what was there to give? There had been no gathering at the cottage after the funeral as there would for a death under normal circumstances, no funeral feast to refresh those who came to mourn, to sustain them on their journey home. Kit and Sarah had discussed it and had decided it would not do, for they, the family of the murdered woman, had gone temporarily to another place though they were present in body, staring at nothing, saying nothing, four black figures hovering uncertainly about the cottage kitchen. They could not be expected to receive callers, to chat softly, to go through the pattern of bereavement which gave comfort to those who had decently laid away a loved one. It was too soon. Indeed would it ever be the right time? They waited, for Jenny, for Lucas, for release from their suffering, and Kit waited with them. Sarah found nothing strange, it appeared, in the daughter of the great house of Chapman, the owner of the Chapman mills, the wealthiest woman in South Lancashire, taking on the supervision and care of a lowly weaver's family. None of them, and none of the men and women, who had appeared from nowhere to see what they could do when the news got about, questioned it, nor seemed to wonder at it, for Miss Chapman was not out of place in the cottage kitchen. She was not grand, nor overbearing, nor patronising. She offered herself simply as another pair of hands, another heart to grieve, another back upon which burdens could be laid, another mind to solve the problem of how to ease the anguish.

'I'll be off then, Miss Chapman,' Sarah was saying softly when the cottage door was flung open and Jenny Greenwood stood there swaying wildly in the doorway. They all sprang to their feet in confusion, even Martha, badly frightened by the violence, for had they not known her well it was doubtful they would have recognised the woman who stood there.

'It was Ellis . . .' she screeched, ' . . . Ellis and the others who were sent to gaol for beating my brother. They did it, they took my boy but it was not them who thought of it, oh no it was not them, for they had not the wits. There was someone else there, I know it . . . behind the curtain, someone else who hated me . . . and her . . .' she pointed a trembling hand at Kit, ' . . . enough to set them on me.' She laughed wildly and Sarah moaned in her throat for surely they were forever cursed in this house. 'Guess, Kit Chapman, go on, guess who it was who had a reason to believe he was badly done by . . .'

'Harry Atherton.' His name was but a whisper on Kit's lips but they each heard it and already Joss and Charlie were reaching for their coats.

'Aye, that's who's got my son . . . *his* son. By God. I've searched these moors, my mind in a turmoil knowing there was something . . . something but not being able to catch it. I was . . . my brain wouldn't function. I didn't care what they had done to me . . . I'll mend, for women do, but my boy . . . they have taken my boy . . .'

'We'll get him back, Jenny. Me and Charlie. You stay here with Mother and Daisy and me and Charlie will take the coach to . . . where does he live . . .?'

'I don't know but she does.'

They all turned to look at Kit, even Martha whose poor mind could not even grasp what they were about and Kit took a step back from the awful snarling hatred which glowered from the three faces of Martha Greenwood's children. Joss had heard Jenny admit to the fatherhood of her son but he didn't care, if he had even noticed. He cared for nothing, not Lucas Greenwood, not Martha, his own mother, not what had gone before which was good in his life, nor what would come when this tragedy was decently buried; not forgotten, but accepted. He wanted revenge, he wanted to expunge his own guilt and shame and here was the opportunity, an opportunity to use his fists on the man who had done this to his family. Not once but twice to beat him into the ground, to do to him, and the others what they had once done to Charlie.

'Where does he live?' He did not use her name and his eyes, though they looked at her face, avoided hers.

'I . . . I can't remember . . . It has been a long time.'

'Where does he live? We can easily find out.'

'Then you must.'

'Tell me or I'll . . .'

'Joss, for God's sake, don't do this. Tell the Peace Officer. Go to the magistrates, but don't . . . please . . .'

Sarah Pickering huddled against the fireplace, afraid as she had never been afraid in her life. There was so much badness here, such malevolence and yet these were decent people and they loved Kit Chapman, all of them. In the past few days she didn't know how they would have managed without her. Once they had called this warm-hearted woman a "stuck up bitch' but she had been a rock to them all and when they were themselves again they would realise it. A good friend to Jenny Greenwood and more to Joss, it was rumoured and by God, she herself had thought in the past few days, if she could give him a bit of comfort now, in any way at all, poor devil, then good luck to her and to him for he'd had a rough time of it with the sweetly vacant woman he had married, God rest her soul. If anyone could pull them all together again it was her for she'd the strength and tenacity not often found in the gentry. Soft they were, most of them, but not this one, no, not this one, and now they were all three of them advancing on her, threatening her as though she had something to do with it, whatever it was they were talking about. God in Heaven, if somebody didn't do something soon they'd be about her and have it out of her one way or another and she'd not stand by and watch it, not Sarah Pickering.

'Stop it,' she screeched, 'stop it, yer daft beggars. What the dickens d'yer think yer doin'? Sit down, all of yer, an' pull yerselves together. Hasn't there been enough violence in this 'ouse . . . Dear Sweet Jesus . . .'

'I only want the address of the man who took my sister's boy, and by God, I mean to have it.'

'How do you know it was Harry Atherton? Jenny didn't see him . . .'

'I know . . . I know, I tell you . . .'

'Jenny, sweetheart, you're not in a fit state yet to . . . make a decision. See, why don't you and your mother come home with me? I'm going back to Greenacres this afternoon but you could come with me, you could all come with me and then, when you are . . .'

Joss Greenwood's eyes narrowed in his ravaged face, grey and lined like that of a man twice his age. They had sunk deep into his head and there was no trace of the handsome good humour, the quizzical interest, the expression of intelligence and compassion which had grown as the boy became a man. There was hatred there and bitterness, a souring of his spirit, a tainting of the goodwill he had cherished towards the men he had led. He had been wild and disorderly in his young manhood, but never brutal. The very air about him had crackled with his anger and contempt for men who had exploited other men but he had always retained his humanity. Now his face was cruel, sullen, baleful with the lust for vengeance which was eating his mind and soul and Kit recoiled from it.

'Joss, for God's sake . . .' Sarah's voice softened as she remembered what he was suffering. 'Joss . . . see, sit down, lad and . . .' but he turned on her so savagely she shrank back against the chimney breast.

'Sit down, *sit down*, with them bastards out there . . . and Lucas . . . they've got her lad and God knows where he'll end up. Let's hope he's dead in a bloody ditch since we all know what happens to pretty little boys, don't we . . . don't we . . .?'

'Dear God . . .' Sarah's voice hissed in her throat and Martha moaned feebly, turning away for she could not bear the expression on her son's face.

'I'll kill them, every last one of them, so help me . . .'

'No, Joss, leave it to the law . . .' Kit's voice was high and wild.

'Bugger the law,' he said, quiet now and all the more menacing for it. 'I've another score to settle with Mr Harry Atherton, an old score . . .' His voice trailed away then he turned to his sister and brother.

'Jenny . . . Charlie . . .?'

In the chair by the fire where she had fallen his mother began to weep.

They had gone, the three of them, striding away up the track which would lead them to Crossfold. Jenny had washed herself and changed the torn and filthy dress she had worn for almost a week, brushed her hair and put on her bonnet and they looked like any normal, decently dressed family, she and Joss and Charlie Greenwood. Charlie, a boy only a day or two ago, his face that of a man now as he took up the sword his brother pressed into his hand, ready to use it though he was no fighter and, if he was

539

honest, badly frightened by what he had heard and witnessed this day in his mother's kitchen.

Martha sat in the same chair not moving until Kit knelt before her.

'What will you do, Martha?' she asked.

'Nay lass, what can I do but wait for them.'

'Will you not come back with me. I could look after you until they return.'

'It's kind of you but this is where I belong. We should all stay where we were put on this earth.'

'No, you're wrong, Martha. We can all move on if we have the wits for it. Charlie will be a great man one day when he has finished his schooling and . . .'

'Joss? Aye, if he can get over this. He's not in his right mind just now, and won't be for a while but he's strong and he'll survive.'

'I'm afraid for him. If he should find Harry Atherton . . .'

'It's not likely a nob like him would be mixed up in the . . . death of . . . well, you know what I mean. And why should he take our Jenny's lad? No, they'll be home soon but they need to be *doing* something, him and Jenny, looking somewhere and Jenny's living on nothing but hope. They'll be home directly and I must be here when they do for I'll be needed. Charlie has to get back to school. To get on with his life. He's only twelve, Miss Chapman and can't be looking back forever, nor our Joss.'

'No . . .'

'He's work to do and he knows it, when the anger's gone. Them words he said . . . he'd not mean them, you know that. He'll not kill anyone . . .'

'No . . .'

'He's wild, hating, and I don't know how long it will be before it leaves him. He loved Mercy, you know that?'

'Yes.'

' . . . and he needs to avenge her, he thinks, being a proper man but when the sense returns to him he'll see that it must be left to the proper authorities.'

'I know.'

'You must be patient, lass,' and with those words Martha acknowledged the bond which existed between her son and this woman.

'Tell them both . . . that I'll be waiting for them . . . when they are ready . . .'

'I will, lass but I can't promise either of them ever will be. They've both suffered a loss, more than they could bear, really. Joss feels . . . well . . . Mercy's brother died because of him, he thinks, and now Mercy . . .'

'I know . . .'

'And my Jenny, she's strong but she loved that boy. I don't know if she'll ever . . .'

'Don't say it, Martha.'

'No. You're a good lass, Kit Chapman, but . . .'

'I know, but I cannot . . . I will wait for them . . . tell them.'

36

It seemed, though she had never in her life worked so hard, that she had more time on her hands than she needed that summer. The summer of waiting. She went alone each day to the mill, working in her office from the time the factory bell rang until seven or eight, nine or ten in the evening, poring over pages of accounts, profit sheets, invoices and bills — dozens of those — from builders and carpenters, engineers and architects, those involved in the construction of her new dwelling houses. She was busy, riding in her carriage out to the almost completed village, inspecting the neat streets in which sturdily built cottages stood, shops, an inn, for the men must have their ale, a church for those of a religious nature, a school, and even a Mechanics Institute which was to provide lectures in technical and scientific subjects, and a reading room and library. There was a vast range of broadsheets and tracts available, pamphlets and popular radical newspapers with a weekly circulation reaching twenty to thirty thousand. With a growing number, already, of working men able to read them; these would be made readily available to those who could not afford to buy them. There was to be an assembly room where functions might be held, a public bath and wash house and a hospital and all to be surrounded by a park, green fields and open spaces where those who worked confined in the mill all week might take the air on Sunday.

But she still had time in which her head was not busy, when her hands were not busy and her thoughts took her over the hills to the village of Edgeclough. They had come home, Jenny, Joss and Charlie Greenwood, she had been told, a week after they had left in the search for Jenny's missing son, Lucas, but they had come without him. Sarah sent word with her son, Jem, who was manager now in Miss Chapman's weaving-shed, that Jenny was grieving, still wandering far and wide in her search, taking no heed of what they told her, going God knows where, disappearing for days on end, turning up only to change her clothes, to kiss her mother and her brother who had returned to school, then to be off again, following the desolate path which led to nowhere, it seemed. Of Joss there was no word for Sarah had none to give.

So time hung heavily and hopelessly on Kit Chapman's hands and there were only so many hours she could put in at the mill. She walked the hills and moorlands with her dogs close to her heels, her only companions these days, they said of her, going nowhere near the village where the Greenwood family lived for something told her not to. She did not know what it was, perhaps a sense, which said they needed to be without her until they had come to terms with their dreadful loss. Not recovered, for would they ever be that, but accepting, and still Joss Greenwood had not come home.

It was September before she went up to the nursery. The

day was wet and her spirits could not face the drifting mist of rain which sighed against her window, the thought of the weary and ever increasing reluctance to confront the lonely walks, the reality that this was to be her life from now on. Without Jenny whose friendship she had come to value. Without Joss whose love slipped through her fingers like water, refreshing and necessary to life but as elusive as the wind. She must have something beside her mills which once had seemed to hold everything she had ever needed. She must or she would become as dry and withered as the leaves which already were falling from the trees beyond the window.

She was drawn that day by some curious impulse to see the child who was alone there now, forgotten, watched over by none but Flora. Flora who still went about the place with a wan, tear-stained face, mourning the boy she had loved as her own and had no time for the silent child who, against Flora's will, was still in her charge.

She rose from her chair and bobbed a curtsey as Kit entered the room. It was quiet now where once a mischievous imp called Lucas Greenwood had romped and roared and stolen the hearts of all the housemaids, empty somehow, and yet did a small ghost still hang about to break hearts as he once had?

Kit felt the tears catch her eyes and a lump she could not swallow come to her throat.

And there was the child.

She remembered the last time. All she had been aware of then was a shadowy face, a mop of hair and two deep set eyes before the sheet had been drawn up to cover them. A small trembling mound cowering away from the danger, the abuse, the harsh words, the careless violence which had been turned on her by all the tall beings she had known in her short life. Instinct, and self-preservation had given her the animal-like reflex that told her that they were to be avoided at all cost. She had been comparatively safe from them beneath the wheels and straps and spindles of the spinning frame, in the dark and filth and waste which, when she heaped it up about her kept her from their frightening eyes, the sounds with which they reviled her, and the lash of the giant's stick. They had caught her though, three giants and after that she couldn't remember what had happened until she had found herself in some strange thing which had contained water. Water like that in which she had often been tipped upside down when she had fallen asleep. They were going to do it again, she realised that of course, and so she had simply sat and waited for it, knowing there was nothing to be done for they always won, always.

She was sitting mutely at the nursery table when Kit entered. Her hair which had been recently brushed was a soft mass of red-gold baby curls and Flora had tied a white length of ribbon to one of them, not very expertly for none of Flora's sisters had ever had such a thing. She wore a little white dress and frilly drawers, white stockings and shoes. She was spooning quite delicately, a rich creamy porridge into her mouth, licking her pink lips with a tongue which flicked in and out like a little cat's. Alone and withdrawn to some place where no one else could reach her, steadily eating the food, the food which had transformed her from a tiny and grotesque parody of an infant human being into a delightfully pretty, still slender but charming little girl. She might have been accustomed to such surroundings, such lovely clothes, to the good food all of her young life, so serene did she appear as Kit opened the door and entered the room but as she did so, beginning to smile wonderingly, for in six months the child appeared to have recovered completely, the little girl's eyes became quite blank, the spoon clattered into her empty plate and she simply slipped downwards until she was completely out of sight beneath the table and the tablecloth which hung almost to the floor.

'Oh no, sweetheart, no, I'm not going to hurt you,' Kit cried out at once, hurrying across the nursery to the table which was placed near the window. She lifted the cloth, smiling, her heart, quite amazingly, warm and gentle for the frightened child, ready to draw her out, to stand her up on her feet, to lead her across the room to the nursery fire and even to lift her on to her own lap, to hold her in arms which had never before held a child. She had known no child but Lucas. She had been carelessly fond of him since he had been a part of Jenny but he had been an exceedingly masculine little boy, spoiled to distraction by Flora and the other maids, loved by his mother whose joy he had been and taking for granted his male dominance of all the women in his young life. But this . . . was different.

She put out a hand to the little girl who was grovelling, her face to the carpeted floor, her hands sweeping wildly, just as though she was gathering the patterned roses with which it was strewn. Sweep and sweep and when she had it all, whatever it was she had gleaned to her, she began to back out, dragging it with her from beneath the table. It was heavy, whatever it was she imagined she carried in her arms for her little face strained and even sweated and Kit could almost smell the fear on her.

'Dear God,' she whispered, 'what is she about?'

'Gathering waste, Miss Greenwood said.' Flora's voice was quite matter of fact. 'She always does it when she's frightened or when she sees someone she doesn't know. Reckons its a new "tackler", I suppose and she'd best be about something before he straps her.'

'But it's been over a year. I thought by now she would be . . . well, I don't know . . . happy, normal . . . She certainly looks it. I don't think I have seen such an attractive child and with a bit more flesh on her bones . . . Oh Lord, now what . . . ?' She stepped back as the little girl scampered from the far corner where she had evidently put the waste and dived back beneath the table.

'She's getting some more,' Flora said. 'Busy as a little bee she is sometimes, fetching and carrying and sweeping, just as though she thinks if she stops she'll get a clout, which she probably did,' she added, 'poor little beggar.' Flora turned to the fire and reached to put on some more coal, evidently so accustomed to the child's ways they were no longer of much interest. ' 'Course she's no one but me to . . . to give her a bit of company . . .' It was said not only sadly, with a threat of tears, but also accusingly, letting Miss Chapman know that Flora could not be blamed for the child's lack of intelligence.

'Well, something must be done. She cannot go on like this. My God, more than a year and she's still living in that awful, fearful world. One would think the kindness you and the other servants have shown her would have made her realise she no longer has anything to fear.'

' 'Appen she needs more than that,' Flora said cryptically, daringly, but Miss Chapman appeared not to hear.

'How old do you think she is, Flora.'

'Nay, it's difficult to say. They all grow at different rates and one child's not like another. Four or five, 'appen.'

'Well, I cannot have this,' Kit said, just as she might to some awkward manager who had gone against her in her own factory. Moving slowly towards the little girl, who was crawling along the floor dragging some unimaginable load behind her, she put her hand on her arm. Immediately the child ceased all movement. Still, still as a wheatear when the hawk flies over, still as a rabbit when the stoat goes by, her silky lashes fluttering in an orgasm of terror as she waited for the blow.

Kit lifted her gently to her feet, then took her hand. It was so cold she gasped but without conscious thought she drew the small, beautifully dressed child towards the nursery fire and the child went blindly, obediently, mindlessly, her fear so great she emptied her bladder into the freshly laundered softness of her frilled drawers. Kit sat down in the chair and the child stood before her, like some sacrificial lamb which knows full well its fate but awaits it stoically since what else can it do? Kit held her cold hands, chafing them between her own warm ones, watching for some change in her expression but there was none.

'Sweetheart,' she said softly, not knowing herself in this new role which the child's despair had cast her in. 'There is nothing to fear here. You are safe with us and always will be. See, there is Flora who looks after you and soon we will have a governess, a kind lady to teach you your letters. Will you not like that?' The child's eyes stared sightlessly into hers and her hands tried to draw themselves from Kit's restraint. But Kit would not let her go. 'See, come and sit on my lap before the fire. You are so cold and we will get warm together. Come, sweetheart, climb on my lap and we will be quiet for a moment.'

The little girl continued to stare, eyes wide, at Kit's moving mouth, a small terrified animal hypnotised by a snake and even when Kit patiently lifted her, placing her awkwardly onto her lap, the little girl sat, stiff as a wax effigy and just as still.

'T'will do no good, Miss Chapman,' Flora said wisely. 'We've all tried it an' all she does is wet her drawers. 'Appen she'll come round after a while when she begins to understand no one's going to beat her or stick her head in a bucket of cold water.' She saw Miss Chapman wince and could have bitten her own tongue because everyone knew such goings on were a thing of the past now at the Chapman mill but Miss Chapman only held the child closer, to no avail, Flora could see. 'Pretty little poppet though, isn't she?' she added.

She was a pretty little poppet and all during the following week, whenever Kit had an hour to spare she went up to the nursery. She would sit at the table and draw the child's attention to the books and games and toys which were scattered carelessly about since Lucas had been considerably indulged by his mother and the little girl would stare at them, politely it seemed to Kit, doing as she was bid when told to sit, to stand, to look at this or that, to hold the 'dolly' or the 'teddy', to put her hand in Kit's, to sit on her lap, obedient as she had been made to be in the factory, but not trusting, ever. She never spoke, or if she did no one heard her and Kit wondered at the hopelessness of employing a governess for she was at a loss as to how the woman could teach the child. She had tried a time or two herself, reading to her out of a book, telling her the tales her own nurse had told her, of elves and fairies, of little people, of magic and far away places, of lovely angels and cheerful animals but the little girl seemed unimpressed until Kit began to see that it all meant nothing to a child who had known only hobgoblins and demons, haunted places where evil lurked and the filth, not only of the mill floor but that in men's minds, but she continued to try, for what else was there in her barren life?

It was several weeks later when she went up to the nursery on her now daily visit, her step slow, her feet dragging and when she opened the nursery door, her determination to break through the child's wall of silence and fixity was missing. She felt low today, her woman's body, it seemed, drying to a husk without the sustaining love Joss had fed it. Five months since she had seen him and she scarcely dare think of him and his hard male body, so great was her longing.

The little girl did not even turn her head to look at her, let alone greet her and Kit sighed in the renewed melancholy which had come upon her today. Five months since the dreadful events at Martha Greenwood's cottage and in all that time there had been not one word of Joss Greenwood. Sarah had told her through Jem, that his mother had received a note or two to say he was well but there had been no clue as to where he was or what he was doing, of how he was living or supporting himself. The fine political career which was to have been his was in tatters, they all recognised, and even his fight for the betterment of the men who had followed him for over ten years seemed to have been swallowed up in his own personal fight for survival.

Parliamentary reform had been called for all over the country and the Prime Minister, Wellington was to resign over it, they said, so opposed to the idea was he, but Lord Grey, heralded as the next Prime Minister was pledging that if he was asked to form a government he would propose a Reform Bill. Joss, she knew, would have been jubilant, since it would transform the franchise in the boroughs and counties and it was calculated that the total electorate would be doubled. Where was he? Did he know of it? Did he care any more?

Kit sighed again as she looked at the child. She was becoming sturdier with every day, the flesh on her limbs glowing with the sheen of good health. Her short crop of curls had grown longer and today Flora had tied it with a blue ribbon, more experienced and with more concern now that Miss Chapman was showing some interest. The dress the child wore, a pretty blue sprigged muslin was already too short as she grew taller. She still collected 'waste' beneath the table, or did when anyone other than Flora entered the nursery, but the unchildlike obedience, the wariness, the rigid acceptance of the kiss Kit gave her, the embrace which she seemed not to understand, indeed to consider threatening in some way, were becoming an irritant to Kit.

'Good morning, Miss Chapman,' Flora said.

'Good morning, Flora, and how are we all today?'

'Champion, thank you, ma'am.'

Kit turned to the little girl, making herself smile, wondering for the umpteenth time why she continued to come up here to the nursery since the girl was unconcerned whether she did or not. Feed her, clothe her, leave her to live in her own private dream world where nothing troubled her and the child would know no difference. She admitted to herself that she had become fond of her but perhaps it was merely because she had no one else to give her affection. Perhaps it was pity, if she were honest but it seemed not to matter. Possibly it would be kinder to let go of her, let her develop, or not, in her own time. She was not educable, that was certain in her present state, and she realised that the secret idea she had carried inside herself for the past few weeks, that she could make this child, her *own* child, the one she would never bear herself, was really no more than a fantasy.

'I think I'll leave the lesson today, Flora,' she said. 'I feel like a walk with the dogs. Those old ones of mine need a bit of exercise,' just as though she needed to excuse herself to Flora. Guilt, she supposed. The guilt of not being able to bring life to this little girl who had been so damaged in her own mill. Who had never been taught to love and so could not accept it. Guilt that she, Kit Chapman, was so soon to give up the idea of trying to teach her. She turned abruptly, on an impulse.

'Put her some sturdy boots on, Flora, if she has any . . .'

'She hasn't any, Miss Chapman. There's only some . . . some belonging to . . .' She could not go on.

'To . . . Lucas . . . ?' Kit's voice was filled with sadness. 'Yes . . .'

'He wouldn't mind, Flora. He was ever a generous little boy.'

'Aye . . .' Flora wiped away a sad tear and neither questioned the way in which both took for granted that the boy would never return.

They walked out of the side entrance into the yard, both of them blinking in the vivid sunlight of the bright autumn day. Kit held the little girl's hand in hers, limp and chill, even in the warmth. She had removed the hat which Flora had jammed onto the child's head, throwing it carelessly to a chair in the passage and the sunlight struck fire from her hair. Their boots grated on the cobbles which lined the yard and the sound carried on the air and from the open stable door on the far side four black bodies hurtled, low and fast, close to the ground, their faces grinning in delight, the stubs of their tails moving furiously. They came towards her, ready to leap and jump, idiotic in their joy, the grace and dignity with which they were normally imbued, lost in their clumsy cavorting.

'Merciful Heaven . . .' One hand shaded her eyes and the other held fast to the child's and she had no time for the hand signals with which she normally controlled the dogs.

'*Down* . . . down I say . . . Barny . . . stop it at once . . . wait a minute . . . Joby, you fool . . . *Stay* . . . stand . . . lie down . . . down Blaze . . .' In her fear for the girl the words tripped incoherently from her lips, making no sense to the dogs who were used to her clear, crisp commands. They were confused, blundering heavily against her skirt, prancing this way and that, rearing up on their back legs, meaning no offence, offering no danger but big and heavy and quite, quite terrifying in their fierce black beauty. Barny, three years old and the buffoon of the four, the clown who loved to play, aware that no danger threatened his mistress turned to the little girl, offering her his laughing face, his sharp white teeth, his drooling tongue, ready to accept the friendship of her hand on his head but she stood as though transfixed, her eyes empty, just as though she could bear no more and had simply gone away.

'Lie down, boy,' Kit said quietly and he did, and so did the rest, settling obediently about the feet of herself and the child and the silence stretched on and on. Across the yard the stable lad stood in anguished misery, telling himself time and time again that it was not his fault. He hadn't been told the little girl was to come with Miss Chapman or he would have held those beggars back until *she* had control of them. Sweet Jesus, that poor little kid, how would she react to it? They all knew her, of course. They had seen her walk beside her nursemaid a hundred times in the garden and sit quietly on the lawn while Lucas, God bless him, played merry hell with Mr Smith's flower beds but Miss Chapman had left instructions that the dogs were to be kept locked up while the children were about.

'Take the dogs away, Dick,' Miss Chapman called carefully, her voice quite controlled, hardly daring to rumple the air which moved about them for fear of sending the little girl further into her trance-like state. If she could just edge her back into the security of the porch, with the door between them and the menace of the dogs, no menace at all really, but horrendous surely to the child, she felt she could encompass her terror. Perhaps she should pick her up and cradle her in her arms, comfort the stiffness of her but that had never worked before and she was afraid to disturb the stillness which had fallen about them.

To her horror Barny stood up. Never, since he was a young puppy had he disobeyed her command. Told to 'stay' he would remain there until he died of it. Through storm and thunder, starvation or a sound thrashing she could guarantee nothing would move him, or any of them, until she gave the command but now he ambled across the few feet which separated him from the little girl and with the unerring sixth sense an animal seems to possess and which told him of her misery he lay down before her and as gently as thistledown nosed at the small hand which hung limply at her side. He licked it, the tip of his tongue just touching her fingers. Not enough even to stir them but her hand jumped and stiffly, probably the first time it had ever done so to another living thing, lifted until it rested on his broad head. It seemed not to know what to do next, lying there like a wilting flower, white against the black, then Barny stood up and his rump moved from side to side and her hand fell off his head so he nosed it again and this time she placed it palm down on his nose, stroking it back across his shining eyes to the top of his head, then, more boldly, across the polished softness of his broad shoulders. She turned her face up to Kit's and smiled. 'Barny good boy,' she said, just as if she was admonishing Kit for reprimanding the dog. 'Barny good boy.'

Kit began to weep. The tears ran across her face and dripped on to the crisp cotton of her bodice and on the other side of the yard Dick felt his own throat close up as the 'poor little beggar' took her first hesitant step from the black world into which she had been born.

Kit was on the lawn, the dogs about her, the child on her lap when Jenny came out of the side door. Someone hovered at her back, a servant eager to announce her, but Jenny waved her away high-handedly, shading her eyes against the sun until she caught sight of Kit. She was wearing blue. A lovely flaunting blue the colour of a forget-me-not and her silk bonnet was a rose garden of cream and palest pink tied with a blue silk ribbon.

She stepped out boldly, knowing quite well every servant in the house had been informed she was here and that all those who could get to a window were staring in horrid fascination at a woman who had been raped, the word only whispered naturally, not by one man but by three. Disgraced she should be since it was well known that only women who encouraged that sort of thing, endured it, and if she had any sense of decency at all she should at least have removed herself elsewhere, or, as most would, have committed suicide.

Her face was not that of the Jenny Greenwood Kit knew. It was a thin wedge, pale and harrowed with the shining grey of her eyes dimmed and sunken into dark, shadowed caverns but the set of her mouth was firm and unyielding. It said she would not weep again, or if she did no one would know of it. That though she had been badly beaten, she was not down and should she ever fall, which was unlikely, she would damn well pull herself up again without any man's hand to help her.

Kit placed the child on the rug then stood up slowly, her heart beating fast, her own face, had she known it, like tallow.

'Jenny?' she said softly, enquiringly, welcomingly.

'I need to work.' Jenny said abruptly and her eyes stared unblinkingly into Kit's begging her to say nothing of the past, not yet, and Kit understood.

'And I need you to work, by God.'

'I can't sit about at home and do nothing, but I want you to understand . . . I might have to go away . . . now and again . . . at a moment's notice . . .' if there should be any news, her eyes said, of the boy.

'I understand. When would you like to start?'

'My boxes are in the driveway.'

'The driveway?'

'That bloody Winters didn't want to let me in.'

'But you came in just the same?'

'Naturally.'

They both managed a tremulous smile.

'May I . . . may I greet a friend, Jenny? I've missed you so much.'

The servants were all made quite speechless by the

spectacle of their mistress enfolding and being clasped in the arms of the woman who had once been her sworn enemy.

37

They settled back together into the companionable routine they had known six months ago, nothing changed it seemed in Jenny Greenwood's sharp and lucid mind, nothing altered in their splendid partnership except that now it was Kit who went up to the nursery instead of Jenny.

'What's she called?' Jenny had asked abruptly on that first day as they shared a cup of tea, still beneath the fascinated gaze of the servants, while the child leaned trustingly against the panting black side of Barny.

It was one of those lovely September days which linger sometimes as autumn moves gracefully towards winter. As warm as June but clear and burnished with a sharpness to the colours which comes at no other time of the year. Up on the hilltops there were shades of gold and red and brown, deepening into purple grey shadows as they ran into the valley. The horse chestnut tree which shaded the two women from the bright sunlight was still green and vigorous and hung all about with fruit and the flower beds were filled with the vivid mass of chrysanthemums, yellow, bronze, crimson and white.

The little girl stood up and ventured a step or two on to the grass, her small feet hesitant, almost as though she was afraid she might damage it in some way. She was still by no means the noisy, carefree child that Kit wished her to be but her curiosity, come suddenly, timidly to life, led her to place an experimental hand on the pattern of Kit's gown, the smoothness of the soap Flora bathed her with, the roughness of the bark on the twisted trunk of the chestnut tree, the softness of her own curls when they were brushed. Looking enquiringly at Kit, still not absolutely convinced that this loveliness about her might not be wrenched from her should she displease, she held Barny's collar and while he slowed his pace to hers, trotted down to the lake to gaze in speechless wonder at the swans which moved serenely on its surface. Since that first incredible moment when she had reached out her hand to the dog she had become a human being, a child with a child's needs and a child's growing trust. Kit did not think she would ever be lively. Perhaps it was not in her nature, even under normal circumstances. How was Kit to know? But she smiled joyfully, her sea-green eyes shining, her gaze marvelling as though the things she saw, she saw for the first time. She loved the flowers and the soft glowing flames of the nursery fire, the lively kittens who lived in the stable, the white clouds, the blue of the sky, the silver moon and stars and the golden sun, the colours and movement of Kit's lovely gowns, the stretch of moorland, the sweep of heather beyond the walls of the house, and Barny!

Kit took her to Jagger Lane to visit Miss Cavendish to be fitted out for new winter dresses, giving rise to another great and overwhelming wave of gossip since what would Barker Chapman's daughter do next, they wondered, and could the child be hers for they seemed extremely close and Kit Chapman held the child's hand, proud as a peacock, just as though she *was*, but those who remembered the incident of Charlie Greenwood's beating, remembered also the child involved and besides, had you ever seen a Chapman with hair that colour?

'Do you know, I cannot seem able to find a name suitable, Jenny. We call her "poppet", Flora and I . . . an endearment, you understand.' On dangerous ground for did not Jenny Greenwood, a mother grieving her son, surely dead, and if not that, lost forever, know only too well about endearments for had she not called him her 'sweeting'?

'Yes, but she must have a proper name.' Jenny's voice was stony and she kept her eyes averted just as though she could not bear to rest them on a child which was not hers. 'Will you adopt her?'

'I had not thought of that, either. This transformation has come about so recently I have still not got a grasp of it. I was . . . it sounds so selfish, so self-absorbed, but I . . . missed you and, to pass the time, I suppose, I began to take an interest in her but it was not until she took a fancy to Barny, and him to her that I was able to reach her . . . but a name? . . . yes, you are right . . .'

Kit watched the child reach out to a leaf which had just detached itself from the branches of an oak tree, drifting lazily down above her head and on to the grass. It might have been some winged being from another world she was so absorbed and she squatted down to study it, the dog beside her, the other three eddying about her in a protective circle. Kit's face assumed a musing expression and her eyes were soft and unfocused.

'A name . . . ?' she said again, ' . . . but what . . . ?'

'Have you not a family name?'

'I don't think so and I can hardly ask my mother. It takes her all her time to nod in my direction if we should cross paths on the driveway.'

'No, I suppose not.'

'It really is curious. There is surely one that is appropriate for her . . .'

'Did you know that in the old days of the movement . . .'

Kit turned to look at Jenny and her eyes were clear and interested.

'What movement?'

'The movement my family is involved in.'

For some reason it seemed Jenny was unwilling or unable to mention her brother's name. It was as though the past, the immediate past was too painful a subject to dwell on, that the future was all that concerned her, the present and the future and nothing else.

'Please tell me.'

'It was the day my father was killed at Peterloo. They marched, all the men of the village and many women too.

556

Charlie and Daisy were babies and my mother needed me at home. I was fifteen and though I longed to go, I couldn't. But they had an emblem . . .' The pain had receded from Jenny's face and her expression was soft, proud. 'They wore them in their hats, the men . . .'

'What?'

'A sprig of laurel. It signified peace and harmony. Perhaps . . . one day we will all know it. Perhaps this child will bring you . . .'

'Peace . . .' Kit sampled the word slowly, a little sadly for it was an elusive thing, her eyes seemed to say. 'Laurel for harmony and peace.'

As she spoke the child turned, holding out the leaf with fingers which said it was the most amazing thing she had ever laid eyes on. She smiled, sharing her amazement with them and even Jenny felt her heart move a little at the child's delight.

'Laurel. That is lovely, Jenny. Laurel.'

And Laurel Chapman walked across the smooth grass towards the two women.

But it was almost the end of October before Jenny spoke of her brother. Though Kit was busy, busy with her mills where she and Jenny went each day, busy with the plans for the opening of her new hospital at which, to the consternation of Crossfold, the Squire himself had agreed to officiate, busy with the employing of a governess for Laurel, there were hours, days even, when Jenny was aware that there was a growing despair in Kit Chapman when Joss Greenwood still did not come home. A grief and loneliness in her that was as great as Jenny's own, a quiet sinking into a kind of apathy which frightened her.

'Tell them both I will wait for them,' she had said to Jenny's mother, and Martha had repeated it each time Jenny came home from her searching, her desperate wandering from town to town.

'Tell them both I will wait for them,' she had said, and she, Jenny had come – for what else was there for her but this woman and this work? – but Joss had not. Kit Chapman was a woman in the shadows. A woman who had remained after Joss Greenwood had left her to go God knows where. Drifting, she seemed to be, waiting for someone who never came, listening for a voice which never spoke, going to her mills each day, moving slowly through the day with often little to say to herself but 'thank you' and 'just as you please, Jenny' and at the end of it, 'good-night' as she languished her way to bed. Ever since Jenny had returned she had been the same and Jenny had been patient with her grieving (for did she herself not know its tearing pain?) until one night at the dinner table, after asking the same question twice with no answer, she had been able to stand it no longer.

'He's not dead, you know,' she said abruptly. 'He's not in his coffin beneath six feet of earth.'

'I beg your pardon.' Kit's eyes had been clouded, her gaze bewildered.

'He would be disgusted if he could see you now.'

'I'm not sure I understand.'

'You know exactly what I mean and this . . . this self-pity is not worthy of you. I thought you were strong, tenacious with the backbone and single-mindedness which would not let you simply . . . give up but I see I was wrong.'

'Jenny . . . !' Her voice was anguished and her expression said she could scarce believe the cruelty of the words Jenny spoke. They were friends and sympathy between friends was taken for granted. Hers for Jenny in *her* heartache and the certainty that Jenny understood Kit's grief. But now it seemed Jenny was ready to turn the knife in the eternally aching wound which Joss's desertion had caused.

'Don't "Jenny" me in that whining voice, Kit Chapman. You knew he had to go, to come to terms with the way in which Mercy was killed, in her death for he sincerely loved her despite her . . . deficiencies. She was like another sister to him and after what they did to her . . . it would not have been . . . decent to turn immediately to you. Give him time . . .'

'I know . . . I know but dear God, I can hardly stand it . . .'

'He is doing what he needs to do . . .'

'*But what is it? Where is he?* My life without him is sterile . . . Dear Lord, if I had realised . . .'

'Stop it! Stop this caterwauling this instant or I swear I will leave this house and find myself a cottage somewhere. You are not the only one to suffer a loss, you know. I have not seen a sorrier face since one of Pickering's lasses lost her kitten in the stream. Wailing and weeping she was, and her a child of eleven and it was not until Isaac promised her another did she wipe her nose and stop her blubbering . . .'

Two pink spots appeared on Kit Chapman's cheeks and she squared her slumped shoulders.

'Are you suggesting I should find myself another lover, Jenny Greenwood?'

'Of course not, but I am suggesting you look about you and see what is needed here and it is not a drooping, miserable creature with a face as long as a fiddle and not a damn word to say for the cat. That child of yours could do with some attention, not to mention the final stages of the hospital. That builder has been to see me a dozen times this week and the draughtsman swears if you do not give him an answer by the end of the week he will take his talents elsewhere.'

'An answer to what?'

'Nay, don't ask me. You're the "maister".'

There was silence then, a silence still quivering with the hurt Jenny had inflicted but there was a feeling of something else apart from that of resentment at being brought to task by a woman who was, though very close to her, surely not qualified to criticise. How dare she intrude on Kit's grief and physical loss of the man she loved? How dare she speak as though that grief was no more than . . . than a child's tantrum at the loss of a kitten, had been her first reaction but creeping into her misery and growing bitterness and indignation was the voice of reason and compassion for Jenny was right and Jenny *did* have the right, as someone who also suffered, to reprove her. Kit's life, and her bed, was vast and cold and empty without Joss in it but it was the life she must lead for now, and she must not inflict her wretchedness on a woman who had enough of her own.

'Where is he, Jenny?' she said quietly at last. 'You must know since you were the last to see him.'

'Aye . . .'

'Can you not tell me what happened? I have not questioned you. I did not want to . . . probe your wounds . . . to make them hurt again . . .'

'They will always hurt until I find my son.'

'Of course . . .' hastily, ' . . . but you are . . .' Kit cleared her throat, aware that what she said might sound trite, patronising and really, could she say she knew the agony of loss Jenny must be suffering, despite her own, but she was constantly amazed at Jenny's composure.

'You are very brave, Jenny,' she said in a low voice.

'No, not at all. I am simply determined. I mean to find Lucas and I cannot do it if I fall to pieces, if I sit down and simply fade away, if I retreat from life and pain and decision making as I often long to do. It would really be very pleasant to just fold my hands and stare off vacantly, as Mercy did, so that I no longer feel anything but who would find my son for me then? And I need money so I must work. I have men to be paid who are searching . . . the factories . . . the mines . . . places where . . . where sweeping boys are employed . . .'

'Sweet Jesus . . .'

'He's small, Kit, so they could use him . . . they could have sold him to . . .'

'*Sold him* . . .'

'Aye, Ellis and the other men . . .'

'Jenny . . . surely not . . .'

Jenny's lip curled scornfully and the look she turned on Kit was filled with contempt.

'You've never really been able to face up to the realities in life, have you, Kit Chapman? Paint it up in pretty colours and what's underneath won't be seen. You know damn well from your own experience that children are used for every purpose under the sun . . .' She threw her head back and her throat worked in a violent contraction as the pictures the words evoked crowded into both their minds. 'I sometimes . . . God forgive me . . . wish I could hear that he is dead so that I should know he is not being . . . abused . . . Dear God, oh dear sweet God, he is only three years old and so . . .'

She swallowed and swallowed, putting up a hand to cover her eyes and Kit stood up violently, barely able to stand the suffering at the other side of the dining table. They had eaten a succulent saddle of lamb, or was it veal, perhaps chicken, neither woman could have said and the silently staring figures of Winters and Ellen still hovered at the back of the room but Kit dismissed them with a movement of her hand and they went gladly ready to spread the news in the servants hall that that hussy had broken at last.

'You went to Harry Atherton's then?' Her voice was harsh and her face as white as the tablecloth, with shock, with pity and with self-disgust at her own stupidity. She had not thought, not in detail of what might truly have happened to Lucas Greenwood. He was dead, she had presumed sadly for why would three ruffians such as Ellis and his cronies spirit him away? Simply for money it seemed. They had wanted revenge on Jenny, and presumably on Charlie for his part in their conviction and to kill her child was surely a cruel enough way to get it, but how much more terrible to take him away and leave Jenny to agonise for the rest of her life on his fate.

Jenny lifted her head and her eyes stared back into the past.

'Yes. We found out where he lived. It wasn't hard, a well-known family like his . . . Atherton Hall, just outside Chester. We went, the three of us, me and Joss and Charlie. The butler ordered us round to the back door. Oh yes, he knew at once we weren't gentry but Joss pushed him aside, you know what he's like. They came into the hall, him and his father and another chap, his brother, I think and when

Harry saw me he smiled just as if he knew what I'd come for. Give me my son, I said. Your son? What on earth are you talking about, woman? he said. I know you were there when they raped me and murdered Mercy, I was screaming, and I saw his father give him a funny look but he was still smiling, enjoying it. Rape! he said. Murder! My dear woman, are you mad? And his father stood there, and his brother, their faces . . . odd, somehow, but behind him, you could see that. You took my son, I said again. *Your* son, Harry Atherton and I'll have him back if I have to kill you for him. I went for him then, tore his cheek to the bone before they dragged me off. But he hadn't finished with me. I have no son, he said. My wife and I have a daughter, yes, three years old and called Elizabeth after my mother. Let me see her, I screeched, beyond reason . . . they had the three of us surrounded by manservants, waiting for the Peace Officers but he only laughed again, holding his hand to his face where the blood flowed. Indeed I will not, for I believe my wife has her in the drawing-room with our guests, and besides she has nothing to do with you. And that was that, as far as he was concerned. Joss was . . . uncertain. He did not know him, you see . . . not as I do and he knew I had been out of my mind . . . and Charlie . . . poor kid. I knew he must not be made part of this again. It made me realise what I was doing to them, to both of them. They took us to the gaol in Chester but the Athertons made no charge and we were released the next day. But I . . . I wanted to be sure . . .' Her eyes had become hooded, withdrawn and strange and Kit felt the prickle of disquiet run down her spine.

'We went back the next day, me and Joss. He was humouring me really. We left Charlie at the coaching inn. They were there . . . in the paddock at the back of the Hall. We had to climb the walls and walk up through some woods . . . the child was on a pony . . .'

'Lucas . . . ? Dear God . . .'

'No. It was a little girl. She had fair curls under her bonnet. I could see nothing of her face but she had on a little dress . . . and her drawers were . . . were . . . She was the same size . . . shape as . . . as . . . but of course . . . being Harry's daughter and half sister to . . . well . . . it was not . . .'

'So you left?'

'What else were we to do? Joss was . . . distraught. I think if we had found Lucas he would have been able to . . . it would have made up in some way for what . . . I had gone through . . . and for Mercy.'

'Why does he feel himself to blame so?'

There was a long and harrowing pause in which Jenny strove to regain her composure, badly shattered by the reliving of that day. Her hands shook and the sweat stood out on her face as though she had been running and she took out a wisp of lace to wipe it away before speaking.

'He was a . . . happy-go-lucky lad. Always laughing and having a joke. Not at all serious like Father. Not a wicked bone in his body but a bit wild, high spirited. He hadn't a lot of time for what my father did. He was enjoying himself too much to be bothered by what others did. He had a way with the girls and as long as he slept in a warm bed and had a good dinner once a day he cared nought for nobody. That is until my father was killed. It changed him overnight. At least, he tried to change into the man my father had been, what my father would have liked *him* to be. I'm not saying my father didn't love him. He did, he loved us all. He loved *all* men and when he went Joss felt the need to take up where he had left off. But in a way he was warring against his own nature. It was in him to be light-hearted and yet he couldn't be. Not with what he took on. And so he became violent, doing what he thought to be right when he wrecked machines and burned warehouses. But he began to realise it wasn't the right way to go about it. And he began to see what it was doing to us. What *he*, with his wild ways, was doing to us as a family. And it nearly defeated him. Perhaps it *has* defeated him . . .'

'Oh no . . . no . . .'

'He doesn't know who he is anymore, Kit. To understand

that his wife was murdered by men who ... because of who we are, because of him, and you, and Charlie and what we are trying to do for all those poor beggars in the factories and mines and sweat shops up and down the country, because of that they hated him and so they got back at him by abusing the women in his family ... and ... taking my boy ...'

'So what is he doing ... what did he tell you ... ?' Kit's cry echoed devastatingly about the elegant dining-room. 'Where is he ... where is he ... and Lucas ... ?'

'Only God knows, and he's not had a lot to do with us for a long time.'

There was a letter the next day come by the stagecoach from Preston to say that a boy answering the description of Lucas Greenwood had been found sweeping chimneys and would Miss Greenwood come at once for the child was barely alive and if he should be her son he would immediately need a mother's care.

She was back within the week, hollow-eyed, thinner somehow, Kit thought, alone and desperate.

'It was not ... ?' she asked fearfully as she led Jenny to the fire in the small back parlour where they increasingly sat as the autumn turned cold and slid towards winter, less formal than the drawing-room.

'No, thank God ... and yet ... if it had been he I could have ... nursed him until he died and known, finally, where he was.'

'Dear God ... what ... ?'

Jenny shivered and put her hands to the cheerfully blazing fire, glad of the warmth and the comfort of Kit's presence.

'I thought the mill children were badly done to, Kit, but this ... this baby, for he was no more than that ... God ...' she covered her eyes, ' ... how we can call ourselves human beings, *human* and, one presumes belonging to *humanity*, of which there is little in the world. If he had lived I would have brought him home ...'

'Of course, we would have found a place for him.'

Jenny turned then to look at her and suddenly her eyes

filled with tears and she began to weep. She shook her head from side to side and Kit, thinking she wept for her son would have gone to her, would have held her, would have done anything to ease her pain for she loved this woman now as she would a sister but Jenny put out her hands and through her tears a smile trembled.

'No ... please, no, it's all right, really ... I swore I would not weep again until I found him and then it would be for joy. These are for you, Kit Chapman.'

'Me! I have no need of your tears.'

'I know. It is just that, after all these years, after all we have said about you, I recognise you, at last, as a truly good woman.'

'Fiddlesticks.'

Jenny went each Sunday to visit her mother and Charlie, striding off alone in the warm woollen dress with a shawl thrown about her as once she had done as a mill girl. She had taken to wearing vivid colours, scarlet and a green like that of an emerald, violet and lavender, lovely as the flower of that name, cornflower blue and turquoise. She flaunted them defiantly, and herself some said, just as though she made the statement her son was not dead; that though he had been taken from her he would soon be back. *She* would find him and bring him back and in the meanwhile she would not wear the drab of mourning. Crossfold said she was mad now, gone off her head after what had been done to her, and most probably, her baby son, charging about the north country at a moment's notice it was rumoured, examining every young boy who came to light and none of them him, of course. But not so daft that she didn't know how to keep on the right side of Kit Chapman, who was also a crank, a childless crank and no doubt Jenny Greenwood was thinking of her young brother, Charlie, for where else had Kit Chapman to leave her mills.

Jenny regained some of her weight when Kit pointed out to her she was no good to anyone if she melted away to nothing in her restless searching, not only for her son, but the return of her peace of mind. She worked hard and late, very often missing her evening meal and picking at a tray the housekeeper left out for her.

'Come home with me, Jenny,' Kit begged her that night as she herself left the mill. 'You should eat properly or you will be ill and then who will look for Lucas?'

'Joss.'

It was so unexpected Kit felt the blood rush savagely to her head, then drain away and she put out her hand to the door handle to steady herself. She had called her carriage and it stood in the yard waiting for her but at the last moment she had gone to Jenny's office to try and persuade her to put away her ledgers, her swatches of the new design John Bamber was to take to London the following week, to turn off the lamps and come home. They could eat a companionable dinner as they seldom did these winter nights, and talk.

'Joss . . . ?' Her voice was low and hesitant for it was many weeks since Jenny had spoken of him and the events which had taken place at Atherton Hall. 'You have heard from him?' Her heart hammered painfully and she had a great desire to press her hand to her breast as she had seen her mother do on many occasions.

'He . . . has been home.'

'Dear God, and you did not tell me.' She whirled about just as though she would dash from the room, fling herself down the stairs and into her carriage and gallop, yes, gallop all the way to the edge of the moorland and then run, skim over the dark, rough, uneven surfaces of it straight into his arms . . .

'Kit, don't . . . don't go . . .'

'I must see him . . . how he is . . .' She turned back, her face quite breathlessly beautiful in her joy. 'How is he, Jenny . . . is he well . . . has he recovered . . . what did he say . . . where has . . . did he speak of me . . . ?'

'Yes.'

'Then I must go . . .'

'No.'

'No, Jenny . . . don't tease me . . .'

'No, Kit, no! He does not want to see you.'

Jenny stood up, then moved quickly round the desk to Kit. She put out a hand for Kit Chapman no longer looked beautiful, nor particularly well.

'Please ... sit down, sweeting.' In her compassion for the stricken woman she called her by the endearment she had reserved only for her boy.

'I don't want to sit down.'

'Let me tell you ...'

'You have just told me.'

'He ... he has taken up his work again. He is so busy. I had meant to tell you more gently but when you said ... well ... sit down ...'

'Stop telling me to sit down.'

'Then I will come home with you and we will eat dinner and talk.'

'What of? He does not want to see me ...'

'Perhaps if you gave him time. He has lost so many months. He has searched for Lucas ... he has many acquaintances all over the north, men who make it their business to look out for abused children, where they can. That is what he has been doing ...'

'You knew?'

'Yes.'

'And you said nothing?'

'He asked me not to ... and I did not want to distress you ...'

'He will not see me then?'

'I ... fear not.'

'Then he is a coward and I am better off without him.'

'He has things which must be done ...'

'Things ... ?'

'Yes.'

It came to her blindingly.

'It's the new Reform Bill, isn't it? I have read about it in *The Republican*. They say that Lord John Russell speaks of converting the House of Commons from an assembly of representatives of small classes and particular interests into

567

a body of men who represent the people. It will mean half a million more people on the national electorate. That there will be an election soon.'

'Aye.' Jenny held her head high and there was a pride about her which Kit had never seen before.

' . . . and they want him for candidate?' she finished softly.

'Aye.' Jenny's voice was sad.

It was clear at last. All these months he had kept away from her. She had grieved for him, mourned him as a wife mourns the loss of a husband and it was his pride, his damned, awkward, stubborn, *male* pride which had kept him from her since he knew they would say he wanted her only for what she could give him with her wealth. The wealth which would allow him to become the man the people wanted him to become. The man to speak for them up in Westminster.

'He is not only a coward, Jenny Greenwood,' turning against even this woman who was his sister, 'but a fool and does not deserve the loyalty his people give him,' she said bitterly. 'I want nothing to do with such a man.'

38

They did not speak of him again and the slight strain which had flared up between them making them polite with one another for a week or two after Jenny's revelation soon ceased in the growing affection and dependency the two women had on one another. Their common interest in the splendour of their new village, already unofficially named Chapmanstown, drew them there whenever they had a moment, to watch the occupancy of each cottage taken up by her mill-workers, to see the well-lit, well paved streets, to visit the school where already those first pupils of her classroom at the mill were teaching others in the 'monitorial' system which worked so well. They were both overcome almost to tears by the bright-eyed, lively interest their visit caused the giggling children, still admittedly, some of them, bearing the humped backs and bowed legs which their introduction to a better standard of living had been too late to eradicate. They were clean, decent, curious to see these two great ladies, not many of them awfully sure who they were but happy to recite their 'adds' and 'takeaways', to sing a song, or show off their new reading skills. There were older boys attending the Mechanics Institute after their day's work, straining, now they had the chance, to 'get on' and over all was a warm air of hopeful prosperity and goodwill.

'Good morning, Miss Chapman,' the women called from their newly 'donkey-stoned' doorsteps, sketching a curtsey some of them for old habits die hard, their eyes placid, their shrunken frames beginning to put on unfamiliar flesh, their children high-spirited, their menfolk men again, and on the site where their old homes had been, Pig Lane, Lousy Bank and Boggart Hole, buildings were being erected, a spinning mill crammed with the new 'self-acting' mules, a weaving-shed with the very latest of power-looms, a carding room, warehouse and printing room where, it was said, Miss Chapman would employ another five hundred or so people when it was complete. She was one of the largest manufacturers in Lancashire now, far exceeding the goal her father had envisaged and they spoke of her with wondering voices since how had she done it with the wages she paid and the subsequent loss of profit she must have suffered?

She spent time in the nursery, getting to know the small girl, Laurel, who, though she could not as yet be said to answer to the name, turned eagerly to Kit when she entered the room. A governess had been employed, a kind woman of thirty or so who had been taught at home by her brother's tutor, well educated and intelligent in a day when women were taught to do nothing but obey their masculine guardian, be he father or husband. She had been faced with the life of the poor relation in her brother's home now that her family was scattered and her parents dead, subject to his wife's whims, or the opportunity to support herself in the only way open to a gentlewoman. She chose the latter.

'Slowly, I think at first, Miss Copeland, for I fear she is somewhat timid.' Miss Copeland had been told the sad story of Laurel Chapman as she now was. 'It is a lot to expect of a child who has been so sadly abused.'

'I'm sure we will manage very well together, Miss Chapman. She has a bright look about her and . . . well . . . I am very fond of children . . .' which proved to be true.

But they did not really need her, Miss Copeland and Laurel. The child became absorbed in the world of learning with which her governess surrounded her. Flora, who had grieved so keenly for her Lucas, now found, just as she was beginning to 'take' to 'Laurel', the child was being possessed by another woman; one over whom she had no authority and though she sat about during lessons, her face truculent, since how that woman expected the poor little poppet to read and learn from such amazingly curious books about flowers of the garden, about trees in the woods and birds in the sky was beyond her. What *good* did it do? As for French, well, the child could barely speak her own language. She was to do arithmetic and to use a globe of the world so that she would know where each country was situated, and what was she, Flora, to do while all this was going on, pray? Sew the child's little dresses, torn hems and such and darn her socks, bathe her and see she was fed and then what?

Kit drifted through the days, busy, always busy from morning until night, up at half past four in the dark cold of the winter's morning, already at the factory as the gate was opened at five-thirty for the first shift workers. And when she arrived home there was an hour in the nursery, coaxing Laurel to accept a hug, a kiss, begging a smile in the slow process of gaining her trust and affection, being ready always to give her own. She would consult with Miss

Copeland, conscious of Flora glowering at their back, on the child's progress which was slow but steady, to listen to the sensible woman's plans for the future and to turn her mind to the increasingly irritating problem of Flora who, after almost two years in the nursery, imagined it to be her personal domain. A schoolroom must be contrived, away from Flora's influence and Flora herself must be found something and soon she would do it, when she could force her mind to let go of the misery which blocked out everything else.

It was some weeks later, a Saturday and at six o'clock the factory bell had sounded its message to those who operated them that it was time to close down the machines until Monday morning. She and Jenny dined in almost complete silence. Jenny appeared to be preoccupied with her own thoughts, her mind far away, Kit supposed, on some increasingly fruitless errand to Liverpool, Manchester, Leeds or Bradford where men still sought her son. She had taken the coach from Oldham half a dozen times in the past three months, on a wild goose chase Kit had heard Flora say quite tearfully to Miss Copeland who had been made aware – by Flora – of the dreadful events of last year.

'Will you be walking tomorrow?' Jenny asked her suddenly.

'I don't know. It depends on the weather. I heard Dick and Frederick discussing the possibility of snow,' but her vague and quite disinterested answer seemed to indicate that really, what did it matter, rain, snow, thunder, if she wanted to walk she would let none of them stop her.

'I'm going to my mother's.'

'Really?' Kit's face was stiff, set away from Jenny, for the mention of Edgeclough was painful and embarrassing to them both. 'But what is unusual about that? You go every Sunday.'

'Yes, but I thought . . .' Jenny shrugged. 'I was merely making conversation, Kit. Both of us are . . . distracted with problems which beset us and really, we should . . .'

'What Jenny?' Kit stretched out her hand to Jenny's

571

where it lay on the polished table and her thin face softened. 'I know I am not a great deal of fun at the moment but . . .'

Silence fell again and Jenny addressed herself to the splendid turbot and lobster sauce on her plate prepared by Kit's chef. They ate without speaking, sipping pale golden wine from crystal goblets, smiling, murmuring to the servants who waited on them, gazing both of them into the candleflames in the centre of the table.

It did not snow as Frederick the coachman had forecast but the next day was grey and cheerless with a low, leaden sky which promised it would do so before long.

'Will you go to your mother's, then?' Kit asked at breakfast.

'Aye. I'll not stop for long if it looks like coming down. She had a cough last week and I want to see how she is or I'd not chance it. And neither should you. Look at that sky. It's as black as the inside of a parson's hat.'

'Oh, I don't know. I fancied walking as far as Besom Hill with you. It's only an hour's . . .'

'Kit, you can't. It would be madness.'

'Besides,' she was saying, 'you are always telling me you should spend more time with Laurel . . .'

'I intend to. As soon as the winter ends I am going to start taking her out with the dogs. I was hardly older than her when I first went out with them . . .'

'Rubbish! You were thirteen or more. You told me so.'

'Jenny! I have not known you in such an argumentative mood for a long time. If I want to go I shall and if I want to stay by my fire, I shall. You should know by now I shall do exactly as I please.'

Jenny sighed as she pulled her thick woollen shawl about her.

'Aye, I suppose so. You were always an awkward beggar.'

It was no more than an hour later when the doorbell rang. She had one foot on the bottom step of the staircase, ready to go up, a book in her hand, one she had loved as a young child and which she thought she might read to

Laurel. She had decided to take Jenny's advice — because it suited her, she told herself — and spend an hour or two before the nursery fire, take the child on her lap with the increasing pleasure both of them were beginning to enjoy in one another's company.

She waited a moment as Winters made his majestic way towards the heavy front door, pondering on who might be calling on her at this hour on a Sunday. At the last moment before the world fell in on her she was tempted to signal to the butler that she was not at home, but then she heard his voice and she could not have moved if a fire had been lit beneath her feet.

'Is Miss Greenwood at home?' he said, and the frozen mantle of paralysis fell about her, shrouding her eyes so that all she could see was darkness, covering her ears so that all she could hear was the thunderous roar of her own heartbeat. Her mind locked itself on the last coherent thought it had, closing about the picture of herself with Laurel settled comfortably on her lap, the lively fire, the pretty kitten, soft and grey and frivolous which was Laurel's dearest possession and which would certainly be expected to share the delight.

He was standing in the hallway when she finally turned, sick and shaking, white-faced, and in the midst of the chaos, curiously angry. Winters still held the door open, his face red and indignant since the visitor had been told *Miss* Greenwood was not at home and yet had still been ill-bred enough to force his way in. The effrontery of the working class was really unbelievable, particularly this family who had been, in his opinion, quite incredibly indulged by Miss Chapman. First the woman and her bastard child, then the boy who was getting above himself, and his betters, Winters had heard, at the grammar school, and now this one, no more than a convicted felon, coming to the *front* door, if you please, like a gentleman caller and asking for his sister, just as though they were as good as anyone.

She said the first thing that came into her head.

'How dare you come here?' Her eyes were a hard and

bitter blue. The aching, anguished recollection of the past months (or was it years, for so it seemed?) pressed against her in great waves of blackness and she wanted to hurt him, hurt him as he had hurt her, over and over again. For on all the joy he had given her he had heaped misery so that the joy was buried, stamped down and extinguished. She had loved him so. Loved him in every way a woman could and when she had held out a hand to him in his desolate loss he had struck it aside and told her, told Jenny to tell her, she meant nothing to him.

'He does not want to see you', Jenny had said and now he was here, like any casual caller, indifferent to her feelings, asking to see his sister.

'Believe me,' he answered her coldly. 'Had I known you were here I would not have come. I wished to see Jenny but she is not here.'

'I live here. Would you not expect to find me in my own home?'

'I was told you walked the moors on . . .'

He turned to go, his eyes blind it seemed, for he almost fell against Winters who still held the door open for him. It had begun to snow and a handful of flakes flung themselves through the open doorway, causing Winters to blink his eyes and step backwards his expression saying quite plainly that it was high time this foolishness was done with. Could the fellow not see that Miss Chapman wanted nothing to do with him and yet he was blundering about like a blind man, unable, it appeared, to get himself through the open doorway. Should he call Dick and Robert, his eyes signalled to Miss Chapman but she had her own fixed on the man's back and on her face was the strangest expression he himself had ever seen. What it meant, he was unable to say but whatever it was it gave her a kind of . . . glow! A moment ago she had been consumed with anger, now, all of a sudden it was gone to be replaced by something Winters did not recognise. Fanciful, he knew it, as he told Mrs Batty later, but he had never seen his employer look quite so lovely.

'Joss,' she said very gently, and their visitor stopped, his face quite blank, not more than six inches from the door frame which he gave the appearance of studying.

'Thank you, Winters. You may close the door and go,' she said, ' . . . no, with Mr Greenwood on this side of it, if you please.'

Winters was tempted to hang about, just on the other side of the door which led to the kitchen for there was sure to be something of interest to tell Mrs Batty. It was nearly a year since the fellow had been here . . . and why? Where had he been and doing what . . . and with whom? But something, some strange feeling in the air prickled the back of his neck and instead he closed the door softly and left them alone.

There was a long and solid silence and somehow she knew it must be broken. Fragments of thought slipped into Kit's head and out again. There was one. It was to do with Jenny; and Lucas! It must be. Nothing else would get him here to this house when the chance that he would see *her* was high. He had come and he had been devastated. He was *still* devastated. Though his voice had been ice-covered, cruel even in his stony politeness, there was in him a volatile tension which had him groping about at the door as though his senses were stunned, *as hers had been*.

She could feel the bubble of joy just beneath her breast-bone and a pulse fluttered delicately at the base of her throat, but she must contain it all, hold her breath, scarce move unless she disturb the fragile emotion which struggled to endure in the hallway, the very feeling from which Winters had just hurried away.

'Why have you come, Joss?' She savoured his name in a voice which was velvet soft, light as air, letting it rest inoffensively inside his head.

'Jenny said she would be here.'

'You have something to tell her?'

'Yes, but it can wait until I see her.'

'Does it concern Lucas?'

'Yes.'

'Joss . . . please . . . can you not tell me?'

He spoke harshly, the effort it took to compose himself very evident.

'I had word of a child . . . she wanted to go herself but she is . . . very tired. I persuaded her to let me go alone. There have been so many disappointments. It was in Clitheroe, a mill child . . . from the poorhouse they said, who matched the description of . . .'

'Of Lucas?'

'Yes . . . It was not him. I came to tell her.'

'I'm sorry.'

Still he kept his back to her, stiff and furious, violent somehow as though his pain and fury might unleash something he wished to keep well hidden.

'Will you not turn round, Joss? Take off your coat and come to the fire. I will order some coffee, it is a cold day and . . .'

'I must be on my way. It is an hour's ride to . . .'

'Please . . .'

'I cannot . . .'

'Why . . . ?'

He turned savagely then and his pain flung itself across the space between them but she did not flinch.

'Because I am afraid I have not the strength to . . . damn you, damn you, Kit Chapman, you are . . .' He bit off the sentence, already revealing too much and she rejoiced but she must not allow him to fight his way through her vulnerable defences and escape again. She had let him go once, told him she would wait for him but he had not come. This time it would be different. This man was hers. She had fought, been wounded and bled for him and by God, *now*, she meant to have him. He loved her still, exultantly she knew he loved her still, but his foolish masculine pride, his passionate certainty that they could never be together, that there was too much standing between them had kept him from her. Curiously, now that she was dead, because of the way she had died, his wife held them apart more certainly than she had alive. But it would not do. He was strong and might fight her, but she was stronger. He was resolute, determined, but she would be more so.

'Please come and sit by the fire. It is only the small parlour. You can tell me what you were to tell Jenny and I will pass it on. Let me send for coffee . . .'

'I cannot stay. My mother is expecting me . . .'

'No, she is not. You know full well she is not.'

His eyes gleamed for a moment in the dim, fire-lit hallway but he lifted his head menacingly.

'You still like to give orders then, Kit Chapman, but I do not take them.'

'So I see.'

She stepped down from the staircase, the book, picked up so long ago – when was it? – still in her hand, and he moved an inch or two from the door, his face guarded but with something in it which was eager to escape, to be let free.

'Jenny was right. She said you were still . . .'

'What, Joss?' Her eyes narrowed and the fire's glow put a softness in them which was exquisitely familiar to him and he moved, mesmerised by her as he had always been ever since he had known her, taking another step towards her.

'Pigheaded!' and incredibly there was a small lift to the corner of his mouth and she smiled too.

'I know, and there are those who call me worse but I have a tough skin and a strong back.'

His eyes drifted over her involuntarily, slowly, and with infinite care she held her breath, wishing in the way of a woman that she had worn a prettier gown, dressed her hair more carefully, not realising that her air of slight informality, unconcern, the drift of loose tendrils about her face and ears, the simplicity of her apricot morning gown gave her the look, not of a lady of fashion, but of soft, careless womanhood.

He turned away from her abruptly. 'I must be going.' He began once more to fumble with the door catch. 'I have to get back . . .'

'Joss, for God's sake leave that damn door alone and turn back to look at me. Let me see what's in your face. Look at mine, I beg you. What we had . . . what we still have cannot . . .'

'Nay, I'll not live on you, Kit Chapman, for that's what you're asking and I'll not turn round and look at you again for if I do I'll be lost,' then he was gone.

She had worked so hard for it and now it no longer mattered. That was the irony of it. No, that was not strictly true for what one had created, built up and strengthened with one's own blood and sinew, like a child in the womb, can never be discounted, nor be considered of no matter. But the mills were a distant hum in her head, a vague, barely distinguishable sound which was drowned by the noise of the pain of her loss. She did not want to listen to it, to any of it, longing to escape from her life for the first time since she had grown to womanhood. And her business was running smoothly and could safely be left in Jenny's capable hands. She might do as she pleased, go where she pleased, walk the moors each and every day, stay in her bed until noon if she so desired for she could now indulge in that wondrous thing known as 'time to spare', 'slippered ease', 'leisure', should she care to take it, but it was strange to her after nine years, unfamiliar and she could not find herself comfortable with it.

What to do then to fill her empty days? What next to strive for? Always there had been a goal. Some objective towards which she must strive. At first it had been her father's attention. Not his love exactly but the need to see approval in his eyes, or even just to make his eyes look at her. She had achieved it. She had become the son he had longed for, that she had longed to be, working beside him and then when he died, in his place at the mills, her mills.

And then Joss. What could she say to herself about Joss that was not already known, loved, longed for, grieved over? She had known hope in the months after Mercy Greenwood had died that somehow, in some way he would turn to her, that at last they could know the peace, the comfort, the joy, the partnership of a true marriage but the very thing which was so dear to her, which she had sweated and wept over was to keep them apart. Was she to choose? Give all she had away so that Joss would not have the barrier of her wealth between them. Could she live on fifty pounds a year in a cottage, could *they*, their love, survive it and she knew it could, but that was not *her* destiny, nor was it Joss Greenwood's. He spoke to many men with his words which were printed in their newspapers but he could speak *for* them in Parliament if he would swallow his damned pride and take what she offered.

In March she went to Southport, spending a lonely few days walking the promenade, staring for hours on end at the wide golden sands and watching the tide come in and out. She drank afternoon tea on the glass covered verandah of the comfortable hotel and ate dinner in solitary splendour, listening quite intently to the small orchestra which played for the entertainment of the diners. She breakfasted on fresh caught Lytham herring, afterwards walking again, wrapped up in her elegant sable-lined coffee coloured cloak, the raw March wind pinching her face, watching the gulls wheel and dive, listening to their lost-soul cries and by the afternoon was on a train heading homewards.

'I thought you were to stay a week,' Jenny said, her eyes careful, hiding the compassion she felt for this pale-faced, sad-eyed woman who had spent her adult life *giving* and had received nothing in return.

'It seems I am not cut out for holidays. I can't quite get the hang of them.'

She lost weight and could not sleep.

'Why don't we have a few days in London?' Jenny suggested in June. 'Perhaps this time we might find it possible to enjoy it.' She smiled, they both did, remembering those days years ago when they had struggled and fought against liking one another, determined both of them, to stay loyal to their own class. 'I really am in need of a new bonnet,' she added, 'and that Monsieur What's-is-name might be glad of our business. What d'you say? Gribb can manage for a day or two without us.'

They bought day dresses with low draped bodices and imbecile sleeves, and evening gowns of extreme *décolletage* with enormous gathered skirts. Pelerine mantles of rose-coloured velvet and peignoirs of silk and gauze, bonnets of *poult-de-soie*, jewelled combs, and Jenny, a *ferronière* which was a narrow gold and jewelled band to be worn low, daringly, about her head and which Monsieur said would be magnificent with her short curls. Shoes and slippers with square toes and rosette trimmings, laced boots of black velvet and satin, coloured stockings and embroidered gloves.

'God knows when we'll wear them,' Jenny said as she preened before her mirror, a green velvet bag with a gold cord dangling on her right arm, and though Kit knew they went through the motions of enjoying this mad spending, the luxury of their smart hotel, the evenings at the theatre, neither of them could wait to get home.

'What is he doing?' she asked abruptly, in August.

Jenny did not pretend not to know who she meant.

'He addresses meetings and political rallies. He writes articles for the newspapers . . .'

'And the candidacy?'

'Is still his if he can . . .'

'Find the money to support himself?'

'Aye . . .' Jenny sighed.

'All that he wants I can give him but he won't let me.'

'It seems not.'

'Then he is a fool,' and her voice was bitter, hopeless.

'I'll tell him so next time I see him.'

'Don't trouble yourself.'

She was sitting on a flat rock, her arms hugging her knees, her eyes staring sightlessly at the valley stretched out below Friars Mere when she heard his voice behind her.

'You were walking here the first time I saw you.'

She whirled about, her face which was already pale

580

and shadowed, losing the last of its colour, only her eyes retaining their striking blue brilliance. They were wide, startled and her first words were concerned, not with the wonder of his presence but the laxity of her dogs.

'How in damnation did you creep up past Joby and Blaze?' she snarled since it seemed that only in anger could she conceal her joy.

'I knew I could count on you for a warm welcome, Kit Chapman, and as for your dogs, they are getting old now, and besides, seemed to find me no threat to you. Indeed they wagged those ridiculous stumps of tails as I walked by them.'

'Damned dogs! I don't know why I keep them . . .' but the colour had flooded now to her cheeks, a rosy glow of something which could only be called hope, surely, for why else would he seek her out, if not with hope for *them*?

But she could not be gracious about it, even as it flooded every hollow space in her body, bringing to life the dreary, twilight world in which she had existed for so long.

She turned away from him as she spoke.

'And what brings you here, Joss Greenwood?' she said, just as imperiously as she had done ten years ago on this very spot.

'You do, Kit Chapman.'

'Really, and what have I to do with you anymore?'

'God only knows, but it seems you do. The truth must be faced that we cannot live apart so if you will be good enough to look at me . . .'

She turned back to him and it shone between them with such brilliance they both gasped with the wonder of it. He held out his arms to her.

'I cannot escape it, my darling. I will have to marry you if only for the sake of those poor wretches down there who depend on me, you know that, don't you?'

'Oh yes.' And with a sigh of thankfulness she moved into them, bringing to life again the warmth and colour of the great, endless fabric of their love.

AUDREY HOWARD

SHINING THREADS

The sequel to *The Mallow Years*

When beautiful Tessa Harrison and her twin cousins take over the lucrative Lancashire mill from their parents, they are plunged into responsibilities for which their luxurious upbringing has ill-prepared them.

For Tessa, there is an added but forbidden attraction at the mill. The foreman, Will Broadbent, with his genuine understanding of the business and its workers could not be more different from the dashing cousins. Yet, like the twins, he is hopelessly in love with this untameable girl. Their love for Tessa will lead one to death, one to the arms of another woman, a third too faint-hearted to take up his rightful inheritance.

And Tessa, the girl who could choose any man she wanted, is forced into more commitments than she could have imagined, before she can be united with the one man she truly needs.

HODDER AND STOUGHTON PAPERBACKS

AUDREY HOWARD

A DAY WILL COME

When Miles Thornley rides into her life, everything begins to change for Daisy Brindle. For the first time she catches a glimpse of a very different life to the one she has always known.

Daisy is a field girl, tramping the roads of Lancashire in a gang of women and children, hired out by a brutal master for stone picking, harvesting, winter work down the pits.

But Miles, heir to a great estate, arrogant and spoilt, who teaches her to love, seduces her and casually casts her aside. He teaches her to hate.

Driven onto the streets of Liverpool, Daisy is rescued by a man of honesty and restless energy, sea captain Sam Lassiter.

First as his mistress and then as his wife and business partner, Daisy comes to enjoy the better things in life. But her unrelenting drive for revenge on the dissolute Miles begins to threaten the destruction of everything she has worked for and achieved. Begins finally to threaten her relationship with Sam Lassiter himself . . .

HODDER AND STOUGHTON PAPERBACKS

AUDREY HOWARD

ALL THE DEAR FACES

Edwardian Liverpool – the greatest port in the Empire, a sprawling, brawling city of poverty and wealth, slum tenements and civic pride, vice and hard-won respectability.

Mara O'Shaughnessy, eighth of thirteen children, longs to escape from the crowded tumult of her family, while her sister Caitlin, quiet but determined, is already, to her mother's horror, involved with the Suffragettes.

Woodall Park, 2,000 acre estate home of Elizabeth and her parents, Sir Charles and Lady Woodall, could have been a million miles away. With their neighbours, the Osbornes of Beechwood Hall, life is lived in servanted ease, country pursuits and suitable marriages.

Yet in the golden years before World War I, Liverpool Irish and English gentry are to become fatefully, passionately entangled . . .

HODDER AND STOUGHTON PAPERBACKS

AUDREY HOWARD

THERE IS NO PARTING

Callum O'Shaughnessy is Liverpool Irish.

Ninth child of a tumultuous, affectionate, mostly devout, sometimes too outspoken family. He has 'got on': working his way up by sheer hard work and dedication to be master of his own ship.

Maris Woodall's family know about ships as well. They own them. Along with their kin, the Osbornes, they live the comfortable life of the landed gentry.

Callum and Maris, from families that seem fated to meet and collide, are so different in class, experience and even age: ill-matched yet passionately attracted.

But, as the Depression years of the 1930s give way to World War, everything around them is in a state of violent upheaval that echoes, and may even swamp, their own stormy relationship.

HODDER AND STOUGHTON PAPERBACKS

AUDREY HOWARD

ECHO OF ANOTHER TIME

Celie Marlow first begins working in the Latimers'
kitchen when she is only ten, learning her art from
kindly Mrs Harper. By the age of eighteen, she has
become a talented cook.

Celie knows her place, and longs only to run a
kitchen as skilfully as her mentor. Until she falls in
love with the wrong man: Richard Latimer, eldest son
of the house. And all their lives change with
frightening swiftness.

Driven from her home, Celie finds unexpected
success in a new venture with Mrs Harper – then
loses everything once more. Thrown on to the streets
of Liverpool, penniless and desperate, she will have
to find her own way.

HODDER AND STOUGHTON PAPERBACKS

AUDREY HOWARD

A WORLD OF DIFFERENCE

Cosseted heiress Jenna Townley is used to getting her own way. And when she meets ambitious young Conal MacRae, she soon knows that this is the man she must marry, despite her father's disapproval.

Their courtship is fiery and their marriage passionate. But their happiness is threatened by tragic and sinister family secrets which refuse to be buried. Is Jenna destined to repeat her mother's tragedy, or can she triumph over the past and keep both the Townley legacy and the man she was meant to love?

Audrey Howard's bestselling novels include *The Silence of Strangers*, *Echo of Another Time*, *The Woman from Browhead*, *The Mallow Years*, *Shining Threads*, *A Day Will Come*, *All the Dear Faces* and *There Is No Parting*, all available from Coronet.

HODDER AND STOUGHTON PAPERBACKS